PENGUIN BOOKS

THREE NOVELS

Isabel Colegate was born in London and now lives near Bath, in Wiltshire, in an eighteenth-century Gothic castle with her husband and their three children. She started work in London as a literary agent. Isabel Colegate is the author of nine novels. *The Shooting Party*, her ninth published novel, was the winner in Great Britain of the 1980 W. H. Smith Literary Award.

Isabel Colegate

THREE NOVELS

The Blackmailer
A Man of Power
The Great Occasion

PENGUIN BOOKS

Penguin Books Ltd, Harmondsworth,
Middlesex, England
Penguin Books, 40 West 23rd Street,
New York, New York 10010, U.S.A.
Penguin Books Australia Ltd, Ringwood,
Victoria, Australia
Penguin Books Canada Limited, 2801 John Street,
Markham, Ontario, Canada L3R 1B4
Penguin Books (N.Z.) Ltd, 182–190 Wairau Road,
Auckland 10, New Zealand

The Blackmailer first published in Great Britain 1958
First published in the United States of America in this collection 1984
A Man of Power first published in Great Britain 1960
First published in the United States of America in this collection 1984
The Great Occasion first published in Great Britain 1962
First published in the United States of America in this collection 1984
This collection first published in Great Britain by Blond & Briggs 1983
This collection first published in the United States of America
in simultaneous hardcover and paperback editions by
The Viking Press and Penguin Books 1984
Published in Penguin Books in Great Britain 1984

Printed in the United States of America by
R. R. Donnelley & Sons Company, Harrisonburg, Virginia
Set in Palatino

CONTENTS

FOREWORD

The Blackmailer was first published in 1958. I had finished it two years earlier but the publisher who had then accepted it turned out to be on the point of retirement, and his decision was reversed by his successor. I can't honestly say that I think that the successor (himself now long faded from the publishing scene) was wrong. Twenty-seven years is a long time to wait for a book to be considered worth reprinting.

In 1958 Anthony Blond paid me a £50 advance against a royalty of 10% on the first 2,500, 12½% on the next 2,500 and 15% thereafter. In 1981, twenty-three years and nine novels later I was paid (by another publisher) an advance of £2,000 against a royalty of 10% on the first 2,000, 12½% thereafter. Allowing for inflation, there doesn't seem to be much in it.

It is said to be harder to find a publisher for a first novel now than it was then. One might expect this to be the case – publishers' costs are higher and no-one likes throwing away their money – but a good many publishers are not too sure about the difference between a good book and a bad book, and not many more can tell the difference between a book which will sell and one which won't. I don't complain about this state of affairs since but for publishers' errors of optimism a lot of us wouldn't get into print at all.

Anthony Blond was full of optimism in 1958 because he had just started his own publishing firm: and, with a war book which was reprinted before publication my novel was his first book. I don't know how many copies *The Blackmailer* sold, but it covered its advance and I think it even went into paperback (a small now-vanished imprint whose director I never met but I remember his

name Frank Rudman with gratitude). *A Man of Power*
which followed two years later and *The Great Occasion*
which came two years after that sold about the same
number of copies and also went into paperback, owing to
the goodness of Mr Rudman who paid me, I think, £100
a time.

People think novelists write fictionalized autobiography; perhaps some do. I think myself that the process
by which one turns one's deepest preoccupations into
fiction is a lot more complicated than that – a kind of
willed dreaming as necessary and as hard to analyse as
the involuntary sort. It's a process I've thought a lot about
since I wrote these three books, but these three I wrote
without thinking because it didn't occur to me not to write
them.

At the time I wrote *The Blackmailer* I was working in a
Literary Agency called Anthony Blond (London) Limited.
It consisted of Anthony Blond and me. I had contributed
£50 towards the initial expenses and was theoretically a
partner. Thus when Anthony in full flood of eloquence
before a dazzled client gesticulated towards me and said,
'I'll get the girl to type the contract,' I would frown fero-
ciously from behind my typewriter. 'Ah,' he'd have to
exclaim. 'I see the girl's not in today. My partner Miss
Colegate may be kind enough. . . .' In fact I was the
typist, though I kept the accounts and wrote readers'
reports, mostly explaining in detail why the typescripts
concerned were quite unpublishable, falling as they did
so very far below the standards set by the world's greatest
literature, which in my ignorance of there being any other
standards I was applying to them. My reports must have
been deeply disheartening.

I married about this time and we were given a Cavalier
King Charles spaniel. My bus journey from Chelsea to
the office behind Barclays Bank in New Bond Street was
more or less the one taken by Judith and her dog in *The
Blackmailer* and by Vanessa in *a Man of Power*. When *a
Man of Power* was published, John Davenport, who had
given it a good review in *The Observer*, telephoned me to
explain that it would have been even better if the Literary
Editor hadn't cut it, and said, 'I see you know the man

who longs for Paris on the top of the 22 bus. . . .' Peripherals do come in, sometimes changed or combined with others to make composites, sometimes almost complete. The man on the 22 bus in *A Man of Power* was complete as far as I knew him, so was the dog in *The Blackmailer*. The publisher who turned down that book was convinced that the character of Feliks Hansecu the publisher in the book was Andre Deutsch; I don't think he believed me when I said I'd never met him. Feliks was based as much as anything on the fantasies of office life in which we used to indulge in our little back room above the Goya Perfume offices with Binky asleep in front of the gas fire and Major Clare and Mr Fitch, our friendly neighbouring dramatic agents, walking through every time they went in or out of the inner room to which ours was a passage. Not only my inexperience but also my incapacitating shyness prevented me from venturing out into the commercial cut and thrust of the literary world. My bolder partner came back with the tales which no doubt provided the information for the character of Feliks. I can't now remember the roots of any other characters, if indeed they were other than fantasies to serve a purpose. It was at the time of the French troubles in Indo-China – there may have been some reported rumour about the siege of Dien Bien Phu which stuck in my mind as a point of departure for a drama.

The late fifties were also the years of the property tycoons. I never met one, but people who did told me afterwards that they thought Lewis was not too far off the mark. I suppose *A Man of Power* is the best constructed of the three books, less tentative than *The Blackmailer* and more modest than *The Great Occasion*. I like it because the funny bits still make me laugh and because a friend of my daughter's who read it recently said that the girl Vanessa was just like she is, which I couldn't have known when I wrote it because she was only three at the time.

I used to think I was rather ashamed of *The Great Occasion*. I had it in my head that I had tried too hard to please; but when I look at it again I don't any longer seem to see the ingratiating smile I must once have caught on the author's face, and it seems to me now to have moments of accuracy in areas where issues are sometimes fudged. On the last couple of pages it fails to convey the excitement of the first glimpse of a whole new group of people, that common, and indeed hard to convey, experience of youth; this weakens the ending because the meeting is meant to be the great occasion towards which one at any rate of the characters was moving all the time – but then those sort of meetings are almost always great occasions only to the people concerned, and look nothing much from the outside. Perhaps, though, I hadn't thought enough about the ending, being chiefly concerned in that book (and it's the only book I've written of which it's true) with technique – simply the mechanics of carrying forward, and maintaining interest in, a number of characters who are not necessarily in the same place but upon whom there is equal emphasis in the scheme of the novel. It was the first book of which I drew a diagram before I started to write.

The Great Occasion was well and widely reviewed; it sold no more, and may have sold less, than the others. I think it made me about £18 over and above the advance and the fee for the paperback rights. I was enormously disappointed. I suppose I had still not seen through that bit they tell you as a child about going on trying and gradually getting better and then everyone being very pleased with you. One or two other inescapable facts of life were brought home to me about the same time (such as that in the course of time one is likely to become thirty); also I began to think for the first time about why anyone writes fiction, and indeed what a work of fiction is. The four novels I wrote over the next ten years were different, more ambitious and more intense, more nervous perhaps. After that I think I changed again. Anyway these three seem to me now to be the ones I wrote instinctively and without difficulty; this makes me remember them with indulgence and feel pleased to see them in print again.

Isabel Colegate

The Blackmailer

1958

1

'BRILLIANT performance,' said the brown man, expansively. 'Masterly, I'd have said. Never thought you'd do it, quite frankly. You must meet all my errant acquaintances.'

'No, I'm sorry. I meant to do better for you,' said Baldwin Reeves, who looked indeed disgruntled and rather puffy in the face. 'I thought I'd get you off altogether; but Fortescue's always hard on motoring offences. We'd have been all right with Lamb.'

'Nonsense, my dear fellow, I'm delighted,' said the other. 'What's a tenner between enemies? I really thought I'd lose my licence this time.'

They paused at the bottom of the steps of Bow Street Magistrates Court. Mr. Parker was just back from a skiing holiday, was off again to the south of France to lose his manly tan in the casinos while the spring crept north. Baldwin had had a hard cold winter, and it showed in his face and his frame of mind. Parker had hit an old woman on a pedestrian crossing on his way home one evening in his new Ford Thunderbird from some boisterous outing with the boys. The old woman had luckily lived, but Parker had a nasty driving record, so Baldwin's case had not been easy. Baldwin disliked, despised and envied his client, but would have liked to have got him an absolute discharge because he was the sort of person whose partisanship was not to be sneezed at.

'I must be getting along,' said Parker. 'Lunching with some old fiend of an ambassadress – ah well, big lunch . . . I really can't thank you enough, really most grateful. See you in the club some time.'

Baldwin thought, rich people are always mean. Outwardly affable, he watched the brown man stride springily away from him toward his car. 'You'd have thought he'd have given me lunch,' he thought, 'and anyway I know ambassadresses too.'

He took a taxi to Fleet Street, meaning to walk down to his chambers in Paper Buildings. It was a cold, bleak, hopeless sort of day, and he had a case coming up that afternoon which he knew he was bound to lose. The taxi put him down in Fleet Street: on his way towards the Inner Temple he went into a pub and asked for a sandwich and a glass of beer.

The place was full of newspaper men and lawyers of one sort or another. Baldwin sat down at a table next to a group of students engaged on just recognisable imitations of a well-known law tutor.

He disliked eating alone. It was partly a question of appearances: he would rather people saw him with someone else, because it gave a better impression and made him seem busy and sought-after; but there was more to it than that. Eating alone reminded him of the bleak years of the beginning of his struggle, of the baked beans consumed in Lyons Tea Shops in those unrelievedly awful days when no one had heard of him, when he looked round at the old women, the shop-girls and the workmen, the intellectuals, the lunatics, the lovers, and thought, with a depth of conflicting emotion which brought tears to his eye, 'I'll show you, you wait, I'll just show you,' and at the same time, 'I'll help you, I'll look after you, leave it to me,' and 'You'll acknowledge me, everyone of you, not a life but will be touched by mine,' and at the same time, 'I will get you out of this, I will give you hope.'

But his own hopes were perhaps not quite what they had been. The struggle was turning out harder than he had anticipated, or if not harder (for he had been prepared for anything) then longer; and there was a bitterness and a doubt of misdirection which he had not used to have. There seemed to be a lack of response, an indifference, at the heart of things, which gave his earlier ambitions, ruthless though he had meant them to be, the aspect of ideals.

Of course this was a bad day, a sour unprofitable day,

to be got through and forgotten as quickly as possible. At least he could have a very small lunch, and that might count as an achievement, since he was greedy though anxious not to be fat.

Finishing his sandwich, he took an exercise book out of his dispatch case and looked at the notes he had scribbled that morning for his big speech the next day. He was nursing a 'marginal' constituency, and reading through his notes his spirits suddenly rose – they were not so bad after all, the agent was sure there would be a big attendance for once, and that television fellow was going to be there so as to have a word with him afterwards; he could do with a television appearance just at the moment.

In this more hopeful frame of mind he greeted with a polite smile the girl who, disengaging herself from the group of now departing students, accosted him with a nervous smile and said: 'Aren't you Baldwin Reeves?'

'You want my autograph I suppose?' said Baldwin, appreciating with his mind's eye the charmingly quizzical lift of his eyebrows.

'Oh well,' the girl said, embarrassed. 'Really, I wanted to ask you about – that is, Lucy Fuller said she knew you – d'you know her?'

'Of course, dear Lucy,' said Baldwin. 'How is she?'

'Oh terribly well,' said the girl, her nervous soft glance sliding away from him. 'She's having a baby. Did you – did you know Anthony Lane?'

'Yes,' said Baldwin, less affably.

'Oh,' she blushed. 'Yes, she said you did. I only met him once, just before he went abroad. I thought he was wonderful. It must have been wonderful to have known him properly, I mean like you did.' She spoke in a rushing series of gentle gasps.

'I see it's not me you admire after all,' said Baldwin sadly. Seeing she still awkwardly stood there, he added: 'Won't you sit down?'

'Oh well really I must go,' she said, sitting down.

'Have a drink?' said Baldwin. She was quite pretty, but her approach annoyed him – its immodesty was too coy. He put her down as a creature of no account: so, for that matter, was Lucy Fuller.

'No thank you,' she said. 'I suppose you don't like talking about it.'

'About drink?' said Baldwin. 'I don't mind.'

'No, Korea,' said the girl. 'I mean, it must have been so awful.'

'Oh yes,' said Baldwin, indifferently. 'Awful.' He began to draw a very bad likeness of her in the margin of his notes.

She looked hurt. 'I suppose you get tired of people gushing about him,' she said humbly. 'Only after all there are so few heroes these days and he is the one person everyone agrees was wonderful. I mean, isn't he?'

'He was a proper hero,' said Baldwin, still drawing. 'A proper hero.'

'You were with him all the time, I suppose – out there, I mean?' she said, her voice a little hushed.

'Not all the time,' said Baldwin, in the same sort of tone. 'There were times when he was where none of us could reach him – times when though we were there he was alone.'

'I see what you mean,' she breathed.

'My poor child,' said Baldwin, putting down his pencil and leaning back in his chair. 'Keep your hero – do you kiss his photograph every night? – but leave me out of it. I am a bad man.'

He suddenly leered at her, an awful base lecherous leer, and leaning towards her with a sort of buzzing sound, pinched her on the thigh. Then he burst into a great shout of laughter.

She stood up, blushing again and quite at a loss. 'Well, I'll – I'll tell Lucy I've seen you,' she said, beginning to edge away.

He waved foolishly, and she hurried out of the pub after her vanished friends. He went on laughing, his horrid gesture having given him a sense of huge release.

'Life's a splendid business,' he said to the small journalist who, passing on his way to the bar, had stopped to stare. 'A splendid business.'

'Come into money?' said the journalist, turning away to ask for a glass of beer.

'No,' said Baldwin.

The journalist came back with his beer. Baldwin knew him quite well in a casual sort of way without being able to remember whether his surname was Harman or his Christian name Herman.

'As a matter of fact I've merely been very rude to a wholly inoffensive girl,' said Baldwin. 'It was unkind, but she unwittingly caught me on the raw, as the saying is. I'm a most resentful person, I'm afraid. I bear malice. Do you? Probably not, I should think.'

'Can't afford to in my job,' said Harman (for it was, in fact, his surname). 'Got to have a rhinoceros hide. How's business? Anything juicy?'

'Nothing much for you I'm afraid,' said Baldwin.

'Nobody's nice confession?' Harman asked. 'A good, hot serial – that's what I want. You know we pay the top.'

'I don't believe you do,' said Baldwin. 'They paid me practically nothing for the only article I ever did for your paper, and then they mutilated it beyond recognition.'

'You must be full of society scandal, the way you get around,' said Harman.

'I only know one scandal, and that's an old one,' said Baldwin.

'How old?' asked Harman.

'Oh, years,' said Baldwin. 'It involves quite a lot of important names, though mainly military ones; it involves one hero and/or one traitor, and could be made to imply that the war in Korea was grossly mismanaged, and that all sorts of people were incompetent. I could make it quite dramatic, spin it out to quite a good length, and apart from anything else I'd be paying off an old score, an old sore score.'

'Write it,' said Harman. 'Write it, for God's sake.'

'Will your paper print it?' said Baldwin.

'How can I say if you don't tell me any more?' said Harman. 'Give me one name, one name involved.'

'Anthony Lane,' said Baldwin.

Harman looked surprised, then nodded.

'Sounds excellent,' he said. 'Excellent. Anthony Lane, eh? You know your facts, I suppose? You were there, of course. . . .'

'How much would they pay for that sort of thing?' asked Baldwin.

'A lot, if it's good,' said Harman. 'Look, write a synopsis, get a bit of authentication – you know the laws of libel better than I do – give me a ring and I'll arrange for you to see Blow, the Features Editor – nothing easier. Now do that, for God's sake. I like the sound of it very much, very much indeed. Anthony Lane, yes. He really was made into a hero, no one's forgotten him – and all that upper-class, smart regiment stuff – yes, I like the sound of some low-down on that very much indeed, just the stuff for us. We'll discuss how I come into it later, eh? I know you're on the level.' He finished his beer and stood up. 'Got to go,' he said. 'Write it. I'll see you get top rates, big money, really big, you take my word.'

When he had gone, Baldwin picked up the pencil which was still lying on the table in front of him, and turning over the page on which he had written the outline of his speech and drawn so unflatteringly Anthony Lane's admirer, he began casually to scribble some other notes. Even as he wrote he was not sure who, if anyone, would ever read what he was writing.

2

H E was a little taken aback when the door was opened by a half-sized man wearing a beret and a mackintosh: it hardly seemed in keeping with the conventional exterior of the house, the clean olive-green door with its glittering brass-work, the rather self-conscious terracotta window-boxes full of frost-bitten primroses.

'Madame is upstairs. If you wait in here I will tell her.' So he was foreign as well as a midget, and perhaps it was one or other of those facts which had embittered him, for the look which he gave to the visitor before stumping out of the room was certainly venomous.

Baldwin looked about him, speculating. This French deformity – was he a servant, or what? He found it hard to imagine anyone wilfully choosing such an unattractive employee. It seemed therefore more likely – and the thinker hardly noticed the paradox – that he should be her lover. Besides, if he were a servant, surely he would be better dressed? The too-large navy-blue beret, the shabby brown belted mackintosh, floppy trousers and short thick shoes seemed by their audacious nastiness to indicate someone who was quite at home. Unless of course he was not a resident there at all, but someone called in to mend the electric light or clean the windows, and whose curious aspect would probably lose him her custom. He hoped so, because a lover, however small, would not suit his purpose; and indeed it seemed the most likely explanation, for the room in which he waited showed no sign of being lived in by an eccentric – nor even, on second thoughts, by a woman, for it was an austere greyish-brownish room with few pictures, many books, and an untidy desk in one corner. It was not, he was pleased to see, a shabby room: there were no outward

signs of poverty. The white paintwork was too clean to
have been done long ago, London dirt being what it is,
and the furniture, though there was not much of it, was
good. On the other hand there was no luxury: there were
no flowers, for instance, and the cigarette boxes were
empty. There were no shiny magazines, no gramophone
or television set, and the Persian rugs on the floor, though
good enough, might easily have come from one or other
of the parents – the Lanes probably, since he had heard
that hers were nothing to speak of – and he noticed, using
a simple means test he had often found valid, that there
was no fitted carpet.

He was still padding up and down the room when the
midget reappeared and said: 'She comes directly. You sit
down.' It was a villainous accent, probably not French
after all, he thought, and was accompanied by a
commanding gesture towards a chair.

'Thank you,' Baldwin said without moving.

The midget waited blankly, and they faced each other,
fat man and dwarf, in deep dislike. A rustle of movement
which raised Baldwin's hopes, making him think she
must be light and airy, frilly and thin as he liked them,
broke the silence, but it was only a dog, a dog who was
light, airy, frilly, but not thin, and who wriggled up to
Baldwin as if they were each others' greatest friends.

'Bertie!' said the midget as if it were some foul impreca-
tion. The dog danced on. The midget in evident rage
seized it by the collar and began to drag it from the room,
the dog protesting with unexpectedly ferocious growls.

'Come out you Bertie,' the midget was saying. 'Sit
down. Come on. Shut up.'

'It's all right, Jean-Claude,' a voice said in the hall.
'Bertie can come with me.'

Jean-Claude muttered something and a girl came into
the room, Bertie behind her.

Baldwin was unreasonably disappointed; for what did
it matter, after all, what she looked like? All the same it
would have been more amusing if she had been attractive;
but he realised at once that she was not his type. He had
expected someone at least rather more distinguished. This
might have been any little Chelsea girl passed on the way

here – flat chest, straight hair, jeans and a sweater, nice eyes, but face too broad, big hands and feet – it was obvious that their relationship could only be a business one.

'So you are Judith,' he said expansively. 'About whom I have heard so much.'

'Oh have you?' she said indifferently. 'You telephoned didn't you?'

'I did, and you were out, and as I was passing on my way back from the week-end I thought I would look in on the chance of seeing you instead of waiting till tomorrow. You don't mind, I hope?'

'Of course not. Have a drink?' She opened a cupboard, and waving at it said: 'Perhaps you'd help yourself. Is it very cold in here? The fire's been going all day but it's still not warm enough, is it? Was it cold in the country?'

'Freezing,' he said. 'I was staying with the Millers – Gavin Miller – d'you know him?'

'No,' she said, without saying that she had heard of him, though obviously she had, because everyone had.

'They have a new central heating system which they're very boring about and which as far as I can see might as well not exist.'

The way in which she was hunched in her chair, one hand holding the dog very close to her legs, made him think she might already be uneasy. The thought crossed his mind that she might even know what he knew – but there was no one who could, or would, have told her, and if she did know she must have guessed. Besides that made no difference, his weapon would be no less powerful.

'Can't I pour out a drink for you?' he asked, thinking, hm, nothing but South African sherry. She refused, but accepted one of his cigarettes, and leaning back in her chair, stared at him for some moments before finally smiling and saying with a small sigh which might have been of resignation: 'So you were with Anthony.'

'I was with Anthony,' he sat opposite her. 'Of course the first thing I must do is tell you how desperately sorry I was that he died, not only because of my own affection for him, but because I knew he had not been married long.'

'Yes, it was very sad,' she said, with detachment, looking down.

'Of course we were all very fond of him,' said Baldwin.

'So many people were,' she said gently, as if anything he might have thought about her late husband was a matter of indifference to her. This was not quite what he had expected, but after all there was a sort of familiarity about it: with Anthony too one's opinions had not mattered because he had been so sure of his own.

'I was his second-in-command, you see,' Baldwin went on.

He understood why she looked surprised, because although he had been only four years older than Anthony Lane he looked more and had besides a certain air of authority.

After a pause she seemed to feel that something more was required of her, and, pulling the dog awkwardly on to her knee, she said: 'I had one letter from there, from where the fighting was I mean. I don't know whether he wrote more – I imagine he was pretty busy.'

'Yes, he was busy,' he said.

The look she gave him amazed him. 'She knows,' he thought. He was aware of two other things, that something in his voice had committed him more than he had meant it to, and that she was, quite simply, in his power. He was so excited that he trembled.

When he had savoured the moment for as long as he felt it wise, he stood up.

'Well, I really only came to introduce myself,' he said, his hands behind his back in front of the fireplace. 'The truth is, this is really more in the nature of a business call than anything else. I'm afraid I was presuming on my friendship with your husband to appeal to your good offices as one of the most successful publishers in London.'

'Oh, you've written a book?' she asked, with the lack of interest he was beginning to expect from her.

'Not a book so much as a newspaper story,' he said. 'Or at least that's how it is at the moment, and that's how

I've presented it to my old friend Blow of the *Sunday News*. But he seemed so excited about it – more so than I'd expected – that it occurred to me that I might very well write it up into quite a startling book; and that's what I thought might interest you.'

'Of course, if it's startling,' she said. 'You've sold it to the *News* then?'

'Well, I've been going into the whole thing,' said Baldwin. 'And one or two people have told me that to sell the serial rights of a book before selling the book itself to a publisher is all wrong – the book loses half its value, and the publisher's not nearly so keen – I don't know whether that's so?'

'To a certain extent,' she said.

'So I'm keeping them hanging about a bit,' he said. 'So that you can have a look at the MS. first.'

'It's non-fiction, I suppose,' she said.

'A true story,' he said. 'A war story. I believe they still sell quite well?'

'Oh yes,' she said, apparently searching for fleas on her dog's broad back. 'Very well.'

'Then if I may I'll leave it with you,' he said. 'And perhaps I may call at your office tomorrow.'

'I'm afraid I'm rather busy tomorrow,' she said. 'Perhaps later this week. . . ?'

'I'll call in tomorrow on the off-chance,' he said. He moved towards the door. 'I really must apologise for having bothered you with all this tonight, but it seemed too good an opportunity to waste as I was just passing, and as you see there is a certain amount of urgency about it because of my having already got Blow interested. But I suppose you must be used to importunate authors.'

She smiled politely, following him out into the hall. Heavy steps stumped up from the basement and Jean-Claude appeared with Baldwin's coat.

'It's funny that I don't remember Anthony ever mentioning your name,' said Judith Lane.

'I only knew him slightly in England,' said Baldwin. 'We never really had much to do with each other until we went to Korea. Circumstances happened to keep us as much apart as two people in one regiment can be until then.'

She nodded, as if she found that only natural. 'You're a regular soldier?' she asked.

'I'm a barrister now,' he said, with an echo of satisfaction in his voice. 'But at the time I had signed on for an extra seven years after the end of my conscription. The seven years expired just after I got back from the prison camp in China. I quite liked the Army in many ways, but I never wanted to stay there for good. It was useful to me, though; it kept me fed for those years and I took my Bar exams in my spare time – all except the last that is, which I crammed for as soon as I came out. That was probably why I didn't see much of Anthony while we were both in London. I was working at my law all my spare time.'

He had been talking partly to cover up his embarrassment over the struggle on which he was at the same time engaged with the midget, who was refusing to let go of his overcoat. As the highest he could reach was about on a level with Baldwin's lowest rib, it had seemed simpler to Baldwin to take the coat away from him and put it on himself, but Jean-Claude, smiling broadly, shook his head and guided Baldwin's hand into one of the sleeves. Baldwin was then in the foolish position of having his coat put on for him by a man who could only just reach above his waist, and as Jean-Claude kept a surprisingly firm hold on the collar he was forced after a moment to give in and bend his knees. Jean-Claude then with much out-blowing of garlicky breath made a great show of smoothing the shoulders and fitting the collar in exactly the right place, keeping Baldwin bent to his own level with the aid of one large hand on his shoulder.

Aware that the girl had watched this exhibition with cool pleasure, Baldwin left rather hurriedly, without shaking her hand, merely saying: 'Then I shall hope to see you tomorrow,' and walking quickly down the street towards the King's Road.

It had gone quite well, he thought as he went, but for the midget. The midget was unbearable.

A little later, Jean-Claude, who had been putting the

dog out, came in with the envelope which Baldwin had left in the hall and held it out to Judith. 'You are wanting?' he asked.

She looked at him. 'It's only something he wanted me to read,' she said, after a moment. 'Leave it in the hall. I'll look at it tomorrow.' But when she went upstairs to bed, she was carrying it under her arm.

Every day there was a moment – every week-day, every working day – when her prepared glance sped between the trees of Royal Avenue to the clock tower of Chelsea Hospital, then the straight view slid sideways and the bus carried her forward. It was a ritual begun in the early days of her marriage, when the assuming of a routine had seemed not merely efficient and adult like being able to cook, but also an enchanted initiation, a form of service lovingly learnt by a religious convert. Happiness had fitted into a framework, whose removal would have taken away half her newly established confidence, though for convention's sake she had pretended to despise it – a convention of being unconventional which it had at the time seemed important not to break. Her slight occasional complaint was also because she did not think it wise for her husband to know the full measure of her content, because she was aware of his tendency to lose interest in what was wholly his, a tendency which she never in the brief course of her married life ignored.

There was now no need for her to pretend that she derived anything but the keenest enjoyment from her morning bus ride to the office. Her code of unconventionality had long since dissolved and there was no one she had to pretend not to adore; so the morning bus usually saw her smiling over the top of her dog's large round head, looking out for each familiar landmark while her mind wallowed in an extravagant day-dream for which the rest of the day was too occupied.

Today the trees were sharply black, or rather that deep dark green which seems blacker than black and which trees usually have in the evening when the light has almost gone, and it was too misty to see the clock tower.

The mist seemed a result of the temperature, like a heat haze only the opposite, rather than a rainy, or dewy, mist, for it was that very cold late February that followed the first brief signs of spring that year. Even on such a morning, a morning too on which she had something to worry about, happiness was too much a habit to be so quickly changed. The familiarities of the routine once loved for reasons now mainly removed had assumed the character almost of childhood recollections, were something like a certain corner of an otherwise unimportant yew hedge or the small patch which was the burial ground of several canaries and rabbits, intimately remembered places with a quality now of revelation about them, only that they revealed the past and not the future.

So she listened with equanimity to the conversation behind her as an elderly lady with blue hair and a neat rubicund man whom she had just rapturously greeted chattered in lively loud stage voices.

'Wimbledon!' the woman deeply fluted. 'My dear, the places they choose! And I have to go to Maida Vale at eight-thirty – eight-thirty! – for *The Rivals*.'

'Wimbledon Common,' the man said. 'On Sunday morning and in a wig.'

'Oh they've forgotten what Sunday is,' the woman lamented. 'A wig?'

'We're supposed to be cavaliers,' said the man, with exaggerated dolefulness.

'The things they do to us,' said the woman in a satisfied tone. 'But oh, I must tell you about the water board. Without a word, without so much as one of those squalid little notes, they cut us off! Not, my dear, because we hadn't paid the bill, oh no, because they were *altering* something. And I said to the man, "If someone should be ill?" and he coolly said, "There's a temporary pump," but had they told us there was a temporary pump? Oh dear me no. Not till four o'clock in the morning did I know there was a temporary pump.'

'You spoke to him at four o'clock?'

'Not spoke to him, no,' the woman answered. 'But heard it. My dear, it was Niagara in the streets, the temporary pump. But till then from the afternoon before I might have died for want of water for all they cared.'

Their conversation rushed on and everyone listened, drawn together, rather, on the top of the bus, by their joint amusement, their joint hope that the two talkers might turn out to be famous.

'Supposing I were suddenly to turn round,' Judith thought, 'and say, "The Water Board may worry you, but I was told last night my husband was what you would call a coward and a traitor – well, that perhaps I knew, but I was told that other people knew, which was worse—'

But as if some echo of the thought had reached her, the elderly actress was saying: 'How awfully brave, those people on the life-boat, did you see? Trying to save those sailors from the wrecked tanker. Wasn't it dreadfully sad? And did you see the captain's telegram? Lost carrying out the supreme duty of saving lives – something like that. Such a wonderful phrase, I thought, the supreme duty. It's a naval expression I suppose. Some of their messages are so wonderful, don't you think, that one reads?'

Judith felt tears ready to fill her eyes at the thought of great duties fulfilled. The fact that her late husband had evidently failed to fulfil his seemed neither here nor there: he had not needed duty, but, to someone who did, nothing could be more satisfying than to carry it out, and she felt a little envious of the men who had died so grandly. A sense of responsibility properly applied could be a great comfort to the applier.

The bus ride was familiar to Bertie too, and at Hyde Park Corner he scrambled from her knee some time before the bus stop. A middle-aged man in a bowler hat said, 'Good doggie, nice little bow-wow,' in a busy portentous way as they went down the stairs.

The Park Lane office of Messrs Hanescu Lane & Co. Ltd., one of the few publishing firms to have been successful since the end of the war, was inclined to arouse as a first reaction from clients a certain amount of distrust; it was unbelievably sumptuous. Baldwin Reeves, when he saw it later, had his fill of fitted carpets. They abounded, and so did flowers and filled cigarette boxes, and wildly expensive modern furniture, white telephones, beautifully bound reference books and good pictures by young little-known painters. There was only one secretary, but she abounded too.

One came first into a peacock-blue room with crimson damask curtains. The carpet there had to be washed once a week by a very expensive firm of office cleaners. There was a huge vase of flowers on a gilt and ebony table, some modern Italian chairs and sofas, some low marble tables. From this room one door led to Feliks Hanescu's office and another to the room where Fisher and Miss Vanderbank sat, beyond which was Judith's office.

The Chairman and Managing Director's room was black and white: black carpet, white armchairs, black desk with a large white extension for telephones, black desk chair. There were black velvet curtains lined with white silk, and white Venetian blinds. The walls were white and were hung with two huge ferocious landscapes and a sketch of Hanescu's head by a famous artist. There was a small white filing cabinet with imitation Sèvres handles in one corner, and a long, low black bookcase filled with manuscripts.

Miss Vanderbank the secretary and Fisher the young man with money worked entrellised in rosebuds. Hanescu had been immovable on this point – Fisher and Miss Vanderbank were to have rosebuds or nothing, and since for Miss Vanderbank the pay was good and for Fisher the prospects, supposedly, alluring, they had of course had rosebuds. Hanescu, quite carried away by the unsuitability of it, had wanted to have gay chintz curtains and armchairs and had even suggested a Welsh dresser for keeping manuscripts in, but here he had been over-ruled and the curtains and carpets were in fact a serviceable dark green, and Fisher's desk, the chairs and filing cabinets were comparatively conventional, though Miss Vanderbank's typing desk was a riot of gadgets.

The argument over Judith's room had lasted for weeks. Hanescu had wanted a William Morris wallpaper, a painted green and white desk (feminine, he thought) and, suddenly, a copper Christ in a pale green alcove. In the end the walls were the colour of bull's blood, the carpet and curtains pale grey and the furniture mahogany. 'This is for the simpler authors.' Hanescu said. 'Up from the country,' and he bought a set of sporting prints for the walls.

Feliks's voice greeted Judith as she came into the office.

'I'm afraid she's in conference at the moment,' he was saying. 'Can I take a message?'

'What is it?' asked Judith.

'Oh wait a moment, I think I might be able to catch her,' Feliks said, still on the telephone. Turning to Judith, he said: 'Good morning. I'll put you through if you go to your office.

'I'll do it here,' said Judith. 'Who is it?'

'Oh no,' said Feliks. 'It's a *private* call. Come on.' He led her through Fisher's and Miss Vanderbank's room, which was empty. 'Honey and flowers,' he said. 'A man with a voice all honey and flowers it is.'

Judith lifted the receiver and her mother-in-law asked her to tea.

'She thinks I'm common,' said Feliks, when the conversation was over.

'It's not that so much as that she fears you have no roots, which is not quite the same thing,' said Judith. 'She likes people to have roots.'

'Oh but branches too,' said Feliks. 'Wiltshire branches, Sussex branches, cadet branches, branches sinister, branches distaff. I have none. I must marry and found a dynasty. Do you suppose Miss Vanderbank would be fruitful?'

'Where are they?' Judith asked.

'I sent them both out to have coffee,' said Feliks. 'I think they're falling in love.'

Feliks Hanescu was huge. The fact was a continual source of irritation to him, for he believed that only little men were great. 'If I had been six inches smaller,' he said, 'I should have been a genius.' That was what he had wanted to be, a genius: having just missed it, he had become a personality instead.

There was nothing small about him at all, except his writing which was illegible because he had once heard that the cleverest people have the smallest writing. He had a large, dark, handsome head, yellowish bright-eyed face and hooked nose. The nose was useful to him for it enabled him when he wished to pass himself off as a Jew, which he sometimes found advantageous from the business point of view. In fact he was neither Jewish, nor, as rumour among the gullible had been known to run, of Rumanian royal blood. His father had indeed been Rumanian – a moderately successful business man who had settled in England and married, in the first flush of his enthusiasm for all that was English, a handsome Sussex farmer's daughter. When it dawned on him that this had been, socially speaking, a mistake, he at once abandoned his wife, and the young Feliks was then submitted to the care of a brisk succession of step-mothers, called from varying social *milieux*, until Hanescu senior in his old age blissfully settled down with the jolly old daughter of an Irish peer. Feliks meanwhile had been conventionally educated at a small public school which by no means deserved the denial he usually accorded it.

Feliks Hanescu Limited had begun in 1947 in a dingy little office in John Street, Bloomsbury, lit mainly by the glowing presence of the enamoured Miss Vanderbank. Eighteen months later it was declared bankrupt. A year after, it re-emerged, its reputation only slightly tarnished and all its debts discharged, owing to the death of Mr. Hanescu senior, who had left his son a modest fortune.

Feliks Hanescu had energy, talent, salesmanship, and an infinite capacity for remembering names. He also had, for the moment, a considerable unearned income. He soon acquired a reputation as an up and coming young man, and a large clientele of ex-convicts, war heroes and deep-sea divers, who, greedily pursued by other publishers, came to him partly because he often caught them before anybody else and partly because they had heard he was good at pushing sales, which was true.

It was Alastair Drudge who had first introduced him to Judith. Alastair Drudge was a plain young red-haired girl who kept Siamese cats and wrote highbrow novels. Feliks disliked her intensely, but he was anxious for his list to be more literary and she thought he adored her. She took him to a party in the Cromwell Road where he glittered and smouldered and ensnared what he hoped were all the new young writers and where someone said: 'There's Judith Fortune – you know, Edward Fortune's daughter,' and he fell in love.

To Feliks Hanescu love and sex were one and the same. Judith, bewildered, studiedly remote and actually fascinated (though this he never knew) rejected his advances. After a time he transferred them to more welcoming objectives and concentrated on conversation. If he had been asked at any time after the first tumultuous month of their acquaintance whether or not he was in love with Judith he would have sincerely denied it, but a more introspective man in his place might have said: 'Yes, a little.' Judith passed through a stage when she rather priggishly condemned him as a charlatan, and then settled down to be his greatest friend.

When she joined his firm she brought the literary tone which he now felt he needed. Her father, Edward Fortune, who had just died, had been a much respected critic, a translator of modern German literature, and a publishers' reader – a serious, learned, kind man, who had advised and been loved by a great number of the writers of his time. His wife Hilda's earnest novels still had their influence and might have had more if they had not been suddenly cut short by her early death when Judith was fifteen.

Judith herself had a critical faculty which served the firm well, and Feliks Hanescu Ltd. began to combine sensational non-fiction with the work of younger, more intellectual writers. It began to be the thing for a new writer to be published by Hanescu.

On Judith's marriage she became a partner, and with some of Anthony Lane's money and most of poor Fisher's they expanded, and moved, to a background of protests from Judith, into the new office. There the firm flourished, even though there were still times when it lived, if not from day to day, at least from month to month.

At the moment their chief hopes were pinned on a book by a white woman who had married an African chieftain, and which had been out for three days.

Judith, remembering this, asked: 'How's that awful book?'

'You mustn't despise your bread and butter,' said Feliks. 'If you mean *Love Is Not Skin Deep*. The booksellers say it's going well, though they haven't asked for more copies yet. Fisher has finally sold the Australian serial rights, after months of feverish negotiation – that's why he's treating Miss Vanderbank to coffee. They've probably gone to Gunter's to stuff themselves with cakes in celebration. So that's nearly everything sold. The film option's definite now and Peters said he thought it very likely they'd take it up. You look worried. Why?'

'Oh this and that,' said Judith.

'You should have no thises and thats,' said Feliks. 'Not when you have me.' He was standing near the window, and happening to look out he added: 'Not when you have Fisher, either, and Miss Vanderbank and that nice-looking plumpish fellow who must be a brother bun-eater.'

'Plumpish?' said Judith.

'Plumpish,' said Feliks. 'Well, they mustn't find us idling so. Stomp's coming in at twelve. I shall send him to you.'

'Who's Stomp?'

'He wrote that horribly technical book about sex,' said Feliks. 'If not Stomp, something like it. He won't be put off by me, and you're so cool with that sort of person.'

'Why on earth did you let it get to the stage of his coming in?' complained Judith.

'I'm so weak,' said Feliks, going back to his own office. 'I'm so weak and you're so strong.'

Judith sat down at her desk and waited for Baldwin Reeves.

He had not really been to Gunters, but had merely happened to cross the road at the same time as Fisher and Miss Vanderbank, and had followed them up the stairs without knowing that their destination was the same as his. When he discovered that it was, he expressed his delight in terms highly flattering to Miss Vanderbank, and asked her which was Mrs. Lane's room.

'I'll see if she's in, shall I?' said Miss Vanderbank. 'She's usually in about this time.'

'Oh don't bother, I don't need announcing,' said Baldwin.

'I think it would be better if I asked her first, if you don't mind,' said Miss Vanderbank, robustly. 'People usually make appointments you see, to see Mrs. Lane herself.' She bounced away into Judith's room.

Baldwin turned to the pale young man who was hanging awkwardly in the background. 'I seem to have been a little brash,' he said. 'Of course Mrs. Lane is very important.'

'Oh she's not *self*-important,' said the young man with desperate earnestness. 'Not in the slightest. But she's awfully intelligent, of course, and we have to, well, in a way, protect her from people who might waste her time, if you see what I mean?'

'I see,' said Baldwin. There was always special treatment for the Lanes. This young man's voice had a familiar ring; it might have been some young subaltern of Anthony's who was speaking. Baldwin's old resentment came back to him; but with a difference, for the wife had not half Anthony's charm or looks. Anthony had commanded even from Baldwin something that was a little like love. Judith's qualities were so much less enchanting that he expected to be able to behave towards her as he really felt towards her, a thing which he had never been able to do with Anthony. At least he had given her something now which ought to have shaken her.

His first thought when he was allowed into her room was that he might have known that she wouldn't be shaken. She was as calm and indifferent as she had been yesterday: if she was a little paler it was hardly noticeable.

'I'm so sorry to burst in like this,' he began. 'Only I thought possibly early would be better than late, since you said you were rather booked up today. I say, I do like your offices.'

'Won't you sit down,' said Judith. She was sitting behind her desk, and the effect was pleasantly unusual: he could imagine new authors being favourably struck.

'I'm afraid I can't quite see your object in suggesting that we might be interested in publishing this MS.,' she said. 'I should have thought it would have been obvious that we were the last people to ask.'

'I thought you might like to see it before it appeared in the paper,' said Baldwin.

'So that it would be less of a shock?' she said. 'Perhaps you're right. You chose a rather melodramatic way of doing it.' She pushed the envelope towards him across the desk. 'Thank you for letting me see it. I don't think there is anything else I can say at the moment, is there?'

It suddenly seemed difficult to prolong the interview. Baldwin said: 'I thought perhaps you might want to know more – more than I have written I mean.'

'Is there more?' she asked. 'You have told me he was a coward, that during the famous siege he was, as you put it, "cowering" in a corner and that he was booed by his men when he emerged. You have told me that in the prison camp he made some agreement with the enemy, and that he gave away a plan to escape as a result of which two of his companions were shot, and that you all condemned him to death and hanged him. What more can there be?'

She spoke in a voice which was completely dry and cold, and yet she brought Anthony to his mind in a way which had not happened for years. Perhaps it was simply the effect of talking to someone who had known him as well as he had.

'You mustn't think,' he said, 'that all the time – after we were captured and so on – we were enemies. That was the extraordinary thing. I mean, not only had he been afraid, but, as I wrote, he was in such a panic that when the order got through to retreat he thought it was an order to stay where we were. He kept begging me to let us retreat, and I refused, because of what he told me this order had been – then when I finally found out, of course it was too late and that was why so many people were killed and the rest of us captured.'

'The people who had issued the order,' said Judith. 'Did they not wonder why it hadn't been obeyed?'

'Everything happened too quickly, you know,' said Baldwin. 'They might not have known anything about it – I honestly don't know. I had one very odd conversation with the colonel, in which I really didn't know what he was getting at, but the truth is, you see, what good would it have done to let the whole story come out, even if they did guess that something had gone wrong? Their instinct would have been to cover it up, particularly as he was dead, and particularly as he had been given such popular acclaim as a hero.'

'I suppose so,' she said.

'But as I was saying,' he went on. 'The extraordinary thing was that by the time we reached China we were all on speaking terms with him again. We'd started off by being, well, pretty contemptuous, treating him as a traitor; but you know he seemed to have so little idea himself of having done anything to be ashamed of, and then he was funny, really very funny, and somehow clowned himself out of a situation you'd have thought impossible. It was his fault we were there, and yet a week after our capture we were all laughing at his jokes, and even – and this was amazing – vying with each other for his good opinion. He seemed so detached, and could at the same time be so attractive, that one longed to make an impression on him. I think he was tremendously relieved that we were out of danger, and also he expected to be free again in a few weeks, and it made him so cheerful that he was even helpful to the rest of us – carried things for people, helped them on the march, all with a sort of carefree condescension; and then his talk was brilliant and he laughed and played harmless practical jokes on the guards so that even they were amused by him. Of course he'd had more rest than we had in the last few days.'

'I suppose he wasn't at all worried about what would happen when he did get back?' she asked.

'I don't think so,' he said. 'We didn't say anything about it for a long time, but later I asked him what he thought would happen to him. He clasped his brow, you know, and groaned, and said how terrible it was; but then he said well, perhaps it would be all right in the end. There were two things I think that prevented him from really worrying. One was his curious fatalism, and the other was his confidence that the power over people that his own charm gave him would never let him down. You might think they'd be contradictory, but the point was that I really don't think he ever made the slightest effort to charm people, so that in a way he could be fatalistic about that too.'

'His charm and his family,' she said. 'Perhaps they even might have got him out of it.'

Her slight smile surprised him. Somehow they were discussing her dead husband as if he had really been Baldwin's greatest friend, as if they had both loved him and were now in admiration and wonder trying to remember for sentimentality's sake exactly how much. This was not what he had meant.

'Then we got to the prison camp, as I wrote,' he said. 'And then things weren't so good – it's all in there. . . .' he gesticulated towards the envelope on her desk. 'And then there was this fantastic trial in the middle of the night, with all the inmates of the prison there, and he was sentenced.'

'Why was he hanged?' she asked. 'And not shot, I mean.'

'We had no guns,' he said. She was far calmer than he was, and he resented that furiously. If she had shown signs of suffering he might have told her that the verdict had not been unanimous, that there had been one vote against it and that it had been his; but as it was he was not going to tell her; it was far too intimate a confession. For the moment he hated her – for being herself, for not being Anthony – he hardly knew which.

'Then you didn't mind my publishing this story?' he said.

'Mind?' she asked. 'I suppose I can't stop you, though I am not quite certain why you want to do it.'

'You are in the literary business,' he smiled unpleasantly. 'You should know the high fees newspapers pay for a good story. This is a very good story – a popular hero, still in the public mind, proved a coward and a traitor? No one's forgotten him you know – practically every day there's something about him in some paper or other, some public speech, people are always telling me how lucky I was to have known him. I don't make much money. Unlike your late husband, I have no private income, nor have I a powerful family. I am a self-made, or perhaps I should say self-making, man. I am at the moment in great need of money.'

'But, surely, couldn't you make it in some other way?' She still looked bewildered.

'Possibly,' he said. 'But this seems, really, the easiest. Unless, of course someone were to pay me not to.'

After a moment she laughed.

'I see, I see, I see,' she said. 'D'you know honestly that aspect of the affair hadn't occurred to me at all. What an innocent I must be. I have been wondering all the time why you came to tell me this, and I never thought of the simple obvious answer, blackmail.'

'Blackmail,' he nodded.

'Surely you should say, "That's an ugly word",' she said.

'Why?' he asked.

'Don't they in detective stories?' she said.

'I hope this is not going to be a detective story,' he said.

'No, I don't suppose a detective would be much good,' she said. 'I might try, though.'

'You might,' he said. 'But then of course I should be forced to reveal the story, which I may say is neatly typed out in a sealed envelope in my office, together with the names of the other eight witnesses, and can be sent off by my secretary to a journalist I know at a moment's notice.'

'But I thought you told me you had already sold it to the *Sunday News.*'

'That was an exaggeration,' he said. 'I had merely sounded them, without committing myself or revealing the story.'

'I see,' she said. 'How you have thought it out. How extraordinary.'

'Well, there it is, you see,' he said. 'I've no doubt in a few years I shall be making money – I fully intend to make a great deal – but for the moment as I say, a few hundred would be very welcome.'

'A few hundred.'

'I had thought of five, for a start. At first I hoped for more, but I understand your marriage settlement from the Lanes wasn't as generous as it might have been.'

'How did you find that out?'

'Oh, I asked about, you know. But I imagine this firm brings in something, or does Mr. Hanescu take all that?'

'I don't get much,' she said. 'I certainly haven't got £500 just like that.'

Baldwin shook his head sympathetically. 'Indeed, who has these days?' he said, sadly. 'Still, no doubt you'll be able to raise it.'

'Well, wait a minute,' she said. 'I may not want to. I may not think it worth it. I don't think I do, from my own point of view. My feelings for my late husband were not based on the fact that the public at large believed him to be a hero – their thinking him a traitor won't distress me.'

'His family?' asked Baldwin.

'How d'you know that I care at all what they feel?' she said.

'I don't,' he replied. 'If you tell me you don't I shall with a clear conscience take my story to the *News* tomorrow.'

'May I have some time to think it over?' she asked.

'Certainly,' he said, standing up. 'Let's say you'll ring me up tomorrow evening.'

'The next day,' she said.

'All right, we'll make it Wednesday,' he said generously. 'Here's my number.' He pulled a card from his pocket. 'Of course if you decide to go away without getting in touch with me, or anything like that, I shall have to sell the story – purely to pay my rent.'

'I'll ring you up on Wednesday evening about six,' she said.

'Right,' he moved to the door. 'I'm sorry about this but I'm sure you understand my position.'

'Oh yes, I understand it,' she said. She watched him without expression as he went out of the room. At the door, he looked back and would have said 'Good-bye', but after a moment's pause he left without saying anything more.

He thought, going down the stairs and out into Park Lane, 'I am a blackmailer.' He had not known, when he had followed Fisher and Miss Vanderbank into the office a short time ago, or at least had not known for certain, that it was in such a capacity that he would emerge. He was not yet quite sure how he liked it, but after all he had wanted to be ruthless and he had wanted to make money, and it looked as though he was going to be able to do both.

Judith went to the office early the next morning, and found Feliks in her room, looking through her letters.

'My own are so boring,' he said.

'Supposing,' Judith said, taking off her coat. 'Supposing, by any chance, *Love Is Not Skin Deep* – I mean the book really did sell – supposing—'

'Hang your coat up nicely,' said Feliks, picking it up from the chair where she had thrown it. 'How you do let down the tone of this office.' And he carried the coat out to the cupboard in the next room.

When he had come back and shut the door, Judith said: 'I want to borrow some money from the firm.'

'You've been gambling,' he said, sitting on the edge of her desk.

'No, I haven't,' she answered.

'But you, so frugal, need money?' he asked. 'I thought you were all right – you were saying so only the other day.'

'I know, Feliks,' she said. 'But this is something unexpected that I've suddenly got to pay.'

'If it's an abortion,' said Feliks, 'I'd much rather adopt it.'

'I don't know how much an abortion costs,' said Judith. 'But I should think this is more, I don't know.'

'How much?'

'£500,' she said.

'Oh God yes,' he said. 'Much more. Well, all right.'

'£500 is what I've got to pay,' she said. 'I can manage about £150 myself. That leaves £350.'

'Take £200 from the firm and I'll lend you the rest,' said Feliks. 'Only don't tell anyone and pay me back before the firm.'

'Thank you very much,' she said. 'I'll pay you back quite soon, really, and the firm. I'll give banker's orders.'

'Don't worry,' he said. 'Don't worry at all. I hate you to be worried. It makes you snappish in the office and then you humiliate me in front of Miss Vanderbank. You're all right, aren't you?'

'Oh yes, I'm all right,' she answered, looking down.

'And don't let anyone know about that £150,' he went on. 'Heaven knows what would become of my reputation if that got out.' It was one of his affectations to pretend to be pathologically mean: some of the stories about this supposed failing were very funny, whether told by his friends, his enemies, or himself.

'I'd better give it you now.' He got out his cheque book, made a few minute indecipherable marks on a cheque and gave it her.

When he went through the other room he said to Fisher and Miss Vanderbank: 'I've just given Mrs. Lane a cheque for £150.'

The pale face and the pink looked up at the same time and laughed obediently.

3

H E said he had to have it in cash. She thought at first this might be merely a pretext for forcing her to hand it over in person, so that he could extract the fullest pleasure from the exercise of his power over her; but later it occurred to her that it must be to avoid leaving any record of his having received the money.

She had already considered carefully whether there could be any hope of catching him out, had imagined policemen concealed behind the curtains and springing out to arrest him at the moment the money changed hands, but these ideas struck her as so melodramatic and unreal that it seemed impossible they should ever become fact. Besides she had the money now, and she had come to think that perhaps she did somehow owe it to someone for her husband's having failed as he had.

She was in this fatalistic frame of mind when she went with £500 to meet him at a coffee bar in the King's Road. She had asked for an extra week's grace in which to collect the money, and by the end of the week she was feeling depressed and rather ill.

It was not that she consciously thought about it so very much – the having to pay £500 and the reason for it – as that all the time it was at the back of her mind, or, as it rather seemed, on the top of her mind, weighing down on everything beneath it, ready to slip into her conscious thoughts the moment there should be room. She had not yet much questioned it, had so far more or less calmly accepted it as simply something else which Anthony had imposed on her, for there had in the past been other lesser situations not altogether dissimilar. In fact the chief emotion aroused by this talk about him, apart from a vague and dreadful sense of brooding doom, of an imminent outburst of either events or emotions, had been one of renewed longing that he might have been alive, anyhow, however disgracefully.

It was six o'clock and the place was not crowded. Baldwin Reeves was sitting in a corner beneath a rather dusty orange tree (it was all Spanish) and looked, particularly in contrast to the group of grubby students who were sitting at the next table, surprisingly proper and pleasant. She had remembered him as fat, untidy and overbearing, and now he looked neat, intelligent and friendly.

When he saw her he got up, folding his evening paper, smiling – they might have been new friends about to spend a delightful evening together.

He, too, was surprised, because she was looking far more sophisticated than when he had last seen her. In a short fur coat which Anthony had given her, a fashionably tweedy dress and high heels, and with her pretty dog, she looked much more interesting than he could have hoped – people turned to look at her.

As he had thought it would, it made a difference. Perhaps this needn't be the brisk formal encounter he had envisaged, after all.

She, however, seemed to expect that sort of meeting, for she had no sooner sat down than she pulled a bulky envelope from her bag and slapping it down on the table in front of him said: 'D'you want to count it?'

'What will you have?' he asked as if she had not spoken.

'To drink? Oh, nothing thank you.'

'Please do,' he said. 'I thought you'd be late, so I ordered this huge mug of chocolate which is already making me feel sick. Do have something.'

'No, really, I won't, thank you,' she said. 'I must go.'

'Have some fruit juice, do,' he said. 'It's really quite good. Melon or something?'

'Oh, well, some lemon then,' she said, feeling that she had conceded something much more important and leaning back gloomily.

'Thank you,' he said, and ordered it. 'Yes, I thought women were always late,' he went on.

'Oh, are they?' she said, indifferently.

There were women, in his experience, who liked to be constantly reminded of their sex, others who pretended to find that insulting: she seemed to belong to the latter category. It made no difference, in his experience, they were all much the same fundamentally; but one might as well observe their whims. He did not then follow up his last remark, but said instead: 'Tell me how you acquired your dwarf.'

'He's not a dwarf, he's a midget,' she said. 'They're different.'

'Oh, are they?' he said. 'And he's a French midget?'

'Yes,' she said. 'He's got a horrid accent in French too.'

'Is that some regional dialect?'

'I don't know,' she said. 'I found him in Paris.'

'Found him?' asked Baldwin.

She smiled. 'In a way,' she said.

As she remained silent, he said, 'Do tell me about it.'

'Oh, well,' she said, looking away. 'I can't be bothered somehow.'

Perhaps the midget was her lover after all. Baldwin wanted to know; but looking at her blank profile he decided to drop the subject and make inquiries elsewhere.

'Have a bun or something,' he said.

She refused, but he, with evident interest, selected for himself two creamy *pâtisseries* and brought them to the table.

'You'll get fatter,' she said coldly.

'I am rather fat, aren't I?' he said. 'But I don't mind being a little fat as long as it's not too much. I don't think it really detracts from a man's appearance, do you, as long as he's healthy? Do I look very fat at first sight, I mean would people describe me to each other, d'you suppose, as "that fat man"? It's hard to tell how one strikes people. Did you think me fat when you first saw me?'

'Fattish,' she said.

'But d'you think I ought to try to get thinner?' he asked. 'Should I diet, d'you think?'

She looked at him in surprise as he waited with apparent eagerness for her answer. Then she said: 'I asked you if you wanted to count the money.'

He looked disappointed. 'You're right, of course,' he said. 'What does it matter how fat I am? No, I don't want to count it. Let's have dinner together. I'll take you somewhere – we'll see how much we can spend.'

'I think you're very odd,' she said. 'I must go now.'

She stood up, attracted the attention of Bertie, whose lead she had let go and who was being fed on lumps of sugar by an enraptured old lady, and began to walk away.

'I hope you have a good dinner,' she said.

A rough wind whipped her as she strode along the King's Road, but even so she thought, approaching her house, that she could not yet go back there, speak to Jean-Claude, eat, read, think. She turned left down Smith Street, finding the wind less violent once she was round the corner, saying to the dog: 'Come on, Bertie, we're going for a walk. You're so lazy,' for he knew where they were and was straining at his lead in the direction of their house, remembering the cats that lurked behind it and his duty as he conceived it endlessly to bark at them.

She had forgotten, however, that Burton Court would be shut. She had thought they might have run in there, thrown sticks and shouted, to relieve the oppression of her mood. She walked instead on and on, quite quickly now, and down Swan Walk and to the river.

There, still bossed about by the wind, she paused and leant on the wall of the deserted Embankment, seeing through the dark night the vague river swirling and saying at last with furious feeling: 'I hate him, I hate him.'

She spoke not of Baldwin Reeves but of her dead husband, and the familiarity of all her sensations, stronger though they were than most she had felt before, made her sob as she said it.

It was a pattern she had been used to – the outrageous demand, the meek obedience to it, the ensuing useless rage. Life had always been like that with Anthony.

After a few incidents, a few of his own particular betrayals, she had thought: 'This must be the end of everything – how can I feel the same afterwards?' but each time it had been anything but the end and each time

she had felt exactly the same afterwards. Later she had
come to believe what had at first seemed to her odd and
rather degrading, that love was not always based on a
similarity of principles, and that it was possible genuinely
to love and even at times to admire someone whom one
could seldom, if ever, respect. She had also occasionally
recognised in herself an emotion approaching a sort of
enjoyment in quietly submitting herself to the distresses,
inconveniences and humiliations which his behaviour
from time to time caused her.

She knew then this evening above the dark winter river
that her fury would soon fade, but it made her for the
moment more rather than less resentful. It was little
comfort to know that an hour or two later love would
have changed her mind.

4

WHEN Judith announced her engagement to Anthony Lane, her paternal aunt, who was rather common, congratulated her on being about to marry 'into a place'.

'I always knew you were meant for something special,' she wrote. 'In spite of your poor mother.'

There was land, there were tenants, employees, villagers, dogs, portraits, plantations. To that extent Aunt Edith Fortune would have been satisfied; but the house itself might have surprised her. It looked more like a church than anything else, a delapidated, deconsecrated church with large haphazard windows later added. It had started as a pele tower, embattled, crenellated, and machi-colated by licence granted in 1280 to Humphry Lane, a Wensleydale farmer. Subsequent generations had added to it until in about 1690, the family prospering, a grander house was begun a mile away, and with its beauty as their setting the Lanes went on from strength to strength. In 1863 the house caught fire, no one knew how, and was burnt to the ground.

The old couple of the time moved into the tower, which was then a farm, and the shell of the other house was left crumbling gently, and not without a bizarre beauty, in the middle of its grand abandoned gardens.

There had never been quite the money or the time or the energy to rebuild it; and now there doubtless never would be, not only because of the turning away of the times from that sort of building but because there were no young Lanes.

The tower house would have looked less bleak had there been a lovely garden, but though the deserted garden of the ruined house a mile away flourished, this one had never been a success, and the Wensleydale moors were everywhere the eye could see.

Judith from the first had accorded the house – Harris was its name – her unswerving loyalty. There was no particular reason for this; the house seemed to her simply to demand it, the house and the old man and his stern feared daughter-in-law.

The real church was in fact two miles away, and they drove to it every Sunday, Sir Ralph Lane, Mrs. Lane, and when she was there – which, the winter Sunday after she had given Baldwin Reeves £500, she was – Judith. They used to walk but then the old man got beyond it.

Mr. Wardle, the vicar, had been there now for twenty years, and the excesses of his youth were far behind him. There had been excesses, of a sort, or so Mrs. Lane would have called them. They had included incense, and bells, and acolytes, and very odd ideas about transubstantiation.

Mrs. Lane had been in Moscow when Mr. Wardle, the former incumbent having died, had been inducted at All Saints, Ribblethwaite. She had returned with her young son after her husband's death in 1936 to find that what she called 'decent English Morning Prayer' had been superseded under the new regime by something called 'Sung Eucharist'. This frankly Popish ceremony involved the co-operation of little Willie Judd and even little Johnny Wilson as incense swingers, bell ringers and general antic-performers (this at least was how Mrs. Lane saw it) and necessitated the presence of a much enlarged choir (and therefore much worse, for how could more than six little boys be expected to sing in tune in a village of only seven hundred?) which was kept breathlessly busy throughout the service, alternately chanting, genuflecting and nudging one another – sometimes to prompt, sometimes to snigger.

It must be admitted that quite a large proportion of the congregation enjoyed it. There was more to watch and though the services were inclined to be rather long it made a nice break when Mr. Wardle changed his vestments in the middle, helped by Willie and Johnny, and all that chanting, though a bit doleful, made a change, and of course the new service did include the Communion, killing as it were two birds with one stone.

On the other hand, a great many people were shocked. It was not at all what they were used to, and they doubted, most of them, with a good deal of head-shaking and mouth-pursing, whether it were right. One or two in fact almost considered going over to the Baptists and taking the bus ten miles to Thorpedale every Sunday, but fortunately Mrs. Lane came back in time to render this drastic course unnecessary.

Her first reaction was that the man must be a Socialist. This was not as illogical as it might seem because for Mrs. Lane religion and class were very closely connected. The Church of England, the Conservative Party and the Landed Gentry were the articles of her faith. Anathema to her were atheists, socialists and, equally, common people with no idea of their places and fast people. That is to say, respectful villagers were on one's side, factory workers and the urban lower middle classes were not; good County families were, worldly dukes and people who spent too long in the south of France were not. She had retained this creed unshaken through several years of more or less cosmopolitan life.

Mr. Wardle, therefore, this brash newcomer (probably an atheist too since he was making such a mockery of religion) must be taught his place. It was not a short struggle, for Mr. Wardle, though weak and sentimental, was also obstinate, nor did he at first realise the strength of his opponent; but in the end, and after some sensible advice from the Rural Dean, he capitulated. Decent English Morning Prayer had come back. The only remaining difference of opinion was over the Creed, which Mr. Wardle sang: on this as on every other Sunday Mrs. Lane's deep voice could be heard through the slightly ragged chanting of the rest of the congregation, firmly speaking out her faith.

She was wearing her church tweeds. They were purplish and though well cut had an air about them of immemoriality. She wore them on Sundays all through the winter, with a fur coat over them on the coldest of days; and in the summer there was a grey coat and skirt which took their place. The unvarying nature of what she wore helped to make going to church the ritual it was at Harris, a ritual about which Anthony had always complained, but which Judith, for whom it was unlike anything she had known before, never ceased to observe with curious enjoyment.

With the tweeds went a felt hat from Lincoln Bennett, bought in 1929, three years after her marriage.

As a matter of fact, Mrs. Lane dressed extremely well, for though some of her clothes were like her tweeds, old and indomitable, seeming to have come from a more privileged age, to be surviving in order defiantly to say, like the old reactionaries they were: '*Then* we knew what quality was,' there were also others. The first time Judith had met her future mother-in-law, Mrs. Lane nad asked her to tea at Claridges where she was staying, and had greeted her in exquisite black with diamonds, looking with her white hair and young face immeasurably distinguished. They had had tea and talked politely and Judith had missed not one of Mrs. Lane's gentle meanings. Judith had enjoyed the encounter, but had had no more idea then than she had now of what Mrs. Lane really thought of her.

Mr. Wardle was not encouraged to make long sermons, and Sir Ralph as they emerged from the damp cold church into the dry cold air remarked that the service had taken fifty-one minutes. Everything he did was timed, because he liked timing things. In the same way he would spend hours over his personal accounts, which he entered in the most complicated possible way in several enormous ledgers, not because he was interested to know what he had spent but because he liked doing accounts. In fact they were so complicated that they were often hopelessly inaccurate, and since he had an unshakable faith in his own calculations he was in a continual state of acrimonious correspondence with his bank manager.

Outside the church they had to wait while Miss Kennedy talked to Mrs. Lane. This happened every Sunday, too, except of course when Miss Kennedy went away, but that was very seldom. Miss Kennedy had huge legs and wore all sorts of gay woolly caps and gloves. She ran the Women's Institute, the Mother's Union, the village Conservative Party and the British Legion.

'Perhaps she has designs on Mr. Wardle,' said Judith as she and Sir Ralph walked ahead down the path.

'It's Dudgeon she fancies,' said Sir Ralph. 'She was Liberal till he came along.' Dudgeon was the constituency's Conservative agent.

'But he's so hairy,' objected Judith.

'That's what appeals to her,' said Sir Ralph. 'That's how they like them. Eh, Vicar?' Mr. Wardle was standing at the gate shaking hands with those of his parishioners as could not sidle past without this greeting. 'Isn't that so, Vicar, um?' said Sir Ralph. 'They like them hairy, eh?'

'Yes, indeed, Sir Ralph,' replied Mr. Wardle, confidently but at a loss. 'In this weather particularly, no doubt. And how long is Mrs. Anthony staying? Back tonight? Ah, dear me, yes, dear me.' He stood awkwardly clasping and unclasping his hands, radiating a Christian goodwill which he had never learnt to express, until Mrs. Lane came up, remarked that the congregation was decreasing again and drove her father-in-law and daughter-in-law briskly away in her new Jaguar.

'Have you ever heard of someone called Baldwin Reeves?' asked Judith in the car quite suddenly.

'Baldwin Reeves?' repeated her mother-in-law. 'Wasn't he a friend of Anthony's?'

'Oh, then you've met him?' Judith said.

'My dear, why look so amazed?' said Mrs. Lane. 'I used to see a lot of them all at one time, you know, when I had the flat and they were all at Wellington Barracks. I can't particularly remember meeting that one, only I remember the name because it was unusual. Wasn't he the one that wasn't quite a gentleman?'

'What's his name?' Sir Ralph asked from the back seat. 'What's the fellow's name? What did you say?'

'Baldwin Reeves, Fa,' said Mrs. Lane, in the tone of reproof she automatically adopted when speaking to the old man.

Her husband Geoffrey had called him Fa and so had Geoffrey's silly sister Kate who had married an American millionaire; now only she used the childish name, making it sound each time as if she said it out of spite. 'A friend of Anthony's,' she went on.

'I should hardly have thought he was a friend,' said Judith. 'He struck me as being anything but that.'

'Fatuous name,' said Sir Ralph. 'Bad enough as a surname. Baldwin – oh, well, I suppose you'll be calling your boy Macmillan, Judith. You'd better hurry or it'll be Gaitskell – ha-ha, Gaitskell. Oh, well, ha-ha, Baldwin. I like that.'

'Judith is not married, Fa,' said Mrs. Lane, icily.

'I know,' said Sir Ralph, tetchily. 'I know that. You don't have to tell me that. I know perfectly well all about it. I'm not a moron.'

'Perhaps he was called after the kings of Jerusalem,' said Judith.

'He got into the regiment in the war I believe,' said Mrs. Lane. 'No, I don't think Anthony did see much of him.'

'I met him the other day,' said Judith. 'That is, he came to see me. He was in Korea.'

Mrs. Lane's fine nostrils quivered slightly.

'Really?'

'Yes, and in the prison camp.'

After a little silence, Mrs. Lane turned to look at Judith then smiled at her, then, looking again at the road, put a hand for a moment on her knee and said: 'You must tell me all about it.'

In moments when they were sharing emotions about Anthony they were quite close: if those moments were to be sacrificed they might find themselves almost strangers.

At Harris Judith's secret knowledge seemed more important than it had in London; for she herself had already known a good deal about her husband's faults, but here she was surrounded by reminders that other people had apparently not known, and it made her look at them in a new light, as one looks at an ill person after a little talk in the passage with the doctor. As one can hardly believe that the patient sitting up in bed with books and flowers and grapes can really be ignorant of the evil already destroying him, so Judith wondered that the woman beside her could have failed to notice the cancer in the cherished body of her family.

For her family – first her husband and then her son – had certainly always been the reason for her existence. It was to her devotion in fact that many of his friends had ascribed Geoffrey Lane's rather unexpected marriage – that and of course her beauty.

Geoffrey Lane had been brilliant, so much so that to Judith he was hardly more than a fable. Clever, handsome, rich, his memory seemed to her that of someone always immensely privileged. He had died young, of cancer, when he was Minister in Moscow.

Though she had never got on well with her father-in-law, Grizelda Lane had come to live at Harris, partly no doubt because it would one day be Anthony's. Anthony had grown up there, and it was one of Mrs. Lane's blindnesses, whether wilful or otherwise, that she had failed to recognise his dislike of the place.

The house, all the same, still held the relics of his childhood. His nursery, untenanted, still housed a lonely rocking-horse; his battered books filled a landing staircase; and downstairs where the coats were kept was still an assortment of scarves and odd caps, Wellington boots and once loved, now meaningless, sticks and stones.

The chief relic, of course, was Nanny, who knew the whole story from the beginning, and who had stood by her bereaved mistress with an aggressive staunchness which had easily withstood Sir Ralph's early attempts to get rid of her. He had given up hope now of her ever leaving. Only occasionally he would say a little wistfully: 'Ah, Nanny, whatever shall we do without you when you go?' but since she was nearly as old as he was, his thoughts might have been of her death, which was certainly more likely than her dismissal.

Nanny's frustrated instincts, which were presumably responsible for most of her gloominess, were given their only outlet by Judith's dog, on whom she lavished in almost pathological profusion the devotion which rightly belonged to a Lane baby. Bertie, of course, having more wit and less supervision than a baby, lost no opportunity of turning this emotion into food, and came back to

London after every visit to Harris in a state of liverish rotundity.

This particular Sunday morning, however, he had not been clever enough to avoid being plunged into a bath as soon as his owner had left for church (Nanny always went to 'early' and walked all the way). They came back to find him sitting very fluffily in front of the fire eating chocolate biscuits and wearing a blue ribbon round his neck.

'Oh, Nanny, d'you think ribbons, really?' Judith said.

'He likes to look nice,' said Nanny. 'Of course, I can take it off if you don't want him to have it. I only thought it would be nice for him to be nice and clean and looking nice, but of course, if you want me to take it off. . . .'

'Oh, no, no, of course not. He looks lovely,' said Judith. 'I only didn't want him to look too sissy.' She sat down beside him.

'Oh, well, if you want me to take it off. . . .' said Nanny.

'Oh, no,' said Judith. 'Don't let's take it off.'

'He doesn't think he looks sissy, do you, my duck?' said Nanny. 'But, of course, if you want me to take it off. . . .'

'What train did you say you were catching, Judith?' Sir Ralph fortunately broke in.

The seven-ten,' answered Judith. There was only one train on Sunday evening, but Sir Ralph never failed to show the liveliest interest in the time of its departure.

'The seven-ten, ah, yes,' he said. 'Seven-ten is it? And that gets you up at about – what – eleven-thirty I suppose?'

'Yes, about that,' said Judith.

'About eleven-thirty?' said Sir Ralph. 'Like me to look it up for you? Make quite sure of the time?'

'Yes, please,' said Judith kindly.

He went to fetch the time-table and when he came back and found her alone he said, surprisingly: 'This fellow Reeves. Nice fellow?'

'Not very, no,' said Judith.

'You know,' said Sir Ralph. 'Your mother-in-law. She was very devoted to Anthony.'

'I know,' said Judith.

'Wouldn't like to hear anything anybody might have said who wasn't so fond of him, you know,' said Sir Ralph. 'Take it hard.'

'Oh, I know,' said Judith looking at him. 'I wouldn't tell her – anything of that sort. . . .'

But his eyes went quickly back to his Bradshaw.

'Seven-ten. Yes, here we are,' he said. 'Sundays only, that's it. Only two stops – King's Cross eleven-thirty-three. Now that's quite quick you know. The eleven-ten train on week-days takes longer I think.' He flicked back the pages. 'Now let's see.'

Judith said nothing, seeing that he was determined to return to minutiae; but it was interesting, she thought, that he should have noticed in what she had said about Baldwin Reeves, or in her voice as she said it, something that Mrs. Lane had evidently quite missed.

Feliks had found a princess. He could talk of nothing else.

'Another one?' Judith said. 'But look at Curtseys and Cuirasses. Look at that awful king.'

'My dear,' said Feliks. 'This one is twenty years younger than Anna Sophia, thirty times more intelligent than the king. And she can write. I asked her for a synopsis on Saturday and here it is this morning.'

Judith took the three pages of adventurous typing which he was brandishing.

'I suppose you promised her a contract on this,' she said.

'If we liked it,' said Feliks. 'If we liked it. She's penniless of course. Read it, Judith, read it. All that stuff about the Kaiser and the story about Curzon. Do admit.'

'You sound as if you had a good Saturday to Monday,' said Judith, who resented the rather inept Nancy Mitford-isms which were likely to result from his smarter week-ends.

He had been staying with one of his most useful clients, Lord Sanderson, whose father (a Lloyd George creation) had among other things built an enormous house in Surrey in the shape of a four-leafed clover. There the present peer entertained with appropriate lavishness, and there Feliks Hanescu, bright-eyed and attentive, was often to be seen 'picking up' as he put it 'threads'.

'No, but Judith, really she's quite fun, this one,' said Feliks, adding encouragingly, 'She lives with a window-cleaner.'

'A window-cleaner?' said Judith. 'How d'you know?'

'George told me, after she'd gone,' said Feliks. 'Awfully handsome, apparently. He was cleaning windows one day, she took a fancy to him, asked him in – and he never got away again. Even you must admit that's quite an achievement for a woman of fifty-two with no money at all and a very nasty house.'

'Well, but she's not going to write about the window-cleaner, is she?' said Judith.

'A really horrid house,' Feliks went on, seeing her interest was nonetheless aroused. 'And she takes in lodgers, but such nice ones, she told me – an Obolenski, such a handsome boy, a Lichtenstein, and a second cousin of King Farouk's first wife, *faute de mieux*, as she puts it. No, but Judith seriously, she has been quite grand, and she does know all these people, and I do think she'd sell.'

'You think she'd look good on the list,' said Judith. 'I know that's what it is. Well, let her write a bit first, that's all I ask, a chapter or two.'

'Oh, certainly, she can do that,' said Feliks.

He went back into his office saying: 'Get me her number, darling, would you?' to Miss Vanderbank, and Judith went on into her own room.

The telephone rang, and the voice she heard when she answered seemed for some reason so familiar that she expected it to be someone she knew much better than Baldwin Reeves.

'What about lunch?' he said.

'Lunch?' she repeated.

'Yes, today,' he said. 'I'll pick you up.'

'I'm afraid I can't possibly have lunch with you,' said Judith, coldly.

'Tomorrow,' he said. 'Oh, no, tomorrow's no good. Wednesday?'

'I'm afraid not,' said Judith.

'Thursday?' he said.

'No, I'm sorry,' said Judith. 'I am afraid I can't have lunch with you,' and she put the receiver down.

She looked into the next room. 'Polly, would you mind not putting that man through again. His name's Baldwin Reeves. I don't want to speak to him.'

'All right,' said Miss Vanderbank, writing down the name in her huge irregular hand.

Judith had no idea what his motives could be in ringing her up. Did it mean that he already wanted more money? Could he seriously imagine that she would accept his invitation?

Apparently he did, for a few days later he rang her up at home with a similar request. Again she put the receiver down, and after that she let Jean-Claude answer the telephone. The next week Miss Vanderbank told her that a literary agent she knew wanted to speak to her, but when she lifted the receiver it was Baldwin Reeves.

'Oh, for God's sake,' she said. 'What is the point of this?'

'I simply want you to have lunch with me,' he said. 'Wouldn't it be simpler if you did?'

'I don't want to have lunch or anything else with you ever,' said Judith petulantly.

Not long after that he walked into the office, asked which was Mrs. Lane's room, and before Miss Vanderbank could stop him strode masterfully past her and confronted Judith.

Judith was discussing children's books with a shy bearded man, who wore sandals, gave the appearance of being intensely intellectual and was in fact the author of a series of books for children from two to six on agricultural implements. *Tommy the Tractor* had been the first. In front of Judith now was *Miranda the Mower*, just out, and on the author's knee his latest manuscript *Herbert the Hedgecutter*.

'So sorry to disturb you,' shouted Baldwin, gaily. 'Do go on. Pay no attention to me – I'm afraid I'm horribly early. I'll just sit down here very quietly – I'm sure Mr. . . . I'm afraid I don't know your name? . . . won't mind?'

'Oh no, no, not at all, so sorry, Graham Wood's the

name, just leaving,' said the author who spoke very quickly.

'Would you mind waiting outside?' said Judith, without looking up from her desk.

'Oh, but the other room seemed so full of activity. I should hate to disturb it,' said Baldwin. 'And if Mr. Wood really doesn't mind. . . .'

'Oh no, no not at all, just leaving,' said Mr. Wood.

'I'd rather you waited in there if you don't mind,' said Judith going towards the door to open it.

Baldwin laughingly interposed himself, 'No, no, I want to see you at work,' he said. 'Please don't make me go.'

'Oh please, not on my account, just leaving, luncheon engagement, business all done, just leaving,' said Mr. Wood.

Defeated, Judith went back to her desk.

'I think we had just finished,' she said stiffly to Mr. Wood. 'I'll keep this one, and you'll think over the idea for the other series, won't you?'

'Yes yes yes, indeed,' he rose uncertainly to his feet, then bobbed down again to extract a neatly rolled plastic mackintosh from under his chair. 'By all means, yes yes, and then the other small point will be I know, your usual promptitude, I'm sure, yes rather.'

'I'll remind the accountant,' said Judith.

'Oh many thanks, many many thanks, no don't see me out, good-bye good-bye, good day sir, good day. . . .' Mr. Wood bowed himself out.

Baldwin shut the door behind him.

'I hope all your clients are as eager to please,' he said.

'What are you doing here?' said Judith.

'I've come to take you out to lunch.'

'I'm afraid I can't have lunch with you.'

'You haven't any other engagement – I asked your charming secretary.' (He had not in fact done this.)

Judith sighed. 'I don't want to have lunch with you and I can think of no conceivable reason why you should want to have lunch with me.'

'Is it so unusual?' he asked. 'For people to want to have lunch with you?'

'It's unprecedented,' she said. 'For someone in your position.'

'Good,' he said. 'I think that's an admirable reason why we should do it. Come on, I've got a taxi waiting.'

He opened the door.

'Ah, this must be Mr. Hanescu. Didn't we meet once with Gavin Miller?'

Feliks, who prided himself on his memory, said: 'Of course, in the House of Lords. Have you seen him lately?'

'Yes, I see a good deal of him,' said Baldwin. 'Now there's a man whose life story you should get.'

'We've tried,' said Feliks. 'Like most publishers in London. I wish you'd use your influence.'

'Oh, my influence is negligible,' said Baldwin. 'But I love using it.'

Judith went to get her coat, with a vague idea that she might slip out before they noticed her, but she returned to find them sitting in the front office, drinking sherry. Her other hope, which had been to make some sort of appeal to Feliks, faded when she saw the friendliness with which they were already treating each other.

'Sherry, my dear?' Feliks asked her.

'No, thank you.'

'Oh, well, I expect you want to get off to your lunch,' said Feliks, getting to his feet. 'What am I doing darling?' he shouted to Miss Vanderbank. 'Talk it all over with Judith,' he added to Baldwin. 'She's the one who makes all the decisions. He's full of ideas for us, Judith.'

'Of course I shall demand an enormous cut,' said Baldwin.

'We always give enormous cuts,' said Feliks. 'That's why everyone loves us.'

Miss Vanderbank approached, as discreetly as anyone could who was carrying an ostentatiously large diary.

'Ah yes,' said Feliks, glancing at it. 'I'm off into the fabulous world of films in ten minutes. It makes publishing seem so genteel. Well, good-bye, have a lovely lunch. What about writing yourself? You do a bit of journalism, don't you?'

'I've got a wonderful idea for a detective story,' said Baldwin. 'I've been meaning to write it for months.'

'Write it, my dear fellow, write it,' said Feliks, and disappeared into his office.

'Well, we must be off,' said Baldwin, rolling his eyes appreciatively at Miss Vanderbank who blushed. 'Come along.'

Downstairs he hailed a taxi.

'I thought you had one waiting,' said Judith.

'I was lying,' he said. 'The Caprice,' he added, to the driver.

'Oh no,' said Judith, 'I have to be back very early. Can't we just have a sandwich?'

'Something light?' said Baldwin. 'Wheelers then,' he said to the driver. 'Not the Caprice, Wheelers.'

Judith stared out of the window.

'How's Bertie?' asked Baldwin.

'All right,' said Judith. 'He won't come out when it's raining so I had to leave him behind. Are you doing this because you like seeing me embarrassed? Does it amuse you to put me into a position which makes any outside observer think I am behaving like a child with the sulks?'

'No no no,' said Baldwin. 'What nasty motives you ascribe to me. Do you always make people account for themselves in this way? Perhaps I just wanted to show you my new suit. Do you like it? Tell me frankly, really, what do you think?'

'It's very nice,' said Judith, without enthusiasm.

'Nice stuff, feel,' he said, holding out his arm. 'Neat, businesslike, not exaggerated, that's what I wanted – but I do think it's quite well cut, don't you? And the hat, what d'you think? Rising young barrister? Or not?'

'Oh, I'm sure you'll rise,' she said.

'Of course I shall,' he said. 'Here we are now. My secretary booked a table.'

'But you didn't know you were coming here,' said Judith.

'Hush!' he said.

There was no table, so they sat at the counter and he offered her oysters.

'Yes please,' said Judith.

'You know, I quite thought you were going to refuse

to eat,' he said. 'One potted shrimp and a piece of toast melba – that's what I was afraid of.'

'I was going to,' said Judith. 'But then I thought I might as well make it expensive for you.'

'Good, good, good,' he laughed. 'That's what I like to see. What about some really expensive champagne?'

'I suppose so,' she said.

He ordered it. 'We must celebrate,' he said.

'Why?' said Judith.

He laughed again. 'Because, as you say, the whole thing's unprecedented. And then, apart from anything else, I am genuinely interested in the publishing business. Tell me about it – I'm completely ignorant. Is there money in it these days? How do you get along as a small firm? Do you have big overheads, is it a risky business? You've been going quite a short time, haven't you?'

She answered at some length. After all, she could hardly sit in silence, and it seemed a safe subject. His comments were intelligent and surprisingly brief – she had thought he would have liked talking better than listening. She found herself interested. Publishing had, especially since Anthony's death, absorbed a good deal of her thought and attention.

He seemed to know most of the books they had published, asked her about their authors, then about agents, and foreign publishing, and films, and books in general, turning out to be well-read and discriminating. Then, when the conversation and the champagne had driven away a little of her furious distrust, he began to make suggestions – ideas that might just catch the tide of fashion and become best-sellers, if someone could be found to write them up, distinguished people whose memoirs might be obtainable, people he knew who might be useful. Then, before she could think he was being too interfering, he asked her advice about his own idea for a thriller, to be based on his experience in the Army in Berlin just after the war, told her the whole plot and aroused her interest to such an extent that she could hardly have prevented herself from offering suggestions.

Only as they left the restaurant did she remind herself that this was the man who was blackmailing her because he knew that her dead husband had been a coward. The fact that she had momentarily failed to behave as if she were conscious of this made her now feel that she had been in some way worsted.

She stood in silence on the pavement while they waited for a taxi, wondering how she could get rid of him for the future, how she could in some way undermine his self-confidence, and make sure that he left her feeling that she, not he, had the upper hand.

She was so absorbed that she failed to notice that one of the passers-by had stopped to greet Baldwin, and when the latter said to her: 'Do you know Thomas Hood?' she thought at first he was talking about the nineteenth century poet, and was going to reply that she had read very little by him, when she saw a thin, brown-haired boy holding out his hand to her. She took it and smiled vaguely.

'How d'you do,' said Thomas Hood, politely.

A taxi drew up and he raised his hat to them again as they drove off.

Judith was still wondering what to say to prevent Baldwin from coming to see her again; but partly through failure to find the actual words, she found that they had stopped outside the office before she had spoken at all.

Annoyed, she got out of the taxi without looking at him, and merely saying good-bye without thanking him for the lunch, walked away. When she got back to the office, she was surprised to find that it was already three o'clock.

5

SERENA DRYDEN was coming out next season. The party her parents gave for her early in March was described, oddly, by Lady Dryden, as 'a sort of pre-*pre*, you know.' In fact, it was not a pre-pre, it was a pre – she had already had a pre-pre – but Lady Dryden was an inexact sort of woman.

Serena's coming-out gave a fillip to the campaign which Lady Dryden had been waging for the last twelve years or more. It gave this indefatigable mother an excuse really to hurl herself again into the fight, in which, since Frances's coming-out four years ago, she had held only ever less powerful weapons. Jane, thank goodness, was married, not brilliantly, but well enough; but there was still Lucinda, still Victoria, still Frances, and now the newest, brightest hope, Serena, whose hair was really golden, not just mousy like the others.

Serena's best friend at school had been Emma Hood – 'very suitable,' her mother said. 'Such charming people and a nice brother and the father dead' – but Emma and her mother being on a visit to some American relations, only Thomas walked his slow way up the wide stairs that evening, greeted his many hostesses with his usual impeccable politeness and settled down by a plate of sandwiches perfectly happy to stand and stare.

The room was crowded; Lady Dryden's parties always were, but there were not a great many people he knew. He talked to one or two of them, had a brief word with Serena, who thought all men impossible until they were forty, and promised several girls whose names he did not know that he would give their love to Emma when he next wrote.

Although his self-possession was often commented

upon as being unusual in someone of his age (and it was usually ascribed to the fact that he had been educated largely in France) he had not yet got over a certain difficulty in looking at the faces of people to whom he was talking, less, probably, through doubt as to what he might see in their eyes as through fear of what they might read in his. This, combined with the fact that one of his eyes gave the impression of being less open than the other, made him look a little sly and also rather tired. He had a deep voice, the volume of which he never seemed quite able to control, so that he appeared afraid of making either too much or too little noise. He spoke slowly, but with a great air of earnestness, enunciating his words badly. He was not tall, but lean and healthy-looking.

When he had finished the plate of sandwiches he decided that the prettiest girl in the room was a fair-haired one in scarlet chiffon who was waving a long black cigarette holder and punctuating her conversation with not wholly successful little twirls on one heel. He made his way across to the window in order to examine her from a different angle. Pleased with her left profile, he approached and offered her a cigarette.

'Oh, my dear, how did you know I was panting for another?' she said. 'How terribly sweet of you. Isn't it too awful? I'm trying to give it up but I simply can't. Could you live without it?'

'As a matter of fact, I do,' said Thomas.

'I know, isn't it awful, so do I,' said the girl, standing on one foot, her gaze darting round the room.

'I mean that I don't smoke,' said Thomas.

'You don't smoke?' she said, her huge blue eyes for a moment resting on him. 'Oh, you lucky thing! But you probably drink frightfully. Men always do.'

'Oh, d'you think so?' said Thomas, politely. 'Don't you drink then?'

'Drink? Me?' said the girl, her eyes again like short-sighted searchlights sweeping the sea of faces. 'My dear, I can't stop. Oh, my God, there's Johnny Whitfield, you'll have to stand in front of me. My dear, how too awful. Has he gone?'

'I'm afraid I don't know him,' said Thomas.

'You don't know him?' she said. 'Goodness, how lucky. It's too awful, I can't possibly tell you what happened. Has he gone?'

'I can't tell you because I don't know what he looks like,' said Thomas. 'Has he got a moustache?'

She burst out laughing. 'A moustache? Johnny?' She stood on one leg, clasping the other slim ankle behind her back. 'You *are* funny!'

A pink-faced young man approached, waving both hands behind his ears, and saying in a mock deep voice: 'Ha-ha, who have we here?'

'Johnny *darling*!' cried the girl throwing her arms round his neck. 'I'm never going to speak to you again after you pushed me into that fountain!'

Turning away, Thomas caught sight of Judith Lane. She was standing, talking, in a corner, where he had not noticed her earlier. In black, and with her dark hair pushed away from her face, she looked, this particular evening, beautiful and rather melancholy. She and Anthony had been suitable 'young marrieds' to be asked to Lady Dryden's parties, and somehow Judith had never been crossed off her list.

Thomas went up to her and reminded her that they had met in the street a few days ago, when Baldwin Reeves had introduced them.

'How clever of you to remember,' said Judith.

'You didn't look at me,' said Thomas, in his serious way. 'So how could you remember? But I looked at you.'

'I'm sorry I was so rude,' said Judith.

'I didn't mean that at all,' said Thomas. 'Are you Russian?'

'No,' said Judith.

'Oh,' he said. 'I've never met a Russian woman, but I always imagined somehow they looked like you. But perhaps they don't.'

'I thought they were fat with bobbed hair and greasy faces,' said Judith. 'I don't know whether that's what you meant.'

'No, not that sort so much,' said Thomas, 'I meant the ones who escape on sledges in the middle of the night all wrapped in white furs and chased by wolves.'

'That's much better,' said Judith.

'In *War and Peace*, though, she had a hairy face, d'you remember?' said Thomas.

'Don't you think it was more in the nature of a soft down?' said Judith.

'Do you read Russian novels?' he asked.

'Well, I don't read them, no, really,' she said. 'I have at various times. I had a passion for Turgenev once, I remember.'

'Oh,' he said. 'Are you married?'

'I was, but my husband died.'

'Good Heavens,' he said. 'How awful. What did he die of?'

'He was killed in Korea.'

'I see. How ghastly.' Impressed, he would have liked to have gone on talking about this, but instead he asked her if she thought Baldwin Reeves was clever.

'Quite clever, I think,' said Judith. 'But not at all nice.'

'No, but still . . .' said Thomas. 'So many young people these days seem to have no ambition. I think they ought to have it, don't you? But they seem to think of nothing but being secure and comfortable and out of trouble. I suppose it's the war. Have you got any children?'

'No,' said Judith.

'I don't like children very much,' said Thomas, comfortingly.

'And are you going to be great?' asked Judith.

'I'm supposed to be going into the Diplomatic Service,' said Thomas. 'But I've got to go to Oxford first for three years. It's an awful bore.'

'A bore?'

'Three years,' said Thomas. 'It's such a waste of time. And then the Army. Oh, I'd better get you another drink.' He took her glass, and walked away, then came back to say, 'Don't go away, will you?'

Lucinda Dryden, passing, asked Judith if she would like to be introduced to anybody.

'As a matter of fact,' said Judith, 'I'm in the middle of a conversation with someone simply sweet whose name I don't know. He's very young, and I'm feeling tremendously grown-up.'

'Oh, Thomas Hood,' said Lucinda. 'I saw you talking to him. He is rather nice, isn't he? Mummy thinks he'd do for Serena.'

Judith said: 'Shall I tell him how wonderful Serena is?'

With this in mind, she asked him when he came back whether he had known the Drydens long.

'Serena's a friend of my sister Emma,' he answered. 'They're both coming out this year, but Emma and my mother are in America until next month.'

'Then you I suppose will be coming out too,' said Judith. 'I mean you'll go to dances every night.'

'I'm going to Israel,' said Thomas. 'Have you ever been there? I've got a great friend whose father's a Cabinet Minister there – he's going next month and I want to go with him, if they'll let me – my mother I mean. I want to see it, I'd like to help – well, I mean, how can I really? – but don't you think it's exciting, starting a new country?'

Flushed, he was desperately anxious that she should share his enthusiasm, that she should treat it without the disapproval with which his mother regarded it. To his relief, she seemed to take it quite as a matter of course, and in his excitement he told her everything he knew or had ever thought about Israel, until, seeing her look round the now gradually emptying room, he said: 'I'm afraid I must be boring you. I'm sorry I went on so long.'

'No, I'm very interested. I should say if I wasn't,' said Judith. 'But I think I ought to go soon.'

'Will you have dinner with me?' he asked. 'Oh, no, you're probably doing something.'

She tried to refuse, thinking he was probably asking her simply because he thought he ought to, and also not certain whether he might not become boring after a time, but in the face of his evident disappointment she asked him instead to come back to dinner with her, and went off to telephone Jean-Claude. It was, after all, a diversion: her life lately had been too full of Baldwin Reeves and the apprehensions and memories aroused by him.

'I ought to warn you that the door will be opened by a midget,' she said on the way. 'People are sometimes surprised. It's like that game that always used to reduce me to hysteria as a child – people putting their heads

round the door where you don't expect them, coming in
on their hands and knees and so on, you know what I
mean.'

'Why do you have a midget?' he asked.

'I found him in Paris,' she replied. 'After Anthony died
– my husband – my mother-in-law gave me some money
to go abroad for a holiday, and she suggested that I should
stay with various people, to take my mind off it. So in
Paris I stayed with some people I didn't know very well
– he was assistant military attaché, and his wife was very
pretty and we went to lots of parties and I hated it more
and more – oh, well, that's neither here nor there. Jean-
Claude was a relation of their cook's, and he was always
hanging round, muttering and complaining, which is
what he does all the time. One day I got into conversation
with him, and it was rather comforting to find someone
who hated everybody even more than I did. He told me
how he hated the French, they were so mean – he's
French himself, of course, and terribly mean – so I offered
him a job in England. That's all.'

In spite of her warning, Thomas was taken aback by
Jean-Claude's usual ferocious manner.

'Are you sure he's safe?' he asked, when the midget
had gone downstairs.

'Oh, he has a heart of gold really,' said Judith. 'At least
I suppose he has. I know very little about him,
considering we live in the same house. He never goes out
or sees anyone. I tried to make him at first, but he says
he doesn't want to. I think food's the only thing that
interests him – it's the only thing he talks about with any
enthusiasm. He has a little stool so that he can reach the
stove. I'm terribly fond of him really, but I've no particular
reason to suppose he likes me, except that he stays here.'

The dinner was certainly delicious, but Thomas was in
that particular respect not the perfect guest he was in
almost every other way. Food to him was merely a necessary means of subsistence. The house in general, though,
delighted him. He noticed everything, and after dinner,
examining her books, asking her about her life, he talked
so much she wondered, much as she liked him, whether
he would ever go.

'You're getting tired,' he said at last. 'I'll go at once.
I'm sorry I've talked so much – I don't usually. I really
don't.'

She was sitting on the sofa with Bertie beside her. 'I've
loved it, really,' she said.

'Do you go out a lot, what do you do?' he asked. 'No,
I ask too many questions, don't I? Do you have lots of
lovers, though, being a widow, I mean?'

'Not at the moment, no,' said Judith, smiling.

'You don't mind my asking, do you?' he said. 'I mean,
I was just interested. Do you not because you think it's
wrong?'

'I don't really want to,' said Judith. 'I suppose I may
suddenly feel a tremendous need for a lover one day – in
which case it will be time enough to consider the moral
problem, don't you think?'

'Could it be me?' he said.

'Who be you?' she said.

'When you need one, I mean,' he said. 'A lover.'

'Oh,' said Judith. 'Don't you think I should be a bit old
for you?'

'No,' he said.

Seeing that she had offended him, Judith said: 'Oh
well, I can't say I anticipate its happening in the immediate future – this tremendous need, I mean – so I don't
think we need worry for a bit.'

'Oh, that's all right,' said Thomas. 'I don't mind how
long it is. I must go now. Would you like me to put Bertie
out for you first, then you needn't get cold?'

'That's a wonderful idea,' said Judith, touched. 'Go on,
Bertie.'

According to his nightly custom, Bertie rolled over very
slowly and lay with his feet in the air and his eyes shut.
Thomas picked him up and carried him, hot and heavy,
out into the street.

It was not until over a month later that Baldwin Reeves
asked Judith for some more money.

He had been into the office several times since she had
had lunch with him, and his friendship with Hanescu

was advancing rapidly, strengthened by the fact that he had obtained for the latter an invitation to a very promising party. Fisher was impressed by him, Miss Vanderbank thought him awfully attractive. When Judith told Feliks that she had reason to believe he was an unpleasant character and that she herself was particularly anxious never to see him again, Feliks showed little sympathy.

'This is not like you,' he said. 'Do you think I can't look after myself? For Heaven's sake, I'm an unpleasant character myself. Perhaps that's why I like Mr. Reeves. If you don't like him, you needn't see him. But he can be useful to us you know – he's got a lot of contacts.'

Judith had resigned herself to hearing from time to time that cheerful voice in Feliks's room, and to passing him occasionally in the outer office. Fortunately his interest in her seemed to have waned; he confined himself to a polite greeting. She kept *The Times Literary Supplement* and the *Bookseller* for reading in the lavatory on the days when he arrived.

She saw Thomas Hood once or twice. He brought his friend David Weitzmann to dinner, a bright-eyed witty boy, the violence of whose opinions about everything she found rather tiring. Thomas's gentler enthusiasms and smaller problems seemed to her much more sympathetic than this boy's sophisticated definiteness; in fact she found herself enjoying the slightly unusual relationship she had with him. Sometimes she felt patronising, often flattered, sometimes he made her feel nostalgic for a time which she had in fact not enjoyed, a time when life had seemed so important and so unfair, when one had worried about one's soul. There were not, after all, so many years between them, but he was at so different a stage that she sometimes felt there were far more. He was simpler than she had been, and more impatient; yet he could on occasions, just as she was on the point of an indulgent laugh, make an observation of such ruthless penetration that she felt she had misjudged him. He could be silly, but even that she rather enjoyed.

One evening she sent Jean-Claude to see a French film at the Classic cinema. From time to time she would insist on his going out, and she found that the cinema was the outing he least disliked. Her first thought when in answer to a knock she opened the door and saw Baldwin Reeves was that he must have known Jean-Claude was out. The thought that he might have been watching the house for days was so disturbing that she let him come in and follow her into the drawing-room before she could protest. She finally told herself that it must be a coincidence: but all the same she did not like to ask him.

He was looking pale, and, rather to her relief, did not greet her with the joviality he affected in the office.

'I'm afraid I must ask you for money,' he said without preliminaries.

'Why?' she asked.

'The £500 didn't go far,' he said. 'I had a lot of debts.'

'How much do you want?' she asked.

'I should like £100 now, and another £300 by the end of the month,' he said.

'I refuse to give it to you,' said Judith.

'Right,' he said, apparently unsurprised.

He drew a large unsealed envelope out of his pocket. 'I shall post this as soon as I leave this house.' He put it back in his pocket and picked up his hat.

'I should like to see it please,' said Judith.

'Certainly.' He handed her the envelope. 'Incidentally, I have plenty of other copies.'

She pulled a thick document out of the envelope. Some newspaper cuttings and photographs fell to the floor. She saw a faded picture of Anthony wearing battledress, leaning against a tank and laughing. She felt sick. Unrolling the document she found a covering letter to James Blow of the *Sunday News*. She skimmed through it. 'Sensational *exposé* . . . name surely not forgotten . . . built up as a hero . . . the scandalous war . . . discomfiture of many people in high places . . . my own reluctance . . . public should know . . . fully documented.' The next page was headed 'Anthony Lane – Hero or Coward?' and several pages of typescript followed.

She handed the envelope back to him.

'I completely fail to understand how you can write anything so appalling,' she said.

'Yes, it's nasty isn't it?' he said. 'I shall try to keep my own name out of it if possible, but I may not be able to.'

She found that he had, quite gently, pushed her back into a chair and given her a cigarette. She looked at him as he lit it.

'You behave so fantastically,' she said. 'That it's quite impossible for me to know what to do. I should like now to have hysterics and throw things at you, but you're so calm, so unlike what you really must be, that I can't do anything. I'm simply bemused.'

'I'll explain myself. It's quite simple.' He had bent down to light her cigarette and now stayed crouching in front of her, talking quickly and rather breathlessly, 'I'm conceited. Rightly or wrongly, I believe myself to be exceptionally talented. All right, I haven't done much so far. I'm thirty-one. I spent nine years in the Army because in 1946 when I signed on for another seven years I was twenty-one and I hadn't a penny. My parents were dead, I had no idea what had happened to my brother. I couldn't afford to qualify myself for a career. So I stayed in the Army and read for the Bar. Now I'm a barrister and doing all right. I'm known to be clever, I'm beginning to be heard of, in another year or two I shall begin to earn some money. I've had articles in weekly papers that get noticed, I know a lot of people, I've fought one election and by the time I've enough money I shall be in Parliament. Already there are people who think of me as a hopeful young Tory. I make speeches, I talk, I write – it doesn't get reported much yet, you wouldn't have heard about it – but it's all building up to something. You see?'

He was now sitting on the floor looking up at her as if with the greatest anxiety that she should understand him.

'Now, I've got to have money. Not a great deal, but some. Without money I can do nothing, I can get nowhere. You might as well be dead as be poor. I'm making a bit, I shall make more. I manage, just, but I need more. You've got some, I know, because of the Lanes. The Lanes are still very rich – I found that out. I know that even apart from whatever Anthony left you you can always fall back on them. I have a means of making you give me some of that money. Frankly, I don't want to publish that stuff about Anthony. I liked him. I hated him, and envied him, but at the same time I liked him – one did. But I shall publish it. Don't make any mistake about that. I shall send this envelope off tonight, unless you give me the money.'

He stood up, and began to walk about the room.

'All right, you say it's a filthy thing to do. It's blackmail. It's wicked. I shall go to Hell. But I don't believe in Hell. Or Heaven. I'm not a Christian at all. I don't believe in immortality. I don't believe in anything. Except myself. So why should I conform to the Christian ethic? I believe it's all here on earth, in one life, and that we are what we make ourselves. So I want to make myself something big, something powerful. For that I want, at the moment, money. To get money, the easiest way at the moment – apart from working for it, which I do as well – is to blackmail you.'

He stood looking at her as she sat hunched in her chair, then he turned away and began to walk up and down again.

'At first I rather enjoyed it. I hadn't known at all what it was going to be like, and I found myself enjoying it. Now I don't enjoy it so much, partly I suppose because the novelty's worn off, partly because I like you much better than I thought I was going to. Also I had anticipated having you much more in my power, and that I should have enjoyed.'

After a pause, Judith asked: 'What was your object in coming to my office, making me have lunch with you, making friends with Feliks. Was that all power politics too?'

'Partly,' he answered. 'Partly I wanted to talk to you. You say how can I take someone I am blackmailing out to lunch. I say why not? I don't know many women like you; I find them frightening, and the small hold I have over you means I needn't be so afraid.' He sat down opposite her. 'So you see the whole thing is perfectly simple.'

'And when you have power?' asked Judith.

He smiled. 'I shall exercise it with as much reason and judgment as I shall by then have acquired.'

'It all sounds very dangerous to me,' said Judith. 'And the result, I should have said, of rather indiscriminate reading.'

She was pleased to see him flush; but all the same there was something impressive about his self-confidence, his energy – she had felt it all the time.

'Nobody ever has enough money,' she said. 'So I presume you will go on blackmailing me for ever.'

'No, no, certainly not,' said Baldwin. 'Only in real necessity.'

'What a comfort,' said Judith. 'Well, I will give you £100 tomorrow if you come here at seven o'clock. I can't give you any more.'

'I must have the other £300 by the end of the month,' said Baldwin.

'I haven't got it,' said Judith.

'Then you'll have to ask the Lanes.'

'That's out of the question.'

He went towards the door. 'I'll be here at seven,' he said.

'You've got to help me, Feliks,' Judith said the next morning. 'You're always saying you're my only friend.'

'My dear, there's nothing I wouldn't do for you.'

It was one of Feliks's mornings for looking literary. Leaning back in his chair, with his feet on his desk, he was dangling an untidy manuscript in one hand and had a pile of several more beside him. He was wearing a tweed suit which was rather too big for him, a big floppy bow tie, suede shoes, and a pair of very large horn-rimmed glasses which Judith had never seen before. He was smoking, with apparent distaste, a pipe.

'I don't know about that,' said Judith. 'I asked you to stop seeing Baldwin Reeves and you paid no attention at all.'

'Ah, but that was for your own good,' said Feliks. 'Obviously I can't do anything that would jeopardise our mutual business interests.'

'Whatever the reason?' asked Judith.

Feliks took his feet off the desk. 'All right, tell me,' he said.

'He's blackmailing me,' said Judith.

'Oh, don't be absurd,' said Feliks. 'I never heard anything so ridiculous. My poor darling, what can you conceivably have done to be blackmailed about?'

'It's nothing to do with what I've done,' said Judith.

After a moment's thought, Feliks said: 'Anthony?'

Judith nodded.

'Good Lord,' said Feliks. 'I suppose he was queer.'

'No, of course not,' said Judith. 'Besides, how could anyone blackmail me if he had been? No, I can't tell you what it was, but it was something some people might be quite interested to know, and which his family would be horrified either to be told themselves or to let other people know.'

'Tell the police,' said Feliks.

'I can't,' said Judith. 'All he's got to do is post the story off to a newspaper. He's got it all ready.'

'It's really news, is it?' said Feliks. 'The police might stop it being published.'

'I don't think they'd have any right to,' said Judith. 'And if they did, you know what journalists are – they'd have seen the story – it would get about. Someone would be bound to print it one day. What's to stop them?'

'I suppose you're right,' said Feliks. 'They made such a fuss about him, of course. He really was a hero. It's extraordinary how people still remember – there was a story about him only the other day in some paper I read. And I suppose he really wasn't a hero at all?'

'Something like that,' said Judith.

'I never really saw him in the part of course,' said Feliks. 'Well, well, well. . . .'

'Don't just sit there and grin,' said Judith. 'What am I going to do?'

'God knows,' said Feliks. 'You'll have to pay him, I suppose, if you don't want the story to get out.'

'Of course I don't,' said Judith. 'Surely I ought to defend his reputation if I can? And besides, his mother would probably die.' She paused. 'I thought perhaps – if you talked to him, without of course letting him know I've told you, but just asking him to leave me alone. I mean he might pay more attention to you, being a man – and he says he wouldn't do it unless he was so poor – I mean he's not completely brutal – I suppose.'

Feliks frowned. 'Is there any point in my making an enemy of him?' he said. 'We mustn't underestimate him, you know. He knows a great many people. He could do me a lot of harm.'

'Oh, but. . . .' Judith started, then stopped. 'Then you can't think of anything?' she said.

Feliks looked embarrassed. 'My dear, I can't honestly say I can. I'll think about it. I really will.'

Judith went back to her room, sat down and cried.

Before long Feliks burst in. 'I've had a brilliant idea,' he said. 'Jimmy Chandos-Wright!'

'What about him?' said Judith.

Jimmy Chandos-Wright was a rich retired criminal whose memoirs they had recently published.

'Have him bumped off,' said Feliks, delighted with himself.

'Oh,' said Judith. 'D'you think so?'

'Of course,' said Feliks. 'Jimmy's boys would do a job like this as easy as kiss your hand. I'll ring him up.'

'Well, but someone might find out,' said Judith.

'Are you kidding?' said Feliks. 'They've done hundreds of these jobs. They don't get nabbed.'

He hurried out of the room, leaving Judith dazed at her desk, and came back a few minutes later to say he had arranged for Jimmy Chandos-Wright to come into the office next week.

'There, you see,' he said triumphantly. 'The whole problem solved.'

'Yes, but I don't know that really . . .' Judith began, doubtfully.

'Talk it all over with him, that's all,' said Feliks. 'You're committed to nothing.'

Halfway out of the room he turned back and, putting a hand on her shoulder, said, 'Don't worry. You know there's nothing I wouldn't do for you, don't you?' He kissed her on the forehead.

'Yes,' she said. 'I know.'

6

I T was Spring, even at Harris. Even at Harris, there were buds and lambs and nesting birds. Even at Harris, the air softened and patches of sunlight scurried in front of the huge cloud shadows across the moors.

The gardens of the other, burnt, house were famous for their daffodils. They grew all round the edges of what had once been the lawn; even the shrubbery was now full of them; they were all over the woods and the lake reflected thousands of them. Later on there would be a carpet of lilies of the valley, and of course there were the rhododendrons. That was what had happened when the place was abandoned.

Nanny had read that it was going to be a bad summer. Every time the sun, a little doubtfully, came out, every time a window was opened or Mrs. Lane went out without her gloves, Nanny said: 'They say this is the only mild weather we shall get this year. They say it's going to be the coldest summer on record, and the wettest. Terrible, isn't it, how the weather's been lately. They say it's nothing to do with the atom bomb experiments, but I wonder. I just wonder, that's all. They wouldn't like it to get about that it was, would they? Naturally they say it's nothing to do with the atom bomb. Naturally. But I just wonder.'

Mrs. Lane gardened, and drove to committees on this and that in her powerful car – she was a Rural District Councillor. She was making, very slowly and with exquisite care, a new set of chair seats in *petit point* for the dining-room, and in the evenings she would sit sewing for hours, in silence. No one knew what, if anything she was thinking.

Sir Ralph, encouraged by the milder weather to loiter

too long in the garden, had a bad attack of lumbago, and gave vent to his annoyance in a ferocious letter to his bank manager.

'I've really caught him out this time,' he said to Judith. 'Fellow can't add. Or else he's trying to swindle me. What's the use of a bank manager who can't add?'

'But d'you suppose he does his own adding?' asked Judith gently.

'Of course he does,' said Sir Ralph. 'What's he for if he doesn't? He's not the Governor of the Bank of England. Of course he does his own adding. Trying to cheat me, that's what it is. He's completely left out a cheque for £50 I paid in last week. Ha. Thinks I'm too silly to notice I suppose. I've written him a snorter, a real snorter. Dignified, but a snorter. Teach him his place.'

He was sitting at his desk in the library, with four large ledgers beside him and two more open in front of him. The reason for this quantity was partly his complicated system of checking and counter-checking, and partly because he believed that it was much safer to have two or three accounts at the bank rather than only one – in some obscure way he felt that it fooled the bank manager.

'Well, of course, it's all a great problem, isn't it, money. . . .' Judith said, looking out of the window.

'Money?' said Sir Ralph. 'One of the most interesting things in the world. And sex, I suppose, and possibly politics. Talking about politics, how's your friend Ramsay Macdonald Jones?'

'He really is a problem,' said Judith. 'Baldwin Reeves.'

'Told you the story about Ramsay Macdonald didn't I?' said Sir Ralph.

'Yes you did,' said Judith.

'Oh. Pity. Problem is he?' said Sir Ralph. 'Making a nuisance of himself?'

'Yes,' said Judith. 'In a way.'

'In the prison camp with Anthony was he?' said Sir Ralph. 'They made them get up early I imagine, there.'

'Get up early?' said Judith. 'I suppose so.'

'Don't suppose they gave them a very good breakfast either,' said Sir Ralph. 'What? Some sort of porridge or something, was it?'

'I don't know,' said Judith. 'I didn't ask.'

'Oh,' said Sir Ralph. 'Like to check that addition for me?' He handed her a sheet of paper. 'She takes away the nibs you know. Still, this is a neat page, a neat month April.'

'It looks all right to me,' said Judith, giving him back his calculations.

'I don't often make a mistake,' said Sir Ralph. 'Anthony not behave well?'

'No,' said Judith.

'I knew him very well, you know,' said Sir Ralph. 'Don't think I didn't. Had no father, of course, poor boy. H'm. Better not tell his mother. Wouldn't like it.'

'No, I won't,' said Judith.

'The trouble is,' said Sir Ralph. 'The trouble is I can't get him to send my statement in on the last day of the month instead of the first day of the next month. I like to keep the whole thing up to date to the day, you see.'

There was silence. Getting to her feet, Judith walked slowly over to the window and stood staring out, waiting.

After perhaps as much as ten minutes, Sir Ralph said: 'I wonder if I could get him to send me fortnightly statements? Might keep him up to the mark a bit.'

After another long pause, Judith said: 'He wants money.'

'Of course he does,' said Sir Ralph. 'That's why he cheats me. But he's got his salary, hasn't he?'

'I meant Baldwin Reeves,' said Judith.

'Oh him,' said Sir Ralph. 'Fatuous name.' He added: 'Money? Why?'

'So that no one shall know about Anthony.'

Sir Ralph frowned. 'Sounds a funny sort of fellow.'

'I've given him £600 so far,' said Judith.

'Oh, no no no,' Said Sir Ralph, with sudden emphasis. 'That won't do at all. Can't have that. You must allow me to regard this completely as my affair. I shall reimburse you for what you have already given him and any other demands you must pass straight on to me. Is that understood?'

'But no, I didn't mean that,' said Judith.

'There's no question about it,' said Sir Ralph. 'Why should you pay? It was my blood, my dear, not yours.'

'I don't want the money back, really,' said Judith, tearfully.

'I've got a new cash book here, a perfectly good one,' said Sir Ralph. 'I shall keep a record of the whole business. Now does this bring you up to date?'

'Well, yes, I think so,' said Judith.

'If he asks for more, let me know at once,' said Sir Ralph, writing busily. 'He'll wonder what all this is about, I daresay.'

'The bank manager will, you mean?' said Judith.

'Of course he will,' said Sir Ralph.

'You can't think of any way out of it, I suppose?' said Judith. 'I have tried to, but I don't see what else we can do.'

'You don't know his mother as I do,' said Sir Ralph. 'You don't, you know. Bad for the Government too. Bad all round. Bad for morale. Besides, you know, disgrace is disgrace, whatever the modern idea may be. We have to defend his honour, for all he didn't himself. Sorry for you, my dear – unpleasant business. Sounds a nasty fellow, Reeves.'

'I'm so glad I told you,' said Judith.

'We'll deal with it,' said Sir Ralph. 'I'll keep an exact record – that's the best thing, I think. He'll wonder, I daresay. Still you've got to keep a check on them – that'll keep him on his toes.' He reached for his cheque book. Judith was not quite certain whether he was talking about his bank manager or his blackmailer.

The dying Othello clawed the curtains of Desdemona's white and crimson bed. His black hand reached her golden hair, his tortured face bore down upon her white serene one; the watchers in the shadows stood motionless; sobbing and singing Othello died, and the curtain fell.

The applause broke, and swelled. The huge cast bowed, and bowed again; then the soloists appeared, Iago, then Desdemona, then Othello.

'They'll get Kubelik up in a minute,' the man next to Baldwin Reeves said, stamping his feet. And there sure enough he was and the man beside Baldwin cried 'Bravo! Bravo!'

Acclaiming again the two principals who, splendidly dressed and grandly smiling, kept up the illusion of being altogether larger than life, Baldwin's eyes filled with tears. The opera itself had been wonderfully moving; for a moment he found the culminating applause almost more so.

On the way out he saw several people he knew, to most of whom he had already spoken in the intervals since he was not a man to hold back once he had seen an acquaintance. He was alone, but wearing a dinner jacket, which made them think, if they thought at all, that he was going on somewhere. This was of course the impression he had intended to give. In fact he took a bus to Parliament Square, and walked along Victoria Street to his flat near Westminster Cathedral.

He was an intelligent man. Judith in her few conversations with him had already discovered this rare quality in him; and because she was something of an intellectual snob it had annoyed her. She would rather not have found her enemy possessed of the quality she most admired.

His behaviour for all that was often far from rational. For instance, his going to Covent Garden in a dinner jacket so that people might not know that his whole evening was in fact to be spent alone was nothing like as petty as some of the ruses to which he would resort in order to impress, or frighten, or otherwise impose himself upon even the least important people. He was unable, or at all events unwilling, to compete on equal terms: he had to be either above or below his rivals. His 'rivals' were of course everyone else in the world. Being below them involved various subterfuges, such as pretending to be completely unable to do certain things which he in fact could do, but badly. For instance, he found certain practical accomplishments, such as driving a car or mending an electric light fuse, extremely difficult. He would therefore make great play with the idea that he found them impossible, and would exaggerate his inefficiency with an appealing air of hopelessness. The same applied to his few social failures. There were one or two people whom he completely failed to charm. Realising this, he would be very rude to them, and then in the same self-deprecating way would tell everyone what had happened, exaggerating both his rudeness and the other person's dislike of him – which had the effect of making him seem disarmingly modest and able to laugh at himself, and of taking the sting out of anything the other person might say about him, he having as it were got it in first.

All these little manoeuvres had been part of his life since his earliest youth. He had been an exceptionally clever little boy. At his grammar school he had been for some time the youngest as well as the poorest boy – his father was a respectable village chemist, but everyone knew that his mother was an invalid and that they had no money at all. Not content with his reputation for brightness, Baldwin had built it up into one of brilliance by concealing the fact that he ever did any work. He would ostentatiously read novels during 'prep.' periods, and play with a white mouse or draw caricatures of the masters in class, so that when he passed all his examinations with distinction his glory was greatly enhanced by the fact that he was known to have done no work at all. In fact, of course, he had worked at home during the night.

Apart from his conceit, Baldwin Reeves had been quite a normal, high-spirited schoolboy, save only in one particular. He very seldom spoke. For one thing, he was overwhelmingly shy. For another, when he was eleven, a boy, rather older than himself, who had been his greatest friend and to whom he had been selflessly devoted, found grander friends and turned against Baldwin, even inciting some of his new friends to bully him. This made Baldwin for some years very bitter against humanity. Then his home life was not happy, his mother being constantly ill and his father's spirit having been quite broken by this misfortune. Also, in spite of his disillusion, he was an emotional boy, and being too young to understand in the least any of his feelings, he was made tongue-tied by them.

However it may have been, his silence, particularly in conjunction with his cleverness, was considered by his masters to be extraordinarily sinister. His perfectly normal naughtiness was made by them into something much more wicked, simply because when they spoke to him about it he would turn completely blank, and none of them ever succeeded in getting a response out of him. This attitude had, of course, its effect on him, and he left school with a definite and flattering conviction that he was damned.

The Army made the great change in him. Sent, by the fortunes of war, into a smart regiment, he learnt quickly – among other things, how to be a gentleman. Again he did well, and again he pretended not to try. There, too, he overcame his shyness, and adopted the habitual jollity which was now second nature to him. He learned to speak better English, and became much more adept at dealing with his fellow men. But he still kept his distance. His women friends were always stupider than he was, and usually common; he had no men friends. He took his Bar exams at an obvious disadvantage, being also in the Army. Pretending to have social engagements which were in fact non-existent was so much a part of his life that he often did it without reason, even half deceiving himself. His ambition was huge, but everything was to be achieved as it were at an angle, not in a straight line.

Lately, for the first time, the points system on which he conducted his relations with other people had been beginning to show its failings. He was now meeting a number of other intelligent people, and the unusual and far from intimate nature of his relations with them made it difficult for him to learn as much from them as he would have liked to. He was quite conscious of this, but did not know what to do about it. In an odd sort of way, it made him insist even more on being always a little different: slightly puzzled, he clung more tenaciously to each little hold he had over anyone.

All this was reflected in his attitude to Judith, over whom he really did have a hold, a hold so strong that, oddly enough, he already found himself being more frank in conversation with her than with anyone else. The fact that he was beginning to doubt whether he really was so different, or at least so damned, made him rejoice in the undoubted unconventionality – to put it at its mildest – of his behaviour to her. For if he was not different and damned then what was he? His self-confidence, though it seemed so vast, was not really strong enough to face a fight on equal terms. Also he was by now attracted to Judith, but here he made a mistake – he thought it was the relationship which attracted him.

The morning after he had been to Verdi's *Othello*, he rang up Miss Vanderbank and asked her to have lunch with him. There were several things about both Judith and the firm of Hanescu Lane which he thought it might be extremely useful for him to know, and Miss Vanderbank had seemed a co-operative source of information.

She, delighted, thanked Goodness she had brought her hat that morning, and tripped happily off to meet him.

She was so easily impressed that he found himself enjoying her company. They had an amusing lunch; he was rather flirtatious and she bridled gaily at each sally. She told him, unintentionally, almost all she knew about Judith, and about the firm.

Miss Vanderbank's only blind spot was Feliks. In spite of everything, including his evident indifference, she loved him. She always had. So when Baldwin asked her about the relations between Judith and Feliks she emphatically, and with a pang of useless jealousy, denied that there was anything between them. Then, as she sometimes did, she became rather sentimental about Judith.

'There she is,' she said. 'So young and everything. And he was so good-looking, the husband, he really was. It's a tragedy really, isn't it? If only she could find a nice husband.' Miss Vanderbank sighed. She had often said the same thing to Fisher in the office, and almost brought tears to the eyes of that sympathetic youth. 'She's so sweet. I'm sure anybody would like to marry her. But of course, I suppose, if you've once been married to someone like him – I mean, he was a hero wasn't he? – it isn't easy to accept a second best. She turns them all

away, you know, and Mr. Hanescu's always saying to
her she should go out more, but she just sits at home
with her little dog and that midget servant. I really believe
they're the only creatures she cares for in the world.'

'Why the midget?' asked Baldwin. 'I thought he was a
most unpleasant creature.'

'Oh, she's fond of him, I don't know why,' said Miss
Vanderbank. 'She brought him back from Paris with her
once, soon after her husband died, and he's been with
her every since. I think he's very devoted to her and that
makes her fond of him, you know.'

'Too fond?' asked Baldwin.

'Don't be ridiculous,' said Miss Vanderbank with spirit.

'Sorry,' said Baldwin, embarrassed. 'I just wondered.'

Feeling that he had lost her sympathy, he changed the
subject, unable all the same to forget the annoyance that
what she had said had caused him. 'What business has
she to be devoted to a dwarf?' he thought later, in the
bus going back to his Chambers.

The thought of the disrespectful little creature lurked
in his mind all day. He worked late, and going back tired
to his gloomy flat he gazed at himself in the mirror, seeing
a slightly dirty face with eyes staring to try to frighten
himself, and said: 'The dwarf must go.'

When Judith went to the office the next day, she found
Fisher uneasily lounging about in her room.

He had a Christian name – it was Henry – but, in so
far as he was known at all, he was known as Fisher. He
was a long thin greenish young man, very polite and sad:
he often sent people flowers, especially Miss Vanderbank,
who was one of the chief causes of his sadness. He was
also worried about his career, because he wanted very
much to be a successful literary man. At Cambridge he
had known happiness, even a modest glory, for he had
quite a considerable talent for play production, and had
put on a series of dramas by Betti, Pirandello, Brecht and
himself, which had attracted some notice; but when he
came to London all that was brought to an end by his
fearsome widowed mother who, suspecting the influence

on her boy of all those nasty acting people had pronounced publishing more suitable, a decision in which she felt strengthened when she saw the nice healthy normal girl with whom he was to share an office.

In the evenings he wrote verse dramas, but since he never attempted a subject less immense than the whole human situation, he found the work very difficult and disheartening. Sometimes he read passages from his plays aloud to a small group of his Cambridge friends, but unfortunately they were a clever lot, who only tolerated him because they hoped one day to have their own works published by Hanescu Lane, and he gained little encouragement from them.

He had inherited from his father, an unromantic but efficient businessman, some sixty thousand pounds, and none of his money sense. A good deal of what was left from his kind and cultural extravagances at Cambridge was invested in Hanescu Lane & Co.

At the moment it was Miss Vanderbank again.

'She's too generous,' he said to Judith, loping about on the pale grey carpet. 'Really too generous. It makes her do things, you know, which she thinks she's too wise to do. But she's not at all – too wise, I mean. This man Reeves, for instance – I don't think she ought to take up with him, I really don't.'

'Has she been too generous to him?' asked Judith, very coldly.

Fisher blushed. 'She had lunch with him,' he said.

'Yes?' said Judith.

'Yesterday,' said Fisher, as if that made it worse.

Miss Vanderbank happening at that moment to come in with some letters, Judith said to her, casually: 'I hear you've been seeing our friend Reeves.'

'Oh! . . .' Fisher, betrayed, turned his back.

'Oh yes,' Miss Vanderbank said, blithely. 'He gave me lunch.'

'Was he nice?' asked Judith, looking through her letters, 'Amusing?'

'Oh yes,' said Miss Vanderbank. 'We talked about all sorts of things – he's so interesting, isn't he? But . . .' seeing her opportunity, 'mainly you.'

'Me?' said Judith.

'Oh, he wanted to know everything about you,' said Miss Vanderbank, happily. 'On and on and on. Said he was too shy to ask you himself. I think that sort of man often is shy , don't you? In spite of that confident manner. Sensitive really.'

'Did he say . . . ?' asked Judith. 'What did he say – about me, I mean.'

'Well, he didn't so much say anything,' said Miss Vanderbank. 'Just sort of implied.'

'Implied?' said Judith.

'Well, yes, implied,' said Miss Vanderbank.

'How very odd,' said Judith.

'Well, I must say, I wondered, when he asked me out to lunch,' said Miss Vanderbank. 'But that's what it was, to ask about you.'

Feliks was shouting in the outer office. 'Where is everyone? Jimmy's here, Judith. In my room.'

'Coming,' called Judith. She smiled at Fisher, who was looking a little shame-faced, and went out of the room, disturbed by Miss Vanderbank's revelations.

When Jimmy Chandos-Wright had been in business, he had had no time for showing off. He had been a largish man in a rather shapeless suit, hard-working, conscientious, and an expert at his job. Only since his retirement had he taken to wearing astrakhan collars and talking as he thought a gangster should.

Most of his life had been spent in burglary. Starting young, he had worked his way to the top. He had imagination, an excellent talent for organisation, and the control over both himself and those who worked for him which is essential in a good crook. There was a time when if you wanted a big job done, anywhere in the world, you asked Jimmy Chandos-Wright (née Green) to do it. He had a reputation for reliability seldom equalled in his particular metier. The police knew all about him, of course, because his work was usually unmistakable; in fact, the morning after most of his coups, not only the police of the world but all the other burglars, blackmailers, dog-dopers, con-men or what you will, opening their newspapers said: 'That's Jimmy.' He was never caught, not in his heyday – there had been times, before he was really experienced, when he had had a spell or two 'inside' – but in his heyday they couldn't touch him.

Nobody knew what he had done in the war: he himself was uncharacteristically shifty about it, but he had certainly made money. Afterwards he did very well on the Black Market, and fixed one or two big deals in scrap which brought him in a nice sum. He lived in Tangier for a time and undertook a variety of commissions for people who were prepared to pay enormously for him to arrange some irregularity or other.

At last, his fortune made and Lucille, his red-haired girl, having always had a leaning towards respectability, they married and went to live in Eastbourne. They bought a yacht and spent a considerable part of the year in Cannes, but the only risk Jimmy took these days was at the tables, where as a matter of fact he had exceptional luck.

Several publishers had tried, without success, to persuade him to write his memoirs, but Hanescu's approach had been sartorial. He had introduced him to his tailor, who made something in wide chalk stripes, much collared and cuffed, which delighted Jimmy, and to his shirt-maker, who produced a succession of silk initialled shirts and a masterpiece in horizontal green stripes. It was probably the offer of an introduction to his boot-maker (he had not in fact got one) which finally won Jimmy for Hanescu.

The friendship thus auspiciously begun had thrived, and when the jolly forty-ish Lucille produced the son who was now his parents' pride and joy, the boy was christened Feliks, and Hanescu, together with a rich Jewish bank-breaker, was a godfather.

'Sandy's your boy,' Jimmy said, when Hanescu asked his advice for Judith. 'Sandy'll do you fine. He's a nice boy and doesn't make mistakes.'

He was wearing a black and white check suit and a yellow waistcoat. 'How beastly you look,' Feliks had said when he came in. 'That's not Denton – he'd rather die.'

'Little fellow in Shepherd's Market – very expensive,' said Jimmy. 'King of Spain recommended me.'

'The King of Spain?' said Feliks.

'That's who he said he was,' said Jimmy.

Feliks had explained that Judith might find it necessary to dispose of somebody. Jimmy, unsurprised, praised the talents and discretion of his friend Sandy.

'He's in dog-doping,' he said. 'But he's not happy there. There's money in it of course, but no scope. He was in Tangier with me, one of my best boys. But it got a bit hot and he came back to something quiet and steady for a time. You'll like him, and he'll be glad of a chance to get out of the rut. He's reliable too – I doubt if there's a better man in Europe for what you want, certainly not in England. I'll give him a ring.' He stretched one large hand towards Feliks's white telephone.

'Oh, but. . . .' said Judith.

'Worried about the price?' asked Jimmy, benignly. 'There isn't a man in London could get better terms for you than I can. What d'you want to pay?'

'I don't really know what the usual thing is,' said Judith.

'He'll probably want a grand,' said Jimmy. 'Of course he's a good man. I know fellows who'd do it for a monkey at the drop of a hat, but then you'd be taking more of a risk. Sandy's a real expert. I'll get it done for less than his usual fee, that I can promise you,'

'The only thing is,' said Judith desperately, 'I'm not quite sure yet whether it will be necessary.'

'All right,' said Jimmy. 'You let me know when you're ready and I'll tip him off. O.K.?'

'Thank you very much,' said Judith

'That's right,' said Feliks, patting her shoulder. 'You let Jimmy know. You'll fix it, won't you, Jimmy?'

'Of course, of course, anything for a friend,' said Jimmy. 'Don't you worry, my dear, there's no risk, not with Sandy. Never slipped up yet, Sandy.'

'I knew we could rely on you, Jimmy,' said Feliks.

7

To a certain extent, of course, Judith was a prig. To a certain, quite small, extent, she was still the scrubbed sixteen-year-old who had commanded the school of which she had been head girl with such devoted efficiency.

Even in her 'intellectual' days, that is to say in the years between her leaving school and her marriage, she had never quite lost that way of looking at things. For instance, though the code she then adopted involved tolerance and even admiration for any sort of unconventional behaviour among her friends, she herself had never really lost her head girl's healthy opinion that 'sex was silly'. This had lasted even beyond her marriage, the principle being only slightly modified – that is to say, sex became silly except with one's husband.

Indeed, it was only in the realm of ideas that she was the free spirit she thought herself. Where behaviour was concerned, where life was to be led, her inclination was towards the safe, the conventional, the duty-guided. Her intelligence, which was not as exceptional as she thought it but was perhaps unusual in a woman, and her eagerness to find a duty whose path to follow, had led her into some strange friendships, into, even, a rather strange marriage; but in spite of everything she had had few moral doubts. Right was right and wrong was wrong. She would not have liked to have heard it expressed by the cliché, but though it perhaps debased her attitude, it more or less summed it up.

With it, she was a fatalist. It was perhaps this last, together with an altogether feminine desire for self-immolation, which made her need to devote herself to a duty, for duty breathed life into the inevitability of events, gave them, if not a meaning, at least something to be suffered for.

Her liking for responsibility was one reason for her liking for Jean-Claude. She wanted dependants. She had enjoyed the days when her widowed father had relied on her; she would have liked to have had a lot of children; in long daydreams she gave herself a kingdom and ruled it with scrupulous fairness and devotion. Jean-Claude was solitary and helpless. He needed to be fed, kept warm, and allowed to cook and clean; that was all he wanted, and Judith, in providing it, gladly assumed him as one of her duties.

When, therefore, Baldwin Reeves after four days of brooding arrived at her house in a self-made rage and ordered her to dismiss Jean-Claude, she was deeply upset. She would rather have paid any money in the world, and said so.

During the last few days, the midget had assumed a disproportionate importance in Baldwin's eyes. The latter's reasoning, being now influenced by various emotions not clear even to himself, was not particularly valid, but it ran, roughly, along these lines. He had found out that to get money from Judith was not hard, but his success had not had what now seemed to be the desired effect on her, for instead of fearing him and acknowledging his power, it was quite obvious that she not only disliked but despised him. She had thawed briefly during one lunch, but had quickly reverted to her usual icy evidence of distaste. He had expected his power to extend to all sorts of aspects of her life: it remained purely financial. This midget had aroused an irritating and unnecessary liking on her part. To force her to get rid of him would show her how much he, Baldwin Reeves, was to be feared, and would at the same time remove the object of, and therefore soon the existence of, this annoying affection.

'I'm sorry,' he said. 'I'm afraid I must insist.'

She had turned pale. When he had told her why he had come there had been a pause, and then, quite suddenly, her face had gone white, and he had thought for a moment that she might faint. It had not occurred to him to change his mind, partly because he felt for some reason as though he had no control now, the whole business simply had to be gone through with: he was obeying orders, even though they were his own.

'Are you not going to give me any reason?' she asked.

'I can't,' said Baldwin.

'But what can anyone have against Jean-Claude?' she asked. 'What can he have done?'

'I'm afraid I can't tell you any more,' said Baldwin. 'I simply want him to go.'

'But what will he do?'

'There are employment agencies, aren't there?' said Baldwin.

'But who'd want a midget?' asked Judith.

'You did,' said Baldwin.

'That's different,' said Judith. 'Besides, he's so ugly.'

'He could go back to France,' said Baldwin.

'Can I keep him until he gets another job?' she asked.

'I'm afraid he must go tomorrow.'

'Tomorrow?' she said, horrified. 'But where will he go?'

'You can give him some money, can't you?' said Baldwin, who had not thought of all these details.

Judith began to walk up and down the room.

'I've told you I'll give you any money you want,' she said.

'I don't want money,' he said.

'You do,' she said. 'You're always saying how much you need money. Or have you found another source of income?'

'No,' he said.

'Why don't you?' she said. 'Why don't you find some more widows with a little money to help me to keep you? Why should I be the only one? I've no doubt you could find plenty more.'

'I don't want to,' he said. 'I simply want you to get rid of the dwarf. I'm not here to discuss money.'

'I want to discuss money,' said Judith. 'I'll give you £500 in three days' time if you leave Jean-Claude alone – and more later. Which would you rather have, £500 or the sadistic pleasure of seeing a harmless midget suffer?'

'Harmless midget suffer,' said Baldwin.

'What about £1,000?' said Judith.

'No,' said Baldwin.

'Anything,' said Judith. 'The house – anything. . . .'

She was pale and obviously deeply agitated, but he felt in a way she should be crying, throwing herself at his feet – then he hoped she wouldn't.

'I must go,' he said. 'And the dwarf tomorrow.'

'No, wait,' she put her hand on his arm. 'Wait.' Would she hit him, he thought confusedly, or throw herself round his neck, or—? 'Wait, isn't there anything you'd rather have?'

He looked at her without saying anything at all, one hand on the door.

'Isn't there?' she said.

The scene became suddenly meaningless to Baldwin. He could hardly remember what it was all about. He wanted desperately to go.

'No, there's nothing,' he said, turning away. 'Nothing at all,' and he went out of the house.

Left alone, Judith sat down to think, to be calm and reasonable and think of a way out, but the whole situation had become so monstrous that her thoughts floundered on the borders of nightmare: she could see no solution. She worked herself up into a rage against Baldwin, for the first time really considering and facing the horror of his behaviour. The rage abated, and left her tired.

Some hours after Baldwin had left, she went downstairs to find Jean-Claude. He was in his small sitting-room, polishing the silver, which was already gleaming, and listening to the wireless, which was turned so low as to be almost inaudible.

'You can have it louder than that,' said Judith. 'It doesn't disturb me at all.'

'S'all right, s'all right,' said Jean-Claude. 'I don't listen.' He turned the wireless off.

There was a silence, broken only by the click of the clean forks dropping into their places.

'Tomorrow,' said Jean-Claude. 'Fish day.' He wrinkled his broad nose. Although he cooked it beautifully, he always expressed the liveliest distaste for all species of fish. 'And for Bertie skin but no bones.' He grinned,

because when he had first come, Judith had had great
difficulty in making him believe that fish-bones were bad
for dogs. 'Dogs eat bones,' he had obstinately repeated,
until Judith had threatened to give Bertie his meals
herself, which Jean-Claude had considered quite
unsuitable.

'Yes,' said Judith. 'Oh, by the way. . . .'

'Yes?' said Jean-Claude.

'I'm afraid. . . .' Judith said. 'I'm afraid there's some
rather bad news. I've got to – that is, things have been
going rather badly, you see, and I'm afraid I shall have
to – it won't be possible for me to keep you.'

'Keep. . . ?' Jean-Claude had not understood.

'I mean that I shan't be able to afford to go on having
you here,' said Judith. 'I only wish I could – I'm very
upset about it – it's not that I don't wish you could stay
for years, but it just – won't be possible you see.'

There was a long pause while Jean-Claude absorbed
this information. At last his evident bewilderment gave
way to a broad smile.

'Ah, I know,' he said. 'It's always the same old money,
money. I know. But look. I wait, I want nothing, later
you get rich, you start to pay me again. I wait.'

'Oh, but you see,' Judith said. 'It's very kind of you,
but I shall probably have to move from here, and go
somewhere smaller where there's no room for you.'

'No small room?' Jean-Claude looked disbelieving. 'You
find somewhere with a small room where I go.'

'Well, I. . . .' said Judith. 'I don't know that I shall be
able to.'

'You try,' Jean-Claude said.

'Well, yes, I'll try, of course,' said Judith. 'But I may
not be able to.'

'Well, then so bad,' said Jean-Claude, shrugging his
shoulders. 'But perhaps yes. And until then I stay here
and we don't worry.'

'Well, the thing is,' said Judith. 'I know it must seem
odd, and I really wouldn't do it if it weren't absolutely
necessary – I mean really it's just as bad for me – only I'm
afraid it's absolutely essential for you to leave tomorrow.'

There was another pause, then Jean-Claude said in amazement: *'Demain? Je pars demain?'*

'I'm terribly sorry,' said Judith. 'I really am. You can't imagine how awful it is for me.'

'You want me to go tomorrow?' he asked again.

'I don't want you to go at all,' said Judith. 'I wish to goodness you needn't. But I'm afraid you must.'

Jean-Claude had put down the fork he was polishing. Now, very slowly, he picked it up again and began to rub it with his chamois leather. 'So I go tomorrow,' he said.

'I'm terribly sorry,' said Judith. 'Of course you'll easily get another job – I'll give you references and everything – and we'll find you somewhere to stay of course.'

'I go tomorrow,' said Jean-Claude, nodding slowly.

'I wish I could explain,' said Judith. 'I mean why it's necessary – it's not that I want you to go.'

The midget shook his head gently.

'I ask no questions,' he said. 'I am a small man. I ask no questions. I go tomorrow.'

Baldwin Reeves was having lunch in the Inner Temple. Sitting next to him was a small, bird-like man called David Saint, whose company Baldwin was generally anxious to cultivate, not so much for its own sake as because of the lordly host of relations by which this otherwise insignificant fellow was winged about.

Today, however, even the relations were not enough to hold Baldwin's attention, which had soon wandered from the complicated and boring details of the Company Law case on which David Saint was currently engaged. He was so preoccupied, in fact, that he got up in the middle of one of his neighbour's sentences, and it was only on turning back to smile good-bye that he realised what he had done and apologised. 'So sorry, old boy, something on my mind. I'd love to hear the end of that – let's lunch here next week— Must rush now.' He hurried out of the Hall, passing in the door two distinguished counsel, one of whom said to him: 'I liked your case this morning, Reeves.'

Usually, Baldwin would have stopped and accepted

this opportunity of getting into conversation with so powerful a man. Today, however, he simply said: 'Oh, thank you, thank you,' and hurried on.

'Hope it goes well,' the Q.C. called after him, then, turning to his companion said: 'He's working himself too hard, that fellow – looks worn out.'

Collecting a bundle of papers which he had left downstairs, Baldwin hurried out into the Strand, hailed a taxi, and giving the address of Judith's house, added: 'Please hurry.'

He had only three quarters of an hour before he was due back in court. He was not even quite certain what he meant to do, but it seemed enormously important to get to her house, and see the midget. Judith herself of course would be at the office.

He rustled nervously through his sheaf of papers. He had meant to have a look at them in the taxi, so as to have one or two points fresh in his mind for the afternoon, but instead he leaned forward to tap on the glass partition and urge on the driver. It was a very old and rattly taxi, and the driver's large back expressed disapproval of this fever for speed. Swearing, Baldwin jerked back into his seat.

They trundled at last down the King's Road.

'Right here,' shouted Baldwin. 'This is it. Turn right.'

Then, when the taxi was half-way round the corner into the street he suddenly battered furiously on the partition, shouting, 'Stop, stop, stop!'

Grumbling, the driver braked, but his passenger had already leapt out, waving his handful of papers and still shouting.

There on the pavement was Jean-Claude, holding in one hand an enormous suitcase and in the other a very small umbrella. Judith had left for the office that morning saying that she would find somewhere for him to stay for a few nights and that on her return that evening she would take him there in a taxi, but it did not seem to him suitable that she should have to take him across London; he thought it better, seeing too how upset she was about it all, that he should leave quietly while she was away at the office. He had packed all his belongings into his one cumbersome old suitcase and clasping his umbrella in his other hand had stumped off with the intention of catching a bus to Victoria.

When Baldwin Reeves, whom he knew vaguely as someone Judith seemed not to like, suddenly appeared in front of him, waving a bundle of papers and shouting incoherently, Jean-Claude, understanding nothing, put his suitcase down and waited.

'Come on, come on, we'll go back,' said Baldwin. He gesticulated at the taxi-driver. 'Go on to number twelve,' he shouted. Picking up Jean-Claude's suitcase, he said, 'Come on, I'll take this.'

'But no,' said Jean-Claude. 'I go the other way.'

There were already a good many cars parked in the little street, and the taxi-driver was prevented from drawing up in front of number twelve by the old white Mercedes which had just stopped there. He went on a little farther, and then got out to keep an eye on his eccentric fare.

Judith, who had just driven up with Feliks in his Mercedes, ran up the steps into her house without looking up the street to where Jean-Claude and Baldwin were arguing.

'I'm so grateful, Feliks, really,' she was saying. 'You'll find him awfully useful, too, I know you will – he doesn't mind what he does. Jean-Claude!' she called down the stairs. 'You may like him so much that you want him to stay longer than a fortnight.'

Going into the drawing-room she took off her coat and, throwing it on to a chair, turned to find Feliks not with her.

'Feliks?' she called. Receiving no answer, she supposed he must have left something in the car, and went to the telephone. She had been trying to speak to Jimmy Chandos-Wright that morning, and had been told that he would be in at two o'clock.

It was with an unconscious relish in the hopelessness of her situation that she had chosen this particular morning to tell him that she would not need his friend's services. She had known all the time that he would have to be told: anything else was ridiculous – murder was hardly even right or wrong, it was simply out of the question. Before the opportunity had been given to her, she would not have known how clear her reaction would be; but in the event she had found the suggestion simply absurd.

'You what?' Jimmy said, when she had told him. 'You don't want him? Baby, you sure are passing something up there. He's a good boy, Sandy. If it's the security angle that's on your mind. . . .'

'No, no, it's not that,' said Judith. 'I'm so sorry to have bothered you but it turned out to be unnecessary after all. If I had wanted it, of course I wouldn't have thought of asking anyone else.'

'Ah, you'd have been making a mistake if you had you know,' said Jimmy. 'I tipped him off there might be something up. He'll be disappointed.'

'I'm so sorry,' said Judith. 'I'm afraid I must go now – there seems to be someone arriving.'

Jean-Claude, whom bewilderment had made even more guttural than usual, was being noisily persuaded by Baldwin to return to the house; following them came Feliks, asking questions; and in the background, detached but watchful, was the taxi-driver.

'All right, all right, I know,' Baldwin was saying. 'It doesn't matter about the train. Come on, for God's sake. I've got to go.'

'But what are you doing?' said Feliks again. 'What are you doing, Baldwin. Do tell me what you're doing?'

'What are you doing?' Judith asked too, but so angrily that Feliks at once stopped his vague questionings, and Baldwin, his hand still on Jean-Claude's shoulder, looked at her in alarm and without answering.

'What are you doing?' Judith said again. The sight of him made her realise what heights of hate she had reached since last she saw him. She was so angry that she felt her nostrils and her upper lip quivering. This evidence of the strength of her own emotion impressed her and gave her a sense of power.

'My dear. . . .' Feliks, who enjoyed scenes but preferred them to be engineered by, and centred upon, himself, approached her cautiously with one peacemaking hand raised.

The intervention broke into Baldwin's stare.

'Well, there he is, there he is,' he pushed the midget forward. 'And the suitcase.' Resuming his air of desperate hurry, he swung the suitcase into the middle of the room, thumped it down and turned to go.

'All right, I want to go back,' he said to the taxi-driver. 'Oh, the umbrella. Here you are,' he held out to Jean-Claude the umbrella which he still held in one hand. The midget drew back. 'No, come on, take it, take it.'

In pressing it into Jean-Claude's hand, Baldwin dropped several of the papers which he was still clasping. He bent to pick them up.

'Got to be back by half past,' he said.

No one else moved or spoke, Feliks because he understood nothing of what was going on and was annoyed because he felt left out, Jean-Claude because it was safer to do nothing, and Judith because she liked to see Baldwin discomfited.

'Must have these things, blast them,' Baldwin said. 'Need them for this afternoon. Can't you be turning round? Oh, he's gone. Is he turning round? Must be there by half past. All right, I've got them.' He went out of the room without looking round.

'Wait,' Judith suddenly followed him, shutting the door firmly upon the silent figures of Feliks and Jean-Claude. 'What are you doing?'

Taking refuge in violence, Baldwin shouted: 'I've brought him back haven't I? What more d'you want?' Realising that they ought not to be overheard he dropped his voice to a fierce whisper. 'What d'you mean, what am I doing? He's here isn't he, for Christ's sake? I can't spend all day messing about here. I'm supposed to be in court.'

'Why have you brought him back?' said Judith.

His motives were inexplicable even to himself. No one was more surprised than he at what he had done. This made him, of course, unreasonably angry with her. Suddenly seizing her by the shoulders, he went on whispering, furiously: 'You've got him, haven't you? You've got your blasted little midget. Now shut up about it. Take him and shut up. Do whatever you like with him – whatever you do do that makes you so fond of him.'

'I'm not, I don't – what do you mean?' she said.

'Stop asking me what I mean,' he began to shake her, bumping her against the wall. 'I don't mean anything. Now shut up. Take him back and shut up.'

'No, stop it, don't, you're mad,' she put up her hands to try and push him away, upon which he stopped and held her in absolute silence, until she laughed, quite quietly, and said: 'No, but really it is funny.'

'I know,' he said, loosening his clasp on her arms, and beginning to smile, as if he could not help it. 'I know, I know, I know.'

The mood having changed, and needing a remark on which to break away from his hold, Judith said: 'I suppose you mean you'll take the £500 instead,' moving towards the front door.

He looked at her in what seemed surprise, then dropping his hands to his sides, said vaguely: 'Oh yes.' He followed her to the door which she had now opened, then, having looked at her again in the same way, ran down the steps saying, impatiently: 'Oh yes yes yes yes yes yes. . . .'

The taxi grunted into movement as Feliks came out of the drawing-room behind her.

'Finished?' he asked.

'Yes,' said Judith.

'Do I understand that Jean-Claude is not leaving after all?' he asked. 'Or is Baldwin instead of me·going to have him? You really must explain yourself a bit, Judith.'

'I'm afraid I can't altogether,' said Judith, turning back into the house.

8

THOMAS HOOD's aunt was anti-Semitic. She was also opposed to vivisection, and a believer in herb cures, but that was beside the point – it was her anti-Semitism which her nephew could not forgive.

He was living, nevertheless, in her house in the Isle of Wight while his mother and sister were in America and their own house was shut up; although as a matter of fact he spent a good deal of time in London and arranged his visits to the Isle of Wight to coincide as much as possible with her absences, which were fortunately frequent. He did have David Weitzmann to stay once when she was there – two days of unrelieved embarrassment and gloom.

When he asked whether Judith might come down for a week-end, his aunt was pleased. She already knew a good deal about her, since even to so uncongenial an audience Thomas had not been able to avoid talking about her, and though at first she had been inclined to think the friendship not suitable, she had lately – without much evidence and mainly because it was convenient – come to the conclusion that Judith was not 'that sort of woman'. There was also the advantage, especially after the trying experience of David Weitzmann, that, as she delicately pointed out to her maid: 'Mrs. Lane is not One of Those.'

The maid, who used that term to denote the homosexual, said with some scorn: 'Indeed, no, ma'am, her being a lady.'

Taking this as a perfectly natural expression of aristocratic prejudice, Miss Hood said: 'Well of course the Lanes are a very good family, and I expect the boy would have married someone nice, don't you?'

Permission having been granted, Thomas then arranged for Judith to come down for the one week-end

The Blackmailer

he was sure that his aunt would be away until Sunday night. 'I'm so sorry, it's the only one she can manage,' he told Miss Hood, untruthfully.

His reason for making this arrangement was partly because he himself found his aunt boring and would rather have Judith to himself, but mainly because he was ashamed of his aunt for being snobbish and unintelligent, and thought that Judith would despise him for having such a foolish relation. In this, of course, he was quite wrong, because Miss Hood was kind and jolly and Judith would have liked her, but he always expected of Judith opinions much more ruthless and uncompromising than her real ones. Also he set himself, in regard to her, an impossibly high standard.

He waited for her alone, then, in Miss Hood's comfortable Victorian house, walking occasionally out into the garden where the mimosa was already over, and wandering once down the lane to where the sea plopped on to the sand with a melancholy he had always liked. Throughout his childhood, this had been the place where his busy parents had sent their children for holidays or when there was for the moment nowhere else for them to go, and the soft sea of the island's northern coast and the stretch of sand where no one came except in August – and even then not in such crowds as went elsewhere, for there were better beaches near – and the strong scent of the ginger plants his aunt grew, and the ugly sweet-smelling house, were all part of his youth and full for him of the nostalgia which at nineteen he felt for the conflicts of sixteen.

When at last he went to fetch the car to meet Judith at Ryde pier head, he was full of quiet reasonable excitement.

Judith on the boat coming towards him was tired and rather cross. She was sick of Baldwin Reeves. She had thought of him almost without ceasing since he had brought Jean-Claude back to her house. He stayed in her mind with a deadly persistence, he was simply there: it was as if they were chained in some dungeon together, out of reach but face to face; to break away was impossible.

The point was that, for a moment in the hall of her house, she had thought he might kiss her and had wished that he would. Afterwards, shaken, she had tried, and failed, to persuade herself that this was not so. That night she had dreamt, dispensing with the subtleties of symbolism, that they were in bed together.

Having had since her husband had died only the slightest and most fleeting of sexual interests in any men, that her desires should now apparently have been aroused by a man she had thought she regarded with loathing seemed to her wicked. Sex and love had never been dissociated in her mind; nor altogether had love and liking, for though she had known Anthony's most serious faults, she would still, she felt, have liked him, in any circumstances, for his charm and wit and understanding: but Baldwin Reeves was a very different affair – he was practically the only man in the world whom she seriously had reason to hate.

Her instinct was to say: 'Nonsense,' but she was too honest to believe it could all be thus dismissed. In that case, the thing must be ignored, repressed, subdued – of course; but secretly her fatalism made her feel that nothing could be done about it, nothing could be avoided, the future was revealed.

She arrived then at Ryde feeling sad, restless and faintly depraved. At the same time she was very annoyed with Bertie, who had behaved horribly in the train because of a couple in the carriage who ate chocolate all the time, and had then escaped from her on the boat, got himself shut in the gentlemen's lavatory and there become hysterical.

'You're tired,' Thomas said in the car. 'You shall go straight to bed with a glass of milk and a biscuit.'

'What, no dinner?' said Judith.

'Perhaps a little if you promise to talk to me and not think of anything else at all,' said Thomas.

'Oh,' said Judith. 'Isn't the food very good?'

'It is rather good as a matter of fact,' said Thomas. 'There's a curious neurotic old cook left over from the good old days.'

'Neurotic?' asked Judith.

'A religious maniac,' said Thomas. 'And methylated spirits. But there's a boat we can go out in if you like. Tomorrow, I mean. Everyone's very serious about sailing here, but of course it hasn't started properly yet. We could fish.'

'Is she a serious sailing woman, your aunt?' asked Judith.

'She's too old,' said Thomas. 'She has rheumatism and puts garlic on it, but she used to sail. She's not here now, though. She's not coming back until Sunday. Didn't I tell you?'

'No,' said Judith.

'It will really be much nicer without her,' said Thomas. 'She's very boring and narrow-minded. David came down, did I tell you? It was disastrous.'

'No, tell me,' said Judith.

She had been thinking on the way down that the week-end would be nice for Bertie, and that it would be good for her too to be out of London, as long as the aunt was not too dull, but now that she had seen him again she remembered that she was fond of Thomas and that his company was always pleasant.

They sailed and fished. The sun shone, though it was still cold in the mornings and evenings. They played tennis, at which Thomas turned out to be very good. They ate a good deal, and played rough games with Bertie on the lawn. Thomas talked.

'Why have I no secrets from you, and you have obviously hundreds from me?' he asked.

'For one thing, I like listening,' said Judith. 'For another, such secrets as I have are either boring or inexpressible, and anyway I sometimes find it difficult to talk to you because I think that you think that I am different from what I am. And then of course you ask so many questions.'

'Which makes you not want to answer?' asked Thomas.

'Which makes me not bother to tell you things because I know you're bound to ask, in time,' she said.

'How are you different from what I think?' he asked. 'Less good?'

'Oh, I should think so,' she said.

'But you needn't worry,' he said. 'I know you're less good than I think, but I still think it.'

When Aunt Susan came back on Sunday evening, Judith was easily persuaded to stay until the next day, and Thomas's confidence after the two days they had already spent together was such that he hardly once blushed for his aunt.

On Saturday morning Judith had written to Sir Ralph to tell him of the need for more money, but once that was done she almost forgot about the whole thing. Even the image of Baldwin Reeves retreated, to emerge occasionally for a moment or two, but without the same oppressive power.

'I'm coming up next week,' said Thomas, when he drove her to catch the boat. 'On Tuesday. I'll come and see you, shall I?'

When she said good-bye to him, Judith kissed him on the cheek. It was not a gesture she was much given to making but it seemed obvious. He looked pleased.

As the boat moved away she leant over the rail to wave to him, the morning being fine and sunny.

Feliks greeted Judith with some petulance when she went into the office.

'All this about my being your greatest friend,' he said. 'And you leave me completely out of your confidence. What's it all about? If it was Baldwin Reeves who was forcing you to send Jean-Claude away, why couldn't you tell me? You told me on Thursday that you'd decided he must go at once, and would I have him for a fortnight, which naturally I said I would. But you know how I hate being left in the dark. You might have told me. Why did Baldwin want him to go, anyway?'

'I've no idea,' said Judith. 'Honestly, Feliks, the whole thing was so complicated and so mad, that I simply couldn't go into it all.'

'Then why did he suddenly bring him back?' said Feliks.

'I don't know,' said Judith. 'I really don't know why he does anything.'

'Is he asking you for money still?'

'Yes.'

'What a monster he is,' said Feliks.

'I don't know,' said Judith. 'Perhaps he isn't. I just don't know.'

'Of course he's a monster,' said Feliks. 'I shall tell him so.'

'You mustn't let him know I've told you about it,' said Judith.

'Of course I shan't,' said Feliks. 'I shall simply tell him he's a monster. Now listen, *Skin Deep* having done so well, and what with one thing and another, I think we ought to have another secretary.'

'Oh, d'you think so really?' said Judith. 'I don't mind typing my own letters now and then, and Fisher's getting awfully good.'

'Fisher's not meant to be a typist,' said Feliks. 'He may look like one, but that's neither here nor there. No, the other night at Gavin Miller's party – now *that* you see after all I do owe entirely to Baldwin Reeves, we mustn't forget that – anyway, there I met quite a nice little girl called Sally Mann, and she seemed perfectly intelligent and wants a job and. . . .'

'Feliks,' said Judith. 'Don't pretend that you don't know perfectly well that her name is Lady Sarah Mann.'

'Well, but Judith,' said Feliks. 'But listen. She could be useful. She really could. She doesn't want much in the way of wages, and if she turned out to be good, you never know, if she's got a bit of money. . . .'

'You think her name would look good on the paper,' said Judith.

'I told her the whole thing depended on you,' said Feliks. 'She's quite clever. Incidentally, this man Ivor Jones – would you like me to have another look at the manuscript?'

'Oh dear,' said Judith. 'I sometimes think we conduct this office in a very unbusinesslike way.'

Ivor Jones was an enthusiastic Welshman whose novel Judith wanted to publish because she thought he would one day write a good one. Feliks, on the other hand, had until then been opposed to it on the grounds that too many of their writers were in the nature of long-term investments.

'I'll think about it,' said Judith, sighing. 'I'll think about it all.'

'You look tired,' said Feliks. 'How are you?'

'Oh, I'm all right,' said Judith. 'Perhaps I need a holiday. What about my going away for a week or two? I haven't for ages.'

Feliks smiled. 'Well, perhaps if we get another secretary . . .' he said.

'We'll get her,' said Judith. 'Where is she?'

'Oh, darling, how wonderful of you,' said Feliks. 'I'll get her to come in tomorrow and you can see what you think.'

Travel was the thing, Judith thought. Even a week-end with Thomas Hood had momentarily taken away her horror of Baldwin. That was the answer, simply geography, simply physical distance. It had been some time since its fascination had worked on her. When she had been younger it had always been on her mind. Not that she was so anxious to see new places – it was the departure more than the arrival which had appealed to her then. Simply to go. She thought again, making her way home from the office, of departure, of trains drawing slowly out of stations, and ships swaying away from crowded quays, of disciplined embarkations on to aeroplanes, of luggage, newspapers and odd encounters, of the infinite variety of individuals even now, even this evening, undertaking voyages.

When she reached home, she found Baldwin Reeves waiting for her.

He had made a fool of himself. The scene when he had brought Jean-Claude back to Judith had been simply absurd. His consciousness of this made him feel, as he always did when the possibility arose of his being laughed at, that the best thing to do would be simply to drop the whole business. He had had £400 out of it, and it was important to know when to stop. He was annoyed by Judith's having, as it seemed to him, insisted on offering him more money in exchange for Jean-Claude. He had come back, then, to tell her that he was not asking for more; and that his plan was simply to get out. The whole thing had become too complicated, and was best forgotten as soon as possible. In a way, he rather blamed Judith for his having turned out to be a not altogether successful blackmailer. It had shaken his faith in himself.

To Judith the sight of him was simply doom; and the look on her face amazed him. She had no idea why he had come, but felt quite convinced that he would never go.

'I came to say,' Baldwin began. 'That there seemed last time to be some misunderstanding about the money. Do you remember?'

'Yes, I remember,' said Judith.

'You seemed to think I wanted £500,' said Baldwin.

'Yes,' said Judith.

'I never said that,' said Baldwin. 'I don't know why you thought I had.'

'What d'you mean?' asked Judith.

'I never said I wanted £500,' said Baldwin.

'Oh,' said Judith.

'I don't,' said Baldwin. 'I don't want it.'

'You don't want it?' repeated Judith.

'No.'

'What? Never? asked Judith.

'I told you the whole thing was only temporary,' said Baldwin.

'Oh,' said Judith. 'Well—' She began to move slowly about the room, nervously picking things up off the tables and putting them down again, moving a cushion, straightening a rug with her foot. Baldwin, standing in front of the fireplace, said nothing. Bertie had hurried downstairs to see about his evening meal.

'Well—' said Judith.

'I thought I'd better tell you,' said Baldwin.

'Yes,' said Judith.

'I'll go then,' said Baldwin, suddenly making for the door.

'Oh, but—' said Judith.

'Yes?' Baldwin paused.

'Nothing,' said Judith. 'I mean I had actually made arrangements – for the money.'

'I see,' said Baldwin. 'But surely, those sort of arrangements are quite easily changed?'

'Yes,' said Judith. 'I suppose so. You mean – it's the end – of the blackmailing I mean?'

'Oh yes yes yes,' said Baldwin, impatiently, going out into the hall.

Judith followed him in silence, and passing him put out her hand to open the front door. He put his hand on her arm to prevent her, then kissed her.

After the first shock, and the first acute pleasure, Judith found herself prolonging the kiss because she could not think of what to say after it. She drew back.

'We understand each other,' said Baldwin, who looked shaken. 'You must see, we understand each other, even when we don't want to. Haven't you felt that?'

Judith, nodding, allowed her head to incline towards, though not actually rest upon, his shoulder. He gave a small moan, and would have kissed her again. The moan, however, had been a mistake: it jarred, and Judith, anyway calmer, suddenly pushed him away.

'No, you must go,' she said. She looked at him for a moment, then smiled slightly – a smile in which she seemed to appeal to him to join. Then she opened the front door and said again: 'You must go.'

After a moment he said: 'Yes, I'll go,' without answering her smile.

He walked away from her quickly, angry with himself, not because of the kiss, which impetuous though it had been he certainly did not regret, but because of the moan he had made, which had been the cause of her pushing him away. She had been quite right, and for the first time he not only admired, he really respected her. It was not the way in which he was used to women behaving, but he was quite aware himself of its having been an insincere moan, and as such an insult to her intelligence. Yet he hated to think she believed him to be altogether insincere; it was merely that he was used to exaggerating his emotions on such occasions, in order by simulating a passion to engender one, both in himself and in the other person. In this case, however, he realised that he had been wrong, and it made him feel rather shabby.

In retrospect his mistake became more and more embarrassing. The hateful little sound seemed hideously vulgar:

it was the sort of thing Anthony Lane would never have done.

The money would be coming all the same – that Judith knew. If there was one person on whom, ever since she had met him, she had relied, it was Sir Ralph.

Her father in his lifetime had been, though rather distant, upright and unfailingly kind; but her mother she remembered as having been hysterical and over-effusive, and there had been no one else, even Anthony, in whom there had ever been any question of her seriously putting her trust. Partly, of course, she was naturally self-reliant, partly the effect on her of her emotional, embarrassing mother had been to breed in her a deep reserve.

With Sir Ralph, however, the reserve, in a curious way, was not there. It was not that she knew him so very well. Their relationship was the artificial but charming one between an old man, to a certain extent worldly, and the pretty girl his grandson had married; but she had felt immediately at ease with him, as if, if revelations had to be made, she would prefer them to be made to him. He had still his old charm, and she found his eccentricities amazingly sane. She was also aware that into her feeling for him there entered the consideration of who he was, that is to say of the people he had known, the houses he had stayed in, the line of similar ancestors. She was outside his world, or what his world had been, not so much even by birth or upbringing as by sentiment, and that made her see it round him as a mysterious but appealing attribute. If she had been told her attitude was snobbish, she would have been furious, but it probably was. There was more to it, however, than that – he was a symbol to her of more than merely a class.

He had a way, a partly defensive way, of seeming vague and forgetful. His great age and his constant state of disagreement with his daughter-in-law had made him now a little sly. Judith was right, all the same, in thinking him worthy of trust: he had never been anything else. Only, now, though the instincts and unquestioning reactions were still there, sometimes the means of putting them into effect, of safeguarding the trust or defending the faith, were lacking.

He had made a note in his little book of the payment to Judith for Baldwin Reeves, and had just sent her the money. One afternoon when his daughter-in-law came in to tell him that tea was ready, he was bent over his books, working out, in anticipation of the next demand, which account could least stand the strain of another payment and would therefore be the most satisfying to use, in order to alarm his bank manager.

'Tea's ready, Fa,' Mrs. Lane said. 'Nanny made it rather early I'm afraid; her watch was fast. Oh, you haven't seen your letters.' She picked up the afternoon post which was lying unnoticed by his desk. 'Here you are – the *Investor's Chronicle* and a letter from the Agricultural people – oh, and one from Judith. Shall I open it? It must be about the week-end.'

'Do, my dear, do,' said Sir Ralph. 'Subtract this from that and there we are. I'll come along in a moment, just got to finish this.'

'Couldn't you finish it afterwards?' said Mrs. Lane. 'You've got all the evening. What's this Judith says? I don't understand. What £500?'

'What's that?' said Sir Ralph.

I'm so terribly grateful that you can deal with the £500, Mrs. Lane read out. *I really believe it will be the last he'll ask for – I'm almost certain of this. You've no idea how much happier I've been about it since I've known you know. I knew Anthony well, always. . . .* 'What is this, Fa?' *though it made no difference to us.* 'What does she mean?' *. . . but you would hardly believe the relief I feel because you understood him too. So you must see how really thankful I am. . . .* 'and so on. What on earth is she talking about? What is this, Fa? What an extraordinary letter.'

Sir Ralph pushed his chair back from his desk.

'May I have it please?' he asked.

He took the letter and gazed at it for some moments in silence. 'Twenty-fourth,' he said eventually. 'Ah yes, let's see, that was yesterday, wasn't it? Is there a postmark?'

'That's hardly important, Fa,' said Mrs. Lane. 'Do you mind explaining what this letter is about?'

'My dear, it was addressed to me,' said Sir Ralph, gently.

'You asked me to open it,' said Mrs. Lane. 'What is she talking about? What is it to do with Anthony?'

'It's nothing, nothing,' said Sir Ralph. 'There's no mystery, it's just a private matter. It's not important.'

'How can it be private when it concerns my son?' said Mrs. Lane.

Sir Ralph looked at her reproachfully.

'Judith and I sometimes correspond, you know,' he said. 'If she talks about her late husband to me, I don't always tell you about it.'

Mrs. Lane looked at him for a moment almost wildly. Then she said: 'So you refuse to answer my question?'

'If you put it like that,' said Sir Ralph.

Nanny's large white face peered round the door.

'Oh, you're here,' she said sadly.

'We're just coming,' said Mrs. Lane. 'You start tea, Nanny.'

'I have started,' said Nanny. 'It's getting cold.'

'Oh come along then,' said Mrs. Lane, impatiently. 'Come along, Fa.'

'You go ahead, Grizel,' said Sir Ralph. 'I'll follow you in a moment. I must just finish this calculation – won't take me a moment.'

Mrs. Lane hesitated, then, shepherded by Nanny, went out of the room.

Sir Ralph picked up a pen in his slightly trembly hand (he always wrote with a relief nib), but he left his subtraction half finished, and sat without moving at his desk. Later Nanny came back and took him, quite firmly, to tea.

9

THERE can be no doubt but that Miss Vanderbank was a dear creature. There was her adored Hanescu flirting about with the new secretary, who looked like a Red Indian but turned out, as Miss Vanderbank freely admitted, to be full of good intentions; and yet, horribly as she suffered, she still performed her duties with her usual bouncing efficiency and most generously watched, encouraged and sighed over what she felt confident was a romance developing between Judith and Baldwin.

'He's taking her out to lunch again,' she said to Fisher. 'And d'you see the way he looks at her?'

'But she's so rude to him always,' said Fisher, who, relieved though he was that Baldwin's attentions had been diverted from Miss Vanderbank, still regarded him with a certain amount of distrust.

'That's just it,' said Miss Vanderbank, wisely. 'That just proves it.'

'Oh,' said Fisher.

He would have been even more puzzled had he seen them at lunch, for Baldwin, who had now decided quite simply to get to know Judith better, in order both to explain to himself the attraction she had for him and to study and somehow deal with challenge she represented, was finding his task difficult, and it was certainly not made easier by Judith, who was never, at the best of times, much of a breaker of silences.

One of his difficulties, curiously enough, was the fact that he felt he already knew her very well. This, being the result of the necessarily intimate nature of the relationship between blackmailer and victim, was an embarrassment rather than anything else. He had resolved to take things slowly, and at first confined their meetings to a series of lunches. For a time he tried to start all over again, and to keep the conversation on the same sort of note it would have had had they only just met; but since, unlike Judith, he was not fundamentally at all a tactful person, this manoeuvre was not successful and he abandoned it.

'What I like about you,' he said once, 'Is that you're not altogether what you pretend. If you were really the good conventional straightforward creature you sometimes seem, would you associate with that scoundrel Hanescu?'

'He's not,' said Judith.

'Not wholly, perhaps,' said Baldwin. 'But mostly. I don't mean to say he runs his business dishonestly, but you know his whole method is – well, shall we say, corrupt?'

Judith defended him, as best she could, but Baldwin laughing, simply said: 'Oh, you won't admit it to me. But I know you admit it to yourself.'

'Do I really seem like that?' asked Judith. 'Conventional and straightforward?'

'Sometimes,' said Baldwin. 'Of course, I've always held that you're less intelligent than you seem – you're well-read and you've got a good clear judgement, and that makes one think there's more behind you – oh, now you're insulted, I love that.'

It was true that she prided herself on her intelligence and hated to have it slighted.

'No, but I think you choose to seem conventional because you wish to be – perhaps it's the Lane influence, I don't know,' said Baldwin. 'You want to seem as if you never have any doubt about what's right or wrong, and yet I think it's only by ignoring a moral problem that you make it seem, both to yourself and to outside observers, as if for you it doesn't exist. It makes you seem strong, but I'm not sure it isn't a sign of weakness. You have too much moral pride: I believe if something upset it, you might find yourself quite at sea.'

'You mean I think myself better than I am,' said Judith.

'Stronger,' said Baldwin.

'And what sort of thing, then,' she asked, coldly. 'Do you see upsetting this false equilibrium?'

'Me, for instance,' said Baldwin. 'I think I might upset it.'

'You?' she said.

'You think I'm bad and yet you love me,' said Baldwin, enjoying his own analysis. 'I think this constitutes a difficult moral problem for you, and one which you are prepared to go all sorts of lengths not to have to face. Of course you knew Anthony wasn't altogether a worthy person, but you apparently got over that somehow. I am a more difficult case, a little too much more unworthy. You don't want to face it. That's what I mean by your equilibrium being upset. You might do something odd and violent. I am not sure, but nothing would surprise me.'

They sat side by side without speaking for some time, then Judith said quietly: 'I am afraid I hate you for being so over-confident and so mistaken.'

When she looked at him after a moment, she was surprised to see that he had turned red and that his eyes were full of tears; but she was wrong in thinking that her reaction had much hurt him, for he had not expected any other. It was merely that thinking about her had suddenly filled him with emotion.

After a pause he said: 'You are like your husband, you know. It's funny, isn't it, that someone so weak of character should be so powerful of personality? I've no doubt he influenced you more than you did him.'

'I'm sure he did. I never knew what were the influences in his life. There were none that I could recognise.'

'Perhaps he was always self-sufficient,' said Baldwin. 'There was something a little cold about it. Perhaps he never loved anybody enough to be much influenced by them.'

'Perhaps not,' she said gently.

Slightly embarrassed, Baldwin went on quickly: 'He influenced me, of course, enormously. The way I talk, I mean the actual words I use, inflexions, intonations, all come from him.'

'I know,' she said.

They talked about Anthony a good deal: neither of them had talked about him much with anybody before. At those times they were not so defensive with each other; but usually their meetings were sharply quarrelsome. Baldwin found them exciting and stimulating, Judith, for the same reasons, frightening. It had not occurred to him that if it was power he was after he might do better by being nice to her. He was delighted to find it out, but she was for the first time really worried by him.

She began to avoid him with more of a sense of oppression and fear than she had ever had while he was blackmailing her.

One evening he came into the office just as she was leaving. 'I was on my way home so I thought I'd pick you up,' he said.

Miss Vanderbank fluttered past in a chiffon scarf, smiling blissfully. Baldwin found himself quite grateful for her so obvious blessing.

They took Bertie into the park. Baldwin had just secured an extremely good brief, in fact he had made what could fairly be considered something of a coup. He would have told her about it, but then somehow he did not tell her, and the fact of his silence gave him pleasure, because he knew she thought him boastful and this was surely a proof to the contrary.

When they reached Judith's house, Thomas Hood was waiting in the drawing-room. Judith was so relieved to see him that she greeted him with too much enthusiasm.

'Oh, Thomas! How simply wonderful to see you!' she cried, and stood smiling delightedly at him.

Thomas looked a little surprised, and then shook her hand, and Baldwin's, in his punctilious way.

Baldwin, on whom Judith's unusual enthusiasm had not been lost, answered without much grace, and sat down aggressively.

Judith suddenly unleashed a flood of idle talk, which was received with complete silence by Baldwin and with a polite response but a look of mild concern by Thomas. Baldwin was relieved when the telephone rang, because it put a stop to this chatter which annoyed and puzzled him.

'Mrs. Lane?' a husky voice said, with so outrageous cockney cum Scottish accent that Judith thought at first it

must be Feliks, who had a liking for that sort of telephoning. She was wrong, however.

'Sandy's the name,' said the voice. 'Pal of Jimmy's –
Jimmy Chandos-Wright – yes, that's it. Said you might
be wanting me for a job. Well, he did say there'd maybe
a spot of delay – I thought I'd just let you know I'm free.
Got a job on next month though. Could fit yours in before
that if you like? No? Quite sure of that, are you? Always
ready to oblige a friend, you know. Tell you what, I'll
give you a number where you can get me, shall I? Then
we can cut out the middleman, eh? Not that I mean I'd
do Jimmy out of his lick – not an old pal like Jimmy – but
saves time, eh? Should you come to be in a hurry, see?'

'Thank you so much – yes – thank you – good-bye. . . .'
She put down the receiver. 'No, really, it's too much,'
she said. 'Too much. I can't bear it.'

'What's too much?' Thomas stood up.

'The whole thing,' Judith said, 'No, I mean
everything— No, really, why should I?'

'Should you what?' said Thomas.

'Anything,' said Judith, 'I mean, really. . . .'

Thomas led her to a chair. 'Take your coat off and sit
down,' he said. 'You're talking nonsense. Sit down. There
you are. You really mustn't get so excited. That's right.'

Baldwin Reeves stood up angrily. 'I'd better go,' he
said. 'I don't seem to be sufficiently soothing. Good-bye
Judith.'

'Good-bye,' said Judith.

As soon as he had gone, she turned to Thomas and
cried: 'Oh, why did you make him go?'

'You are in a state,' said Thomas. 'What shall I do for
you?'

'I'm sorry, Thomas, I really am,' she said. 'Oh dear,
how awful of me. I don't know what it is. I ought to go
away or something.'

'What you want,' said Thomas, 'Is a nice quiet holiday
by the sea, with plenty of fresh air, exercise and good
food. Isn't it? So we'll go down to the Isle of Wight
tomorrow. Aunt Susan's away and you can do whatever
you like. I'll ring up tonight and say we'll be there in time
for tea.'

'Oh, d'you think so?' said Judith.

'Of course,' said Thomas.

'Well, yes,' said Judith. 'It is kind of you. No, I don't want a handkerchief thank you.'

'Bother,' said Thomas, putting it away.

'Why?' asked Judith.

'I often imagine you crying and me comforting you,' said Thomas.

'Oh do you?' said Judith. 'I'm sure it's not in the least like this.'

'Yes, it is,' said Thomas. 'Only you cry more.' He went to telephone his aunt's house.

In the morning Judith told Feliks that she would like to take advantage of the new secretary's presence to take a week off, and they went down to the Isle of Wight.

It was warmer than before. There were a few little sailing boats fluttering about the sea, and one great lovely schooner stretching new sails. The trees were all out and some early azaleas. The daffodils were already over. On the sheltered part of the beach, two or three groups of children built sand castles, and three more fortunate ones daily galloped past on tubby uncontrollable ponies. Farther along it was rocky and deserted. They walked there one day, and Bertie chased seagulls and fell into the sea. After that he began to like it and took to sea-bathing with an enthusiasm astonishing in one so luxury-loving. Judith was happy and guilty – guilty about Thomas, about Baldwin, about herself. Baldwin still lurked in her mind, and his presence there made her feel all the more strongly that there was something in what she was doing now, in her respite, in Thomas, to be snatched at while there was still time.

'You're better,' Thomas said. 'Aren't you?'

'Yes,' she smiled.

'You remember you were going to let me know when you felt like love?' he said.

'Was I?' she said.

'Of course,' he said. 'I think it's probably about now, don't you?'

'No, I don't think so,' she said. But she let him kiss her, and the love which she recognised in him touched her, and made her realise how much she needed it, how much difference already, in spite of her other unhappiness, his love had made to her. She meant to feel ashamed of herself, but somehow could not, and returned his kiss.

He got up, took her hand, and led her out of the room. 'Where are we going?' she asked, but he did not answer and led her upstairs to her bedroom.

'You can put your clothes on that chair,' he said, shutting the door. 'And I'll have this one.'

She meant to laugh, or protest, or ask questions, but before his solemnity she said nothing, but undressed quietly and got into bed.

After that the figure of Baldwin Reeves did not retreat but became less menacing. She felt it all to be only a suspension of time, but she could not deny that for the moment she was happy, and that everything Thomas did helped to make her more happy.

Thomas himself was wholly in love. Obscurely he felt he should not tell her: he hardly knew why – it was perhaps an attempt at what he felt was sophisticated behaviour, perhaps a dim fear which he would not yet admit to himself that words might show up the difference in their states of mind. So sometimes tears would run down his face and though he might sob, or hurt her, or stare enraged into her eyes, he still said nothing. Partly, of course, he did not know the words. His experience of love, though it was more extensive than that of his contemporaries who had not been brought up, as he had been, abroad – that is to say, though it included having once been to bed with a woman – had not taught him its vocabulary. He could say 'darling' but when he once said 'my darling' he blushed furiously and never tried it again.

Judith never knew the extent of his feelings. She realised that he loved her, that he was very moved, that he had known nothing like it; but she never knew how all his life was now in terms of her, how he quite took it for granted that when he had been to Oxford he would marry her and live happily ever after. If she had thought she might have known, but she was, after all, fairly self-centred, and besides she did not want to think.

She was relieved that Thomas's questionings seemed to

have come to an end, and that he said nothing about the future, nor did it occur to her that this was because he imagined there was no doubt about it. Sometimes lying beside her in the big spare bedroom he simply laughed, thinking about it. She would ask him why and he would refuse to tell her. Then she would take him by the shoulders and say: 'Tell me, tell me. . . .' and he would kiss her again, sometimes too roughly, so that she had to stop him, and then he would be sorry. Then he would make love to her again more gently, and then quite suddenly he would be asleep.

Behind his confidence there did lurk a small uncertainty, but he wanted to be confident, and nearly all the time he was.

They stayed longer than a week. Judith rang up her office, but was unable to take business problems in the least seriously. Hanescu, talking to her, sounded a little puzzled: indeed she spoke as if she were in Timbuctoo, not ninety miles away in a big Victorian villa in the Isle of Wight. But Aunt Susan came back, Thomas's mother and sister had finished their visit to America, and nothing could wait.

They travelled back to London and parted at the station, with peace of mind on Thomas's part and a great sense of loss on Judith's. She took a taxi to Chelsea, and as it turned into the street she saw the familiar figure of Baldwin on her doorstep. He was asking when she would be coming back, and she saw him, having been turned away by Jean-Claude, come down the steps and walk into the King's Road, preoccupied, passing her taxi without noticing who was in it.

10

'I'M going to ask you a question,' Mrs. Lane said. 'To which you needn't of course reply if you don't want to. But I feel you will, because I don't think, really, we've many secrets, have we?'

She was smartly dressed, as she always was, in London, and had had her hair done that morning – it was naturally wavy and fitted her fine small head in blue-grey exactitude. Her dark eyes bent their kind distant smile on Judith, a smile as controlled and calm as all her other manifestations.

A little frightened, Judith said: 'Of course we haven't.'

'No,' said Mrs. Lane, leaning back in her chair and accepting a cup of tea. 'It's just that poor old Fa – well, you know, really he's a bit past.'

Already anxious about what was to come, Judith wished her mother-in-law would not look so grand. Harris, Heaven knew, was shabby enough, yet for some reason Mrs. Lane always made Judith feel the little Chelsea house was hopelessly inadequate.

'He likes to make a mystery out of things,' Mrs. Lane went on. 'I suppose it's because, poor old thing, he hasn't much to occupy him these days.'

'No,' said Judith, now sure of what was coming.

'It was just a letter which he asked me to open for him,' said Mrs. Lane. 'One of yours. And there was some mention in it of Anthony, and a sum of money, which I didn't quite understand, and when I asked him he became so secretive that I thought the best thing was to ask you. I didn't want to worry him about it.'

'No, of course not.' Judith paused. 'Well, as a matter of fact, it is something, not really – well, which you might not like.'

She looked at the woman sitting opposite her. There seemed to be so much strength in her face that Judith wondered whether she had not been foolish in not telling her before.

'If you want to know, of course I'll tell you,' she said. 'I didn't before because it's rather unpleasant.'

'If it concerns Anthony I should like to know it,' said Mrs. Lane.

'Well,' said Judith, reluctant to remind herself. 'I suppose I must.' She sighed. 'Anthony wasn't a very brave man. You probably know that. He had many more important qualities and it doesn't alter the fact that we all loved him. But the reports of how he behaved in Korea were not quite truthful.'

'They were perfectly well authenticated,' said Mrs. Lane.

'Somebody who had been with him the whole time came to see me,' said Judith. 'And told me the whole story – about how frightened Anthony had been. . . .'

'Frightened?' said Mrs. Lane. 'I imagine they were all frightened.'

'Somebody else had to take over the command,' said Judith. 'And Anthony kept back the order to retreat because he thought it was an order to stay where they were. And then in the prison camp some of them were treated very badly. Anthony gave away a plan to escape and so someone was shot. Anthony didn't die of wounds as it was said. He wasn't wounded.'

'He was shot trying to escape?' asked Mrs. Lane.

'He was killed by the other prisoners,' said Judith. 'Because he gave away their plan to escape and one of them was shot by the guards.'

Mrs. Lane put down her tea cup.

'Who told you this?' she asked.

'Someone who'd been with him,' said Judith. 'He blackmailed me, saying that he would make a public scandal out of it by telling the whole story to the newspapers. So I had to give him money.'

'Was it the man you told me about ? Reed?' Mrs. Lane asked.

'No no, not him,' said Judith. 'Another man.'

'But this man Reed was with him,' said Mrs. Lane. 'He can deny the story.'

'Reeves,' said Judith. 'He said the same thing.'

'He was jealous,' said Mrs. Lane. 'He was always jealous. I knew at the time. He should never have been allowed in the regiment.'

Judith, who had not looked at her mother-in-law while she was speaking, now raised her eyes and saw that Mrs. Lane had turned a yellowish white. She did not meet Judith's eyes, but turning her face away said: 'Why did you not tell me at once?'

'I didn't want to tell you,' said Judith. 'I couldn't see any point in upsetting you.'

'Upsetting me?' said Mrs. Lane. 'Upsetting me? What an extraordinary thing to say. It doesn't upset me in the slightest.'

'It doesn't?' said Judith, amazed. 'Then you knew – we all knew – oh, how strange!'

'Of course I knew my son,' Mrs. Lane said. 'I knew him better than anyone else. I was the only person he cared for. I knew him, and I know him now.'

Judith said nothing.

Mrs. Lane went on, in a hard rasping voice that trembled frighteningly.

'I know that no amount of slander can make any difference. He was always brave and true and honourable – all his life. He came of a decent family, and he upheld its traditions. It was unthinkable to him to do anything dishonest. He was an English gentleman.'

Judith gave a sort of moan.

'You know it as well as I do,' said Mrs. Lane, in her new voice. 'How dare you take our money to pay some slanderer for his lies? It was wicked of you, wicked. The man must be punished. I shall go round to the War Office at once – yes, now.' She stood up. 'I'm going to put a stop to it at once. What is the name of this man? He wasn't there at all. I knew all of them who were with Anthony. What is his name?'

Judith got up too. 'Please. . . .' she began. 'Please don't do anything rash. I have thought so carefully about whether anything could be done. . . .'

'What is his name?' said Mrs. Lane.

'But please,' said Judith. 'It won't do any good.'

Mrs. Lane suddenly seized her by both arms. 'What is his name?' she said wildly. 'What is his name? What is his name?'

'But I can't tell you, I can't,' said Judith. 'He didn't tell me who he was. He wouldn't say.'

Mrs. Lane began to shake her. 'You'll tell me who he is,' she now spoke in a sort of screaming whisper. 'I'll make you tell me. I daresay you thought it all very fine to get money out of an old idiot like that. Didn't you? What did you do with the money? Did you keep it? Did you make the whole thing up?'

'No no stop,' said Judith. 'You mustn't say that. I know how awful it is. I was horrified too.'

'So you were horrified,' Mrs. Lane was still gripping Judith's arms. 'You were horrified. Oh yes. Of course. You thought it was a good way of getting money didn't you? Was it for this man, or did you make the whole thing up yourself? He's your lover – you hatched the plot between you. You've always been after our money. That's why you married Anthony. I knew at the time you didn't care for him.'

'Oh don't don't,' said Judith. 'You mustn't say that, you don't mean it.'

Mrs. Lane suddenly let go of her arms, pushing her violently away.

'You never understood him,' she walked away from Judith. 'You wanted the money, the position. I knew. How could you understand that sort of man, who was a gentleman and came from a good family? This could never have happened, never, when I was young. Nobody would have believed you then. The world's changed. People have no sense of values, no decency, they're all out for what they can get. Our sort of people get pushed aside by all the lies and ingratitude. The Welfare State – it's just a means of sheltering these liars and slanderers and upstarts. I brought Anthony up in the old-fashioned way, to be what his father was before him.'

She suddenly stopped, and turned fiercely round.

'If his father had been alive this would never have

happened,' she said. 'He would never have allowed it. He wouldn't have allowed the marriage. He'd have seen Anthony married to someone who could understand him, someone of his own sort.' Tears began to run down her face, which did not change its expression of fierce despair. 'I spent my whole life in bringing up Anthony to be what he was. My whole life. My husband died of overwork for his country – they don't do that now. They have a five day week, holidays with pay, pensions, free this, free that. But my husband and my son died for them. They don't do anything for widows and mothers, do they, in the Welfare State? They don't do anything for me, do they? I have to live out my miserable life in that horrible uncomfortable house with a gaga old man, and who cares what becomes of me? I don't get anything for it. They don't do anything for old women, do they? Who ought to be being looked after. But who cares for what I've done for my country – both my brothers were killed in the war. But they don't do anything for old women. There's no sense of values. The young are so selfish. . . .' her voice mercifully began to die down.

'I know,' said Judith quickly, urgently wishing to put an end to this horrifying tirade. 'I know how you feel, I really do. . . . Look, do come and sit down.'

'You don't know anything,' said Mrs. Lane. 'You're selfish and hard like all your immoral generation. Why should I sit down, here, in your house, when you're a traitor to everything Anthony died for?'

Judith said gently: 'You needn't of course. I'm sorry. I didn't know there was all this bitterness in you – I never really knew what you were feeling, but I never imagined, I never dreamt, it could be this.'

Mrs. Lane was now leaning against the wall in an attitude of exhaustion, still very pale.

'You think I'm just a bitter old woman,' she said. 'You wait. You'll see. I've been patient. I've done my duty. But who cares for an old woman? I'm ugly. I'm often in pain. What do I get back for what I gave? Soon I shall die, but who'll care about that? I'm just a useless old woman in a world that's made for money, and war, and power. Nobody believes in what I believe in now.'

'But you must believe it,' Judith was trembling with shock and with desire to persuade this unknown frantic being out of its despair. 'You don't believe it any more. You haven't thought lately, you've forgotten what your faith was – it wasn't like this. It was strong and valid once. It was a faith in humanity and God, and. . . .'

'God!' said Mrs. Lane, jerking herself away from the wall and sitting slowly down in an armchair. 'What do you know about God? You're all atheists, your generation. Our God doesn't exist any more. You saw to that.' She took a small handkerchief out of her bag and blew her nose violently. 'What do you care about Anthony?' she then said. 'You never had any children. The modern generation don't believe in children. I know.'

The door was suddenly opened and Jean-Claude's ugly sane face looked in. 'You heard not the bell?' he asked. 'Is Mr. Reeves.'

'Oh Baldwin,' said Judith, as his figure appeared in the dark of the hall, behind Jean-Claude. 'Look, I've something to show you here, before you come in. . . .'

Outside the drawing-room she shut the door, and led Baldwin half way up the stairs, out of earshot.

'Listen, I've had the most terrifying scene with my mother-in-law,' she said quickly. 'About Anthony. I had to tell her – she found out – I can't explain now. But she went absolutely frantic, she won't believe it, she thinks I made it up to get the money – I can't tell you how awful it was. She's almost mad.'

'What can I do?' asked Baldwin. 'D'you want me to go?'

'No, we'll go in in a minute,' said Judith. 'It's better, I think. If she's alone with me she'll only start again. But she knows you were with Anthony. She doesn't think you're the blackmailer. I told her that was someone else; but she's very likely to talk to you about it.'

'What do you want me to say?' asked Baldwin.

'You must tell her he was a hero,' said Judith. 'It doesn't matter what she thinks of me. Tell her that.'

She led the way back into the drawing-room.

The arrival of a stranger had induced Mrs. Lane to make the effort necessary to calm herself. She was sitting

quietly, looking at an evening paper. Judith introduced
Baldwin, and he began to make polite conversation while
Jean-Claude cleared away the tea things. Judith, suddenly
tired, leant back in her chair and allowed Baldwin to take
over the conversation. She had to admit he did it well,
talking entertainingly but uncontroversially about
theatres, the traffic problem, this and that. The look of
strain lessened on Mrs. Lane's face, but after a time she
took advantage of a brief pause to say, with her polite
smile:

'Wasn't it you who was in the same regiment as my
son Anthony?'

'Yes, that's it,' said Baldwin. 'I remember coming to
your flat in Hyde Park Gate once with him. Have you still
got that? It was so nice, I remember.'

'No, I gave it up,' said Mrs. Lane. 'I don't come up to
London a great deal now. My life is much quieter without
Anthony. We were so much together, you know.'

'Yes, of course,' said Baldwin. 'You live up in Lancashire, then, do you? Or is it Yorkshire?'

'Anthony was a wonderful son to me,' said Mrs. Lane,
without answering. 'There aren't many people like that
nowadays. They always say it's the best who go, don't
they?'

Judith, checking an impulse desperately to agree, went
over to the cupboard in the hope that an offer of a drink
might change the subject.

'Didn't Judith tell me,' said Mrs. Lane. 'That you were
with Anthony most of that terrible time?'

'Yes, I was,' said Baldwin.

'You'll forgive me if I say I think that was a privilege?'
said Mrs. Lane, smiling again.

'It was,' said Baldwin. 'Anthony had immense charm.
I very much enjoyed knowing him. He had a lot of
friends, of course. I wonder if you ever see any of them.
Do you remember Charles Finnigan, who came with us
to the flat that day?'

'Some of his friends were rather odd,' said Mrs. Lane.
'Some were jealous, and wanted to detract from his glory.
He died a glorious death, you see.'

'Yes,' said Baldwin. 'But Charles was always one of his

most outspoken admirers. I just wondered whether you knew what he'd done after the war. His family lived in Leicestershire somewhere, I think.'

Miraculously, Mrs. Lane did know the Finnigans and could be persuaded to talk about them. In fact the conversation flowed on comparatively smoothly until she said, addressing Judith for the first time since Baldwin's arrival: 'I'm afraid I must go. The Digby's are back from Washington and very kindly asked me to dinner, and I shall have to change. I'm looking forward to seeing them again. Thank you so much for my tea. No, don't bother to see me out. Oh, my coat – thank you so much, Mr. Reed. I'm glad to think you knew Anthony. You know, mothers are foolish, I'm afraid, and I'm awfully proud to think he was a hero.' Again the wild smile, and she shook hands with Baldwin, though not with Judith, and was gone.

'Oh oh oh,' Judith sank into a chair. 'That was awful, terrible, frightful. . . .'

'She will convince herself again that he was a hero,' said Baldwin. 'She'll really believe it before long.'

'But what can her life be like?' said Judith. 'I had no idea, no idea. You don't know the bitterness she revealed, the horror. Bitterness against everything. Oh, such despair. . . .'

Baldwin sat down opposite her, and looked at her attentively. 'It's not easy to be old,' he said.

'But I had no idea,' said Judith. 'That's what's so extraordinary. Was she always like that, do you imagine?'

'Probably it was once quite an admirable pride,' said Baldwin.

'What are you doing here?' said Judith. 'I forgot about that. I couldn't bear another scene.'

'I'm very reasonable really,' said Baldwin, smiling. 'Very reasonable. If you like I'll go away, but I'd rather not.'

'No, it doesn't matter,' said Judith. 'Besides I'd rather not be alone – life's too alarming, suddenly.'

'What a confession,' said Baldwin. 'You admit that you'd rather have me than nothing – I never dared hope for as much as that. No, I mean it – it was a moment of weakness of which I won't remind you, but I am pleased.'

'But look,' said Judith. 'All this is your fault.'

'I know,' said Baldwin seriously. 'Of course I know. I want to talk to you about it, and about some other important things, but I thought perhaps not now?'

'No, not now,' said Judith. 'After dinner.'

'After dinner,' said Baldwin, noticing that she was committing herself to spending the evening with him.

'How did she find out?' he asked later.

'She opened a letter I wrote to the old man,' said Judith.

'What did it say?' asked Baldwin.

'Oh, it mentioned the money and so on,' said Judith. 'He paid it you see. The £500 came. I knew it would, and now you say you don't want it.'

'No,' said Baldwin. 'Send it back. I never knew you'd told him.'

'You told me to, don't you remember?' said Judith. 'I hadn't got that amount of money myself.'

'Oh,' said Baldwin.

'So now I'm to send it back?' asked Judith.

'Yes,' said Baldwin.

'Well, you have got into a mess, haven't you, over this?' said Judith.

'Yes,' said Baldwin.

'I can't think what you were doing really,' said Judith. 'And it was very dangerous. You might easily have gone to prison.'

'Perhaps that was what appealed to me about it?' suggested Baldwin.

'I don't think so,' said Judith.

'No,' said Baldwin. 'I think it was jealousy of Anthony among other things. He got away with so much, you know; and then I felt he was even getting away with that, when I came back and found him a public hero. And you looked a bit like him, in a way, as if you might be equally unassailable. That made me want to tell you – yes, nasty I know. I knew it was nasty at the time. The thought of blackmail came second.'

'You felt that gave you a reasonable excuse for making

the revelation which was to humiliate me?' asked Judith, coldly.

'Possibly, possibly,' said Baldwin. 'I don't fool myself. I did it only because I'd not thought of anything legitimate which might serve to further my ambitions.'

'You still think that?' asked Judith.

Baldwin looked embarrassed. 'It's a – a theory which might have to be modified,' he said. 'In practice.'

Judith smiled.

'But you can imagine feeling the power,' he said, with some vehemence, looking at her. 'The power in you. Imagine feeling every day more confident in it, knowing it's growing and time is passing, and not being allowed to use it.'

'There's humility,' said Judith. 'The most tiresome, and the most often misinterpreted, of the Christian virtues, I know, but still there it is.'

'I have no humility and no patience,' said Baldwin. 'Perhaps you would care to teach them to me.'

'I don't think I can teach you anything,' said Judith.

He was not prepared to argue with her now. He smiled and said: 'You taught me how not to be a blackmailer.'

'I should have thought you were quite a successful one,' said Judith.

'You mean the money?' he said. 'You must tell me which was his and which was yours, so that I can return it.'

'And that, of course, will make everything all right?' said Judith.

'I know, I know,' he said. 'I told you. I made you tell him. And the mother.'

'She'll never get over it,' said Judith. 'And he is a simple man with simple principles who – what an awful thing to have done, what an awful thing.'

'Yes,' said Baldwin. 'It was irresponsible. You know I wish you hadn't told him. I never really thought you would.'

'How was I to get the money?' said Judith. 'And there you were, waving that foul document in front of my face. No, you can't shift the blame.'

'I wasn't trying to do that,' said Baldwin. 'No, I accept it all. But it makes it difficult. He knows it's me, of course?'

'Yes,' said Judith.

'Yes,' he said. 'No, I really wish he didn't know. I really wish he didn't.'

'Why?' said Judith. 'What does it matter to you?'

'It makes things difficult,' said Baldwin. 'Especially in view of the proposition I was going to make to you. You're fond of him, aren't you?'

'What proposition?' asked Judith.

'You respect his opinion, don't you?' said Baldwin. 'He's your family, more or less, only you're more sentimental about him. Isn't that so?'

'I suppose so,' said Judith. 'It's my home, very much. There's no reason why it should be, now, but it still is.'

'And you go up for a lot of week-ends,' said Baldwin. 'And you really rather admire your mother-in-law too. And there's old Nanny, and the house, and the village.'

'Did I tell you this?' asked Judith.

'Not in so many words,' he said.

'What about it?' she said.

'I'm afraid if we got married it might mean a break with them,' he answered.

There was a pause. 'I should have thought that was a contingency which was hardly likely to arise,' said Judith, eventually.

'You don't face facts,' he said.

'Facts?' she echoed.

'The fact of – no, don't be angry – the fact of what exists between us,' he said. 'Please don't ignore it. But we should get on very well. We're the same sort of person. Together we should be much more of a force than apart.'

'You're thinking of power again,' she said. 'You think I might help you to be successful – a wife might be useful to your career. I'm to be nice to the right people, have them to dinner, open fetes and jumble sales when you stand for Parliament.'

He smiled. 'You'd be rather good at it,' he said. 'You'd hate it, but funnily enough you'd really be quite good at it. No, you know I don't mean only that: you want to pretend I mean that so that you can work yourself up into a rage and think how despicable I am, but there's more to it than that, and I know you know it because you always know what I mean. That you can admit – aren't I horribly clear to you?'

'I suppose so,' she said.

'Look, you know how you find the world,' he said. 'Remember that scene tonight with Mrs. Lane. You know how sometimes madness seems to be on every side. You see it on people's faces in the street. Or illness. You think everything's fine with people and then there's some little lie and the whole thing's gone to pieces. Sometimes you think the only people who aren't impossibly shifty or mad are the very very stupid, or the ones who are dying. But you and I, to each other, are different. We're reasonable, we're of the same mind – we haven't altogether proved it, but we know it. We do, you know.'

'I don't,' said Judith. 'Nor do I think all that.' She was thinking of Thomas, but rather as if he were dead.

'You think I'm bad, you know,' said Baldwin, after a pause. 'With reason, no doubt. But what about you? You seem, in some curious way, to have come to think of yourself as a Lane – not a member of the real Lane family, because after all we both know the very great weaknesses of that – but a sort of idealised Lane, upholding the old traditions, rooted firmly in your county past, a part of English history. . . .'

'No,' said Judith. 'Nonsense.'

'Now morally,' said Baldwin. 'I'm the first to admit you're a good deal better than I am, but you can be unscrupulous too. What about your behaviour to Thomas Hood? How's that been?'

'What d'you mean?' she said.

He paused, then said: 'Well, we won't go into it. All I mean. . . .'

'Yes we will,' she said. 'What about Thomas Hood?'

'No, you looked guilty,' he said. 'It doesn't matter.'

'Yes it does,' she said. 'What are you talking about?'

'Oh, my dear, what do I know about it?' he said. 'I've seen you together that's all. I've seen him, after that time you went away for so long I know you used him as an escape from me. I know the state of mind you were in. I can see he's in love with you, as you are not with him, and that you know he's very young and quite unable to deal with you. I can only think your behaviour rather ruthless.'

Judith's eyes filled with tears but she said nothing.

'He can't help, you know,' said Baldwin. 'It's no good pretending things are other than they are. That's why I think we ought to get married.'

After a pause, Judith said: 'Apart from anything else, you've already pointed out that it would mean the end of any sort of relations with the Lanes. That makes it out of the question for me.'

'Will you try one thing?' said Baldwin. And if it fails you shall decide as you like. Take me up there for a week-end. She doesn't know I was the blackmailer. I'll return the money to you, so that you can pay him back before we go there, and we'll explain to him somehow that it was a mistake and I'll see if I can improve the situation. Just let me try. After that, if you really want it, I'll give up.'

'You really will?' she said.

'Yes,' he answered.

'I suppose I could,' she said, slowly. 'If you insist. I could ask anyway. Yes, I suppose I could.'

'You will then?' he asked.

'Yes, I will,' she said. 'All right. I will.'

Thomas's mother and sister came back from America. He went to meet the boat train at Victoria.

On the station he bought two yellow rosebuds, one for each of them. When he had come out of the shop he stood uneasily between platforms six and seven, holding the flowers and wondering if the gesture were not rather affected. He decided it was. He would rather keep them and give them to Judith; but he could hardly greet his mother and Emma holding flowers which were not for them. If he shortened their stalks, he might almost put them in his pocket; but then they would probably be squashed. Could he, perhaps, out of the two pieces of paper in which they were severally wrapped, make them into one uninteresting parcel which would escape his mother's notice?

Engrossed in this problem, he began to walk towards the platform at which the boat train would arrive.

A moment later he saw Baldwin Reeves. He would have preferred not to have spoken to him, but Baldwin had already seen him, and breezily accosted him.

'Ah Thomas!' he said. 'Where are you off to? I'm on my way back from a case in the suburbs – you've no idea what lurid lives they lead there. What charming flowers.'

'I'm meeting my mother,' said Thomas. 'She's coming back from America.'

'I wonder how it will have affected your nice sister,' said Baldwin. 'They've been there several months haven't they?'

'Three,' said Thomas.

'Seen anything of Judith Lane lately?' said Baldwin.

'Yes,' said Thomas.

The proud monosyllable annoyed Baldwin. Not having altogether meant to, he nevertheless found himself saying: 'We're getting married you know.'

Thomas looked surprised, and politely interested.

'Congratulations,' he said.

Baldwin was embarrassed, and would have liked to have withdrawn his remark.

He went on rather abruptly: 'Yes, we're going up there next week-end – tomorrow in fact. Well, I must be going – see you later.'

'Up where?' asked Thomas.

'To Harris,' said Baldwin.

'Oh I see,' said Thomas, with more interest. 'Is she a friend of Judith's?'

'Is who a friend of Judith's?'

'Your – that is, the person you are marrying?'

'But I am marrying Judith.'

They stood without moving, Baldwin half turned away and Thomas amazed.

'I don't understand you,' said Thomas, eventually.

Baldwin moved his feet awkwardly. 'I'm afraid I've been a bit premature in telling you,' he said.

'No, no.' said Thomas. He paused a moment, then went on firmly: 'But there's a mistake. You're wrong.'

Baldwin smiled uneasily, annoyed again. 'I'm not, you know,' he said.

'You can't marry Judith,' said Thomas, with finality.

'I can,' said Baldwin. There was another pause.

'Judith is my mistress,' said Thomas.

Baldwin turned red. 'Even so. . . .' he said.

'She told you?' asked Thomas.

'Well. . . .' said Baldwin.

'How can you marry her, then?' said Thomas.

'Look, I'm awfully sorry about this,' said Baldwin.

'How can you marry her?'

'What do you mean, how can I?' said Baldwin. 'Of course I can.'

'I don't understand,' said Thomas.

'I'm sorry,' said Baldwin. 'I should have left it to her to tell you.' He stood inadequately, not knowing what to say but not thinking of telling Thomas the truth, that he had simply made the suggestion to Judith. This was because, though he felt genuinely sorry for Thomas, it seemed to him out of the question that he should lose face in front of him by going back on his original assertion: he was also by now convinced that it would soon become a fact.

'Well, I must be getting along, you know,' he said. 'Sorry about all this. Silly of me to say anything about it. Anyway – we'll meet soon. Good-bye.'

But Thomas, though almost as outwardly composed as ever, was in the grip of the most bitter emotion of his life. Out of it he said, suddenly and loudly as Baldwin began to walk away, 'I want you to have these.'

He held out his two yellow roses, stiffly, at the end of his arm. Baldwin stopped, but looked at him in silence. Thomas pressed the roses into his hand, stared into his face a little wildly, and in a moment had disappeared, running through the crowd towards the way out of the station.

11

Tʜᴇʏ went to Harris. It was May and bitterly cold. The wind from the north swept through Wensleydale and Wharfedale, whisking away, it is true, the rainy edges of the deep cloud that lay over the Lake District, but bringing with it a bleak unseasonable cold.

The central heating was turned off on the first of April, regardless of the weather. The huge boiler, which, antiquated, wasteful and marvellously powerful, kept the draughty house warm all through the winter, finished its task the moment March was over, and though for several years now, such had been the slowness of our northern spring, there had been protests, discussions, even decisions, nothing had ever been done, and the central heating still went off on April the first.

Nanny was even against fires after that date. There was no reason for this. She suffered from the cold as much as, if not more than, most people; but she had always been very mean with other people's property. Fires were lit, however, because Mrs. Lane insisted on it, but Nanny had various methods of sabotaging this course of action. Looks and sighs and mutterings went unnoticed, so she attacked the fuel supply. She would intercept Florence, the maid, a gentle shy girl from the village, and volunteer to carry the refilled coal scuttle into the drawing-room; then she would leave it outside. She would also seize any opportunity she had when left alone in that room to push the wood basket into a dark unaccustomed corner. When anybody complained of the lack of fuel, she would say briskly (or as briskly as she ever said anything): 'Well, do you really think it's cold enough? I hardly think it's really cold enough, you know.' And then occasionally the fire would be allowed to go out, and Nanny would be left with a sense of righteous victory.

This campaign took up most of her time for the few weeks after the central heating was turned off. They were probably the happiest weeks of her year, for in them she felt the mental stimulation which is the reward of the overworked.

Feliks came with them. It was his first visit to Harris: neither Anthony nor Judith had ever been much given to asking people there; and it was perhaps partly the feeling of achievement his having finally got there gave him which made him so extravagantly delighted with the place. He was eulogistic at meals, thereby immediately forfeiting the regard of Mrs. Lane, Sir Ralph and Nanny, who could none of them believe him to be sincere.

Judith knew that he was, and was glad after all that he had come. He had asked himself, unable, he said, to bear the humiliation of Baldwin's having been asked before he was; and Judith, quite unable to explain why Baldwin was coming at all, had half-heartedly agreed. As it was, though, he was an asset, for though Mrs. Lane was charming to Baldwin, it was an uneasy, over-laboured, charm, and Sir Ralph had retreated into age and silence.

Judith tried to talk to him, but could get nothing out of him. He had found a canvas bag in some old cupboard. It was a relic of the days when he had had, for a year or two, a passion for sailing, and had raced an eight-metre with startling success, but it seemed to have hardly been used.

'This is going to make things much easier for me, much easier,' he said. 'I shall be able to take all my things out to the turning-round-house.'

There was an old creaking summer-house in the garden where he liked to sit when it was warm enough. The trouble was that it very seldom was warm enough, and he spent a good deal of time packing his 'ditty-bag' with all his account books, his writing materials, his scarf, and anything else he thought might come in useful – glue, a dictionary, a compass – and taking it out into the garden, only to be told, or to decide for himself, that he was bound to catch a chill. He would come back again and unpack. Then a shaft of bright sunlight would come through the window, the sky would be briefly blue and the whole process would start again.

'You did understand about the money,' Judith said. 'That it all came back?'

'Yes, yes indeed,' said Sir Ralph. 'I think I've sorted that out all right. Took some doing, but I've got it clear now. Haven't had my this month's statement, though, of course – I daresay he's made a muddle of it.'

'You see it was all a mistake,' said Judith. 'About Baldwin, I mean.'

'I'm not going to take a dictionary today,' said Sir Ralph. 'What on earth do I want a dictionary for?'

'*The Times* crossword?'

'Oh,' said Sir Ralph. 'Oh yes. You may be right. The crossword. But this is a German dictionary.'

'You see he never meant that, at all – it was my fault really,' said Judith. 'I was so frightened – when I heard, I mean – it was really my idea to give him money. . . .'

'I will take it,' said Sir Ralph. 'I will take it. You never know, do you? And besides, I like dictionaries – always have liked them – even German ones. Never ought to be without a dictionary.'

'But you do understand?' said Judith.

'What's that?' said Sir Ralph.

'I want you to understand about the mistake about Baldwin Reeves and the money and Anthony,' said Judith. 'It's very important to me that you should.'

'Do you know what the Vicar's Christian name is?' said Sir Ralph.

'No,' said Judith.

'I was listening to what you were saying,' said Sir Ralph, apologetically. 'Only it reminded me that I didn't know the Vicar's Christian name. On account of Baldwin being such a funny name for a fellow. Really a very funny name.'

'D'you like him?' asked Judith.

'Wardle?' said Sir Ralph.

'No, Baldwin,' said Judith.

'Oh yes yes yes,' said Sir Ralph. 'Very much indeed.

You like everybody when you get to my age. Except Nanny. What about this, eh? This string. . . .'

'I wanted to talk to you about Baldwin,' said Judith. 'I thought you might be able to help.'

'Ah, as to that,' said Sir Ralph. 'I think I will take this string. I might want to do some gardening. Yes, I know, I know. I'm an old man you know, Judith, we mustn't forget that. I'm really an old, old man.'

'Oh I didn't mean,' said Judith, 'to bother you.'

'You could never bother me, my dear,' said Sir Ralph, smiling at her. 'But don't you worry. There's a point, you know, when one must let oneself grow old, just as there's a point when one must let oneself die. It's difficult to know when they're reached – very difficult. I don't want to read out there, do I, as well? I've got my accounts. Still, I might as well take a book, just in case.'

'What about a rug?' asked Judith.

'A rug. Yes,' said Sir Ralph. 'Though it really looks quite warm out there. Still there's no harm in taking a rug. Don't you worry my dear. There's nobody I wish better than you, nobody at all. No, don't bother. I can carry it. Gets a bit heavy, though. D'you know I think I will leave that dictionary behind after all?'

Mrs. Lane said to Judith: 'How charming Anthony's friend is.' That was what she had made him in her own mind – Anthony's faithful friend, courageous witness to the heroism of his superior officer – and as such she talked to him endlessly of her son. He let her do it, hoping it might make her look less ill.

He was interested besides, in hearing anything about Anthony. This odd hard house had been where he had lived and Baldwin's feelings about him were refreshed by it; in fact, Mrs. Lane's memories being all coloured by her state of mind, he found the house a more rewarding source of information about Anthony than his mother was.

'Did Anthony like this house?' he asked Nanny.

'No,' said Nanny.

He had lived here though. He had walked into this cold

room, thrown down a coat or a stick, lain in this chair, been a light-eyed boy in the nursery.

'He was a boy, like all boys,' said Nanny sourly, in answer to his queries. 'They're all the same, boys.'

'All?' said Baldwin.

'Well, he had a way with him, that's all,' Nanny admitted. 'He was up to all the tricks I will say. I never knew a child like him. Not but what he was like all boys. They're all the same, all boys.'

'You mean he didn't like washing?' Baldwin asked. 'That sort of thing?'

'He was a clean boy, that I will say,' said Nanny. 'Not a sissy but always looked nice. Lovely complexion he had, all through school and everything, I remember. But untidy! You'd have needed three of me to clear up after him. Did he ever take off his coat without throwing it on the floor? And books and paints and pencils and forever taking off the dogs' collars and losing them.'

'Oh dogs,' said Baldwin. 'Was Bertie one of them?'

'Retrievers he had,' said Nanny. 'He always had retrievers. It was she liked this kind. He had retrievers. And bones all over the house and never did he hang up a coat of his own.'

'But when he married,' said Baldwin. 'Then of course it must have been different.'

'Nothing could change him,' said Nanny, with satisfaction.

'No, I daresay nothing did,' said Baldwin. 'Did you go to their wedding?'

'I went to London for it,' she said. 'We all went to London for it. There's many would have given a lot to be in her shoes, though she suited him, I will say she suited him well enough. And the nursery now, the nicest room in the house, he used to say.' This admission, rashly made to a stranger she did not wholly trust, seemed at once to strike her as having been a mistake, for she began to mumble in a vaguely qualifying way.

'I can see he broke a lot of hearts,' said Baldwin unkindly.

'Well, I must be getting along,' Nanny said. 'They're all the same, all boys. Well, I must be getting along.' She bustled out of the room, quite as if she had something to do.

Later Baldwin walked up into the nursery, and found that the wide windows and some pale sunshine in which the dust danced made it what might well have been the nicest room in the house.

There was an ink-stained desk in the corner at which Anthony had presumably sat. In the thin face the light brown eyes had scanned, bored, the unrewarding country from this window: the voice had been here, had insulted, probably, that doting old Nanny; all those familiar movements had been made in this room. 'Oh, Baldwin,' he might have said, turning as if he had been waiting for him, 'Oh, Baldwin,' and made some demand on him, with which he would have without question complied.

The room had the look very much of being uninhabited, which made Baldwin feel quite simply the desolation of being dead, no matter how many demands might have been made, and acceded to, how much love willingly or unwillingly claimed.

As he went out of the room he vaguely registered it as being the one in which he and Judith were least likely to be disturbed, should it come to that. He did not go into the question of whether or not the fact of its being the room most still reminiscent of Anthony had anything to do with the pleasantness of his picture of Judith's seduction there. It was all too complicated.

The next thing now, it seemed to him, encouraged by his success with Mrs. Lane, was to charm Sir Ralph.

At first he surveyed him cautiously but with confidence, a military expert inspecting a beleaguered garrison which could not hope to hold out much longer. It was simply a question of finding the weaknesses in the ancient walls, of executing the campaign with the most possible dash and bravado. But in some extraordinary way the citadel remained impregnable. Through lunch, tea, dinner, the garden, the cold summer house, the draughty library, the campaign was waged, and failed.

At dinner Baldwin had all his forces out. Hardly a name in public life for the last fifty years but was evoked to help his cause. (You must have known So-and-so – he

was a friend of mine.') Some or other variation of this
method had usually worked in the past. There was nearly
always a snobbery somewhere, of however rare a variety,
through which an assault could be made. Here there was
either none or one so vast as to imply: 'Of course you
know all the right people – otherwise you wouldn't be in
my house.' Baldwin could not make up his mind which
was the case, but nor could he believe that this tried old
method would not somehow prove applicable in the end.
Like a general with too many victories to his credit, he
had become inflexible.

Advice on gardening and estate management ('Gavin
Miller was telling me the other day that at Longdon – I
expect you know it – he's turning over more and more to
timber. Soft woods, of course'), on the Stock Exchange,
on tax evasion and on the desirability of litigation ('I hear
you're having some difficulty with a tenant farmer') all
provoked the same polite, vague and increasingly irrelevant replies. The recent years of Sir Ralph's life had been
quiet: his daughter-in-law's animosity was so much a
habit for both of them that it had assumed a sort of
propriety in his estimation, and by the few people outside
his family whom he did see he was treated with deference
but not taken seriously, not listened to much, but
humoured, as a well-known eccentric, so that conversationally he had had things pretty well his own way. He
found the battery to which he was now exposed – and
by someone of, as far as he could remember, the most
regrettable character – unusual and altogether unwel-
come. He retreated a little further into the refuge of
apparent feeble-mindedness.

'Didn't you once own an eight-metre, sir?'

'Ah, we can't all be spacemen, Mr. Baldwin.'

'No, indeed. I'm sure I should prefer the Solent to outer
space. I spent a good deal of time last summer on a rather
nice converted six-metre belonging to a friend of mind.
He keeps her in the Hamble.'

'Nanny, I think Mr. Baldwin would like some bread.
The Hamble, yes, how delightful.'

'His name is Mr. Reeves, Fa,' said Mrs. Lane.

'You kept her at Cowes, I suppose?' said Baldwin. 'No,
I won't have any bread thank you.'

'No, no, Good Heavens no,' said Sir Ralph. 'We lived
in London then. We never went to Cowes except for the
sailing.'

'Oh,' said Baldwin. 'They're lovely boats, of course,
aren't they? But awfully expensive to keep up. Paget,
whom I met the other day, was telling me he doesn't
think he'll be able to afford his much longer.'

'Nanny, did you give Mr. Baldwin some bread?' said
Sir Ralph.

'No, I won't have any really, thank you so much,' said
Baldwin.

'He doesn't want any,' said Nanny.

'Really?' said Sir Ralph, apparently surprised.

'No, really, thank you,' said Baldwin. 'Was he in the
class when you had your boat – Paget, I mean?'

'We had a wretched vet here once,' said Sir Ralph with
sudden animation. 'Absolutely without the most elemen-
tary knowledge of hygiene – a filthy fellow. If you had a
sick animal you could be quite sure it would catch something far worse if he came to see it. He was covered in
germs. I used to make him stand in a bucket of Lysol
before I'd let him into the stables.'

'Oh did you?' said Baldwin.

'His name was Paget,' said Sir Ralph.

Afterwards Judith said to Baldwin, 'I think he likes to
be left alone really.'

'Oh no, he's a splendid old thing,' said Baldwin. 'I
enjoy talking to him. We shall get on very well.'

Judith had not imagined him thick-skinned. If she had
not known whether or not she wanted him to succeed
with Sir Ralph, she had certainly not known how much
importance she would attach to the outcome of his effort.
She had not expected to see him fail so dismally at his
own game. She thought it a discreditable game, but that
did not seem to alter the fact that she preferred to see
him succeed at it.

Success in fact had come to be what he stood for in her
mind, a man whose unscrupulous charm no one could
resist. When it was successful the unscrupulousness could

not discount the charm; indeed in Judith's eyes, she now began to realise, it had in an unreasonable sort of way rather added to it; but when, face to face with this frail defender of some other faith, Baldwin's confidence faltered and he began to bungle, Judith found herself shocked. She began to wonder what it was that had seemed so powerful about him.

Baldwin, however, had sniffed the breeze of victory. Mrs. Lane, with whom he had anticipated the greatest possible difficulty, had fallen without a fight. The old man, in spite of a certain foolish reluctance, was bound to succumb before long. And then new, and not uninteresting, vistas opened.

There was Harris, for instance. Married to Judith, he would probably be asked to take the place over, perhaps even before Sir Ralph's death. It would be a little difficult to manage, with Parliament, but they would be able to work something out. There would be some Lane money to help, and possibly Judith might have to spend a good deal of time up there while he was in London. The idea of being a country gentleman had never appealed to him before, but here in the north country there was a sort of rough practical feudalism among the Lane tenants which he had never come across before in his country house visiting, which tended to concentrate on the southern counties, and he began to see a sort of dignity in taking part in that way of life.

Any doubts he may have felt about Judith, about whether he was rash to allow himself to feel so strongly about her, about how much Anthony was involved in what he felt for her, about whether she would ever trust him, were dissolved in this mood of optimism. Of course she was in love with him, of course she would be useful to him, of course he was going to be a tremendous success.

By lunch time on Sunday he had convinced himself that Sir Ralph was more or less won: it was simply that his manner was naturally surly.

Judith, feeling tired because she had stayed in bed so late that morning, was talking to Feliks who had been jealously reading the book reviews in the Sunday papers.

'I suppose Peter Flower's your Member here?' said Baldwin.

Judith looked up and would have spoken, but Sir Ralph said: 'Peter Flower, yes. Silly ass.'

Judith turned back to Feliks.

'A wonderfully safe seat, of course,' said Baldwin.

Sir Ralph said nothing.

'One hears rumours that he's going to retire, but he never seems quite to bring himself to the point,' said Baldwin.

'Retire?' said Sir Ralph. 'Yes, he's retiring. Sent the committee a letter the other day. Good riddance. That's what we all thought.'

'Really?' said Baldwin. 'It's not officially announced yet, is it?'

'No,' said Sir Ralph.

'Nice seat for somebody,' said Baldwin.

There was a pause.

'I wonder if they've got anyone in mind,' said Baldwin. 'A local man, I mean.'

'Aren't any local men,' said Sir Ralph.

Baldwin, encouraged by the fact that Sir Ralph seemed for once to be paying attention to the conversation, said cheerfully and as it were jokingly: 'There's me, of course.'

Feliks looked up. 'Surely you couldn't abandon your faithful following in wherever it is?' he said.

'I could,' said Baldwin. 'I'm due for a safer seat anyway. There's not much hope of winning that one back now.'

'I can't quite see you in the part of the country Member,' said Feliks.

'D'you know, I was only thinking this morning how much it would become me?' said Baldwin. 'I like this country. One feels one can breathe up here.'

'What a good idea,' said Mrs. Lane, quite suddenly, from the end of the table. 'Don't you think so, Fa?'

'Excellent, my dear, excellent,' said Sir Ralph.

Baldwin, surprised but delighted at the way things were going, began to take it all the more seriously.

'Of course the rest of the committee would have to know who I was,' he said. 'I'm on the Central Office list, but then I think these far-flung constituencies are often predisposed against a Central Office recommendation before they've even seen him.'

'Yes,' said Mrs. Lane. 'Suggest Mr. Reeves to Elliot, Fa.'

'He is a neighbour of ours,' said Sir Ralph to Baldwin. 'A charming fellow. He goes in for pheasant farming. He's just started it.'

'I thought you disliked him, Fa,' said Mrs. Lane. 'But if you're on good terms with him now all the better. It makes it easier for you to suggest Mr. Reeves to him as a suitable candidate.'

'Candidate?' said Sir Ralph. 'Do you wish to take up pheasant farming, Mr. Baldwin?'

'No, not exactly,' said Baldwin, thinking it might be wiser to change the subject for the moment. 'It must be very interesting though. Does he do it on a large scale?'

'A very large scale,' said Sir Ralph.

'Mr. Reeves wants to stand for Parliament, Fa,' said Mrs. Lane, persisting. 'Why don't you suggest to Elliot that he should succeed Peter Flower?'

'Oh, he's thought of that,' said Sir Ralph. 'He'd make a complete ass of himself.'

'Not Elliot,' said Mrs. Lane, 'Mr. Reeves.'

Sir Ralph said gently, 'Mr. Reeves knows why I am unable to recommend him to any position of trust.'

Judith, who had been waiting for this, had not guessed that it would be administered so directly. After a moment of admiration for the old man, she found her eyes full of tears. She had not realised until that moment how much she had wanted a husband.

Nanny, seeing her tears, brightened, and looked round the table optimistically. Perhaps something was going to happen.

Mrs. Lane turned pale. However vague her suspicions, they were there, and she knew that they threatened her life. She put a hand up to her hair and said vaguely: 'If Anthony – if only Anthony could have had the seat. . . .'

Baldwin thought, 'I could have sworn he'd forgotten all about the money.' Catching sight of Judith's tears, he thought, 'She's crying for me. That's good. I'll take her away from here.' He felt full of tenderness for her.

Feliks, feeling out of it, thought resentfully that he

might have enjoyed the week-end more if the train fare had been less.

After lunch Baldwin, feeling now that to have lost the Lanes was nothing if he had gained Judith, led her firmly off to the old nursery and said, 'Now we can talk.'

'What about?' said Judith.

'What would you like to talk about?' he said.

'Oh nothing, nothing,' she said.

'Thomas Hood is more fortunate than I,' said Baldwin.

'Oh, Thomas,' she said.

'Can you dismiss him so?' asked Baldwin.

'I used Thomas as an escape from you,' said Judith. 'You know that and you know how pleased you were because you felt that through Thomas my fall had been accomplished, I had been brought low, I could no longer fool myself I was any better than you. I know I treated Thomas badly, but it seems to me that is a chance we all take all the time. Anthony distressed you, you me, I Thomas. But Anthony's is the only victory because he is dead. For us the process goes on, and for the moment is reversed because we are neither of us as wicked as we should like to be. Thomas is making me feel guilty, I shall make you unhappy because in the course of engineering a seduction which was to be the conquest not only of me but of Anthony you have fallen slightly in love. Also of course the seduction has failed.'

'I see I have a lot to learn from you,' said Baldwin. 'You make my attempts at ruthlessness seem naïve.'

'I am only being reasonable,' said Judith.

'What a destructive quality reason seems to be,' said Baldwin. 'Has it failed, the seduction?'

'As you say, reason is destructive,' said Judith.

'You know, I quite thought you – how shall I say it? – reciprocated my feelings,' said Baldwin.

'I did. I do.'

'But you resist them?'

'What we feel for each other is really a passion for power,' said Judith. 'We want to destroy each other by making the other fall in love with us – we challenge each other, that's all. You want to revenge on me the fact that

you loved Anthony, I on you the fact that I sometimes
hated him. But reason, as you say, has destroyed it all.'

She faced him with a sort of subdued excitement which
he could not quite understand. Finally he said: 'I believe
I once congratulated you, do you remember, for combi-
ning so much passion with so much stability. But now I
see they are more closely connected than I thought, and
the passion was for the stability – is it possible to be
passionately stable? I suppose you would think me hysterical if I asked you whether you had a heart?'

'A heart?'

'Whether you love anything.'

'I suppose discipline is a part of love?' she asked. 'It's
a long time since I had to put love into practice, so I find
it hard to remember. All the same, there are things I love.
Perhaps you are right in thinking one of them is stability
– or could you call it God?'

'No, I don't think you could,' said Baldwin. 'But you
are quite up to date. Isn't God rather the thing these
days?'

'I believe He is among the very young, but I don't know
much about that. Thomas talks about it sometimes.'

'I told Thomas I was going to marry you,' said Baldwin.

'Why?'

'I thought I was. Also it gave me pleasure. I was jealous,
you see.'

'Poor Thomas.'

'But you can tell him it's not so.'

'No.'

'No?'

'No, I shan't tell him – not yet at any rate. It would be
better to leave it.'

'You don't need him now you are disposing of me,'
said Baldwin.

'I was thinking of him. But perhaps there is something
in that.'

'And I'm to accept defeat so humbly?'

'What else is there for you to do?'

'Nothing,' said Baldwin. After a pause he said, 'Is this
all because I was snubbed by your husband's
grandfather?'

But that was something which, for once, she did not feel capable of going into.

'I suppose he may have had a little to do with it,' she said. 'And Anthony, too.'

'Oh, I can't compete with Anthony,' he said.

It had begun to rain. They stood at separate windows, looking out on to the wide moors.

'I miss him, all the same,' said Baldwin.

12

AFTER the panel game, Baldwin usually got a little drunk on beer. He liked neither beer nor being drunk, but it was what he seemed to need in that particular situation. The long slow intake and the resulting blur – he found no exhilaration in beer-drinking – the dreariness of the particular pub in which he chose to drink, the failure of its inmates to arouse in him the faintest flicker of interest, soothed him, and provided the soporific he needed after the intense and irritable liveliness of mind brought on by the exercise of his wits. He exercised them to good effect, and could be called, as far as television was concerned, a success. Already he was in the process of arranging to appear regularly in a discussion programme, with the aim of furthering what he regarded as his serious career, the political one.

All this led to his greeting more amiably than usual an unimportant advertising agent called Charlesworth whom he met in Victoria one evening. The man offered him a drink and Baldwin accepted, because though he had already had his post panel game fill of beer, he was in no particular hurry to go back to his flat. Also he felt like talking, and Charlesworth, being, he considered, of no account, was the sort of person with whom he found it easiest to talk freely. They went into a pub.

'How do the constituents like their candidate's television fame?' asked the advertising agent, with rather sycophantic jollity. 'Going down well, I daresay?'

'With some, with some,' said Baldwin, looking round with unshaken contentment. 'With some.' He smiled benignly. 'And how's the advertising world? Not that I want you to tell me.'

'Oh, not so bad,' said Charlesworth. 'My trouble is. . . .'

'No, no, I said don't tell me,' said Baldwin. 'Advertising is a perfectly revolting profession.'

'I don't know that I'd go as far as that,' said Charlesworth, a little uneasily.

'Yes it is, it's revolting,' said Baldwin, happily. 'Take politics, take industry – take journalism, like my friend Herman here. . . .'

'Harman ' said Harman. He had been sitting at the bar not far away and had come up to join them.

'You're always in pubs, Harman,' said Baldwin.

'I know,' said Harman.

'You strike me as a lonely fellow,' said Baldwin, pleasantly. 'I don't believe you have any friends.'

'I haven't,' said Harman.

'How very admirable,' said Baldwin, whose sleepiness was beginning to give way to a sort of serene enthusiasm.

'What about that story?' asked Harman. 'The one you were going to write and I was going to take you to see Blow about?'

'I gave up the idea,' said Baldwin. 'I got side-tracked somehow.'

'You know they're making a film of the Lane incident, don't you?' said Harman. 'Are you in on that?'

'No,' said Baldwin.

'Not?' said Harman. 'I should have thought you'd be getting a fat fee as an adviser or something of the sort. They must be crazy not to have got hold of you. Why don't you do something about it?'

'They approached me,' said Baldwin. 'But I was unable to accept their offer.'

'Oh,' said Harman, thinking quickly. 'You mean because you're expecting an election this year?'

Baldwin laughed loudly and clapped him on the back. 'You old newshound,' he said.

Harman, who was a small man, winced and spilt some of his beer.

'What do you think I'm paid for?' he said irritably. 'There must be a good reason for you to pass up the money and prestige you could make out of that affair now. But don't worry. Don't tell me. I'll read it in the newspapers, I don't doubt.'

'I could, I suppose, have made some honest money out of it,' said Baldwin. 'How odd. Or fairly honest. But one must live in the future, not the past, don't you agree? And I don't feel that I am destined to make my mark in films.'

Harman shrugged, unappeased.

Baldwin began euphorically to think of the fields in which he was destined to make his mark, surveying the smoky saloon as a drunken emperor might benignly watch the soldiers he was tomorrow to lead to further glories carousing after a victorious battle.

'Have the other half,' said Harman.

'How simple life is,' said Baldwin, pushing over his glass. 'When one has faced the fact of one's solitude. For the true solitary, ambition has no limits. I feel splendid. What would you most like to see me do?'

'God knows,' said Harman, disapprovingly. 'I leave it to you.'

For a moment Baldwin paused, suddenly gazing through the mists of his intoxication into a not unfamiliar abyss where loneliness and failure monstrously loomed; then looking solemnly at Harman he said with resolution: 'Yes, leave it to me. I'll think of something.'

'Of course you will,' said Charlesworth, suddenly and heartily. He had been eyeing a blonde on the other side of the room and paying no attention to the conversation, but now beerily remembered that Baldwin was a useful man to keep in with.

'Oh shut up,' said Baldwin.

Fisher and Miss Vanderbank were having an early lunch. They had taken sandwiches into Green Park, and Bertie had gone with them for the exercise. He scampered from group to group (it was sunny and the park was full) licking the faces of lovers and stealing the sandwiches of typists, taking the bread from the mouths of pigeons and a bar of chocolate gently but firmly from the hand of a justly enraged child. Miss Vanderbank shrieked prettily, but he ignored her. Fisher, embarrassed, had to pursue him.

'I wonder if it won't be me you finally marry,' said Hanescu.

'I don't think so, do you?' said Judith.

'You ought not to remain childless – that horrible Nanny made me think of it. Motherhood would suit you. And then of course I like the idea of founding a dynasty, like all self-made men.'

'I'm a great rejecter of experience, you know,' said Judith. 'Perhaps I'm wrong.'

'The experience of Baldwin might have done you good, though not as much as it would have done him,' said Feliks. 'But then I don't think you need experience. I think you knew it all when you were born. We won't have Nanny in the house, of course. How angry the Lanes would be if we married. I'm afraid there's a certain stratum of society in which I shall never be accepted – not the highest of all, I'm all right there, but the next. Ah well, we mustn't be morbid about the Lanes, either of us.'

'No,' said Judith.

'And you could do a series on bringing up children,' said Feliks. 'And I daresay we could fix you up with one of the better Sunday papers. Child guidance, that's the sort of thing.'

'Miss Vanderbank would hate it,' said Judith.

'We could fix her up with Fisher,' said Feliks. 'A double ceremony. It would be an excuse for redecorating the office.'

'I don't know about that particular excuse,' said Judith. 'But I'm sure you'll find another. In which case I insist on abolishing those rosebuds.'

'You're quite right,' said Feliks. 'I've gone off wallpaper anyway. We'll have paint in wonderful colours. Let's plan it. Have you got a piece of paper? I need a new desk. Substances – we must have more substances. Pink for Fisher?'

Judith smiled, comfortably assuming a familiar role.

'Certainly not,' she said. 'Anyway, the whole thing sounds far too expensive.'

A Man of Power
1960

1

'**H**E can't have been a great man because he achieved nothing,' said Ruth.

There was a smell of central heating and ink, of wooden walls and Miss James's unsuitably exotic scent. We were discussing Cromwell. I was jealous of Ruth because I suspected her, probably wrongly, of being less intelligent than I was, but knew that she appeared more so. She was efficient, self-confident and fattish. She was only in Switzerland for health reasons: next autumn she was going to Oxford, having already passed the entrance examination. I could imagine how she might have impressed the interviewers with her sound opinions, her sober judgments, her solidity. Flightiness was altogether alien to her, whether of mind or body; she would be serious and hard-working all her life.

I envied her, because, having been badly educated, I had a sort of nostalgia for learning, and admired it out of all proportion. I should have liked the idea of myself as a Greek scholar or a mathematician, but since I had no grounding in either of these subjects it seemed to me, by the time I reached the age at which the desire became apparent to me – about sixteen I suppose – to be too late to do anything about it. I did suggest to my mother that I should go to a university, but she became unusually severe. 'Darling, where girls are concerned those places are (a) immoral, (b) a needless expense, (c) a complete waste of time.' I seldom argued with my mother.

There was certainly nothing immoral about Mme. Rabat's little establishment. We talked about sex a good deal, in a manner three parts priggish and one part secretly licentious, and we all fancied ourselves in love with our ski-instructor, but that was all. Some of the girls did claim to have had experiences of various sorts – a French girl in fact was said to have had an abortion – but these revelations were always made in confidence to particular friends, and I was never among the favoured few. The stories reached me only at second or third hand, by which time they had acquired a tinge of the fabulous, which seemed to dissociate them from everyday life. As to needless expense and waste of time, I was not much aware of them then; though now it seems to me that they were both there in excess.

Miss James taught us history and was the worst of our teachers, because she was over-emotional, and so despised mere facts that those she did give us were mainly inaccurate. She had been engaged to an Italian before the War and he had become a Fascist, upon which she had refused ever to speak to him again – that at any rate was her story. We assumed that it had led to her taking to drink or drugs, but we had no evidence on which to base this opinion, other than that of her ravaged appearance. She constantly drew our attention to the fact that her life had been ruined, in order, I think, to give herself an aura of romance in our eyes. In this she failed, because we found her ugly. She was an over-made-up, a ruined blonde; and so we laughed at her love story.

'And what does Vanessa think?' she said, leaning forward to gaze at me intently, as if something dramatic hinged upon my answer. 'Ruth says Cromwell was not a great man, because he left no permanent mark behind him. What do you say?'

I did not often take part in this sort of discussion, mainly because I had at that time very few opinions on any subject at all and was terrified that this might be discovered – I had thus, paradoxically, gained a reputation for 'deepness' – but some book or other on Cromwell had impressed me, and I mumbled that I did think him great.

As I had feared she would, Miss James asked, 'Why?'

'Because he believed in tolerance,' I said weakly.

'Why, Van, how ever could you?' said Mary, the American, shocked. 'He was a wicked dictator.'

Here, fortunately, Miss James intervened in an attempt

to modify this view, and I was able to sink again into the pleasant state of mental numbness in which I had been earlier. I thought vaguely about what I was going to have for tea – I was greedy about cream cakes, though not fat – and about the ski-instructor, and about the letter I owed my mother.

After a time I heard Ruth again advancing her views about Cromwell's inefficacy. The rest of the group, in so far as they were interested at all, seemed impressed. Irritation was beginning to stir in me, when suddenly Miss James banged her fist down upon the table and cried out 'No, no!' in her ringing contralto. We shifted uneasily in our seats, prepared for the sort of wild harangue with which she often strove to instruct us.

'You're a materialist, Ruth,' she said. 'A narrow legal-istic materialist. You're the sort of person who's got us where we are. If there'd been more *heart* in people we shouldn't have the atom bomb, there'd have been no Hitler, no Mussolini to smash a generation's hopes of personal happiness.' She paused and looked round at the five unresponsive faces, an orator making sure she held her audience. 'Why was Cromwell great?' she then apos-trophized us, raising one nicotine-stained, scarlet-tipped hand dramatically into the air. 'Because he *was!*' She banged the hand down on to the table. 'Because he was. He had a great soul. He loved what he took to be right, and he loved liberty of conscience more than anything. He could have really enforced his will on the people if he had wanted to, but he didn't want to – that's why he was an unsuccessful dictator. Vanessa can grasp that. Ruth can't.' I looked down modestly, though not without a quick glance at Ruth, who to my gratification was scowl-ing. 'He was an honest man,' Miss James went on, looking from one to the other of us as if she expected us to break into a cheer. 'An honest man. And a man on a big scale, with huge anxieties and gigantic loyalties, a man with a proper self. That's why he inevitably attracted power – he couldn't help it. There aren't men like that nowadays. What would he think of the piffling nincompoops you know? There's no place for a big man today. What can they do? If they exist at all they're made petty neurotics by their environment; they turn into criminals or business men. They can't be leaders any more because the world doesn't want them. The world only wants fanatics with ideologies or comforting hypocrites with pipes and golf clubs – the true hero, the humanistic hero, is finished. Lucila, define for me the difference between an idea and an ideology.'

Lucila, the Spanish girl, who hardly understood English, looked blank, but Miss James could not wait.

'Think about it,' she said. 'Ask Ruth. And think what you would do if you had been born a great man. Women, of course, have only one function. It is. . . ? Ruth?'

'Reproduction,' said Ruth, sullenly. We could all have answered that one, for we had this particular lecture about once a week.

'Reproduction. Good,' said Miss James, 'and if that is thwarted, they are failures, half-women. You look embarrassed.' This was hardly true: we were quite used to her. 'But that's all I am. I am a half-woman. I am honest about it. Like Cromwell I am honest. I had my chance and Mussolini took it away from me. I have told you about that.' She looked down at the hands, modestly. 'I am an old woman now.'

'Oh, Miss James. . .' said Ruth, politely.

'You're young,' she said. 'You're all young.' She clapped her hands commandingly. 'Go out and reproduce. Fulfil your function. Reproduce.'

She smacked together the books on the table in front of her and getting up said in a tone of exhaustion, 'Think about it.' She turned to go, then paused and said, 'Write me an essay on the modern hero. And you, Vanessa,' she pointed a finger at me. 'Put some heart in it. You know what I mean?' And with an inexplicably roguish smile at me, she left the room.

Relieved that the approach of tea-time had made her outburst briefer than usual, we went up to our rooms to change into an assortment of more or less experimental 'après-ski' wear, and made our way down to the village.

It was a small ski-resort, not yet fashionable. We always went into the same café because we knew we were likely to find Philippe there.

Philippe was our ski-instructor, the one with whom we were all in love. He was the youngest of the instructors and the best-looking in a thin shy way. Our behaviour where he was concerned was amazingly immodest, considering our careful upbringing and the fairly strict supervision under which Mme. Rabat kept us. Of course it was harmless enough, and perhaps Mme. Rabat, who was indeed a worldly creature beneath her façade of genteel prudery, let us flirt with him as a matter of conscious policy.

We used to crowd round him in the café, or when after the morning lesson we ate our packed lunches in the chalet at the top of the slope, touching him and laughing, looking at his mouth and his long eyelashes, each claiming his attention, each secretly convinced we were the one he loved. Walking beside him, one would stumble so that he had to put his hand for a moment on one's arm; fumbling with stiff ski-bindings one would pray for the moment when, laughing at one's clumsiness, he would crouch down and his brown fingers would flicker at one's feet, on a long run one would wait for the moment when one could genuinely claim to be tired and in need of his help. We would never have dreamt of behaving in such a way with any other young man. I suppose it was the clear definition of status which made it possible – not that we ourselves would have recognized that at the time, for we were quite sincere in our passion. He knew his job too well to take advantage of it. We were rich young customers who had to be given our money's worth of flirtation as well as of instruction in skiing: he did it very nicely.

I suppose I was happy in Switzerland. I seem to myself now to have been too ignorant and thoughtless to know what happiness was; but then each year my last year's self seems in retrospect embarrassingly silly, and there was certainly no reason why I should not have been happy.

We were healthy at least. We slept so well, and played about on the mountains in the sun, and ate enough, and were not allowed to stay up too late. We complained, of course, about the restrictions of our life, and mocked at

Mme. Rabat for her snobbery and her pretensions and wished we could have spent the evenings with Philippe in one of the bars in the village.

There were two little groups of us, the better skiers and the less good. I was one of the better. Our group was perhaps eight or ten strong – the whole establishment was so small as hardly to merit the name of 'finishing school', a fact which seemed to make it more rather than less expensive. We lived in a pretty house belonging to Mme. Rabat who was of aristocratic lineage. She it was who was responsible for our manners and general deportment.

Miss James was the only English member of the staff: all our other lessons were in French. I can only suppose that Madame Rabat employed Miss James, the peculiar nature of some of whose advice to us she must have known, because, not being very clever herself, she had decided that Miss James was brilliant, if erratic; and indeed I suppose there was, beneath that shattered exterior, the ruins of a brain. Unfortunately her views were expressed in a tone so unsympathetic and surrounded by so much egocentric nonsense that we none of us realized at the time that many of them were worth taking seriously.

I had learnt to ski when I was very young, about seven, before the War, when my mother took me to St Moritz one year. That made it easier for me to learn again after the War, and I had had two winter holidays in Zermatt when I was still at school in England. By this time, then, though I was still slow and not in the least dashing, I had a good enough style to be allowed into the better class, the class which considered itself infinitely more worthy of Philippe's attention than the inept creatures who made up the rest of the establishment. We were allowed to go on long runs; sometimes, at weekends, taking the whole day. It was on one of these that I had my first meeting with Mrs. Lewis Ogden.

We had seen her before, for she had been staying for about a week at the one really smart and expensive hotel in the place, and we had watched her closely and made a good deal of speculation and comment, for we were intensely interested in the way of life of the very rich. It was all part of our keenness to learn about the more worldly aspects of grown-up life, which fascinated us and about which we tended to assume, even to each other, an airy self-confidence which we were far from feeling.

We had heard of Lewis Ogden because lately his wealth had become such as to merit reporting, not merely on the City pages of newspapers, but on those of more general interest; but we had no idea how he had acquired his millions or what he did to make them go on growing. Later I came to know a good deal about the business side of his life, but at that time all we knew was that it was something to do with take-over bids and property deals. We had none of us ever had any reason to be interested in him, which was why when Philippe told us one day that he had spent the previous afternoon teaching the wife of our famous English millionaire to ski, we had difficulty in remembering anything about him; but a millionairess was definitely worth observing and, Philippe having pointed her out to us, we were delighted when she later came and sat at the next table to ours at the café where we went for tea.

She was alone, which limited our opportunities of finding out about her, since there was no conversation at which we could eavesdrop. She was very quiet – quieter even, I mean, than most people by themselves. She had changed from her ski-boots into soft fur ones, and she slipped into her seat without a sound and ordered chocolate and two cakes. She ate and drank slowly and without even the chink of a spoon against a cup. As soon as she had finished she called for the bill in a quiet but nasal and not very attractive voice, paid without smiling, and padded from the room, closing the door gently behind her.

'A fairly unassuming piece of leopard skin, all things considered,' said Serena.

'That's only what she throws on to keep warm,' said Mary. 'She still had her ski-pants on.'

'She doesn't look Jewish, does she?' said Serena.

'Is she?' I asked.

'Oh, surely,' said Serena. 'I'm sure she is, and they always marry each other.'

'I don't think she's Jewish,' said Mary. 'Is she Jewish, Marie?'

'No,' said Marie.

Since Marie was a Jewess – a rich, pretty, French one – this was taken as final.

We saw her once or twice after that, and decided that she was a disappointment. She was always alone, always quiet, always simply dressed. Since she must obviously be common, her husband being self-made, we had been hoping for some entertaining errors of taste – huge diamonds pinned to her anorak, her Christian name in gold on her skis. There was nothing like that. There were not even any of the things we should have admired – oysters flown from England and carried, with the greatest difficulty, up the mountain for her lunch ('he might be sent down again for the red pepper'), a Rolls-Royce to meet her at the bottom of the cable railway, whence it was at least five minutes walk to the hotel, insults to inferiors, or the flashing of wads of notes to avoid queuing for the ski-lifts. Fortunately for us, she did not even do what any one of us in her position would have done at once – hire Philippe for a fortnight's individual and unremitting tuition. As a matter of fact, she needed it, for she ski'd very badly.

We had been on a long run one day, and were skiing down through the woods to the village. The path was narrow and icy, and Lucila who was a frankly cowardly skier and I who preferred to think myself merely cautious let the others go on ahead and took it slowly. Philippe, knowing that we knew the descent well, did not wait for us until he reached the bottom.

Lucila was even slower than I was, and about halfway down I sat on a bench in a little clearing beside the track to wait for her. When she came up she sat down beside me and immediately began a long and breathless account of the sufferings of the peasants on her father's land as a result of a failure in the water supply. This seemed to me to be completely uninteresting, and since I knew that she herself felt nothing but distaste for the lower classes of any country, and more particularly of her own, I could only assume that she was talking to me about something so boring to both of us because she found me difficult to talk to. This depressed me, because it was one of my continual anxieties that I was not so forthcoming, easy and gossipy as the others.

Lucila spoke in little soft gasps, very quickly and in ludicrous English. I listened in silence, staring at the white slab of the opposite mountain through the trees.

A figure skidded round the corner, went off the track into the deep snow and jerked to a stop. It was Mrs. Lewis Ogden, neat and nervous in her well-cut trousers. Without looking at us, she stamped her way back on to the path, pushed off cautiously and passed us, looking uneasy and cold.

'He is not quite good,' said Lucila, giggling.

'We'd better go,' I said. 'They'll be waiting. She'll stop at the next corner and we can pass her there.'

There was a steep little run, however, before the next corner, and she had fallen at the bottom of it, having left the track and apparently run into a tree.

'Are you all right?' I called patronizingly as we passed. She made no reply and did not seem to be making any effort to get up, so I stopped and went back. She was lying awkwardly, half buried in snow. She turned her head as I came up to her, and said, 'I think I've hurt my leg.'

'Let me take your ski off,' I said, pleased at this interesting turn of events. 'Which leg is it?'

'The left one,' she said.

'I shall have to dig to get at it,' I said. 'There, now you can sit up. I'll take the ski off, then you can see if you can move it. There, now try.'

'I can't,' she said, evidently in pain.

'I'll go and get help,' I said. 'You stay here, Lucila.'

'Ah no no no,' said Lucila, rolling her eyes. 'Is darkness falls. I am not able to be in the dark since a child.'

'Nonsense,' I said. 'It won't be dark for hours. You know I ski much faster than you.'

'I go, I go,' she said, turning back to the path. 'I go tell Philippe. You wait.' She set off with determination.

I turned back to Mrs. Ogden and smiled. 'Lucila is afraid of the dark,' I said. 'But she'll send someone up here quite quickly. It's not at all far to the village.'

She did not answer my smile, but said awkwardly: 'I'm sorry to give you this trouble.'

'It's all right,' I said. 'Here, have my scarf. Wouldn't you be more comfortable if you could lie down altogether?'

'I'm all right thank you,' she said.

'I hope it's not broken,' I said. 'Perhaps it's just a bad strain. Is it the first time you've ski'd?'

'Yes,' she said.

'It's bad luck hurting yourself the first time,' I said. 'Of course I think it is the most dangerous time really, when you're just learning. Were you having lessons?'

'Yes.'

'Philippe took you one afternoon, didn't he?' I said. 'The good-looking one. But then I think you went to someone else. Philippe's the best really. Didn't you think he was awfully good?'

'Yes,' she said.

'You're staying at the Mont Blanc, aren't you?' I said. 'We saw you there the other day. D'you like it?'

'Yes,' she said.

I began to feel inadequate.

'I don't suppose they'll be long now,' I said. 'They'll bring the blood-wagon – it's a sledge, and one of them skis at each end. They're awfully good at it.'

She did not speak.

'Does it hurt now?' I asked, sympathetically.

'No,' she said. 'It's all right.'

'I suppose you're insured,' I said.

'Yes,' she said.

'Were you going to stay long?' I asked.

She put her head in her hands and began to cry, quite quietly.

After a pause, I said: 'I'm terribly sorry. I thought you might want to talk.'

'I do,' she said, and went on crying.

Her hands were big and businesslike, with unpolished almond-shaped nails; but otherwise she was small and thin. Her black hair had fallen over her face, and she trembled slightly with grief as the tears ran through her fingers and melted the snow in tiny patches; but there were no sobs. Even in what was evidently anguish she was curiously silent.

After a time she sat up and pushed her hair away from her face.

'I'm sorry,' she said. 'I'm afraid this is very boring for you.'

So she knew that I had been looking forward to finding in our chance encounter some food for gossip, something to tell the others.

'It's all right,' I said.

Her face was broad and pale, pleasant enough but unmemorable. As I had noticed, she made very little impression in the ordinary course of events; but here alone with her I began to feel I could trust her.

'Mountains are rather awful, aren't they?' I said, tentatively. I thought it would be a good idea to make her talk.

'Yes,' she said, and began to cry again.

I was now sitting beside her on the snow. It was beginning to get cold. A feeling of desolation, which was not altogether unpleasant, descended on me. Although I had no idea of the reason for her distress, which was obviously a result of something more than simply her accident, I began to feel that I was myself somehow concerned in it. It was as if I had once known what she was crying about but had forgotten, only remembering that it was sad for me too. This made me feel much closer to her, as if we had something in common to regret: this something seemed bitter and irrecoverable, a failure, a lack, an absence.

She seemed to stop crying after a time, but she did not raise her head. I heard her sigh, and put out my hand to touch her knee. Gestures of that kind have never come easily to me, and even at the time I was slightly surprised at what I had done. She put one hand on mine, without moving or looking at me, and we stayed like that until Philippe arrived, with one of the other instructors and the sledge.

I heard later that the leg had been broken, but not badly, and that a car with a uniformed nurse in it had driven up to collect her the next day. She had told the people at the hotel that she was going to a clinic in Geneva where she would stay until she was well enough to travel back to England.

2

My mother's mews house was painted pink, the door and window frames white. The window boxes and the pink and white tubs outside the door were beautifully kept. Two sturdy young women came in a van every week or so to tend them: I believe they were immensely expensive. My mother was extravagant though in fact not rich. Her interior decorating business was run at a small loss.

Some time during the summer succeeding my winter in Switzerland, the summer during which I was the gloomiest and most ill at ease of debutantes, Alexander Leithen became our lodger. He paid four guineas a week for bed and breakfast. The bed was a riot of quilted chintz roses, since my mother had only just redecorated the room and had designed it at the time for female friends, and the breakfast was excellent. It was cooked each morning by the charlady Mrs. Simmons, with simple faith that she knew what a man liked to eat. There were always eggs and bacon or kidneys or sausages and a great deal of toast and coffee: in the winter there was porridge. Alexander never felt well enough to eat it.

In the days before he had a job he would emerge late from his room, greenish-white and shaky, though shaved and neatly dressed, would gulp down three or four cups of black coffee, and leave the house without having been able, even had he wished, to say anything coherent at all. When, later on, he had to be in his office by ten, his early morning appearance was even more frightening; but Mrs. Simmons, against all evidence, persisted in her belief that he 'liked a good breakfast', and often in order not to offend her I would eat it myself, since my mother and I were only supposed to need coffee and toast.

I once suggested to my mother that Alexander's rent was perhaps rather high since he spent so little time in the bed and so seldom ate the breakfast, but she replied that she earned it by the trouble she was put to to collect it. It was true that, though there were days when it appeared all at once in cash after some gambling party, there were far more often weeks and weeks of evasiveness, of cheques given and received in a spirit of mutual scepticism as to their being eventually cleared, and of cold, distant bearing on the part of Alexander, who always held it against people that he should owe them money.

After having left the house in the morning, he would sometimes return to bath and change, in which case I might or might not see him, but quite often our next meeting would be at a party in the evening, where he would appear full of energy and sparkle, the antithesis of the pale creature who was again to creep from his room a few hours later, his evening having ended very late and very drunkenly. His stamina must have been tremendous, for this was the pattern of his life for years.

At first I rather disliked him, but even then it was more in theory than in practice. In fact, in spite of my disapproval, I always found him sympathetic. He was one of the few people I could talk to about myself without difficulty or affection, and as a result I did so a good deal, without, however, eliciting any similar confidences from him. He seldom mentioned his own affairs to me: from time to time he would admit to a liking for this or that girl but even these admissions were made discreetly and I was never invited to follow the course of the friendship in any detail. Very occasionally he would make some reference to his father, usually simply to observe that the latter had or had not sent him some money. His father was a politically active Viscount, his mother the daughter of a Duke: they were apparently efficient and powerful. I thought the father charming when I once met him, but found her alarming. They did not approve of Alexander's way of life, but their protestations, the jobs they found for him, the means, financial and otherwise, they took to persuade him to mend his ways, appeared to make no impression on him at all.

He worked intermittently for my mother's interior decorating shop, on a commission basis. I never could make out that he did anything very much, except introduce clients, some of whom were more satisfactory than others, and occasionally drive about in her little yellow van, which had Essex Cowper, Decorations, in flowing script on its sides. She had, however, by this time for one reason or another obviously 'taken him up', which was useful for him, because in spite of everything my mother was still able to exercise influence in all sorts of fields.

What precisely 'everything' was I am still not sure, but there was 'something' – and I had been vaguely aware of it for some time. My mother was a famous beauty. At forty-five she had the look exactly of that: one would never have mistaken her for anything else, for an actress, for instance, or a model, or simply an unknown: one did not need to have seen her photograph in all the fashionable magazines to be reminded of it when one saw her in the flesh. Her beauty was regular and without flamboyance. Her complexion was pale, her hair deep brown, her nose and mouth flawless, her eyes fine and sad. Her sublimity was only in her perfection: she was a perfect statement of something one knew already and had heard expressed a hundred times by a *cliché*. She was tall, and inclined towards calculated under-dressing. Her movements and her voice were delightful and she had an aura of sophistication which I have never seen equalled.

I had adored her as a child, without seeing a great deal of her, and if lately I had come across slight difficulties in being her grown-up daughter, had suspected, possibly, certain calculations on her part for which I had not been altogether prepared, all this made no difference to the powerful effect on me which her beauty had – largely by the way in which it seemed to put her in a world of her own, where different rules applied – or to the unquestioning submission with which I accepted her right to rule my life. I do not know what it was in my early upbringing which still made me do things simply because she told me to, or whether it was merely that she was strong

and I was weak, but however much I might criticise or
complain, we both knew that there was never in the end
any question but that I would do whatever she wanted.

The 'something' I have referred to, however, and of
which I had been becoming lately increasingly aware, was
to be found in the attitude towards her – and therefore
towards me – of some of her friends and all her relations.
Some inborn obtuseness – certainly no adult's anxiety to
shelter me – had kept from me for many years the fact
that my mother was considered by some people to be
shocking. Our more pompous relations certainly thought
her so, and so did the parents of my school-friends, who
were a dismally respectable lot. Though her friends were
naturally not so disapproving, at the same time the existence of this opinion, even though held by others, made
a difference to their own attitude. It had the effect, for
one thing – and this was another of my recent discoveries
– of making them treat her in a sort of off-hand way which
her beauty, her intelligence (for she had that as well)
and, more than either of those, her reserve, her stand-
offishness, her way of really not, in public, much letting
her hair down – although she was, I suppose, fairly free
of speech – might not have led one to expect.

It was true that though she would now and then
express mild disapproval of one or other of her friends,
nothing they did ever seemed to surprise or shock her.
At the same time I never saw her behave in a particularly
unconventional way herself, and I could not decide upon
what this evident reputation for, at least, 'fastness' was
in fact based; apart from the inescapable fact of her having
had four husbands. Two of them had died, the first and
the last; she had been divorced from the other two, one of
whom was my father. The last had been Tommy Cowper,
whom she had married when I was ten and whose name
I had taken, as a result of my own most urgent wish.
Quite why I had wished it I am not sure, since I had
never particularly liked him. He was noisy, stupid and
kind, and he was killed in a motor race four years after
they were married. My own father lived in Rhodesia. I
could hardly remember him, and he took no interest in
me. He was, I believe, rich, but he gave my mother very

little. She had had various money-making schemes, none of which had been altogether successful – these I suppose had also shocked the relations. Her interior decorating business had lately become rather fashionable and her prices were enormous.

In spite, as I have said, of this reputation, whatever exactly it was and whether or not it was deserved, my mother was still likely to be extremely useful to any person or cause she cared to adopt. Whatever her relations may have thought of her, they recognized her as one of the family. She was well-connected by birth and by marriage and she had been beautiful and fashionable for a long time; this gave her an influence: to describe it exactly, to go into all the ramifications of the means of its operation, would be beyond me, but it was usually quietly at work on something or other, whether it was a question of a job for a friend, an eligible young man to take her daughter out, an import licence for French wallpaper, an item of gossip to be kept out of the papers, or someone to stay with in the South of France. Not having seen a great deal of her, through being at school and spending the greater part of my holidays with her brother and his family who lived quietly in the country, I had never grown quite used to it, and the fact of there being a friend or connection to fix every situation was still a surprise to me.

Perhaps to anyone on the look-out for irregularities, my mother having taken in Alexander Leithen as a lodger might have seemed unusual; but then I lived there as well, and so, on and off, did a curious assortment of successive foreign female students who helped in the house with varying degrees of inefficiency, so I suppose the arrangement could not really have been called improper. It certainly never occurred to me that it might be. My mother needed the money, and Alexander had been the first person in need of accommodation whom she had met after deciding to let the spare room. I think she hardly knew him then, but he had a way of inviting confidences if not of inspiring confidence in the general meaning of the phrase, and he soon became absorbed into our lives. In no time my mother was discussing everything with him, especially me; which oddly enough did not annoy me, touchy though I was on that subject. The idea that he was perhaps not the most suitable person to consult upon the upbringing of a young girl did not occur to any of us.

It was Alexander who found the Acme School of Business Training.

A friend of my mother's had had a daughter who had died of flu. This tragedy – not that I imagine it would have been any consolation to the bereaved parents – had had one minor beneficial repercussion. The death having taken place after the girl had combined a full-scale 'Season' in London with an apparently arduous course of training at a School of Floristry, my mother had decided that for a débutante to concentrate on anything other than social life was to endanger her health, and I had therefore been able to put off for several months the decision as to what I was going to do. Towards the end of the Season, however, my mother began to bring up the subject a good deal.

'We really must decide what you're going to do,' she would say, adding rather hopelessly, 'Isn't there anything you want to do?'

There was nothing I wanted to do.

'Couldn't you get married?' she said.

'All the men I know are foul,' I said.

'I suppose there must be some nice ones somewhere,' she said. 'Perhaps I should have sent you to Oxford after all. But then they'd be too young for you there. It's a complete mystery to me where they are, the nice ones. You could marry for money, I suppose, quite simply. There's Johnny.'

'He's got no roof to his mouth,' I said.

'You can't have everything,' said my mother, but without conviction. 'Well, then, what about modelling? Everyone seems to do it these days and you'd make lots of money. Your figure's perfect for it – they have to be thin and shapeless – and your face is lovely if only you'd bother about it a bit and not look so exhausted all the time. They cover it with make-up anyway. Do try that.'

'I can't walk,' I said.

'No,' said my mother. 'But you could learn. Look,

follow me.' She did a good imitation of a model displaying a dress. I tried to copy her but failed.

'Pretend to be acting,' said my mother. 'Show off a bit. You're so bound up with yourself. I suppose one is at your age.'

'I can't act,' I said.

'Oh, darling, I've seen you in school plays. Everyone said how good you were as Rosalind.'

'Well, I was,' I said, pleased.

'There you are then,' said my mother. 'But of course you don't photograph well, do you? What about working in an antique shop? I don't mean you should work for me, because you ought not to be too much under my influence. You do want to be independent, don't you?'

'Not particularly,' I said.

'Oh,' said my mother. 'You are sweet. I could easily get you a job in an antique shop though.'

'They'd want me to type,' I said.

'It always seems to come back to that,' said my mother. 'You'll have to learn to type.'

'I should hate that,' I said.

'You'd hate anything,' said my mother reasonably. 'We'll ask Alexander what he thinks.'

This dismissed the subject for the moment, Alexander not being immediately available. Consulted later on, he too came down on the side of typing.

'You can't get a decent job without it,' he said, quite as if he had tried. 'Even if you don't use it, you have to know how to do it. And they teach you all sorts of other useful things at those places, like book-keeping for instance, and filing.'

'Then you really would be useful if you came and worked in the shop,' said my mother, 'if you could do book-keeping. I have to pay Miss Thorpe nearly ten pounds a week. I'd pay you too of course but not so much because you'd still be learning, gaining experience.'

'I suppose I could work in a book shop,' I said.

'Book-keeping,' said my mother, patiently, 'has nothing to do with books.'

'I know,' I said, 'but I wouldn't mind working in a book shop, and you have to type for that too. I asked someone.'

'I think that's an excellent idea,' said Alexander. 'It's just the sort of thing you might find interesting. We'd better find out about secretarial colleges.'

We found out about secretarial colleges. The situation was not encouraging. We had apparently left it too late for me to get into any of the reputable ones that autumn. Alexander suggested that I should take a correspondence course, but my mother objected to that on the grounds that I should never get any fresh air. The subject was allowed more or less to lapse until one day Alexander came back from fetching some furniture in the yellow van and announced that driving through Fulham he had passed a house marked 'Acme School of Business Training'.

The next day I was going to stay with someone in Scotland, but my mother and Alexander drove off to Fulham. My mother was going abroad the following week, and I should not see her again until the end of the month, so she wrote to me in Scotland.

The man who runs it seems very pleasant and responsible. the letter said, *and I am delighted with the whole idea. It will give you an opportunity to widen your horizons by meeting some people not of your own class.*

3

COLIN DAVIS was the only person who was nice to me about Mr. Higgins's speech. That was how I came to know him. Otherwise I might have passed my whole brief career at the Acme School of Business Training without doing more than exchange an occasional 'good morning' with him.

Mr. Higgins remains a mystery to me. I have never been able to imagine what his life was really like, what he did when he was alone, whether he was unbalanced or perfectly sane. He lived in a flat on the top floor of the shabby Victorian house whose first two floors were taken up by the Acme School of Business Training. The third floor was the office of a Literary Agent called Heywood. This latter was a small, quiet, middle-aged man of an eminently respectable appearance, who came in punctually at ten o'clock every morning and left at five. About one o'clock the smell of burnt toast, or, more depressing still, burnt milk, would float down the stairs and indicate that he was lunching. This shabby and out of the way side street seemed an unsuitable place for an office of that sort, since he could hardly have hoped to rely solely on local talent, and indeed during the whole time I was there I never saw a client or a secretary or for that matter anybody at all going up to see him.

One might have thought that these two evidently solitary human beings, Mr. Heywood and Mr. Higgins, working in the same building, boiling I believe at more or less the same time their separate kettles for tea three or four times a day, passing each other regularly on the stairs, might have been drawn together, have looked in on each other for a talk now and then, or at least in passing have mentioned the weather, or the cricket score, or inquired after one another's health; but as far as I know their only exchange was the regular one which occurred every time they met. 'Ha, Heywood,' breezily from Higgins, and 'Morning, Higgins,' briskly from Heywood. The latter usually quickened his pace on seeing Higgins, and looked even more busy and efficient than usual, so it may be that something had once come between them, some question about the rent, or the burning of the toast.

Higgins was a fat but springy man with an organizing air: he might have been a scoutmaster had he looked healthier, or a bank-manager had he looked less dishonest, or even a bishop but for his grin – a grin which was almost permanently stretched across his features, exposing huge brownish teeth and creating an atmosphere of uneasiness rather than expressing the *bonhomie* which was no doubt intended.

How or why he had started the Acme School of Business Training I have no idea, but his attitude towards his pupils was half that of the Master of some secret sect to his disciples and half that of a rather old-fashioned and ladylike welfare worker. He appeared to have tremendous faith in the importance of what he was teaching us. The outlines of the shorthand code were revealed to us like an alphabet of the occult, with reverence and urgency. If we showed signs of boredom – which happened fairly often because no one could make shorthand interesting – he was shocked and hurt. 'If you don't care to learn,' he would say, 'go. We don't want you here. We only want people who understand the importance of their work. What you learn here matters to you and to the world. A sound business training is a sound training for life.'

And he would walk between the rows of clattering typewriters, his fat hands urging us on as if we were conducting a symphony.

I think that in spite of his slightly shifty appearance, which was mainly a result of his grin, he may in fact have been perfectly sincere and worthy. At the time I thought him sinister and odious, partly because of the speech, but now that I come to think of it he may at least have been a truly happy man. Everything I ever saw or heard of him certainly bore out the supposition that he had his faith, a faith which will probably never falter, and of which the chief article seemed to be 'Blessed are the shorthand-typists for they shall inherit the earth'.

He seemed to be interested in our moral welfare, and would give us little talks on citizenship and helping our neighbour and being good in general. The arrival of a new pupil would nearly always result in a dissertation of this kind, which was delivered in a calm, gentle, yet admonishing, voice. When Colin Davis arrived, which was the term before I did, the fact of his being the only boy there gave rise apparently to a talk on Sex, extracts from which were frequently on the lips of those who had heard it.

My initiation was even more embarrassing, for me at any rate, since I had then no idea that these speeches were a regular feature of life at the school and were privately laughed at by the students. The subject on which my arrival inspired Mr. Higgins to expatiate was Class.

Fortunately the whole school was not there. I had arrived late, Hardcastle Street being practically impossible to find, and one class was already at work under the supervision of Joyce, Mr. Higgins's bouncy, games-mistress-type assistant.

There were I suppose about ten or twelve people sitting with their notebooks on their knees in the stuffy little room into which I was led by Mr. Higgins, who had welcomed me in baronial style on the doorstep. They were all girls except for Colin. My general impression was one of overall seediness and weediness: I later realized that this was not at all a true impression, since one or two of the girls were definitely pretty, most had good figures and only a few were badly dressed. I think what gave me the idea was the incredible dinginess of the room, the naked electric light bulb which was needed to supplement the weak grey light from the uncurtained window, and the mingled smell of girls and gas, dust and deodorants, which was born on the over-warm air.

With some ceremony Mr. Higgins presented me with a notebook and a pencil (I had not thought of bringing one of my own, which was what one was meant to do) and introduced me to the front row of girls. 'Susan and

Doreen, Avril, Pauline and Rita,' he said, waving one benevolent hand at them. 'And this is Vanessa, everyone. We're all on Christian name terms here, Vanessa, as you'll soon find out. We're a friendly little company and we hope you'll like us. Now take a seat at the end there and I'll just try and outline to you one or two of our aims.'

I sat down obediently. Mr. Higgins perched informally on the edge of the table facing us.

'First of all,' he said. 'We're all keen on our work. We love it, and we give it all we've got. After the class I want you and Janet here, who's our other new girl this term, to come and see me separately and we'll have a talk about shorthand and all that it means. The others know it already.' He spread his great grin over us and slid more solidly on to the table. 'Secondly,' he went on, 'we're all equal here. There's no favouritism, no special treatment for anybody. But that's not to say that we're unaware of social differences. We may think that they don't matter, that they get submerged here by something bigger, our common task; but that's not to say we don't believe they exist. That would be just silly, wouldn't it, to say that? Now, what I'm getting at is this, I had a talk with Vanessa's mother and father when they came here to see me, and they agreed with me that Vanessa and all of you girls could have a lot to learn from one another. Vanessa, it seems, has led a fairly sheltered life to date, and we're to help her to learn a little more about the way things go, and as for all of you, I want you to observe Vanessa carefully.' He swayed from side to side like an elephant in line; the table creaked. 'We must keep our sense of proportion, of course. That's one of the most important rules in life. But don't let us mistake pride for a praise-worthy lack of snobbishness. Let us be humble in order that we may learn. The spirit of the age is against Vanessa's kind, but that's all the more reason to learn from them while they remain. Vanessa comes of a very ancient family, girls, and whatever you may feel about man being born equal there can be no doubt but that it shows in her face and in her bearing. She has the look of someone born to command.' I shrank back, horrified, into my chair. 'Look at that face, those hands – you'll find that you can always tell a lady by her hands. And her nose. That nose has adorned the faces of great men and women through the ages, princes, prime ministers, generals, poets, and courtesans.' At this, fortunately for my own state of mind, I began to laugh, and hid my face in my hands.

'Ah, Vanessa,' said Mr. Higgins, in a tone of gentle reproach, 'that is one of the things we shall have to teach you. Life is not always a joke, not for all of us, you know. We haven't all had your opportunities for laughter.' He plomped off the edge of the table, and surveyed the group before him in silence for some moments. Finally he said, 'Well I shall say no more now. All I shall say to you is, don't shut your hearts. I shan't shut mine.'

He walked slowly round the table, sat down at a chair behind it, and said with a startling suddenness, 'Mussel!'

Everyone round me immediately began to write busily in their notebooks.

Mr. Higgins looked at his watch and after I suppose a minute said 'Stop!' I discovered that everyone had been writing 'mussel' in shorthand and that a girl called Jane had written it eighty times, which was considered good.

There is no doubt that Class is a bad subject. There had once been a rich girl at the school and Mr. Higgins had talked about Money, but that had caused no offence, the Sex talk had of course been a great joke, and there had once been a girl there who had been to a Borstal institution, which had given rise to a talk on Morals, which had given the girl in question considerable prestige. But Class was frightful. If I had been outraged by Mr. Higgins's talk, so had they. They did not, however, blame him for their feelings; they blamed me.

Except when it was absolutely essential, no one spoke to me for a week, all conversation stopped as soon as I came into a room, and when I left the school in the evenings the groups dawdling round the entrance turned their backs on me. I was quite incapable of dealing with the situation. Every time I made some sort of overture and tried to start a conversation, the precise tones of my accent sounded agonizingly in my ears. Once I said to the girl sitting next to me, 'I say, have you got a rubber?' and she said 'Fraytfully sorry, Ay hevn't, ectually.' If only I could have laughed, but I was too paralysed by my embarrassment and guilt. I longed to abase myself before them, assure them that I felt myself in no way superior (which would have been three parts true), that anyway the whole thing was purely superficial and incidental, and that I thought Mr. Higgins a terrible fool, but apart from the fact that I was temperamentally incapable of such action, I had read in a book about coloured people that they despised one as much for being too eager to please them as for being too arrogant, and I thought that the same might apply to these people.

As it was, however, my purpose was probably served by my appearing so obviously wretched and miserable throughout that first week. I arrived the following Monday determined to leave at the end of that week; but at lunchtime I found Colin Davis at my elbow saying 'Come and have a coffee'. I said that I should love to, and we walked outside together.

'There's the Mecca up there,' he said, pointing, 'and Daly's that way. Most people go to Daly's but the other's quieter, so you can take your choice.'

'You decide,' I said.

'It's you that's born to command,' he said. 'Come on, then, we'll go to the Mecca.'

After that everything was all right.

There were several of the girls having coffee at the Mecca too. They came over to talk to Colin, and I found it quite easy to join in the conversation. Within a few days my position had completely changed. I never felt embarrassed with any of them again and they in turn soon treated me without constraint. Later on Mr. Higgins's speech was sometimes referred to jokingly, but I do not think it was ever held against me again. Because we were roughly the same level in shorthand and typing, I became part of a small group consisting of Colin and four of the girls, of whom Avril was the liveliest: we usually had lunch together.

Of all the people in that little room who had seemed to me at first sight to look weedy, Colin was the only one to whom in fact the adjective could truthfully be applied.

He was small and pale. His sharp irregular features, his extreme thinness, his straight pale brown hair of which a wisp hung over his forehead to be irritably tossed back from time to time, his fidgetiness and his hunched bony shoulders, all combined to convey an impression of under-nourishment and ill health. On the other hand, he was always well-dressed and particularly clean; he washed his hands often and smelt of expensive soap.

Although his appearance was at first sight against him he was curiously attractive: the girls told him he looked like James Dean. His odd nervous energy may have had something to do with this. He was seldom still; he could hardly bear even to sit through the course of a meal but would abruptly stand up and begin to walk round the table, talking all the time, or would tip his chair backwards and forwards dangerously, then turn it round and sit astride it, leaning his arms on the back. He talked a great deal, breathlessly and with a nasal Cockney accent which he tended to exaggerate. He could be extremely funny, usually in a rather savage way, and when he had made a successful joke he was delighted with himself: a too appreciative audience went to his head and he became facetious or too unkind. He was a great enemy of capitalism, successful business men were his bogeys, and he would often hint at some secret knowledge of the hideous machinations of I.C.I., 'the big insurance companies', and also, incidentally, the Archbishop of Canterbury. He seemed to follow the news closely in the newspapers and on television but one wondered why he bothered to do so since he evidently believed very little of what he read or heard, and despised anyone who was taken in by such instruments of propaganda.

The girls did not much sympathize with his bitterness, and treated it on the whole with kindly ridicule, changing the subject whenever he became too vehement. Avril seemed to be his generally acknowledged favourite among them, and it was she whom I asked about him one day when he was away with a cold.

'What's he doing here?' I asked her. 'Why does he want to learn shorthand and typing – doesn't he want to do an ordinary job?'

'Oh, Colin,' said Avril. 'He's a funny case, you see. He's had all sorts of jobs. He was in films for quite a while – a cutter or something like that – but he's never stuck at anything. Then he got offered a job as a private secretary by some important man – he was going to pay him a terrible lot and take him round the world and everything – only he wanted him to be able to type. So he decided to learn. I think his sister pays. She seems to be the one with the money, but he doesn't talk much about his family. He won't stay here, though. I'm sure he'll leave before the end of the course. I tell him he should stay now. It's a soppy thing for a man to learn but if he's started he might at least finish it.'

'Have you met her?' I asked. 'The sister, I mean.'

'No,' said Avril. 'I met his mother once. The sister's married, I think.'

This sister certainly seemed to play a fairly large part in his life. Soon after my conversation with Avril, he began to talk about getting a flat of his own, and being sick of living with his mother: it appeared that the sister had offered to pay for it.

One day I went with him to see a flat off the Fulham Road which was on my way home. It was a large basement, and the sitting-room looked out on to quite a pleasant garden. The people who owned the house seemed nice and the rent was not high. Colin, however, would only say that he would think it over, and when we left he was scornful about it: he had apparently envisaged something grander.

'I want something in the West End proper,' he said. 'One of those ritzy bachelor apartments with a lift and central heating, and all done up.'

'I don't think that's at all your sort of thing,' I said.

'Well, it's not,' he said. 'No. But you ought not to see that so easily. I want it to be my sort of thing. It will be my sort of thing. You'll see. Besides, what is my sort of thing? That dreary basement? Or my mother's filthy hole?'

'Is it a filthy hole?' I asked.

'Not altogether, no,' he said. 'But I think it is. And cats everywhere, stinking the place out. It's on the first floor and she's got a plank out of the window for the cats to get down into the yard, because she's too old to go up and down stairs letting them in and out all day. There's this one Smarty, he's so fat and old he can hardly stagger up the plank – he's the one that stinks because he's the tom – and one day last week he fell off on his way up and hurt his leg; you've never heard such a fuss. I said he ought to be put down and she had hysterics. Now there he sits on a cushion in front of the fire and she brings him hot milk every five minutes. She hasn't got enough to do that's her trouble. I tell her she ought to go out to work.'

'How old is she?' I asked.

'About seventy,' he said. 'She looks a hundred, though.'

'It seems a bit old to work,' I said.

'She doesn't need to work,' he said. 'She's got more money than she knows what to do with. Tell you what, we'll go and look at some flats on Saturday, some really good ones. You'll come with me won't you? You could help me a lot. This Saturday. Where shall we meet?'

'You could come to me,' I said. 'Not too early.'

'I'll be there at ten,' he said.

My mother and Alexander were both away that weekend. Punctually at ten o'clock Colin appeared on the doorstep, looking as always dapper and fidgety, and accompanied by Avril, looking shy. At that time we had a Spanish girl living with us, who was supposed to do various domestic duties in return for her keep: she went to English classes every day. She was extremely idiotic and thought of nothing but sex. She let them in, wriggled her huge bosom a bit at Colin, and flounced off to her room to repaint her face.

'Is that your sister?' said Colin, looking after her appreciatively.

'No,' I said. 'D'you want some coffee?'

'Don't you have breakfast late?' said Colin, sitting down comfortably. 'Who makes it for you?'

'Mrs. Simmons,' I said.

'Have some coffee, Av,' he said. 'Sit down and make yourself at home. We'll need some more cups.'

Avril blushed and sat down. I went to get the cups.

When I came back I found Colin prowling round the dining-room, examining and touching everything.

'Nice I must say,' he said. 'Can I see the rest after?'

He sat down again and drank some coffee, then lighting a cigarette said, 'Come on, can we see? Or is your mum still in bed?'

'She's away,' I said. 'Look wherever you like.'

He covered the whole house minutely, missing nothing, exclaiming with delight and only occasionally criticising. Avril padded quietly after him, agreeing with him and still rather subdued. My mother is very good at her job. The house was once two large mewses: now it has four bedrooms and two bathrooms upstairs, a small dining-room and kitchen and a big drawing-room downstairs. She has decorated it extremely well, resisting almost everywhere the temptation to overdo it.

'This is the sort of thing I want,' Colin said. 'This sort of place. I suppose it's terribly expensive. Your mother must have got marvellous taste I must say.'

Flattered, I followed them on their tour. My mother's bathroom delighted them – she had allowed herself to be luxurious. When they came to Alexander's room, Colin said, 'Who sleeps here?'

Alexander is not only an immaculately tidy person, he also has very few things. There was a bottle of hair oil on the dressing table; some letters on the desk were covered by a book; but otherwise the room bore no sign of being regularly inhabited.

I answered, 'No one.'

I do not know whether I said this because it suddenly crossed my mind that Colin, always anxious to think the worst, might assume that Alexander must be the lover of either my mother or myself and that I should not be able to persuade him to the contrary, or because I was pleased to see someone usually so sceptical evidently impressed by our apparent wealth, and therefore did not want him to know that we had to have a lodger. He had developed a way, only half mocking, of treating me as if I were innocent, didn't know much about life, wouldn't understand anything nasty: perhaps it was something to do with my rather liking that attitude which made me lie to him.

'It's the spare bedroom,' said Avril, as if he ought to have known.

Colin said that it was a nice chintz for a bedroom and went downstairs. We went out to look for a flat: he had a list from a house agent.

We looked at three, one in Eaton Square, one in Knightsbridge, and one in Mount Street. They were all very small, the Eaton Square one being possibly the nicest, because it had not yet been decorated. Looking out of the window on to Mount Street, Colin, whose ebullience had faded early, said, 'They're all terrible. What do I want a flat for anyway? Just tell me that. What am I going to do in a flat? Give a ball? Stuff myself down the wastemaster? Or what? I can't afford it anyway. The whole thing's only a game. O God. What a bloody waste of time. Let's go.'

We followed him obediently into the lift.

'But I thought your sister was going to pay, Col?' said Avril, distressed. 'And that you were fed up with stopping at your Mum's.'

'She was. I am,' said Colin. 'But she's not going to. And I belong there don't I, with my dear old mum? No place like home, you know.'

As we got out of the lift, Avril shrugged her shoulders at me and said, 'He's off.'

We followed him into Park Lane. After some moments of hurrying along in silence, he made an indication with his head and said, 'Here, follow me.'

'What d'you think we're doing?' I said loudly.

'O.K., O.K., come on,' he said. 'I'm going to show you something.'

He led the way towards a grand and beautiful house which had several company plates outside its door.

'Oh, Colin,' said Avril. 'Wherever are we going?'

'Shut up,' he said. 'Come on.'

He led us briskly past a shining Rolls-Royce which was drawn up before the entrance with a chauffeur reading a newspaper at the wheel, up the steps and on into the house. There was a commissionaire's desk at one side of the hall, but it was deserted. The house was very quiet: it was late on Saturday morning and I suppose all the typists had gone home. The November sunshine, which had seemed bleak outside, looked warmer here, struck a pillar between which the window dust danced, and from another window crept up two steps of a fine fragile staircase which curved up into apparent darkness.

'What's the idea, Colin?' Avril asked in a nervous whisper.

'Oh, I often come here,' said Colin airily.

'Go on,' said Avril disbelievingly.

There was a blur of voices from behind a door. Immediately Colin seized us by the arms and pulled us into a corner by the staircase.

'Shut up for God's sake,' he said. 'I don't want him to see me.'

The door was opened hurriedly and a small boy came running out with a piece of green paper in his hand, and disappeared through another door at the back of the hall. 'Urgent rate,' a voice called after him.

The door opened again as another voice said impatiently, 'I'm late already.' A man in a black overcoat came out followed by two other men, who looked worried and carried dispatch cases.

'I did telephone through to say you might be delayed,' one of them said.

'We can settle the other thing on Monday,' the man in the overcoat was saying. 'Get Fisher round here. You'd better give him lunch, and I'll see him afterwards.' His voice, though not at all deep, was particularly clear and strong.

The chauffeur had jumped out of his seat and stood holding open the door of the Rolls. The man in the overcoat hurried down the steps, putting on his hat as he went, and got into the car. The young man who had telephoned followed him; the other, who was older and grey-haired, stood watching them drive away, then turned and walked quickly away in the other direction, frowning and looking at his watch.

A voice above us said, 'Looking for someone?'

We turned to see the commissionaire coming downstairs towards us, looking suspicious.

'It's all right, thanks, we've seen him,' said Colin confidently. 'Come on.'

'Just a minute,' the commissionaire said behind us.

'Oh, Colin,' Avril said a little breathlessly. 'Whatever was the point in all that?'

'I know him, that's all,' said Colin.

'Who is he, then?' I asked.

'Not the sort of person you ought to know,' he said.

'Oh, do tell us who he is, Col,' said Avril.

Colin said nothing.

'Why is he not the sort of person we should know?' I asked.

'He just isn't,' said Colin.

'Why did you show him to us so proudly then, if you're not going to tell us who he is?' I said, annoyed.

'I'm not proud of him,' said Colin.

'Why did you insist on our seeing him then?' I asked.

'I didn't,' he said. 'I wanted to see him and you happened to be with me.'

'I think it's perfectly ridiculous to be so secretive,' I said.

'Oh, shut up, you two,' said Avril. 'Let's all go and get a sandwich.'

We ate some expensive sandwiches. Colin had become morose, and I was still angry with him. Avril and I talked about clothes. Afterwards we got on to a bus. At Knightsbridge I left them and went home.

4

M Y mother and I spent Christmas with her brother Vere and his wife. My mother was bored but I was pleased to be there.

They lived in a solid Georgian house in Somerset: it forms a little group with a church and some stable buildings. My mother finds Vere and Ann dull. I suppose they are; but sometimes a desperate nostalgia fills me for that house, and to a lesser extent for them. Before Tommy Cowper died we lived in the country, and after that I spent a large part of my school holidays with Vere and Ann. The house in Somerset was the place I chiefly thought of as being where my real life was lived: for a short time, later, its position in my mind was usurped by the house my mother made Lewis Ogden buy on the edge of Salisbury Plain; and there was another time, a few years earlier, when we had had a converted oast house in Kent for the weekends; but mainly my allegiance was to Coombe, its smell and look, the garden, the long clear water, the loud birdsong in the still air, the trees, the gravel, the sun through the open door – all this was what I secretly, with no clear idea of what I meant but with all the same a sense of loss, had some sort of faith in: so that, having arrived and exchanged greetings, I walked out into the garden and breathed in the air and thought, 'Now then,' as if I were going to do something. I never did anything, but I always felt that if I stayed there long enough one day I should.

This time I thought how much I should have enjoyed bringing Colin and Avril there. They had come to be almost my closest friends, although there were whole regions of my life from which they were excluded, and of theirs from which I was. Seeing them every day, however, and occasionally in the evening or at weekends going to the cinema with them, had made them very familiar and easy to be with: I suppose they and Alexander were the people I found it easiest to talk to. I had a few so-called friends among the girls with whom I had come out, but I never felt much at ease with them, perhaps because we were in too competitive a position; and my relationships with the young men who from time to time took me out to dinner, or to the theatre, were at that time wary.

Of course there could have been no question really of taking Colin and Avril to Coombe. Vere and Ann would have been horrified by my having such common friends. Not that I mean to condemn them particularly for that. I always felt that they had chosen their conventionality wilfully, not merely accepted it without thinking. They farmed on quite a big scale and took an active part in local life – Ann was chairman of the Women's Institutes of the County, and Vere was a Deputy Lieutenant. They seemed fond of each other and had a son of thirteen and two daughters of eight and ten. They were not, I suppose, a clever or amusing family, but all the same there may have been a tinge of envy for their stability in my mother's insistence on their boringness. She was, of course, perfectly charming to them the whole week that we were there, and had brought wonderful presents for the children; but she was relieved to get back to London.

My mother, unlike me, has an immense quantity of friends, many of them I think probably fairly close. Although I would say that the impetus in these friendships comes mainly from the other people, who fall victim to her beauty and strength of personality, she is very kind and thoughtful about anyone she has accepted. I could never understand her continued kindness to Betty Carr. She is usually impatient of foolish people, but of Betty, if I complained about her, she would simply say, 'Oh well, dear old Betty, I've known her a long time.'

Betty Carr introduced Lewis Ogden to my mother.

I came back from work one day not long after Christmas to find them all three sitting in the drawing-room.

He was standing by the fireplace holding a glass of sherry. He was fairly tall, but narrow-shouldered. He had a look of great seriousness. His face was thin, he had large light blue eyes and thick but neat black hair: he would have been extremely good-looking but for his mouth which was slightly crooked and not well-shaped. He wore a dark suit, white shirt, black tie and expensive-looking suede shoes.

My mother said, 'This is my daughter Vanessa. Let me introduce Mr. Lewis Ogden to you darling.'

I had expected him to have a deep voice, more because of what I had imagined of his character than because of what I had seen of his appearance, and I was surprised to find it light and pleasant when he said, 'How d'you do.' As he did so he smiled in, I thought, too obviously charming a manner. His eyes remained cold.

I would have said something then about my having met his wife in Switzerland had it not been for Betty Carr, who, perched nervously on the edge of the sofa, said with a slightly proprietory air, 'I'm trying to persuade him to be interested in the Easter Ball. I don't think I've succeeded yet though.' She gave a giggle and took a gulp of sherry with a great jingling of charm bracelets.

Betty is well-meaning, kind and generous: she is also annoying to a degree quite out of proportion to her faults. It is not merely that she is stupid. She is incredibly tactless, and will find the wrong thing to say in a situation where one might have thought that there could have been nothing wrong to say. She also fidgets all the time and has a thick neck. Her face is pretty but one forgets this after the second time of meeting her. She has had a certain amount of bad luck in her life, having married a peer who was killed in the war, since when she has lost a good deal of money through injudicious investment; she now spends most of her time looking after her senile father, an extremely unpleasant retired Civil Servant. She was obviously pleased with her discovery of Lewis Ogden, though at the same time evidently nervous of him. I noticed immediately that his manner to her was as off-hand as was conversant with politeness. A little later I noticed that the same was true of my mother's manner to him. I could see no obvious reason for this, and could only conclude that he must have offended her before I arrived.

'You're going to be on our Junior Committee aren't you darling?' Betty said to me.

'Oh,' I said, helplessly. 'Am I?'

'I'm afraid you'll be angry with me, Betty,' my mother said. 'I've had one of my sudden stern fits and told Vanessa she mustn't do any more charity work till she's passed her exams.'

'So you have,' I said, smiling gratefully at her.

'Oh, naughty Essex,' said Betty. 'You are unkind. D'you really mean that?'

'I'm afraid so,' said my mother gently. 'But I'm sure you'll find plenty of others.'

'Oh, I am miserable about that,' said Betty to me. 'I was counting on you. I've got your friend Annabel, and little Kate Flower, d'you know her? And I thought Louise Ardingly – would she do it d'you suppose?'

Thankful for my own release, I allowed myself to be drawn into a discussion of possible Committee members. My mother and Lewis Ogden began to talk about, for some reason, public school education: I suppose the subject had developed out of the fact that the Charity Ball in question was in aid of some children's charity. Listening as well as I could at the same time as carrying on my conversation with Betty, I heard my mother venturing some rather Left Wing opinions which I had not suspected her of holding.

'It was all very well having an *élite* education when you had an *élite*,' I heard her say, and something about 'propping up an obsolete hierarchical system'.

Ogden who had moved little since I had come into the room, put down his glass and turned towards her. I heard his clear voice quicken with interest. It sounded like a man of twenty-four speaking – I mean from the tone of his voice – and I longed to ask Betty how old he was. The idea of a young millionaire seemed romantic.

'I wish I could agree with you,' he was saying. 'I do agree that without the abolition of the public schools you won't get equality in this country – you won't ever get over the accent difficulty for one thing, which is one reason why this is the most class-conscious country in the world. But I've lost my faith in equality. The thought of people being born equal seems to me even more frightful than I once considered the thought of their being born unequal. But the fact is, of course, that they aren't born equal at all, in intelligence, or value to the community, or, surely, worth as human beings. And if that's so, oughtn't the best to be educated as such? The thing is to select the best; and whether the present system does more or less get them, as well as quite a number of others, I don't know. I think it does.'

I noticed with interest that his own accent, though nearly perfect, was not quite without fault.

'But darling you're not listening,' Betty said to me. 'Do. You see, I've been so stupid and left the whole thing so horribly late. The thing is I did start in the autumn, when we fixed the date, and I got a lot of preliminary work done, but then Daddy was so awfully ill again, poor darling.'

'I'm sorry to hear that,' I said, thinking how foolish a woman of forty sounded talking about 'Daddy'.

She started to describe his illness. Ogden was talking about Secondary Modern Schools.

'But however good they may become,' my mother said slightly aggressively, I thought, 'parents will still consider it shameful if their children don't get into the Grammar Schools.'

'You know you are looking awfully tired,' Betty suddenly said. 'Half asleep, poor lamb. Essex was quite right. You're working too hard. Isn't she, darling? I was saying how tired Vanessa was looking.'

I felt Ogden's light eyes on me. I thought he was probably annoyed at having his discussion with my mother interrupted.

'D'you want to go and have your bath darling?' my mother said. 'What time's your party?'

'Now,' I said. 'I think I will if you don't mind.' I got up and, smiling in the direction of Betty then of Lewis Ogden, said, 'Well, good night.'

As I went out of the room I heard Ogden begin to say that he ought to leave. About five minutes later, on my way from my room to the bathroom, I heard a taxi stop in front of the house. I paused to listen, wondering who it was, and heard Isabella the Spanish girl open the door, and a taxi-driver explain to her, with some difficulty owing to her bad English, that he had come in answer to a telephone call. I waited to see Lewis Ogden leave. I heard him say good-bye, then he came quickly out of the room, through the front door and into the taxi, putting his hat on his head as he went. I immediately realized that I had seen him before.

I ran downstairs in my dressing-gown.

'Darling!' Betty greeted me enthusiastically when I went in. 'Your mother's a genius, an absolute genius! I know he wasn't going to do it for me but she's made him buy tickets – yes, darling, it was all your doing – and once he starts being interested who knows where it will end? But wasn't it rather a brilliant idea of mine to bring him here, honestly? And who'd have thought he'd have been so presentable, don't you think so, Essex?'

'How old is he?' I asked.

'Forty-five,' said Betty. 'I looked him up. But doesn't he look younger?'

'Much,' I said, disappointed. 'What else do you know about him, Betty?'

'My dear, nothing!' said Betty. 'Sue Lawton met him at a business dinner – Chris is something to do with one of his companies – and happened to tell him about this charity and he seemed interested, so she asked him in for a drink yesterday to meet me and he really didn't seem at all keen then, and then I said well he must meet our very best and most wonderful patron, *you*, darling. And I told him all about you, you know, and how wonderful you were, and I think he seemed to have heard of you, and anyway he was awfully interested about your father and everything – of course they're bound to be awful snobs these people, but what I can't get over is that really he's not very common is he? I mean really not obviously? One would know of course that there was something not absolutely . . . well, I mean that he wasn't *quite* one of us – but I think it's amazing. And yet of course he's come from nothing.'

'Has he?' I asked.

'Oh yes,' said Betty. 'Well I mean I think so. I mean they all have. He was a builder's assistant or something. There's a wife too – she'll come, of course, won't she? But Sue said everything's very much what he says, not her.'

'I know her,' I said.

When Betty had run through the gamut of emotion from amazement and delight to envy and reproach at this piece of information, my mother said, 'I believe I remember you telling me something about that. Wasn't it in Switzerland?'

I told them how she had broken her leg and that she seemed quiet and harmless. I did not say anything about how she had cried while I sat beside her in the snow, partly because it would have given the gossip-loving Betty so much pleasure, partly because I should have found it difficult to describe.

'Also,' I went on, 'a boy at the secretarial school – you know, Colin, Mummy, I've told you about him – knows him. I don't know how. He once pointed him out to me.'

'That does interest me,' said my mother. 'Why should Colin know him? Does he like him?'

'No,' I said.

'How wonderfully mysterious,' said my mother, looking pleased. 'He's a bit of his past. Could he be an illegitimate son, d'you think?'

'He might be,' I said. 'Or it could just be that Colin once worked for him and was sacked. Or, wait a moment, Avril once said something about a rich man who wanted him to be his secretary. D'you think he's queer and made a pass at Colin?'

'And now Colin's blackmailing him,' said my mother.

'Oh, how awful!' wailed Betty. 'Oh, I do think that's awful! Oh, Essex, ought Vanessa to have that sort of friend?'

'We were only joking, Betty,' said my mother. 'Do go and have your bath, Vanessa.'

I went. I was very late for the cocktail party, which had evidently not been a very good one, and was almost over by the time I arrived.

The first person I saw was Alexander. I was relieved to see someone I knew, and pleased that it should be Alexander, because I had not seen him for well over a week, during which time he had been in bed when I left in the mornings and had not appeared at the house until after I was asleep in the evenings. I immediately went over to him and told him about meeting Lewis Ogden.

'What a splendid find,' he said in, to my surprise, a rather sneering tone of voice. 'We mustn't let him out of our grasp.'

'We've hardly got him in it yet,' I objected.

'Your mother will see to that,' said Alexander. 'Your wicked, wicked mother.'

'Oh, was she thinking of that, d'you think?' I said.

'Doesn't anyone when they meet a millionaire?' he said.

'I don't know,' I said, faintly annoyed.

He laughed and said, 'No, no, your mother was only interested in him because he's an interesting man, naturally.'

'Well, of course she was,' I said. 'Besides, as a matter of fact she wasn't at all polite to him.'

'In fact I think you're both in love with him,' he went on, paying no attention to my interruption. 'I can't think why you don't fall in love with the same people more often. The answer of course is that neither of you ever do fall in love with anybody, ever.'

'Oh, nonsense,' I said.

'Well, who are you in love with now?' he said. 'Mr. Ogden? Your lower-class boy friend from the dear old Acme? Me?'

'I don't have to be in love all the time, do I?' I said.

He paused a moment and then said, 'Of course I always really wanted your mother to be a shocker. It's only right and proper that she should be.'

'What are you talking about?' I said.

'Nothing to do with you,' he said quite kindly. 'Would you like to have dinner with me? I offered to take that small girl over there, but I'd rather be with you so I'll ditch her. I'm going to a gambling party afterwards. D'you want to come?'

'No, thank you,' I said.

We left to have dinner. On the way out we met our hostess who was coming upstairs with some other newly arrived guests. I tried to explain to her why I had been so late, why I had not said 'how do you do' to her when I arrived and why I was leaving already. I found this difficult.

Alexander was amusing at dinner, and I felt flattered at his asking me since I knew that his financial affairs were in one of their uneasier periods. Halfway through the meal he suddenly said, 'You know I'm terribly fond of you and your mother. I think you're wonderful people to live with and I hate the thought of anything that could conceivably bring it all to an end. I expect that's why I was probably rather mean about your Lewis Ogden. It was silly of me but you do understand, don't you?'

I was immensely touched at his consideration in telling me this, particularly because it was not at all the sort of thing which he, usually the most indirect of people, was given to saying; I was also surprised, since I had thought him far more detached, in regard not only to us but to everything, than this confession implied.

I immediately said, 'But of course I didn't mind – not that I thought you were mean about him at all. Anyway I'm sure if you'd been there you'd have seen there wasn't anything like that, nothing that could have seemed a threat to anything.'

Only after I had reassured him did I wonder what he had meant. I tried to remember whether I had told him that Lewis Ogden was married; I was certain that I had. I did not open the subject again since Alexander seemed to consider it finished. After dinner he dropped me at home and went on to play cards.

A long time after this I said to my mother, 'Why were you so rude to Lewis when you first met him?'

She thought for a moment, and then said, 'I suppose it was instinct. I felt he would find me more interesting if I was cold instead of gushing like Betty. Also I knew at once that he felt something about me because of my being who I was. That's why I thought it would be more inter-

esting if·I expressed opinions opposite to those I might
have been expected to have.'

'How clever you are,' I said.

That was in the summer, in Italy.

The morning after my dinner with Alexander I arrived
at the school to find Mr. Heywood and Joyce in conversation at the foot of the stairs. I was, as usual, late.

'Why does he think I insisted on having two instruments put in up there?' Heywood was saying in a tone
of complaint. 'The major part of my business is done on
the telephone, the major part. Authors can't be bothered
with letters, they're not a businesslike race, you know.
No, they just lift up the telephone and talk to me – far
less trouble. The only things I get through the post are
the contracts, and the cheques.' There was a note of
defiance in this last phrase.

'I know, Mr. Heywood. Of course I understand,' Joyce
was saying, looking like a brisk young undermatron. 'It's
just his manner. He's the same with all of us.'

'I mustn't keep you,' said Heywood, at the sight of me
waiting to pass them. 'Well, all I say is good manners oil
the wheels of life, don't you think?' He looked from Joyce
to me for verification. We agreed. 'Ah well,' he sighed. 'I
suppose we can't hope for more than one ray of sunshine
about the place.' Here he gave Joyce a mildly roguish
look, then said again, 'Ah well. Back to the grindstone,
I suppose,' and walked slowly up the stairs, humming
slightly, very neat and small.

Joyce giggled, before he was out of earshot.

'What was the matter with him?' I asked.

'It's the way Higgins gives him his letters,' Joyce said.
'Heywood says he hands them to him with a supercilious
look. There are so few, you see.'

'How sad,' I said. 'Can't you write a book, Joyce, and
make his fortune?'

'Not likely,' she said. 'I say, aren't you late? You'd
better hurry, he's in there.'

I went upstairs and into the room where Mr. Higgins
was teaching shorthand. He gave a short talk on punctua-

lity but seemed in good humour, possibly because of his recent humiliation of Heywood.

I had lunch with Colin, Avril and a large quiet girl called Mary.

As soon as I had sat down, I said, 'Why were you so mysterious about Lewis Ogden that time, Colin?'

Colin looked annoyed. 'How d'you know about him?'

'Oh, I didn't recognize him at the time, but I know him quite well really.' I said this because I was afraid that Colin might still be secretive about his connection with Ogden, and thought there was less chance of his being so if I claimed to know all about him.

To my surprise, however, Colin said at once, 'Oh God, I might have known it. He's my flipping brother-in-law, that's all.'

Avril gasped. 'You might have told us,' she said. She looked, I thought, surprisingly horrified.

'But Colin, you mean that's your sister?' I said. 'His wife?'

'You mean you know her too?' said Colin, looking even more disgusted.

'I met her in Switzerland,' I said. 'She broke her leg.'

'That's right,' he said. 'That's her. If I'd known you knew them I wouldn't have said anything about them.'

'But why not?' I asked.

'Oh, I don't know.' He rubbed his forehead, looking worried. 'The whole thing's a bit of a muck-up.'

'But isn't she happy, then, Colin?' Avril asked.

'Happy?' he said. 'Of course she's happy. Wouldn't you be? She's O.K. We'll go and see her one day. Come on, have some more coffee.'

'How did she meet him?' I asked, in spite of the fact that Colin obviously did not want to go on talking about her.

'She was his secretary,' said Colin. 'There's hope for you yet, girls. She was a bloody marvellous secretary, did it for years. Then she married him.'

'That's the stuff,' said Mary. 'Isn't it, Avril? Just wait till we get our shorthand up to a hundred and twenty.'

'Yes,' said Avril. 'That's right.'

But she was not at all in her usual cheerful lunchtime

form. I could not make up my mind whether this was simply because Colin remained depressed or whether she had some reason of her own for seeming worried. I began to feel that I had somehow made an error of taste by bringing up the subject of Lewis Ogden; the least I could do was to let it drop.

On the way back to school Avril and Colin walked together; I followed with Mary. Avril offered him some chocolate and when he refused she made him keep the bar for later. He laughed and did not want to take it but she insisted. They walked hand in hand until we got to the school.

5

'H E was a war hero,' said my mother. 'That's bad don't
you think?'

'Why?' I asked.

'I never trust anyone who's had a good war,' said my
mother. 'Charlie Trentham knows all about him. He told
me last night.'

'What else?' I said.

'He was a political firebrand before the war,' she said.
'He's evidently forgotten all that now hasn't he? But he
was an ardent Socialist, always making furious speeches
at Hyde Park Corner, that sort of thing. Then the war
came, when he was still very young – he was the youngest
Colonel in no time. He did something terribly brave in
one of those smart places like Crete or Yugoslavia and
was wounded and invalided out. Then he worked in the
Ministry of Supply – that's where he made all his useful
business contacts, and at the end of the war he started
buying up property while it was still cheap – as simple
as that. Now he apparently has all these hundreds of
companies – it's not only property now but all sorts of
different financial schemes – and he really is a millionaire.'

'Is he Jewish?' I asked.

'Evidently not,' my mother said. 'Charlie didn't seem
to know much about his origins except that they're said
to be humble. Apparently he leads a quiet life and doesn't
throw his money about. Charlie says he has a terrific
reputation for working and wears out all his
subordinates.'

'Is he honest?' I asked.

'He must be pretty sharp, I should think,' said my
mother. 'But Charlie says his reputation's good. He's a
friend of quite a lot of politicians – he met them in the

Ministry of Supply – but only does business with them I think, no more politics.'

About a week after Betty Carr had brought him to see us he asked my mother and me to have a drink at his flat in Portman Square. It was in a large expensive block which smelt of central heating and carnations.

His own flat was large, carpeted throughout in pale green, and curiously lacking in individuality. It was like an expensive suite in a hotel hired out for entertaining. There were about a dozen people already gathered in the drawing-room, of whom neither my mother nor I knew any. They gave an impression of middle-age, wealth and sobriety: I immediately assumed that they were all business friends. They none of them looked particularly at ease.

We were led into the room by a cross-looking parlour-maid. Lewis Ogden came over to greet us. His smile struck me as more genuine this time: when he said, 'How good of you to come,' I felt as if he really had been afraid that we might not. The elaboration, however, with which he drew us into the room, gave us Martinis and took us over to meet his wife, seemed exaggerated, as if he were over-acting his part.

'Jean, I want to introduce Lady Essex Cowper to you,' he said. 'And her daughter Vanessa.'

She was standing with a large dark woman, looking exactly as I remembered her, quiet and uneasy. She was dressed very plainly in black. I had been prepared for her to be embarrassed on seeing me, for she had not struck me as the sort of person who would be well-disposed towards anyone in front of whom she had burst into tears, but to my surprise a look of intense pleasure came onto her face.

'But how wonderful to see you again!' she said to me, shaking hands rather perfunctorily with my mother. 'I never thought I should. I wanted to thank you, but they insisted on dragging me down to that wretched clinic, and then of course I realized that I'd never known your name.'

'Oh, you know each other then?' Ogden said, not looking particularly pleased.

'She practically saved my life in Switzerland,' said Jean, still delighted.

'Really?' he said. 'You must tell me about that.' He turned away to introduce my mother to someone else.

'No, but really I felt ever so guilty about never thanking you,' said Jean.

'But I didn't do anything,' I said. 'Is your leg all right now?'

'Oh yes, quite recovered,' she said. Suddenly she looked as if, her first pleasure having passed, she could think of nothing to say.

'The funny thing is,' I said, 'that I only realized a few days ago that I know your brother too.'

'You know Colin?' she said, pleased again. 'But how could that be? In films?'

I explained about the Acme School of Business Training. If I had wanted to keep up the favourable impression I had evidently made at our first meeting I could hardly have done better than turn out to know, and like, her brother. She immediately began to talk about him, about how she wished he would settle down and get a steady job, how she was sure if he'd only gone on in films he could have been a director, how he'd always been bright but so nervy, how of course lately one or two things had been too easy for him and perhaps it wasn't good for him – perhaps that was her fault and she hadn't been wise – and would I tell him how she wished she saw him more often.

I believe she would have gone on indefinitely had Ogden not come up and said to her reprovingly, 'Aren't you going to introduce Vanessa to any of these charming young men, Jean?'

She looked flustered and began to apologize.

'No, but I'm so pleased to see your wife again. . .' I began; but he had already led up to me the only man under forty in the room, whom he introduced as Peter Grindall. I was conscious of Jean behind me being quietly chivied off about some hostess's duty: I began to think that I disliked her husband.

I asked Mr. Grindall whether he knew the Ogdens well.

'Heavens, no,' he said. 'I'm only an office boy, more or less. It's a tremendous honour for me to be here at all. In fact, to be honest, I've been wondering all evening why I was asked. Now I think it must have been to talk to you.'

'I expect it was,' I said. 'He seems to work that sort of thing out. Tell me about him.'

'I know very little,' he said, looking round to make sure that Ogden was at the other end of the room. 'I lead such a humble existence I hardly ever see the great man himself. As a matter of fact no one in the firm is really – well, a friend of his exactly. He works at a terrifying pace when he is there, everyone's scared stiff of him.'

'Isn't he there much then?' I asked.

'Oh, he leads this tremendous tycoon-style existence you know,' he said. 'Rushing about, secretaries everywhere, flies in, flies out, New York, Johannesburg, I don't know.'

'Is he nice?' I asked.

He looked shocked, then said in a low voice, 'How can you be nice if you're a tycoon?'

I said, 'You don't sound like a very devoted follower.'

'Well as a matter of fact,' he said, 'I shan't be there much longer. I've got a job in Canada, and I'm emigrating.'

He did in fact look rather like a poster encouraging emigration, his ruggedly handsome young face turned towards the Land of Opportunity. I said something to that effect, which he did not seem to think funny. We talked seriously about Canada for some time; then I asked him to tell me about the other people in the room.

'The fat man your mother's talking to is Clive Haddon,' he said. 'A Conservative M.P. who's just been on a trade mission to Moscow. The large dark woman is his wife – very dull. The small man talking to her is my immediate boss. He is very clever and L.O. rather likes him I think. The very dark man is the head of a building society which L.O. has something to do with. He's extremely shrewd and has done terribly well in the last few years. The fair woman is his wife – she's Swedish, was a model. I must say I thought she was rather terrific until your mother came in. I don't know any of the others – oh yes, those two talking to each other are both stockbrokers. And the man talking to Mrs. Ogden now is Sir James Wilson, a big merchant banker. His wife's not here.'

At that moment Lewis Ogden detached the merchant banker from Jean and introduced him to my mother. Jean remained standing awkwardly beside them. I approached, partly to talk to Jean, partly in order to wait for an appropriate moment to suggest to my mother that we might leave.

As soon as she saw me my mother said, 'Oh, darling, yes we really must go. We're so late.'

'You can't go already,' cried the merchant banker, 'I shall be heart-broken. I've only just managed to persuade Lewis here to introduce us and now you say you must go! But look here can't I drive you anywhere? I've got my car just outside.'

'I'm so sorry,' my mother said. 'We've got a car. But thank you.' Smiling at him, she moved towards Jean.

'Thank you so much,' she said, holding out her hand. 'We have enjoyed ourselves.'

'It was so kind of you to come,' said Jean, as if she meant it. 'And I was thrilled to see Vanessa again.'

I felt relieved: I think I had been afraid that Jean might appear inept beside my mother.

'I'm so glad we're to meet again on the twenty-fifth,' my mother was saying.

Jean looked blank. 'The twenty-fifth?' she asked.

'The Easter Ball,' said Lewis Ogden, who had been hovering watchfully beside them.

There was a pause; everyone remained smiling, as if they were waiting for a photographer.

Then Jean said, 'Oh, yes, of course. How silly of me. We shall look forward to that so much.' It was perfectly obvious that this was the first time she had heard anything about it.

As soon as we had left, I said, 'How monstrous of him not to tell her about that. I'm sure he's perfectly terrible. Don't you think so?'.

'I don't know,' said my mother. 'I suppose so. It may

be, of course, that she likes it that way. She looked a
simple sort of creature.'

'She's quite nice, though,' I said defensively. 'I know
she's not exactly your sort of person, but she really is
nice. And I'm sure she hates him.'

'Oh, d'you think so?' said my mother.

'Well, he's not very nice to her,' I said, 'and Colin
doesn't like him. I'm sure she hates him. In fact I think
everybody does.'

'Pretty hellish other people weren't they?' said my
mother stepping out of the lift past a couple waiting for
it, who stared at her.

'Yes,' I agreed, following.

'I'm sorry, though, I really am, about the Easter
what'sit,' she said, as we got into the car.

'Yes, what was all that?' I said.

'He said couldn't we join up for it,' she said, sounding
slightly guilty. 'And was so keen, and said Betty'd made
him buy ten tickets and wouldn't we ask eight friends
to join his party and bring our own party and all sit
together.'

'But you never go to those sort of things!' I said.

'Well, I know,' she said. 'But I somehow found I'd said
we would.'

'But it'll be so boring,' I said. 'And they're always so
expensive, those things, by the time one's finished. We
can't afford it.'

'I know,' said my mother.

'Can't you tell him you made a mistake?' I said.

'Well, not very well,' she said. 'Besides we're to ask all
the people and he's paying for ten tickets.'

'Isn't he asking anyone?' I said.

'No.'

'But they'll have a miserable time,' I said. 'The Ogdens
I mean. Oh, poor Jean. I know you're going to be beastly
to Jean.'

'Of course I'm not going to be beastly to Jean,' said my
mother. 'I don't know why you have this protective thing
about her. And you can ask anyone you like. Haven't you
got anyone you want to ask?'

'Of course not,' I said. 'You know I never have anyone I want to ask.'

'He'll buy all the champagne,' said my mother.

'What on earth does he want to do it for?' I asked.

'That's the mystery,' said my mother. 'Here we are. I'll drop you here so that I can turn round. You don't mind walking the rest of the way, do you?'

'No,' I said, getting out. 'Have a nice time.'

She was going out to dinner. I went home and boiled myself an egg.

The following Saturday morning we had a late breakfast in our dressing-gowns and decided who to ask for Ogden's tickets for the Easter Ball. Alexander was gloomy.

'I'm not at all happy about it,' he said. 'Not at all. I know what it is. I'll be landed with some wretched deb at the Tombola and it'll cost me five pounds. Yes, I know he's paying for everything but I can't ask him for that, can I? I can't go up to him at the end of the evening and say, "Thank you for everything, oh and by the way there's a small matter of what I had to spend at the Tombola." I might do it earlier I suppose. "Well, just off to the Tombola. . ." sort of thing, or, I know, "Can I buy you a Tombola ticket, sir?" What about that?'

'No,' said my mother.

'Well, I don't know,' said Alexander. 'It seems to me we've got to learn how to deal with this fellow. It seems to me he's going to be a feature of our lives for quite some time.'

'Why?' I asked.

'It's perfectly obvious to me that he's fallen in love with your mother,' said Alexander. 'And is consequently, quite simply, going to support us all.'

'Oh Alexander,' my mother said. 'You've never even met him. He's not at all the sort of person who falls in love with people just like that.'

'Besides he's got a wife,' I said.

'Besides he's got a wife,' repeated my mother.

'Well, I don't know,' said Alexander. 'Perhaps he's in love with Vanessa then.'

'Of course he's not,' said my mother. 'He's just interested in us. Now do, for God's sake, think of someone to ask.'

A few weeks later my mother rang up the Ogdens to tell them who was coming and to ask them to meet us all at our house for a drink first. Alexander and I were sitting in the same room: he had just mixed a Martini. I was going to the theatre with a young man who had not yet arrived to pick me up. My mother and Alexander were going to spend a quiet evening working out the accounts of the shop: apparently it was nearly time for the books to be made up for the year, which meant that the accounts had to be up to date. My mother had put on enormous horn-rimmed glasses for the purpose.

Lewis Ogden answered the telephone and said that his wife had gone away for a few days.

'I wonder,' said Alexander, in a disbelieving whisper.

When they had finished discussing the plans for the dance, he asked my mother out to dinner.

'There you are, there you are, what did I say?' Alexander whispered loudly.

My mother refused.

'Accept, accept,' hissed Alexander.

My mother said good-bye.

'I'm sure he heard you,' she said mildly to Alexander.

'You're mad to refuse,' he said. 'You should have gone.'

'I didn't want to,' she said. 'Besides it will make no difference.'

'No,' he said, looking at her, 'it will make no difference. Well, there we are. But, look here, this is getting serious. Isn't it time you asked him to give me a job?'

'Don't be ridiculous,' said my mother sharply.

'No, no, I mean it,' said Alexander. 'I've got to get a job, you know. I can't go on much longer without. And it follows the classic pattern, doesn't it? Do ask him, Essex. Next time you have dinner with him.'

'You're being absurd,' said my mother, looking annoyed. 'What time's your theatre, Vanessa?'

'I don't know,' I said. 'But I think this is Robin.'

I had heard a car draw up outside, and a moment later the doorbell rang. My mother seemed relieved, and greeted Robin with more warmth than usual.

The next morning I told Colin that we were going to a charity dance with the Ogdens. He said, 'Jean won't enjoy it. She doesn't like parties.'

'Does he?' I asked.

'I don't know what he enjoys,' said Colin.

'Why do you dislike him so much?' I said.

'Oh, I don't know,' said Colin evasively. 'I don't know that I do dislike him. Funny you saying what does he enjoy, because I don't believe he enjoys anything. He has this thing about books, but I never saw him read one – except Greek, and Jean says he can't understand a word of it. He has the English translation on the opposite page.'

'He reads Greek?' I said, surprised.

'Pretends to,' he said. 'It's only a pose. Makes people feel small.'

'You do dislike him, though, don't you?' I said.

'He's wicked,' said Colin. 'That's all.'

Much later Lewis Ogden told me that during these weeks he bought all the old copies of the *Tatler* which had photographs of my mother in them. If ever he was driving within a few miles of where we lived, he told his chauffeur to go via our mews. I suppose sometimes we may have been sitting there talking about him and the big car may have slipped quietly past, with him sitting straight in the back, his evening paper lowered so that he might see our front door. He had all the known details of her past life, and of her family relationships, looked up and given to him. They lay on his desk among the few important papers he kept there in a tray: when anyone came to see him he would move the tray on to a side table so that he faced his visitor across a completely bare expanse of mahogany.

6

As time passes I find it easier to remember Jean. If one has been close to someone's death one remembers them for a time as being always dying, and thinks of all their life in terms of its last moments, so that their name means 'the person who died', 'the person who was in their death agony'; only afterwards does one begin to remember that they had an existence apart from their dying. This other existence gradually assumes more importance in one's memory. The last of their physical changes, however frightful its accompanying circumstances may have been, becomes something less terrible in the light of a whole life.

Trying now to remember her as she struck me at that time, it still seems to me that even then she bore the marks of doom. That is one way of putting it. One could say that her personality seemed likely to lead her into unhappiness; but it was more than that. Other people might have tragic potentialities in their characters; only Jean could with such an infallible touch exploit these potentialities to their very limits. The doom was probably all within herself; it needed no stroke of fate; it was a case rather of predisposition on her part than predestination on the part of Providence. Jean had such a predisposition towards disaster as to be exasperating.

It cannot always have been so. She must have been a success at her job before her marriage. Lewis Ogden was not an easy man to work for unless you were good: if you were, he was fair and could even be inspiring. Even though she worked for him in his earlier days, first at the Ministry and then when he started up on his own, he must always have been an exacting employer. He once told me that Jean was the perfect secretary. I can imagine she would have been neat, quick and unobtrusive, but I cannot imagine her meeting emergencies with decision, or acting on her own initiative in all the small crises which must necessarily have arisen. I suppose that by the time I met her she had lost her self-confidence. Perhaps that was one of the things she was mourning when she wept on the mountainside.

If during these few months when I came to know her quite well, I, who because of that scene in Switzerland and because of Colin had come to defend her cause with passion, found her sometimes maddening, how much more so must he have done ever since her position changed from that of secretary to that of wife. Her gloominess, her unwillingness to hope, did not offend me because I could to a certain extent sympathize with them; but he had a fundamentally optimistic nature and must have found her congenital depression hard to understand. It was the sort of thing which he might not have noticed in a secretary, and which later on in a girl he was hoping to marry and who was desperately in love with him might have seemed a rather touching melancholy, to be dispelled for ever by their marriage. But it was something far deeper-rooted than that; and I know that it was a shock to him to find that out. Where her fatalism did seem to me to go too far was when it led her to assume the worst in any situation, meeting disaster far more than halfway, and with the object not of taking steps to change the course of events, but simply of getting the business of accepting defeat over as quickly as possible.

So many times she must have said to herself, 'Then he won't come,' when only a telephone call or the sign of an effort on her part was needed even then to make him come. How many misunderstandings there must have been in their five years of marriage which she had simply accepted as meaning that he had ceased to love her, instead of taking any action in order to clear them up.

She could hardly have been less fitted to be the wife of an ambitious man. Even since their marriage he had made considerable advances in wealth, power and scope of interests, and she was quite unable to keep pace with him. The effort required in social intercourse was beyond her. Not only would she have found it extremely difficult to make, she also considered it actually wrong. She felt that people ought to accept her as she was if they were going to accept her at all: she hated the idea of playing a part. She thought it presumptuous to try and talk about things of which she knew nothing; she made a positive principle of being unassuming, the more so because she was keenly conscious of the criticism to which the mere fact of her being so rich exposed her. Making it clear that she was not 'on the make' seemed to absorb all her social energies. She was too honest to indulge in small talk merely for the sake of keeping up a conversation, and she could not see it as a means of establishing communication. She had also unfortunately very few subjects on which she really could talk. She was interested in the theatre and had always seen all the latest plays, but she read very little, was not interested in politics, and was ill-informed about current affairs.

At the party for the Easter Ball she was a failure, while he was a success.

From that evening dated what he later in self-mockery called 'my Society period'. It was Alexander as much as anyone else who had seen to it that among the people we asked were several of my mother's friends who entertained a good deal, whether because, as in the case of the two married couples, they had debutante daughters, or, as in the case of a young Frenchman and an unbelievably handsome middle-aged South American, their diplomatic positions obliged them to. His object was to please Jean. I told him that he misjudged her but he would not believe me.

'It is absolutely impossible that she should not want to rise socially,' he said. 'And if she doesn't we must make her. Because *that* will compensate her for the fact that her husband is going to make a fool of himself over your mother, *that* will be the only reason why she will encourage their friendship. Thus we shall be able to keep her happy while we enthrall him.'

'I suppose you're joking,' I said doubtfully.

'Oh, don't worry,' he said. 'Your mother will keep it all within bounds. I hope.'

We had asked, then, the Marwoods and the Poores. Lady Marwood was a relation of my mother's, handsome in a hefty Charles II style, extremely sociable, foolish and gay, generous though I suppose fundamentally selfish, quite an amusing conversationalist in a gossipy sort of way. She had quarrelled wildly with all her children and was only on speaking terms with the youngest girl for whom she was planning a season of some magnificence. Lord Marwood was rich and interested chiefly in cattle. The Poores were in their early forties, and both intelligent. He was good looking and a very successful Q.C., she was small and bright and witty, a member of a literary family. They were Roman Catholics and had a great many children of whom the eldest girl was just grown up. We had also asked two girls of my own age; Robin Taylor, the Frenchman and the South American made up the party.

It is hard to imagine the impression we corporately made on the Ogdens. To Jean I think we were nothing more or less than a collection of people whom she did not know. She probably took in only her immediate neighbours at dinner, of whom Charles Poore was too clever for her and Lord Marwood too unfamiliar a type; and Alexander, whose polite attention she rather suspected.

As for Lewis, Alexander said the first time we danced together that Lewis was thrilled with the whole thing. I suppose this must have been true. It was some time before I could quite believe that Alexander was right about Lewis's social ambitions. When I did believe it I could not see how anyone could fail in some degree to despise him for it. That was because I did not then know what it was that he expected of us. Nor did I fully appreciate the difference between the life the Ogdens had up till then been leading and the world my mother represented.

The dance was at the Dorchester. My mother and Jean had arranged the seating for dinner in consultation beforehand. My mother had suggested modestly that Lewis should sit between Lady Marwood and Elizabeth Poore, but Jean had insisted that my mother should sit on his left with the South American diplomat on her other side and Elizabeth Poore beyond him. I was sitting between Robin Taylor and Charles Poore. I could not make up my mind whether it would be better to try and draw the latter's attention away from Jean altogether, which was obviously the course which she herself would have preferred, or to try and make the conversation general. If I turned to talk to Robin I was conscious of uneasiness on my other side: Jean was proving at her most unresponsive, and the situation finally resolved itself into Poore and Lord Marwood talking to each other across Jean, occasionally managing to draw a monosyllabic comment from her.

She was wearing a rather fussy dress, whose pale colour accentuated her own pallor. She was not looking well. On the other hand if you looked at her twice you could not fail to notice her good skin, her pleasantly shaped face and her sweet mild smile: the trouble was that the first impression she made was not such as to encourage a second look: she was not good at presenting herself in the evening.

I could hear Lady Marwood's high voice talking to Lewis Ogden. 'One's simply got to have a lead roof because of the radio-active fall-out. I've had the whole of Marwood re-roofed. Reggie was livid but I said we've got to think of the children. You may not mind being sterile at your age, I said. Of course the thing is that Reggie's violently pro-Russian.'

'Really?' said Lewis Ogden. 'I should hardly have suspected that.'

'No, people don't, you see, that's the trouble. But he says he'd rather be a Communist than dead. Isn't that the most dangerous kind of argument? I refuse to accept that those are the alternatives. It's all very well for Reggie. He'd probably get on splendidly in a Communist state, he's always been good with servants. But I should be the most fearful misfit.'

The South American diplomat was describing to my mother a house he had recently stayed in in Ireland – 'and the whole of the ceiling was a vast inverted shell. . .'

Caroline Mason, opposite me, was saying to Lord Marwood, 'Daddy had a wonderful bull but he sold it.'

Robin beside me said, 'You always listen to other people's conversations.'

'I know,' I said. 'I read other people's letters too. Do you?'

'I used to read Andrew's,' he said. 'But the whole thing got too much for me. They were too horrific. I couldn't sleep at nights.'

Andrew was the young man with whom Robin shared a flat. He had a tremendous reputation for disreputability. I asked Robin to tell me about his latest rumoured exploit which involved an heiress, a gambling debt, and a fabulous diamond. The whole story proved to be a fabrication.

I could hear Alexander talking rather cleverly to Elizabeth Poore about a recent exhibition of paintings. He was saying exactly what she herself had been about to say, and which probably bore no relation to what he had really thought about the pictures, which in fact I remembered him having said that he found very boring; but she looked pleased enough.

Lady Marwood had begun to gossip to the Frenchman about mutual acquaintances in Paris. Lewis Ogden was talking to my mother.

My mother on her best occasions assumes an evening lustre which few can equal. She was wearing a dress of an elegance so startling as to show off to the full the dazzling self-confidence of her beauty; she also wore her diamonds. There was no doubt that Ogden responded. Everything about him expressed the pleasure and stimulation he found in her company. I could not hear what they were talking about since neither of them had such carrying voices as Lady Marwood's, but to my anxious imagination they had the look of two people set apart on some negotiation of their own. He had a powerful stare, and bent on her as it now was it gave their conversation an air of urgency, possibly of conflict, which belied their smiles.

I saw Jean watching them, but with no evident concern. All the same I was relieved when the arrival of a man selling raffle tickets distracted her attention. A few moments later she moved away to dance with Lord Marwood, and immediately afterwards Charles Poore asked me to dance.

He began to ask me about the Ogdens.

'Tell me about them,' he said. 'Are they your mother's latest discovery? I think I see her point about him although I haven't had much opportunity of talking to him. But I found her pretty hard work.'

Tired of defending Jean, I told him as briefly as I could what I knew about the Ogdens, and changed the subject. I saw my mother and Lewis dancing, and told myself firmly that the whole business was no concern of mine.

I believed this for I suppose about an hour and began a mild flirtation with the Frenchman. Then came the scene in the cloakroom. I came back from a dance to see an empty chair next to Jean's, and sat down in it. She was on the point of going to the cloakroom and I said that I would come with her, because I was feeling the heat. She said that she felt tired, and we had some conversation about late hours and how they affected us. She went into one of the lavatories, and I was combing my hair when Lady Marwood and Elizabeth Poore came in together. Lady Marwood was saying in her bright carrying voice, 'That's what I said to Essex. It's always the wives that give them away. It's harder for women of course.'

Seeing my face and my gesture towards the lavatory door, she went on breathlessly, after only a slight pause, 'I mean you know women never are so good at that sort of thing are they? I mean, at games. So I said to her, absolutely, I said my dear if you can't play bridge don't try. It's not really a woman's game, don't you agree?' She smiled at me triumphantly.

I said that I did agree.

'Bridge is such an intelligent game,' said Elizabeth Poore, helpfully.

It was no good. Jean came out of the lavatory. I knew, we all knew, that she had heard. She knew that we knew.

When we went back to our table there was fortunately an empty chair next to Alexander. I sat down in it and as soon as I thought Jean could not hear told him what had happened and asked him to be nice to her. He immediately went up to her and asked her to dance, and in fact hardly left her side until the Ogdens left, which was not until an hour or two later. He showed no sign of being bored with her, and talked with animation most of the time.

I was so touched by this that when Robin said to me, 'Alexander seems much struck with Mrs. O.,' I answered with sincerity, 'Alexander is the most wonderful person in the world.' It took me some time to explain away this spontaneous remark, since Robin insisted that it was so unlike me that it could only mean I was seriously in love.

Then, of course, it had to be Jean who won a raffle. She was so painfully embarrassed at having to walk up and collect it, and she brought it to Lewis like a dog with a ball. It was a shapeless piece of nylon fur, and she brought it to him as he sat smiling his cold smile between my mother and Caroline Mason and held it out to him and said, 'There, look, it's rather nice, isn't it?' in her nasal voice and with her hurt look. He got up and put it round her shoulders. My mother stood up too and admired it, then walked round the table and said to Charles Poore, 'I've been meaning to talk to you all evening. I want to ask you something. I know it's the sort of thing people pay hundreds for your opinion on, but there's this wretched client of mine. . .' and she went on to ask his advice on a point of law.

Jean sat down next to Lewis. A moment later he asked her to dance. Nothing in his behaviour to her had fallen short of the polite; indeed it was too polite, too stiff. I felt that she must know he was annoyed with her for having made my mother move.

Jean must have told him while they were dancing that she was tired, because after that he danced once with those of us with whom he had not already danced and then left with her, although it was early.

When he danced with me, I wanted to talk to him about Jean, to say how much I admired her, or to mention Colin, whom I did not know whether he knew that I knew. Alternatively I wanted to be brilliant and scornful so that he should see that I despised him. In fact I was silent and awkward. I found him alarming, and I think that he was probably wondering what sort of thing I usually talked about. He made some remarks about the band and asked me whether I enjoyed dancing, all with his searching serious air. Held correctly in his arms, staring bleakly at his left shoulder, I found myself for some reason in the grip of the most hideous shyness. I answered him in freezing monosyllables, imagining all the time what would happen if I suddenly tripped and fell down, dragging him with me, or said something obscene, or began to scream at the top of my voice and could not stop.

After the Ogdens had left there was a perceptible lightening of the atmosphere at our table. Alexander suggested that we should go on to a night club. The South American tried to persuade my mother to come, but failed, and we left them with the Poores and the Marwoods.

I should have liked to have stopped thinking about the Ogdens then, but I found that everyone else wanted to go on talking about them, about how rich they were, how dull she was, how much taken with my mother he was, with apparently endless speculations about their past, present and future. Morosely, I drank a good deal of brandy and watched the Frenchman's inclinations being transferred to Kate Flower, who was being quite funny and malicious.

A large party of Alexander's friends whom I knew slightly came into the night club soon after we arrived. One girl was being pursued by the Press because she had left her husband, and pretended to suspect everyone of being either a reporter or a private detective or her husband in disguise: I found this extremely tiresome. Alexander began a long and involved argument with a fat frightened-looking man; it was something to do with money and they were insulting each other outrageously but without apparent venom. I asked for a glass of water and found it extremely difficult to persuade a waiter to bring me one: I was annoyed with Robin for not being more aggressive with the waiter. One of the girls among the party of Alexander's friends fell asleep. The Frenchman drank a great deal and became more and more amorous. He and Kate were to be seen struggling in an undignified manner on the dance floor. After a time Alexander left, with two other men and the girl who had left her husband. She said she was taking them to a party in Soho. Robin, who was showing no signs of enjoying himself, insisted nevertheless that he did not want to leave. Finally I persuaded him to drive me home. He complained all the way because Alexander had not paid his share of the bill.

7

THE Ogdens sometimes went to Brighton for weekends. They stayed in a hotel and Lewis went for long walks by the sea, very fast and breathing deeply. The rest of the time he read intensively, mainly in the classics. Sometimes he would begin to talk to Jean, perhaps at dinner after a day spent in reading and walking, and he would talk late into the night, occasionally about some particular business negotiation, but more often about his ideas, about politics, morals, philosophy: he would sometimes expound a case to her with tremendous passion, a passion more or less wasted since she always agreed with him. He seemed to need these occasional outpourings of the results of his speculations; I have heard them too. After some days of tiring work, they were his form of relaxation; he felt much better after them. A furious political argument lasting far into the night would have the effect of making him begin the next day refreshed and renewed. His own theory about this was that he was fundamentally lazy and needed constant intellectual stimulus in order to achieve anything. He said that it was having to overcome this exceptional laziness which had made him a success. I suppose this fits in with certain psychological theories but as I never saw any signs of the laziness he laid claim to I never really believed in his explanation.

He was born in a suburb of Liverpool, where his father worked as a chemical engineer. Newspapers always tended to exaggerate the circumstances of his childhood: he had certainly not been brought up in a slum. His father, according to Lewis, 'made a profession of humility' and was so modest that he once refused the offer of a slightly better though not very responsible job because he did not think he would do it well enough. I thought that

Lewis was hard on his father's memory. I once said to him that he sounded an almost saintly character, with his renunciations, his lack of mercenary considerations, and his anxiety not to think himself better than his neighbour. Lewis, however, insisted that it was all the mark of a disappointed man, a man too proud to admit that he had failed, who therefore had to pretend that he had not tried; he said that when Lewis had begun to be a success – even when he was doing well at Manchester University – his father was bitterly jealous. Anyway he seems to have provided a background of extreme dreariness. He had very little money and was himself apparently only inter-ested in his stamp collection, which was a rare one; so that he sent Lewis to a small local private school, which was cheap and bad and where he was not at all happy. Lewis always bore a grudge against this school, not only because it had taught him so little but because he said that it had taken away his ability to enjoy himself and that it had taken him twenty years after leaving there to get it back again. I doubt whether the school deserves all the blame for this, because I feel sure that he can never have had a sufficiently spontaneous nature to have been good at enjoying himself. Nor in fact can the educational standard have been quite as low as he made out, for he immediately did well when he went to Manchester University, where he took a first-class degree in science.

His mother went mad when he was ten, for which he never forgave women. It was perhaps too much emphas-ized to him that the reason for her madness was a physical one, to which all women of her age were liable, for it gave him the idea that women were by nature of their sex neurotic, nor did he regard this purely as a misfortune; it seemed to prove to him the basic inferiority of women. Perhaps I misjudge him in this. It certainly did not appear very much in his ordinary dealings with women, except that in general conversation he would nearly always rather talk to a man; but it was an attitude which any disagreement with a woman would certainly tend to lead him back to. Perhaps, however, it was less a certain belief than a fear.

He was very thin in those days – I mean in his

Manchester University days. I found an old photograph of him once, showing a young man of intense earnestness, with a large Adam's Apple: he was handsome, though less so than he became later. His forehead was broad, his eyes large and honest-looking, his nose fine; only his awkward mouth gave his face a slightly crooked slant. He was, he told me, extremely talkative and dogmatic. Politics were his great enthusiasm, and he spent much of his time in debating societies or doing active Socialist canvassing or work in social settlements. He belonged to a sort of clique of serious Left Wing young people in Manchester: the only thing apart from politics which interested them was music. They went to a great many concerts and Lewis was enthusiastic about Wagner: this seemed curious to me because when I knew him music bored him, especially opera. They also went, he said, on reading parties in the Lake District, or walking tours further afield. The friends he had then had completely passed out of his life. Indeed, he only spoke of this pre-war period with the greatest reluctance. I think there were two reasons for this, neither of them being that he was in any way ashamed of it: one was that he was living at home during this time – having no money to go anywhere else – and did not care to recall the boredom and irritation of his relations with his father; the other was that he was secretly ashamed of having given up all political allegiance. He also told me that in fact his relations with the companions of those days, though they discussed everything between them with the greatest of freedom, were never particularly close, and this I can believe because the small complications of friendship bothered him: he took the whole business sometimes too seriously and sometimes not seriously enough, through lack, I suppose, of some sort of talent. It may be that he was never sufficiently interested in other people except in so far as they impinged upon his own existence. Though I heard many people at various times speak of him with admiration or respect – especially people who had known him during the war – I never met anybody who could truthfully have been called a friend of his.

It does not seem that in those early days he was necessarily the moving spirit in his group. He was evidently among the most violent in his opinions, and he also – and this he did remember with pride – spoke well at political meetings; but he does not seem to have been thought of as a leader. It was the war which changed that.

When he first told me that he had enjoyed the war I was horrified. The general, though vague, opinion among people of my own age was that war, even apart from the threat of recent fearful weapons, was something to be avoided at almost all costs; the idea of pacificism was far more congenial to us than anything more conventionally patriotic, and the thought of anyone actively enjoying war was extremely immoral to me. I could see, though, that the war had given Lewis opportunities that he might never otherwise have had, had widened his field of experience and enabled him at a comparatively early age to wield a power which it would probably have taken him years to attain in other circumstances. What did surprise me was to learn that he himself saw the whole thing in terms which seemed to me impossibly out of date – in terms of heroism, of personal glory, of inspiring communal courage.

'But it can't have been like that,' I said. 'In nineteen fourteen perhaps, and the first rush of all those young men to France, and the way they were all killed, but not this war?'

'I don't mean to say that there were no terrible or shocking moments,' he said. 'And obviously there were places where it was nasty to be, and I was lucky. All I say is that there were also tremendously exciting moments, and moving ones, and satisfying ones.'

'But wasn't it disillusioning?' I said. 'Didn't people crack under the strain? Wasn't it all sordid and humiliating? What about all those books I've read?'

'I never saw much of that sort of thing,' he said mildly.

Perhaps because I so obviously would not understand he told me little about his war experiences, except that authority came to him very quickly and that he liked it. He had, of course, been in some of the more romantic theatres of war. I tried to imagine him going out over wild bare hills on a raid, leading his faithful followers, clasping his hand-grenade and sniffing the wind from Siberia; but I failed. All the same it must have happened, because he was given a medal for it.

Office life, of course, had made him less healthy by the time I met him, which made it harder to imagine him in those circumstances. He went everywhere in his big car and only walked on his weekend visits to Brighton, which were becoming rarer at the time I met him. He once went so far as to arrange to go on a cure at Aix-les-Bains with another rich business man, but he put it off at the last moment and went to Italy instead.

Most of what I know about Lewis Ogden's business life I learned from Alexander. What it all really amounted to I don't know. I see him sitting at his great desk, or at a conference table, L.O., his silence, his listening, his brief emphatic pronouncements. He would take pleasure in outlining with precision a position, a problem, the state of a certain company, the effect which a certain course of action could be expected to have; he would take pleasure too, certainly, in snubbing an over-eager subordinate, or exposing a foolish argument. As to the rest of it, how is one to say what it all meant? To me, now, it seems the reasonable behaviour of a man whom authority became; to some it seemed ambition at its most single-minded, power-lust for its own sake; some said that he was bitterly jealous of possible rivals and was determined to the point of mania to rule his empire in solitary dictatorship; others – including Alexander at one period – that it was his inability to deal more than most superficially with the whole question of personal relationships which left him in an isolation which he did not seek. I never knew for certain what Lewis thought of it all, how conscious or unconscious some of his behaviour was: I don't think he always knew himself.

My mother and I did not see the Ogdens again for some time after the Easter Ball. Easter itself intervened. I had two weeks' holiday from the typing school and went down to stay with Ann and Vere. My mother went to

Deauville with several friends, but sent me a postcard to say that she was bored and was coming back. A few days later she turned up at Coombe in the little yellow van with Alexander driving.

I was coming back to the house after taking the dog for a walk when I saw them drive up to the front door. I was unaccountably filled with apprehension and unwillingness to meet them. As I was extremely fond of my mother and had by that time become attached to Alexander I could find no explanation for my feelings unless they might be a premonition of some bad news which my mother was bringing. I walked round the garden for some time trying to imagine what this could be, but when I finally went into the house I found them having tea with every appearance of peace of mind.

'Has something happened?' I asked my mother.

'Of course not,' she said, surprised. 'What sort of thing? I must say, you do look well, darling, doesn't she? You ought not to go to bed so late in London, you know.'

'I don't go to bed nearly so late as either of you two,' I said equably.

Vere said 'Ha!' and Ann looked at him nervously. I had evidently confirmed their worst suspicions about my mother's way of life. Realizing this and seeing that my mother looked slightly annoyed, I at once began to ask her in the friendliest way about her visit to Deauville, so that at least they should see on which side my loyalties lay. I think my effort was probably wasted; nor were Vere and Ann pleased when Alexander, whom they had never met before, spent the next day in bed claiming he had a headache.

Soon after our return to London, Colin said to me, 'Jean's ill. She wants you to come with me one day to see her.'

I asked what was the matter with her, but he did not know: he thought it was nothing much.

Early May was warm. Even London smelt of summer, of mown grass and lime trees, the petrol fumes overlaid with the smell of flowers. We went by bus one Saturday afternoon to see Jean in the flat in Portman Square. The bus was full. Near us was a neatly dressed, portly, small man with a reddish face and rheumy eyes. He looked respectable and businesslike; he looked sober, but I suppose was not, because he was talking to himself, quietly but audibly, in an excessively doleful manner. He was talking about Paris, but since he could not pronounce his 'r's it sounded like 'Pawis. Pawis I ought to be in Pawis. I love Pawis. Pawis for art, Pawis for . . . Pawis. Ought to be in Pawis.' Nobody in the bus was paying the slightest attention to him. I saw a tear creep down the side of his nose; his lament did not pause while we remained on the bus. The woman sitting next to him, who seemed to have no connection with him, gazed stolidly out of the window.

'Why does no one notice?' I said to Colin,

'English,' said Colin.

'Perhaps they don't think it odd,' I said. 'Perhaps they're all saying it, but he's the only one saying it aloud. Or if not Paris, they're thinking of Spain, or New York, or Heaven, or Milford Haven.'

'Aren't you full of fancies?' said Colin.

Jean's flat was cold and anonymous: she had had boiled fish for lunch. She was lying in a big bed covered with eau-de-nil quilted satin; she looked cold and anonymous too, but seemed pleased to see us. Almost her first words were, 'He's in Paris.'

'Unlike our friend on the bus,' said Colin.

'It was urgent business,' said Jean a little defensively. 'He's coming back tomorrow night.'

I asked her what was the matter with her.

'One of these viruses,' she said. 'Temperature and so on. It's nothing really, but depressing. They say it's always depressing.'

She had a neat pile of new novels by her bed, and another of shiny magazines. I looked at the magazines while Colin talked to her; then he found a Chinese Chequers board and we played this uninteresting game for the rest of the afternoon. A maid brought in tea. Jean became quite animated over the Chinese Chequers. I had never seen her relaxed and laughing before.

A few weeks later my mother told me casually one morning that she had had dinner with Lewis Ogden the night before and that Jean was still ill. I said nothing, but felt my resentment against him growing. It had already been fanned by Colin, who now talked about him more freely, admitting that he thought Lewis not only neglected Jean but took pleasure in making her feel her inferiority. He also called him vain and cold, and ascribed to him all the vices he associated with the capitalist, greed, dishonesty, unscrupulousness and lust for power.

8

I T sometimes seems as if events foreshadow themselves, or as if preliminary rumblings of circumstance precede a great upheaval. The upheaval does not always follow; the murmurings die down, Vesuvius will not erupt this year; but the next time the indications lead somewhere, the stirrings are followed by one particular big incident, and the rumours justify themselves. I feel that the episode of Mr. Heywood comes into this category.

I was hurrying along from the bus stop, having been up late the night before and smoked too much, having also made the mistake of eating Alexander's egg for breakfast, when I saw him. He appeared quite suddenly at the window of his office on the second floor. He seemed to be standing on the window sill, or perhaps on a table just inside the window, the lower half of which was open.

He looked exactly as usual, his black hat and overcoat, his neatness, his dispatch case. This last, as I watched him wondering what he was doing, he bent to put down at his feet, then – the whole thing seeming for the moment perfectly inevitable and to be expected – he bundled himself out of the window and neatly and blackly plopped on to the pavement below.

For a moment he did not move, flat on his face on the pavement, and nor did I, standing some yards away from him. I became vaguely aware of some agitated figures far away at the end of the street, and then suddenly Mr. Higgins came running flabbily out of the house, his mouth pushed out in front of his face like the trumpet of a daffodil, expressive of what seemed to me at that moment an exaggerated concern. Joyce hurried efficiently after him; faces appeared at the lower windows of the house; a small crowd seemed now to be approaching up the street. As I began to move, so did Heywood. He twitched. Mr. Higgins and Joyce together turned him over on to his back. I was by now close enough to see his face, and noticed not so much that it had blood on it as that he looked surprisingly different without his hat, which had fallen some yards away.

He opened his eyes and saw Mr. Higgins bending solicitously over him. He began to scream. At first I thought he was screaming with pain, but almost immediately I realized that it was not pain but rage. The particular high piercing note of it, not like a man-made sound yet expressing an anguish far beyond the range of an animal, seemed to strike a sort of dread in the hearts of the crowd which had gathered: they stopped, faltering, a little way away, so that Higgins and Joyce bending over the fallen Heywood, and I myself standing behind them, made a separate group. Higgins and Joyce too seemed momentarily paralysed by the screams. Then Higgins pulled Heywood into a sitting position. 'It's all right, old chap, all right now. Let's just see if anything's broken, shall we? That's the way. We'll have you inside in a jiffy.'

He began to pull Heywood's arms and legs about in a business-like way. Heywood, though his voice was still unrecognizable, became more or less coherent. It appeared that he was pouring a stream of abuse at Higgins.

'Now, now, old fellow,' said Higgins soothingly. 'Come along, we'll get you inside. Let's see if you can walk, shall we? Joyce and I will support you,' adding to Joyce quite loudly. 'He's raving. Gone off his head.'

'Come along, Mr. Heywood,' said Joyce, briskly. They supported him under his arms and dragged him to his feet. He was silent for a moment, and the ten or twelve people who had now collected surged forward with helping hands, and a murmur of suggestions, inquiries, and observations as to the shocking, amazing, dreadful and unusual nature of the incident.

Heywood seemed unable to support any weight on his right leg, but held up by Joyce and Higgins, he hopped towards the house, dragging it after him. As he got to the door, he suddenly began to jerk convulsively and try to pull himself out of their grasp.

'I'm not going back, I'm not going back,' he shouted; then began to scream again, 'You stopped me, you stopped me, damn you and blast you to Hell, it's all your fault, I won't, I won't . . . you. . .' and he again began to abuse Higgins, pouring out a volume of obscenity and blasphemy of which one would never have dreamt that he would have been capable, howling his rage and frustration at his failure to kill himself.

Later an ambulance came to take him away. He had apparently broken a leg and some ribs. I left the school soon after, my year's course completed: he did not come back while I was there. I never saw him again, nor heard what became of him. We supposed that the loneliness of his dingy office, where the telephone never rang and where only circulars and bills were scornfully delivered by Mr. Higgins, had seemed to him not worth living for: if there was more to it than that, we never heard the story.

My mother seemed to be seeing a certain amount of Lewis Ogden at this time, with or without Jean: there was some talk of their buying a house in the country, which my mother, of course, would decorate. One evening they came to dinner and Alexander persuaded Jean that she ought to take a villa near Amalfi in July.

Jean said that she had been to Capri, but had never been further south than Naples. He began to tell her how much she would like this particular villa, which belonged to someone he knew.

The dinner party had been a success. It was the first time I had seen Jean since her illness, and I was pleased to see her looking so much better. When I realized that Alexander was encouraging her interest in the villa with the idea that we all might be asked to stay there, it seemed to me a fairly harmless way of taking advantage of Lewis's money.

A few weeks later my mother told me that it was all settled, that Jean was going to spend the whole of July there, with Lewis coming and going as business allowed: we were of course asked to stay.

The summer in London seemed long. There were parties, but I still had not learnt to enjoy them. We took an exam at the Acme School of Business Training, and left on the assumption that we had passed it. I missed the last day of term by staying in bed with a cold. It was perfectly genuine: there was a virulent summer cold going about, and I had a temperature of 101°; but Mr. Higgins obviously thought it was merely an excuse and was not at all pleased when I rang him up, partly, perhaps, because it meant that the audience for his farewell speech would be, however slightly, diminished. He said, disapprovingly: 'Of course, I wish you all the best for the future, naturally. All I do say is, don't forget what we've tried to teach you, what we stand for here. Don't forget that, Vanessa. And don't be afraid to give. You've got to give in life. You haven't been our most co-operative pupil, that I will say, just by way of warning, but let us know how you get on, at all events. You should be able to land a very interesting and rewarding position with your opportunities, Vanessa, and remember if you've any young friends we can help just send them along. We'll be here. We'll be carrying on.'

Colin came in later and told me about the farewell speech, which had included some lengthy observations about death, apropos of Mr. Heywood's attempt to achieve that condition.

Then he got up rather abruptly and said, 'Well, cheerio. See you sometime.'

'In Italy,' I said. 'D'you know when you're going?'

'I'm not,' he said.

Jean had made him promise to go and stay with them. He had made a great fuss about accepting, saying that he wouldn't fit in and would be made a fool of, but had finally agreed. Thinking that he had now gone back on this, but deciding not to gratify him by becoming involved in a display of temperament, I said merely, 'Oh.'

'Jean's not going either,' he said. 'She's ill again.'

'What?' I said. 'What's the matter with her?'

'I don't know,' he said. 'Same thing, whatever that was.'

'In that case she's mad not to go,' I said. 'She'll get better there. It's just what she needs. What's Lewis going to do?'

'He's going without her,' said Colin.

'But I thought he was going to be too busy to be there for more than a few days,' I said. 'What's the point of taking the wretched house at all in that case?'

Colin shrugged. 'To entertain you and your mum, I imagine,' he said.

'I shall go and see Jean,' I said.

'Do,' he said. 'It won't do any good. Well, enjoy yourself.'

'What are you going to do?' I asked. 'Have you got a job?'

'I'm going back to films,' he said. 'Something big.'

'You'll come and see me,' I said doubtfully.

'Sure,' he said. 'Sure. 'Bye now.'

I got out of bed when he had gone and stood at the window to watch him walk away. His hands were in the pockets of his trousers and he dragged his feet sulkily. Irritated, I went back to bed. After a time I began to feel depressed, thinking that I might never see him again.

When I went to see Jean I found her, as he had foretold, immovable.

She said that she had been ill again and that her doctor had advised her not to travel, but that she had persuaded Lewis not to give up the Italian holiday, which she was sure would do him good: she meanwhile would go into a nursing home for a complete rest. She did not look ill, apart from her pallor, and was not in bed. We talked of this and that. I felt inadequate and got up to leave as soon as I could.

'It's no good, Vanessa,' she said then. 'I know why you came. I appreciate it, you know I do. But I can't compete, that's all, I just can't.'

She smiled apologetically, sitting quietly in her chair.

'Compete?' I said.

'With your mother,' she said.

'Is it a question of competition?' I asked, knowing that it was.

'Of course it is,' she said. 'He's told me everything.'

'Oh,' I said.

'That's he's in love with her,' she said. 'Not in so many words, I mean. But he talks of nothing else. He adores her. He thinks she's what he's been looking for all his life, and her friends too, and the life you all lead, and the way you talk. You don't understand how different it all is, what it means to him. I always knew it would happen one day.'

'What would happen?' I said. 'I don't know what you mean. Why are we different? We're not clever – what about the people he knew before, all those M.P.s and things that were here when we came for a drink that time – they're much more worthwhile than we are. What does he think we are?'

'I don't know,' said Jean. 'Natural leaders or something. Colin says he's a Fascist. It isn't that, though. Don't think I blame him. It's ever since he lost Socialism.'

'I must say I never thought of anyone liking us for political reasons,' I said.

'He's got so much power now,' she said. 'I see all these people cringing before him. And all the money we have. I think he wants to excuse it to himself.' She looked worried, trying to justify him to me.

'But how do we come in then?' I said.

'You prove that the *élite*'s really worthy of being an *élite*,' she said. 'So that it's all right for him to belong to it too.'

'Oh, God,' I said.

'Of course, really he needs friends,' she said, 'that he can talk to, like he can't to me. But he has to have a theory for everything.'

'But Jean, if he only wants friends,' I said, 'can't you come to Italy? You don't mean that it's because of my mother that you're not coming?'

'Oh no,' she said. 'I need a rest.'

Her confidences were evidently over. She would say no more; nor could I persuade her to come to Italy.

Alexander went to Cannes with some friends, and joined us at Lewis's villa a few days after we arrived. My mother had made him promise to come alone, and he did. Later we found two of the friends staying in Positano. My mother paid their hotel bill and they moved into the villa.

The villa was on the top of a cliff high above the sea. One had to lean over the terrace to see the cliff; otherwise the view was simply of the amazing blue sea and the sky and the distant islands. It had once been a monastery which had for some reason been abandoned: a rich South American had bought it, converted about half the building into a house and pulled down the rest. The terraces of the garden contained an orange grove, and vines and bougainvillaea and brightly coloured climbing geraniums. The rooms were still cell shaped, but though it was sparsely furnished the house was luxurious. The South American had sold it to an old Italian countess of literary leanings, whom Alexander had met when he was staying in Rome with some Embassy friend of his.

There was a courtyard now where half the house had been. It was full of sunlight, and almost unbearably bright at the time of year when we were there. There were wide steps leading into it from the door of the house, down which one expected some grandly cloaked tenor to come singing, so operatic was the scene. In fact Lewis came down them to greet us, wearing a grey flannel suit and dark glasses and looking not at all relaxed.

Our first day with him was constrained. He seemed to feel that Jean ought to be there. He apologized for her absence so often and with such evident sincerity that I was more than ever convinced of her mistake in staying at home. We walked and talked, but he seemed worried that we might not be going to enjoy ourselves. He was anxious to arrange expeditions, to Pompeii, Herculaneum, Paestum, said there was so much he wanted to see, asked if we had read this or that book, seen the Naples museums, remembered the passage in Virgil about the Cumaean Sybil. My mother used her not very profound knowledge of Ancient Roman history to good effect; in no time he seemed to be planning an advance course of classical reading for her. I found his conversation exciting but strange: there were no jokes in it and he was not ashamed of seeming proud of his learning.

The day after our arrival he left, with more apologies, for an important meeting in London. He promised to be back by the week-end, but later wrote to my mother saying that he could not rejoin us until the following week.

By the time he returned, Alexander had been with us a week, but had not yet revealed the presence of his friends at Positano. My mother had repeated several times her warnings about the importance of Alexander's not filling the villa with a lot of disreputable hangers-on; he had denied that he had any such intention.

It was hot. I covered myself in oil and looked with satisfaction at my brown body. My arms and legs, usually a source of mild shame to me because of their length and thinness, now pleased me. I looked at them as I sat on the terrace, drinking before dinner: the smell of my expensive sun oil lingered, in spite of my bath; I stretched out my hands and looked at my brown wrists. I was worried about not being able to expose either my bottom or my bosom to the sun, but when I had confessed this to Alexander he found a small stretch of shingle which was concealed from the rest of the beach by a big rock, and for half a hour a day he kept watch with his back to me on the top of the rock so that I could lie there completely naked.

'It seems a waste when nobody's going to see them,' he said.

'I don't like the idea of being patchy,' I answered. The little stones were hot all the way down my back: the thought of sharing my pleasure in my body with someone else seemed attractive. I could not remember having felt so simple before.

With Lewis away we did nothing but sit on the beach or swim. My mother looked extremely beautiful and managed to remain white without inconvenience. She sat in the shade in an enormous hat reading Herodotus and attracting a good deal of attention. Being unusually lazy, she was completely happy. Back at the villa the three of us ate delicious meals prepared by the Italian countess's cook and drank large quantities of wine. Our meals were very funny, especially in the evenings: the absent Lewis, or the wine, or the days of sun, supplied somehow between them the fourth person we kept congratulating ourselves we did not need to stimulate us. The telephone never rang, London was forgotten, we seemed to have no secrets from one another, no existence except in common; suspended on our balcony in the immeasurable dark blue sky as in a bubble or a moon there seemed to be nothing we could want except each other and all we had to talk about.

The effect on me of the sun on my body explains I suppose why I became suddenly obsessed by Lewis on his return; that was the next dream into which I drifted. It lasted, I suppose, all the time we were in Italy.

Lewis came back looking tired. It seemed as if he talked solidly for two days. When he was called to the telephone we sat in exhausted silence, hearing the peculiar sharp carrying note of his voice in the distance, until he came back, already before he was in the room picking up the conversation where he had left it. All fears of our being bored seemed to have left him: it evidently did not occur to him that we could be anything but fascinated by what he was telling us. To some extent, largely as a result of this conviction of his, we were; and the whole negotiation in which he had been involved, the first stage of which he had just successfully concluded, became vivid to us in spite of our ignorance, generally speaking, of the matters he described. The names became familiar to me, and evoked personalities, some of which I later discovered to be quite unlike the real ones, the issues seemed immensely important, the victory one in which I shared. I pictured Telford, the simple industrious north country-man who had built up his own small textile firm, and Oldfield his workman, now dead. Oldfield's name I had to ask for – no one seemed very interested in him. He had, however, it appeared, made some tiny technical alteration to an ordinary spinning machine which was to have the effect of very much reducing the labour needed to operate it: the new process had been used for some years by the little firm of Telfords, who had finally, after long experiment, perfected it.

'I had lunch with Manning of the F.B.I.,' said Lewis, as if it was a name we should know, 'an old friend of mine. He happened to mention a little trouble which had just started with the Trade Union involved about the cutting down of employment which the spread of this thing would set off. So I rang up Telford, and saw him the same day. You'd like Telford,' he told my mother. 'He's the best sort of English business man. He started his own firm with practically nothing. It's still very small, but wonderfully run – they certainly work there, I've never seen anything like it. And he had the imagination to see what this invention meant right from the first. But of course he hadn't the capital.'

Telford had been on the point of selling his process to the biggest textile firm in the country. 'I was just in time,' Lewis said. 'But I had to get the means of mobilizing the thing. What was the point of having something as revolutionary as that in one's hands simply to sell it and make a quick profit? But to develop it, to promote it, to put it into use in a really big way, to change the whole scene in the textile trade. Of course Robey's aren't all that big, but they've got the mills and they're a well-established old firm.'

Robeys was the textile firm in which the finance company through which Lewis operated had bought the controlling interest, after negotiations of an immense complication, which Lewis seemed to have thoroughly enjoyed, with the three Jewish brothers who owned it. And there he was, through Robey's and Telford's about to revolutionize the textile trade.

Alexander asked him in more detail about the machines. It was one night at dinner. Lewis sent for a pencil and paper and made diagrams; from that he went on to the other technical processes involved in the manufacture of textiles, then to their marketing and use, with a wealth of statistics and a good many sentences which began, 'What people don't realize. . .' or 'What no one seems to have understood. . . .' I became frankly bored and tried to talk to my mother about something else. I noticed that

Alexander's interest did not seem to flag. My mother said, 'You've been interested in the textile trade for some time then? I mean before this particular venture?'

'I never gave it a thought until my lunch with Jim Manning,' said Lewis. He was as proud of all his new knowledge as of his readings in classical literature.

Telford was the man about whom we heard most. Lewis had evidently been much impressed by him, and was relying on him more or less to run the business for him in Manchester. He was coming out to Italy to talk to Lewis the following week.

'Of course he has no charm really,' Lewis said, beginning to lose his confidence in our all immediately liking him. 'It's just that he's an interesting character and rather brilliant at his job. But I suppose you won't have much in common with him.'

It was perhaps anxiety to provide us with more congenial fellow guests which made him so immediately invite Alexander's friends from Positano to stay at the villa, though Alexander said his reasons were snobbish because one of them was a prince.

Alexander, I must admit, managed the whole thing very well. He got us all to Positano for lunch without arousing any suspicions, though my mother and I understood everything as soon as we came upon Leopold von Radwitz and Marcus Edge sitting elegantly on the beach, knowing as we did that they were among the penniless of Alexander's friends and that he had been with them in Cannes.

The formality of mutual amazement over, Alexander introduced them to Lewis, and they invited us all to lunch.

'We eat up there,' Leopold said, pointing to a nearby restaurant. 'The food at our hotel is foul.'

'The thing about our hotel,' said Marcus, 'is the flies. You must come and see them afterwards. I mean, for someone keen on that sort of thing it's a fascinating study. Every sort of fly you can imagine. All over the walls. They sleep on your bed – terribly heavy sleepers, you have to wake them up before you can get out of bed.'

'When did you arrive?' Alexander interrupted, rather

sternly, evidently thinking that Marcus was overdoing it at this early stage.

'Monday,' said Leopold. 'We went to see Simon on our way. He's doing all right, really very very much all right, living in tremendous style. He behaved very badly to us though.'

'Leopold made a pass at her,' said Marcus.

'That was the excuse given, yes,' said Leopold. 'In fact of course he's just mean with her money. It was only a token pass, a mere politeness. It made him uncomfortable seeing us eating there: it was a very ungenerous attitude.'

Marcus now turned to Lewis and said, 'D'you know Rapallo? That's where we've just been staying, with a friend of ours.'

He went on to talk about Max Beerbohm. Leopold nodded with approval, and giving Alexander a smile of pride in Marcus's prowess, lay down to sunbathe.

He was vain, with reason, about his torso: it was beautiful, though his face was like a sad bird's, his sleek black hair forming feathers behind his ears. He belonged to the Baltic aristocracy. How genuine his pride of ancestry was I was never quite sure. Certainly he knew his own family tree and those of his erstwhile neighbours by heart, but that was in order to put it to good use as a means of impressing the people on whom he wished to sponge: I believe he was too intelligent to be other than cynical about the whole thing. Apart from his birth, and the necessity to which his financial situation put him to make it work for him without respite, his main concern was with his health. His wild hypochondria seemed so unlikely in one so young and healthy that it was generally looked upon as a pose, but I think it was in fact quite genuine. He was always a slave to the latest pill, whose influence on him was enhanced by its extreme expensiveness; he was usually on some new régime involving the keeping of peculiar hours and much time spent in exercises. His present one included the drinking of milk every few hours, which caused inconvenience wherever he went but more particularly in Italy, where, having overcome the difficulty of obtaining it at all, he then insisted on its being boiled for exactly three minutes.

His health, the finding of a means of subsistence apart from actual work, of which he had long ago decided he was simply incapable, and the pursuit of young heiresses, generally attended by the most fearful misfortunes and humiliations which he would later describe at length, kept him fairly busy. He had now taken on another, self-imposed, task, that of stopping Marcus Edge smoking. As the latter had even less money than he had it was quite easy to ration him: the trouble was that he was adept at begging them from other people.

Halfway through his conversation with Lewis, Marcus said, 'I say, you haven't got an English cigarette by any chance have you?'

'No, no, absolutely no,' Leopold sat up. 'He's not to have one. Don't give him one. He's had five already this morning. This man is a slave to tobacco. The first thing he does in the morning is to reach out for his cigarettes. He's killing himself – and also, more important, me, since we're sharing a room.'

'Sorry,' said Lewis, putting back his case.

'It's absolute nonsense,' Marcus said. 'It's only because he thinks the room doesn't smell sufficiently attractive when he brings in those vast women he has to have. They're too fat to have any sense of smell anyway.'

'Marcus,' said Leopold, warningly.

'My dear, I have my designs,' said Marcus complacently mystifying everybody. 'I do admit Italian cigarettes rather stick in the curtains. But then we haven't got any curtains.'

We bathed before lunch, leaving my mother and Lewis sitting on the beach. We swam round the corner of the bay to another little beach. There Marcus explained that Leopold's interest in his smoking habits might have struck Lewis as too solicitous and he had therefore hastened to reassure him as to the purity of their relations by describing Leopold's heterosexual activities. It seemed over-subtle, but he was convinced that he had saved the situation. I lay beside them happy because they were talking about Lewis.

Since his return I had thought of no one else. My mind was flooded with him, I felt heavy with the weight of my

imaginings. The fantasies on which I endlessly dwelt were
of so purely dreamlike a quality as hardly to affect my
actual relationship with him at all. The peculiar drowsy
erotic state of mind in which I found myself seemed to
require no action: I did not expect my dreams ever to
come true. I allowed myself to believe he had a faint
unconscious fondness for me which only wanted some
romantic chance to turn it into passion; at the same time
I saw the whole thing so little in terms of reality that had
the romantic chance arrived I should have been incapable
of taking it. I did not know whether my feeling had started
as a result of my being impressed by his more assertive
and powerful manner since his return, or whether it was
because in my liberated sun-struck mood the strength of
his personality had simply seduced me, for I had not
noticed his physical attraction before. There were times
when I wished I could throw off my feeling, when it
became oppressive; but on the whole I accepted it without
much question, and certainly with no thought as to its
implications as far as my mother, or Jean, or even Colin,
were concerned: I suppose it was more of a schoolgirl
crush than anything else.

Our lunch in Positano was a success because Marcus
set out to interest and amuse Lewis, and did. He was still
intelligent, in spite of having spent the last ten years of
his life drifting aimlessly from one Mediterranean resort
to another, with the help of a succession of patrons.

He was ugly: his mouth was large and loose and he
sometimes had a faint streak of nicotine up the side of his
face. His only form of regular employment was to make
up immensely difficult crossword puzzles for a highbrow
periodical. He was always late with them. He would sit
on the beach composing them, a cigarette in one corner
of his mouth and his hands trembling from the after-
effects of a night of drinking. He was the most completely
detached person I have ever know: I must also confess
that he seemed the happiest. The neuroses of the rootless,
the morally insecure, the vicious, seemed to have left him
untouched. He drank because he liked it, and counted it
worth the hangover. He liked conversation but by no
means required it to be brilliant: he would spend hours

in the company of some sozzled expatriate on the chance of a free cigarette or two without ever appearing bored. He was without malice. An odd assortment of people counted themselves his friends, but he would never himself seek them out: it was they who from time to time said, 'I wonder what's happened to Marcus Edge? Is he still in Taormina?' and found him, in his latest situation, a little nearer to physical wreck perhaps, but more or less unchanged, his crosswords his only link with the life he had left. These friends were beginning to wonder now how long his way of life could last, dependent as it was upon a more or less constant supply of benefactors, and to look for the signs of incipient bitterness in him, to listen for the first regrets: they never came. Perhaps he felt the great decision had been made years before when he stayed on in Cannes instead of going back to Cambridge, where he had been for some time because he was unfit for war service and where he was supposed to be making a brilliant career; and was still in the state of self-satisfaction of a man who has made his choice. Anyway to all appearances he remained happy, undemanding and intemperate.

Lewis liked him, and let him talk, and afterwards asked Alexander whether he thought his friends would care to move into the villa for a few days, since they were finding their hotel so uncomfortable.

When it had been arranged that they should, Lewis expressed his pleasure, and said, 'Let's take a taxi then and call at your hotel for your luggage on our way.'

'Oh well, yes, how sweet of you, the thing is. . .' Leopold began. 'That is, shall Marcus and I run up there and collect it and perhaps Alexander could help us? I mean it's not exactly on your way. You'll help us won't you, old boy?'

'No, no, of course we'll take a taxi,' said Lewis. 'You don't want to carry your luggage all the way back here.'

'We can easily walk, it's so near,' Marcus went up to my mother and put his arms around her. 'Perhaps Essex would like to come too? Darling Essex, my oldest friend, you'll walk up with us won't you to see our funny old hotel and its funny old proprietor?'

'But Leopold, you told me. . .' Alexander said. 'I mean, look here, I did say. . .'

'Ran out, old boy, ran out,' said Leopold quietly to him. 'Relying on Simon you see. Simon let us down.'

'Of course we'll take a taxi,' said Lewis again.

'I had no idea, no idea, I promise you,' said Alexander anxiously to my mother.

'I'll walk up with you, Marcus,' said my mother, tight-lipped. 'Come on. Don't you bother, Lewis. You and Vanessa wait here. I'll go with these creatures. Alexander can come too, to carry the heavy luggage.' She led the way up the hill, followed by the three men, bickering amongst themselves.

I believe that Lewis had no idea of what the conversation had been about or that my mother was now going to pay Leopold and Marcus's bill in order that they might leave their hotel and move into his villa.

As soon as they had gone he turned to me and said, 'How intelligent Marcus Edge is. Tell me about him.'

9

LEOPOLD did not drink, because of his health but Marcus
and Alexander were seldom sober the week after our
visit to Positano. There was an apparently endless supply
of alcohol at the villa, and as they were both capable of
being drunk quite quietly, Lewis, if he noticed it at all,
could not have found it actively objectionable. Alexander
turned his peculiar greenish colour and smiled a lot;
Marcus sweated.

My mother was furious and divided her energies
between trying to conceal their state from Lewis and
speaking about it with unusual but hushed ferocity to
Alexander.

Leopold pursued Amalia, the statuesque Neapolitan
housemaid, and complained about Lewis, to whom he had
taken a dislike.

'He's too solemn,' he said. 'I don't trust him. He's so
elaborate and stand-offish. I believe his operations are
more sinister and illegal than you imagine – or else he
has a secret vice.'

'You're jealous because he's not your discovery,' said
Marcus. 'I think he's a charmer. I love people to be
serious.'

'Nonsense,' said Leopold. 'He's as bad as an American.
And when he's *not* an American, you see – that's when
it becomes sinister. I've told Essex she should be careful.'

'My dear, she hardly needs your advice,' Marcus said.
'If ever anyone were capable of handling a situation. . .'

'I don't know,' said Leopold. 'I don't know. Sometimes
I wonder whether this time she might not have met her
match.'

'No, no,' said Marcus. 'What you can't believe is that

someone so sharp over business can be so naïve over other things – that's the paradox. He is though.'

'He'll learn,' said Leopold. 'One day, quite suddenly, he'll learn. Then we shall all be out.'

'We may be out,' said Marcus. 'But she won't.'

'As for Alexander. . .' said Leopold.

'You're over-complicating the situation,' said Alexander. 'Millionaires like to spend money.'

'Don't tell me he knows all about you,' said Leopold.

'Shut up,' said Marcus.

'Oh,' said Leopold. 'Well, then, do you enjoy Henry James?' He turned suddenly to me.

'Quite,' I said.

'Have you read *The Awkward Age*?' he asked.

'Yes,' I said.

'I think it's one of his most perfect,' said Leopold. 'And such a situation – the daughter suddenly grown-up and what to do about all the fast talk after dinner. Don't you see yourself rather as Nanda?'

'Not at all,' I said. 'Besides I don't know anyone who is in the least likely to regret my lack of innocence.'

'I don't believe you're as un-innocent as you think you are,' said Leopold.

'How do you know how un-innocent I think I am?' I asked coldly.

'Do shut up, Leopold,' said Marcus. 'If your mediocre powers of analysis must be exercised turn them on to this heavily-built man climbing up the steps here; finding it hard going too, stopping for a rest, mopping his brow, on he comes, determined. Now, who do you think he is?'

'A man from Interpol,' said Leopold. 'Come to ask Lewis if he'd mind answering a few questions about the latest consignment of heroin via Marseilles.'

'Travelling salesman,' said Alexander, moving aside a trailing frond of bougainvillaea to stare a little glassily over the edge of the balcony. 'He's going to put one of those coupons through the door saying 6d. off your next packet of Washo.'

'Somebody from the Conservative Central Office to offer Lewis a peerage in return for £100,000 for the party funds,' said Leopold. 'Or, no, I think he's one of Lewis's agents, his Neapolitan agent, an undercover man, ex-commando, quick on the draw. That's clever bluff you see pretending to be out of breath. He's really as fit as anything, lean and sinewy, a nasty long scar on one cheek. It's clever make-up, the red nose.'

'I think he's a car salesman,' said Marcus. 'Delivering a brand new Continental Bentley. How lovely. What do you think, Van?'

'I don't know,' I said. 'I'm going to sleep.' I pulled the canopy of my deck chair down over my face.

'Perhaps he's Lewis's business friend,' said Alexander. 'Brunel.'

'Telford,' said Leopold.

'He doesn't look forceful enough,' said Marcus.

In fact it was David Smart, and Marcus was quite right about his being a car salesman. I knew this perfectly well, but I had no idea what he was doing there, and preferred to leave it to my mother to find out.

He belonged to a period in my mother's life which seemed, fortunately, to be over. In fact, it may well have been I who put an end to it, by coming to live with her permanently and having to be 'brought out': but I remember before that, staying with her in the holidays from school and finding David Smart in the house a good deal, brought, I think, in the first place by Betty Carr. There was often another man with them who I think was in the Navy, or had been; there was also sometimes a little perky woman who laughed a lot and kept a flower shop somewhere in Kensington. I remember my mother once or twice saying to me, rolling her eyes as if at the horror of it, 'Now we're all off to an afternoon drinking club,' but whether they really were or not I never knew. David Smart was always nice to me and gave me some stockings for Christmas and took us to the cinema quite often: my mother said, 'Dear old David, one can't help being fond of him – he's awfully kind, you know.'

I never knew how it was that this little crew had either begun or ceased to be her intimates, because all this was at a time when I was not seeing a great deal of my mother, what with school and spending so much of my holidays with Vere and Ann because of the country air. Certainly

I had seen none of them since I had been living permanently with my mother.

I heard his heavy step approaching along the balcony: he had climbed up the steps through the garden instead of going round by the road and arriving at the front door.

'Anyone about?' he called.

I stayed without moving under my canopy, wondering how long I should be able to bear the heat there. I heard Alexander say, 'Well, no, I don't think there is really.'

'Oh oh, oho,' said David Smart, in a tone of alarm quickly changing to one of jollity. 'I didn't see you chaps. I say, you look comfortable. Wouldn't mind changing places, I must say, after that steep climb. Make you work for your *vino* here, what? But you must be wondering who I am.'

'Not at all,' said Alexander, politely.

'Ha, ha,' said Smart, 'That tells me where to get off, eh? The fact is I'm looking for someone called Essex Cowper. Is she around, d'you know?'

'Essex! Essex! Friends!' called Alexander faintly.

'Oh, well, not to worry,' said Smart. 'I mean if she's having a siesta or something. I'll hang on. The funny thing is I just happened to see her in the distance earlier on today. She is staying here, isn't she? I thought so; I asked around you know. I was sure it was her, but I was too late to catch her. Haven't seen her for an age, old Essex, thought I must look her up. Jolly nice hole this, I must say. Is it hers, d'you know?'

'It's mine actually,' said Leopold languidly. 'I'm Lewis Ogden the well-known millionaire.'

'Are you really?' said Smart, impressed. 'How d'you do? Hope you don't mind my barging in like this, only she and I are old friends don't you know and I thought I must look her up and have a chat about the old days.'

'Quite,' said Leopold. 'I'll go and call her.' He sprang to his feet with sudden vigour, rather frightening David Smart, and began to walk with springy steps towards the door of the house. Half way there he stopped and breathed in and out very slowly four times. 'It's all in the breathing,' he said. 'It's all a matter of lung control, don't you agree?'

'Rather,' said Smart keenly. 'Oh yes, breathing exercises, I know like these Indian fellows, what?'

'I'll come with you,' said Marcus, rising unsteadily to his feet and then sitting down again suddenly. 'Got to do that bloody crossword. Who's got my pen? Oh, Christ, it's leaked, it's melted, oh, my God, it's all over my shirt.'

'No one's going to notice, you're filthy already,' said Leopold helping him to his feet again.

'Nonsense I had it washed,' said Marcus, hurt. 'It's all your fault, if you'd leave that wretched girl alone we'd all get our washing done.'

'I'm coming too, I'm coming too,' said Alexander. 'Wait for me.' He got up then said to David Smart, 'Have you met Miss Brigitte Bardot by the way? I'm afraid she's asleep at the moment but I expect she'll wake up soon.'

I lay silently under my canopy, furiously hearing their three uneven footsteps retreating. I thought it unlikely that they were going to fetch my mother.

'Oh, I say, how d'you do?' said David Smart. 'What luck meeting you. Well, yes, anyway when you're awake, sort of thing, which I hope you soon will be, what?' He gave a hearty laugh, then there was dead silence. I suppose he was pondering his best move to wake the sleeping sex kitten. After a time he began to cough loudly, and then to sing, badly, snatches from Neapolitan songs. Into this noise and my own immobile rage there broke to my surprise the slightly lisping voice of Leopold, saying, 'Frightfully sorry, Essex is away for a few days staying with friends on Capri.'

'On Capri?' said Smart, surprised. 'What, since this morning? Oh, I say, what a let-down. You are sure, aren't you? Well, yes, I mean, of course you're sure – but you know I mean you didn't say anything about it before. . . .'

'Frightfully sorry, forgot,' said Leopold.

'She left awfully suddenly,' came Alexander's voice. 'At a moment's notice really. An old friend rang up.'

'It seems I'm out of luck,' said Smart. 'When's she coming back, d'you know?'

'She didn't say,' said Leopold.

'Actually I thought of making a trip to Capri myself one day,' said Smart.

'Really?' said Leopold. 'You ought to look her up. She's staying at the Morgano Tiberio with some people called Sludge.'

'Sludge?' said David Smart.

'Sludge,' said Leopold.

'Oh, I see,' said Smart. 'Well, I'll hope for better luck there, then. Give her my love will you if I don't catch up. with her? David Smart's my name. I say, mind if I sit down half a mo' before I start the downward climb?'

'Good God, it's half-past three,' said Alexander. 'Terribly sorry, old man, this is where we have to wake Brigitte for her rubber of bridge – we play every afternoon, you know. I'm afraid we shall have to ask you to leave.'

'Before you wake her?' he said. 'Bit hard, isn't it? So near and yet so far, I mean, don't you know?'

'I'm terribly sorry, but it's as much as our lives are worth,' said Alexander. 'She's here for a rest you know – she's just had a nervous breakdown and she can't bear strangers.'

'If you wait in the piazza about noon tomorrow you'll see her going past on her way to the beach,' said Leopold. 'We'll try and introduce you – can't promise anything of course but we'll do our best.'

'That's jolly nice of you, I must say,' said Smart. 'I shall look forward to that.'

'It's easier going if you go out the other way,' said Marcus. 'Then you can walk back by the road, instead of all those steps.'

'Oh, I see, O.K., thanks a lot,' said Smart. 'See you all tomorrow anyway. We might have a drink together, what?' I could imagine him looking wistfully towards the well-loaded drink table.

'We shall look forward to it,' said Leopold.

When he had gone I emerged from under my canopy and said. 'Poor man.' They were all three lying back in their chairs again.

'You're always on the side of the underdog aren't you?' said Leopold. 'It was frightful cheek coming up here like that.

'Mama might have wanted to see him,' I said. 'She may be furious.'

'What d'you mean?' said Leopold. 'She told us to send him away. She'd seen him arrive and heard everything he said. Apparently he'd once tried to sell her a car, that's all, he didn't really know her at all. Frightful cheek.'

'Oh,' I said. 'I see.'

'You'd never seen him before, had you, Vanessa?' said Alexander.

'No,' I said. 'Never.'

Later on I seem to remember there was an odd joke or two about the incident which my mother did not encourage; but I never asked her why she had lied. It might have been that she was ashamed of him and did not think he would fit into Lewis's view of her, since had she allowed them to meet she could hardly have concealed the fact that David Smart had once been a close friend; or it might have been that she saw it as a defence measure on Lewis's behalf against another potential sponger. I did not understand it, but it seemed to me to be no concern of mine.

The next day my mother and Lewis and I went on an expedition to Paestum to see the Greek temples. I remember it as a day of pure happiness. Lewis lectured us in the museum, and in the temples became emotional and could not finish a sentence of speculation as to whether or not it had been malaria which had emptied the ancient town. My mother looked at him very kindly then and I felt grateful at the thought of her being fond of him. The roses bloomed between the ruins. We picnicked by the sea where for once there were waves, blue white-topped ones in which we swam.

We returned to find a telegram from a friend of Alexander's, called John Miller, who had been supposed to be arriving that day, to say that he was unavoidably detained in Tangier. Alexander, Marcus and Leopold, having exhausted the subject of what could be detaining him, were beginning to feel bored at the thought of his not arriving. Leopold had already begun to complain that there were not enough friends about! They were all three waiting for us in the shade at the top of the steps outside the front door when we returned in our hired car.

'Has something happened?' I asked.

'No,' they said.

'Telegram from John,' said Alexander. 'Not coming.'

'A bore in a way,' said Leopold.

'Hot, isn't it?' said Alexander. 'Have a nice time?'

'Lovely,' said my mother. 'You look what one might call at a loose end, you three.'

'Did you bathe today?' asked Lewis.

'Not really, no,' said Alexander.

'You mean you just sat here all day?' said my mother.

'In a way,' said Alexander.

'What a bad host I am,' said Lewis. 'I don't provide enough entertainment.'

'That's nonsense,' said my mother. 'Anyway you offered them a wonderful trip to Paestum which they simply refused.'

'Seen it,' said Alexander, looking guilty. 'Lovely isn't it?'

'I did a lot of useful work on my crossword,' said Marcus. 'Ah, that's a good sound.' It was the distant roar of a powerful car engine changing gear. The throbbing approached.

'It's coming here,' said Leopold, excited.

Into the courtyard swept a gleaming Mercedes sports car, and stopped abruptly. The man at the wheel raised a hand in salute, picked up a roll of documents from the seat beside him, swung out of the car and bounded heavily up the steps. He was large and thick-set, with a red face and thick black hair. He was wearing a luridly coloured Palm Beach shirt.

Ignoring the rest of us, he went straight up to Lewis, slapped him on the back, and said in a strong Lancashire accent. 'Here we are. I've got your bloody drawings for you.'

'Good,' Lewis said. 'Essex, may I introduce Mr. Telford?'

He gave us a comprehensive and totally uninterested glance, said, 'Pleased to meet you,' then turned back to Lewis and said, 'I'm in a muck sweat. I'll have a wash and then I'll show you the plans. I had a bloody awful drive.'

'Yes, come along, do,' said Lewis. 'Did you bring the other estimates? This way.' They went into the house.

Marcus and Leopold immediately went down to look at the car. Alexander remained at the top of the steps looking dazed but happy.

'Terrific,' he said. 'Fantastic. Fabulous.'

'Alexander, for God's sake,' said my mother, 'pull yourself together.'

'Isn't he wonderful?' said Alexander. ' "I've got your bloody drawings. . ." I want to be like that. Why can't I be like that, Essex, with that car and everything? You know you've only got to say the word.'

'Oh, stop whining,' said my mother.

'You know you've always wanted me to make something of myself,' said Alexander.

'I can't remember having made such a flight of fancy,' said my mother. 'You must be thinking of someone else.'

'I don't believe you love me any more,' said Alexander.

'I suggest you go and sober up before dinner,' said my mother.

'Come with me,' said Alexander, 'and help me. Don't look so cross.'

'Go on,' said my mother.

When he had gone, she said. 'He's so tiresome when he's drunk. I wish to goodness Marcus and Leopold would go.'

'I thought you liked Marcus,' I said.

'I do,' said my mother, 'but not here. And the Marwoods are coming.'

'The Marwoods?' I said. 'Heavens, we'd better get them out before then.'

'I know,' said my mother. 'I think Alexander had better go as well.

'He'll be all right when they've gone,' I said.

'Lewis doesn't think much of him,' said my mother.

'Oh,' I said. 'I don't think he likes me much either.'

'You?' said my mother. 'Of course he does. He's always saying how beautifully you move. I can't think why. No one's ever said it before.'

'Move?'

'What's called an awkward grace,' said my mother.

'Actually it's rather clever of him to see it. Of course he's sentimental about youth. But he thinks Alexander's a bad example of inbreeding – which is ungenerous of him since it's exactly his breeding he likes about him.'

'Is he still such a snob?' I asked.

'It's more complicated than that,' said my mother, 'though that's what it amounts to. It's interesting really. He expects an awful lot of us, you know, I mean of you and me and one or two others. It's a little frightening.'

'Does it matter so much?' I said.

'It matters to him,' said my mother. 'I know you think I'm only after his money.'

'I never said so.'

'Of course it is nice, I know, being here, and all that,' my mother went on. 'I would like it if he bought a house and let me do it up. Of course I don't ignore all those aspects. On the other hand there is something very definite he wants from us and which we can give him. I mean that he knows so little about people and we can teach him and introduce him to people and make interesting friends for him, the sort of people he really deserves.'

'Do we know them?' I asked.

'You are a little damping,' said my mother. 'Don't we?'

'People Lewis deserves?' I said. 'I don't know.'

'We can supply him with something he needs,' said my mother.

'Does he need Alexander and Marcus and Leopold?' I said. 'Does he need us? He's got Telford.'

I don't know why I spoke with such sudden bitterness; or what emotion exactly it was which filled me. I felt tired and hopeless.

My mother said, 'Don't you like him then?'

I said, 'Oh yes.'

It came out very calmly. Even so I looked at her nervously in case I had given away everything.

'Well, then, it is very simple,' she said. 'We have something to offer him. The best of human relationships are based on fair exchange.'

'I don't believe they are,' I said, 'and I don't believe it's so simple. Or that you are.'

'What d'you mean?'

'Well, isn't he in love with you?' I said.

'Oh, in a sort of fairy-story way I suppose he is,' she said.

'And Jean?' I asked.

'What about Jean? I shall do nothing to offend your precious Jean. Isn't it you who sees things in too simple terms?'

'Perhaps I do,' I said. 'I don't know. I don't know anything about this situation. Is it a situation? What situation is it?'

'It is a situation,' said my mother. 'Not an uninteresting one. But don't let it worry you.'

We stood for a moment in silence in the shadow of the doorway, looking down into the bright courtyard where Leopold and Marcus still peered and marvelled at the dangerous car. I was filled with anxiety.

My mother said, 'I shall have a bath. Why don't you bring your blue dress along afterwards and we can see what we can do with it?'

So later I went to her room with a dress I had had made and which did not fit. My mother had a dressmaker who was cheap because although she sewed well she was ignorant of style: she made beautiful clothes for my mother because the latter with great trouble and firmness instructed her exactly. I was too vague and lazy to achieve the same success. My mother's room was cool and white. We looked at her clothes and decided what new ones we each needed. I put on my blue dress and she began to improve it.

The developments of the next few days delighted Leopold: the place was suddenly overflowing with people.

Some American friends of my mother's arrived first, but they only stayed one night because they were flying back to New York the next day. They were followed by the Newcomes, and later by the Marwoods and Kate Flower.

After the Newcomes arrived we saw less and less of Lewis, who did not always appear even at meals. I think this was not because he disliked the Newcomes but because he felt that there were now enough guests to entertain each other, and he had work to do with Telford. In fact he seemed to like the Newcomes well enough: they were both intelligent sympathetic people who could talk about anything. Kitty Newcome flirted with him which seemed to amuse him. My mother said to me hopefully. 'It seemed such a good opportunity for Lewis to get to know Mike. I want him to give him a job later on. He hardly earns anything at the moment and Kitty does like money.'

As soon as they arrived Leopold began to pay Kitty the most elaborate attentions. He said she was such a lovely blowsy old thing and so funny – the description would have displeased her because she had been peachily beautiful until recently and was still convinced of her fatal charm; but she pronounced Leopold a darling and gossipped with him endlessly. She and Mike both drank almost as much as Alexander and Marcus and became noisy with them, but funny, because they were both unusually good at talking. Mike was healthy and handsome and devoted to Kitty, who chose rather than he did the pace of their life. I liked him, probably because he seemed to like me.

The Newcomes changed the tone of things. I became more of a spectator than before. They were at least twelve years older than me and had shared with my mother a past of which I was ignorant; also I did not feel myself up to them conversationally. Another alienating factor was the presence of Tim Anderson, whom Alexander had discovered staying not far away, and who now seemed to have most of his meals with us. I thought him odious. He had been working in Rome as a film extra, which for some reason had necessitated his dying his hair an odd shade of red, and he was on his way to Sicily to join some young man whose tutor he was supposed to be. He had a big heavy face and spoke in an offensive drawl. He went out of his way to be as rude as possible to everyone, evidently as a matter of principle and pride, for he would often recount at length the stories of old insults, and always repeated the rudeness of the moment several times in case anyone had missed it. He seemed to have a reputation, for Leopold and Alexander, at least, laughed at everything he said, and I therefore concealed my dislike for fear they might think me stuffy.

Then the Marwoods arrived, bringing Kate Flower. Leopold and Marcus had to leave because there was no longer room for them but we had one lunch all together before they left – the Marwoods, the Newcomes, Kate, Tim Anderson and an elderly Italian Count he for some reason had in tow that day – fourteen of us in all. I made a fool of myself by having a quarrel with Tim Anderson.

I suppose I was first of all annoyed because when we went to lunch we found that another table had been brought in and laid for five, because there was not room for all of us at the marble one we usually used. My mother suggested that I should sit there and settled Kate, Alexander, Leopold and Tim there too. Lewis looked over from the big table and said, 'Ah, I see the young things have a table of their own,' putting on a benign paternal look which annoyed me.

Tim began a futile pantomime about being a baby and having to wear a feeder, at which Alexander sniggered, with what seemed to me a deplorable lack of discrimination. So that I began the meal in a bad temper.

It was the first time that day that I had seen Lewis, who had appeared only just before lunch with Telford, and had looked, I thought, slightly taken aback for a moment at the number of people drinking on the terrace. I wanted to sit at his table so as to hear him talk and know in what mood he was. Sometimes he was preoccupied and brusque with everyone except my mother, sometimes he talked in an artificial although controlled manner which was 'making conversation'. He had not lately talked as he had when my mother and Alexander and I had been alone with him. I liked him best when he was lecturing us, looking keen and didactic, but the quantity and extreme talkativeness of the company were now hardly conducive to monologues, except the sort which Marcus made lateish in the day and to which nobody listened.

Marcus was now talking to Telford. He and Alexander had both apparently decided to develop an admiration for

Telford because of his forcefulness and efficiency and the way he swore all the time. It was fortunate that they had because it prevented Tim Anderson from trying to insult him. Leopold disliked him wildly, but everybody else simply ignored him: with so many people there, it was quite easy to do, and on the whole he tended to appear only for meals, eat hurriedly and often leave before everyone else had finished. I noticed that he seemed to drink quite as much as any of them, especially at lunch time, but it appeared to have no effect on him whatsoever. Kitty had tried to talk to him but got no response: Lewis told my mother that he disliked women although it was believed that he had a wife somewhere. I could hear his voice now telling Marcus something about motor racing. 'Bloody car blew up right in front of me – buggers had mucked up the brakes. . . .'

I daresay Lucy Marwood was horrified. It was not at all what she was used to. They were on their way to join a yacht cruising round the Greek Islands, and were to spend two nights with Lewis before leaving for Brindisi.

'I thought Lewis was overdoing it a bit when he asked them,' my mother said. 'I know they asked him to their dance and so on but they really are a couple of old bores.'

Their daughter was already on the yacht and had asked Kate Flower too, which was why she was now travelling with the Marwoods. Kate had changed within the last few months, and was no longer the lively little bouncing debutante she had been. She had become rather arty and wore her hair very long and her skirts very short. A friend of hers was making a film and she was going to be in it. It was all going to be shot in the Kings Road and was highly symbolical: she was sure it would start her on a fabulous film career. It may of course have been a very good idea and her friend a serious man; only because it was Kate I suspected the whole thing of being bogus, which was ungenerous of me and made me more irritable than ever. She held forth about it all at some length and the three men seemed enchanted. I sat in silence listening for Lewis's voice.

He was sitting between Kitty and Lady Marwood, and I noticed that he seemed to be talking exclusively to Kitty, so perhaps he too had decided that Lady Marwood was a bore. He was talking about some book: they seemed to be arguing; he looked alert and responsive, almost as he did when he was talking to my mother. Lady Marwood was talking to the old Italian about deer-stalking. Lord Marwood did not seem to be talking at all, but Mike Newcome and my mother and Marcus, whom they had distracted from Telford, were building up some fantasy which sounded funny but which I could not properly hear. Altogether their table looked much more amusing than ours.

Tim Anderson finally turned to me and said, 'And what do you think, sitting there so silently, you little sphinx, you?'

'What about?' I said.

'Not listening, eh?' he said. 'Longing to be with the grown-ups, aren't you? I know that feeling.'

'No I was just sleepy,' I said, meaning to smile politely.

'I'm sorry our conversation is such a soporific,' he said.

'Vanessa's always half asleep,' said Leopold helpfully. 'It's part of her charm.'

'Lovely sleepy charm like a cat,' said Tim Anderson and began to stroke my arm.

I ate some salad quickly and said, 'Well, of course you know all about films, don't you? I mean, having just been in one.'

'The Tony Curtis of tomorrow,' he said with a self-satisfied smile. 'Don't you think I'm like him?'

'Well I suppose so,' I said. 'In a way.'

'In what way?' He asked as if the question were of great significance. He took hold of my hand and squeezed it fattily.

'Sex appeal, of course,' said Leopold.

Tim Anderson squeezed my hand again and said, 'D'you really think I've got sex appeal, mm?' He looked round the table to see if Kate and Alexander were watching – which they were not. 'Kate,' he said, 'Vanessa thinks I have tremendous sex appeal.'

'I don't,' I said, trying to remove my hand from his grasp.

'Now don't be coy,' he said, moving his hand on to my arm. 'Of course you do.'

I suddenly said very loudly, 'For Heaven's sake leave me alone.'

Everyone had heard. I stared furiously at my plate in a sudden silence. I heard Kitty's deep voice saying, 'Scuffling among the young ones,' and then conversation seemed to start again.

Tim said, 'What a little wild cat.'

I said nothing.

Leopold started to speak but Tim interrupted to say, 'You were asking for it, you know. Don't pretend that isn't just what you're after, my dear.'

I got up and left the room. Everyone watched me go. When I got to my bedroom I slammed the door. I suppose they all heard that too. I was trembling with rage. I banged my hand furiously on the edge of the chest of drawers for some moments, hurting it; then I found myself able to cry, so I lay on my bed and sobbed noisily. After that I began to feel a fool, and cried because I had been so childish and Lewis must have thought me silly.

I lay there for sometime and was almost asleep when Alexander came in.

He said, 'Come and have some coffee.'

'I don't want any, thank you,' I said.

'You oughtn't to let Tim annoy you,' he said. 'He's only rather an ass.'

'How can you like him?' I said.

'He's a nice man really,' he said. 'Women often don't like him – he is silly with them sometimes; but he's a simple good-hearted sort of person basically, hopelessly inefficient about life.'

'Oh, Alexander. . .'

'Really. I've known him for ages. Anyway, he's going soon. And so are Leopold and Marcus. You'll come and say good-bye to them, won't you?'

'Not if he's there.'

'I'll try and make him go before they do,' he said.

'You could come and tell me when he's gone,' I suggested.

'O.K.,' he said, and went away.

I lay there a little longer, feeling grateful to Alexander; then the door opened very quietly and Kitty Newcome's big white face with its pretty mop of golden curls peered in at me.

'My dear,' she said hurrying in as soon as I looked up. 'I had to come. I do so understand.'

I could see at once that she was fairly drunk. She sat down at the end of my bed and blinked her huge blue eyes at me.

'It's rotten, isn't it?' she said, looking enormously sympathetic. 'Isn't it all rotten?'

I sat up and said firmly, 'I was rather silly, I'm afraid. But it's all right now.'

'But I do so know,' she said. 'I do, I do. I've been through it all. Of course you're terribly attractive. I expect there's someone you're frightfully in love with, too, isn't there?'

Embarrassed I said, 'Well, I suppose so.'

'I know it sounds like one's grandmother,' she said. 'But do be careful, darling. Don't throw it all away. I was so in love, but so in love, with my first husband, but I had no idea – I mean it was quite meaningless our marriage, I was so unfaithful. And now of course Mike and I are frightfully happy – we quarrel a bit but that's only because I'm often so disagreeable, really hellish to live with, and he's very sweet and calm really, and we laugh at all the same things and all that and of course I'm proud of him because he's so good-looking, don't you think? He thinks you're wonderful incidentally. And there we are, and your mother was only just saying to me that she thought we were the happiest couple she knew, but the thing is, poor darling, he's impotent.'

'Oh, God,' I said.

'We've tried everything, absolutely everything, but it's no good. It's one of those psychological things – it's all to do with his mother. She's been so awful, too. She can't bear me and she was terribly against our marriage and now she's convinced that it's me who can't have children because of having led an immoral life. And I keep saying to Mike, "But tell her. Tell her it's you. Tell her you're impotent, and that it's her fault." But of course he won't.

He keeps saying to me to go on and go to bed with someone else and I say I won't, I'm too much in love with him and so on and anyway I've had sex, I mean honestly I probably have had more than my share, by and large. Not that I mean to say we don't have any sex at *all* in our marriage. . .'

'Oh,' I said.

'No,' she said. 'I mean there are *some* things one can do. But God knows I mean we've been married two years now and he keeps telling me to go on and do it. Anyway what I meant to say to you, darling,' stretching out one pretty white hand towards me, 'is that I do understand – I mean about all the problems. My trouble really was that I was too easy-going. It's no good, you've got to be tough with them, really tough, don't let them have it all their own way, especially someone like Tim Anderson. Of course he is attractive, but one's got to admit he isn't frightfully suitable. Of course in a way I suppose Essex is a tiny bit naughty bringing you here at all just this very moment. I suppose Alexander is supposed to provide the alibi. Heaven knows he is the most accommodating young man I've ever heard of. Still, really I think she might have waited until the divorce is through.'

'Divorce?'

'Of course it's so easy to give opinions about how other people should bring up their children and everyone does say how well Essex manages with you. Well, I mean, you do get on wonderfully, don't you? Which is everything. I never felt that I could possibly tell my mother a thing. I would have waited for the divorce myself all the same.'

'What divorce?'

'His, of course.'

'Alexander's?'

'Lewis's, darling.'

'Oh, yes, I see.'

'Still, I know what it is,' she went on. 'When one wants someone one wants someone. In fact if that's what it is I'm glad to see it happening at last for Essex. I never really thought she was in love with any of the others. Of course he's madly in love with her. I'm terribly happy for you all.'

'I don't know that it's all quite as fixed as you seem to think,' I said.

'Isn't it though?'

'I don't think so.'

'Don't think I mean to pump you,' she said. 'Essex will tell me all about it when she wants to, and I don't want to hear before then.'

'Did she tell you Lewis was divorcing his wife?' I asked.

'Not in so many words, no,' said Kitty. 'I think it was Betty Carr who said something about it when I saw her last in London. D'you mean he's not going to then? Oh, my dear, I am sorry. Is he a Catholic or something?'

'No,' I said. 'Perhaps he doesn't want to.'

'Doesn't want to?' she said. 'Oh no. Essex has never made a fool of herself over a man yet. She won't start now. Or will she?'

'Why don't you ask her about it?' I said. 'I'm sure she's much more likely to tell you than me.'

'I suppose she is. How funny it must be to have a daughter. Anyway you're very lucky to have such a wonderful mother – she adores you too.'

That embarrassed me. I had never considered the question of my mother's feelings for me.

'But really,' Kitty assured me. 'Everyone knows what a lot you mean to her. So there you are – you've got so much, my dear, and those heavenly legs too. D'you know, we must see a lot of you when we're back in London. I'm always in need of girls for one thing. Everyone I know is married or something. Will you come and have dinner with us often?'

'I'd love to,' I said.

'Well, I'll leave you,' she said. 'But I didn't want you to feel neglected or that no one was interested.'

'It was very kind of you.'

'See you later,' said Kitty, 'd'you know I think I'm going to go and lie down for a bit too.'

She went out leaving me with food for thought.

I decided that there might well be nothing in what she had said about Lewis getting a divorce. It was quite probable that she and Betty Carr had decided between them that it must be the case, and it was even possible in spite of her disavowal that her intention had been to pump me; but I found it sufficiently disquieting that it could be an assumption which people were obviously making. I decided to tell my mother: then it occurred to me that Betty Carr and Kitty had doubtless already asked her what her intentions were with Lewis – why had she not given them an unequivocal answer? I began to worry, and lost myself in a maze of uneasy speculation. Incidentally I wondered whether Mike were really impotent or whether Kitty might have made that up in case I might be falling for Mike, who it seemed was prepared to make a pass at me – and why should it all be his mother's fault? And what had been the real reason for Kitty's coming to see me? Once I had started there was no end to my doubt, and then at the back of my mind I was bothered by the pale figure of Jean.

I had changed into a clean cotton dress and was combing my hair when there was another tap on the door. I thought it was Alexander and said, 'Come in.'

It was Lewis.

It seemed ridiculous.

'I've had so many visitors,' I said.

'I didn't realize that,' he said, surprised. 'What a lot goes on in this house. I'm glad to see you're all right. I was worried about you.'

'I'm sorry.'

'No, no,' he came in, speaking gently. 'I'm rather an absent host. You know I don't know who half the people are who come here. Perhaps I ought to be more careful about that – young Alexander's friends and so on. It's a great responsibility having you and your mother staying here. I believe I haven't been taking it seriously enough.'

I said nothing for a moment partly because I was surprised and partly because the first thing which came to my mind was some sort of explanation about 'young Alexander's friends' being no revelation either to my mother or to me, and this I thought I had better suppress.

Then I said, 'I've never enjoyed staying anywhere so much. I liked the expeditions we did most, but I like seeing a lot of people too. I just get cross sometimes.'

'Yes, of course,' he said. 'We all do that. Tell me, d'you ever see your father?'

'My father?' I said. 'No. He lives in Rhodesia.'

'Yes, I see,' he said. 'I wondered. It seems a waste for him to be missing knowing you.'

'Why have you been thinking about him?'

'I have been thinking how nice it would be to have a daughter,' he said. 'I have been seeing you and your mother and your remarkable relationship, and thinking how well you both manage it and how intelligent you both are, and so I have been wondering whether I myself should manage so well in a similar situation – if I had a child, I mean. There.'

'I see.'

'I'm sorry you're going soon,' he said. 'I've enjoyed your visit. What are you going to do when you go back to London?'

'I shall have to get a job, I suppose,' I said. 'I don't know what – a secretary or something.'

'Can I help you to find one?'

'No, I'm too bad, I really am,' I said. 'Wait till I get a little more efficient.'

'Will you ask me then?'

'Yes,' I said. 'Are you going to divorce your wife?'

He hardly paused before he said, 'I don't know. Why do you ask?'

'Someone told me you were,' I said. 'Someone – not important.'

'Listen,' he said. 'I haven't discussed the possibility with anyone at all, even myself, least of all myself.'

'Not with my mother?'

'Certainly not with your mother.'

'I'm sorry I asked you,' I said. 'It worried me when I heard it, I can't explain why. I'll forget about it now.'

'I thought of going down for a swim,' he said. 'Everyone else seems to be asleep. Why don't you come?'

I said, 'All right,' and turned to take my bathing suit off the window ledge where it was drying.

He said rather vaguely, 'Don't worry. Don't worry,' as he held the door open for me.

As we went down to the beach he was silent, but I was

thinking that everything was all right because it was not true about the divorce and he liked my mother and me, both of us, quote ordinarily, and here I was going to swim with him, one of his quick, purposeful bathes, not the sort of lounging about in the sea and sun which I usually did; and we should walk back to the villa together, talking, and everyone would see. Even if they said, 'How nice of Lewis to be kind to poor Vanessa,' I should not care because I should feel that they were wrong and we should be walking side by side.

Lewis said, 'You're happy now,' looking surprised.

'Of course,' I said.

10

Soon after our return to London my mother said to me, 'Lewis is getting divorced.'

'What?' I said.

'Darling, don't look so horrified. I know you've always thought that I had something against Jean but I assure you that the first I heard about it was last night. He said they've been thinking about it for some time and have finally both decided it's the best thing – so it's not at all a question of him being nasty to her.'

'He'd never said anything about it to you before?' I asked.

'Never,' she said. 'He had talked about Jean a little and about their difficulties – that he'd married her without knowing her properly, that they'd both expected something else of the other and so on – but nothing more.'

'I see.'

'May I say, if you won't bite my head off,' she went on, 'that I do honestly think it's good thing for him? I can't help finding her completely dreary, and Lewis is an exciting person whatever you may have against him – not that you do have things against him now do you? – and he deserves someone a little better than that.'

'I suppose so,' I said.

I had started work in a secretarial agency in Knightsbridge. It was run by a very efficient Pole called Madame Sobiska: for the first three weeks I had to go and work in her office so that she could check on my secretarial prowess, then I was allowed to be sent out on simple undemanding jobs. She liked an atmosphere of bustle and achievement round her, and to be treated herself as if she were a tycoon. She wore a neat black tailored coat and skirt and a white blouse; her hair was beautifully done and blueish; she always had a bunch of expensive flowers on her desk and wore a good deal of scent, to bring in I suppose a note of femininity. She had a husband somewhere in the background and they lived in Hampstead. She talked a good deal about expanding the business and cornering the market and staff problems and my girls. I think she saw herself as a sort of American-type superwoman: perhaps she was.

I soon fell into the routine, learnt to take telephone messages in a hushed responsible voice, and pad quickly about the office with an air of urgency and respect. This pleased her and made up to some extent for the fact that I found it difficult to be there on time in the mornings.

It was dull working in the office, but more interesting when I was sent out to different people. On the whole it tended to mean taking someone's place when they were away for a fortnight's holiday: this could be boring but was never long enough to become desperate. There were also bed-ridden old rich women dealing with their week's correspondence, travelling businessmen or Americans, occasional authors, script-writers or television stars, and once a large American lady who was something to do with a ballet company and gave me a gigantic tip. It was sometimes quite amusing, and well-paid considering my lack of experience. I found it all rather tiring and often had to ring up from my bed to say in a brisk voice, 'Mme. Sobiska's Bureau here. I'm afraid our Miss Cowper may be a few minutes late this morning. She was detained at the office.' The clients never seemed to mind.

I had not seen Colin since my return from Italy, which made it easier for me not to think about the Ogden divorce. I did not want to think about it. I was afraid that my mother might, consciously or unconsciously, have played more part in it than she was prepared to admit: I was also afraid that Lewis might be being unfair to Jean, and though my peculiar passion for him seemed, to my relief, to be fading now that I saw so much less of him, I still wanted to be able to like him.

It began to be autumn and the leaves fell and the evenings brought a little mist. It was the time of the year at which I most liked London. On the strength of the fact that I was now earning some money, my mother and I went and bought some expensive clothes. I found that, being no longer quite so unreasonably young, I could dress better: I decided to try to be beautiful, and also to be tidier. I turned out all the drawers and cupboards in my bedroom, re-arranged the room entirely and resolved to go to more concerts. I joined the Chelsea Public Library and made an enormous list of philosophical books which I wanted to read.

Our extravagance over the clothes made it necessary for my mother to ask Alexander for his rent, which he had not paid for several months. This led to the usual hurt coolness on his side and we saw little of him for the next few weeks. At the beginning of October he went to stay with his parents in Scotland: they gave him some money on condition he found a job by Christmas.

'Seriously, would you mind if I asked Lewis?' he said to my mother. 'I know him well enough to ask him myself now. I know he's not keen on me, but I only want something quite menial and I shan't mind if he turns me down.'

My mother said nothing for some moments. Alexander had paid the rent a day or two earlier; and today for the first time we were given to understand that he was prepared to overlook our error of taste in having asked for it. He had appeared just after I got back from work, carrying some bottles of gin and whisky and shouting for us. 'I'm going to take you out to dinner. We're going to have the best meal we've had in our lives.'

I was in the bath, but I got out and came down in my dressing-gown. My mother was supposed to be going to a cocktail party. 'Now I shan't,' she said. 'How lovely. Where are we going to eat?'

The taxi she had ordered arrived, and Alexander sent it away, over-tipping the driver. He came back to pour out drinks and we began to make plans. I was afraid that when he started to talk seriously about jobs the evening might be spoilt, but after a pause my mother said, 'I think perhaps it might be better coming from me.'

Alexander said nothing.

'I'm lunching with him on Wednesday,' she said.

Alexander said, 'If you're sure. . . ?' and she nodded.

After that they both seemed lighter of heart, as if the decision had been a relief. They insisted that I put on one of the smarter of my new dresses, and we went out to dinner.

By the end of the meal I was feeling tired because I was still not used to working all day; so that when Alexander said that he wanted to go to a night club I said, 'You two go. I should fall asleep.'

'Nonsense,' Alexander said. 'Of course you must come.'

'No, really, I've eaten too much,' I said. 'You go.'

'I'm too old for night clubs,' said my mother.

'I know Essex wants to come,' said Alexander. 'But can't we persuade you, Vanessa?'

I insisted that I was tired and my mother finally agreed that I had been looking pale lately. They dropped me at the house and went on. I found an envelope pushed through the door on which had been scrawled, *Where are you? Come and see me at Tom Jones, Records, Pimlico Road. Colin.*

I wrote him a postcard at once saying, *Will come on Saturday morning,* and posted it before I went to bed.

Tom Jones, Records, was a very small shop near the top of Ebury Street. In front of it was a stand full of shabby old books: there were more of them in the window, with a few bright long playing record jackets scattered among them in a haphazard way. It was almost impossible to see the inside because it seemed to be full of people.

I went in cautiously and found that there were in fact only three men and a girl in there, all looking through the piles of second-hand records which were stacked about on various pieces of tumbledown furniture. It was only the unusual smallness of the room which made it so crowded. There was no sign of Colin. I walked towards the back of the shop and found a door which led into a dusty little room containing a desk and a typewriter, two cats and several hundreds more old gramophone records. There

was no one there. I opened the only other door I could
see and found a bathroom. In it was Colin, wearing a
smart dark suit and shaving with an electric razor.

'Oh, there you are,' he said. 'Have you had breakfast?'

'Yes,' I said. 'It's eleven o'clock.'

'We can have some coffee, though,' he said.

He came back into the little office, shut the door into
the shop, which I had left open, and bent down to light
a gas ring which was concealed by the desk. He put a
kettle on to it, then opened a large cupboard in the wall
and took out two cups, a tin of Nescafé, a half-pint bottle
of milk and a packet of sugar. There was nothing else in
the cupboard.

'What does this remind you of?' he said, spooning the
Nescafé into the cups. 'The old days at the Acme School
of B.T., with poor old Heywood burning the milk in his
wretched office? Do you wonder he did himself in, or
tried to?'

'Why don't you put some of the books in the cupboard?'
I asked.

'We'd never be able to find them,' he said.

There was a knock on the door.

'Oh, God, some half-wit wants to buy something,' said
Colin. He opened the door and said, 'Terribly sorry, the
machine's broken.'

The young man in jeans said, 'Machine? What
machine?'

'The record-playing machine,' said Colin. 'So you can't
try any of the records, I'm afraid. It'll be back on Monday
though.'

'Oh,' said the young man. 'I just wanted to see Tom
Jones.'

'He won't be back till this evening,' said Colin. 'After
five.'

'Tell him Alan came,' said the young man, 'and I'm free
for Tuesday but I can't get the car. I'll come round this
evening if I can.'

'Who's Tom Jones?' I asked when he had gone.

'My landlord,' said Colin. 'I live upstairs. I help down
here now and then – more now than then you could say
at the moment. I just finished a job, you see, on a film.

Silly bastards decided not to make it after all – at least it wasn't really their fault, they couldn't get the money – took them three months to find it out, though, during which time I got £20 a week for doing nothing.'

'Does he ever sell anything?' I asked.

'Yes,' said Colin. 'It's easier when they can listen to the records.'

'There seems to be an awful lot of them,' I said. 'Records, I mean.'

'They come in all the time you see,' said Colin. 'He always takes them, that's the trouble. He can't bear not to because they always need the money so badly.'

'Has he got a lot of money then?' I asked.

'No,' said Colin. 'He's a stupid sucker, that's all. Have some more of his lovely Nescafé.'

'Did that young man want to sell him records, then?' I asked, holding out my cup.

'Shouldn't think so,' said Colin. 'Probably to do with anti-H. bomb meetings. They go about in this rackety old car saying down with the bomb and save the children and everything through a loudspeaker which is always going wrong. Nobody listens.'

'D'you go?' I asked.

'Sometimes,' said Colin, looking slightly guilty. 'Anything to annoy the Government.'

Feeling that I had to get it over, I said, 'Colin, what about Jean?'

'Jean?' he said. 'Oh, Jean's fine. They're getting divorced, you know.

'I know,' I said.

'You would,' he said. 'Well, there it is.'

'But is she all right?' I asked.

'Of course she's all right,' he said irritably. 'Like I said, she's fine. The whole thing was her idea.'

'The divorce?' I said. 'It was her idea? But that's all right then.'

'I said it's all right, didn't I?' he suddenly shouted. 'What's happened to you since I saw you? Brain gone soft or something? I just said it's all right.'

'Sorry,' I said.

He began to pull the drawers of the desk in and out

with some violence. 'Why isn't there anything to write with?' he said.

'I've got a pen,' I said.

'I'd better leave a note,' he said, taking it. Then he said. 'No, I'll be here at five, I'll see him,' and gave it back to me.

'How's Avril?' I said, changing the subject.

'She's all right,' he said. 'Poor old Av. Haven't seen her much lately.'

There was a silence. He looked depressed. Fortunately there was another knock on the door, this time from a girl with a pony tail who wanted to buy two records.

The sale seemed to put Colin in a better humour.

'You look lovely,' he said when she had gone. 'I forgot to say before. More . . . whatever the word is.'

'Old?' I said.

'Old,' he said, and laughed. 'Let's shut the shop and go for a walk or something. I'll take you to see Jean one day, don't worry – not yet though.'

After that I saw Colin regularly again. He seemed to be making no effort to get another job. There were still occasional hints about the big things he could do if he wanted to, but they were fewer than they used to be. It seemed that Tom Jones was having an influence on him, but I could not make out quite in what direction, and I did not meet Tom Jones until much later. Colin referred to him a certain amount in conversation, mostly in passing, as having been with him on this or that occasion, but sometimes more directly and usually with a slight note of irritation, as being a fool, for all his supposed intelligence, or as putting up with too much from casual acquaintances or from life. I think at that time Colin himself had not made up his mind what to think of him, and was not prepared to discuss him with me until he had, since with me, even more than with most people, he was always afraid of making a fool of himself.

So we did not talk about Tom Jones, or about Jean, or about Avril; but otherwise were as good friends as we had ever been, which pleased me. I had been afraid that

Colin might like me less after we left the common ground of the typing school.

Alexander began to work in a minor capacity at the head office of Ogden Enterprises three weeks after my mother had agreed to speak to Lewis about it. He seemed to be being paid a good salary but I could not make out exactly what it was that he did: he seemed to be genuinely puzzled on this score himself. Whatever it was it was apparently too hard work. He complained endlessly, about the hours, the tea, the tube journey, the insolent office boys who quibbled about stamps for private letters, the sexy scornful typists, the noise. I did not expect him to stand it for long. I saw him setting off each morning, his face a transparent greenish-white, his eyes glazed, his suit impeccable; and each evening expected to hear him say he would never go through it again. The very fact of having at last given in and begun to work for his living seemed to have strengthened him in a resolve not to give up any of his old pleasures. He went to bed as late, and often as drunk, as ever; once or twice in fact he did not seem to sleep at all but slunk in about eight in the morning after gambling all night, changed into his City suit and crept neat and spectral on to the nine o'clock tube train.

'And Lewis?' I asked. 'Now that you see him in action, in his own empire, what is he like?'

'I never see him,' he said. 'Oh, once, coming out of the loo. I was going to be sick so I couldn't wait.'

'Sick?' I said.

'I sometimes am,' he said. 'He doesn't go through my department much. It doesn't seem to be on the way anywhere.'

My mother and Alexander seemed to be on particularly good terms about this time, which I was relieved to notice because I had thought in Italy that she might be beginning to be bored by him. Lewis, on the other hand, seemed to be less in her life than recently. I thought this might be because she was being tactful about his divorce. There was a newspaper story about it one day, laying emphasis on Jean's humble origins and the fact that they had married in the early days of his success, pointing to the conclusion that he had dropped her on the way up. I did not think it particularly offensive; but when I read it I slightly regretted that I had arranged to go to the cinema with Colin that evening.

He came round to collect me from the mews, a thing he rarely did but had announced his intention of doing this evening because it was on his way to the cinema. Neither my mother nor Alexander was in.

To my relief he did not seem much disturbed by Jean's publicity, and said it could have been worse. I offered him a drink, thinking that if Alexander were to arrive back from his office this might be a good moment to introduce them, which I had not yet done.

Alexander did arrive, but with Lewis.

Aware of my own complete ineptitude I said in a bright nervous voice, 'Oh, Alexander, this is Colin Davis. And you know each other, of course.'

I could not look at Lewis, but knew that he was standing very still. Only later did I learn that he had been afraid to see my mother for the last few weeks because he was not sure into what new relation the definitely established fact of his divorce would put them. He had waited in his car outside his own office to see Alexander leave in order to be able casually to offer him a lift home: he had been afraid that if he telephoned my mother she might find an excuse not to see him, because it seemed to him that it must now be obvious to her that he meant eventually to ask her to marry him.

All this was completely outside my knowledge. I had no idea why he was there.

Alexander offered Lewis a drink and began to talk in an easy and effortless way about the economics of record-producing companies. While admiring this performance, I was completely unable to contribute anything to it, and Lewis and Colin would only answer monosyllabically when he directly addressed either of them.

After what I suppose was only a few minutes of Alexander's gallant monologue, I managed to say, 'We were just going to the cinema. Perhaps we ought to go,' and stood up.

'Yes, perhaps we ought,' said Colin.

I moved towards the door. 'Well – we'll probably see

you later.' As he followed me, something – perhaps the proximity of Lewis as he passed him – must have made Colin change his mind. I am sure he had meant to follow me quietly, but then he stopped and said, 'Spitting in my sister's face in public seems to suit you. You look well on it.'

A little silence.

'I wouldn't have put it quite like that,' said Lewis stiffly.

'Oh no?' said Colin. 'I haven't your advantages of education of course. How would you have put it?'

'Colin. . .' I said.

'I know, I know, I know,' he turned on me. 'It's awfully bad form, absolutely not done. But it's done by me. I'm not one of you. I'm not a tight-laced lump of etiquette like all your smooth boy friends. Nor is he. You can fool them, can't you?' He turned back to Lewis. 'You can make them think you're so charming, so interesting, so prepared to pay quietly for their lovely company. Just let them wait. I've seen some other things. I can remember you yelling at my wretched mother the time she said you'd get to think Jean wasn't good enough for you, the time you said we were all too bloody humble, the time you said you'd make Jean so that everybody knew she was good enough for any of them. She wouldn't play your filthy game, that's all. You couldn't do it. You couldn't turn her into what you wanted her to be, a scheming, cheating, dishonest lie of a woman. Now you think you'll get one that knows the game better, don't you, one that's been born to it?'

'You'd better go,' said Lewis. 'You're making a fool of yourself.'

'Oh, don't let's talk about who's being made a fool of,' said Colin.

'Please come,' I said, seizing his arm. He was trembling.

'You don't realize, you don't know,' he said to me. 'You don't know what you're in for with this man. You aren't a match for him, any of you, you don't know what toughness is, not his kind you don't. He'll break you all, he'll break every one of you, like he broke my sister.'

'I don't remember you as being quite so melodramatic,'

said Lewis. 'But then I understand you've been in the film business recently.'

'You offered me a job once d'you remember?' said Colin. 'You wanted to draw me in too, didn't you, and make a schemer of me too? Don't like to remember that now I daresay, now that you think you've thrown off Jean and her family as if they never existed.'

Lewis said in his strained voice, 'You are completely ignorant of the reasons for the end of my marriage. Your behaviour is interfering and hysterical. I think you ought to see a doctor.'

Desperate to get Colin out of the room, I had half dragged him to the door. 'All right, all right, I'm coming,' he said shaking off my hand. 'I don't want to stay – why should I? It makes me sick to be in the same room with that sort of stuff.'

At last he came with me.

Outside the house he said. 'You'd better go back.'

I said, 'If you hadn't lied to me and told me that Jean was all right and that the divorce had been her idea, I would never have run the risk of that stupid scene.'

'I ought to have known he'd be here,' he said.

'Does Jean feel as you do?' I said.

'I don't know.'

'Is she unhappy?'

He turned his face towards me in the light from the doorway and said, 'She's ruined.'

I did not know what he meant but the word sounded full of horror.

He began to walk away from me down the Mews.

Suddenly furious I shouted, pointlessly, 'What charming manners your friend Tom Jones seems to teach you.'

His yelled 'Shut up!' came howling back to me down the mews.

I went up to my bedroom. A few minutes later I heard Lewis leave the house and get into his car, which drove off. I realized that his chauffeur must have heard everything Colin and I had said.

I stayed in my room, because I did not want to talk to Alexander about Colin, whom I knew to have appeared in the worst possible light. I was hurt that Colin should have done it, miserable at the thought of Lewis's rage, with Colin, with me, even perhaps with Jean, and alarmed to think how little I knew him. I was too angry with Colin to be afraid that he might have had some right on his side, but simply the reference to those episodes I had never heard of, that former life which I found so hard to imagine, frightened me.

Before long I heard my mother come in. I imagined Alexander telling her what had happened. It seemed a long time before she came up the stairs and into my room.

'I hear there's been a scene,' she said. She was looking tired.

'It was ghastly,' I said.

'Was Lewis upset?'

'I think so, yes,' I said. 'Of course I had no idea he'd be here.'

'No,' she said. 'I don't know why he came.'

'He didn't lose his temper,' I said. 'I mean he was – controlled.'

An odd look crossed my mother's face; perhaps it was admiration. It looked like pleasure.

'I don't want you ever to ask that young man here again,' she said.

It did not strike me as an unreasonable request.

'All right,' I said. 'Of course, I shall see him again.'

'That's different,' she said. 'He must never come here.' Then she added: 'Of course the lower classes are very emotional.'

Long afterwards on the hill above his house in the country, Lewis talked to me about that evening, among others. He told me that after leaving the mews he stopped the car near Hyde Park, got out and told the chauffeur to drive home. He walked into the Park, which was still open although it was already dark, and passing the furtive or abandoned couples on the benches or the grass he walked quickly away from the road, then turned left towards Kensington Gardens, along the Serpentine, which was covered by a light mist lying low on the water. He walked until he was no longer angry.

When he had decided that his marriage to Jean was finished and she had agreed to divorce, he had taken into account the fact that the actual process of the separation and the settlement would be attended by various annoyances. He was prepared to put up with Colin's outburst as one of these, and treating his anger as a purely physical thing he very shortly rid himself of it.

When he was calm he asked himself again how much of the failure of his marriage was his fault, how much his hopes of marriage to my mother were based on his eagerness to gain the advantages she would bring him, and how much his money and his power, to which already – though they were still increasing – he had become completely accustomed, were 'corrupting' him. He felt that he had failed Jean only by not understanding himself well enough to know before he married her that he did not love her. He could not see that there was anything more complicated in the affair than that. He also felt that he loved my mother; because of her rare beauty, intelligence and mystery. He was aware that the latter was partly a result of her social standing, her birth and connections, and certain attributes she had gained from her environment; but the existence of this factor as so small a contributory cause of his passion did not seem to him to detract from the passion itself. He saw it as the romance of his life. He felt that the development of a relationship with so fine a creature must provide the intimate rewards he knew himself to lack: at the same time he felt that she would never submit her whole personality to him with the demanding subservience which he had come to think of as a characteristic of many women but most particularly of Jean. Again, as against that, he said to himself, 'Of course I want to possess her, to make my mark on her, to grasp at all her pride, to humble her; but then it is always like that in the early stages of love.'

He knew that Colin had seemed foolish and that my mother was not likely to be turned against him by such hysteria. He was therefore able to dismiss Colin as someone insignificant and over-emotional.

I think that must have been one of the times he said to himself that nothing and no one should stop him from using himself to the utmost. In that phrase he understood himself to include the functions of love and companionship, but it was a solitary man's resolve.

When he told me this, or some of it, later, I asked him whether he had been angry with me that evening. He said, 'No. I don't believe I thought about you at all.'

11

'I AM so much the perfect secretary,' I said, pleased to find my mother and Alexander both ready to listen to me, 'that all the clients are simply falling over each other to steal me from Madame Sobiska and have me all to themselves for ever.'

'Impossible,' said my mother.

'Their intentions are not honourable,' said Alexander.

'They are,' I said. 'Mr. McHughes is being joined in Brussels by Mrs. McHughes to whom he is very devoted, also by Miss Bea McHughes who is to study the viola at the Conservatoire.'

'What are you talking about?' said Alexander.

'Who is Mr. McHughes, darling?' asked my mother. 'Is he the television one?'

'No, no, he's the insurance one,' I said.

'But I thought you said he was so boring,' said my mother.

'He is,' I said.

'And he's offered you a job?' she asked.

'The thing is, he likes my being so English,' I said, 'and putting his letters into grammar and being so cold when people ring up. Also it doesn't matter about my shorthand because he never remembers what he's dictated so I can make them up.'

'How clever of you, darling,' said my mother. 'But you can't go to America. It's too far.'

'He wants me to go to Brussels for three months,' I said. 'He's starting an office there and he wants an English secretary, and I know something about the business now; and then he'll find one over there. He offered me an immense salary.'

'You must go,' said my mother.

'Why not?' said Alexander. 'Brussels is a pretty fiendish place, that's the only thing.'

'I know,' I said. 'I don't think I want to go anyway. I just thought it was rather impressive being asked.'

'I think you ought to go,' said my mother. 'It's good for you to see places.'

'I don't know where I'd live,' I said. 'He wouldn't arrange that, you see.'

'But we know someone in Brussels, surely?' said my mother. 'Yes, of course, Lydia Holmes, Henry's first secretary or something – *en poste* as Lydia would say. She'll find somewhere suitable – it's just the sort of thing she's good at. She'd probably have you herself – it's only for three months.'

'But I don't like her, do I?' I said.

'She's quite harmless,' said my mother. 'Rather stupid, that's all.'

'She admires Essex, too, that I remember,' said Alexander.

'Admires me?' said my mother.

'Thinks you're such a glamorous friend to have,' he said.

'Aren't I?' she said.

'Oh, dear, those are the ones that never like me,' I said.

'I shall write to her,' said my mother.

So it was arranged. Lydia Holmes wrote to say that I could share a flat with such a nice girl who worked at the embassy and wouldn't my mother come and spend Christmas with them so that we could be together. Mme. Sobiska took it all quite calmly, collected a large agency fee, and told me to come back in March.

Before I left I went to Tom Jones's record shop to look for Colin.

There was a violent wind, and the huge white clouds trundled about the sky like cart-horses at the sight of a train, so that sudden patches of brilliant sunshine burst through and one was dazzled and buffeted at the same time, and newspapers and leaves hurled about the Pimlico Road and people ran from shop to shop as if it were raining. The wind rushed me into the still darkness of the little shop. I saw nothing for a moment, then a white face disclosed itself between two piles of books. It was Jean's and it looked, as Colin had said, ruined.

I felt intensely embarrassed; but for a moment only, because her expression immediately changed. She smiled and came forward, seeming delighted to see me; and nothing in her behaviour thereafter bore out my first impression.

'Colin's out,' she said. 'He'll be back, though. It's awfully nice to see you again. How are you? You're working I hear from Colin.'

'Yes, I'm going to Brussels,' I said. 'For three months. I'm going on Monday. Are you staying here?'

'In Colin's flat upstairs, yes,' she said. 'I spend quite a lot of time in the shop. No one else ever seems to. They're an odd lot. Have you met Tom Jones?'

'Colin's never let me,' I said. 'I've often wanted to.'

'He's awfully odd,' Jean said. 'Beard and so on. Doesn't say much except when you really talk to him. Kind enough – he's letting Colin have an extra room upstairs so that I can stay for a bit, while I'm looking for a flat. Colin likes him, you know. He's made quite a difference in his life in a way, and yet I think he's a bit ashamed of him – Col is, I mean – he's still got this idea that he ought only to know people who are on the way up – you know, people in television, that sort of thing, making money and in smart flats.'

'Isn't Tom Jones on the way up?' I asked. 'Politics, or something?'

'No, no, he's far too crazy,' said Jean. 'Here's Col, look. And whoever else? I must say there's plenty of variety here.'

Colin came in with an enormous African of so ferocious and alarming an aspect that I wondered whether Tom Jones's activities might not be more dangerous and sinister than I had supposed.

He was introduced to us, greeted us politely but with what I took to be an assassin's smile, and disappeared upstairs. Colin, Jean and I went out to lunch.

'Is he going to kill somebody?' I asked. 'That black man?'

'Not so far as I know,' said Colin. 'He's going to be a

Law student. He's a very mild sort of person really. He's just staying with Tom until he can find a room. He's a friend of another Nigerian Tom knows.'

'I thought perhaps Tom Jones was some sort of revolutionary,' I said.

'Oh, Lord, no,' said Colin. 'He's not at all violent.'

'Oh,' I said 'That's all right then, I suppose.'

'Of course it's all right,' said Colin. 'Come on, tell us about this Brussels trip.'

I told them about it. Jean seemed interested and happy. After lunch she said she must go back to the shop, and Colin walked part of the way home with me.

'Jean seems all right,' I said. 'In fact I've hardly ever seen her in such good form as she was today.'

'Nor have I, hardly,' said Colin. 'The thing is, she's terribly keen on you, didn't you know? It was you that cheered her up. She thinks you're a sort of angel, so good and kind, poor old Jean. So mind you live up to it. Actually I will say she's better lately. She's going to find a flat and get a job.'

'Will she be poor then?' I asked.

'Poor?' said Colin. 'He's given her a fortune. A fortune. Far more than he need have done. Didn't you see it in the report of the case in the paper?'

'I think perhaps I heard something about it,' I said. 'Somebody said something about it being a tax wangle.'

'It's not,' said Colin. 'It's conscience money. But we won't talk about that. I meant to say, I see you've forgiven me for making that scene. Which is decent of you. Tell you what, Jean and I'll come over and see you in Brussels one weekend, what about that? What is there to do there?'

'Nothing, everyone says,' I said. 'But do come. I really wish you would. I shan't have any friends.'

I don't know why it took me so long to believe that Primrose Elliott was a friend. I kept looking out for flaws in her. Even she herself said, after I had been in Brussels sometime, 'How distrustful you are.'

She in fact had far more justification for suspecting me,

because I had been introduced to her by Lydia Holmes, whom she did not like and who had said to her, 'She's Essex Cowper's daughter, you know, and absolutely the top socially. It ought to be very interesting for you to make friends with her and she might introduce you to someone really nice. In fact she's just the sort of person you might find a husband through, because they move in a very cosmopolitan and interesting set and probably know lots of the sort of people who might like you – you know, older, and tired of pretty girls.'

This horrible woman was a cousin of Primrose's mother and a great organizer of the British colony in Brussels. She was the daughter of an earl and though not much liked was generally respected and even admired: she was fashionable and quite amusing, both qualities rather lacking in diplomatic circles in Brussels at that moment. Our dislike of her was the first point of contact between Primrose and me.

Primrose was nearly thirty and not pretty. She was calm and intelligent, but I suppose someone like Alexander would not have found her particularly amusing. She was engaged to a zoologist who was on an expedition in South America. They were going to get married when he came back in a year's time. She had studied music for years before she started working in the Foreign Office, and wanted to be a composer. We went to concerts together: they were the best thing about Brussels – otherwise, as everyone had warned me, it was a dull town. All the same I became fond of it because I was happy there. Primrose's flat was a comfortable, light, modern one at the end of the Avenue Louise, near the Bois de la Cambre, in which we used to walk and have long conversations of the sort I had not had with another girl since leaving school. Primrose was very solid and tolerant and hopeful in her ideas. She accused me of assuming a fashionable disillusion which was not genuine, in which she may have been right.

Lydia Holmes did not approve of Primrose's penniless zoologist, and was always trying to interest her in alternatives: that was where I was suppose to help.

Later on Primrose said to me, 'I don't think you are the

top socially. Lydia is simply dazzled by your fast-set life and your mother's publicity.'

This annoyed me and I found myself trying to explain to her that my mother could be very smart indeed if she wanted to, which made Primrose laugh at me. In that respect she was odd; she was one of the very few people I had met who did not like my mother. That was partly because of the episode of David Parker.

David Parker was the Military Attaché. He was forty-five, handsome and a bachelor, and therefore much sought-after. He was known to be susceptible where girls were concerned, though his passions were usually short-lived, but even so the fact of his being apparently at once and completely bowled over by me caused a stir in the tight little reed bed of the British community in Brussels. I found him boring, vain and thick-skinned, and the grati-fication of having made such a conquest lasted only a week or two. Nothing would put him off, however, and he loaded me with flowers and presents and hangdog looks. One of our attempts to get rid of him involved the pretence that I was in love with someone else, who was very jealous and did not like me to go out with other men. Having invented this person we found ourselves developing him into a character so odious that anyone less gullible than David Parker must have seen through the deception. His name was Valentine and he was more or less the 'He' of advertisements. He always brought me those chocolates with such lovely centres, and liked me to wear the latest scent, and wore certain socks, ties, shirts, drank the latest drinks, and had a heavenly tweedy smell. He had definite and fatuous views on everything under the sun and we quoted him at length with wild laughter which I suppose David Parker thought was girlish giggling only to be expected at the mention of the beloved's name. None of this had the desired effect. He would not be diverted.

At Christmas my mother came over and stayed with Lydia Holmes. She arrived in a cloud of excitement, presents, talk and laughter, and enraptured everyone she met, including and most particularly David Parker.

Lydia gave a party for her, and the next day several of

us went out to dinner together. On both these occasions
his obvious enslavement was widely noticed.

Afterwards I said to Primrose, 'It looks as if my mother
has relieved us of David Parker. But what d'you suppose
he'll do when she's gone?'

'I don't know,' said Primrose. 'Is she always like that?'

'Like what?' I asked.

'I mean – does she like him?'

'Good Heavens, no,' I said. 'My mother's the most
easily bored person in the world.'

'Why did she encourage him then?' asked Primrose.

'I suppose she thought it was funny,' I said. 'Actually
I didn't think she did encourage him.'

'Oh yes,' said Primrose. 'In that night club, and
everything.'

'But people always behave like that about my mother,'
I said.

'All your boy-friends too?' asked Primrose.

'It's not like that at all,' I said. 'Besides, people always
do think she's wonderful – it's only natural. It doesn't
mean anything to her.'

'Doesn't it ever annoy you?' said Primrose.

'No,' I said.

'I'm always telling you you're much nicer than you
pretend,' said Primrose.

'You don't know her at all,' I said. 'She's awfully nice
to me, and never leaves me out of things, and really she
is much better than anyone else. Look how we all woke
up here in Brussels just because she came. She's a terribly
good mother to have.' I remembered with embarrassment
that she had perhaps rather ignored Primrose.

'Well, anyway, I wonder whether we shall have David
Parker back on our doorstep when she goes,' said Primrose, 'or will he throw up everything and follow her back
to London?'

He was back on our doorstep two days later, un-
abashed, and carrying a small white kitten in a basket.
Primrose told me afterwards that I should never have let
him in, because his behaviour during my mother's visit
made a good excuse for refusing to see him; but I wanted
the kitten. Its name was Marius and it was fine and soft

and luxury-loving. Most days I took it to the office in its basket.

January and February were cold. The snow was thick in the Bois, and in the streets the slush made it even harder to fight one's way through the crowds on to the steamy trams. The flat was warm and Marius could hardly be persuaded to leave it.

In March I delayed my return to London by another month. The work in the insurance office was quite hard and not particularly interesting, but I was happy in Brussels and for some reason reluctant to go back to London. One day I had a postcard from Lewis Ogden saying that he was coming to Brussels on business the following Friday and would I have dinner with him.

I went to meet him at the Hotel Métropole where he was staying. He was sitting uncomfortably in a chair too small for him, reading a paper and looking tired – a tired businessman in a hotel lounge drinking a whisky and soda. We went to a restaurant where he ordered a meal in bad but efficient French and told me that he wanted to marry my mother. And now that he had simply said it, I could not remember why it had once seemed such an alarming prospect.

'I hope you'll be able to like the idea,' he said. 'I believe we can all lead quite an interesting life together.'

And I began to see how interesting life would be, and how rich we should be, and how much we should travel and meet people and buy things.

'How free you can be when you've got enough money,' I said.

He laughed and said, 'Thank you for referring to it. Of course it gives you freedom. You can do anything you like if you're rich enough, even give it all up and go and live on a desert island.'

'Will you do that?'

'No,' he said. 'I love it. I love my work. It's the most exciting thing you can do in the world today – except perhaps be a successful scientist, but that's so rare, and anyway the chances are one discovery will have to last you a lifetime. In the sort of business I do there's no end to it: there are new things to be achieved every day, and the power and freedom that the money brings you are incidentals, at the time anyway. The negotiations, the scope of the big schemes, the personalities, the practical politics of it all, as well as the ideas, the imagination, the theory – it's the most stimulating life in the world, and don't you believe anyone who tells you otherwise. And do you know, incidentally, who's beginning to see that? Your friend Alexander.'

'Alexander?' I repeated.

'I thought you'd be surprised,' he said. 'I took him on to please your mother, because she asked me to, being an old friend of his mother's and so on. And there are always certain people who are impressed to see someone of his sort in the office. I thought I might find a use for him now and then, but I never thought much of him. But something's happened to him lately. I had to see a certain amount of him over something – this thing I'm over here for as a matter of fact, an industrial machinery deal – and I saw the change happening to him as he began to see the possibilities. He's not without imagination. So I'm letting him do a bit more now and keeping an eye on him. It will be interesting to see what happens.'

'I'm so glad,' I said. 'I'm sure he'll do well, if he really does get keen. I suppose he probably never has been, on anything, but he's more – I know he's more reliable than he seems. . . .'

'I think you're probably right,' he said. 'But then a lot of you people are like that – you like to pretend to be altogether flippant and worthless when you're not really.'

'A lot of us are,' I said seriously.

He smiled. 'So are a lot of us. Or do you think I am that common phenomenon these days, the man without a class?'

From there it seemed easy to talk about his youth and how he had made his money. I was delighted that he should be talking to me like this and liked him better at that moment than anyone else in the world. That was the first time he told me about his life in Manchester and his Socialism, and how he had lost faith in it.

'It achieved so many of its aims,' he said. 'In fact most of them. Which means that the Socialist movement is a completely different one now, and the people who think it isn't are the most ineffectual of the lot. And then, that being so, those principles I'd thought so important and unalterable ceased to apply as my own life changed and the scope of it widened so enormously – the scope of my life I mean. But I feel a certain nostalgia for the old faith now and then.'

'Would you ever go into politics now?' I said. 'On the other side?'

'I've been thinking of it,' he said. 'I believe your mother would like it – she'd be superlatively good at it. It would mean giving up a lot of my business though, which I shouldn't like, but it would be a new field. I don't pretend I'd be very much use to the community. Indeed I'm far more useful at the moment, providing employment and sending all those taxes to the Exchequer. And of course success in the House of Commons depends on all sorts of odd things which one can't possibly gauge beforehand. I might be a complete failure there. But it would be interesting. I think one would probably have a feeling of being very much more in on things, in the centre of it all, than I am at the moment.'

'People say, though, that it's not what it was,' I said, 'that you're at the mercy of the Party Whip, and all that.'

'One would have to get beyond that stage,' he said. 'There might be a few years of drudgery. But I should have the advantage of believing in the system, of not thinking there need necessarily be any loss of integrity involved. I believe the country's not so very badly run, either, that the top people, the really top ones, on the whole deserve to be there. . . .'

'Oh, Lord,' I said. 'Does anyone else?'

He smiled.

'If they don't, it seems to me that I should have a tremendous advantage,' he said. 'Faith is a useful quality. Don't you think your mother would rather be married to a Cabinet Minister than a mere industrialist?'

'I expect she would rather you were both,' I said.

'I haven't asked her to marry me yet,' he said. 'But I shall now. You've heard about the house she found for me?'

'She told me at Christmas,' I said. 'You'd just bought it I think.'

'It's a lovely house,' he said. 'It was a piece of luck that the man was a friend of hers and that she heard he wanted to sell it before it came on the market.'

'Yes, wasn't it?' I said, thinking that she need not have taken so much trouble over the commission since she was now to be so rich. 'And she's making it beautiful, isn't she? She wrote me a long letter about it.'

'She does like the house, doesn't she?' he said eagerly. 'Yes, she's being very clever about it; but at the same time she's doing nothing too exotic, I shan't feel out of place there. I'm looking forward very much to its being finished. I hope it will be ready by the time you come back.'

Then he changed the subject and began to tell me what I should be reading, and was evidently favourably impressed at what I already had read: he promised to send me some books when he got back to London. He suddenly laughed and said, 'In a funny way I feel I know you better than I do your mother. One always feels conscious of great reserves in her. It's part of her attraction. I'm rather afraid of her.'

'A lot of people are,' I said. 'But they're quite wrong because they don't know about her kindness.'

He took me back to the flat in a taxi and I went upstairs in a state of great happiness and did not go to bed for a long time but walked about my room repeating our conversation and thinking about the future. I wrote a letter to my mother telling her that I thought Lewis was wonderful and that she would be making a terrible mistake if she did not marry him; then I decided it was sentimental and tore it up.

Four days later a parcel of books arrived for me with a letter from Lewis saying how much he had enjoyed our dinner. The next day I had a letter from my mother in which she said:

I am thinking of marrying Lewis Ogden. Would you be very upset? I think it would be a good move and you could give up your job. Please send me a telegram telling me whether I should or not.

I sent a telegram saying 'Of course you must.' I don't know whether it would have made any difference if I had said 'Don't', but I felt it was nice of her to ask me.

12

I came home to find a small crowd of women scattered about the drawing-room in attitudes of attention, furs and diamonds, little hats, holding glasses of sherry and about to be addressed by Betty Carr. A few well-dressed youths were among them, outdoing them in cosy helpfulness.

I went upstairs and found my mother in bed.

'I couldn't face it so I said I had a cold,' she said. 'It's the One-armed Orphans or something equally depressing. One of Betty's committees. Have a drink. How are you?'

'All right,' I said. 'You look well. How's Lewis? Is Alexander still living here?'

'Of course. Why should he not be?'

'I don't know. I just wondered. What about the house in the country? Is it finished?'

'More or less, yes. Lewis is going to give an enormous party there, before the wedding. It's pretty. A dream, in fact. I don't think I'm going to want to live there though.'

'Not?' I said, surprised.

'I don't like the country,' she said. 'It's so terribly crowded; and full of machines. You might as well go for a walk in a factory.'

'You could move further away – Scotland for instance.'

'Yes, that's what I thought. Scotland. I shall be a capricious wife, full of expensive whims.'

'Are you going to like it?'

'I shall like the expensive whims. How I shall like being a wife I don't know. It's so long since I've been one.'

'But you've been one quite often.'

'That's true. But I don't know that quantity helps. All

marriages are exactly the same. Which reminds me, what about you?'

'Me?'

'Marrying. I was wondering if you might marry Alexander. I should like to keep him in the family.'

'I don't suppose he'd be very keen,' I said. 'I daresay he'd be quite a nice husband, though. And Lewis told me he thought he was going to do well in business.'

'That's the trouble,' said my mother. 'In a way.'

'Have you been working too hard?' I asked. 'You don't look as well as I thought you did.'

'I probably have,' she said. 'It's high time you came back. You're my good angel – my good daughter anyway. Don't listen to my nonsense. The Kensington harpies will go in a minute. What shall we do this evening, just by ourselves?'

My mother had a new car, a neat and shining little Fiat. In it we drove to Mowle, Lewis's new house on the edge of Salisbury Plain. Lewis was in Manchester but was to join us the following day.

'I shall tell you nothing about it at all,' my mother said. 'You must come on it quite unprepared.'

In fact by the time we reached it she had been unable to resist telling me a certain amount, and I was expecting the best, and my expectations were fulfilled.

It was a late seventeenth-century house built by some local architect much under the influence of Inigo Jones, and made an immediate impression of complete agreeability.

'You see what some idiot did to the windows,' said my mother, as if she were running down some much praised child for fear of seeming too proud. 'Those hideous big panes – but only on this side – and the hall is ghastly, that I must warn you; it's the worst thing about the whole house. Someone in the last century tried to make it look grand and made it much bigger than it was meant to be and put in absurd mock marble pillars. But this is the drawing-room – really rather pretty – and here in the dining-room there's some quite good George I panelling; but now come upstairs, the best thing of all is at the very top.'

She whisked me through the bedrooms and up to what should have been an attic but which in the eighteenth century had been made into a library, a long low room taking up most of the top of the house and surrounded by formal bookshelves. She had had it painted simply white and curtained the windows in some heavy deep blue material; the floor was polished, and there were Persian rugs, and two huge eighteenth century globes of which my mother was proud.

'It's nice, you must admit,' she said. 'This is very much Lewis's room. Of course it needs more furniture, and yet in a way it suits him better like this, all bare. This is where he comes and paces about dictating to his machine and ringing up his underlings at seven o'clock in the morning to frighten them.'

'Seven in the morning?' I said.

'Oh, he gets up at five,' said my mother. 'All great men do. Didn't you know? It's the very least attractive thing about them I always think.'

Lewis and Alexander arrived the next day just before lunch and I immediately noticed the changed relation between them.

I was in the garden when I saw the big car stop in front of the gates, as the Italian manservant ran from the house to open them: he must have been watching for it because he was out of the door before the chauffeur could move from his seat; then he ran back again as the car circled slowly round the sweep of gravel and drew up in front of the house, and was there, wreathed in smiles, as the chauffeur opened the door for Lewis. As I saw the two black-coated figures get out of the car and go into the house, I was reminded of the time when I had hidden with Colin and Avril in the hall of Lewis's office to see him leave. Alexander might have been the young man with the dispatch case who had hurried into the car with him: he had the same look of alert respect.

Coming in from the garden, I found Lewis greeting my mother, and could think of nothing to say to Alexander but 'You've got a new hat.'

'You're quite right,' he said. 'Absolutely right, as always. What about you? Have you got a new hat?'

'No,' I said.

'Did Telford say he'd spend Sunday night here?' Lewis said to Alexander. 'Or Monday?'

'Sunday,' said Alexander. 'Before the meeting.'

'Sunday,' said Lewis, turning back to my mother. 'I do hope that's all right.'

'Of course,' said my mother, without much enthusiasm. She walked past Lewis to greet Alexander with what seemed to me an odd formality.

At lunch it became apparent to me that Alexander had progressed enormously in Lewis's esteem, and that he was flourishing in the new situation, and that my mother definitely disapproved of it. Why this last should be so I had no idea. I thought it must be the result of an obscure and unreasonable jealousy, and that she had liked Lewis to be interested only in her. It was true that a fair proportion of his conversation at lunch was directed at Alexander; but the emotion I ascribed to my mother was so untypical of her that I wondered again whether the wedding preparations and the organization of the party which was to take place at Mowle the following weekend were not becoming too much for her.

Lewis was more awe-inspiring again. In Brussels he had seemed somehow, perhaps because he had been tired, to have shed some of his personality, to have been quieter and altogether less overpowering. Here it was all back, the endless talk, the charm, the display of knowledge, the elaborate politeness, all the special habits and the restlessness. He had nothing but boiled fish for lunch while the rest of us ate well, and he was twice called to the telephone. The second time he sent Alexander to answer it, who came back saying, 'I told him to get in touch with Josephs. He only wanted to know who to deal with about the contract.'

'I'm so sorry,' Lewis said to my mother. 'We came straight from Manchester this morning and didn't call in at the office. Miss Walker must have told one or two people who couldn't wait till Monday that I'd be here.

Tell me about this party. I don't seem to have done much about it – and it was my idea too – how's it going?'

'The whole thing grows more and more elaborate every minute,' said my mother. 'I should think you'll hate it. Everyone's accepting, needless to say. The Press keep ringing up too, with the usual inane questions.'

'What a bore for you,' said Lewis, concerned. 'Alexander can deal with them next time – he always knows what to say to them.'

'Oh, does he?' said my mother. 'How does that highly-paid P.R.O. of yours – what's his name, Lloyd? – how does he take that?'

'It keeps him on his toes,' said Lewis. 'Owens, yes. He's all right really. I want you to walk round the garden with me and show me the improvements. Oh, yes, coffee, all right. And Vanessa really likes the house? I knew you'd like the library best.'

He and my mother walked out into the cold early spring garden, very handsome and distinguished together, and I was left with Alexander, to whom I at once turned and said, 'I want to know about your conversion.'

'There's nothing to tell,' he said. 'It's a conversion, as you say, and that's all there is to it. I'm working hard, go to bed early so as to be on time at the office – it's too dreary.'

'Why on earth d'you do it?' I asked. 'Are you going to make a fortune?'

'No, the truth is, it isn't dreary at all, not to me,' said Alexander. 'I've never had such an interesting life, and it gets more and more exciting every day because I'm more and more with Lewis. Lewis is fabulous. Fabulous.'

'Why?' I asked.

'He's brilliant,' he said. 'No one can compare with him for grasp and imagination. His memory's phenomenal. He doesn't care how hard he works, in fact he's only happy when he's got about five really big schemes all starting at once. He's not dishonest as I used to think he must be. He gets there first by thinking quicker, that's all. Everything about his methods I absolutely admire. You might think he'd be too impatient, but you'd be amazed how deep his knowledge is. He doesn't make hasty judgements about things, or situations – though he does about people. He's not nearly so good about people, not that he's taken in by fools or confidence tricksters, or that sort of thing, but motives, what you might call human nature, he'll stumble over now and then, and that does occasionally affect some business issue. But I admire him more and more every day, as I say.'

'I see the change,' I said. 'I certainly do. I'm glad. I'm sure it's a good thing. Lewis told me when he came to Brussels in January that he thought you were going to be good.'

'I think he's beginning to trust me more,' said Alexander, 'but I still feel I'm very much on trial. He only took me on at first because Essex asked him to – he thought nothing of me at all but he thought I'd be happy to hang around for a bit looking aristocratic in the outer office until I got sick of it. He thought I'd leave of my own free will after a few months – he's told me so. The only trouble is your dear Mama.'

'She doesn't seem very keen on you and Lewis getting on so well.' I said. 'I can't quite make out why.'

'The trouble is,' he said, 'if she decides it doesn't suit her she'll get at Lewis and try and persuade him to drop me. I know her. How much difference that will make to him I don't know.'

'Why shouldn't it suit her?' I said.

'That's difficult to say,' said Alexander. 'I'm never honestly quite certain, you know, how much to say to you. You have a way of nodding quietly as if you know everything and suddenly there you are all horrified youth. It's very attractive of course but it makes it rather difficult to talk to you about your mother.'

I said nothing, and after a pause he said, 'You knew, I'm not happy about this marriage.'

'Why not?' I asked.

'I sometimes wonder whether she quite realizes what she's doing, but I can't talk to her like I used to, she simply flies into a rage with me. Perhaps that's because she does know.'

'Know what?' I said.

'Well, you know, I keep coming across examples of

what you might call his business ethics,' said Alexander. 'His private life I don't know so much about. I gather he behaved fairly badly to his first wife, but then the real mistake was in ever marrying her – and as I said his fault is that he finds ordinary simple human beings hard to understand. And I suppose he's a selfish man. Though I don't know, he's generous enough, and very fair to the people who work for him. Admittedly they don't generally much like him, but that's because he can't help being rather distant with them except over strictly business matters – he simply doesn't know how not to be. But he's very fair, and scrupulous, and loyal. Honestly. Since I became interested I've asked a lot of people about him and I've been back through some of the files in the office and found out an awful lot about him and what he's done; and I promise you that where he's been ruthless – which God knows he can be – it's been with people who've tried to cheat him first. No, you're laughing at me, but I promise you. . .'

'I'm not laughing at you,' I said, 'it's only such a change from what you used to say about him. I believe you absolutely. But surely that's a good thing? Why does it make you worry about their marriage?'

Alexander got up and walked towards the window. Looking out from my chair behind him I could see my mother and Lewis in the distance walking slowly across the lawn towards the house.

'I don't thing that she's being fair to him,' said Alexander. 'I don't mean that she ought to be wildly in love with him, or even that she ought not to be marrying him for his money. But she's not prepared to give up a single thing for him, not a thing, or change her life in any way to suit his. She wants to have everything she had before, and him, and his money, and everything he's giving her. It's too – too shabby, for Lewis. Can't you tell her so? You're the only one she pays any attention to, over that sort of thing.'

'But what ought she to give up?' I said. 'I don't understand you. I don't see that there's anything she need give up. Her shop? But Lewis doesn't mind that and it amuses her. Besides she probably will give it up after a bit. And what else is there? Putting money on horses or something? What d'you mean?'

'Oh, well,' Alexander sighed. 'Perhaps some of her friends.'

'That's ridiculous,' I said. 'You've just told me how wonderful Lewis is because of his loyalty, and now you say my mother ought to give up her friends when she marries him. I never heard anything so ridiculous.'

There was a pause, then Alexander turned away from the window and said, 'Yes, it must sound silly. I can't quite explain what I mean. This house for instance. It's really been a good old racket for half her friends; practically every piece of furniture or material you can see has meant a nice little commission for somebody, without Lewis knowing anything about it. But it isn't only that. I'm not sure that your mother knows what she's about, or even that she really knows what Lewis is like – but Heavens above they're two intelligent people, old enough to deal with their own problems, so I don't know why I have to be so gloomy about it. You've lots more to tell me about Brussels. And what's this I hear about smuggling a cat?'

'I smuggled him through the customs, that's all,' I said, 'in a big handbag. I'll never do it again. I nearly died of fright. But I couldn't bear to leave him behind or send him to some awful kennels for months – he's such a nice little cat, white. I left him in the Mews with the Spanish girl: I thought Lewis might not like him, although he's quite housetrained.'

'I'm sure he wouldn't mind,' said Alexander. 'You must ask him. Isabella will probably eat him.'

'There was plenty of other food in the house,' I said.

Lewis and my mother came in just then and Alexander explained to Lewis about Marius.

'But you should have brought him,' Lewis said at once, 'or doesn't he care for the country? I tell you what, Telford's driving down tomorrow for the night – he shall pick up Marius and bring him down. What about that? I'll go and ring him up.'

I began to bathe in the comfort, in the atmosphere of lovely ease my mother spread about the house, in Lewis's charm and approval. He treated me now with greater familiarity than before our meeting in Brussels, as if that evening had lengthened our acquaintance by as many months as hours. Alexander said, 'Lewis likes you. He can say nothing but nice things about you. You must encourage him to talk to you – you'll find him good value.'

'I should hardly have thought he needed encouragement to talk to anyone,' I said.

'He has different levels of conversation, though,' said Alexander. 'You'll find out.'

'I think I have found out,' I said. 'But don't worry. I won't let slip the opportunity to improve my mind.'

'I haven't become a pompous bore since I got interested in my job,' said Alexander. 'I haven't. So shut up.'

On Sunday afternoon I went for a walk with Lewis. He liked long walks, but this time we turned back at the top of the slope beside the house because we saw my mother's car drive up to the front door.

She had left after lunch to see the Ryans who lived about ten miles away and who had promised to put some people up for the night of the party; and when we saw her driving back so soon, Lewis said, 'She can't possibly have been there and back in the time. Perhaps she's forgotten something.' We waited on our little hilltop looking down on to the sheltered house but no one seemed to move there.

'She's had time to fetch a list, or whatever it might have been,' said Lewis. 'I believe she's decided not to go after all. Shall I go back and bring her? I know she'd like to come with us.'

'I'll come back with you,' I said.

We began to walk back the way we had come. At the bottom of the hill there was a gate which led into a walled garden, which in its turn led to the garden proper and the house. I suppose Alexander, whom we had left dozing over the Sunday papers, had told my mother that we had just left, and they must have assumed we had gone for one of Lewis's usual walks, which seldom lasted for less than two hours.

We came up unobserved on the soft grass outside the drawing-room window and saw them standing in front of the fire, kissing.

We seemed to watch them for a long time, while they only slightly swayed. I suppose both of them had their eyes shut, otherwise they must have seen us. Their kiss seemed not so much loving as infinitely knowledgeable; a whole lifetime of intimate intensity seemed expressed by it. My mother's body was arched backwards, her hair falling away from her rapt face, while he seemed to lean on her as if from some far greater height, drawn by her like Narcissus to the irresistible cold pool.

I felt a hand on my arm, and in obedience to it moved away, and round the corner of the house. I felt nothing but terror, and could think of nothing to say. Lewis led me to the dining-room, where he poured some brandy into a glass and gave it to me. I swallowed it and coughed. Then I began to be afraid that Lewis might think I had known about Alexander and my mother all the time, and I began, 'I didn't. . .' but could not finish the sentence. I started again 'Perhaps. . .' meaning to say that perhaps it had suddenly happened just now by some chance and for the first time, but I did not have the conviction to finish that sentence either.

Lewis said distantly, 'I've just remembered I have some letters to write. We'll finish the walk another day.'

'Yes,' I said.

He opened the door for me, saying vaguely as I went out, 'Don't worry,' as he had done in Italy when I had asked him about his divorce.

I spent the rest of the afternoon in my room trying to imagine Alexander and my mother in bed together and wondering whether they had laughed at me. I imagined them rolling about on her bed in all the abandon the kiss I had seen implied, and thought of their cries and kisses and afternoons behind locked doors. The curve of my mother's body had had a look of avidity, and it seemed to me that vast regions of shame and fear and secrecy must hide the members of one's own family from one, from everyone perhaps except their lovers. How could I

have been said to have known her, to have known either
of them, when I had not known that?

Probably everyone in London except me had known for
months. Certainly now that I saw things in that light it
was perfectly obvious that they had been having an *affaire*
since very soon after Alexander became our lodger – all
sorts of little incidents and remarks, whether made by
either of them or by outside observers, bore it out. I
reproached myself furiously for being so obtuse: I always
was, it was in my nature. Perhaps if I had lived more
with my mother in my childhood instead of being packed
off to dull relations for the holidays I might have known
better what to expect from the world of grown-ups; but
even so the experience of the last two years would have
been enough for most people. Of all my attributes the
one I was most ashamed of was this thick-headed ability
to be shocked.

I wondered whether the concealing of their relationship
from me had made them bored with me: I supposed they
must have been glad when I went away because then
they could move into the same room.

Only when I had exhausted myself with these pictures
did I remember to think about Lewis.

I went downstairs to find my mother and Alexander
having tea in the drawing-room with a large fringed
woman who turned out to be the wife of a painter who
lived nearby. My mother, having once met her in London,
had come across her walking along the road and had
made her promise to come to tea on her way back from
some visit to which she was then on her way. My mother
had then abandoned Mrs. Ryan and returned to the house
to make ready for this unexpected but promising source
of help. This large round-faced woman with her fringe,
her bangles, and her eager smile, was an heiress – this
my mother had remembered – and lived with her poor
but worthy painter husband in some style in her old
family home. Even as I came into the room she was saying
happily, 'Well, I suppose at a pinch, if they don't mind
roughing it, we could put up about twenty.'

'Oh, Vanessa, look, it's too wonderful, she's solving all
our problems,' my mother cried. 'This is my daughter

Vanessa. She's being too wonderful, darling, and saying she can put up twenty people. Have you ever heard anything so kind?'

The painter's wife gave a sort of amber glow and accepted a cigarette from Alexander. Nothing had happened.

Lewis did not appear for tea, but there was nothing remarkable in that since he had not done so the day before. My silence was not noticeable because my mother and Alexander were concentrating on the painter's wife, whose name was Moyra Ramage, and who was herself breathlessly talkative. She talked about the party, the people she was to put up, the house, her own house, her husband's work and how good it was, her own pottery and how bad it was, her small children, her cats, her tame hare, the shocking opinions of the local Tory Member of Parliament, her interest in amateur theatricals, her garden. Then she left, with repeated protestations of boundless hospitality, and her strong sandle-shod feet bore her down the drive.

'What a very hellish person,' said my mother.

'I rather liked her,' I said truthfully.

'Oh, darling, you are too odd,' said my mother. 'Are you feeling all right? You looked terrible when you came in but I didn't say anything because of her. Have you got a headache?'

'I'm all right,' I said. I found myself unable to look at either of them, as if I were guilty, which in a way I was.

I went upstairs again until just before dinner when the roar of his car announced the arrival of Telford.

He was standing in the hall as I went down, holding Marius in his basket, and shouting, 'Lewis! Lewis! Where the hell is he? I've got his cat here. It's peed all over my car. I'll have to get new covers. He can bloody well pay for them. Where is he anyway?'

'It's my cat,' I said, 'and I'm sure he didn't pee all over the car, at least he never has before. Perhaps you frightened him by going so fast.'

He went even redder in the face with embarrassment and said, more quietly, 'I was only having Lewis on. He's a nice cat. I mean it. Here he is. Pretty hot stuff, this place, isn't it – the house I mean. Where's the old man, d'you know? In the Turkish bath or something?'

'I can't offer you that, I'm afraid,' Lewis said, coming down the stairs. 'You'll have to make do with the common sort if you want a bath before dinner, and take a big whisky and soda with you to console you. Angelo will bring one up. Come along and I'll show you the way.'

I took Marius out into the dark garden, where he scratched delicately in the new rosebed.

Dinner was no more than slightly uneasy, which might just as well have been put down to Telford's awkwardness with my mother as to any tension between her and Lewis; and after dinner the three men went up to the library because Lewis said they had something to discuss.

'You're sure you're all right?' my mother asked me, when I said I was going to bed early.

'Of course,' I said.

'You're not worried about my marrying Lewis or anything are you?' she said. 'I thought you were pleased, but since he's been down here with us you seem to have gone rather quiet.'

'Of course I'm pleased,' I said, 'that is, if you are. If you really think it's a good idea.'

'I can't see why it shouldn't be,' she said.

'You don't think he . . . well, you know how you said to me once that he thought about you in a fairy-story sort of way, and then you remember how we used to talk about him?'

'You mean plotting to get him to pay for things?' she said. 'Letting people sponge off him, without his realizing? He doesn't mind that, you know, he expects people to be after his money – it flatters him in a way. I think we understand each other very well. He knows all about me.'

'Oh, does he?' I said.

'Don't sound so surprised,' she said. 'He's no fool, Lewis. He may like to have romantic ideas about some things, but he's a perfectly down-to-earth person really, otherwise he wouldn't be where he is. I don't quite know what you're getting at, but if you mean which is pretty insulting of you – that Lewis may have romantic illusions about my character, I'm sure he hasn't.'

'No, I didn't mean that, of course I didn't,' I said. 'I don't know what I meant really. Anyway I'm sure it's all all right. I'm only going to bed because I'm sleepy. It must be the Hampshire air, or Wiltshire, or wherever we are.'

I went upstairs with a new thought, that Lewis might have already known of the existence of the *affaire* between Alexander and my mother, which would explain why he had apparently taken that afternoon's revelation so calmly. This seemed to me incomprehensible, but not impossible.

All the same I went on waiting for something to happen; but the next morning Lewis left for London with Alexander and Telford without apparently having said anything to surprise or annoy my mother. I watched her say good-bye to him affectionately, and then to Alexander, and was amazed at all their casual calmness.

The following day my mother and I drove back to London; and still nothing had happened.

13

O N my return from Brussels I had been to see Madame
Sobiska, to tell her that I was not going to work for
her any more. She gave me a long angry talk about letting
people down and being irresponsible and flighty and said
that I should never get anywhere unless I could learn to
stick to something.

'I don't really know where I want to get to,' I said. 'So
it's a little hard to know what to stick to.'

'That's not at all the point,' she said. 'The point is to
stick to something, it doesn't matter what.'

I said that my mother needed help with arranging the
flowers in her new house in the country, and Madame
Sobiska said 'Pah!'

The result was that I had nothing to do and wandered
endlessly and without direction about the streets, my
thoughts turning round and round but to no end either.

I went one day to Tom Jones's shop to look for Colin,
but found only a small boy who knew nothing of either
Colin or Jean, but said that someone else was living
upstairs. I wrote Colin a note and left it in an envelope
in case the elusive Tom Jones should know his address,
and a few days later had a reply from Manchester:

I'm working on a TV job up here, he said. *Stinking awful
hole. I'll be back soon. Jean's all over the place about your
mum marrying her late husband. I told her she ought to have
known it but it seems she never believed it and takes it hard.
I think she's gone back to Mum which is plain crazy but Tom
Jones would know. I may not even stay till the end of this job
as I can't stick the North and the long love affair with the
whirring cameras is drawing to a sticky close, so I may see
you in about a week.*

The letter came the day my mother and I went down to Mowle to prepare for the party which was then only two days ahead, and I decided I would ring up Tom Jones and try to get in touch with Jean as soon as I got back to London.

The situation between Lewis, my mother and Alexander seemed unchanged and I could only believe that Lewis must have known about the *affaire*, must even, I supposed, be prepared to condone its continued existence. I spent the weekend before the party alone in London, pretending to my mother that I was going to the theatre on Saturday night because I could not make up my mind how to behave to them all.

On the way down I asked my mother about the party, the plans for which I had not heard in detail.

'I wondered when you were going to take an interest,' she said.

'I'm sorry,' I said. 'I'm afraid I haven't been much help.'

'There was nothing to do,' said my mother. 'Though there'll be plenty these next two days. I thought we wouldn't have many people to stay the whole weekend. It's really too much for the Italians, even though they'll have help. They'll have an awful lot to do for the party, especially as we are having food. So only Mike and Kitty Newcome are coming on Friday night, which means we'll be six, and then the Spencers for dinner on Saturday, and six others to be provided with beds for that night. Johnny Spencer's arranged the band, of course, because he's so good at that sort of thing – apparently they're marvellous, Alexander's heard them. And as for the guests, well, they're the only fly in the ointment.'

'Who are they?'

'Not very many,' said my mother. 'Just friends. I thought it was such a good idea at first since the post wedding party's got to be rather a pompous one. I thought we'd just have amusing people we really wanted to see, and no bores, but the trouble is there are going to be no restraining influences and I've a nasty feeling that people are going to behave badly and Lewis won't like it. On the other hand quite a lot of them know him now and no longer think it doesn't matter what they say or do because isn't it fun, here we all are sponging off a *nouveau riche* millionaire, and then food will be a stabilizing influence. Actually I've asked a lot of your friends because Lewis likes seeing young people at parties.'

'Who?' I asked.

She spent the rest of the journey enumerating the guests and discussing them and I began to think that after all it might be amusing and that perhaps I might enjoy my position as the future step-daughter of the house, even though I was myself secretly uncertain as to how secure that position might in fact be.

Lucy Logan was the first arrival: that was an auspicious beginning.

She was a new discovery of Alexander's whom none of the rest of us had met. We had heard of her, because she had a certain following, and we had read of some of her exploits in the papers. She had really only emerged as a personality during the past few months, while I had been in Brussels, though I remembered her faintly as a some-what strange-looking débutante the year before.

We came out from dinner to find her standing in the middle of the hall, her luggage beside her, rather as if she had been waiting – for some time – for a train. She was small and painfully thin. Her shining straight mouse-coloured hair was parted in the middle and reached down to her waist; moving one heavy curtain of it aside from her face, she peered out at us with a perfectly self-possessed smile. She wore black stockings, laddered, a very short black overcoat, and apparently nothing else. Her eyes were heavily made-up and she wore no lipstick.

'You must be Lucy Logan,' said my mother, moving towards her.

'I'm afraid I must be early,' she said. 'Or late.'

Alexander, who had been holding the door open for us to leave the dining-room, now saw her and came forward to make some introductions.

'How did you get here?' he asked her. 'I thought the Webbs were bringing you.'

'I came in my bubble,' she said: 'I thought it might be useful to have it here.'

Looking out of the windows we saw that there was indeed a tiny white bubble car sitting outside the front door.

'I'll get your luggage out,' said Alexander.

'It's all here,' she said.

'You had to carry it in yourself,' said my mother. 'I'm so sorry. I can't think what can have happened to Angelo.'

'I just walked in, I'm afraid,' said Lucy Logan. 'I didn't ring. I don't know why.'

She declined the offer of food but said she would like a bath. Alexander carried her luggage upstairs. It consisted of an enormous portable gramophone, a large box of records and a diminutive attaché case. As she followed my mother across the hall to the staircase she put one hand slightly before her and touched the pillars as she passed them so that she gave the impression of feeling her way from pillar to pillar; but at the staircase she seemed to recover and skipped up it in little darts behind my mother.

'Drunk already,' hissed Kitty Newcome.

But when Alexander came downstairs again, and could be questioned on this point, he said, 'Oh, Lord, no, she never touches alcohol. She's incredibly short-sighted, that's all, and won't wear her glasses.'

'And what about the luggage?' Kitty asked. 'Was that really a gramophone? And hasn't she got any clothes?'

'They're in that little case. She takes the gramophone everywhere because she has to have it in her bedroom. She likes to have it on the whole time, with the latest hit tunes. Most of the time she dances to it.'

'She dances most of the time?' said Kitty. 'But doesn't she ever see anybody then?'

'Oh, yes, it all goes on at the same time,' said Alexander.

'And eating and sleeping?' said Kitty.

'She hardly does,' said Alexander.

We were having coffee upstairs in the library because the downstairs rooms were sparsely furnished in readiness for the party, and as we went up we heard the throb of music from Lucy Logan's room. Kitty turned to me and said excitedly, 'My dear, it's the New Woman. How too fascinating. We can't possibly compete.'

Much later, when we were all downstairs waiting for people to arrive, she reappeared wearing a short mauve skirt and a black *décolleté* sweater: she still had on the black laddered stockings.

'I do love your stockings,' said Kitty.

'They're tights,' she said, briskly lifting her skirt to show the truth of this statement.

Delighted, Mike Newcome moved over to her and rather ponderously asked her what she did in London.

'I do social work in the East End,' she said. 'D'you think there's any lemonade anywhere?'

Mike hurried off to get her some and Kitty murmured to me, 'You see, he's fallen for her already.'

Then Moyra Ramage, looking flustered, led in her large, and to her unknown, party. Her husband turned out to be a pale donnish figure who had however a gleam in his eye and seemed to be enjoying himself rather more than she was. Their party included Kate Flower, who was wearing black stockings which did not suit her nearly so well as they did Lucy Logan, and Leopold von Radwitz, whom I had not seen since we had been in Italy. I began a conversation with him but found it hard to follow because he was already exceedingly drunk: he went off to dance with Moyra Ramage, who looked even more uneasy.

The band, which consisted of six apparently hostile West Indians, was good, and the floor became crowded as more and more people arrived. By twelve o'clock the party could have been said to be going with a swing. I could see my mother glancing anxiously at Lewis as they stood by the door greeting the last arrivals, and thought that the fears she had expressed to me in the car coming down were probably going to be realized. Whether people had felt they needed more alcoholic encouragement than usual before they could face the drive from London, or whether it was something to do with the feeling which seemed to be abroad that we were there to celebrate my mother's triumph in capturing her millionaire, or whether again it was simply the 'Good old Essex, she doesn't mind anything' attitude which I had never been able to understand in relation to my beautiful and aloof mother, or whether it was pure chance, the fact remained that someone was vomiting in the rosebed before half the guests had arrived, and the supposedly stabilizing influence of the large quantities of delicious food came far too late.

I moved over to talk to my mother.

'How is it?' she said. 'I'm going to move away from here in a minute. I don't think anyone else is coming. Or are they? Who's this?'

Four nondescript looking men in good and rather similar suits were giving their coats to Angelo.

'My dear, who on earth are they?' said my mother. 'They look like private detectives.'

'They are,' said Lewis, going into the hall to greet them.

There was a shadow of genuine anxiety behind the mock alarm in my mother's eyes as she turned to me and said, 'What can he mean? D'you suppose they're business friends?'

But now a big black-haired man was arriving shepherding before him two brilliantly pretty girls. Their greetings to my mother were cut short by three or four young men who rushed eagerly up to him saying, 'Harry! How splendid to see you. My dear fellow,' and more quietly, 'Are we going to have a game? Brought the chips I hope? What about it?' and 'James will play. Longford's here. Johnny Shell will play.'

My mother said, 'It might keep Lewis amused. He likes gambling. Come with me and see if we can persuade a few more people to go through into the other room and eat.'

I followed her, but almost immediately a handsome man whom I hardly knew appeared at her side saying, 'Darling, am I finally going to be able to talk to you? Come and dance,' and they went off together.

I danced with Alexander. We talked about Lucy Logan, who had been dancing without pause all evening. She moved in a peculiarly angular and twitchy way in time to the music, giving an occasional hop or skip, or going for a moment or two into an ordinary jiving or rock and roll motion, talking some of the time but mostly just smiling a fixed but amiable smile.

'She's nice, you know,' said Alexander. 'In spite of being an interesting phenomenon. You'd like her. Kate Flower's gone off though, hasn't she? I used to think her rather attractive.'

'Mr. Ramage the famous painter still does,' I said.

'Yes, that's true,' he said. 'I hadn't noticed that. Yes, they are going it, aren't they? Leopold's in a bad mood. He seemed to be picking a fight with Johnny Spencer but someone stopped them.'

A bearded person in a green open-necked shirt trod heavily on my foot. When I had recovered I asked Alexander who he was. 'God knows,' he said. 'Your dear mother did her usual fatal thing of saying airily to people, "Bring everyone".'

'Why is everyone so drunk?' I asked.

'Oh, are they?' he said. It seemed a natural state to him: I noticed he was looking greenish himself. And then I found I had a sort of affection for his various pallors, and thought how very well-known he had seemed to me, and so I stopped dancing rather abruptly saying, 'I promised to send some people through to eat,' and went into the crowded dining-room.

It was already fairly full and I had been there for several minutes before I noticed Moyra Ramage sitting by herself in a corner with a plate of fruit salad on her knee. I went over to talk to her.

She was wearing a yellow mohair sack dress which made her look enormous but not unimposing. She immediately began to tell me how much she was enjoying the party.

'This part of the world has never known anything like it,' she said. 'It's going to be wonderful having you as neighbours. I was just sitting down for a moment's pause. I've been terribly greedy about the food, too. It's heavenly.' I think she meant that. She went on about the house, and how beautiful it was, and about the panelling. 'I was enjoying being able to have a quiet look at it. It's lovely of course, isn't it?' I agreed that it was, and she went on to say again how lovely it was and how she wished there had been some in their house which was the right period but, alas, all the panelling had been taken out. She was not thinking about the panelling but about her pale husband next door with Kate Flower's hot young body pressed against his in the safety of the stirring crowd on the dance floor. And instead of all those compliments, she meant, 'Why do you have to come here and lure away my husband with your drink and your frivolity, and your hateful corrupt town bodies, when he needs rest and quiet for his work and someone who Understands his Art, and can bear his children and bring them up to run barefoot in the fields and tame wild hares. . . .'

I wanted to say that I knew what she meant, that I knew about those sort of torments, but I did not know how to, and so we sat side by side eating fruit salad and talking about the panelling.

Fortunately we were observed by my mother, who introduced John Miller to Moyra Ramage, which, since she had been his dinner hostess, reminded him of his obligations and he asked her to dance. Mike Newcome then came up to complain that Lucy Logan was dull, stupid, rude and affected: she had evidently not responded to his advances. I danced with him for some-time, until he led me out into the garden and tried to kiss me. We were interrupted by the Spencers, who were bickering because she wanted to go home and he didn't. Johnny Spencer and Mike began a conversation about cars, and I left them on the pretext of having to see whether the band were being given drinks.

As I came into the drawing-room I noticed that Kate Flower had been detached from Mr. Ramage and had just finished a dance with one of the sober-suited men whom Lewis had said were detectives. I went up to them, hoping to find out some more about him, but as I approached he left her, apparently to fetch her a drink. I asked her who he was.

'I was just going to ask you,' she said. 'I didn't hear his name. He works in Lloyds or something. He seemed quite nice.'

'Someone said he looked like a private detective,' I said.

'My dear, I hope he's not,' she said, looking alarmed.

'I was wildly indiscreet. You don't really think he is, do you? What would he be doing here? Seeing that no one steals anything? In that case it wouldn't matter what I said, would it? Oh, dear.'

'What did you tell him?' I asked. 'All about your love life?'

'Not mine, exactly,' she said. 'But it couldn't matter, could it? I mean detectives aren't interested in gossip are they?'

'Who did you gossip about? Lewis?'

'Well, not him so much,' she said, looking embarrassed. 'Oh, dear. I always talk too much when I'm drunk.'

'I suppose you talked about my mother?'

'Well, yes,' she said. 'But everything I said was common knowledge. You don't think he was from the Press, do you?'

'Did you talk about Alexander?'

'Of course, that's what I meant,' she said. 'But after all everyone's been talking about it. I mean, since she got him the job and then got engaged to Lewis and then went on living with Alexander. But it would be libel if they printed it, wouldn't it? I mean, how could they put it?'

'I'm sure he wasn't from the Press,' I said. 'And of course he's not a private detective, that was only somebody's joke. Actually I think I've seen him before at my mother's parties.'

'Thank God for that,' said Kate. 'You are naughty. You terrified me.'

'You're having a wild success with the famous painter,' I said.

'It's too embarrassing. He won't leave me alone,' said Kate, looking gratified. 'He wants to paint me.'

'Is that all?' I said.

'My dear, you have got coarse,' she said. 'It must be Brussels.'

'All those bloated burghers, yes,' I said. 'Anyway, here he is coming back to you.'

Mr. Ramage, a hectic flush now garnishing his pale cheeks, approached and brusquely asked Kate to dance. As soon as they reached the dance floor he folded her into a clamped embrace. She rolled her eyes at me over his shoulder, but seemed to be enjoying it.

I looked at a clock and found to my surprise that it was not yet one: it seemed much later. The party looked as if it had been going on for hours. The dancing was either vigorous or amorous, mostly the former, there were one or two male figures in attitudes of slumped abandon round the walls, and there seemed to be a good many small quarrels going on. Two very young pink-faced men whom I knew vaguely but whose names I had forgotten were arguing sweatily in a corner about some disagreement which had started at the *chemin de fer* table in the other room, and I saw Mike Newcome and Leopold involved in some sort of dispute. They were both flushed and talking loudly, Leopold's black hair now flopping over his forehead. He looked the more drunk, Mike the angrier. Finally they went out of the room together and one or two others followed them anxiously, I suppose with the idea of preventing a fight.

'Where's Lewis? Have you seen him?' My mother suddenly appeared beside me. 'I haven't seen him for hours.'

'Nor have I,' I said.

'Do see if you can find him anywhere,' she said. 'And tell him I'm looking for him.'

'He'll turn up, don't worry,' said the same handsome man, whose name I could not remember. 'I want to go on dancing with you.'

'Oh, John,' she said, as if she were bored with him. They moved off all the same among the dancers, and he was brushing back her hair with his hand because it was untidy and laying his cheek against it while she shut her eyes, looking faintly irritated.

Later I went upstairs to my room. It was the first bedroom one came to, a little room before one reached the upstairs landing. My mother had made it pretty and it had a tiny bathroom of its own and a lovely view from its window. I had turned on the light before I realized that there was someone in there: I turned it off quickly without seeing whose bodies they were on the bed. I heard a gasp, and a muffled man's voice saying, 'It's all right.'

As I came out again, shutting the door behind me, Lewis passed me on the stairs. He was going down hurriedly, looking stern, and did not see me. I followed him slowly, wondering where to go, and wandered aimlessly into the now half-empty dining-room: noticing Moyra Ramage talking to a man I did not know and looking tired I avoided her because I could not think of anything to say to her, and went out into the hall again.

Suddenly, to my surprise, I heard the strains of 'God Save the Queen' played in a slightly uneven manner, as if the band were not quite sure of the tune. They played it loudly and slowly, however, so that there could be no question of anyone not hearing it.

A large angry figure in dark glasses appeared in the doorway of the dining-room. 'What the Hell's that?' he said. A discontented rumble seemed to wander over the groups of people standing in the hall. Then one of the pink-faced young men came hurrying out of the drawing-room saying, 'It's "God Save the King". He's stopped it. I saw him telling the band to play it. He's stopped the party. It was him.'

'Who, for God's sake?' said the big man irritably.

'Ogden,' said the youth. 'Lewis Ogden. He told them to play, "God Save the King".'

Someone behind me said, 'It's only half-past one. I thought we were going on all night.'

'It's a bit hard,' said a girl, 'coming all this way. . .'

Everyone seemed to be making towards the drawing-room. As I followed I saw Kate Flower and Mr. Ramage hurrying down the stairs. Kate was looking calm, but he seemed feverish and ruffled. I supposed they had been in my room. I saw Moyra Ramage approaching them from the other end of the hall as I went into the drawing-room. I was just in time to see my mother go up to Lewis as he stood near the band. She looked angry but I could not hear what she said; and then I saw them go out of the room together. I followed them as best I could through the crowd of disgruntled people which had now collected and came up with them at the back of the hall in a small passageway near the door leading to the kitchen. They were talking in quiet angry voices: my mother's face was white in the semi-darkness.

'If you choose to be so absurdly melodramatic about it,' she was saying.

'You'll go,' Lewis said firmly. 'All of you.'

My mother turned as I came up and walked past me, apparently without seeing me. I heard her say sweetly to someone behind me, 'Too sad, isn't it? We ought to have warned you – but Lewis is working so hard at the moment. Sweet of you to come. . .' and then she swirled upstairs and out of sight.

I was still standing facing Lewis, who had not moved. He said, 'I've told them all to go,' and walked past me. I saw Alexander running upstairs after my mother.

Slowly people began to leave. The band packed up; the bottles of champagne were carried out of sight: Angelo, looking bewildered, was carrying coats about. Then I noticed the sober-suited men again. They were moving quietly through the crowd, chivying people towards the doors. I saw one of them supporting Leopold, who was holding a blood-stained handkerchief to his cheek, out of the house and into a car, and another came up to the pink-faced young man who had been so agitated by the sight of Lewis telling the band to play the National Anthem, and who was standing near me.

'Excuse me,' he said, deferentially but firmly. 'I've been asked to see that everybody's all right for transport. Have you got your car?'

'Yes, yes, I've got a car,' said the young man, irritably.

'Oh, good. Perhaps I can help you find your coat, and the rest of your party.'

'Well, yes, O.K., O.K.,' the young man said, going towards the coats. 'We're all here. Except Mr. Shell. You can find Mr. Shell if you must do something.'

And then a moment later Johnny Shell came wandering out and the man hurried up to him to say, 'Excuse me, sir, I've been asked to tell you that your party are ready to leave and are waiting by the car.'

And so, gradually but efficiently, the reluctant guests were persuaded to leave. I saw Lewis going round and speaking to each of the people who had been supposed to be spending the night at Mowle, and realized that they were being turned out too. I did not hear what he was saying to them, but they seemed to be taking it fairly calmly. I went upstairs to pack.

So we were out. Months ago in Italy, Leopold had said, 'One day he'll learn. Then we shall all be out.' 'We may be out,' Marcus Edge had said. 'But she won't.' Marcus had been wrong. We were all out, even my mother.

As I went upstairs, I came face to face with her. She may have been waiting for me. She looked white and bleak.

'I'm going to pack,' I said.

'You're not coming with us,' she said sharply. 'You're far too dangerous a person to have around. You'll have to find somewhere else to spread your harm.'

'What do you mean?' I said.

'Don't look so innocent, for God's sake,' she said. 'The one thing I never thought you'd be is so bloody deceitful. I suppose you've known about Alexander and me for months and waited to choose your moment to spring it on Lewis, ruining everything for everybody. What a little teenage monster I've sprung after all.'

'I didn't tell him,' I said. 'Besides, he knew before this. He knew two weeks ago.'

'He did, did he?' she said, most venomously. 'And how do you know? He told you I suppose? Asked your advice? I see. Oh, God help you, Vanessa. All I say is keep out of my way now, just don't let me see you for the next few weeks, just keep out of my way.'

'But I . . . where shall I go?' I said.

'How do I know?' she said. 'Why didn't you think of that before? What do you expect me to do? Forgive you or something?' She broke off and turning quickly ran back up the stairs. Looking round I saw Lewis approaching.

'She thinks you told me,' he said.

I nodded.

'I'll tell her,' he said, and went on up the stairs.

I went into my room and sat on my bed without moving.

After some time Lewis tapped on the door and came in.

'She won't believe me just at the moment,' he said. 'I think you'd better stay here for the night.'

'Oh, I can't,' I said.

'Yes, you can,' he said, 'and in a day or two she'll realize her mistake.'

'You don't want me,' I said. 'You want us all to go.'

'Of course I want you,' he said. 'It will be all right. You go to bed. Don't worry.'

He went out again.

I stayed sitting on my bed. I heard feet passing my door going downstairs: someone banged a suitcase against the wall: no one came in, and gradually the sounds faded and no more cars started in the drive. Images danced through my mind. The insistent music still echoed there and the dancers gyrated, embracing, in my mind's eye: I saw the angle of my mother's head as the man John murmured into her hair, and Alexander looking at her across some girl's untidy head burrowing into his shoulder: and Kate and Mr. Ramage, my bed still warm from the heat of them, and Moyra Ramage talking about the panelling with her big dog eyes speaking of other things, and the black-haired man sweating over the shemmy shoe and someone shouting 'Banco' and the pink young men whispering about cheating, and the little dark girl whose dress had fallen off one shoulder and whose half-exposed breast looked faintly grubby as she bickered with a young swaying man at the foot of the stairs, and the two other girls I had seen in the bathroom, one holding the other's head and saying, 'It was all that whisky after dinner: why don't you put your finger down your throat?' and it all led back again to my mother and to that kiss all that long time ago, to those two twisting bodies and all they had conjured up.

Much later I heard a step on the stairs, which faltered outside my door and then stopped. There was a pause, while I hoped he would go away, while I prayed he would come in; then there was a knock.

'Come in,' I said.

314

'I saw your light,' said Lewis. 'I hoped you would be in bed, and asleep.'

'Sorry,' I said.

He sat down on a chair. 'They've all gone,' he said.

'Oh,' I said.

'I had to do it,' he said. 'I couldn't let them stay.'

'No,' I said.

'It's been an unfortunate episode I'm afraid,' he said. I noticed that he did not look unhappy, but alert and wakeful, as if he had been enjoying himself.

After a long pause I said, 'Why did you wait so long? After we saw them I mean?'

'I wanted to find out the extent of my foolishness,' he said, 'before doing anything rash. It suddenly seemed that I was the victim of a plot, and I had to find out its extent. Those men you saw tonight told me everything I wanted to know.'

'I see.' I thought of Kate Flower's conversation. 'You waited for them upstairs – that's where you were all the time, up in the library, waiting for their reports. How strange somehow, waiting up there.'

'How else could I find out where I stood, what I was?' he said. 'They told me how all those people saw me, in what manner I was being used, and what was common knowledge about – the people concerned.'

I remembered what Alexander had said about Lewis being ruthless to people who had tried to cheat him, and asked, 'What will you do to them – to the people concerned?'

'My dear,' he said. 'Nothing. What could I do? Except come to my senses.'

'They aren't bad. . . .' I began hesitantly.

'Of course not,' he said. 'The fault was all mine. In expecting something quite different.'

'I didn't know about it,' I said.

'I won't ask you anything,' he said.

'I didn't know,' I said.

'I know you didn't,' he said. 'I'm sorry. I'm afraid this has been upsetting for you.'

'No, no. . . .' I said.

We sat for some time in silence.

'Won't you go to bed?' said Lewis.

'Yes,' I said, without moving.

I felt waves of self-pity beginning to mount in me.

'There were people on my bed,' I said, 'I came in and found them. The bed's warm.'

'When did they go?' he said.

'With the others,' I said.

'That was some time ago,' he said. 'I'm sorry about this. Please don't let it distress you. It's only one way of looking at things you know, what you're thinking now – it's not the whole picture.'

'No, of course not,' I said, still staring at the floor, stiff with tiredness and tearfulness.

'I shall go out of the room now,' he said firmly. 'And come back in ten minutes, by which time you must be in bed.'

He left. I undressed and got into bed. He returned carrying Marius.

'I found him wandering about,' he said, giving him to me and sitting down on the edge of the bed. 'I know very well what you are feeling but it won't always seem so bad. There is that way of seeing people but it's only a facet. I don't want you to worry. Nothing's going to be so very changed.'

I stroked Marius. All those bodies came back to my mind, the couples shifting, mouthing, the note in the voices; and at the same time I wanted to throw myself into Lewis's arms, and because it was me and because it was Lewis it seemed to me to be quite different.

'Now you must go to sleep,' he said, 'and don't worry. You can stay here as long as you like, naturally. Good night.'

'Good night,' I said.

14

THE time that followed is quite detached in my memory from what happened before or after. It was an interlude, bearing no relation to reality, a pause in time which only someone still a stranger to responsibility could have relaxed as I did, lolling idly in the apparent safety of my solitude and Lewis's protection.

That Sunday I saw him only at meals, and we did not talk about what had happened. There was no silence or constraint because Lewis could talk endlessly about general subjects without seeming to be doing it only to avoid more dangerous topics. In the evening he told me to stay at Mowle for the time being, and that he would try to speak to my mother while he was in London. I said that I might go back to Brussels for a time and would write to Primrose.

'That might be a good plan,' he said, 'but don't do anything in a hurry. I'm leaving early in the morning and shall be back on Friday night. It's possible you may hear from your mother in the meantime.'

'I may,' I said, 'but she didn't seem likely to change her mind very quickly. Anyway I'll write to Primrose to see if there would still be room for me in her flat. It's very kind of you to let me stay here.'

'No, no,' he said. 'I feel responsible. I precipitated all this into your life.'

'I don't want to be on your conscience,' I said. 'I'm all right. Especially here.'

'You can keep an eye on things for me while I'm away,' he said. 'See if you can't make them finish that lily pond this week. And you can do some more sorting out of the books if you like.'

He was gone by the time I came down the next

morning, and I spent the week there alone, wrapt in comfort and peace and the sudden spring weather and my dreams of Lewis and of a future which should be like this for ever. I wandered round the garden and watched the lily pond being rebuilt and the daffodils coming out and the crocuses dying and the newly planted cherry and almond trees beginning to blossom. I spent hours in the library among Lewis's books which he had not yet sorted out and which I made intermittent attempts to divide into categories. I was so idle and well cared for that I found myself spending happy hours improving my appearance and my clothes, lying in long luxurious baths, changing carefully for dinner though no one saw me except Angelo who served me and Marius who lay on his cushion at my feet. I was perfectly happy.

I heard nothing from my mother. Letters began to arrive for her. They looked like 'thank you' letters from people who had been to the party. I did not forward them because I could not think they would give her much gratification. On Friday morning Lewis telephoned to say that he would be back in time for dinner.

He arrived looking tired. I could see the effect working pleasantly on him of the house, the warmth, the welcome from me.

He told me that Alexander had been waiting in his office when he arrived on Monday, to beg him not to sack him. He had admitted to having taken the job on false pretences but had told Lewis of his interest in it now and of his conviction that he could be useful.

'That's true,' I said. 'He told me all that before there was any question of his losing his job. He likes it. He wants to be like you.'

Lewis looked pleased, and said, 'I'm keeping him. Of course he's useful. There's a big site bang in the middle of London which I'm thinking of buying. He's involved in all the negotiations and he's good at it. Besides, there's another thing that's come up – this textile machinery – I might be going to develop it in the States through a company there in which I have an interest. If things go as I mean them to I shall go over there for some time in the summer and I'd like to take Alexander with me and

leave him there for a couple of years to work on that end.
It would be invaluable experience for him if he's really
aiming at big things. Of course, I know there's another
aspect.'

'What's that?' I asked.

'As regards your mother. . . .'

'You mean she'll lose Alexander?'

'Yes.' He sighed. 'I wonder how glad I am to take my
revenge. It is a revenge. She loses what she thought to
gain from me, and Alexander too. Well. . . .'

'You mean that's why you'll keep him?' I asked.

'No,' he said. 'But it might be. It so well might be that
in some very small measure perhaps it is. At least that's
how, say, your friend Colin would expect me to behave.
Isn't that how he'd see it?'

'Colin is prejudiced,' I said. 'It's all part of his politics.
He thinks capitalists must be wicked.'

'Do you?' he said.

'No,' I said.

He laughed, and said, 'Tell me about the lily pond. Is
it progressing? Shall we turn it into a swimming pool
instead?'

In the morning a pale blue Zephyr convertible arrived.
Lewis took delivery of it with delight, genuine in spite of
his awareness of his own performance as the great man
showing his childish pleasure in simple things. The man
who had brought the car down was overwhelmed by the
magnificent charm of it all, and Lewis smiled at me so
that I felt I was sharing in his game; and then he told me
that the car was to be kept at Mowle as something useful
to run about in. 'You can use it of course as much as you
like.'

I said that I was not sure that I drove well enough and
was afraid of doing it some damage.

'We'll go for a drive now,' he said, 'and you shall try
it. I've just got a couple of telephone calls to make.'

He came out later looking pleased and saying, 'Today's
going very well. Now we can forget all about business.'

'You told me you never did,' I said.

'Then I shall try for the first time today,' he said. 'Shall
we drive to Bath?'

'It's miles,' I said.

'I drive fast,' he said.

We went to Bath, and had lunch there. Lewis hurried through the lunch so as to see the Roman Baths and the Cathedral and the Assembly Rooms before we drove back. We drove slowly through the Spring evening agreeing that none of the houses we passed compared with Mowle.

At dinner I felt sufficiently familiar with him to ask, 'Did you mind very much, about my mother I mean?'

'My pride suffered,' he said, as if he were simply interested to discuss it, 'very badly, and something else, some sort of foolish idea I had which was hopelessly, ridiculously, wrong. You'd hardly believe how wrong it was, because having lived so much more familiarly with people than I have you probably know far more about them. But I didn't realize that then. I don't think anything more fundamental suffered. Perhaps it would have been better for me if it had.'

I said nothing, pleased because he seemed to be saying that he had never been in love with my mother.

'I don't feel I have to worry about it here,' he said. 'My pride, I mean, or the loss of that idea. Which is funny really considering how much the house was hers.'

I did not feel I had to worry either. If someone had said. 'This isn't really happiness,' I might have believed it, or 'You're not in love you know,' I might have agreed. I no longer felt I had to give a name to my state of mind, or question it at all. I simply accepted the situation, the delight and isolation in which I found myself.

Before he left on Sunday evening, Lewis said, 'Incidentally the Press have been ringing up a certain amount. They seemed to know you were here, and Alexander told them you were cataloguing my library. You can refer them to him again if they get on to you. If you hear from Primrose, there's no need to hurry out there unless you particularly want to.'

I said nothing, not knowing what to say.

'I like having you here,' he said. 'There's no need to hurry away.'

'No,' I said. 'Thank you.'

'I'll see you on Friday,' he said, as he got into the back of his big car.

The next day my mother rang up. I did not at first recognize her voice. She began to speak immediately, sounding urgent and strained.

'Vanessa, you've got to do something. You're the only person with any influence. He's got to drop Alexander. Make him do it. Tell him anything you like – tell him the truth. That's all I mean. Tell him the truth – you know. It's not hard Vanessa, just tell him that Alexander started the whole thing – he did, you know how he plots, you heard him, you told me only the other day how shocked you were – well, tell it to Lewis, tell him. Alexander started everything. He came here to this house because we were short of money and didn't know what sort of person he was, battened on us, seduced me. . . .'

'Oh no. . .' I said.

'Seduced you then – I don't care what you tell him. Anyway I thought he was quite different, he misled me, tell Lewis, got a hold over me. . .'

'No. . .'

'Stop saying no. Tell it in your own words, only tell it. It's true. He behaved monstrously. Forcing me to get him a job with Lewis, blackmailing me. . .'

'Did he?' I asked.

'I was afraid he might,' she said. 'Anyway the point is Vanessa – Oh, why are you so hostile? Don't you understand?'

'But what am I to do?' I asked.

'Make him get rid of Alexander,' she said. 'It's ridiculous that he should keep him on after what's happened. Stop him taking him to America. . .' To my complete amazement she began to sob. The sound came harshly over the line and filled me with horror instead of pity.

'But surely,' I said, 'wouldn't it be best if he did go, if that's how you feel about him – if they both went? Then you could forget all about the whole thing.'

'Forget?' she sobbed. 'How can I forget? Oh, God, how little you understand. I need him, don't you see? For God's sake when it's so easy for you why can't you do something about it?'

'But I'm afraid he never – I mean, isn't it all over?'

'No, no, how can it be all over, so suddenly. You don't understand. We're lovers.'

'Oh,' I said.

'What are you saying "Oh" for? Put it some other way, then, if you want to. It's no use pretending to be shocked. You know that's what the whole thing was about. You told Lewis yourself, for Heaven's sake. All I'm asking is that you should now save something from the wreck you've made.'

'You mean it's Alexander you want?' I said. 'Not Lewis?'

'Yes, yes, yes, of course.'

'I thought you were talking about Lewis.'

'What d'you mean? When?'

'When you were saying you needed him.'

'Oh, Vanessa,' she began to laugh hysterically, 'really, honestly, for the schemer you've shown yourself, aren't you a little obtuse?'

'I didn't scheme,' I said.

'Look, for Heaven's sake,' she said. 'We can't discuss that now. No, Lewis doesn't matter at all. He was just a mistake, an idea which didn't work out. But Alexander does matter.' She was no longer sobbing but her voice sounded strained, a tone higher than usual and immensely tired. 'I'm not young, Vanessa. These things didn't matter in the same way when I was. But at my age you don't have so many chances.'

'You mean you're in love with Alexander?' I asked.

'Oh, dear, you are so blunt,' she said. 'What can I say? You don't know anything. It's never just love. Alexander is good for me, he amuses me, he keeps me young, I want him. Why shouldn't I have him?' Her voice began to quaver again.

'But then, for that, another person might do as well,' I said, trying to be reasonable.

'Oh, my Christ, what have I done to deserve this?' she suddenly yelled. 'What are you? Why are you being like this?'

'I'm not, I'm not,' I said quickly, 'I'm only trying to find out how things are. You see Lewis told me that Alexander had been to see him to say that he liked working with him and wanted to stay, and that he was going to keep him. I don't see that there's much I can do.'

She was now very cold.

'I've told you what you can do. You don't want to do it, that's all. Lewis has always liked you. I suppose you are in love with him and that's why you've turned him against me. In that case he'll no doubt be flattered and touched, so it would be quite easy for you to turn him against Alexander. At least you could try.'

'But if Alexander wants to stay with Lewis?' I began.

There was a pause, then the tired voice went on, 'That is the reason why I'm having to appeal to you in this way. Can't you see how humiliating that is for me, in view of the way you've behaved and the state. . .', a wild quaver suddenly, 'the state of our relations now, when I used to think . . . I'm your mother, Vanessa, your mother. . .'

'Please believe me, I never told Lewis anything,' I said. 'Please. I didn't even know myself until a week or two ago. I had nothing to do with his finding out, nothing.'

'What does it matter?' said the voice. 'What does it matter? I just asked you to do something for me, but if you can't, or won't, that's that.'

'I'll try,' I said. 'I will try.'

'Good-bye,' she said.

I walked slowly out into the garden, which had already in a few weeks acquired what might have been a year's load of associations, was full of my walk with Lewis across the lawn to look in through the window on my mother and Alexander, and the night of the dance on the dark terrace, and my wanderings of the last week, my private dream.

For a day or two I did nothing but turn over and over in my mind this new concept of my mother. I had never imagined her weak or in need before: as for what I now condemned in her, it had seemed her opposite. I could not name what it was that I condemned, and which I suppose was some lack of dignity more than anything else, but I knew that I did condemn it and this frightened me. Then there was the idea quite suddenly of her being depraved, of her being an ageing beauty craving for young lovers, and this was even more new. If she had been angry at the loss of what she had hoped for from Lewis I should have recognized her more easily, but that she should sob, should wail, should sound so old, for Alexander, that was amazingly strange. Then there was the fact that I was her daughter. I still could not tear my thoughts away from myself, and so I thought of my feeling for Lewis and wondered whether I were hereditarily over-endowed with feelings of luxury and concupiscence and whether I should have a long chain of lovers and end an aged harridan buying young men. I looked in the mirror and thought of my face grown old and thought, I am her daughter. At the same time I felt huge reserves, huge untapped tanks of loyalty and love, heavy in me, and saw my devotion creeping round Lewis quite sure and green; but I thought, I must not trust it, I must hide it, I must wait, perhaps for years. And then I thought, perhaps it's a bad thing, this 'love', something to be ashamed of, not good as we have been taught, but that was exciting, and made it all seem easier to bear; and so that thought in its turn must be suspect. So the days passed until Lewis's return.

One day a reporter rang up. He said he wanted to confirm that the engagement between my mother and Lewis had been broken off. I said that I knew nothing about it, and suggested that he telephone my mother.

'And do you yourself expect to see your mother within the next few days?'

'I don't know,' I said. 'Probably.'

'You're returning to London, then?' he asked.

'Oh yes,' I said. 'Some time.'

'Not in the immediate future though?'

'Well, I don't know exactly. . . .'

'You expect to go on staying with Mr. Ogden?' he went on.

'Mr. Ogden is in London,' I said. 'I'm cataloguing the library.'

'Mr. Ogden has an extensive library?'

'Oh yes.'

'How many volumes I wonder? Could you give me an idea?'

'I don't know, I'm afraid,' I said.

'And are you using any particular system for cataloguing the books?'

'Any particular system?' I said. 'No, not really. I mean, just by subjects, and chronologically.'

'I see,' he said.

'I'm sorry I can't be more helpful,' I said. 'Goodbye.'

The conversation worried me slightly, but I did not think I had said anything indiscreet.

Lewis arrived earlier that Friday, in time for lunch.

'I wanted to see the garden,' he said.

After lunch we went for a long walk.

'I never dreamt this place would be such a joy to me, such a refuge,' he said extravagantly, looking down on the house from the hill. 'I shall spend more and more time here.'

'You may get tired of it,' I said.

'I don't think so,' he said.

This time we began to talk about me. He asked me about my childhood, the schools I had been to and how much I had seen of my mother. I told him about my Uncle Vere and his wife, and how much I liked their life, though my mother found it boring. Then, the next day, we had a conversation about Jean; and afterwards I said, 'And now we've covered everything,' and Lewis, whom I had expected to laugh, said quite seriously, 'Yes. I'm glad.'

It was then that he told me about the perfect secretary Jean had been, and how he had thought that she could be a perfect wife, in just the same unobtrusive, efficient, unfailingly mild way. 'Of course it was a bad basis on which to marry anyone,' he said. 'Because that's not what one wants of a wife. And even then her extreme submissiveness, not just to me but to life in general, and her willingness, I think even her eagerness, to be hurt and to suffer in silence, had begun to annoy me, but I thought they would pass. I hadn't realized how fundamental to her whole nature they were. Nor how obstinate she could be at the same time. I know you thought I made Jean unhappy. I suppose I did, but she was unhappy before, she's temperamentally unhappy – I suppose the word is morbid. I don't know whether anyone could make her happy, but I rather doubt it. For one thing it would need someone as extremely gentle as she herself, and I don't know whether such a person exists. Anyway if there were a pair of them the world would ruin them in no time.'

Sunday was our last day. The morning was fine, but in the afternoon it rained. One of the Sunday papers had a paragraph saying that my mother and Lewis had announced that they would not now marry.

'A close friend of Lady Essex's told me that she and Mr. Ogden were still friends, and that Vanessa Cowper, Lady Essex's *ex-débutante* daughter, was staying with Mr. Ogden in Wiltshire at the moment. Miss Cowper said on the telephone a few days ago, "I have no particular plans for returning to London at the moment. I am cataloguing the library here. I do not know how many books there are. I am following no particular system in cataloguing them." Lady Essex said last night that she did not expect to see her daughter for some time.'

Lewis swore when he read it, and seemed unwilling to let me see it when I asked what it was. Then he handed it over, and watched me as I read it.

'I'm afraid it's my fault,' I said. 'I shouldn't have talked to that man on the telephone. But it doesn't look too bad, does it? Does it matter?'

'She shouldn't have said she didn't expect to see you,' said Lewis.

'She can't have known why they were asking,' I said. 'Otherwise I'm sure she'd have stopped them putting this in. It's the sort of thing she can always do. I'm sorry.'

'What for?' he said, rather angrily.

'Well, I mean, perhaps it's a bad thing, for you,' I could not quite understand why he seemed so upset.

'For me?' he said, getting up from the breakfast table. 'No, of course not, of course not.'

He went out of the room. A little later I wandered out into the garden because the sun was shining, and he followed me from the house. We walked together towards the rose garden.

'I'm afraid I've been selfish in keeping you here,' he

said. 'I believe perhaps until the whole thing blows over you would do better to go.'

'Yes,' I said, quite calmly. 'I will. It would be better.'

We walked in silence for some moments.

'Where will you go?' he asked.

I thought, he doesn't want me to go, but looking away said quietly, 'To Brussels.'

'I wish you needn't go,' he said. 'Damn the newspapers. Do you want to go?'

'No,' I said.

'No,' he said. 'I don't want you to go either.'

We walked on.

'Let's not think about it,' he said in a more normal tone. 'Let's forget it now, just for today. Can you do that?'

'Yes,' I said. 'I think so.'

'Well, then, we will,' he said.

But we had taken another of our unmapped journeys towards each other; and the day passed in a haze of things unsaid, movements not made, issues avoided; a day of waiting. In the afternoon it began to rain heavily. Lewis stayed with me in the drawing-room instead of disappearing upstairs to work as he usually did. We had tea and afterwards sat in front of the fire without much conversation. At dinner we talked idly, mainly for the sake of Angelo; but afterwards we sat in the drawing-room in silence, and at last stared at each other.

Lewis got to his feet and said stiffly, 'I believe I ought to write some letters,' though he made no move to leave the room.

I said, 'Primrose will let me stay with her for a bit. I might take a job there again.'

For some reason I had stood up when he did, and now he took one of my hands and held it in both of his. After a moment he bent down slightly and lifted my hand so that the back of it touched his forehead. His skin felt soft and hot. Then he put my hand carefully back at my side and turned towards the fireplace.

'Yes,' he said, looking into the fire. 'Perhaps it would be best. You'll want to let her know you're coming, which means you can't go before Wednesday or Thursday. I've got to go to London early tomorrow morning and I'm spending Tuesday night in Manchester. I was supposed to stay on Wednesday too but I can get all my business done that morning. Then I can come down here on Wednesday night and take you to the plane or boat or whatever it is the next morning. Would that do? I want to see you before you go.'

'Yes,' I said.

'Vanessa, I believe I am afraid to talk to you,' he said, turning towards me again. 'I'm so afraid of doing some damage. Perhaps by Wednesday I shall be able to be a bit more coherent. I think I'll go upstairs and do some work now, and then I'll see you on Wednesday. Will that be all right?'

'Yes,' I said.

He went to the door, and paused there.

I said, 'You will come, before I go?'

For the first time he smiled as if he were happy.

'Of course I'll come, of course, of course, of course. Good night.'

He had gone the next morning before I woke up. I could hardly push my thoughts beyond next Wednesday, but I wrote to Primrose telling her to expect me on Thursday and walked down to post the letter, thinking only that Lewis had looked so shaken, had stared at me so intently, that he must love me, that we were in love.

The telephone was ringing when I came back into the house. I lifted the receiver and heard Jean's voice saying, 'Vanessa? Is that you, Vanessa?' She sounded more hurried than usual but not otherwise different.

'Jean,' I said, 'where are you? In London? I came to see you at the shop but you'd left.'

'I've been living with my mother,' she said. 'As a matter of fact I'm not far away from where you are at the moment. Vanessa, listen, I had to phone you. I read the paper. Are you with Lewis then?'

'I'm here, yes,' I said. 'Lewis has gone to London this morning.'

'I see,' she said. 'But it's all over between him and your mother?'

'Oh yes,' I said.

'I suppose then, well, I mean, all those fancy ideas he

had, about the aristocracy and such, they're all finished too?'

'I suppose so,' I said. 'I think they probably have been for some time, I don't know.'

'He'll be just as lonely again, then,' she said.

There was a pause. I was wondering what she meant. The thought flashed across my mind that she might be hoping he would need her again. But he had never needed her.

'The papers put it in a funny way,' she said. 'Does it mean, your still being there, does it mean you. . . ? Well, I used to think you were like Colin, disapproving of Lewis.'

'I didn't know him then,' I said.

'You mean are aren't on my side any more,' she said.

'On your side?' I asked. 'But, Jean, have you got a side? I mean, I thought – Colin said you were glad about the divorce. I thought it was all over ages ago. . . .'

'Yes, it's all over,' she said.

'But what do you mean, I'm not on your side?' I said. 'Of course I'm on your side. But I'm not against Lewis.'

'But you're under his spell,' said Jean. 'Not like you used to be.'

'I'm not under his spell,' I said. 'I've been through all that. I've know him a long time now. I'm not under any spell. I just. . .'

'You mean you're in love with him.'

I said nothing, feeling foolishly happy because the words had been said.

'You're living with him there, then,' Jean's voice went on, wondering.

'I'm going to Brussels on Thursday,' I said. 'I'll be there for weeks probably. I only stayed on here because my mother didn't want me in her mews after the quarrel with Lewis. That's all.'

'But you love him. You just said so.'

'I didn't say so,' I said. 'But anyway what's wrong with people loving each other? There's no changing of sides involved. I don't know what you mean.'

'Loving each other,' Jean said. I could not tell what expression there was in her quiet voice.

'Jean, I can't talk on the telephone,' I said. 'If you're near, why don't you come and see me? Lewis isn't here.'

'Yes, I might come,' her voice sounded farther away now. 'I might come. I'll ring you again.' The receiver clicked.

She was staying at the Bear Inn in the village, half a mile away, but I did not know that until later. While I was walking that afternoon on the hill above the house, still in my dream, my private world, she was not far away, striding through the fields and woods for miles without pause, to return exhausted at the end of the day. We might have met, though I suppose it would have made no difference if we had.

15

TUESDAY was the Italians' evening out. I had told Mrs.
Hodge, who usually cooked the dinner on Tuesdays,
that she need not bother to come that day, and had boiled
myself an egg and gone up to bed early. It did not occur
to me to lock any of the doors before I went up.

I had not yet undressed when I heard the front door
bang. I suppose it was about nine o'clock. I thought, he's
come a day early, and ran to the top of the stairs. A figure
was lurching across the hall, reeling stupidly between the
pillars. I thought, it's some drunk who's got in, what a
fool I was not to lock the door. When she reached the
foot of the stairs I saw that it was Jean. Clutching at the
banisters, she leant on them heavily and was sick.

Without moving, I watched her begin to climb painfully
up the stairs, still clawing and reeling. Halfway up she
vomited again; and then again. I thought, Lewis's staircase, and then, Lewis is lost to me. She had not yet seen
me because her head was down, but she came on towards
me. After a moment I went down to meet her.

Her face was greenish-white and covered with sweat.
She said, 'I had to see you. It was a mistake.'

I took her by the arm and helped her towards my room.

'What was a mistake?' I asked.

'To take the things,' she said.

'What things?' I asked, thinking for a moment that she
must have stolen something.

'The pills,' she said.

'Oh,' I said. 'I thought you were drunk.'

She stopped to grasp the banister and retch, then she
said, 'I took half a bottle of aspirin.'

'Come in here and lie down,' I said.

I put her on my bed and covered her with a blanket.

'I'm going downstairs to fetch you a hot water bottle and some tea,' I said. 'Don't move till I come back. Here's a towel and a sponge.'

'I want to talk to you,' she said.

'I'll be back in a moment,' I said.

I ran down and put a kettle on to boil. Then I picked up the telephone and asked the operator to put me on to the nearest doctor. A maid told me that Doctor Murray was out but was expected back at any minute.

'Please could you ask him to come to Mowle House?' I said. 'I think it's rather urgent. Someone's taken too much aspirin.'

I went back into the kitchen, made the tea and filled two hot water bottles and took them up to Jean, who was lying where I had left her, pale and shivering, but without apparently having been sick again. She had washed her face.

'Drink this,' I said. 'The doctor's coming.'

'The doctor?' she said. 'Oh, what have you done? What doctor?'

'I rang up the nearest doctor and asked him to come,' I said.

'You didn't tell him why?' She half sat up in bed and clutched me by the arm. 'Vanessa, you mustn't tell him what happened, you mustn't tell him I did it on purpose, I shall be sent to prison. You mustn't, Vanessa, please, please. . .' She began to cry quietly but hopelessly. 'You get sent to prison for attempted suicide, honestly you do. Promise not to tell him.'

'I only left a message with the maid,' I said. 'I didn't say anything about suicide.'

'Listen,' she said with desperate earnestness. 'Don't tell him. Let me talk to him and tell him what I want to. It's my affair. Please promise.'

'All right,' I said reluctantly.

'Even if he asks you,' she said. 'Please, Vanessa, swear it.'

'I won't tell him,' I said.

She lay down again, and I held out the cup of tea.

'Drink this,' I said. 'You'll feel better.'

Her eyes filled with tears but she drank it.

'You're cross with me,' she said.

'I just want to make you better,' I said.

'I think it's over,' she said. 'I got it all out of my system. I'm sorry I made such a mess.'

'What happened?' I asked.

'It doesn't matter,' she said, turning her face away.

With an effort I said, 'Please tell me. I was only trying to be efficient and to think what to do. I didn't mean to seem unsympathetic. Why did you take the things, what were you doing? How did you get here?'

'I ran all the way, as soon as I decided to stop taking them,' she said. 'I've been staying in the village. In the pub. I've been there since Sunday.'

'But why?' I asked.

She paused so long that I thought she might not answer at all, and then she said, 'It was since I saw that in the paper about you and Lewis.'

'You mean you were in the pub when you rang me up?' I asked.

'Yes,' she said. She suddenly turned on her side to face me. 'It's not good enough, Vanessa,' she said fiercely. 'It's not good enough. That's why I did it.'

'What's not good enough?' I said.

'Everything,' she said. 'Nothing. Nothing's good enough.' She sighed, and went on in an exhausted tone of voice, 'I was spoilt, you see, brought up soft, that's what I think. Our mum spoiled us. Everything that happened she was there to put it right. You don't know, not with a mother like yours, or any of her friends. There was nothing she wouldn't do for us, for Col and me. D'you know she never let me do a spot of house work to help her, or cooking? She did everything. And bad things that happened – well, she just told us they weren't bad, everything was all right really, everyone was kind and nice, there was nothing to worry about. Oh, you think it's soppy probably. Col did, of course, as soon as he grew up, and then he broke away. But I depended on her for everything, I did really, right up until I married Lewis. Then of course it was no good any more.'

The tea had made her cheeks less violently white. I pressed her to drink some more, and said, 'Go on.'

'Oh, you know all about me and Lewis,' she said. 'I suppose I wanted him to be kind and protecting like Mum, I don't know. I never wanted to be his equal. But I tried to be a good wife and I loved him. I thought that was all you had to do. It isn't, though, it isn't even a start, but it should be, shouldn't it? I don't understand the world, Vanessa, honestly there just doesn't seem to be any place I could ever be at home in, not since I left Mum. I don't seem to be any good, somehow. I tried going back to her, you know, when I heard Lewis was marrying your mother, but of course it was too late, it didn't work any more. And then I read it was all over between Lewis and your mother and it was Lewis and you now.'

She was breathing heavily and seemed very tired. I suggested that she ought to sleep.

'Look, I was killing myself,' she said, 'and I stopped halfway through because I realized I wanted to talk to you. Now I'm here what do I want to sleep for?'

'You sound quite like Colin sometimes,' I said. 'Shall I get Colin to come?'

She did not answer that, but soon went on, 'You were the only one. That's what I thought. The only one ever to be on my side, to be like me. There used to be Colin, but he hasn't been the same, not for years, not since I married Lewis really. Perhaps I was wrong ever to think that about you. I thought I was wrong when I read about you and Lewis, and after I talked to you on the telephone. that was really what made me want to finish the whole business. I thought there was no one I could ever talk to again, no one who'd understand, no one who wanted life to be like I want it to be, just simple and easy. But then I thought halfway through, after I'd made up my mind to do it – I spent all yesterday walking and walking trying to make sense out of things – and then halfway through I felt I wanted to talk to you, to explain why I was doing it, and then I thought, well, if I want to talk to someone that means I don't want to die.'

I was silent, trying to think of the proper reassuring thing to say.

'It seemed you were in on the game, too,' she said.

'When I read that bit in the paper. Even if it wasn't true what they implied, that you'd stolen him from your mother, it didn't make much difference. It still meant you were in on the game. Anyway, you knew I still loved him.'

'I didn't,' I said. 'I didn't know that.'

'Didn't you?' she asked, almost hopefully.

I thought for a moment and then said, believing it to be the truth although I now think it was not, 'Perhaps I did know.'

'Yes,' she said.

She was silent for so long that I thought she must have fallen asleep. Her face was turned away from me again, and I stood up to lean over her. I saw that she was not asleep, but lay with her eyes open, crying silently.

She turned to look at me and said restlessly, 'It isn't good enough, is it? You do see it isn't?'

I sat on the floor beside the bed and held her hand.

Then I said, 'All the same, really, I don't think you need have tried to kill yourself.'

She did not answer. Eventually she said, as if from a great distance, 'If I'd had a child. . .' I did not know what to say. We stayed sitting there in silence for a long time; then I heard the door bell.

As I stood up Jean roused herself to say, 'You promised, Vanessa, you promised to let me talk to the doctor. You promised you wouldn't say I did it on purpose. Even if he asks you, Vanessa, you swore it.'

'I won't tell him,' I said.

'Don't tell him my name,' she said. 'I'll be Jean Davies.'

Doctor Murray was a wizened little Scotsman, agreeably gruff and grumpy. I apologized for bringing him out late but said that I had been worried about a friend who had come to see me after dinner and had been taken ill. He peered without much interest at the remains of the vomit on the stairs, and asked how much aspirin she had taken.

'I don't know,' I said. 'I haven't asked her a great deal about it because I thought she'd better rest. I gave her some hot water bottles and some tea and she's been asleep most of the time since I telephoned you.'

He grunted and said. 'She didn't take the dose here then?'

By this time we had reached my room and I led him in saying, 'She'll be able to tell you better than I can.'

Jean immediately struggled to sit up in bed, and began to speak with startling animation.

'Oh, doctor,' she said. 'I think it must be appendicitis.'

I thought that the doctor looked doubtful, but he sat down and said, 'Tell me what happened.'

'I suddenly had the most terrible pain in my right side,' said Jean breathlessly. 'It was such agony that I took eight aspirins because I sometimes have very bad headaches, so I'm used to large doses. And then, the idiotic thing was that, after I'd taken the dose, the pain was still so bad that I took another eight forgetting that I'd taken the first lot. It really was silly. So when I realized what I'd done I ran up here to ask my friend to help me, and then when I was nearly here I started being sick.' She lay back again on the pillows, apparently exhausted.

The doctor grunted and said, 'I'd better have a look at you.'

I went out of the room and down into the hall to wait for him. I walked up and down at the foot of the stairs. He seemed to be taking a long time. It seemed to me most likely that he would simply say that she must spend a few days in bed, and that in that case she would have to stay here, and I should have to ring up Lewis to tell him not to come down.

At last the doctor came out, closing the door quietly behind him. 'I think I ought to get her into hospital,' he said.

'Hospital?' I said, alarmed.

'Oh, I don't think it's anything too serious,' he said. 'But she complains of this acute pain in her right side. I can't see any sign of an inflamed appendix, but since she says she still feels the pain and that it's very severe, I think I ought to have her under observation for a day or two. It seems the only sensible thing to do, since I'm not entirely happy about her. It may turn out to be quite unnecessary and we can send her home after she's had a good night's rest, but it's better to be on the safe side.

Can I use the telephone? I'll get an ambulance. She's in a pretty exhausted state after that overdose and she'll be more comfortable in an ambulance.'

'It hasn't done any harm then?' I asked.

'The system was able to reject it,' he said. 'There was no need for me to do any more. She'll be all right now. It's just the shock to the system, you understand.'

'I see,' I said.

'It seems to have given her a fright,' he said. 'She seems in quite a distressed frame of mind. She'd told you about the way she took the overdose, I suppose?'

'Yes, more or less,' I said.

'The same as she told me?' he asked.

'Yes,' I nodded.

'You don't know of any reason, I suppose, why she should have wanted to do it on purpose?' he asked hesitantly. 'She's not been depressed lately?'

'Oh no,' I said. 'No, I'm sure she wouldn't do it on purpose.'

'Fine,' he said, sounding relieved. 'That's all I wanted to know. I'll get the ambulance now.'

He went off to telephone and I went upstairs to Jean. The curious vivacity she had shown in front of the doctor was gone. She lay still and white again, reminding me for a moment of the time Colin and I had been to see her in the flat in Portman Square after she had been ill. 'A virus,' she had said. 'They say it's always depressing.' Lewis had been in Paris, and we had played Chinese Chequers.

'I'll get hold of Colin,' I said. 'I know it will help. We'll both come and see you and it will be like that time we played Chinese Chequers and you laughed so much. You remember.'

She did not answer.

'You'll feel better soon I know,' I said. 'Perhaps you've been ill again, like you were that time. Perhaps it's the same virus.'

She still did not speak.

'You don't mind going into hospital for a day or two?' I said.

She shook her head slightly.

'It won't matter at all if they find you haven't got appendicitis,' I said. 'They'll just keep you there for a couple of days and then let you out without knowing what it was. And the rest will do you good. I'll lend you a nightdress. Here, I'll put it in this bag with some washing things and a comb, and I can bring you anything else you want tomorrow.'

'Thank you,' she said.

'Had you taken more aspirin than you told him?' I asked.

'Yes,' she said indifferently.

'Have you really got a pain in your side?'

'No,' she said.

'I'll go and see if he's got the ambulance,' I said.

I found the doctor in the hall. He said that the ambulance would be here quite soon. I offered him a drink and he accepted some whisky. When I had brought it to him, he began to ask me about who lived in the house, and about Lewis, so that to escape his questions I went back upstairs again and sat with Jean. She was still motionless and silent. There seemed no point in staying with her, and after some time I left her and went to fetch a bucket of water and a cloth to clear up the mess on the stairs.

I scrubbed furiously at the carpet, seeing it through tears. They must have been tears of rage. I could only think that Jean had ruined everything, that everything in the world seemed covered with this vomit.

When the ambulance arrived, I followed the two stretcher bearers upstairs. When she saw me Jean said weakly, 'Don't bother to come with me.'

'Of course I'll come,' I said.

As I got into the ambulance beside her, the doctor said, 'I'll be following in my car. If you can keep her talking that will be all to the good. She'll be better to stay awake for the time being.'

One of the ambulance men explained to me cheerfully that he would be sitting in front beside the driver and that I was to tap on the window if I needed anything.

Jean lay with her eyes shut, encased like a mummy in a thick roll of grey blankets. As the ambulance started I asked, 'Are you all right?'

'Yes, thank you,' she said.

A moment later she turned on her side, and with some difficulty pulled the blankets up to her face so that it was almost completely covered.

'The doctor says it takes about half an hour to get there,' I said conversationally.

'I know,' she murmured into the blankets.

He had told me to talk to her, but I could think of nothing to say. I sat in silence, gazing out of the window at the night. I knew that my strongest feeling was one of resentment, and I was afraid that if I spoke I should betray it. She seemed to sleep all the way to the hospital.

They carried her in still covered with blankets. A nurse was waiting with a trolley on which they laid the stretcher. The nurse said to me, 'I'll just show you to the waiting-room and then I'll take her up in the lift.'

I waited by the entrance as she turned to the head of the trolley which had already been wheeled some way away from me. I heard a quick gasp, there was a moment's whispered consultation with the ambulance men, and I heard one of them say, 'We'll get her upstairs.' They went away, the nurse walking beside the trolley. There was a pool of dark liquid on the floor behind them, and a trickle of it following them. In a moment another nurse came hurrying back from the direction in which they had gone, and showed me to a waiting-room.

'Is she all right?' I asked.

'I don't know. I haven't seen her,' she said. 'The doctor will be down in a minute. I'll bring you a cup of tea,' and she bustled out again.

I wondered whether Jean had been sick again, perhaps had some sort of haemorrhage as a result. But surely I should have heard her? Could she have had a nose-bleed – something to do with the shock?

After a long time the nurse brought me a cup of tea and said, 'Doctor Murray's just coming down to see you.'

I drank the strong tea and waited.

When the doctor came in, the nurse came too, and stood alert and starched rather close to me. Perhaps they thought I was going to faint.

'I've brought you some bad news,' the little doctor said in his Scottish voice. 'Was Miss Davies a relative of yours?'

'No,' I said. 'What's happened?'

'Then she has no relatives in the district?' he asked.

'She has a brother in London, that's all,' I said. 'But I think he's in Manchester. What's happened?'

'Well, as I say, it's bad news,' he said. 'I'm afraid the patient passed away a short time ago.'

'Passed away?' I said loudly.

'Yes,' he said.

'But when? How? I don't understand.'

'She was dead when she arrived,' he said. 'I'm afraid she had taken her own life. She had cut the veins in her wrists in the ambulance. She was carrying a razor blade.'

'In the ambulance?' I said. 'But I was sitting beside her.'

'She had covered her face with the blanket,' he said. 'Naturally you'd have thought she was sleeping. Now, there's no need for you to reproach yourself. Even a trained nurse might very well not have noticed what was going on.'

I had been sitting beside her.

'It was all over by the time she reached hospital,' he was saying. 'It's a most unfortunate thing and I'm afraid it must be a shock for you. Of course, I'm pretty sure now that she must have tried to do it earlier with the aspirin, but she wouldn't admit it and insisted she thought she had appendicitis. I had to take that in good faith for the time being. Most unfortunate. Of course if we'd known she'd tried it earlier we could have taken precautions to see she didn't get another chance.'

'Yes,' I said. 'Yes, of course we could.'

She had hidden under the blanket, and in the hot darkness drawn the razor blade across first one and then the other wrist, and bled to death, because I had been her last hope and had hardly even tried not to fail her.

'Now I'm going to drive you home,' said the doctor. 'I suggest you get straight to bed. I'll leave you a sleeping pill. And on you way you can tell me how to get in touch with the brother.'

I believe the nurse pressed another cup of hot nasty tea into my hand; and then the doctor drove me back in his little car and gave me some pills to take and told me again not to worry, that there was nothing anyone could have done.

Some time later I took Marius and went out to start up the blue Zephyr. Then I remembered my clothes and went back into the house and packed them all, leaving nothing. The roads were almost empty and I drove fast, so that I suppose I must have reached London soon after one o'clock in the morning. I drove straight to the record shop to look for Colin.

I rang the bell and it was answered immediately by a large figure wearing an overcoat with the collar turned up and bedroom slippers.

'They're none of them here,' he said.

'Where's Colin?' I asked.

'Colin?' he said, peering out at me. 'Oh, Colin. He's in Manchester.'

'Can you give me his address, please?' I said.

'Yes, I think so,' he said. 'Come in.'

I followed him through the dim shop into the office beyond. The piles of books and papers which were usually on the desk had been added to those already on the floor and the desk itself was covered with a blanket. There were several dustbin lids in one corner. It was rather cold.

The big man lit the gas ring and put a saucepan of water on top of it.

'I'm sorry if I seemed rude,' he said. 'I thought you were one of my boy's girls. They've been in a bit of trouble this evening and I thought one of the girls might have come after them hoping for more excitement. I've got Colin's address here somewhere I know.' He began leafing clumsily with his large hands through a pile of papers.

'Are you Tom Jones?' I asked.

'Yes,' he said. 'Here we are.' He pulled a letter out of the pile. 'If it's not too urgent, though, why don't you come back the day after tomorrow? He'll be here then. He's given up the job in Manchester.'

'I want to see him tonight,' I said, taking the letter. 'Thank you very much.'

'So you're going to drive to Manchester,' he said.

'I must,' I said. 'I must see him. Besides, I've nowhere else to go, particularly.'

He opened the cupboard, took out two eggs and dropped them carefully into the saucepan. Then he sat on the desk and said, 'It's a long drive.'

He was not fat so much as chubby, if that adjective can be applied to someone so big. He looked healthy. His face was moon-shaped and full-lipped. He wore glasses. He had large well-shaped hands which he did not move much; as he sat opposite me they hung heavily between his knees.

'I know it's a long drive,' I said.

'You expected to find him here?' he asked.

'Yes,' I said. 'I knew he'd been working in Manchester but I thought he might be back. I had a letter from him saying that he didn't like the job.'

'Are you that girl with the mother?' he asked.

'Yes,' I said.

'His sister used to talk about you,' he said. 'Jane, Joan, Jean. Jean.'

'She's dead,' I said.

'I'm sorry to hear that,' he said. 'Does Colin know?'

'No,' I said.

'She stayed here for a short time when he was living here,' he said. 'Worked in the shop a bit.'

'I know,' I said. 'I came here once when she was here.'

'Would you like a boiled egg?' he said.

'No, thank you,' I said.

'Do you mind if I eat them?' he said, getting off the desk. 'I didn't have time to have anything earlier. Perhaps you'd like some coffee?'

'No, thank you,' I said.

Moving quickly and quietly for a big man in a big overcoat, he spooned first one and then the other egg into two pink egg cups. These he put on the desk, pushing back the blanket which covered it; then he drew up a chair and, sitting down with his back to me, started to eat with concentration. When he had finished he sat in silence, his chin on his hand, having apparently forgotten all about me. Jean had said something about his not speaking until he was spoken to: remembering the description I wondered why he had shaved off his beard. I decided that I must go, now that I had Colin's address; but the longer I sat there the more difficult it became to break the silence. I still felt compulsively that I must find Colin, but the anti-climax of not finding him here had numbed me. I began to feel I had been sitting there for ever, staring at this broad unhelpful back. With an effort I stood up, but instead of leaving I said, 'It was all my fault, about Jean. That's why I must tell Colin.'

For a moment I thought he was not going to speak even then. Finally he said, without turning round, 'Was it?'

'Yes,' I said. I told him why it was my fault, in some detail.

When I had finished I said, 'I'm only telling you all this because Colin isn't here. I meant to tell him.'

'Yes,' he said, 'I'm afraid it will be a shock to Colin.'

'I only wanted to tell him to get it off my mind,' I said quickly, realizing that this was so. 'I wanted to ease my conscience by telling him and letting him be angry with me.'

'Quite,' said Tom Jones.

I began to feel afraid of myself. He turned to face me.

'Listen,' he said. 'You must rest. As early as possible in the morning I will ring up Colin, tell him what has happened, or some of it, and get him to come down here at once. As to you, I must not bother you with idle comfort, but you must remember that Jean was a person with pronounced suicidal tendencies, and also that very many other people as well as you are to blame. She was here, for instance, working in my shop for quite a long time, and I was too busy with my own absurd affairs to do more than barely notice her. As you saw, I couldn't remember her name. We'll talk. We shall have plenty of time to talk later on. In the meantime, where are you going to sleep?'

'I suppose I might be able to get into my mother's house,' I said. 'She won't be very pleased to see me though.'

'You could sleep here,' he said. 'But the trouble is these wretched boys are here. They're from a club I know and the silly fools had to come up to the coffee bars in the

Kings Road and get into a fight, so I've got half of them sleeping upstairs – they missed the last bus of course – that's why I'm trying to sleep down here. There is a camp bed up there which I tried at first but it's too small for me. You could have that, but it would be in the same room with three Teddy boys.'

'I don't mind,' I said.

'They are asleep after all,' he said. 'And I shall have to get them out long before you wake up. They've got to get home.'

Following him upstairs I said, 'I needn't have bothered you. I mean, I was looking for Colin. . . .'

'Hush,' he said sternly, perhaps because he did not want to wake the sleeping Teddy boys.

He signed to me to wait and went into one of the two bedrooms, from which he quickly emerged carrying an enormous striped pyjama jacket which he pressed into my hand. Then he led me into the other bedroom and pointed to a camp bed in one corner.

'Go to sleep,' he said.

The light from the door fell across the pillow of the other bed. Disturbed by it, a boy's head moved. As the white face turned I saw a dark bruise covering one cheek. He opened his eyes and his hand went to his cheek. Then he saw us standing in the doorway. He smiled delightedly and said:

' 'Ullo, love.'

'Hullo,' I said.

When Tom Jones had shut the door I took off some of my clothes but not all because I thought the boy might be watching. As soon as I got into bed I fell asleep.

16

A LEXANDER took me to the inquest. I rang him up from Tom Jones's shop the morning after Jean killed herself, and asked him to tell Lewis what had happened.

'I can't see him,' I said. 'He was going to come down to Mowle tonight and take me to the boat for Belgium the next day, but I can't see him now. I shan't go to Brussels because I must see Colin first.'

Alexander drove me to the inquest in the blue Zephyr, which he was afterwards going to take back to Lewis. He arrived at the shop in a taxi, looking neat and formal in a dark suit. He gave me a note from Lewis which I read in the car. It said, *I am deeply and desperately sorry for what has happened. Of course you're right not to want to see me. Alexander will tell you that we have put forward our trip to the U.S. Please tell him if there is anything at all I can do. Please take care of yourself.*

I had been frightened at the thought of the inquest, but when it came it was all quite simple. The Press had not heard about it, and there were very few people there. The Coroner was a kind old red-faced man who simply wanted me to confirm that the deceased had been in a depressed state of mind and asked me if I knew of any particular reason. I said that she seemed to feel that she was a failure, but that I had not been able to understand what it was that was really worrying her. He did not cross-examine me at all closely about what she had said or whether she had admitted to having tried to kill herself earlier with an overdose of aspirin. He announced briskly that he found she had committed suicide while the balance of her mind was disturbed, and passed on to the next business. The whole thing only took a few minutes.

As we got into the car to drive back to London Alexander said, 'That's over. Now what?'

'Can you take me back to the shop?' I said.

'You're going back there?' he asked.

'I must,' I said. 'I must wait for Colin.'

Colin had disappeared. Tom Jones had told him about Jean's death on the telephone, and he had said he would come to London at once. So far he had not turned up. I had rung up his Manchester landlady and been told that he had left immediately after the telephone conversation with Tom Jones.

'You'll go on staying with this chap Jones?' said Alexander.

'I've promised to look after the shop for a week,' I said. 'He suggested it as soon as I told him about the situation with my mother, and that I wanted to wait to see Colin instead of going to Brussels. He said there was something he had to do which would take him away for a week and he's been waiting till he could find someone to look after the shop. So he went off, I don't know where to. He's a bit mysterious.'

'Yes,' said Alexander. 'Of course, you ought to be a bit careful, you know.'

'Why?' I said.

'I don't know much about him,' said Alexander. 'He may be a fairly harmless sort of crank but I know he's had one or two brushes with authority. You want to be careful how much you become involved; or know what it is before you become involved in it.'

'Oh, that's something I shall always do now,' I said. 'At the moment he seems to be busy about boys' clubs more than anything else. Though he did say something about a magazine. I like him rather.'

'Boys' clubs sound on the right side of authority anyway,' he said. 'I've nothing particularly against him. I just want you to be careful. Listen, even if you stay there for a bit, and work for him, go and see your mother soon.'

'Will she want to see me?' I asked.

'Of course,' he said. 'She's been in rather a bad way lately. Oh, I don't mean anything terrible, she hasn't gone to pieces in any dramatic sort of way, but after all things seemed to be going pretty swimmingly for her and now it's all bust up and everybody knows it. Friends have been pretty foul as they always are. So have I, let's face it. She needs you, rather. You're good for her. You could go back and live there and go on doing whatever you liked – she wouldn't object to anything you wanted to do.'

'But would we get on?' I said. 'I mean, it could never be the same.'

'No,' he said. 'If it could, I might not be so keen for you to go back. But you're free now. You'd never be her slave again, or blind to her limitations. You'd never, probably, turn into the sort of person there was always the possibility of your turning into. There wouldn't be any danger for you. Of course if you found you got on each other's nerves you could always leave. But I don't think you would. She's very clever, whatever you may say. She'd know the situation, and adapt herself and not impose on you, or at least I think she would. It wouldn't be like her if she didn't.'

'I don't know,' I said.

'Try, some time,' he said. 'I'll write to you there from America. You know we're going next week? Well, I shall write to you at the Mews, then you'll have to go and see her to get the letter.'

'I could go when she was out,' I said, 'or get someone to forward it. How long are you going to be in America?'

'Two years if all goes well,' he said. 'Lewis a few months.'

'Did he mind, about Jean?' I asked.

'I think he was very distressed at the way it happened,' said Alexander.

'Has he said anything to you, ever, about me?' I asked.

'No,' said Alexander.

'If he does, will you tell me?'

'All right.'

'Whatever it is?'

'Yes,' he said.

After a pause I said, 'All this spoilt everything. Jean's suicide, I mean. Now it's all foul. It wasn't before.'

'No?' said Alexander.

'I'm afraid it must all have been a mistake,' I said. 'It must have been wrong.'

'What must have been wrong?' asked Alexander.

'What I thought about Lewis,' I said. 'Did you know?'

'Not really,' said Alexander.

'It wasn't anything really,' I said, 'I mean nothing happened. It was only just beginning to turn into something. Was I very silly, d'you think, to think of it?'

'No,' he said.

'But after Jean it's all no good,' I said. 'I know he'll think that too. But if he says anything. . .'

'I'll tell you,' he said.

'I know that you. . .' I began. 'That is, I wouldn't say anything about it if I didn't know that you like him too.'

'I know,' said Alexander. 'I do.'

Colin came back that evening. I had been to the cinema, and came back to find him drinking Nescafé in the office. I went to the cinema because I did not like spending the evenings alone in the shop, trying to read or playing the gramophone, while Jean died over and over again in my mind and I waited for the telephone to ring and Lewis's voice to ask for me.

When I came in Colin looked up and said, 'Well, here we are. Nescafé?'

'Yes, please,' I said. I sat down and said, 'I hoped you'd come soon. I didn't know where you were.'

'I've been around,' he said, pouring the boiling water into the two cups. 'So old Jean did herself in.'

'Yes,' I said.

'She never got the hang of things, at all, did she?' he said. 'Daresay she's better out of it.'

I said nothing, and after some time he said, 'So you were there. Mucky I suppose. Tom said you thought it was your fault for not trying to help when she came to you, but I'll tell you something. With Jean, you never could do anything with her when she was in that mood. I know.'

I was grateful.

'Of course,' he said, 'though that's true, what I say, it's not what I thought at first. At first I thought it was everybody's fault, not just yours, the whole lot of them – Ogden, your mother, the whole lot. That's why I wandered about you know, didn't come here, felt I couldn't see you, sort of thing. But of course it wasn't as simple as that. Anyway you're in the same boat as me, more or less.'

'Yes,' I said.

'Anyway, what the Hell?' he said. 'She's O.K. I've thought of doing the same thing, these last few days.'

'Oh no, Colin,' I said, 'you haven't. You're not like that, however much things seem black to you. You'd know what I mean if you'd seen Jean then. She was ill with despair, it was an illness. You haven't got it, Colin, I know you haven't.'

'No, O.K., I haven't,' he said, nodding quickly. 'We'll be all right. We'll be all right, you and me. We'll stay here. Tom's a good fellow, you'll find that out. We'll stay here, with him. He'll give us a few jobs to do and we'll get on with them, just quietly, not trying anything too difficult, eh?' He lifted his cup to his mouth with hands which trembled violently. 'We'll be O.K.,' he said, 'We'll just stay here, and hide. We'll keep out of things and hide. We'll be O.K.'

Even so short a time after Jean's death I knew that I did not want to keep out of things and hide. But I said, 'Yes, of course. We'll stay here.'

Colin put down his cup carefully on the desk, came over to where I was sitting on one corner of it and put both his hands on my shoulders. Shaking me very slightly, shutting his eyes in some sort of effort, he said, 'We'll be O.K. We'll be O.K.' Then he put his head on my shoulder and cried.

I put my arms round him and kissed his head. In a moment it was over and he was quite calm. We finished our Nescafé and talked about Tom Jones.

Every day until the day he and Alexander left for America, I waited for a sign from Lewis. I told myself that it would not come, that his note made it clear he was relieved at my decision to avoid him, that it was the best thing, that I should have to refuse to see him even if he did ring me up because everything was spoilt and finished: all the same I waited. Once or twice I nearly went to his office, in the hope of seeing him go in or out, perhaps of talking to him, pretending to be passing by chance; but the fear of seeing a look of boredom, irritation or embarrassment cross his face at the sight of me prevented me. Until I knew that they had gone I felt immensely tired, and when I brushed my hair it fell out in handfuls; but after that I began to feel better. I stayed in Tom Jones's spare bedroom, working in the shop.

Tom Jones seemed busy. Every time he saw me he said, 'We must talk,' but we never did. He told me that a magazine with which he was connected and which I had heard of though never read was going to be run from the office; he asked me to help with it and said that if I liked the job and the people, I could take over from the secretary who was leaving to get married in a month's time. 'They'll pay you far too little of course, but you'd enjoy it and it's very much worth doing. It's a good paper. I'll tell you all about it when I get back.' And he wandered off again in his preoccupied but unhurried way and somehow never did tell me all about it.

'He'll calm down next week,' said Colin. 'It's this commission or whatever it is on juvenile delinquency. He's giving evidence, or rather a long statement of his views, to which of course as usual, since as usual they're crazy, nobody's listening. You'd think he'd be used to it by now, but it seems to upset him just as much every time he gets ignored. He'll be back to normal next week, sitting around for hours with nothing to do, jabbering.'

Colin had gone to live with his mother, but came to the shop every day. He said he had to be with his mother until she got over Jean's death, but I felt that if I moved out of Tom Jones's spare bedroom he would move in, which was one of the reasons why I went to see my mother not long after I knew that Lewis and Alexander had left for America.

I saw a letter from Alexander waiting for me on the

table as soon as the new foreign girl opened the door. She was more formal than the Spaniard, and asked me politely, 'Who shall I say it is?'

'It's all right, I'll just go in,' I said, picking up the letter and putting it into my bag.

I went into the drawing-room and found my mother with Betty Carr.

'Oh, there you are, darling,' said my mother. 'Have a drink. There's a martini there.'

I poured myself out a drink and sat down. I could see from the fluttering excitement in her eyes that Betty Carr knew every detail of the situation, and I felt my old irritation that my mother should pour her troubles into such silly ears.

'Tell us all about your inflammatory friends in Pimlico,' said my mother.

She was smartly dressed – they both looked as if they were going out to dinner – and of course she was beautiful, but her perfectly white face seemed to me a little more gaunt than usual, her beauty less serenely confident.

'You make them sound so interesting,' I said.

'Aren't they?' she asked.

'In a way,' I said.

'We're going to see a terribly forward-looking play about incest,' said my mother. 'Betty knows the author's first wife and says it's all true. Why don't you come with us?'

'I think I've got to get back really,' I said.

'We're going with two international crooks Betty picked up in a bar,' said my mother.

'Oh, Essex, what nonsense,' Betty began, but my mother cut her short and said, 'I tell you what, Betty, you could go on ahead in case they're waiting for us. I'll follow you in two minutes.'

Betty got to her feet obediently and left, complaining, 'I know you'll be late. Do try and be in time. I wonder if I ought to leave you. You will promise not to be too late?'

When she had gone my mother said, 'Oh, well, poor old Betty, I really do find her rather restful, I don't know why. Now tell me how things are with you. I heard about that poor woman. It must have been horrid for you. You'll have to forget it very quickly, and all that whole incident. It was a mistake, the Ogden episode.'

'Yes,' I said.

'And now the wretched man's gone roaring off about his business, leaving us all in ruins,' said my mother cheerfully.

'But it was our fault Lewis ruined us,' I said. 'It wasn't his fault. We weren't up to him at all. He couldn't help ruining us. I'm so sure about Lewis now. That's why Colin and I can never be quite such friends as we were, because he'll never understand how wrong he is about Lewis.'

'Yes, well, I daresay you're right,' said my mother, looking surprised by my vehemence. 'Anyway, as for what I said to you on the night of that party, of course I was in a rage and talking rubbish,' she said. 'I shall have to go or Betty will never forgive me. I hope you're staying?'

'I don't know,' I said. 'I wasn't sure whether it would be a good thing.'

'My dear, of course it's a good thing,' she said. 'It's quite comfortable here, after all. As for Jones, if that's what's worrying you, haven't I always wanted you to be more independent? You know I shan't think of interfering. You need hardly see me if you don't want to. I'd like to have you here though, just to know you're about. See what you think anyway. Come a little later if you like. I really must fly.'

I helped her on with her coat.

'They aren't really international crooks,' she said. 'I wish they were. They might be more amusing. Still I'm not flying so high these days.' She kissed me on the cheek and said, 'Good-bye darling. See you soon. Get Lola to give you some food if you want some before you go. There's lots about.'

She left, turning to wave from the door.

I opened the letter from Alexander, and skipped through it until I found what I was looking for.

I had a conversation with Lewis the other day, he wrote,

*which started with his giving his views about English Society
life – you know how he holds forth – and that led to the people
he met through your mother, and finally to her. Of course,
for obvious reasons, we didn't discuss the episode as frankly
as we might other things, but he did say something about
what a mistake the whole thing had been. 'Anyway,' he said,
'the daughter was the only one who was any good, not the
mother.' I said you were wonderful, or words to that effect,
and he agreed. Then I said I knew you were absurdly loyal.
He knew what I meant and said at once, 'Oh no. Such as that
was, it must be over. I could only do her more harm, and
anyway she needs quite another sort of person, not merely a
younger one. Besides, my Society period is over.' Then he
changed the subject, quite firmly. He said it as if he meant it.
I know this is what you wanted me to tell you.*

It meant that I was not to hope. But I should always
hope.

I went out of the house and walked to the nearest bus
stop. I waited there for a few minutes, but as no bus
appeared I began to walk. The April evening was not cold
and I walked all the way back to the shop. Suddenly my
immediate future seemed quite clear and uncomplicated.

I should go back to live with my mother, for as Alexander had said I had nothing to fear from her any more.
I should never be in her thrall again. If after what I had
now seen of her, I found irritation or disapproval or even
pity coming between us I could always leave, but I
believed I should not need to, she was too tactful and
realistic. My other experiment would be with Tom Jones,
and it might or might not be successful. For Colin, Tom
Jones was now simply good and right and so was everything he did. Colin was too truly a pessimist to be
prepared to do much about this conviction of his. He
only wanted to crouch in Tom Jones's shadow, a heathen
seeking sanctuary in what he felt to be a holy place. I
knew that I was different, and that if I came to think as
Colin did I should want to be more positive about it; but
I did not know whether I ever should think as he did and
in a way I doubted it, because my sort of scepticism was
very different from his.

Tom Jones at least was something of a mystery, something to be found out about, and there was a hope – surely there was a hope – that through him I might find a life less futile than was offered by Madame Sobiska's Bureau, or my mother's antique shop, or Betty Carr's charity committees. I did not know; but it was worth trying.

I began to feel happy. And then for a moment I was able to face the fact that Lewis and I would never be reunited, never live happily ever after; but only for a moment, and then I began to dream again, of cables from America, new reports from Alexander, sudden confrontations, the big car drawn up outside the record shop and the figure in the back behind the evening paper, watching for me.

As I went into the shop I met Tom Jones coming out.

'How are you feeling now?' he said, staring at me earnestly.

'All right, thank you,' I said.

'Good,' he said. 'We must talk.' He began to walk away.

I laughed. He turned to look back, his big face surprised.

'Why are you laughing?' he asked.

'We are always just going to talk,' I said.

He smiled and coming back towards the shop said, 'Then let us talk now.'

The Great Occasion

1962

1

Aᴛᴛᴇʀᴡᴀʀᴅs, when he looked at the photographs, he
noticed that his morning coat was getting tight. There
was a wrinkle of strain when the button was done up.
The button might be moved, that was all it needed, but
no one had done it, no one had told him it needed doing.
Impossible to suppose they had not noticed; they had
simply not been interested enough, had seen no reason
to bother about it. It was such a little thing, one of his
daughters could have done it in a moment, if only it was
the sort of thing they ever did do. It distressed him,
afterwards.

At the time, though, he felt pleased, because it was a
sunny afternoon and he was conscious of being handsome. Susan, unlike most brides on their wedding day,
was not looking her best. She had a cold sore below and
slightly to the left of her mouth, partially concealed by
make-up – well, really quite successfully concealed, you
would only notice it if you were fairly close. Her face was
pale and the corners of her mouth were tight, so that they
were tucked into her cheeks a little, as they always were
when she was being obstinate about everything. There
was a head of Pallas Athene where the corners of the
mouth disappeared in just that way into a small particular
roundness of the cheeks. There it was touching, not, as
he found it in Susan, irritating. But then there was a faint
stirring in him of the feeling that only his family could
arouse, an uncomfortable mixture of pity and embarrassment, hostility to the outside world for hurting them,
hostility to them for hurting him by being hurt; an anguish
really. Susan had always been subject to cold sores on
important occasions.

The fact remained she was looking plain. This was a

357

comfort to him because then it did not matter so much that she was throwing herself away on this fearful Wing Commander. The photography finished, he led her into the church.

But there is Angel, he thought, she'll show them. She was sixteen and should have been, surely, at the awkward age. She was draped in white and wearing leaves in her hair, a conventional bridesmaid; only she was simply beautiful. No one can deny that, he thought, however they may pretend they pity me for being without a son. No one I know can offer anything to match that little piece of creation. I did it. She'll show them.

They were all looking handsome, he thought, pushing back his shoulders ready to march up the aisle, as the bridesmaids fell in behind; even Charlotte, fourteen and solid, all that gold hair scraped back behind her leafy head-dress, had a sort of calm proportion, just suggesting but not too obtrusively the presence of strong passions. He knew the passions were there, and sometimes he thought the strongest might be a passionate dislike of himself, but for the moment he was not thinking about that. He was thinking how nice they looked and how proud of them he was. Selina's round face on her long neck looked surprised as usual but quite pretty for a nine-year-old, and looking down the aisle towards them from the front pew was Penelope, her face a presentiment of Angel's, her hat the height of fashion. He was pleased with the way she had taken to dressing since her marriage.

'Praise my soul the King of Heaven,' they sang, and he began to move forward, his heart swelling. Oh dear, thought Susan, Father's going to cry.

They are all here and here we go in procession and another of my daughters has become a woman and I am giving her in marriage. There's old Crump, and Ogilvie – decent of him to make the effort, he must have only got back from West Africa this morning. They have turned out in force, my colleagues, their wives, smartly dressed too. They've really made an effort; shows what they think of me. Fortescue – should he not have been put nearer the front? – that ass Logan, sweating as usual though it's

not hot, Rose, Mrs. Rose, now there's a pretty woman;
and how beautiful they have made the church. That was
Penelope, she had organized the flowers; had organized
the Wing Commander into paying for them too, because
she said the bridegroom always paid for the flowers. I
would have paid, he thought, I'd pay for anything they
wanted, let them do the thing in style, nothing's too good
for them. And we march, and they shall have splendour,
and music, and everything shall be grand. We are only
so small a part of the procession, of the millions upon
millions upon millions, but everyone shall know which
part of the procession is ours, because of the flags, and
the trumpets. He laid his left hand over Susan's, which
was on his right arm, and without feeling the slight with-
drawal there led her to the steps of the altar. But Heaven's
above, the Wing Commander's mother. It must be a practical joke. No one could possibly look like that. In the first
place she was obviously a man; and then her clothes –
what could she be thinking of?

'Who giveth this woman to be married to this man?'

He held forward her hand, and bowed, and went back
to sit beside Penelope.

'You're looking very nice,' he whispered loudly.

'So are you,' she answered, smiling and patting his
hand. He was pleased. Penelope had always been the
most responsive of his daughters. He smiled across her
head at Ham, who gave a neat little nod. Penelope was
under the mistaken impression that a mutual admiration
and respect existed between her father and her husband.

The service proceeded with comfortable majesty. Penelope looked critically at the bridesmaids, who were standing close to her pew. She had designed the dresses
herself, and supervised their making, because Susan had
no idea about that sort of thing, and she was pleased to
notice how cunningly Charlotte's breadth was glossed
over by the pleating of the chiffon, not that she could
ever be expected to look her best in pale colours. Penelope
could just see the small bunch of red roses she was
carrying, and noticed that it was trembling violently. Poor
Charlotte, she thought, I suppose she's falling in love
with the Bishop.

Charlotte was falling in love with the Bishop, but quite
slowly, because her mind was also occupied with the
tragedy of Susan's marriage. She thought the Wing
Commander was a brute, a great coarse brute who told
dirty stories and had an offensively mannish smell. She
was sure Susan was only marrying him to get away from
Father and she thought it would be better to kill oneself
than do that. It would be better for Susan if she were to
be struck dead, now, by a thunderbolt. Oh God, she
prayed, send a thunderbolt and kill her.

Selina, behind her, and conscious of her feelings, felt
the weight of her own responsibility. She knew she was
the only person who was aware of Charlotte's state of
mind, and felt it was her duty to look after her, but did
not know how best to do it, except by being there, and
feeling, though less violently, the same. It would be so
awful if Charlotte made a scene, shouted out to stop the
wedding, or started to cry, that terrible loud rasping
crying she sometimes did, not like a human being at all
really, but even less like an animal because an animal
would never be able to suffer as much as that. Selina
wished she could warn Angel to be prepared for Charlotte
to do something awful, but Angel would never believe
her.

Angel, anyway, was in a dream of happiness. The
music, the people, her own clothes, the flowers – lucky
Susan to be getting married – perhaps she would have a
baby soon. Angel hoped a lot of people would talk to her
at the reception: she knew she was going to enjoy this
wedding much more than Penelope's.

They were going into the vestry for the signing of the
register and the kissing. Susan's signature was shaky but
her father wrote firmly, Gabriel Dobson, with a flourish.
He liked writing his name. He had to give his arm to the
Wing Commander's mother and walk her down the aisle.
He began to feel depressed. Why did Susan have to make
such a bad marriage? All these people were probably
feeling sorry for him. He wished the whole thing were
over and could be forgotten.

'I'll organize transport shall I, sir?' said Ham, unnecessarily officious, the more so since he must have known that transport was organized already.

The reception. 'Your lovely daughters . . . such a heavenly service . . . he looks so *sensible* . . . you're looking very fit, how's business? . . . another married off, eh? That's it, you'll have them all five off your hands before long . . . But *Angel*, my dear, so *exquisite*! . . . how dear Hannah would have enjoyed it . . . such pretty dresses . . . of course Penelope did so awfully well for herself, one could hardly expect them all to keep it up and we did owe so much to those Battle of Britain boys . . . congratulations, old boy, they're a fine-looking lot of girls . . . so *tragic* their dear mother can't see them . . . at least he looks *kind* . . . don't you adore weddings? . . . I want to have a word with you some time about this new issue. Can we lunch? Next week? . . . How proud of them all you must be . . . such ages since we met . . . poor motherless darlings how they must pine for her, how you must all pine for her the lonely evenings, I know it all the . . . I say, old boy, you've got a beauty there, the eldest bridesmaid, a real beauty that one . . . such a lovely service . . . what a pity poor Hannah can't be here . . .'

It was flattering, amusing, he saw a few people he had not seen for a long time; but after a little he began to feel tired. He wished they would not talk about Hannah. He had nothing he really wanted to say to any of them. It occurred to him that he had no friends. There was Ogilvie to be looked after, though, and pretty Mrs. Rose: he knew how to play his part.

'The Shores are here,' said Selina to Charlotte.

'How frightful,' said Charlotte.

'They're wearing hats,' said Selina.

'Oh,' said Charlotte.

The Shores were approaching, having shaken hands with the bride and bridegroom. First came the large horsey parents, then the large horsey girls. The girls were objects of intense admiration on the part of Charlotte and Selina, because of their brilliance at riding, and their general air of independence and manliness.

'Ha! The bridesmaids!' cried Mr. Shore, hurrying up to clasp Angel warmly by the hand.

'What pretty dresses,' said Mrs. Shore, scanning the crowded room feverishly for friends, or champagne, or the way out.

'Hallo,' said the girls.

'Hallo,' said Charlotte and Selina, both turning red in the face.

After a pause, Selina said, 'How's Sailor Boy?'

'He's all right,' said the Shores.

'Oh,' said Selina. 'How's Arcturus?'

'Actually he's got a bog spavin,' said Belinda Shore.

'Oh,' said Selina. 'How awful.'

'At least the vets thinks it is,' said Sarah Shore. 'We're giving him cold compresses.'

'Gosh,' said Selina.

The Shores then moved on, in the wake of their parents, and were succeeded by an interfering person called Aunt Beatrice, who questioned them closely about their education.

'A lot of children go to boarding school at nine these days,' she said. 'It seems too absurd for Selina to be all alone with Miss Martin now that Angela and Charlotte are at school. I shall talk to your father about it. Wouldn't you rather be with the other children, Selina?'

'No, thank you,' said Selina, politely.

'She sees plenty of other children in the holidays,' said Charlotte firmly. 'And Miss Martin has to be there anyway, because she's Father's housekeeper. Father has to have a housekeeper.'

'It seems curious to have a housekeeper who is also a governess,' said Aunt Beatrice, but more faintly, alarmed by Charlotte. 'But who am I to tell whether she's being properly educated? I shall have to ask Father Arnold. I shall bring him over to have a talk with you.' And she moved purposefully off into the middle of the crowd.

'Who's Father Arnold?' asked Selina.

'Some frightful monk,' said Charlotte.

'Oh,' said Selina, impressed.

' "G-r-r, there go, my heart's abhorrence,
Water your damned flowerpots, do,
If hate killed men, Brother Lawrence,

God's Blood, would not mine kill you," ' said Charlotte, rather loudly.

'I know,' said Selina, nodding.

Angel was talking to Ham, and blushing because he was paying her elaborate compliments. She liked it but wished he would not go on because after a certain amount of it one had to answer and she did not know what the proper answer was.

'Oh, Ham,' she said.

'Old Shore had to be dragged away by his wife,' said Ham. 'He held on to your hand for at least five minutes.'

'He's awful,' said Angel.

'Come with me and I'll introduce you to some attractive young men,' he said, taking her arm. 'They've all been longing to meet you.' He wheeled her off, purring quiet politeness, smooth and calm and polished as an expensive car. She went, delighted to be so piloted, and shook hands with young men, and smiled, feeling wonderful.

Penelope was pleased to see Ham being so sweet to Angel. She liked him to be proud of his sister-in-law; but there was Susan to be organized; the cake must be cut if the couple were to be away in time to catch their aeroplane to Jersey. The Wing Commander had always spent his holidays in Jersey and wanted to take Susan to his favourite hotel. Susan had of course agreed, although it was November and she would hardly be seeing the place at its best.

Susan had a round face and downy cheeks, brown straight hair and anxious eyes. Her forehead was broad and high and she had tiny well-shaped hands but she was not beautiful. She had Charlotte's solidity without whatever else it was that Charlotte had which made people look at her, even when she was fourteen. Charlotte had the air of someone who would have to be taken into account. Susan could be ignored. Susan was gentle. She looked as if she might be afraid of hurting people, but really afraid, afraid that if she hurt them they might scream and scream so that the whole world would disintegrate.

When they were alone together, she and Bill, the Wing Commander, she cried. That was after the speeches, and the changing upstairs, with Penelope being bossy and the three children rather sweet and excited, and the coming down, feeling for the first time really happy because the step was taken and they were going away, and the waving and her father's kiss on her forehead and the noisy goodbyes. She felt the reaction begin the moment the big sick-making car pulled away into the stream of traffic. Perhaps it was something to do with the way her father had shaken hands with Bill, his assumed heartiness and obvious dislike. Not that she minded her father despising her husband – she had never expected him to approve of anything she did – but it made her feel more isolated, for after all none of them approved, not even Angel who was usually so kind. She was relying solely upon her own judgement. Through all the difficulties and delays (her father had made them wait six months in the hope that she might change her mind) she had had only her own instincts to support her, and if they should be proved wrong she was lost, because everyone could say, 'We told you so.' She began to cry a little, but the act of crying loosed all sorts of further emotions, and she threw herself into Bill's arms, sobbing and groaning.

'Come along, come along, what's this!' he said kindly.

'I'm so miserable, I'm so frightened, you don't know how frightened I am all the time,' she cried. 'They're all so awful, I hate them so. Will you look after me? Shall I be all right with you? You will be kind to me? You don't know what I'm like. You don't. Will you be kind to me?'

'Of course I will, silly girl,' he said. 'Don't fuss. You'll be all right with me, don't you worry. Come on, sit up now. The driver'll think I'm abducting you. Don't you worry. It's the best thing you've done in your life, marrying me.'

He patted her comfortingly.

'Tell me who all those funny people were, come on,' he said.

She was timid, dependent. He liked that.

'It's all right then?' she said, seeking more reassurance.

'Of course it's all right,' he said confidently.

After the wedding Gabriel went to see Lisa Parnell, who was in bed with a cold.

She lived in Trevor Square, in a nice little house, full of pretty things, the prettiest of which he had given her. Her collection of objects of virtu was now of some value, and when she needed a little money for anything in particular he would arrange the sale of some of it for her and see that she got the best price. It was a happy arrangement. It gave him the opportunity to spend a pleasant amount of time in sale rooms, galleries and his favourite kind of shop, to enjoy being known to the dealers and treated with respect as a man of taste, and to show, as often as not, a profit on his deals, which was flattering to his discernment as well as financially gratifying to Lisa. In this way he was able to contribute towards her expenses without offending his own delicacy. He had done well for her, especially on Fabergé, of which she had a nice little collection, and the prices still seemed to be rising. There were one or two pictures too on which he was anticipating a good level of appreciation, though time alone would show.

The taxi drew up in front of her blue door. He paid the driver and rang the bell. The door was opened by her cynical Spanish girl and he went straight up to her bedroom. It was warm and full of flowers. She was sitting up in the big pink bed, wearing a soft lacy bed-jacket and her pearls. He felt a momentary shock because she looked so ill. Then he went towards her with his hands outstretched.

'My dear,' he kissed her on the forehead. 'How wretched for you. Has the doctor been?'

'Oh yes, it's only some silly germ,' she pushed him gently away. 'You mustn't catch it. And now tell me about the wedding. How did it go? And give yourself a drink. Behind you, on the table. How did it go? You were wonderful of course.'

'I was?' he said. 'Oh yes. I was. But no one else was up to much. The girls looked pretty, the bridesmaids. But poor Susan, God knows what sort of a life she'll have with that fellow. Why did she do it? Can you tell me that?

You're a woman. Why does a girl fall for a fellow like that?'

'I haven't met him, you know,' she said. 'He doesn't look very attractive, from his photograph, certainly. What else about him? He's terribly common of course.'

'It's not that so much,' he said. 'I don't mind people being common . . .'

'Oh, darling,' she interrupted. 'Not at all?'

'Well, hardly at all,' he said, pouring out a whisky and soda. 'No, seriously, I mean, half the people I do business with are common as hell – I say half – three-quarters is more like it. I don't mind that.'

'But they don't marry your daughters,' she pointed out.

'No,' he said. 'But there are a lot of them I wouldn't mind as a son-in-law. They've got ambition. They're getting somewhere. That's what I can't understand about this fellow Groves – he's got no ambition. Retired from the air force at forty, and d'you know what he wants to do? Keep chickens. Somewhere near a good golf course.'

She laughed, then coughed. 'Poor darling, that is a bit hard for you.'

'That's a nasty cough you've got there. Are you looking after it?'

'Yes, yes, I've hundreds of pills. Oh dear, poor Wing Commander.'

'Poor Susan,' he said. 'Not that she's ever seemed to want much out of life. At least I've never known what she wanted. But then they don't tell me.' He looked aggrieved, large in his bedroom armchair.

'And she looked pretty?' asked Lisa.

'Not very,' he said. 'Angel did. Angel looked very beautiful. Everyone said so. And Penelope was well turned out.'

'What was she wearing?' she asked. 'You can't remember of course. And Hamilton?'

'Now this will surprise you,' he said. 'That rat, that slinking white rat, has been adopted Conservative candidate for Blagton. Safe seat, by-election in December.'

'No!' she exclaimed. 'It's definite?'

'They knew today,' he said.' Would you have believed it?'

She was all amazed, ready to listen to his grievance, share and thereby soothe his resentment. For seven years, since a year after Hannah's death, she had been like that. She was soft and pretty and worldly. Her love of luxury and her foolishness, which was tempered by a certain acuteness, were endearing faults which only increased her dependence upon him. She was what he needed. She helped him to relax, encouraged him by her tender and unfailing interest, listened to him. He told her everything. It was important to him that he should be able to tell everything to someone. He told her about his business worries, his boredom, his troubles with his daughters, and even, going back, his troubles with Hannah, for there had been a few, not many, but he told her all about them. And now she had to have that look on her face which he had seen before, on Hannah's face; but she only had a cold, for Heaven's sake?

'What did the doctor say it was exactly, this germ?' he asked.

'Don't fuss,' she said. 'At least do, because it's sweet of you, but not too much. It's a sort of flu which is going about, Asian flu or something. You have a high temperature for a few days, that's all. Really, you oughtn't to stay, you don't want to get it. Just tell me about Ham and then go. Will you gargle when you get home?'

'Of course it's the name, and all that,' he said. 'It's more or less a family seat. It still makes a difference, you know, that sort of thing. There was a faction against him, apparently, with a local candidate they were very keen on, but the others won the day. Penelope may have helped. She'd be a very good candidate's wife. But I ask you – that rat – without an idea of his own in his head.'

'Perhaps that's what they like about him,' said Lisa.

'I daresay,' he said gloomily. 'He'd say anything to please anyone.'

'Well, I suppose there's something rather nice about it,' she said. 'The family link, I mean.'

'Oh, no,' he said, moving angrily in his little chair. 'That's family. They haven't been any good for generations. Look at that brother. He's just a bugger, lives with some lout in Wales, keeping monkeys. And Ham's got as much moral fibre as an ape.'

'The truth is,' she said, kindly, 'you're jealous.'

'Of course I'm jealous,' he said violently. 'I'm furiously jealous. Why should that nincompoop have what I haven't had, just because he's better born? Of course, it's my own fault. I don't blame anyone else for it. If one's a failure, it's always one's own fault.'

'You're not a failure, Gabriel,' she said, genuinely surprised. 'Oh, darling, you have been depressed by this silly wedding. Of course you're not a failure – how can you say such a thing after all you've done?'

'But I should have done more,' he said. 'I should have done far more. I should be doing more now, there should be more in the future. I'm only sixty. I should be at the height of my career, not going down.'

'But you're not going down. What can you mean? You've got more directorships than you had before, there's this British Industries business. You're always busy . . .'

'These things are nothing,' he said. 'I could do them in my sleep. I often do, I'm too bored to keep awake. It's not enough for me. I could be doing more, things which really mattered. I'm not using all my faculties to the full, Lisa, I'm not working at my highest pitch.'

'You surely don't want to work hard all the time?' she began, then immediately seeing that that was not the right line to take she said, 'But you've got money, darling, and power. You had to work for those things, they weren't left to you by a family. You've certainly got them now. You mean that Trade Adviser job was more important?'

'Yes, yes, I'm going down,' he said. 'Then I was working at full pitch. I should have known, you see, I should have known when I was young and gone into politics. That's where the prizes are.'

'But you did, I thought,' she said. 'I thought you tried politics.'

'I fought one seat, yes – but that should have been just the beginning of my training. That's what old Sir Robert meant it to be. Then I married Hannah.'

They were silent; then he said, mildly, 'Hannah was too intelligent. She couldn't help making fun of party politics. And I wasn't really happy about some of the things the Conservative Party stood for in spite of Sir Robert. I suppose something of my father's attitude had sunk in, though I thought I was rebelling against all he stood for. And then politics took me away from her too much, and she was so rude to the constituents, and we were so busy with other things.'

'Wouldn't you rather have had what you had with her than have spent all your life in politics?'

'But what have I got to show for it now?' he said sadly. 'Not friends. The friends were Hannah's. They've dropped off now. What have I got to show for it?'

'Well, darling, to be a little vulgar,' she said sensibly. 'Rather a lot of money.'

'I haven't got much money,' he said. 'It all goes in taxes and on the children and the house and all that.'

'Anyway,' she said, rather briskly because he often talked for quite a long time about how little he had. 'I don't think you'd have been a great success in politics. You're too violent.'

He was shocked.

'Violent?' he repeated. 'But I am . . . I am the most reasonable person in the world.'

'No,' she said decisively. 'I don't think you are a reasonable man. I think you are a . . . a passionate man.'

'Oh well, well, as to that . . .' he was amused. 'As to passion . . .' He gave her a roguish look. Then he laughed. 'So that's what you think of me? An old man of sixty?' He was flattered.

'Now you must run along,' she said, seeing him restored to cheerfulness. 'You really must, or I shall be in trouble. The doctor made me promise not to see a soul and to spend all the time asleep.'

'My dear, you should have told me.' He stood up at once, concerned. 'I've tired you, talking about myself as usual. Really that is naughty of you not to have told me. I'll go at once. Now is there anything you want, anything particular?'

'No, nothing really, you're so sweet. I'll just go to sleep.'

He made her pillows comfortable and poured her out a drink of barley water. She lay down. He looked at her with distress. 'Now you are not to be ill for long, you're not to. I shall come tomorrow evening and you must be looking much better or I shall be angry. I'll ring you up in the morning. You go to sleep now.'

'I will. Don't worry,' she smiled up at him. 'Good night, my darling.'

He was fond of women. He needed them, for all sorts of reasons. He had known a lot of them very well. He knew their faces and could tell at first sight not only whether they were happy or not, but whether they were in love, or pregnant, or dying. But it was silly to think that the drawn withdrawn look on Lisa's face, which she had tried to hide with her usual liveliness, must be the same look as Hannah had had in that gloomy hospital with the bombs dropping all round it. Lisa had a high temperature, that was all. He went back to his flat and took two sleeping pills.

The next day when he telephoned, the Spanish girl told him that she had found Mrs. Parnell very ill in the morning and that the doctor had come and taken her to hospital. She did not know which hospital. The doctor was out but he found out from the secretary that Lisa was at St. George's. He rang up but the Sister was too cautious to tell him anything. He could not get hold of her doctor. He rang up his own doctor who arranged for him to be allowed to see her for a moment, asleep under drugs, breathing heavily, her face unfamiliar and shining with sweat. He left a message for her doctor to telephone him and went to his office. Later the doctor telephoned to say that a lung had collapsed. He saw her again for a minute in the evening, looking no better.

Late that night the doctor telephoned to tell him that she was dead.

2

SUSAN woke up screaming, her head full of death.
This is it, this is the truth, she thought, seeing in a fearful white light the turning twisting burning falling bodies, and seeing their great gaping mouths aghast at it, and their heads bursting open, great blisters forming on the skin, and the children's eyes full of blood, and holes where their soft hair used to be, greenish purplish ghastly holes, and the white pulses beating the agony and fear, and the rat-like scurrying figures foraging among the ash, dragging half-severed limbs across the morass, and the twisting of the broken bodies, and the slowness of the release, the dreadful delay before the foul sick evil thing that was oneself lay still.

'Oh God oh God how long?' she shrieked, turning about, wracked, in her bed.

'I am here, I am with you.' Bill put his arms round her, waking in perfect control of the situation. 'It was only a horrid dream.'

'No, no, it was the truth,' she sobbed. 'It was the truth. It will happen, I know, I know. Oh I wish it would happen and be finished with. Why isn't there any God?' she wailed. 'Why were we ever allowed to believe there was? Why were we taught to hope?'

'Now, dear, as to that, there are many opinions, as you know. Now have a nice drink of water. There, that's better. Now, you don't want to start worrying about these things in the middle of the night like that.'

'Why isn't there a God?' she wept, already half soothed.

'I happened to believe there is,' he said with quiet confidence. 'We all have our different innermost beliefs and I am the last person to suggest that we should all think the same about everything, but I happen to believe that Jesus Christ was sent down to earth to bring us all a message of hope. And I believe that you and I, if we go forward hand in hand, in all humility, may become partakers in that message.'

'Oh,' said Susan. 'Oh dear, do you think so?'

'I am sure of it, my dear. But don't let's talk about it any more. You leave all that side of it to me, I'll do any worrying that has to be done. Now the first thing I do tomorrow is to get you some sleeping pills.'

'It was so clear though,' she said. 'Like a vision. Oh, Bill, it must be true, it must be going to happen . . . all those people . . . oh, Bill . . .'

'Hush now. It was the macaroni cheese. We'll have no more cheese in the evenings. Just something light, and then a hot drink and a sleeping pill. And I think we might ask the doctor to give you a tonic too. You're a bit under the weather all round.'

'I expect that's it,' she said, beginning to relax in his embrace. 'I never have been healthy, I'm afraid. And I know I've got a weak heart, though the doctor said I hadn't. But doctors are often wrong, aren't they?'

'They sometimes make mistakes, yes, dear. We'll take you to see another one. Now you just put your head there on my shoulder and you'll soon drop off to sleep again. That's the way.'

Selina and Miss Martin were in the wood. Selina had a small chopper and a large pair of gardening gloves, and boots and trousers, and a thick sweater. She was slowly dragging a small elder branch towards the pile which was later to be a bonfire. She was bored and cross because she wanted to go to the henhouse and write her book.

Miss Martin could not believe that the children did not like working in the garden with her. They had told her, quite kindly, that it bored them, but the idea was so inconceivable to her that she had been unable to absorb it; and still on sad cold November afternoons she would press Selina's little axe into her hand and say heartily, 'Come on now, we've got a lot of clearing up to do.' Selina would usually look resigned, but occasionally rebellion would gleam on her face, and then Miss Martin would say, 'We'll have a bonfire,' or in the spring, 'We'll plant bulbs.' These two activities were supposed to be the children's favourites: indeed they were, because bonfires were always amusing, and planting bulbs could be satisfying, because there was a little tool which lifted out a piece of earth like a castle pudding and then you put the bulb in and pressed the castle pudding back on top of it; but none of that was enough to make up for the fact that gardening took them away from their own affairs, which were far more important.

'But you can't spend the whole afternoon shut up in a henhouse,' said Miss Martin. 'Not now, anyway. It's far too cold.'

'It doesn't feel cold in there,' said Selina.

'Of course it's cold, it must be,' said Miss Martin. 'It will make your chilblains worse.'

Selina made a great fuss about the chilblains on her toes and rubbed vinegar on them every night.

'It won't,' she said angrily. 'It's these boots that make my chilblains worse, and wearing two pairs of socks in them.'

'But you wear your boots in the henhouse,' said Miss Martin.

'I know, that's what I mean,' said Selina. 'It's the boots, not the henhouse. I ought to have proper shoes.'

'But they'd let the wet in,' said Miss Martin. 'Then you'd have a cold as well as your chilblains.'

'Well there ought to be other shoes that don't let the wet in that aren't boots,' said Selina, taken by violent loathing of her boots.

'You can wear galoshes if you like,' said Miss Martin. 'I always used to wear galoshes when I was a child but I thought they'd gone out these days.'

'I don't want to wear galoshes,' said Selina.

'Couldn't you write your book after tea, in front of the fire?' said Miss Martin.

'Of course not,' said Selina, shocked.

'I wouldn't read it,' said Miss Martin.

'I couldn't possibly,' said Selina. 'I have to write it there. And anyway, that's the time for reading.'

'Well then I know what,' said Miss Martin. 'Just finish that one little bit in front of you and then go. It won't take you long.'

'All right then,' said Selina. She began to drag a rather large branch across the deep wet leaves towards the bonfire.

Miss Martin turned back and attacked the undergrowth with a sickle. 'Not sharp enough,' she said. 'This thing needs sharpening.' She laid about her vigorously until a branch whipped up and hit her in the eye. 'Bugger,' said Miss Martin.

'I'm-so-sorry-darling-how-naughty-of-me-don't-ever-use-that-word-yourself,' said Selina.

'Bloody hell,' said Miss Martin, in pain, pressing her hand to her eye.

'Will you be blind?' said Selina.

'Of course not,' said Miss Martin.

Miss Martin's language was bad, because for years before she had come to the Dobsons she had been personal assistant to a Press Lord, and she had picked it up from him. The children hated the Press Lord and put their tongues out when they saw anyone reading his paper, because he had betrayed Miss Martin. At least only Selina put her tongue out now, because Angel and Charlotte had gone to school and though they had changed very little it had been enough to stop them, putting their tongues out at the Press Lord's paper.

Miss Martin had come to them in 1943, soon after their mother's death. She was forty-three herself and had just faced the fact at last that the Press Lord would neither marry her nor be faithful to her nor even long rely upon her for affection or advice or loyalty. Her sister, who was the headmistress of a big girls' boarding school, had asked her to go and live with her and teach some of the younger children (since she was a natural teacher of small children though not a trained or qualified one) but she had hesitated to commit herself, and had then, answering an advertisement on an impulse, become the Dobson's housekeeper and governess. It had appealed to her as something that needed doing, and she had only meant it to be a temporary expedient; but seven years later she was still there and showed no sign of leaving. When she had arrived, Selina had been two, Charlotte seven and Angela nine. She had guided those three with remarkable success through their first years of motherlessness: even Angel could now remember very little about her mother's death. Penelope had been seventeen and at school. She was sensible and calm and had easily made friends with Miss Martin, without entering into any very deep relationship with her. Susan was fifteen. She had suffered the most, as far as Miss Martin knew, and had been the most unapproachable, partly because her school influences were stronger than her home ones. One of Miss Martin's many objections to the school to which the Dobsons were sent was that it had proved disastrously incapable of helping Susan in any way when her mother died. Miss Martin would have liked them to go to her sister's school, which she believed to be good because it was run according to the ideas and beliefs of her own family, which she shared. The family was one of Cambridge dons and scientists, and only her fatal affaire with the Press Lord had prevented her from being one or the other – that, and a certain deep laziness.

Her laziness was one of the reasons why she had settled down so happily with the Dobsons, for though a certain organizing capacity was required the house was comfortable and adequately staffed, and her life, especially when only Selina was at home, was easy, and left her plenty of time for reading and gardening. The garden in fact owed a great deal to her energy and devotion, because it was too big for the one gardener they had, and Gabriel himself was interested rather in contemplating than in cultivating his garden.

The relationship between Miss Martin and her employer had settled down into a state of amicable disagreement. Miss Martin thought him an old rogue, and he found her slapdash and insufficiently respectful. He knew that he could rely on her unfailing devotion to his children and her sensible management of his household, but his consciousness of this debt only made their relationship more uneasy. He knew that she thought him a bad father: it made him feel that he must convince her of the importance of his work and the unavoidability of its keeping him away from his children. At the same time her criticism annoyed him; he felt that she did not understand him, that she had lavished affection and sympathy on the motherless children but spared no thought for the widowed father. So he snubbed her at meals, scoffing at her opinions, and was conscious of the children siding with her against him, and became more loftily scornful, and later felt guilty, and brought her books from London.

'I've finished now. Can I go?' said Selina.

'Yes,' said Miss Martin. 'I'll shout when I'm going in to tea.'

Selina crossed the field which separated the wood from the house, stopping on the way to feel in her pockets for a carrot for her donkey. He saw her stop and came hopefully towards her, but she found her pockets unusually empty and walked on. Frustrated, he followed her, butting her back with his big furry head.

Selina would have liked a pony, a proper pony like the Shores', but no one else in the family except Charlotte was interested in ponies, and Miss Martin said that horsey girls were a bore, so Selina rode the donkey, James, who had a cunning way of kicking people sharply on the knee with his near hind leg when they were trying to get on his back. She was quite fond of him, and usually content to go for rides during which there was no question of his going any way but his own. The part of Lincolnshire where they lived was sparsely populated and they seldom met anyone on these rides; but when occasionally she caught sight of the Shores a field or two away, cantering correctly towards her, she would drum her heels into James's hard sides and make for the nearest cover. Once they caught her: she had never even told Charlotte. James had refused to move and she had dismounted and was pulling him as hard as she could towards the hedge. He had stuck his feet into the ground. She heard the Shores' hoofbeats approaching. She was breathless and nearly in tears when they swept up and stopped, their ponies jigging about prettily.

'You in trouble?' Belinda asked.

'Is he being obstinate? Shall we give you a lead?' said Sarah.

Scarlet and panting, Selina said, very loudly, 'It's all right, thank you. I just got off to go to the lavatory.'

'Oh, that's OK then,' said Belinda.

'We'll hurry on then,' said Sarah.

With a cheerful wave of their crops, they jingled off. Selina was left to comfort herself with daydreams in which she found a beautiful wild white horse and tamed it and won all the prizes at the White City and the Shores asked her if she could possibly get them tickets.

Now, however, crossing the field, she was quite well-disposed towards James and promised to bring him a carrot later. She passed a stile which led over the fence on to the drive and went round a longer way and over another stile which was nicer, and through a gate under an arch into the stable yard. It was a little way from the house and enclosed by a high stone wall. One end of it was paved but grass grew over the other two-thirds. At the paved end were two loose boxes and a large building which had housed a machine for making electricity before the house was connected with the main supply. There was a door in the wall opposite the entrance which led to the woodshed, which was big and dark with piles of sawdust in it and a grindstone which you turned with a handle. At the other side of the rectangle were four or five ruined loose boxes full of stones and rubble and nettles and sometimes cats having kittens. Next to the woodshed was an opening which led into another smaller enclosed area which contained a large wood pile and a henhouse and led in its turn to the kitchen garden. The kitchen garden was let to a man who lived in a cottage on the other side of it (this was part of Gabriel's 'cutting down on expenses'). In the summer the children stole his fruit. The wood pile was a good place for houses. The children had all had houses there at one time or another, sometimes all five of them together, more usually in rival groups. Last winter Selina had left two of Charlotte's books out there for a week and they had gone mouldy and Charlotte had pulled her hair and she had screamed. This winter Selina was using the henhouse.

There had not been any hens in it for years. James and the prolific cats, and a fat black spaniel who came out to chase them, were the only livestock now to be seen in the stableyard. The henhouse was an old-fashioned one, rather like a half-sized sentry box. It had probably been used either for broody hens or for fattening up cockerels. There was a shelf at one side where Selina could sit quite comfortably with her feet against the opposite wall, and a.another shelf at the back for keeping things on. Light came from the door, a third of which was open and covered with wire netting. The smell of hens had gone and had been replaced by the smell of damp wood and dead leaves.

Selina settled herself on the shelf and began to write.

This settling down to write gave her great happiness, the going away from everyone else into a place of study, where her writing materials were waiting; the writing materials themselves, the clean page of the notebook, the two sharp pencils and the rubber; the feeling of beginning to work. She never went on working very long, and often most of the time in the henhouse was spent in drawing faces and aimlessly thinking about fame and glory and cheering crowds, but she usually left it with a feeling of achievement. What she wrote was not of much importance, even to her. It depended entirely on what she had been reading, and was sometimes quite a fair imitation; but as her rate of production was slow the influences appeared to succeed each other with surprising rapidity and this made the narrative jerky.

When it began to grow dark Miss Martin collected her tools and walked back to the house.

She was halfway across the darkening field when she saw Gabriel's big car coming up the drive. There was a long tree-lined drive up to the house, through fields which had once been a park. The house itself was a solid mid-Georgian block, built of brick and bare of architectural features, but with a certain space and calm inherent in its proportions. Instead of going on to call Selina to tea, Miss Martin turned towards the front door and went to greet him.

He was looking pale.

'I'll have tea in the library,' he said. 'I've got one or two papers to see to.'

'Won't you have it with us?' said Miss Martin. 'Selina will be so sorry.'

Gabriel was annoyed: she was criticizing already. He said solemnly, 'A very dear friend of mine has just died. I am not a fit companion for children.'

'I'm so sorry, how sad for you,' said Miss Martin with sincerity.

He had already walked into the house, but he turned back to say, 'I brought you *The Grandeur That Was Rome*. I thought you might like to read it to Selina.'

'How kind of you,' said Miss Martin. 'She will be pleased. She's awfully keen on the Romans at the moment.'

'I know,' said Gabriel. 'That's why I bought it.'

Miss Martin went to tell Selina that her father had arrived. 'Go and say hallo to him and then come and have tea. He's not having it with us because he's sad about a friend of his who's died.'

'Oh good,' said Selina. 'I mean, good that he's not having tea with us. I'm sorry about the friend, of course.'

Penelope and Ham were driving up from London to spend the weekend with her father.

'I wonder what Selina will say,' said Penelope.

'Hardly understand I should think,' said Ham.

'Oh yes,' said Penelope. 'Children know all about the facts of life these days.'

'Facts of life? Oh you mean the baby. I thought you were talking about the constituency.'

'No, silly. Anyway Selina would understand perfectly about the constituency too.'

'You said that when we got engaged, you know. "I wonder what Selina will say," you said.'

'Did I?'

'Yes. And she was six or something. What would you have done if she'd said you were mad to marry me?'

'Oh I didn't mean that. I didn't mean I wanted her

advice. I just wanted to give her a surprise. I thought she might be pleased.'

'Dear baby sister . . .'

'Oh, Ham, you like her too really, you know you do.'

'She's spoilt of course.'

'Of course. But only a bit. I do wonder what will happen to her. I mean, it's extraordinary to be young, in a way, isn't it?'

'Poor old thing. When did middle age set in?'

'No, but I mean, to go through it all, the business of being young. I suppose it's wonderful. I hated it.'

'Hated being young?'

'Well, not really. Some bits of school I quite liked. But being the eldest was a bore somehow. And then I didn't enjoy the bit before being married. I know I should have. But I just wanted to get on with life and get married and be properly grown up. Silly, really – I mean, an awful waste.'

'Everybody wastes their youth.'

'You didn't. All those women and everything.'

'What makes you think that womanizing is going to be confined to my youth?'

'Well, at least you enjoyed yourself. Look at Susan.'

'Yes, well, she didn't celebrate her youth much. Perhaps she'll settle down into a happy middle age.'

Penelope sighed. 'I doubt it. I don't think she loves Bill. She just thinks he's safe.'

'I don't think all the opportunities are lost when you've stopped being young,' said Ham. 'I hope not anyway.'

'No,' Penelope agreed. 'But afterwards it's different. It's all on another scale. Youth is the great thing, the great event that nobody realizes is happening at the time, or even if sometimes they do, it so seldom comes to anything, things go against them, they make a mistake, something goes wrong, and they're left all bitter and old. And it goes on happening all the time, all these new people, millions and millions. So I just wonder what Selina will make of it.'

'What a philsopher maternity is making of you. Not what one expects of your Cambridge education. Talking of the little darlings lining up to take the plunge into life, what about Angel?'

'What about her?'

'I was thinking. Do you think it would be nice if we brought her out next year?'

'Brought her out?'

'Yes. A season in London, chaperoned by you.'

'Well, but surely . . . I mean, the flat's not big enough.'

'We could move to another. There's hardly room for the baby in that flat anyway, and I'll be an M.P. by then. We'll have to raise our standards a bit.'

'I'm sure Father wouldn't allow it. He's awfully against that sort of thing, it's his Puritan ancestry or something. And you know how mean he is, he'd never pay up. It's awfully expensive, surely?'

'We needn't do it on a very grand scale. And we'd do it with him, of course. He might enjoy it. He's probably lonely since your mother died.'

'I don't think so. He's always so busy. Anyway I remember when I was seventeen he told me that he and Mummy had talked it over and decided that none of us was to be brought out, because it was a waste of time and money and not in tune with the modern world and we were all to be trained for careers. Quite right, too.'

'That was in the war. Things have changed – the social revolution has turned out not to be so revolutionary after all. There's a Conservative Government. All the deb business seems to be back in full swing. And anyway, you talk about careers, that may be all very well for the rest of you, but what can Angel do, except look beautiful?'

'Oh, but she's perfectly intelligent. She passed School Certificate.'

'Only just.'

'She could be a model.'

'Wouldn't it be nicer to have a year of parties and then marry a duke?'

'She could marry a duke anyway.'

'Then why waste time being a model? It's very hard work. No, marriage is going to be her career. I'm sure of it. You may be content with a penniless second son, but Angel might get something very much better than me.'

'Well, of course, I do believe marriage is the best thing for a girl, and helping her husband in his career rather than having her own. I've always thought that. But I don't know that Angel's going to find a better husband by being a deb.'

'I'd be surprised if she married Wing Commander Groves.'

'Well, so would I. It's against the law. Unless Susan died of course.'

'You know what I mean. You father was furious about that marriage. Now's the time to work on him, tell him that Angel mustn't make the same mistake.'

'I suppose there's something in it.'

'Of course there's something in it. And I'm not just being altruistic about Angel either. I'm thinking about us.'

'Us?'

'Of course. I shall be in Parliament. Isn't it going to be rather pleasant if instead of being just a hopeful young M.P. with a wife and a baby and a tiny flat, I'm responsible for the deb of the year? Angel's going to be a beauty, remember. And if your father pays we shall be able to entertain in a way we couldn't afford to do otherwise. It all helps you know.'

'Oh no. Really?'

'Yes, yes, it does. Just a little. We shall make a mark we shouldn't make otherwise. Other things are important naturally, more important no doubt. But this would pay off. You'd see.'

'Well, but you'd always be in the House of Commons. It's supposed to be such hard work, I thought. All night sittings and all that.'

'I don't mind not sleeping, you know that. And one can slip away easily enough and be back for the Division. Anyway, that's where you'd be so important, as the hostess. You know how good you are at that sort of thing. It's a challenge, my dear. Accept it.'

'There'll be the baby.'

'Your father will have to pay for a nanny. You'll be looking after Angel for him.'

'I suppose it might be a good thing.'

'Well, don't worry about it. See what you think. There's

no wild hurry to decide. Only if you do think it's a good idea, I think you ought to raise it with your father. It would look better coming from you.'

'Yes. Yes, I suppose it would.'

At Christmas there was a scene. They were all there, Gabriel, his five daughters and two son-in-laws, and Miss Martin.

The scene came about because Charlotte and Selina did something terrible.

They were in the library one day when Gabriel was away. Selina was reading, at random, Boswell's *Life of Johnson*. She was not interested in Johnson but liked the book, which was a slim red leather volume, printed on India paper. Charlotte was looking through the drawers of her father's desk for a map because she wanted to go on a bicycle tour of East Anglia: instead she found a drawer full of old letters and diaries and began to read them. The diaries were small engagement diaries, and consisted mainly of entries like, 'lunch K. 1 o'clock', but the letters were more interesting.

'I've found a lot of love letters,' she said.

'How awful. We mustn't read them,' said Selina, dropping her book and hurrying over to Charlotte.

'They're from Mummy,' said Charlotte.

'Oh don't read them, please,' said Selina, blushing.

'I'm not going to silly,' said Charlotte. 'Look at this lot. Who was Janet, do you think?'

'Oh don't,' said Selina.

'Here's a huge bundle. Who's Sir Rt. Sutton?'

'Oh, you know, the man who took up Father when he was young, and brought him into his business and all that.'

'This says, Marriage 1925. Here's another one signed Robert. What thick paper. " . . . My continued support in all you do. You know I have great hopes for you in your political career, and I believe Hannah will help you because she is so beautiful and charming. I do hope and trust she will share your faith and enthusiasm. As for the business, I meant what I said the other night. I'm getting old. I want to hand over to you, quite gradually and along the lines we discussed over dinner, because if you're handling things I can retire with a quiet mind." I wonder what happened about that? The great hopes didn't come to much did they? I say, you know, his parents must have been awfully peculiar, Father's I mean. They refused to have anything more to do with him after he started working with that man Sutton because they thought capitalism was immoral.'

'It wasn't that, I thought,' said Selina. 'It was because he volunteered for the Army in 1914 and they were pacifists.'

'I wonder if any of these are from them,' said Charlotte, turning back to the drawer.

'They probably couldn't write,' said Selina.

They giggled nervously.

'Of course they could write,' said Charlotte. 'She was a school teacher.'

'Only Sunday school,' said Selina.

'Oh was it?' said Charlotte. 'But he was a clergyman, he must have been able to write.'

'Not a proper clergyman, only a Baptist or something,' said Selina.

'He never talks about them, does he?' said Charlotte. 'I suppose he's ashamed of them.'

'He doesn't talk about being a prisoner in the First War either,' said Selina. 'He probably didn't like them, that's all. He quarrelled terribly with his father. Martin knows about it, she told me. His father was very fierce and puritan and believed in poverty and no singing and dancing and he slaved away among the miners, bringing them salvation. And Father ran away to make his fortune.'

'He sounds marvellous,' said Charlotte.

'I don't think he does at all,' said Selina. 'I'd have run away too. They saw his mother sometimes I think.'

'I know, I remember her, very vaguely. She had a piece of velvet ribbon round her neck and a funny voice.'

'Fancy keeping all these letters, in bundles like this, with dates on.'

'Perhaps he's going to write his autobiography,' suggested Selina.

'How could he, he hasn't done anything,' said Charlotte. 'Here's a long bit he's written on one lot, "I found this bundle in my darling's desk two days after she died. May 13th 1943. They are all the letters I ever wrote to her." '

'Oh please don't read them,' said Selina.

'I'm not going to,' said Charlotte. But one of the letters had slipped out and was open in her hand. They read the first few lines.

'My dearest darling, So you wrote to me in your new blue dressing-gown. If I'd been there I would have opened it to kiss your darling breasts and you'd have had no time for writing letters . . .'

'Oh put it away, put it away,' cried Selina, scarlet with horror and embarrassment.

Charlotte stuffed the letters back into the drawer and shut it.

'Other people's love letters really are rather embarrassing,' she said grandly.

'Yes,' said Selina. 'Aren't they?'

They went back to their chairs and picked up books, pretending to read them.

'I suppose I ought to tidy up that drawer,' said Charlotte. 'Or he might see someone's been in there.'

But then Miss Martin came in, cross with them for being late for lunch, and they left the library with her, and afterwards simply forgot that the drawer of letters bore evidence of their guilt.

It was several days before Gabriel, opening that drawer in mistake for another one, saw that the letters had been tampered with and tidied them up, thinking it must have been one of the Italian servants who wouldn't have understood what they had read anyway, and locked the drawer.

At lunch there was a good deal of noise, Charlotte was being teased, Selina had a fit of the giggles. They forgot for the moment that there seemed to be a certain coolness between Ham and Bill Groves, and that Gabriel had been in a state of brooding ill-humour all the holiday. Their good spirits made him suddenly, without expecting to do

more than modify their gaiety by letting them know that
he was always on the lookout for treachery, say, 'Have
any of you children been looking in the drawers of my
desk?'

There was silence. He looked round the circle of
bewildered or indifferent faces until he came to Selina's,
which to his amazement was bright scarlet.

'Selina?' he said.

Selina said nothing.

'Selina!' he said.

'Yes, no, I mean it was a mistake,' said Selina, not yet
crying but with tears in her eyes from blushing.

'Good God!' he said in a voice of disgust.

'It was me,' said Charlotte, who had turned rather pale
and was sticking out her jaw as if she expected to be
struck on it. 'I did it. It was nothing to do with Selina.'

'You too?' he shouted. 'I might have known it.'

'But what were you doing, Charlotte?' said Penelope
helpfully. 'Were you looking for something? Pencils or
something?'

'I was looking for a map,' said Charlotte.

'We wanted to go on a bicycle tour,' said Selina.

'Oh what a good idea, I went on a bicycle tour once,'
said Susan hurriedly.

'You didn't, Susan, it was a walking tour,' said Angel.

'Be quiet,' said Gabriel, whose face was trembling. 'That
wasn't the map drawer, was it, Charlotte?'

'No,' said Charlotte.

'What drawer was it?' said Gabriel, through his teeth.

'Just a few old letters,' said Charlotte, trying to sound
bored.

'Just a few old letters,' shouted Gabriel, banging his fist
on the table. 'You take my life and pass it through your
ignorant stupid smutty little fingers and say it's a few old
letters. The most sacred secret intimate documents of my
life and you take them and giggle at them in your ignorant
schoolgirl way. . . .'

'Perhaps Charlotte and Selina had better go to their
rooms. They've been very naughty,' said Miss Martin,
hoping to avert the storm.

'And what did you do about it?' said Gabriel, pointing,

a shaking finger at her. 'You didn't stop them did you? What do you think I pay you for? That's what it is, it's being without a mother that's made them what they are – hard, hard and cold, all of you – small hearts, small minds, smutty, curiosity, ingratitude . . .' His face trembled so violently that it looked as if it might disintegrate. He gave a dry sob. 'Ingratitude, ingratitude,' he said.

Bill Groves stood up.

'This seems to be rather a family matter, sir,' he said. 'I think I'll go and smoke a pipe.'

'Sit down, you ape,' Gabriel, flapping both hands at him. 'You're a member of the family, aren't you? You can't run away. Is that what our gallant air force did in the war? You wouldn't have got away with it then, would you? Even though Susan now tells me you were on the ground staff because you had flat feet. Waited till after the wedding to tell me that, of course. You're all the same, all of you. All trying to deceive me.'

'I didn't say flat feet and I said for part of the war,' said Susan crisply.

'We're sorry,' said Selina.

'Sorry?' he shouted. 'What good does that do? The harm's done, isn't it? You've done the thing haven't you? When I think of what I do for you. I give you everything, everything, my beautiful house, an expensive education, expensive weddings – do you know what they cost me, those weddings? – and God knows what I spend on your clothes, your allowances, your holidays abroad, your train fares. You have everything, everything – do you realize how few children in this country today have what you have? A beautiful garden, pets, playthings, gramophones, my beautiful library. And what do I get? Treachery, Deceitfulness. Snooping. You were snooping, at my private letters, giggling and sneering at my letters to your mother and hers to me. Let me tell you . . .' again the shaking finger. 'There isn't one of you, no, not one, who can understand that relationship, who can truly know what it was, no matter how much you snoop and sneer. None of you comes anywhere near her, none of you is fit to, fit to . . .' The tears were now pouring down his cheeks. He dabbed at them furiously with his napkin.

'We didn't read them, we didn't,' said Selina. 'We saw a letter from Sir Robert Sutton, that's all, and we read that.'

Gabriel said in a more normal voice, 'Those are all my private papers, and nothing to do with any of you.'

Penelope took the opportunity to say, 'Shall we go into the other room?' lunch having been over for some time.

Gabriel stood up.

'They ought to be punished,' he said irresolutely to Miss Martin.

'They certainly ought and I'll see to it this afternoon,' said Miss Martin briskly. 'Come along now, Charlotte and Selina, come upstairs with me.'

When they were upstairs she said, 'How silly you were. Now for your punishment you must work in the wood for an hour this afternoon. There's a lot of clearing up to be done there.'

'I won't,' said Charlotte, and ran into her bedroom and banged the door.

Miss Martin said through the door, 'I'll just take Selina then. You can come out when you're feeling better. You'll have a much worse punishment if you stay in there brooding all afternoon.'

Selina and Miss Martin had quite a pleasant afternoon in the wood and as they went in to tea Selina said, 'We didn't read Mummy's letters and only one line of his to her.'

'Of course you didn't,' said Miss Martin. 'And now you've finished the punishment I should forget about the whole thing.'

But Charlotte would not forget. She went about in a state of suppressed fury for several days, and told Selina that as soon as she was sixteen she was going to leave school and become a famous actress and never see her father again.

Gabriel went to sleep over *The Times* crossword after lunch. He dreamt that he was in bed with Hannah and woke up feeling sexually excited and extremely miserable. Before dinner Angel came in and said that Penelope and

Ham would like to play bridge after dinner and would he play with them as she, Angel, had been practising and was getting quite good now. This mollified him a little, and at dinner Ham asked his advice about a political question and then Penelope, choosing her moment, said, 'Well, we haven't had a row like that since the one about the date of the Jewish sabbath when Charlotte hit you on the head with a plate. Do you remember that one, Father?'

'That was quite different,' said Gabriel. 'She simply refused to accept a fact, which I verified from several books of reference.'

'You were even more angry though,' said Angel.

'Unreasonableness is extremely annoying,' said Gabriel, with a slight smile.

It was a famous incident in the family, grown more astonishing by much re-telling.

'You were pretty frightened when she came at you with that plate,' said Penelope.

'It was a most disgraceful exhibition,' said Gabriel, and began to laugh. He shook all over. He put his big head back on his big shoulders and shouted with laughter. 'It was quite disgraceful,' he shouted, and tears of laughter rolled down his cheeks.

Charlotte looked at her plate and smiled reluctantly. Bill Groves looked shocked. The others were all laughing. The evening was saved. Afterwards they played bridge and Gabriel gave Angel advice about the game and was pleased with the progress she had made.

Bill Groves thought the whole episode had been in very bad taste. He never forgave his father-in-law.

3

ANGEL drove down with Roger Martin to see Charlotte act in the school play. When they got there they found that she had been replaced by her understudy because she and another girl had been to the cinema one Saturday afternoon and that was against the rules.

Charlotte was outraged: they had certainly hit her where it most hurt. She was to have been Rosalind in *As You Like It*, and thought she would have been very good. She had imagined all the parents rising to their feet in a storm of applause, and the English mistress, whom she loved, running through the cheering crowd to shake her by the hand. Now all this had been taken from her.

Angel and Roger Martin arrived with bags of cherries in an open car to find her in her most smouldering state of mind. She had been told that she must watch the play, because to refuse to do so showed that she cared more for her own honour and glory than for that of the school.

'Of course I do,' she said furiously, repeating this news to Angel. 'I don't care tuppence for the honour and glory of the school, filthy stinking foul unnatural hole, I wish it would fall through the earth and everybody be killed before it should have any honour and glory. In fact I'm jolly glad I'm not in the play because then everybody will think what a bad school it is when they see how bad Mary English is as Rosalind.'

'But how boring to have to watch it when you're not in it,' said Angel. 'Boring for all of us. We only came to see you. We don't want to see Mary English. I remember her. She had huge teeth and something wrong with her bosom.'

'That's right,' said Charlotte. 'Miss Brace says she has a beautiful speaking voice.'

'What's wrong with her bosom?' said Roger Martin, polishing his dark glasses with a silk handkerchief.

'She has three,' said Angel in a fearful whisper.

'No, really? How amusing,' said Roger Martin.

'I'll go and see if I can get round Miss Brace,' said Angel, who had been looking forward to showing off her new found sophistication in front of her former headmistress.

Miss Brace was a personality. She was seventy-five. She had wild white hair scraped into an unruly bun, a Churchillian delivery and a sarcastic tongue. Her subject was Divinity.

Her father had been a headmaster of Rugby, and she would have liked her school to be as like his as possible; but while teaching the girls the importance of sport, team spirit and academic success, she concealed a secretly snobbish heart and her favourite Old Girls were not the teachers, the doctors, or the research workers, but the ones who had married well. This was a prejudice she would never avow, and girls and staff equally were treated with scorn if they were seen to show interest in such inferior pursuits as sewing, cooking, child care or the improvement of their own appearances. There was a famous occasion when a pretty young biology mistress came to Prayers wearing lipstick and the deep voice barked from the dais, 'Child, go and wash that paint off your face!' No member of the staff was allowed to wear make-up.

Parents on the whole were impressed by Miss Brace: she was so rude to them. They thought that a personality so vigorous must have a stimulating and educative effect on their children. She herself subscribed to this view, but in most cases it was wrong, because her personality was too strong. It imposed itself, it drove all before it, including such tender shoots of being as might be sprouting in the souls of the children in her care and which were turned back and grew in again like toenails meeting a shoe which was too small. There was a mousy little history mistress who played no part in school life outside the classroom. The girls listened to her lessons because they seemed less dull than the others, but they never much noticed her as a person. Nobody was in love with her, nobody had a hate for her. Even quite stupid girls did well in the history examinations. Miss Brace said, 'History is the easiest subject,' because she did not understand Miss Welch's unselfishness.

The standard of teaching, apart from Miss Welch's was not as high as Miss Brace's policy required. This might have been a result of the scarcity of good women teachers, or of Miss Brace's bullying of her staff, or of her anxiety to keep their salaries as low as statutory requirements would allow, or of the cold inaccessibility of the particular part of the Suffolk coast which she had chosen for her school.

Miss Brace liked Angel. She had once read in a book that 'the best mother has a favourite child,' and this had confirmed her theory that the best school mistress had favourite pupils. Angel had been a lovely favourite – so pretty, and on the whole, unlike her tiresome sister, so good. Angel had enjoyed being at school and thought Miss Brace quite a sweet old thing as long as you teased her a bit. Charlotte was as temperamentally incapable of teasing her as she was of obeying her rules.

Angel ran along the passage to Miss Brace's room and burst in with swirling skirts and a smell of expensive scent. Miss Brace felt as if her heart first leapt, and then melted – it was quite painful – and she plodded forward on her fat flat feet to kiss her former pupil on both cheeks.

'Well, you have grown up,' she said, opening her blue eyes very wide and looking at her over the top of her spectacles: Angel knew this as her benign expansive look, and felt warmly toward her in return.

'How lovely to see you, how are you?' she said, laughing happily. 'How's the school? It all seems just the same. It's lovely lovely lovely not to be here!'

'Well, it isn't lovely lovely lovely not to have you,' said Miss Brace. 'We only have your naughty little sister who causes us a lot of trouble. But how pretty you've grown – and such a pretty dress – and we read all about you in the papers, at this or that fashionable affair. And what about the secretarial course? Gone by the board I suppose?' This with a mock stern look.

'Of course,' said Angel. 'But only till the autumn, then I'm going to do it seriously.'

'And you enjoyed your three months in Paris?' said Miss Brace. 'How's your French?'

'Magnifique,' said Angel. 'It was lovely. Paris is marvellous.'

'And now you're enjoying yourself, being frivolous?' said Miss Brace, indulgently.

'Oh yes, every minute of it,' said Angel, in her new, slightly affected voice. 'Everyone thinks I'm mad. They all go to all these dances and things, getting more and more bored and blasé about them, and there am I always laughing my head off – silly really. Poor Charlotte, Miss Brace, she's so upset about this play. Of course it was terribly naughty of her to go to the cinema like that, nobody ever did it in my day. But she's so miserable.'

Miss Brace swept the benign look off her face, and replaced it by the very grave one.

'I'm worried about Charlotte,' she said. 'She's one of the most anti-social girls we've had, and that's very difficult to deal with. It seems impossible to make any impression on her. It amazes me that anyone so young should be so hard.'

'She isn't really hard, I'm sure she isn't,' said Angel, winningly. 'It's just that she feels so strongly about everything. Couldn't she possibly be in the play?'

'No', said Miss Brace. 'She must be punished. She must be made to realize that she has a contribution to make. She's too proud for a child of fifteen. That's why I've said she must watch someone else play the part.'

'Oh,' cried Angel, tragically. 'I believe it might break her heart. Supposing we did something really improving, like taking her to a museum, couldn't we miss the play then?'

Miss Brace smiled at her. 'It's very naughty of you to ask me,' she said.

'Oh please, please,' said Angel. 'And when I marry a duke I'll send all my twelve daughters here and they'll be such a credit to you.'

Miss Brace laughed and smacked her playfully on the

bottom. 'Run along with you, child,' she said. 'I oughtn't to allow it, but off you go.'

'And we can miss the play?' said Angel.

'Yes, yes, you can miss it,' said Miss Brace. 'It's a pity, we've got a good cast this year . . .' but Angel had waved her hand and swirled out of the door and was running along the passage, which girls were forbidden to do. Miss Brace sighed, and thought how sweet she was and how well she had turned out. It was naughty of her to say that about marrying a duke. Still, it would be rather fun if she did.

They did not take Charlotte to a museum. Instead they had a picnic on the beach, and afterwards Roger Martin bathed, but the girls said it was too cold for them. Charlotte asked Angel about him.

'He's a sort of paid informer for gossip columns,' said Angel, who was lying face downwards on a rug, sunbathing. 'Isn't it a frightful thing to be? He's a great friend of Ham's and often puts bits about him in the paper – good publicity – and Ham does useful things for him. All rather sinister really. Isn't he frightfully good-looking, don't you think?'

'Yes, except he looks rather ill,' said Charlotte.

'That's terribly attractive,' said Angel with authority. 'Lots of people are madly in love with him and he treats them all frightfully badly.'

'Does he treat you frightfully badly?'

'Of course not. I'm not in love with him.'

'Is he in love with you?'

'Oh, I should think so,' said Angel in an exaggeratedly bored voice. 'Everyone is.'

'Angel!' said Charlotte, shocked.

Angel laughed. 'I was only teasing you. I don't know whether he is or not. I don't think he is. He hasn't asked me to marry him yet anyway.'

'Do they all do that?'

'Oh yes,' said Angel. 'Well, actually, only two people really have, absolutely outright you know, but quite a lot have hinted and that sort of thing.'

'And what do you say?' asked Charlotte, impressed.

'I say, 'Can't we just be friends?' said Angel. 'It's so funny, you should see me.'

'Collecting proposals?' said Charlotte. 'I can't imagine it somehow.'

'Oh, you'd never do it, you're much too serious,' said Angel. 'It's only a game, you see, really.'

'Do you let them kiss you?' said Charlotte.

'Oh yes, all the time,' said Angel. 'It's awful.'

'All the time?' said Charlotte, amazed.

'Well, no, what I mean is,' said Angel. 'It is rather awful in a way because it really doesn't mean anything at all. And when I think – do you know, the first time I was kissed I thought we were engaged practically? And now as a matter of course I kiss anyone who takes me home or people at dances or anyone really, and it doesn't mean a thing.'

'Do you like it?'

'Sometimes. It depends on the person. Sometimes it's ghastly. And sometimes of course they want to go much further.'

'And do you do that?'

'Oh, no. I've never really wanted to, for one thing. And then I think people know whether you will or not and don't try if you don't want to. Everyone knows the girls who do, of course. It's rather bad luck on them, I suppose, because then they must be doing it all the time. People are always doing it with Roger. Do you remember that girl Faith Dunbridge who left the year before I did?'

'Yes,' said Charlotte.

'Well, she went to bed with Roger.'

'How do you know?'

'He told me. He tells everyone that sort of thing. It would be fatal to go to bed with him I should think. He said she was terribly over-sexed.'

'No! How extraordinary. She didn't look a bit like that.'

'You never know. I think I must be rather under-sexed, but I suppose it's different when you're really in love.'

'Some people never do fall in love.'

'I'm sure I will, I do hope it will be soon,' said Angel. 'Wouldn't it be lovely to be married?'

'No, I think it would be perfectly ghastly,' said Charlotte. 'Imagine being tied to somebody for the rest of your life!'

'You're different. I think it would be lovely to be tied.'

'But not to Roger Martin?'

'I don't think he'd be a good husband,' said Angel. 'I suppose it might be all right if he was in love with you. But I'm sure it will be different when I meet the person I marry. The awful thing is you can't help leading all these people on in a sort of way, I mean just till they say they're in love with you or ask you to marry them or something, and then of course you stop. Is that very awful, do you think?'

'Yes. I think it's terrible. You must be a flirt.'

'Yes, I suppose so. But it doesn't matter really does it? I mean everyone knows it's only a game. And they are so funny!'

'I suppose it's all right for you, because you're not. But will you stop when you're married!'

'Of course! The absolute first minute! Of course I will!'

When they had taken Charlotte back to school, Angel and Roger Martin began the long drive back to London. On the way Roger suggested that they should spend the night with his mother who lived in Suffolk.

'She's a fearful bore,' he said. 'But it might be nicer to drive up in the morning.'

'I'd love to, if you think it would be all right with her,' said Angel.

Mrs. Martin turned out to be a cosy little woman, not at all the sort of person Angel had expected. She was the widow of a prosperous director of a large bank, and lived very comfortably in a large imitation Queen Anne house with a pretty garden. She was keen on interior decoration and floral arrangements: the house was full of gilded cherubs and the latest thing in thistles. Her son evidently despised her, but this did not appear to worry her: she was more interested in the local literary circle and a little luncheon club she had just started. Angel found her comfortable to talk to, and loved the girlish bedroom to which she showed her. It had a little Victorian bed with white muslin drapes and pink ribbons on it, and pink and white painted furniture and a thick white fitted carpet. Mrs. Martin lent her a frilly pink nightdress.

Angel was brushing her hair when Roger came in to say goodnight to her.

'Goodness, look at all these frills and things,' he said. 'My senses swoon. What do you think of my dear old bourgeois mum?'

'I think she's sweet,' said Angel.

'Isn't she just?' he said.

'Do you come here much?' she asked.

'Not if I can help it,' he said. 'It's all just the teeniest weeniest bit too comfy for me. Live dangerously is my motto.' He took her in his arms.

'I don't think you live a bit dangerously,' said Angel. 'Not really.'

'How we despise each other,' he said, and kissed her hard. Angel drew her face away and rested it on his shoulder.

'I don't despise you,' she said. 'I like you.'

'Like me?' he said, putting his hand under her chin to raise her face to his once more. 'Good heavens, no one's ever done that before. We'll have to do something about that.'

He pushed her gently back on to the bed and kissed her again.

'Hadn't you better go to bed?' she said.

'That's what I had in mind,' he said.

'I mean your own bed,' she said.

'In a minute. Don't worry.'

'No, honestly, please, Roger.'

'It's all right, I won't hurt you. Don't worry,' he said, pushing aside the frilly pink nightdress to reach her breast. 'Darling, you like that, I know you do. Oh God, how beautiful you are. You like this, say you like it. Relax, darling, I won't hurt you.'

'But, Roger, I don't really want to . . .'

'Darling, trust me, just trust me. I won't hurt you.'

Angel shut her eyes.

After a time he said gently, 'Naughty girl. You've been teasing me.'

'What do you mean?' she said.

'Teasing, teasing, teasing everybody.'

'I don't understand.'

'You're not a virgin, my little honey-bunch.'

'What do you mean, Roger?' she said, pushing him away. 'Of course I am. I've never been to bed with anybody.'

He held her face between his hands and looked into her eyes. They filled with tears. 'I don't understand,' she said.

'It's all right,' he said. 'Some people are born like that or it happens riding, or playing hockey, or whatever it is girls do. Don't worry. It's nice for you.'

'Roger,' she twisted away from him. 'I feel terrible. Could we stop a minute?'

'No,' he said firmly. 'Not now. Not ever. Shut up. I want you. Don't you know what that means? I suppose you don't, poor little soft thing. Now shut up and keep still.'

Angel shut her eyes again.

Nothing very terrible seemed to happen.

Afterwards Roger fell asleep. She pushed him aside and slid under the bedclothes. Soon she fell asleep too.

There was no one on her bed when she woke up in the morning. She dressed, feeling worried, and went down to breakfast. Roger was there, so much the same as ever that she soon forgot to be embarrased with him. She began to feel better.

They drove back to London. On the way she decided that the whole business of sex was a lot of fuss about nothing: this gave her a certain feeling of emancipation. He was quite kind and polite. He dropped her at Penelope's house, and said, 'Goodbye, darling. I like you very much. See you soon.' Then he drove away.

She was glad he had not said anything about marriage: she thought it would be hateful to be married to him.

Charlotte walked along the cliffs into the wind, which

was blowing saltily in from the sea, making the waves thump on the stony beach below, and the seabirds shriek drifting on the gusts of it. The conversation she had had with Angel about men was worrying her, and she was not sure why. Jealousy, disapproval, shame, fear? She did not know. She was embarrassed by the thought of Angel being kissed by a man, that was one thing, and she supposed it was no wonder, because she was her sister, and there was a weight of inherited and acquired tabus against thinking of one's own family in physical terms at all. For instance, the thought of Gabriel with a woman filled her with shame and disgust and yet she should not pretend that there was anything basically wrong in the idea of her father having sexual urges. But her conversation with Angel had been more personal than that. It had made her think of what she herself might be doing in a year or so's time. It filled her with doubt – but doubt that it was a good thing to do, or doubt that she would be any good at doing it? She shared a dormitory with a girl who kept a notebook in which she wrote down the names of the boys who had kissed her. There seemed to be an awful lot of them already, and one of them had a cross against his name because he had been the best.

Charlotte strode along the cliff-top thinking could that be all she was aiming for, all the agonies of one sort or another leading only to the list of names in the notebook, and the cross against the one that kissed her. But the aim of my life is not, she thought with violent scorn, to be attractive to men. It is – to be, to reach – but now, that was better, she could feel that she was getting a little nearer to the idea of what it was that had to be reached. Quickening her step along the cliff top she thought, yes, that's it, of course I am different from Angel, Angel does not know that there is anything to be reached. But I do. It is this truth at which I guess when I am at my best, when life is leaping in me, when my mind is thundering with thought, when the smell of the sea and the grass, and the colour and sound and size and beat of them are exploding around and within me and my feet that pound the earth are the feet of millions and of me, and the air I gasp for feeds the strength of the will in me, the will which sweeps me with all my faculties clear and singing with apprehension towards the truth. And Rachel Bredon keeps a list of boys who have kissed her. Charlotte laughed, flexing her fingers to feel the power in them, thinking, oh my brothers, of Keats and Swinburne and Samuel Palmer, and thinking, what is this power, this energy, what shall I do with it?

At the end of July Penelope left Angel in London, and went up to Harkwood to rest.

There had been the election, the baby, then the bringing-out of Angel. She was white and thin. Also all sorts of things which she had never had to worry about before had recently become vast anxieties. She worried about the baby, who was four months old and in the care of a nanny, paid for according to plan by Gabriel. The nanny was large, starched and inflexible, and blamed the baby's continual crying on Penelope, because he was not breast-fed. Ham had told Penelope that the baby would have to be bottle-fed because otherwise she would not be free to concentrate on Angel's career as a debutante, but she had been prepared to start feeding him herself and wean him early. When it came to the point she found herself unable to do this, and so incurred the lasting disapproval of Nanny. Her consciousness of this disapproval exacerbated the guilt which she felt at not really very much liking her baby. She had meant to like him, had fully expected that she would, but when he came he was so ugly and cried so much that she found herself unable to care for him. Sometimes he smiled at Nanny, and sometimes at Angel, but it seemed to Penelope that he did not much like his mother, and this made her nervous.

Ham was kind about it, and said that he hated women who were silly about babies and that it was much more important that she should be a good companion to her son later on; but all the same it worried her.

She worried about Angel, too, because she thought she had become rather silly and wondered whether Ham was careful enough about the people to whom he introduced her, because really she, Penelope, did know that at heart Angel had always been an awful fool, and Ham seemed unable to understand this.

Another thing which worried her was that she had ceased to believe in God. She mentioned it to Ham and he shouted with laughter. 'Goodness, what a case of arrested development,' he said. 'It happened to everyone else at fifteen.' But it had not happened to her at fifteen. She had gone on going to church all through her three years at Cambridge, not with fervour exactly, but with confidence. She liked the Church of England, and thought it sensible and not exaggerated or in anyway suspect – unlike the Church of Rome – and she liked the familiarity of the prayers and psalms, and thought that without faith one would be bound to fall into the sin of despair. And now that was what she felt she had done – lost her faith and fallen into the sin of despair, and there was no one to help her. She had never had the habit of confidence in Miss Martin, fond of her though she was, and now more than ever she seemed to her too optimistically removed from real life. Her father was away, Charlotte's holidays had not yet started and anyway she was to spend the first week of them in Cornwall with a school friend. Only Selina was there, and Penelope, who was usually so fond of her, as the youngest, the clown, was beginning to find her a bore. The world in which she lived seemed so much her own that Penelope feared she was becoming whimsical and blamed Miss Martin for encouraging her.

After tea every day Miss Martin sewed and Selina read aloud, and Penelope, who was afraid of being alone and had quite lost the habit of reading herself, had to sit through it.

Lars Porsena of Clusium
By the Nine Gods he swore
That the great house of Tarquin
Should suffer wrong no more.

Selina read with verve but rather fast. She also skipped indiscriminately so as to get on to her favourite passages.

Alone stood brave Horatius,   [she rattled]
But constant still in mind;
Thrice thirty thousand foes before,
And the broad flood behind.
'Down with him!' cried false Sextus,
With a smile on his pale face.
'Now yield thee,' cried Lars Porsena,
'Now yield thee to our grace.'

Round turned he, as not deigning
Those craven ranks to see;
Nought spake he to Lars Porsena,
To Sextus nought spake he;
But he saw on Palatinus
The white porch of his home;
And he spake to the noble river
That rolls by the towers of Rome.

'Oh Tiber! father Tiber!
To whom the Romans pray,
A Roman's life, a Roman's arms,
Take thou in charge this day!'
So he spake, and speaking sheathed
The good sword by his side,
And with his harness on his back,
Plunged headlong in the tide.

'I'm sure Emily Brontë would never have read anything so bogus as Macaulay's *Lays of Ancient Rome*,' said Penelope irritably.

Selina looked crushed.

'Nonsense,' said Miss Martin. 'She might well have admired them. The Brontës had very bad taste. Go on, Selina.'

'I don't think I will,' said Selina with feigned indifference.

'Oh do,' said Miss Martin.

'No, I've read enough,' said Selina. 'I think I'll just go for a walk before I go to bed.'

When she had gone Miss Martin said mildly, 'It does get her out, the Emily Brontë phase . . .'

'Get her out?' repeated Penelope.

'To tramp the moors, alone with her faithful dog,' said Miss Martin.

'But surely it can't be good for her, all this make-believe?' said Penelope.

'I should have thought it was, rather,' said Miss Martin. 'It isn't exactly make-believe, it's just falling rather violently under the influence of a succession of historical personages. It keeps her busy. She's never bored.'

Sensing a reproof, because she knew her own boredom had been evident for the last few days, Penelope said crossly. 'But if she's so busy with all these historical personages how can she have any time to get used to real life?'

'What is real life?' said Miss Martin whimsically. 'Anyway she's only ten.'

'She'll have to go to school soon. Then she'll have to adapt herself to real life,' said Penelope.

'Ah, now that I do know. The one place where real life isn't, is a girls' boarding school,' said Miss Martin. 'Anyway I hope your father will put off sending her for as long as possible.'

'Oh dear, what do you think about boys?' said Penelope, who did not really want to quarrel with Miss Martin. 'Julian's down for Eton but I'm not at all happy about it. How do you think one should educate a boy these days? Ham says . . .' And she was off on to another worry, little Julian's education.

Selina had wandered out into the warm damp evening, wishing that Penelope had not become so thin and cross and that Charlotte would come back, because Charlotte, in theory at least, was always on her side.

She went through the stable yard towards the kitchen garden, meaning to climb along the wall, which was high and dangerous, but on the way she looked in at the henhouse and read through the last few paragraphs of her book. She could see at once that it was not going to work. It would be better to start again, with new characters and a different situation; so she drew a heavy line under what she had written and turned to another page, on which she wrote 'CHAPTER ONE'. Then she realized that she was not ready to start the new book, because she had not thought about it enough, so she waited idly for a few minutes, and then she wrote, carefully, for her writing was beginning to look quite tidy:

> Still let my tyrants know I am not doomed to wear
> Year after year in gloom and desolate despair
> A messenger of Hope comes every night to me
> And offers for short life eternal liberty.
>
> He comes with Western winds, with evening's wandering airs,
> With that clear dusk of heaven that brings the thickest stars:
> Winds take a pensive tone, and stars a tender fire,
> And visions rise, and change, that kill me with desire.

She read the two verses aloud, twice. They were not what she had read when first she had discovered the poem: they had become her own, and possessing them gave her a sort of power. She read them again, and her body throbbed to the sound of her own voice. She began once more, but that was a mistake, the magic had gone; she put the book and the pencil back on the shelf and went out of the henhouse, bolting the door carefully behind her.

She slipped through the gate into the kitchen garden, stole an unripe cooking apple, and climbed back into James's field without being seen. She ate the apple and gave the core to James. Miss Martin came out to tell her that she was late for bed.

'I wanted you to be punctual tonight because your father's coming back tomorrow,' she said.

'Why on earth should that mean I must go to bed punctually tonight?' asked Selina.

'So that you look healthy tomorrow,' said Miss Martin. 'And not tired.'

'But I always look healthy,' said Selina.

Penelope could not sleep until the early hours of the morning.

She went downstairs again after she had been lying in bed for some time, and walked about in her dressing-gown. It was not cold. The moon was very bright, making the garden look elaborate, ready for a masquerade. She went into the library and looked for a book to read, but nothing appealed to her. She began to regret having read so little lately. She had somehow given it up after leaving Cambridge, and now only kept up to date with politics. There she was often better informed than Ham. She read the pamphlets he was sent as well as the newspapers and the weeklies and the propaganda from the Conservative Central Office. It was useful to Ham, but now, desolate in the moonlit library, it seemed to her awfully silly, for of course he could look after his career well enough on his own without her anxious earnest futile help.

'I am as bad as Susan,' she told herself.

For it was Susan who suffered from depression and feelings of inadequacy, not Penelope, Susan who thought that no one loved her, or that she had cancer, or perni-cious anaemia, not the disciplined efficient Penelope.

'But perhaps she has no more worries now,' thought Penelope, imagining Susan being endlessly comforted by the Wing Commander. She could not see him as being particularly comforting herself, but Susan evidently did find him so. Penelope had been to see her a month or two ago in a little house on the edge of a common near Byfleet and she had said she was happy and looked as if she meant it.

'But Ham is quite comforting too,' said Penelope aloud in the empty room.

She had not married him for comfort, nor yet exactly for love; but more with the idea of doing something constructive, because beneath his docile and flippant exte-rior she had been aware of a relentlessness in the pursuit of certain ends. He was ambitious, though she was not quite sure even now whether she knew the springs of his ambition, and she knew that she could help him, and felt that to help him would be right. She looked on the marriage as a contract to regularize that arrangement, because though she was generous she had not a loving heart. She required her rights, and in return took a very serious view of her own obligations. She felt she had done well over these: she had produced a son, worked hard at the election, done what Ham had requested about Angel and their splash in London society. Only she was filled with this awful ill unease: it felt like something worse than overwork. She hardly dared to think that it might be anything to do with Ham – with his using Angel for ends of his own? Making friends with the wrong sort of people in politics? He seemed to spend his time with what seemed to Penelope rather insignificant plotters and intriguers: she could not feel they were the people that really mattered. But then, after all, everybody liked Ham.

'Perhaps I'll talk to Father,' she said.

He was coming back tomorrow, and he did know quite a lot about the world, about affairs in general. She had not often asked his advice about anything: indeed she did not mean to be so specific now. She simply thought that a talk, a real talk, which covered politics and conscience and ambition and duty, might help her to clear her mind, and give her back what she seemed to have lost, her sense of direction.

'He likes Ham too,' she thought. 'Of course he will be able to help.'

Then she went back to bed.

Gabriel came back ebullient.

Hope and vigour had taken the place of the depression he had felt after Lisa's death.

He had been to Paris for a week on business.

'You must get Ham to take you over there for a weekend,' he said to Penelope. 'It would do you a world of good. Let me know when you're going and I'll tell you where to eat.'

He had spent the previous weekend with some friends who had taken a house for the summer at Bembridge in the Isle of Wight. The friends were rich: Gabriel had met him through business, and the relationship had progressed rapidly. Gabriel was delighted to have been asked for the weekend; he very seldom stayed away.

'It's a charming place, Bembridge,' he said. 'You should

get to know it. It would be nice for Julian later on. Of course this is just the children's holiday for the Biddles. They're going to Greece themselves in September. They take a house in Bembridge every year. It's an amazing place, rather snobby of course, full of people one knows – that nice Mrs. Mahon was there, the one whose daughter was at Angel's dance, and all sorts of people. The Biddles say it's not what it was before the war, because undesirable elements have crept in, but it seemed very nice to me. There's sailing of course, you more or less have to do that, but it's rather amusing. Fairly expensive, I suppose. The Biddles have a cruiser and a Redwing, a beautiful boat – Brian's fearfully keen on racing, never wins – and a couple of Fireflies for the children, exquisite little boats. That's the way to do it; but then of course they must be very rich indeed. There was rather a charming little woman staying there at the same time as I was, a Mrs. Probert – Rosalie Probert – a widow, awfully amusing. You'd like her. Amazingly good in a boat, too. I thought of taking up sailing a bit. She gave me one or two useful tips about it, didn't seem to think I was too old, funnily enough. I thought it might be amusing to have a little boat, something one could sleep in for a weekend, keep it on the South Coast somewhere. Little Mrs. Probert could give me a hand at first. Sarah Biddle actually suggested we should share it, Rosalie Probert and I, I mean, but I thought that was most unsuitable. Heaven knows what else I should be expected to share with her.' He gave an earthy laugh. 'Not that I should object, far from it, but still, I didn't think it was the right basis on which to start. But I shall certainly ask her advice. And it will be nice for you children.'

'The advice?' said Penelope.

'The boat. Though I daresay you could take a tip or two on other things from her. Delightfully turned out, she was, all weekend. I do like a woman that makes the most of herself. Still, I must say you're very good in that respect yourself, Penelope, except that you look pretty much below par at the moment. Not having another baby, are you? No? Good. Women often do immediately after the first. They seem to be particularly fertile at the time. Or else it's something to do with the mistaken theory that it's impossible to conceive while breast-feeding. But then, of course, you're not feeding Julian yourself are you? Or should one not discuss these things in front of Selina? I always forget how young she is.

Selina blushed, hating him.

'Of course I hope I shall have another grandchild eventually,' he went on to Penelope, adding in a foul French accent. 'Un pour l'amour, deux pour la beaute, et le troisième gâte tout. That's the saying. Not that it happened in our case, I'm glad to say, though of course we might have stopped earlier if we'd managed to produce a son. Ah, well, who knows, it's not too late yet, I may still get an heir.'

'May you?' said Penelope, rather superciliously.

'Of course I may,' he said. 'Why not? Old Nigel Stone fathered three boys after the age of seventy-five.'

'But he was a joke,' said Penelope, unwisely.

'That's as may be. He happened to be a doddering old fool with no teeth. In fact I still don't believe he did it himself. But I'm only sixty-two. Besides I've always seemed young for my age. No one at Bembridge last weekend would believe I was a day over fifty – not that I tried to make them. So why not? I might easily get married again, to some nice pretty little person who could comfort me in my old age. None of you will take care of me when I'm old, you won't want to be bothered. You'll just be waiting for me to hurry up and die so that you can get your hands on my money. I know you all, all the same, every one of you.'

'You have come back in a horrid mood,' said Penelope. 'It must be the sea air.'

So she did not have her talk with him; and a day or two later returned to London. Angel was not there: she had gone to stay with a new friend of hers called Simon Reeves. The Parliamentary session had come to an end and Ham had accepted an invitation for them both to spend a week in the south of France with Harry Fieldman, a rich business man who was another fairly new Member. This week of sun and comfort cured Penelope of her depression for the time being.

Gabriel did not share a boat with Rosalie Probert; but he shared a bed with her, or rather a sofa, in her comfortable little flat near Holland Park, one warm night in August a week or two after their first meeting.

He had not expected it to happen so soon. They had had lunch together one day. She had been immaculately pretty and rather more flirtatious than she had been in the Isle of Wight. She had told him how unhappy she had been with Charlie Probert, and had managed delicately to imply that he had been brutish in bed. Gabriel found this exciting, but she quickly changed the subject and asked him with keen interest all about himself. It was a successful lunch.

A week later he took her to the opera at Covent Garden. They sat in the best seats and had champagne and smoked salmon sandwiches in the intervals and dinner at Boulestin afterwards. Gabriel enjoyed himself very much. The opera was *Tosca*, of which he was fond, and which made him cry. The dinner was nostalgic, and reminded him of the time when a friend of his and Hannah's had taken them often to his box at Covent Garden, and they had used to dine at Boulestin afterwards. They had once heard the whole of *The Ring* and their companion had been so knowledgeable and helpful that they had found the experience stimulating. It had been some time in the nineteen-twenties and the friend was dead now.

Towards the end of dinner Rosalie grew becomingly flushed. Her skin was rather dark, and she was now slightly sunburnt. She seemed to take on a more opulent look as the evening wore on, less neat and bright, more warm and glowing. It was very satisfactory.

As they left the restaurant and she came to him near the entrance where he was waiting for her (she had gone to powder her nose) he noticed that her eyes for all their brightness looked tired and were surrounded by lines; but he put that down to an unflattering light. 'Besides,' he thought without resentment. 'You can't have everything at my age.'

He put his arm round her in the taxi. She pressed herself warmly against his side, but as he bent his face towards her she placed two fingers on his lips and whispered. 'Not yet.'

Pleased, he leant back in the taxi, and remained in silent self-congratulation until they reached her flat.

Upstairs in her small beige sitting-room, she poured out two large whiskies and sodas and disappeared with hers into another room, saying, 'Make yourself at home. Put something on the gramophone.' He did not put anything on the gramophone, but wandered round the room for a few minutes, looked at a shiny magazine – there were no books – noticed the number of plants in pots, the absence of pictures, the superfluity of cushions; and then suddenly she was back in the room, stark naked.

Momentarily taken aback, he quickly recovered, put down the shiny magazine and advanced slowly towards her, feeling a pleasant surge of appetite.

'How do you like it?' she said, posing for him. She turned round, and wriggled her hips. 'The back view's good too,' she said.

'I like it very much,' he said, smiling lustfully.

She pressed herself against him, undoing his tie.

'I'm more used to being the undresser than the undressed,' he said, archly.

'Not here,' she said. 'House rules.' She pushed him back on the sofa and undid his shirt. He tried to kiss her.

'Don't be impatient,' she said. 'You shall have all you want in a minute. I knew you'd be greedy. I can always tell.'

She undressed him. He helped her, thinking, who'd have guessed she'd turn out like this, but not averse to the pleasures offered.

Then she was on him. He had to use all his strength to push her down beside him. 'I like to do some of the work myself,' he said.

Obscenities began to run through his brain. Little bitch, he would hate her and hurt her and leave her. If this was what she wanted she should have it: he joined battle.

He hated her with all the strength in his body. He had a good deal of strength in his body, even now. When he had finished with her he thought, tomorrow I shall feel ashamed of the pleasure I have felt. He lay beside her, wondering how soon he could leave.

Apparently she had other ideas: she was already stirring invitingly. At first he could not believe she wanted more already, but it seemed she did. He was now beyond pride, so he sat up abruptly and said, 'Enough is enough.'

'Not for me it isn't,' she said with a soft laugh.

'It is, you know,' he said. He disengaged himself, stood up and pulled on his trousers.

She still lay naked on the crumpled sofa.

'Poor old thing,' she said unkindly. 'Too much for you was it?'

He went on dressing in silence.

'And I thought you were going to be so good at first.' she said. 'Still, I suppose you're getting a bit past it.'

He could not look at her for shame and loathing.

'I like these things ordered with a little more delicacy,' he said stiffly, picking up his coat.

'Delicacy is it?' She began to laugh, but he did not hear what more she said, because he went out of the flat and banged the door behind him, leaving her alone on her tousled sofa.

There were no taxis about. He seemed to walk a long way. He found himself in a broad tree-lined street, with big white houses set back in their gardens. It seemed an endlessly long street. He could no longer keep his thoughts silent. Oh God, what was this agony in his heart, merely because some wretched woman had turned out to be sexually insatiable? But Hannah, but Lisa, he cried silently, my loves, my sweet gentle modest generous loves, or other women at other times with whom I shared something which had nothing to do with shame: oh loves, where are you now? I gave you my secret, my treasure, we shared its joy, we worshipped it together, you in your lace and frills and pearly-scented flesh, I in my strength and golden manhood. Has it all gone then with everything else I loved and valued? I am old, it must be that.

I am old, I am old, I am old, he cried to himself, marching from tree to tree down the broad street. Oh, Hannah, oh, Lisa, who sheltered me, how could you leave me exposed to this vulgarity, this obscenity, this putrefaction which is old age? It seemed he could smell the decay rising in his body. Sickened, he clasped one of the trees and leant against it, feeling its firmness against his own throbbing insubstantiality. Oh, Hannah, oh, Lisa. He was wildly unhappy.

4

SELINA went to school at the beginning of the winter term of 1953.

There had been what amounted to a family consultation about it, in the autumn. They were all, except Susan, at Harkwood for a weekend, the weekend before Charlotte was due to go back to school.

'Selina ought to be going too,' Gabriel had suddenly announced.

Penelope had said, 'I agree. She never sees anyone else of her own age.'

Angel said, 'I expect she'll love it.'

Charlotte said, 'I suppose she'd be all right. Jill Holbrook's sister's coming this term, and Pat Graham's, I think. They're probably both quite nice.'

Selina said, 'I'd rather like to go.'

Miss Martin said, 'She's only eleven, younger than any of the others when they went,' and 'I do think Wood Hall is much more of a school for older children. They don't bother much about the little ones,' and 'She'll be very much better educated if she stays at home until she's thirteen, and anyway the home influence is much more important than the school one for girls,' and 'It would be such a pity if she were to be turned against school just by being sent too young,' and 'My sister never recommends boarding school for girls before thirteen and after all she is in the business,' and finally, 'I really can't put it too strongly. I think it would be a terrible mistake.'

Selina went to Wood Hall in January, in her new uniform, accompanied by a trunk load of woollen vests and navy blue knickers and carrying a new lacrosse stick. Before she went Miss Martin gave her a brief account of the human reproductive system, because she thought it might be talked about among the girls. Miss Martin's description was rather technical and as it meant nothing at all to Selina, being unrelated to anything in her own experience, she forgot it the moment Miss Martin changed the subject.

Miss Martin waited anxiously for their letters. Charlotte wrote, 'Selina seems to be all right though rather silent. Unfortunately I don't see much of her because the Junior House is in the village and we hardly see them.' Selina wrote, 'I am in a room with four other people. They are called Ann Lawrence, Elizabeth Wright, Jill Tomlinson and Mary Daly. They seem quite nice except for Mary Daly. Miss Hope seems quite nice. We don't see Miss Brace much. I think I shall like it here when I am used to it.'

Miss Martin wrote to Selina three times a week. Selina wrote back twice a week, on Wednesdays and Sundays. Most of her letters ended, 'I still quite like school. Lots of love from Selina.'

Miss Martin told herself she was a fool: of course Selina was perfectly happy.

There were not many girls in the Junior School. They had glasses of milk and thick pieces of bread and butter for supper at seven o'clock.

The first evening Mary Daly sat on a table and said to Selina, 'There's a girl here called Daphne Sparks who has horrid stripy greasy hair. We all hate her and if you speak to her you'll be tied to a tree in the garden and have brambles pulled across your face.'

'All right, I won't then,' said Selina sensibly. 'Why d'you hate her?'

'She wets her knickers,' said Mary Daly. 'Do you know what the Curse is?'

'No,' said Selina.

'She doesn't know what the Curse is,' said Mary Daly.

Several people laughed. There was a group of girls talking in one corner, but most of the others had gathered round Mary Daly.

'Fancy your mother not telling you,' said Mary Daly. 'She must be daft.'

'My mother's dead,' said Selina.

'So squish to you, Mary Daly,' said a pretty fair-haired girl called Brigid Knight. 'Here, have another piece of bread and butter. This is all we have for supper. Isn't it mingy?' She held the plate out to Selina.

'Sally Carpenter's mother's dead too,' said a fat little girl.

'Shut up,' said Brigid Knight.

'I only meant they might make friends,' said the fat girl, injured.

'Anyone who makes friends with Sally Carpenter ought to be in a loony bin,' said Mary Daly.

'Here, come on, you new girl,' said a squat girl with permanently waved hair who looked like a little middle-aged housewife. 'I've got to take you to your dormitory.'

'I'll take her,' said Mary Daly. 'I'm head of the dorm. Come on.'

When she had shown Selina where to keep her clothes it was time to go to bed. Selina was not wearing her navy blue school knickers, and Mary Daly seemed to think this was very funny. She picked up the white ones which Selina had just taken off, and danced round the room with them.

'Catch!' she cried to Ann Lawrence, a little ratty child who obediently caught them and threw them on to Elizabeth Wright who had round cheeks and fat yellow pigtails and shieked with nervous laughter.

Selina got into bed.

'Do you know what your parents did before you were born?' said Mary Daly. 'They went off into a wood and they lay down on top of each other and then they kissed each other in a special way, not like ordinary kissing but putting their tongues right inside each other's mouths, and then . . .'

'Look out!' hissed Elizabeth.

Matron came in, a plump and amiable person.

'No more talking now,' she said. 'Settling down all right, are you, Selina? I expect it seems strange at first but you'll soon get used to it. Are they looking after you all right?'

'Yes, thank you,' said Selina.

'Yes, Matron,' said Mary Daly. 'I've shown her where to put her clothes and told her what to do in the morning.'

'That's right, Mary,' said Matron. 'We'll all help her, won't we, because she's our only new girl this term. They usually come in the autumn, you know,' she said to Selina. 'At the beginning of the school year. So you're our only one this term. Good night all of you, sleep well.'

'Good night, Matron,' they chorused.

Miss Brace said to Charlotte, 'How is your solemn little sister getting on? Miss Hope tells me she hasn't managed to get much out of her yet.'

'I think she's all right,' said Charlotte. 'I don't know that she finds all of the other children exactly easy.'

'She's been rather solitary, hasn't she?' said Miss Brace. 'She'll have to learn to mix. Miss Hope is very good with them.'

Charlotte had become acceptable to Miss Brace. She was not exactly a favourite, but she fitted into the scheme of things, because she had become that recognizable figure, the eccentric artist. A new art mistress had accomplished the change last term: under her guidance Charlotte had painted the backcloth for a form play. After that her view of things was transformed, and she decided she would be a great painter instead of a great actress. Her father, who had sworn that she should never go on the stage, was relieved by the change, and had agreed that she should go to an art school after a year in the sixth form: he had been encouraged by the art mistress's enthusiastic estimate of her talents. Miss Brace now saw Charlotte as making her contribution after all, for communities did have artists. So now there was an excuse for her lateness, untidiness and insubordination: it could be indulged as an expression of artistic temperament. Showing parents round the school Miss Brace would say when they reached the art room, 'And our art mistress has great hopes of one of our girls in the sixth. She really seems to be extraordinarily talented, and we're hoping it will last. She did the scenery for one of our plays quite beautifully.'

Now that she felt no pressure from Miss Brace, and having achieved a certain amount of freedom by reaching the sixth form, Charlotte passed her time happily enough, her time-table adjusted so that she could concentrate mainly on the theory, history and practice of art. For the first time she felt in no particular hurry to leave school.

Sometimes when she was alone in the art room, Selina would come in and stand beside her.

'I just want to stay here a moment,' she would say.

Charlotte was aware of the damp cloud of unhappiness she brought with her, but could think of no comfort to offer, except to point out that the first term was always foul.

Sometimes out of her heavy silence, Selina would say, 'What shall I do?' breathing rather heavily and looking the other way, 'What shall I do?' in a strangled voice.

Charlotte laughed at her, kindly, because really it was impossible that anyone should look so unhappy. Charlotte could not recognize her decisive, self-possessed, busy sister. Her whole body seemed to have drooped and grown smaller, her hair and skin to have faded. Her school uniform was unbecoming; her tunic was too long because Miss Martin had thought it would be better to buy a size too large. Her whole aspect was one of exaggerated dolefulness.

'You can manage,' said Charlotte. 'I know it's awful but it does get better.'

'I know,' said Selina, nodding. 'I know I can manage. It's just that I'm never alone. I would like to have some time to be alone.'

'You get more time to yourself later on,' said Charlotte. 'At least I suppose not really until you're in the sixth form.'

'That's too long,' said Selina, turning away to make a horrible face which stopped her from crying.

'Don't you like any of the others?' said Charlotte.

'Yes, but they don't like me,' said Selina. The idea of being disliked was quite new to her, and that she might be disliked not for any particular action or attribute, but simply on sight, for being new, horrified her. She felt helpless. She did not know what one was meant to do in such a situation.

'It's just that it's so cold,' she muttered.

'Haven't you got another jersey?' said Charlotte. 'Most people wear two.'

'My other one's dirty,' said Selina.

'I'll lend you one of mine,' said Charlotte. 'It won't matter if it's too big. Come on.'

On the way to Charlotte's dormitory they met the Senior School matron.

'Now then, what's this?' she said briskly. 'Junior School are now allowed upstairs in Senior School. You know that, Charlotte, don't you?'

'I was just going to lend her a jersey,' said Charlotte.

'We have no borrowing or lending of clothes here, now do we?' said Matron. 'Goodness me, you must see your sister knows the school rules, Charlotte. You sixth form girls should be setting an example to the younger ones. Now get along downstairs both of you.'

'Can't I just get her a jersey?' said Charlotte. 'She's cold.'

'It's against the rules, Charlotte, I've just told you,' said Matron. 'I'll speak to Miss Hope and see that Selina writes home for another jersey to be sent to her.'

'Gosh, how kind,' said Charlotte sarcastically. 'I'm sure that makes Selina feel warmer at once.' She marched angrily off down the passage, followed by Selina.

'Charlotte, come back here,' called Matron. Charlotte ignored her. 'I shall report you to Miss Brace for insolence,' said Matron.

'Silly old fool,' said Charlotte. 'No one pays any attention to her. I'll bring you a jersey in prep tonight. You'd better go back now.'

Selina hurried back to her own house, impressed and encouraged by Charlotte's contempt for authority.

Miss Martin came down for half term. She stayed in the Cherry Tree guest house in the village. It was rather uncomfortable and full of low-voiced groups of parents and children.

Selina had a bad cold. Miss Martin bought medicines and food and they spent most of the weekend in front of the gas fire in her bedroom. Charlotte made sketches of Miss Martin and complimented her on her bone structure. Halfway through Saturday afternoon, Selina, her head under a towel, inhaling Friar's Balsam, felt a sudden release of tension all over her body, as if she had taken a strong painkilling drug. Emerging, flushed, a few minutes later, she began to talk, not about school but about everything else, and shouted and laughed and made jokes and ate a great deal. Miss Martin gave a sigh of relief and put her earlier misery and silence down to her cold.

On Sunday evening the silence returned, but it was only natural that she should feel sad at the end of the weekend. Miss Martin went to speak to Miss Hope, the head of the Junior School, before she left.

Miss Hope was a kindly old person who had been living in the village, taking an active part in local life, for some time before Miss Brace asked her to look after the Junior School. Miss Martin immediately liked her, but after a very little conversation decided that she knew nothing at all about little girls and so began to dislike her intensely because she saw her as a danger to Selina.

'You don't find your lack of training and experience a disadvantage then?' Miss Martin asked in the friendliest of tones.

'No, on the contrary,' said Miss Hope. 'That was Miss Brace's idea in appointing me – so brilliant, Miss Brace, don't you think? – she said to me, you'll be able to see them as individuals, not as guinea pigs. No, the only disadvantage to me personally is a financial one, since naturally I couldn't expect Miss Brace to give me the same salary as if I were a trained person. But from the point of view of running the school, I really think it's an advantage because we do try and make a home-like atmosphere here rather than a school one. For instance the children have as little supervision as possible – of course we're very careful of their health and so on, but in their free time they play in the garden quite on their own. We like them to develop their personalities in their own way. Of course we're short of staff as well. This part of the school really is run on a shoe-string.'

'Do you think it's wise when they're so young?' said Miss Martin. 'I mean, for instance, are they kind to each other?'

'Good heavens, yes,' said Miss Hope. 'Of course there's the usual rough and tumble, they have to get used to that, but you must remember that all these children here are nice girls from nice homes.'

'Even nice girls do nasty things sometimes, when they're children,' said Miss Martin.

'Oh goodness me, what a gloomy point of view,' said Miss Hope. 'I can assure you no nasty things go on here. They're a particularly nice little group at the moment. I hope your Selina will soon fit in very nicely. I'm sure she hasn't got nasty ideas either, though of course growing up in the more solitary way that she has she's not quite such a straightforward happy child as I should like. But I'm sure she'll settle in and become a little more responsive than she is at the moment. I've put her in a dormitory with a particularly nice normal girl called Mary Daly who will help to bring her out of herself. Of course she's ahead in class which is a disadvantage.'

'A disadvantage?'

'It's better if they're all at the same stage, you know,' said Miss Hope. 'Then they can be a real class and feel themselves part of it. She's had too much individual tuition. It's put her ahead. But I expect she'll soon level down to the others.'

'Oh, yes. That will be nice,' said Miss Martin gently.

'Yes, well, now if you'll excuse me,' said Miss Hope. 'It's time for prayers. We have longer prayers on Sunday evening and join in a hymn or two. The girls love it.'

'I'm sure they do,' said Miss Martin.

Walking back to her car she said aloud, 'What the bloody hell does she think we send them to school for, fatuous old cow?' but when she had driven a little way she reminded herself that she had too many causes for jealousy to be fair about the school; and calmed herself with the memory of Selina's face, laughing in front of the gas fire, eating digestive biscuits and butter.

'It's a thing we always do to people who suck up to the staff,' said Mary Daly, twisting a skipping rope round Selina's wrists. 'We have to, it's a rule, it's not that we like doing it.'

She tied the skipping rope firmly round the trunk of a small tree.

'Now try and get loose,' she said.

Selina tried.

'I can't,' she said.

'Good,' said Mary Daly. 'Bring the brambles, Liz.'

There were six others girls there. They had cut long pieces of bramble out of the hedge at the bottom of what Miss Hope only too truthfully called 'the Wild Garden,' and now they began in pairs to pull these backwards and fowards across Selina's legs, as if she were part of the tree and they were trying to saw it down. It was difficult to do, because the bramble branches were too limp for them to be able to put much pressure behind them. Also most of the girls were frightened and did not pull hard. It was some time before they managed even to draw blood and when they did, Elizabeth Wright said, 'Hadn't we better stop now?'

'We haven't done her face yet,' said Mary Daly. 'Come on, Ann, pull with me, up here across her face.'

'Oh don't, Mary,' said Elizabeth in a frightened voice. 'Miss Hope will see the marks.'

'She'll say she tripped and fell into a bush,' said Mary Daly. 'Won't you, Selina?'

Selina did not answer. Her eyes were shut. She felt two sharp scratches on her face.

'Oh, come on, do let's stop,' said a voice.

'All right, back to the lawn everybody,' said Mary Daly.

'Aren't we going to untie her?' said Elizabeth Wright.

'Of course not, we never do,' said Mary Daly. 'You'll stay there all night and then you'll die of pneumonia, you know.'

Selina believed her.

A long time later Elizabeth Wright came back and untied her. It was nearly dark and Selina was very cold.

'They've been looking for you,' said Elizabeth, whispering although there was no one near. 'What will you say?'

'I don't know,' said Selina, through chattering teeth.

'Come on, we'll go through the form-room window,' whispered Elizabeth. 'She'll be livid with me for setting you free but I had to.'

'Thanks,' said Selina.

'It's only Mary Daly, you know,' said Elizabeth. 'She's always like that with new girls. It'll be all right next term. Why don't you cry? She stops when they cry.'

Selina told Miss Hope that she had been for a walk in the garden and had forgotten the time: also she had walked into a bush in the dark. Miss Hope made her learn two verses of Wordsworth's 'Ode to Duty' and told her to try and remember that she was part of a community now and could no longer live for herself alone.

Elizabeth Wright was particularly active in the pillow fight which took place the following night because she wanted to be restored to Mary Daly's favour. The pillows had books in them and were all aimed at Selina. Once Elizabeth whispered in her ear, 'Cry,' but she could not do it.

Angel went to see Susan in the spring. It was a sunny day and she rang up from London and said, 'Can we come to lunch or something? I'm with a man called Boy Cunningham.'

While Susan was talking to her on the telephone, Bill shouted, 'Tell her to start now, then we can have a drink at the club before lunch.'

Susan passed on the message.

'I wonder who Boy Cunningham is,' she said later to Bill.

'Sounds a racy sort of name,' said Bill. 'One of the usual young bloods, I suppose.'

'I think it sounds a bogus name,' said Susan. 'I wonder

if we've got enough for lunch. Angel always does everything at a moment's notice.'

When the crunch of gravel from the neat semi-circle in front of the house announced the guests' arrival, Bill looked out of the window and said, 'Nothing bogus about that car anyway,' but a moment later he was in the kitchen, aghast and stammering, and loudly whispering that Susan must 'do something'.

'What's the matter?' said Susan. 'Why don't you open the door?'

'Susan, look here, for God's sake, what are we going to do?' he gabbled. 'The fellow's black. Black as your hat. It's one of these blacks. In a Continental Bentley.'

'No!' said Susan. 'Oh, no! How terribly funny. Trust Angel. Oh, dear, can they eat pork?' She took off her apron and walked towards the door. Bill seized her arm. 'But, Susan,' he said, 'have we got to have him in the house, sit down with him?'

'It will be all right,' said Susan. 'I'm sure he's perfectly nice if he's a friend of Angel's.'

She opened the front door and Angel came in with her usual rush, kissed them both enthusiastically, then said she was dying to go to the loo. Susan took her upstairs.

In her little chintzy bedroom, white-walled and immaculately tidy, Susan said to Angel, 'You are naughty not to tell us he was black. Bill nearly had a fit.' She was feeling pleasantly stimulated by Angel's arrival, for though she liked her life to be quiet it was agreeable to be in touch with a larger and more dangerous world occasionally, as long as one could quickly retreat again into one's own security.

'Oh, didn't I say? How awful,' said Angel, combing her hair. 'I quite forgot. I always think people know everything that I know. Isn't it silly?'

'What a lovely dress,' said Susan. 'You look awfully ill though. Are you all right?'

'It's just London, horrid old London,' said Angel. 'You are so lucky to live in the country, sort of country anyway, and have this dear little house and everything. It's so tidy and clean and white, like a hospital almost. Goodness, look at all these pills and things.' She was washing her hands and looking at the shelf above the basin. 'My dear, it really is like a hospital. Of course you always were a hypochondriac. Or is it Bill?'

'No, they're mine,' said Susan. 'I don't know why there are so many. I always seem to have some sort of ache or pain, and Bill makes me go to the doctor every time.'

'He oughtn't to encourage you,' aid Angel, drying her hands. 'You know there's nothing wrong with you. Why don't you have a baby?'

'Bill thinks it might not be good for my nerves,' said Susan, then added hurriedly, 'No, it isn't really that, honestly it isn't. It's just that everything's so nice as it is, and we're so happy, I'm afraid of changing it. There's no hurry after all.'

'I'd hurry,' said Angel. 'My absolute dreamiest dream would be to have twins nine months after my wedding day.'

'Why don't you get married then?' asked Susan.

'Oh, I don't know, it never seems to work out quite right,' said Angel. 'I only seem to know such horrid people, or something. The only one I really do like is queer. Isn't it awful? Still, I'll make it one day, don't worry. We ought to go down. You'll love Boy, he's terribly funny and gay. He's a real old-fashioned playboy. His father's something fearfully grand in Nigeria and he's stinking rich.'

They were now halfway down the stairs. At the bottom of the stairs was a room which was half a hall and half a sitting-room and in which there was a bar. Bill and Boy were standing beside it, holding drinks.

'We were talking about you, did you hear every word?' said Angel, putting her arm through Boy's and resting her head on his shoulder.

'Every word,' said Boy, giving her a smacking kiss on the cheek. 'But I knew you were after my money anyway.'

Bill shuddered visibly and turned quickly to the bar. 'A glass of dry sherry for the ladies?' he said in an unnatural voice.

'Could I have a Bloody Mary or something?' said Angel. 'Sherry always makes me feel sick, I don't know why. Or whisky would do. But I thought we were going to your club, Bill.'

'I thought perhaps we wouldn't bother,' said Bill. 'It's nearly lunch-time anyway.'

'Oh do let's,' said Angel, trying to be nice to Bill. 'I would like to see a real Surrey golf club on Sunday morning, or is it Sussex? And I know Boy would like to, it's an English phenomenon surely?'

'I think perhaps another time,' said Bill embarrassed.

'Really? Oh dear, I am disappointed,' said Angel. 'Anyway, Boy might not be here another time. He's going home quite soon.'

'Perhaps, all the same, another time might be wiser,' said Bill, furiously convinced that Angel was embarrassing him on purpose.

'I think your brother-in-law means that they don't allow niggers in his club,' explained Boy kindly.

'Really?' said Angel, surprised. 'I never thought of that. Why didn't you say so? Oh, I suppose it would have been rude. Fancy that. I thought it was only Jews.'

'There's a dash of Jewish blood in my veins as well,' said Boy. 'And you know what else? A Scottish missionary, a couple of generations back, white as snow he was, and took a fancy to my great-grandmother. So how about that? A Scottish Jewish nigger. You don't see many of those around the Surrey golf clubs on a Sunday morning.'

'Oh, don't be silly,' said Angel. 'You went on for hours last night about your pure Hausa ancestry or whatever it was. He's a terrible liar,' she said fondly to Susan.

'The black man doesn't know the meaning of truth,' said Boy, grinning gaily. 'He only says what he hopes will please.'

The visit was not a success. Even Angel noticed it. Bill was very angry. He had had, for a moment – the moment when Susan had opened the front door – good intentions. He had meant to try and be polite. But the fellow had turned out to be insufferable, insolent, uppish, far too well-dressed, and disgustingly familiar with Angel: he was deeply upset by the whole incident. Susan, depressed by his obvious displeasure, retreated into silence, and

Angel and Boy talked about their mutual friends, who seemed to be innumerable and curious, and as soon after lunch as they reasonably could, they climbed back into the scarlet Continental Bentley and drove away.

Bill turned to Susan.

'Your sister Angel must never come to this house again,' he said.

'Oh, Bill, please, it's only because she's so thoughtless,' said Susan. 'And anyway he's going away soon, they said so.'

'There'll be others,' said Bill, grimly. 'You don't understand. I shall have to tell you, though I'd much rather not. Once a white woman has slept with a black man she can never sleep with a white man again.'

'Why not?' said Susan, horrified.

'It's not the same thing,' he said solemnly. 'It's like doing it with an animal. White men are no use to them after that. They have to have blacks. They become insatiable. I've seen it happen.'

'But how ghastly,' said Susan. 'I'm sure she doesn't sleep with him, though. I mean, Angel isn't at all like that really.'

'Of course she does,' said Bill. 'A man can always tell. He had a proprietary look about him. Good God, when I think of it. . . . No she must never come here again. She's put herself beyond the pale.'

'But she is my sister,' said Susan, distressed. 'Oughtn't we to help her?'

'Your duty lies here, with me,' said Bill solemnly. 'I am your family now.'

'I shall write to Penelope about her,' said Susan.

'I think that's an excellent idea,' said Bill. 'And now I think you should go upstairs and rest.'

'Rest? But I'm not tired. I thought I'd write that letter.'

'You look pale,' he said. 'It's been a horrid experience for you.'

'Do I?' said Susan. 'Oh, well, I suppose I am rather tired. I will then. I'm sorry Angel bothered you like this.'

'It's you I'm worried about,' said Bill. 'You shouldn't be exposed to that sort of thing. Now you go up and lie down and I'll bring you up a nice cup of tea later on.'

'Three cheers for the good old British Empire,' said Boy Cunningham, driving very fast indeed.

'Do shut up,' said Angel. 'It's nothing to do with the British Empire anyway. It's just Bill, and I'm sorry about Bill, but honestly I didn't know there were people who thought like that. My father doesn't and he's terribly keen on the British Empire. He'd take you to his club any day. Or do you think perhaps he wouldn't?'

He laughed. 'You're a nice girl. Anybody ever tell you that?'

'Everybody,' said Angel. 'All the time, sadly, like you.'

He left her at Penelope's house in Chelsea, because she said she felt terrible and would go to bed, but when she went in she found Roger Martin waiting in the drawing room. Ham and Penelope were away in the constituency but Nanny had let him in.

'I haven't seen you for ages, so I thought I'd drop in,' he said. 'There's no food in my flat either and I thought there might be some here.'

'There probably is,' said Angel, lying back in a chair. 'Go and have a look.'

'I didn't mean this minute,' he said. 'Later I will. Have a drink.'

'No thanks,' said Angel. 'Anyway Ham locks the cupboard when he goes away.'

'I broke it open,' said Roger. 'I never heard of such a thing. Locking the cupboard indeed. Ridiculous. That brother of his was here when I came.'

'Toby?' said Angel. 'Oh where is he, has he gone? I do wish I'd seen him. What was he doing here?'

'I don't know. He left when I arrived. He doesn't like me.'

'No, he can't bear you, quite rightly,' said Angel. 'He doesn't like Ham much either, he says his driving forces are envy and malice. At least he once said that and then tried to go back on it, but I think it's what he really thinks. That's why I wondered why he was here.'

'Perhaps he came to see you.'

'Oh, I do hope so,' said Angel. 'I like him better than anyone else in the world. He said I could go and stay with him in Wales.'

'With the boy-friend?'

'Yes. He's called Fergus.'

'Fancy that. How's your love life these days?'

'Busy. Boring.'

'Boring?'

'It's always the same, isn't it?'

'Is it?'

'I mean the whole thing,' she said. 'Meeting a person, falling for them, everything going wrong. Next stage, you're enemies, or too embarrassed to speak, or friends in a very ghastly way like you and me.'

'How many times have you been through this process?' asked Roger. 'Simon Reeves? Who else? Mr. Cunningham?'

'No, not him, I only met him last night,' said Angel. 'Lots of other people, but why should I tell you? Let's go to the cinema.'

'All right. I haven't got any money though. Have you?'

'No.'

'I'll go and borrow some from Nanny,' said Roger.

Selina kept a diary in her second term at school. It was a way of marking the passage of time, but she was too ashamed of her feelings to write them down, and the diary was accordingly rather dull.

'Better day today,' she would write, or 'Bad day,' without referring to what it was that made the day better or worse and which was simply the fluctuation of her homesickness and fear.

'Worse day. Letter from Martin.

'Better. Mary Daly was sick in maths and went to the sick room.

'Better day. Played leap-frog on the lawn with Charlotte and two friends of hers. They were nice. Had to learn sixteen lines for not being with the Juniors in playtime.

'Worse. Mary Daly better.

'Worse. Terrible. Very, very bad day indeed.

'Still bad but getting a bit better. Only three weeks till half-term.'

The term was marked by the sudden departure of

Daphne Sparks. Daphne Sparks was a large girl, plain and greasy-skinned, the perpetual butt of Mary Daly. The first day of term Mary Daly said, 'You've grown a bosom in the holidays, Daphne Sparks.'

'I haven't,' said Daphne Sparks, flushing and turning away.

'Yes you have, I can see it,' said Mary Daly. 'I saw it wobbling when you ran up the stairs. You ought to wear a BB. Your mother should have bought you one.'

'No, honestly, I haven't,' said Daphne. 'Honestly, Mary.'

'Why are you so feeble about it?' said Ann Lawrence. 'There's nothing wrong with having a bosom.'

'I know, I just don't want to talk about it,' said Daphne, putting on an oddly unattractive look of modesty.

'Run up and down,' commanded Mary Daly. 'Go on. Run up and down and we'll tell you if it's wobbling.'

'I don't want to,' said Daphne.

'Go on, run,' ordered Mary.

Daphne obeyed, and made an ungainly run across the lawn.

'Do it again,' said Mary. 'You're holding yourself stiff. Let yourself go. There it is, it is wobbling. I saw it.'

She threw herself with wiry strength on to the flabby Daphne, knocked her down on to the grass and began to tear at the front of her tunic. 'I can feel it, I can feel it,' she cried.

Selina felt a sudden rush of excitement. She screwed up her face, intensely anxious for Mary's fingers to push aside the tunic and reach the flesh beneath, so that they could all feel it, and scratch it and squeeze it and hurt it.

'Now, girls, not too much romping!' cried Miss Hope, approaching them from the house. 'Have you all done your unpacking?'

Mary Daly jumped up. 'Yes, Miss Hope, I've done mine,' she said.

'Well done, Mary. What about you others?'

'I haven't,' said Selina untruthfully, and ran back into the house as fast as she could.

A few weeks later Mary Daly decided to bury Daphne

Sparks, so they dug her a deep grave at the bottom of the garden. It took them several days.

'We're digging your grave, Daphne Sparks,' Mary Daly would say.

When it was deep enough, Daphne was led to it. She obediently lay down in it, and stayed there without a sound or a movement while they covered her with earth. This complete lack of opposition, caused in fact by paralysing fear, made the whole episode something of an anticlimax. They left her, and went back to their form room for the evening prep period. When Daphne was missed, no one confessed to knowing where she was. Half an hour later Elizabeth Wright stood up.

'Yes, Elizabeth?' said the mistress who was taking prep.

'Daphne Sparks is buried at the bottom of the garden,' said Elizabeth in a rush, white in the face.

It caused a tremendous scandal. They were interviewed separately by Miss Hope, who was deeply shocked, and collectively by Miss Brace, who made one of her rare visits to the Junior School to give them an impressive lecture on morals.

Daphne Sparks was kept in the sick room until her parents came to take her away. As they were leaving Mary Daly ran up to Daphne (though they had all been forbidden to speak to her) and pressed half a bar of chocolate into her hand.

'Good luck, Daphne,' she said fervently. 'I hope we'll be friends one day.'

The Sparks parents, and Miss Hope, were touched. Daphne looked at her with eyes dulled by fear and misery. Before she got into the car she unobtrusively dropped the chocolate.

Selina was no longer Mary Daly's victim: she had become her enemy. She was beginning to form a group of her own, with Elizabeth Wright as her lieutenant. At first they were not openly hostile to Mary Daly and her group. They merely moved about together, apart from the others, and chose not to come under Mary Daly's jurisdiction. This annoyed Mary Daly, and one day she laid ambush for them behind the coal shed and there was a brisk fight, which resulted in dirty clothes and a certain amount of enquiry from Miss Hope, who was now keeping a closer watch on their activities. After that it was open warfare, and Selina began to feel the pleasures of power. She had become a gang leader. She could say, 'We will line up here and attack as they come round the corner. Elizabeth stand here, Judith here. Raise your sticks,' and be obeyed instantly. She could frighten new girls, and impress her personality on her followers, so that they adopted her way of speech and hastened to forestall her opinions. The new situation did not make her much happier, because she had still no friends; she was obeyed because she was making a stand against Mary Daly, but she did not feel herself liked. She was never now without an uneasy sense of there being a deep danger somewhere very close: this was not so much because her gang was often the loser, as because of the unfamiliarity of the attributes she was beginning, without recognizing them, to develop, guile, sadism, secrecy, the spirit of competition, the lust for power which was really the struggle for existence. The conflict between Mary Daly and Selina Dobson and their rival groups became too obvious and too disruptive. At half-term Selina was moved up into the next form.

She could hardly believe her good fortune. She could not follow the lessons at first but the mistresses were kind to her and it was generally considered to reflect to her credit that her behaviour had been so bad as to have necessitated a step so unprecedented. Her pleasure and relief came not only from the fact that she now saw much less of Mary Daly, but also from the presence in her new form of Brigid Knight, whom she had admired since the first evening at school.

Brigid Knight was a tall, thin, twelve-year-old with long bony legs on which, in the winter, she wore knee socks with garters which had a little woollen tab showing under the top of the sock. Everybody wore knee socks until they were thirteen but only Brigid had those sort of garters. In the evenings when they changed out of school uniform she wore Fair Isle jerseys and hairy tweed skirts, or in the summer faded gingham dresses, rather short. She had curly hair, fairer on top than underneath, and usually untidy. She was gap-toothed and had a wide smile and a helplessly loud laugh. She was good at games and could run very fast. She had long bony fingers and bit her nails. She had a particular, embarrassed way of bending her head down so that her chin was as close in to her neck as possible, and looking up bashfully before giving way to her wide reluctant smile. She was untidy, forgetful and cheerful. She had a pony at home, and her desk and the locker next to her bed were covered with photographs of him and of her three brothers. She was popular, and had a particular friend called Morag. She did not speak much to Selina at first; but Selina loved her. For the next year her life was taken up with this love.

5

GABRIEL Dobson was known to be an honest business man.

It was Hannah's money which had made him free to indulge his honesty, as well as his acumen. When he married her, in 1925, being thirty-five himself, he had been managing director of a firm which owned collieries round Nottingham, but soon after his marriage old Sir Robert Sutton, his benefactor, died, and conflicts arose within the firm, where Gabriel had always been resented as the favoured outsider. When a merger was proposed with another company, he was glad to take his compensation and leave. He used Hannah's money to make more. He was shrewd and clear-sighted, and a man of imagination: he had one or two failures but more successes. His investments did well. He put money and work into several companies which needed development, a small company manufacturing mining equipment, another which made textile machinery. He became a useful man to have on boards, one whose advice on business problems generally was esteemed.

In 1940 he went into the Ministry of Economic Warfare, where he came to wield considerable power.

After the war, more official positions became available to him; he advised the Government on various aspects of foreign trade, headed a Royal Commission on labour relations.

The fact that all this was made possible, in the first instance, by Hannah's money caused no embarrassment between them, because Hannah was one who might have been thought largesse personified. She was a huge, beautiful, witty woman whose influence on Gabriel changed his character, at least during her lifetime. As a young man

he had seen himself, perhaps romantically, as a ruthless
seeker after power. His father's crime in his eyes was not
then, as it came to seem to him later, his sternness nor
the narrowness of his views, but his complete ineffective-
ness. A few people were grateful to him, a few admired
him, but his church was never more than a quarter full,
he was poor, unknown and totally insignificant. When
Gabriel had been offered a job by Sir Robert Sutton and
had accordingly given up his plan to be a schoolmaster,
his father had spoken to him at length about the evils of
capitalism and the corruption of those in power.

'What good can you do by railing against them?' the
young Gabriel had said to himself afterwards (he had not
bothered to answer his father at the time). 'One should
go in there, use them, be one of them, preserving all the
time one's solitude and scorn and indifference.'

He had gone on thinking that until he met Hannah, his
resolution strengthened by three years in a prison camp
in the 1914 war. It was all changed by her. Solitude, scorn
and indifference melted before her intense participation in
everything she did, just as ruthless will to power seemed
meaningless as soon as she laughed. He learnt pleasures
he had no time for before. They had together what they
both thought was a good life. It seemed more important
to him than anything else, and somehow as things turned
out it involved his giving up politics. Before his marriage
he had been a Conservative candidate and he had fore-
seen a great future for himself in Parliament: even while
Hannah was still alive he had regretted it, had thought
of it as something he still might do, one day when he
had time. Only now that his son-in-law had started what
looked surprisingly like a successful political career was
Gabriel obliged to face the fact that it was too late for him.

It made it worse that it should be Ham who brought
this home to him, because he despised and distrusted
Ham. He could not imagine how he should seem to be
doing so well: he had been made Parliamentary Private
Secretary to quite an important Minister very soon after
his election, and he gave a definite and irritating impression of being in on things. Going to lunch with him in
the House of Commons was for Gabriel an exercise in

mortification. The mere fact of Ham's belonging there was annoying. The policemen greeted him with a deferential familiarity which Gabriel would have found most gratifying, he dashed authoritatively through doors, walked briskly along the corridors, smiling a greeting here and there, enjoying himself, knowing his way around.

'Ah, Maitland,' people said, or 'I see you got your question,' or 'Coming to the Committee? 10.30 I believe.'

He slapped the back of a shambling old fellow who seemed to be waiting for someone, and said loudly as they walked on, 'I have lots of good friends on the other side, you know.'

Gabriel had come to ask him about a Bill which was coming up for its Second Reading the following week, and which concerned the granting of export licences for light machinery. One of the firms in which Gabriel was interested was likely to be affected by the Bill, and he was anxious that Members of Parliament should support it.

'Of course I can help,' said Ham. 'I know just the man to get on to about it. We'll see if we can find him afterwards. He should be about.'

'It would be very kind,' said Gabriel.

'Nonsense,' said Ham. 'I'm delighted to be able to help.'

It was true, he was delighted. He thought his father-in-law was pompous, self-important, and priggish, nor would he ever forgive Gabriel's searching and scornful investigation into his financial standing when he became engaged to Penelope. He knew that it annoyed Gabriel to receive this small assistance at his hands, and so it pleased him to give it.

Gabriel suspected this reaction and it irritated him. After all he could easily have approached the matter through someone else, he knew plenty of more important Members of Parliament. He had done it through Ham to please Penelope.

After lunch Ham fetched a certain Mr. Pratt down from the library to talk to Gabriel. He was planning to speak in the debate and expressed himself eager to hear Gabriel's views. Ham left them alone together and Gabriel's spirits improved. Mr. Pratt asked him to meet him again later to discuss all the implications of the Bill more fully, because he had to go to take his seat. Gabriel watched the Speaker's procession. He decided he needed a holiday. He would go to Venice in the spring; but should he go alone? He would take Angel, she had never seen Venice. He had a board meeting at three. At least he was busy: it was not as if he were finished, by any means.

Ham was lolling on his seat not listening to the anyway almost inaudible Under Secretary who was answering questions. He was working out his father-in-law's earned income and wondering how much of it he saved, and whether, therefore, the amount of the capital to be inherited by his daughters on his death was likely to be increasing. They had left £10,000 each by their mother, but the rest of her money had gone to Gabriel for his lifetime. Ham was short of money. He had £500 a year of his own, but he had given up the not very rewarding job which he had had in a stockbroker's office and so was only earning his salary as an M.P. He had not been able to find the sort of job which he had imagined would be easy to find as a Member of Parliament, something part-time where the name 'The Hon. Hamilton Maitland, M.P.' would look impressive on the writing paper. Gabriel never gave money to Penelope. Ham thought this very mean, since he must know that they needed it: he ought from time to time to press a cheque into her hand saying, 'A little something towards expenses.' He could well afford it but he never did. They had done quite well out of Angel's season. Gabriel had paid for all the entertaining and most of Penelope's clothes as well as Angel's; but he was a selfish old thing and it was unlikely now that the season was over that he would do more than pay a small rent for Angel to stay in their house. He would have to ask Toby again.

He disliked asking his brother to lend him money. In fact he disliked his brother. He always had. As children they had fought, and Ham soon found out that although he was two years younger he could always make Toby cry. Toby cried a lot as a child, and was afraid of the dark and of guns and big dogs. He liked beetles and fishes and butterflies and all the very small insects that live in grass. He was supposed to be 'difficult' but he was loved: everybody loved him, especially their mother, and everybody accepted without question the principle that he came first in everything because he was the eldest son. That meant that he inherited not only the title, but most of the money, of which there was not anyway a great deal. Ham considered that Toby had proved himself in every way unworthy of his inheritance. He lived a solitary life in their old home in Wales with various animals and a beautiful boy. Occasionally he would turn up in London to buy books or equipment, or he would disappear abroad for months on end. This life of what Ham considered cowardice and selfishness still had not robbed him of that air of security, of being cared for, which Ham passionately resented.

Toby had been in London more than usual recently and had been seeing a certain amount of Angel. It was an incongruous friendship, but Angel claimed to adore him. Ham was not easy about this. It had crossed his mind that for Toby, the wilful outlaw who should have been rejected by decent society, to end by marrying a more beautiful sister of his own wife's would be another unfairness. He thought it unlikely that Toby would marry anybody, but odd things did happen and he did not like the idea. He knew Toby to be in London at the moment, and he thought perhaps a hint or two aimed to destroy his view of Angel might be wise. He would ask him to lunch, borrow some money (Toby never refused, which made it somehow more galling) and casually imply in passing that Angel's character was quite unsuited to Toby's: he could infer that she was a nymphomaniac – after all she almost was, if Roger Martin was to be believed.

An attendant brought him notice of a telephone call. It was Penelope, breathless, asking him to come home because something serious had happened. He went home.

Penelope was waiting for him, walking up and down in the drawing-room, white and worried.

'Angel has just told me that she is going to have a baby,' she said.

Ham almost laughed. The news came so oddly after his recent thoughts.

'Silly little fool,' he said slowly. 'Good Lord. I didn't know she was as silly as that. Where is she?'

'Upstairs, resting. She doesn't seem particularly worried. Just surprised.'

'Who is it?'

'Roger Martin, she says.'

'It would be. Why not one of the others? Is she sure?'

'Yes. He doesn't know. You'll have to tell him, Ham. They must get married at once.'

'Get married? Does she want to?'

'No, she says she can't bear him, but I'm sure it's only because of this. I'm sure he could persuade her.'

'If he wanted to.'

'But he must want to, surely?'

'Must he?' said Ham. 'Besides, do we want it? He's not much of a catch. He's penniless and obviously never going to do any good.'

Penelope sat down.

'I thought he was your greatest friend,' she said. 'And how, for heaven's sake how, can you talk about a "good catch" now? She's going to have a baby.'

'Does she want to have it? asked Ham.

'Well, not exactly, no. I mean, it's not the ideal way of doing it, is it?'

'She doesn't have to, you know.'

'She said that,' said Penelope. 'She said she could have an abortion, quite calmly. Really she is too peculiar.'

'And what did you say?' asked Ham.

'I said that I would never allow it. She seemed rather relieved. I said if they didn't get married she could stay here with me and have the child and I would look after them. Obviously I said that. I would have said it anyway, but all the more so because she was living with us when it happened. It's our responsibility. We haven't looked after her properly.'

Ham looked out of the window in silence for some moments.

'My dear,' he said, finally, turning round. 'I don't think you have quite understood the situation.'

Angel went into a nursing home near Harley Street. Pregnancies were terminated on the top floor. It was all quite comfortable. She was convinced that it was the best solution, and she was grateful to Ham for having arranged everything so calmly; only she cried for all of the four days she was there. The nurses said it must be something to do with her glands.

Ham mentioned the incident to Toby. Toby telephoned Angel and arranged that she should go to Wales as soon as she came out of the nursing home.

Simon Reeves paid for the operation. Neither Ham nor Roger Martin had the money at the time, and by cross examining Angel they worked out that, allowing for a certain amount of inaccuracy on the part of the doctors, it was just possible that he might have been responsible.

Penelope took on herself all the guilt for the whole affair. She had argued with Ham until four o'clock in the morning, until her throat was sore and her bones ached. She had cried. She had accused him of callous immorality. Shocked by his knowledge of how to arrange the details, she had accused him of having murdered hundreds of little Julian's half-brothers and sisters. She had been unreasonable and desperate and passionately in earnest. Ham had not once lost his temper. Afterwards she had to admire him for that. He had been patient and reasonable. He had repeated over and over again that it would be detrimental to his career if his sister-in-law had an illegitimate child in his house, that he could not force Roger to marry her if neither of them wanted it, that that would be no foundation for a happy marriage, that Angel herself did not want the child, that it should be done properly and would make no difference at all to her health and future child-bearing capacities.

Penelope had thought that there was nothing she could do to prevent it, but afterwards she wondered whether the right course might not have been to tell her father, deeply though it would have shocked him. She spent a long time in an empty dark church, looking at two candles which were alight on the distant altar, and thinking, 'I have assisted at the murder of a child,' but nothing happened. She could not pray and her mind became no clearer. When she left she felt that God had not forgiven her: but then she was no longer sure that He cared.

Angel had her hair cut before she went to stay with Toby. She thought that as he did not care for women the shining swinging length of her hair as she used to wear it might be repulsive to him, so she had it cut very short, and was afterwards pleased with herself for having taken so positive a step. It fitted neatly round her head and pointed in to the nape of her neck; it gave more emphasis to her face which was thinner now, revealing more than ever the extreme perfection of its shape.

She travelled by train to Wales and took a taxi from the station. They drove for some miles through wild country until they came to a high iron gate with an ugly little lodge beside it. Here the taxi-driver stopped and refused to go any farther. A long avenue led across the park, disappearing into a wood. There was no sign of the house. The taxi-driver shouted, and eventually an old man appeared from the lodge. When the situation had been made clear to him through the gate, which the taxi-driver would not allow him to open, he volunteered to ring up the house.

Angel began to feel cold. It was March. There were daffodils under the trees beyond the iron gate, but the wind was cold. Angel sat in the taxi and waited. The driver explained for the tenth time that he was a married man and could not risk being eaten by wild animals.

'Nobody goes beyond this gate,' he said. 'Not the milk nor the post nor nobody.'

Angel began to think that Toby had forgotten he had asked her, or had not meant it; then a cloud of dust appeared from the wood, moving rapidly. It was a jeep, driven fast along the sandy drive, with two men in it, and two black panthers running easily beside it. His worst fears realized, the taxi-driver whipped Angel's suitcase out of the boot, pocketed her money without looking at it, and drove off as fast as he could. Angel was left standing outside the gate with her suitcase at her feet. The old man hurried to let her in as the jeep drew up, the panthers standing watchfully at a distance. Toby jumped down and took her case.

'I am so sorry,' he said. 'I should have found out what train you were coming on and met you. They won't come in because they're afraid of the animals. This is Fergus. Jump in.'

Angel had only seen Toby in a tweed suit before. It was old and shabby and it had not occurred to her that it might be his best suit, or indeed his only one. Now he was wearing a blue French peasant's shirt and a filthy pair of trousers. He smelt slightly of raw meat. His face, a gentler and more open version of Ham's, was disguised by a day's growth of beard.

Fergus perched behind them in the jeep, embarrassed by Angel. He thought Toby had been naïve to have asked her and to have thought that she would make no difference to their lives. He knew women. She would be organizing them in no time, complaining of his cooking, insisting that they put sheets on their beds. He scowled into the wind.

Toby had made Fergus come with him in the jeep in order to make it clear to Angel that he was a friend and not a servant. He remembered that Angel could be tactless and foolish, and for the moment he forgot why he liked her or why he had asked her to stay; no one had stayed in that house for ten years. Even visiting zoo experts only came for the day. He had been wondering all morning how he could have done anything so rashly against his principles as to have asked her. He drove very fast, out-speeding the panthers, in order to avoid conversation.

The drive was two miles long. After the narrow strip of woodland it curled round the side of a hill and disclosed in a hollow the enormous house. It was really a castle, battlemented, slit-windowed and self-consciously asymmetrical, built in 1865, with fifty bedrooms. Attached to one side was a small cathedral, once the family chapel and now semi-ruined. There was a neglected terrace on the other side, behind which unfolded a vast romantic view of woods, hills, valleys, and the distant sea.

It was so unlike Angel not to greet all this with a stream of more or less inane exclamations that Toby, slowing down for her to see it, turned to look at her. She was blinking. There was something in the tenseness of her nostrils, in the way in which she sat, rather exaggeratedly at ease in the windy uncomfortable jeep, which made him realize that she was shy, that she was trying not to be too girlish, that she was anxious to make a good impression. There were marks of strain too on the fine face, round the mouth and eyes.

He stroked the back of her head. 'I'm glad you got here safely,' he said. 'Now you shall see our cats.'

He led her round on to the terrace. Most of the windows on this side of the house opened into immensely long wire runs. Ham liked to present his brother as a maniac, who lived the life of a recluse, protected by ferocious wild animals; but this was not quite the case. He kept a small private zoo, and was much respected by various experts on animals. He was the only person under whose care a certain sort of Siberian lynx had been known to breed in captivity, and zoos from all over Europe would occasionally send him difficult animals with which they had not the time or space to deal. The only unusual thing about this particular zoo was that the animals lived in the house. All the downstairs rooms except for the library and kitchen were cages for animals, who could jump out of the windows into their runs. The vaster pieces of Victorian furniture which Toby had been left had proved unsaleable and so the cages were unconventionally furnished. Leopards crouched on walnut commodes, a lioness slept on a huge four-poster bed and marmosets climbed over a whatnot. The animals which lived upstairs were small and more or less tame, a pair of flying squirrels, the marmosets and a rather vicious sort of African rat which had not proved a great success. There were fifteen animals in the house at the moment. They were looked after by Toby, Fergus and the son of the old man who lived in the lodge. The house and garden were not looked after at all. Fergus did most of the cooking. He had come to Toby several years ago as a bear-keeper, and was handsome, gentle and extraordinarily good with animals. There were no bears now, because apart from the upstairs animals, Toby only kept larger members of the cat family.

Angel found them rather smelly at first. The vastness of the house, however, prevented the smell from reaching every corner. The library in which they mainly lived was fairly free from it. The room was forty yards long. At one end, lost in the gloom, lurked a grand piano which Toby played. The fireplace was the size of a small room, and in front of it was a stool covered in red brocade which might have served as a rather hard bed. There had once been twenty-four large Persian rugs on the floor, but Toby had sold them and now there were bare oak boards with one or two pieces of rush matting on them and a number of stains, varying in size according to the species of animal which had relieved itself.

Apart from the difficult cases which had been sent from other zoos, most of the animals were more or less tame, that is to say they had established a relationship of trust with Toby and Fergus, who nevertheless still treated them with respectful caution: the two black panthers were the only ones who were allowed to wander freely and they had been brought up from birth by Toby.

'I had no idea,' said Angel as they walked round. 'I didn't know there was all this. Ham never told me.'

'Ham, hasn't seen it lately,' said Toby. 'He doesn't approve, not unnaturally. It's not his sort of thing at all. Here we walk quietly because we have a very miserable tiger. She's only been here a day or two. She was going to have cubs and the zoo she belongs to were very pleased because it was going to be the first lot they'd had, and then she lost them. They were doing a lot of rebuilding there and it's thought the noise upset her.'

'Poor darling,' said Angel.

The tiger gave a blood-curdling roar.

'She's fierce at the moment,' said Toby. 'She'll calm down, I expect. They usually do here, they have so much space and quiet and no one stares at them. Now this is the last and best thing. Here is the mate of that panther you saw before, and she has two cubs, a month old, one black and one spotted. The spotted is male and is called Tom because we go through the alphabet and we've got to T, and the black one is female, and we've broken the rule, a thing we've never done before, and gone back to A and called her after you.'

'Oh the darlings.' Angel sank dotingly to the ground

in front of them. 'How could anything be so adorable?' Her resolutions about showing restraint and not being silly about the animals fled. 'I don't think anything ever has happened to me so absolutely utterly marvellous as having her called after me. How could you think of something that would make me so happy? She's fabulous. She's so beautiful. Oh how I wish I could be as beautiful as that. Oh could I hold her do you think? Or perhaps later on when they know me a bit? Oh would she let me hold her baby, do you think? Oh, Toby, I love it here, can I stay for ever?'

She did not take over the cooking, because she did not know how to cook; but she helped Fergus in the kitchen and he taught her how to make one or two simple dishes. It was several days before she asked him if he thought it would be all right if she swept out the library occasionally, and most of her time was spent either looking after the two cubs or working in the garden, where she cleared paths, cut branches off trees and uncovered several shrubs and plants which had been concealed by undergrowth and were about to flower. This activity was interspersed with long intervals of lying in the grass. In the evenings she and Fergus played backgammon for enormous stakes while Toby wrote letters or played the piano. She read the complete works of Mrs. Molesworth which she found in the library. They listened to concerts on the wireless. Sometimes Toby sang songs by Schubert or Richard Strauss in a reedy tuneful baritone. They went to bed early because they had to be up early to feed the animals. The spring sunshine began to be warm, the air to smell of spring; the panthers ran through the wood like legendary beasts, on grass starred with flowers. After some time Angel wrote to Penelope to say she did not know when she would be coming back to London.

Penelope told Ham. Ham told Roger Martin. Neither Ham nor Roger Martin were pleased: they had their different reasons for being jealous. Nothing needed to be said, or hardly anything. One day a small paragraph appeared in the gossip column of a daily paper: 'ROMANCE? Ex-deb-of-the-year Angel Dobson, nineteen-year-old daughter of wealthy industrialist Gabriel

Dobson has been staying for some weeks with Lord Trent, thirty-five-year-old animal lover, until recently something of a recluse. "Toby's never cared for girls before," said a close friend of the family. "We are all wondering whether there will shortly be an announcement." '

Angel read it, and thought simply that Roger must be running short of material. She did not mention it and Toby did not read it, but that afternoon two reporters came to the lodge and were frightened away by the panthers. The next day's paper made a big story of it, the fierce animals, the mad peer, rumours in the village, the fact that no one dared to go beyond the lodge gates, an interview with the taxi-driver, the fact that Toby lived alone with Fergus, that no one had stayed there for years, no comment from Ham, from Penelope, from Gabriel, from an unknown voice that answered the telephone at Lord Trent's residence and subsequently left the receiver off.

A telegram arrived from Gabriel to tell Angel to come home to Harkwood immediately. It did not reach her until the evening because they left the receiver off the telephone; the telegraph boy brought the telegram to the lodge and the old lodge-keeper was out until six o'clock.

'I'll have to go,' said Angel.

'Yes,' said Toby. 'I'll take you to the station tomorrow. What are the London trains, Fergus?'

'There's an 11.15, the one you usually go on,' said Fergus. 'Seems a shame to me.'

'It's all my fault,' said Angel.

She thought Toby was annoyed by the publicity because he had been silent since the telegram came and had seemed almost relieved at the prospect of taking her to the station, but he said, 'My dear, why should I mind? The panthers keep the brutes out. They can spend months in that frightful pub in the village for all I care. As for my reputation, it's improving every minute. But if your father sends for you you have to go. Perhaps you could come back when it's all blown over.'

He remained silent and worried all evening, and when Fergus had gone to bed he stood up quickly and began to talk.

'I must tell you, Angel, that life is not so simple as you think it, it is a great deal more simple.' He began nervously to pace up and down. 'It is simply this, that we are here for one thing only, one thing. We are not meant to be happy or good or miserable or bad, or to try to be important or to make up music or anything like that. These are meaningless gestures of independence, we are meant to reproduce ourselves and then die. We are creatures of Nature and nothing else, there is no other meaning to life, no other meaning at all. And Nature is not good or bad, it is merely endless. The process is endless and senseless and repetitive, also eternal and immortal. All the immortality you will ever have is that a hundred years from now some wretched little spacewoman will have a beautiful nose, a nose like yours.'

'I should like that,' said Angel gently.

'You are so humble it breaks my heart. You are like that cat out there with her cubs. You only want to submit yourself to the forces of Nature. You are more beautiful than she is because every movement you make is informed with a spirit and an intelligence far superior to hers, but like her you only want to be used and when you have been used, rejected. And in the interval sit in the sun, or plant a flower, or comb your hair.'

'But if it is as inevitable as you say, isn't it better to want it?'

'Yes it is better to want it, and at the same time it is unbearable,' he said. 'Unbearable because it is so senseless. Or perhaps unbearable because I am excluded.'

'Then what do you want?'

'I don't want anything,' he said angrily. 'I want nothing. I want no part in it. I want to be one of Nature's dead ends, leading nowhere. I want to have nothing to do with the process, it is senseless, meaningless, cruel, cruel, cruel. I am a mistake, I reject it, I am not strong enough to take part in the struggle.'

'If you think it so hateful why do you keep your leopard and her cubs? Why don't you reject her?'

'Because how can I help feeling a tenderness for her? As I do for you, only a hundred times more so. I mean, a hundred times more so for you.'

'But then,' said Angel carefully. 'If we feel a tenderness for each other, should we not stay together?'

'No, no, no, no,' he said, still pacing backwards and forwards. 'Because I could not undertake such a relationship, for one thing. I am not able to, it would be simply a question of giving and taking pain. I have never had what one might call a serious, grown-up, responsible relationship with anyone and I never can. My whole soul shrinks from it, the stress of it would send me mad. Anyway we could never marry, because I am impotent.'

'Of course you are if you believe all this,' said Angel. 'Anyway the truth is I don't much like that sort of thing.'

'But you want children.'

She hesitated. 'Well, yes,' she said. 'I do.'

'So, then . . .' He stopped by the piano and stood looking at her across the long dim room. He spoke with bitterness. 'So you must get married, fall in with that low form of love, that bargain, that contract that should never need to be written down, and be a wife and get your rights, your position, your security, your children, and give in return your services in the house and in the marriage bed, and your face to be a possession and your voice to bolster up some idiot's self-esteem. All that is nothing to do with me. Nothing to do with me. All I can do by loving you is hurt you a little, as I am doing now.'

'Is that all I can do for you?' said Angel sadly. 'Hurt you?'

'Yes,' he said.

'I will do whatever you like,' said Angel, her eyes on his face.

But he turned away. He began to play the piano, briskly.

She cried, far away on the sofa. Then she went up to bed, and cried more. She heard him playing the piano on and off all through the night, but she did not dare to go downstairs because she was afraid of the look of pain which would cross his face at the sight of her.

In the morning he drove her to the station. There were several reporters and photographers. Toby ignored them, and kissed her goodbye. The next day there was a photograph of them on the front page of several newspapers,

looking at each other just before they kissed. Angel cut it
out and kept it.

Gabriel had recently been interviewed on television in
a programme dealing with labour relations, arising out of
a recent strike in the motor industry. The interview lasted
eight minutes and he came across very well. He bought
a television set on which to watch the recording of the
programme, and installed it in what used to be the
nursery. Angel watched it almost the whole of every
evening.

Gabriel and Miss Martin were shocked. They were not
used to the phenomenon of television and thought it a
danger to young minds because it might stupify them into
a state of non-thinking: it distressed them both to realize
that that was exactly what Angel hoped of it.

'It appears to me that she was in love with the fellow,'
said Gabriel. 'And that he was no use to her.'

Miss Martin was knitting a jersey for Selina. 'It's a
bloody nuisance,' she said irritably. 'Men are shits.'

'I wish you would moderate your language,' said
Gabriel mildly.

'Sorry,' said Miss Martin. 'What can we do for her?'

'She won't talk to me,' said Gabriel. 'I've tried, but I
can get nothing out of her. I've been most tactful, haven't
said a word about what's happened, but it's no good. She
won't talk to me at all. I'm taking her to Venice in a
fortnight's time, but she hasn't even said anything about
that. Not that I expect gratitude exactly. I mean, I've told
her that I'm taking her because I want a companion, but
after all not many people get a free holiday in Italy,
staying in the best hotels, just like that, you know.'

'I'm sure you'll find she'll relax when you get there,'
said Miss Martin. 'I think it's the best possible thing for
her.'

He sighed. 'They're a great responsibility,' he said.

Later Miss Martin went upstairs to see Angel, who was
watching the Cisco Kid with the curtains drawn because
it was still light outside. Turning the sound down slightly,

Miss Martin said, 'I wish you could be a little nicer to your father about this trip to Italy.'

'I am nice to him about it,' said Angel distantly, her attention still on the television.

'Not very,' said Miss Martin.

Angel said nothing. The programme seemed about to end, so Miss Martin waited.

'Oh news, I can't bear news,' said Angel, jumping up to turn it off. 'Except for one of the announcers and it isn't that one. It's the only thing I turn it off for, news.'

She went back to the sofa, lay down and reached for a cigarette. Miss Martin did not speak.

'Oh, Martin, yes, well . . .' said Angel, after a moment. 'Of course I know it is kind of him.'

'He is anxious for you to enjoy it,' said Miss Martin.

Angel drew on her cigarette. 'It will be hellish,' she said. 'I can never think of anything to say to him. What can we talk about?'

'You can ask him about things,' said Miss Martin, encouragingly. 'He is very well-informed, a wonderful person to travel with. And he enjoys travelling, it stimulates him, he is at his best.'

'Isn't grateful a really feeble thing to be?' said Angel. 'I don't suppose anyone has ever been grateful to me. I'm glad. It's a very milk and water feeling, don't you think? I am grateful to you, though. I will try to be nice to him. I know it is mean of me to be so dull, to make no effort. But I feel mean and dull. Aren't you glad you haven't got any horrid children to be mean and dull with you?'

'No,' said Miss Martin.

'Oh, Martin, Martin, you've got us,' said Angel, rising with a return of her usual manner and putting her arms briefly round Miss Martin's neck. 'Now I must go and find some whisky. When the news comes on that means it's time for drinks.'

6

CHARLOTTE leant against the black front door, waiting. in front of her four uneven steps led down to the pavement beside the area railings. There were two Vespas parked in front of the house. They belonged to the two Greek musicians who lived next door. On the other side of the road was a pub, on a corner, with a large Victorian inn sign creaking a little in the wind. The pub was nearly always empty. Sometimes behind the frosted glass window of the bar she had seen the proprietor's face, staring, moon-like out for hours at a time: in the summer his flabby form would heave itself with some difficulty, for he had a wooden leg, out of a first-floor window on to the flat roof above the bar, turning to pull a deck-chair after him. There behind the peeling cream parapet he would sit and sleep until it was time to open the bar, observable only from the Moulds' bedroom window.

Charlotte lodged in the basement of the Moulds' house near World's End in Chelsea. She had a bedroom, and a kitchen which was also a bathroom, and a separate entrance, to which as often happened she had forgotten the key, so that she had to wait for Clara Mould to come back from shopping, or taking the baby for a walk, or whatever it might be. It was nearly evening. She had put her painting materials down at her feet, beside the sooty geraniums growing in the terracotta urn the Moulds had brought back from Italy the year before last. She had worked hard at the Art School that afternoon, as she always did because of her deep enthusiasm, and now she was agreeably tired, leaning against the door, her head back, staring at the creaking inn sign. When Clara Mould came and let her in she would go to her little kitchen and make herself baked beans on toast, and tea. She would have a bath, change into her other pair of trousers, take a number 11 bus to Charing Cross, and walk across the bridge to the Festival Hall where there was a concert she wanted to hear.

She looked along the street opposite her, which joined the one in which she waited, to see if Clara was yet in sight. There was a tree in that street: it was blacker than black in that light. The house on the corner opposite the pub was smarter than the others, painted white with a yellow front door. The tree was behind it, marking its superiority. The street in which the Moulds lived was wide. The houses were shabby, and at the end there were a few prefabs built on a bombed site and not yet replaced. Children played in the street in front of them. Charlotte could hear them shouting. The traffic roared in the King's Road, but none of it seemed to come down their street. A boy on a bicycle wriggled his way rapidly past her, drawing a violet veil behind him; that is, as he passed, the evening turned from white to violet without ceasing to be translucent. Everything was palely violet, the silent pub, the neat house and the shabby ones, the dark tree, the group of children the length of the violet street away. Charlotte leant her head back against the door again, and saw the sign of the inn impossibly clear against the pale sky. She breathed, from deep inside her but carefully, feeling her arms tingle and the breath rise in her and rise until it broke into her eyes in tears.

'Oh dear,' said Clara Mould's soft voice. 'I am sorry. You must have waited a long time.'

She was at the foot of the steps with her pram, her big pale face concerned.

'No,' said Charlotte, pushing herself away from the door and stretching.

'You looked so tired as I came up.' Clara put the brake on the pram and hurried to unlock the door.

'I was thinking how could I possibly be so happy,' said Charlotte.

'That's all right then. I am glad you're happy, and know it. It's fortunate to be able to recognize it at your age.'

'Don't you?'

'Oh, I do now. But I didn't recognize any of my

emotions until I was thirty. I knew they were emotions of course and usually very uncomfortable, but I didn't know what name to give them. I expect I was a late developer.'

'I used to feel uncomfortable about music,' said Charlotte.

'Oh music,' said Clara, humping the pram up the steps while the baby laughed appreciatively. 'I hated music until I was eighteen. It seemed almost wicked. And yet I don't think I minded how much books made me cry. I suppose it might be that books are less physical, they don't make you want to move. Though I do move now when I read poetry. I don't think I have ever felt anything deeply about a picture. I don't much care for the visual arts. I may be only saying that to annoy you.'

'Don't you ever feel about colour as you do about music?' said Charlotte

'No,' said Clara, lifting out the baby who now began to whimper. 'My eye is not trained. Also I really rather distrust art, it is so often anti-intellect. Be an angel and get me a couple of nappies from the cupboard. Art is so much in favour these days which is another thing against it. On the floor, yes. There, now you can have a good kick. Isn't he fat?'

Charlotte tickled him and he laughed. He was a good baby.

'I thought music and mathematics went together,' she said.

'They do, I believe,' said Clara, putting a kettle on to boil. 'But I am not really a mathematician.'

'But when I answered your advertisements you were correcting proofs of a book about algebra,' said Charlotte.

'Only a Junior School text-book,' she said. 'I am an amateur.'

'Does your husband dislike art, too?' asked Charlotte.

'No,' said Clara, pouring rose hip syrup into a mug. 'Though he makes rather unartistic buildings. Would you like some tea?'

'I'd love some.'

'Do you eat enough? I often wonder whether you do, but I haven't liked to ask you. There are all these articles in the papers about young girls who only eat sandwiches for lunch.'

'I eat baked beans,' said Charlotte. 'Have you seen any pictures by a man called Smith Pennington?'

'I don't think so, though I've heard of him. He's well thought of, isn't he?'

'I saw a picture of him the other day, just one, in a gallery. A huge huge landscape. I thought it was the most wonderful picture I'd ever seen.'

'Why?' asked Clara.

'I don't know. The colours. But really, there was some sort of mystery about it. I could have looked at it for ever. I'm going to look at it every day until someone buys it. It's very expensive, so perhaps no one will.'

'They like them expensive,' said Clara. 'He's a friend of a friend of ours who thinks he's very good too. You should meet him, the friend I mean. He's often here.'

'Oh could I?' said Charlotte with enthusiasm.

'Of course.' She picked up the baby and began to spoon rose hip syrup into his mouth. 'Give yourself some tea,' she said.

Their sitting-room was grey and brown, with some purple cushions. They were the colours in which Clara Mould seemed mostly to subsist and into which she infused a particular, if somewhat austere, warmth. There was something peculiarly unchanging about Clara Mould. Even after so short an acquaintance Charlotte felt that she could be relied upon never to wear anything else but some combination of that brown and grey and purple, never to voice any opinion that was not similarly a variant upon the reliable tones of her mind – not that this limited the opinions, it merely coloured them – and they would be delivered in the same gentle pedantic voice, which could never be personally unkind and could imbue the mildest of trivia with an air of final truth. Her husband was an architect. They had no money because he would not compromise with his clients and so had very few. He was esteemed abroad and wrote articles for foreign magazines: they were usually both of them bent over papers, for she did proof-reading and editing for a publisher. Charlotte would see them through the window before she went down to her basement, bent and busy and untidy.

They seemed to personify something of the freedom and the ideas about right conduct which had come with her leaving school and coming to London. They were Socialists: she violently approved of that. She saw little of Angel or Penelope in London and had refused invitations to meet their friends. She spent a good deal of her time when she was not at the Art School alone, walking through the streets without particular aim, or leaning on the wall of the Embankment, gazing at the river, or sitting in the Chelsea Public Library, in the reference section, reading. She had not dared to believe that her father would allow her to live alone, but the Moulds had produced references and he had said nothing beyond that it seemed an unsavoury part of the world, and that she had better come home every weekend to get some clean air.

'Our friend John Mason is in America,' said Mrs. Mould. 'But we'll ask him round when he gets back and he shall tell you about Smith Pennington.'

Charlotte went to look at the picture as often as she could, until one day it disappeared from the gallery. She could not say what she felt about it, either in ordinary language or in the new art language which she was learning from her fellow students. It was her private revelation of something she had begun to guess already. One day she would paint like that. One day she would talk to the man who had painted it. The picture, and her idea of the painter, became part of the new truth. When she looked at the picture a few years later she found it was the only one of his which had become meaningless to her because it represented so completely a whole phase of her life which was over.

Penelope was giving what Ham called a 'hen lunch' when her father telephoned to ask them to Harkwood for Easter.

'The Biddles are coming,' he announced with elaborate casualness. 'They're rather charming and I thought it would make an amusing weekend. I rely on you to play the hostess. Myra Biddle does that sort of thing so awfully well herself.'

'Yes, of course, Father. Would you like me to come the day before to help Martin a bit?'

'Well, perhaps that might be a good idea. Yes, I'd be very grateful – if Ham doesn't mind, of course. I knew I could rely on you.'

When he had rung off, Penelope said, turning back into the room. 'What a surprise. He's actually asked someone to stay. It's unheard of.'

'He must be branching out into a gay old age,' said Jane Macadam, who knew him slightly. She had been at school with Penelope; and looked rather as if she were still there, a fresh-faced untidy senior prefect, with a flowered hat incongruously perched on the back of her head. Her husband was a noisy back-bencher with agricultural interests, who thought it rather endearing when his wife spoke disparagingly of 'wogs,' 'yids', 'blacks' and 'oyks', although he was aware that there was a ferocity behind her use of these terms which he did not share, despite his keen adherence to what he would have called 'the good old Party Line.'

Then there was Celia Mander. Her venom was chiefly reserved for certain other Conservatives wives, but she knew this attitude to be incorrect and so spoke with amazing malice and hostility of 'the other side'; no one would have believed that her heart was not in it. She was pleased to have been asked to lunch by Penelope, whose looks, clothes, and excellent lunch she admired. She herself was always beautifully dressed. She had recently been photographed as one of London's top hostesses and had been quoted as saying, 'I always ask husbands and wives separately, they are so much better company apart,' and was wondering whether she dared start putting this precept into practice. She did not much care for the fourth member of the party, who seemed to be having some difficulty in keeping awake. This was Caroline Cope, the well-born wife of a well-born Junior Minister. She despised Mrs. Mander for trying so hard for things which were not due to her by right. She found politics a bit of a bore but was used to them; she liked horses and gardening and was friendly and well-meaning within the bounds of her assumptions. She liked a good meal and rather a lot to drink.

'The Biddles are everywhere,' she said. 'They're frightfully rich. He's head of some big concern, I can't remember what. He's pretty crooked I think, though no one says so.'

'I thought he had rather a good reputation,' said Celia Mander. 'John met him at a lunch, and said he seemed very able. She's terribly attractive, I think, don't you?'

'I think they're jolly nice,' said Jane Macadam. 'It's such a relief to meet a rich business man who's not a Jew. Not that your father is, of course.'

'I don't think Father can compete with the Biddles,' said Penelope. 'Not by any means. Have some more coffee, Caroline? Now what about this canvassing? We must all rally round and help Laura. Could we arrange a rota, or something? It's only Balham, after all – I mean, not far away.'

'Of course we must help,' said Celia, keenly. 'These local government elections are much more important than people realize.'

'I wish I could,' said Caroline. 'But I'm not coming up to London next week because the garden's in such a mess. Anyway you're all much better at that sort of thing than I am. Just a tiny brandy then, darling, how lovely.'

Susan was sitting in her garden when her husband brought her father's letter out to her. The spring sunshine was warm. They had made a sun-trap in front of the summer house, a small paved area with some expensive garden furniture, and one or two wrought iron tulips to put glasses in. Bill called it Susan's present to the house because she had paid for it.

She was reading a novel by Georgette Heyer, and Minou their new Siamese kitten was asleep on her knee. She wished the day would go on for ever; when she read her father's letter her first feeling was that perhaps it might. He had written, 'Perhaps after all we might fix a

later weekend for your visit. I had forgotten that I had
asked some friends, a Mr. and Mrs. Biddle, and it would
make us rather a large party. Poor old Martin gets fussed
about the catering, and anyway I don't suppose Bill would
find the Biddles particularly congenial. Would Whitsun
suit you?'

'Oh I am so glad,' said Susan. 'Then we can just stay
here quietly.'

'Well, but it's all very well.' Bill was discontented. 'We'd
been asked, you know. I bet he asked these people Biddle
after us.'

'You know you find weekends there a strain,' said
Susan. 'And I can't bear them. Father becomes more and
more selfish and overbearing every day. He doesn't need
us. Why should he go on trying? He's never liked me.'

'Nonsense,' said Bill. 'I'm sure he's not lacking in the
proper paternal feelings. It's just that he's a difficult man
to get on with, that's all. But we don't want to break with
him completely, now do we? I mean, good Heavens,' he
gave a jolly laugh. 'He might cut you out of his will, or
something.'

'I shouldn't mind,' said Susan.

'Sometimes I think you overdo the humble act, dear,'
said Bill gently. 'Surely that was rather a foolish thing to
say?'

'But why?' she said. 'What do we want that we haven't
got? We do perfectly well on your pension and my income
from the Trust. Why should we want any more? I don't
want anything to change, anything at all. I'm happy for
the first time in my life, the very first time. Why can't I
be happy, Bill, why do you keep making me worry about
things?' Rather to her own surprise, she burst into tears.

'Now, now.' He knelt beside her, his large face
drooping with kindness. 'Don't cry. I put it badly. All I
meant was that I didn't want you to lose touch with your
family altogether, that's all I meant. And if you don't
make a bit of an effort, people soon drift away. They're
all busy you know, and rather selfish as you say, and
then, you know, they don't really think I'm of much
account, I'm afraid.'

'But they're so wrong, they don't understand,' she

cried. 'I need you to be like that. I hate them, because they're so, so oppressive. They are people of account. I don't want to be like that. Oh, I know I am a coward.'

'No, no, we know what you are,' he said. 'You're a neurotic. And we know why, don't we? Because of your mother's death and those things that frightened you as a child. Now would you like me to get some more of those books from the library, and read them to you? Which one did you like the best?'

'Adler, really,' she said. 'But it seems silly. Angel would be furious.'

'She doesn't understand,' he said. 'All I want to do is to help you to understand yourself.'

She sighed, her brief emotional storm over. 'I'm afraid nothing will stop me getting worse and worse,' she said, smiling.

'We shall read together and try to help you,' he said. 'And in the meantime I think you should accept your father's invitation to go there for Whitsun instead of Easter. It's no use being proud about these things.'

When Selina read her father's letter saying that she could not have Brigid Knight to stay until after Easter because of the Biddles, she said, 'How mouldy.'

'It doesn't really matter,' said Brigid. 'I can go to Morag. She was livid anyway because I was going to spend all the holidays with you, so it's probably just as well. They're going to Exmoor or something. It might be rather fun.'

Brigid's father was in the Army, stationed in the Middle East, and it was not thought wise for Brigid to join him for the Easter holidays because of the political situation.

'Would you rather stay all the time with her?' said Selina. 'I mean, you don't have to feel you have to come to us. I mean, we never do anything at all interesting at home, and there's no one there and nothing to see or anything.'

'Don't be silly,' said Brigid, giving her a thump on the back. 'You know I'd rather be with you than stinky old Morag.'

Selina, rightly, did not believe her. Brigid liked both her friends and usually preferred whichever she was with at the moment. Selina cared only for Brigid.

Angel was very thin and had begun to follow extremes of fashion in her dress. She had become aggressively elegant, accentuating her angularity. A large part of each day was spent in making up her face, the result sometimes seeming to betray a satirical intent.

'I have a worm,' she groaned, exaggeratedly despairing in front of the mirror.

'A girl at school had worms,' said Selina.

'I was speaking metaphysically,' said Angel.

They were all in Angel's bedroom, all that is, except Susan, because this was the weekend from which she had been excluded. They had to go to Angel's bedroom if they wanted to see her in the mornings because she never came out of it until lunch time.

'Oh rose thou art sick,' said Charlotte. She was sitting by the window, her strong gold hair half concealing her bent face as she scribbled sketches. 'The invisible worm, that flies in the night, hath . . . hath . . .'

'Hath thy life destroyed,' said Selina.

'I thought he had, the brute,' said Angel.

'I think we're all like that,' said Penelope. 'To a greater or lesser degree. All tending to depression. It's something to do with Mummy dying.'

'And Father being a brute,' said Charlotte.

'You were nearly grown-up when she died,' said Angel to Penelope.

'I was in my impressionable adolescence,' said Penelope.

'I think it's our physical constitution,' said Angel. 'We've inherited hers. We're all going to die young.'

'No, we're not,' said Charlotte. 'The only one who's a real depressive is Susan, and she's never been anything else.'

'I think she's going mad,' said Angel. 'Bill encourages her. If she's mad she's even more helpless. He carries that thing some men have about helpless little women to extremes. Perhaps he's mad too.'

'He couldn't possibly be anything so interesting,' said Charlotte.

'I don't think madness is interesting,' said Penelope. 'Not once you're over the borderline. You become irrelevant, as if you'd flown to another planet.'

'I once wrote a poem about a worm,' said Charlotte.

'Recite it,' said Selina.

'No,' said Penelope.

'Yes,' said Angel. 'I like Charlotte's poems.'

'I've forgotten it,' said Charlotte.

'Of course you haven't,' said Selina.

'It's very bad,' said Charlotte. 'I wrote it a long time ago.'

'Come on,' said Angel.

Charlotte recited her poem, in an impressive monotone.

'Heart soul body mind
Meat and bread are
For this Love's worm
Intestines to brain consumed
Veins liver lungs
Worm grown so large at last
My skin holds no more.

So were there terracotta walls of clay to crumble
And this proud worm to be set free,
Then might it not superbly settle on your shoulders
In a grey garment soft as ash?

And you then would walk on all enshrouded
By this unseen not intangible cloak
Warmer to your soul and moving body
Than all the tens of thousand flannel petticoats
Of long dead long unloved factory women.'

'Oh I like that very much,' said Angel.

Selina gave an abrupt shout of laughter. 'I think it's funny,' she said. 'The one I like is the one about wronged Antigone's unblemished shoulder.'

'Are you in love?' asked Penelope.

'Of course,' said Charlotte. 'But I wrote that before I was in love.'

'Who are you in love with?' asked Selina.

'A painter called Smith Pennington,' said Charlotte. 'He's rather famous.'

'But how marvellous. Where did you meet him?' said Penelope.

'I haven't met him yet,' said Charlotte. 'But I shall. I know all about him. I've seen a lot of his pictures and photographs of him and talked about him a great deal with a friend of his.'

'Oh really you are too maddening,' said Penelope.

'I think it's better to be in love with someone you don't know,' said Selina. 'Then they themselves don't play any part in it, loving or not loving you. It's much safer.'

'Oh she is so experienced,' said Angel, not unkindly. 'A whole lifetime of loving is behind her.'

'Perhaps they're going to be great lovers then, Charlotte and Selina,' said Penelope. 'I suppose they might be. It seems odd. So few people are. I could never be.'

'Don't you love Ham?' said Angel.

'Not in a great love sort of way,' said Penelope. 'Just as a husband, someone to be loyal to.'

'I couldn't love Ham,' said Charlotte. 'There'd be nothing to get hold of, he's so slippery.'

'Oh, Charlotte, you don't understand at all,' said Penelope. 'Just because he's not your sort of person doesn't mean he never has an important thought. He's very serious, much more so that one might think.'

'Now she's being loyal,' said Angel. 'What would you do if he did something terrible, something you really thought was wicked, would you be loyal then?'

'I should have to be,' said Penelope, seriously. 'Though I might have to decide what would be the most loyal thing to do. But I can't see the situation arising exactly.'

'Well, I must get dressed,' said Angel, who was still in her dressing-gown. 'How are the Biddles this morning?'

'Vile,' said Selina. 'He thinks he's the most wonderful thing that ever happened.'

'And here are we, all worrying about our worms of doubt and despair,' said Angel, with a sigh.

'Nonsense,' said Charlotte. 'I'm not worrying in the least. I am full of nothing but strength and appetite.'

'Gosh,' said Angel, stretching. 'Lucky old you.'

Gabriel was thinking that action kept one young. Travel, movement, stimulation, new schemes, risks: he had great hopes of his association with John Biddle.

His holiday in Venice had done him good. He felt well and energetic, ready for work. Angel had been sweet in Venice, had seemed to enjoy herself in a quiet way. He had been proud to take her about with him because she looked so pretty. Everyone said so wherever they went, and he had thought really for fineness and delicacy there is nothing to compare with what a man feels for his daughter. They had not communicated much; but then the young were odd these days.

He was proud of all his daughters, except Susan. He liked the look of them, sitting round his table at meals, and thought how favourably they must impress the Biddles. They were irritating of course, and their conversation was foolish: at the same time it had a certain brightness. They are rather distinguished, my daughters, except Susan, he thought with mild amusement. Nothing anaemic about them, though, a shot of good red middle-class blood from my side. And brain. That comes from my side. Hannah was a clever woman, but the rest of her family was half-witted. They get their brains from me. And then a sudden discontent broke in on his complacency. Why didn't they use their brains, why didn't they get anywhere, why did they make stupid marriages, waste themselves? They should have been boys. Or perhaps they were too well-bred after all, too restrained, too conventional, they had nothing to fight against. They were spoilt. He had spent too much money on them, that was it. But Biddle was asking him something, wanted to finish a conversation they had had earlier, had been thinking about it, he said.

'Let's take our coffee into the library,' said Gabriel.

'If the ladies will excuse us,' said Biddle, bowing to them. The ladies looked at him with varying degrees of coldness. Ham was holding the sugar bowl for Myra Biddle.

'I don't want to rush you,' said Gabriel, sitting down in the library and offering Biddle a cigar. 'It was simply that you mentioned your interest in anything new just about the time this thing came up. I can give you a few more figures now, by the way.'

'Good,' said Biddle, accepting a cigar and pulling his armchair up close to Gabriel's so that their conversation took on a confidential aspect. 'You know my position. I need to expand my interests, not have all my eggs in one basket. It's a big basket of course but then there are a hell of a lot of eggs.' He gave two rapid jerks, indicating mirth, and went on, 'I've told you about Mansel, but there again I don't want to become too much dependent on what I do with him. You want a lot of irons in the fire, you know, when you start going in for this speculative stuff. Now, Baker Boles has a good name.'

'It's a good business,' said Gabriel. 'It's a little run down at the moment, that's all. It needs money and some new energy. They brought me in as chairman mainly in fact to get these things for them, since I told them quite frankly that I had neither time nor capital to spare myself, but they were very persistent and were kind enough to say they wanted my advice and so I took it on. I found that fundamentally it's a very sound business indeed. There's only one other firm which provides serious competition. It's a specialized thing, as you know, this particular sort of printing machinery. This other firm, the rival, is a new one, without the good will and tradition and so on of Baker Boles; but since there is this challenge, now is the time – very much so – for Baker Boles to get a move on and not get left behind. As I told you there is really no controlling interest at the moment. It was a family firm and has been left between four members of the family. They don't get on, and two at least would I know be willing to accept a decent offer and sell out.'

'That would be a *sine qua non*, as I said before,' said Biddle. 'I'm not interested unless I can have a controlling interest. You see my point.'

'Of course,' said Gabriel. 'I should not have let our

conversations get this far if I didn't feel fairly confident of being able to persuade them to agree to that. Now I've got some balance sheets here which you may care to look through.'

Biddle grunted, pushing himself deeper into his chair and taking a big puff at his cigar. He stretched out his hand for the balance sheets. It was a broad, short-fingered hand, with a few red hairs on the backs of the fingers. His complexion and his temper were bad; his one passion was for money, for the commodity itself, not for what it could buy. He was single-minded in his pursuit of it, shrewd in his manoeuvres to effect its increase, supremely confident of his values, not kind to his wife. He unfolded the balance sheet with deliberation, an expert in his field.

'Good cigars, these,' he said, beginning his scrutiny.

Ham was in the garden with Myra Biddle.

'Why can't Moulton get my daffodils to look like that?' she was saying. 'I don't believe my gardener knows anything about gardening. But then as I don't either, how can I ever be sure?'

She gave a helpless, pretty laugh. She was half Swedish, tall and blonde but fragile. Since she had no confidence in anything about herself except her looks, she needed to be constantly reminded of them. She fed on compliments and pined without them. Ham gave her a feast, having discerned that in her view enough was not as good.

When he had compared her to a daffodil, to the disadvantage of the flower, he said, 'What are your husband and my father-in-law up to this weekend? Are they plotting a coup, I wonder, to shake the business world to its foundations?'

'But of course,' said Myra. 'John never thinks of anything but business.'

'What is it this time, I wonder?' mused Ham, without appearing more than mildly curious. 'I don't think my father-in-law has anything much to do with the engineering world.'

'Oh, but my dear we are expanding,' she said. 'We

don't want to have all our eggs in one basket. It is a big basket but there are a lot of eggs. We are going in for everything you can think of, property, magazines, printing machinery, imported textiles, plastics, everything, but it's no use asking me anything about it because John never tells me anything, and if he does I don't listen, because I simply haven't enough brain to understand about business.'

'Nonsense,' said Ham. 'You're too modest. What you mean is that you're too intelligent to bother about business, in which you're quite right. But I daresay that's what they're talking about, printing machinery. My father-in-law has been trying to raise money for a firm. I know, because he told me about it. I dare say it would be quite a good investment for your husband.'

'No, that's one thing I do remember,' she said. 'Printing machinery is someone else, because he came to stay for the weekend and I rather liked him. A young man called Harvey Oldham. Do you know him?'

'No, but why did you rather like him?' said Ham. 'What sort of young men do you rather like? Describe him to me. I am jealous of him already.'

Later Ham made a telephone call to Roger Martin in London. He asked him to find out about Harvey Oldham and his relations with John Biddle.

That evening Roger Martin telephoned Ham to tell him that Harvey Oldham's firm was the only serious rival to Baker Boles in the field of specialized printing machinery; that Harvey Oldham was a bright young man, and that from certain highly confidential sources of Roger Martin's there seemed every reason to believe that he was either about to be backed by John Biddle, or was already in that fortunate position.

'The old shit,' said Ham, in a tone of admiration.

He could not manage to be alone with Biddle until the following afternoon, when Gabriel was sitting in the sun doing *The Times* crossword, and Myra Biddle was watching racing on television with the curtains drawn. The four girls and Miss Martin had disappeared. He saw

Biddle wandering off into the garden, his hands in his pockets, bored. Gabriel was not a good host except for guests who liked to be left to themselves.

Ham followed him and offered to drive him round to see the beauties of the neighbourhood. Biddle refused.

'I get too much driving as it is,' he said. 'It's good for me to take things easy for a couple of days like this. I find this flat countryside a bit monotonous, though, don't you? Of course neither Myra nor I are really country people, if you know what I mean.'

'But you go to your house in Sussex most weekends?'

'Oh yes, yes, when we can. Just to get a bit of peace, you know. Not that we do get any peace, because the place is always full of people.' He sounded gratified, however, by this state of affairs. 'Myra is a great one for entertaining.'

'I hear you had a friend of mine down there the other day. Harvey Oldham. Awfully nice, don't you think? And keen, too. I mean, on the ball, and all that.'

'Oldham? Oldham? Oh yes. Some young man Myra picked up I believe.'

'Funnily enough,' pursued Ham. 'I was given the name of his firm as a hot tip on the Stock Exchange. Oldham's Printing Machinery. My source told me you were taking it over. Not that I should dream of being anything but absolutely discreet. I haven't actually bought any shares.'

'I don't know where your informant could have got that story from,' said Biddle, coldly. 'Of course these fellows looking out for a quick gamble are always starting rumours. If they know you've had someone down to your house for a weekend they get all sorts of ideas.'

'He's rather good, as a matter of fact, this fellow,' said Ham. 'He's done some quite useful things for me in the past. And for my father-in-law too. We have an arrangement by which I usually pass on to him any good tips I may get. I don't know whether I shall in this case or not. Those were the daffodils your wife was admiring so much yesterday.'

'Myra's a great one for gardening,' said Biddle.

The daffodils stirred in the faint wind. The two men

walked towards the wood, hearing the sound of Miss Martin's axe in the distance.

'The lake is rather pretty at this time of year,' said Ham. 'I always think it's such a pity one doesn't see it from the house.'

'I suppose it is,' said Biddle, absently.

'Of course, anyway, Gabriel would probably think it disloyal to buy Oldham's shares, even to make a quick profit,' said Ham. 'He's in the same line, with this new thing of his, Baker Boles, I don't know whether you've heard about it?'

'He mentioned it,' said Biddle.

'And they are of course direct rivals,' said Ham, speculatively. 'The only rivals, in fact. So I daresay if he bought the shares in his own name there'd be a bit of a frisson in Oldham's, because of course anyone who gained control of both could absorb one of them if he felt so inclined, so that the other could have what would amount to a monopoly of the business.'

'Quite,' said Biddle.

They walked on in silence.

'Do you know,' said Biddle. 'I think perhaps I wouldn't mention that tip to your father-in-law just yet. We both have his best interests at heart, and we shouldn't like to see him make an unwise investment, should we? They're rather tricky, these things, you know.'

'Yes,' said Ham. 'Of course, if it would help you in any way, I certainly won't say anything about it to him.'

'I think perhaps that would be the best policy,' said Biddle. 'For all concerned.'

They reached the lake. On the other side of it they could see Miss Martin at work. She raised a hand in greeting. They responded, and turned to walk round the lake.

'I've been wondering,' said Ham. 'Whether there might be any interesting openings . . . I mean, one gets the merest pittance as an M.P., and I've been looking round for something I could combine with it, that wouldn't take up too much time. Some sort of directorship or something, which would give me a decent salary.'

'Ah well maybe I can help you there,' said Biddle, with

forced cordiality. 'There are one or two things I can think of that might fit the bill, companies I have an interest in, you know. In fact it often suits me better to have a nominee on their boards rather than take it on myself. Come and see me in London. Could you lunch one day next week?'

'That would be very nice,' said Ham, bringing a slim blue leather diary out of his pocket. 'Wednesday or Thursday?'

'I think Friday's my only day if I remember right,' said Biddle. 'I always keep Friday free for things which come up.'

'Let's make it Friday then,' said Ham. 'There's only one more point – rather embarrassing, I'm afraid . . . I wouldn't bother you with it, only that you've been so kind. I'm going to have to increase my overdraft next week, in fact I ought to go and see my bank manager about it on Monday. Do you think perhaps. . .? It would be a great help to me if you could put what you've just said in writing – gives me a leg to stand on, don't you know? And perhaps if we could actually put in a figure for the salary? Just to pacify the bank manager, you know.'

'Quite,' said Biddle, with a creaking smile. 'I always believe in having everything in writing myself. Then you know where you are.'

'Exactly,' said Ham. 'That's what I always say. If it's in writing, you know where you are.'

7

CHARLOTTE met Smith Pennington in May at a cocktail party in the House of Commons.

It happened in this unlikely setting because the man giving the party was both a collector of modern pictures and the father of an eighteen-year-old daughter. He had recently bought a Smith Pennington and so had met the painter and liked him, and he had asked Charlotte to please Penelope whom he also liked. Smith Pennington had come because he usually did accept invitations; Charlotte had come because Penelope had insisted.

'It won't involve you in anything you don't want to get involved in, I promise you,' she had said. 'All I want is for you to meet some new people, or just some people, in fact. There might easily be your sort of people there. She's not a debby sort of girl at all, she's quite intelligent. Please, Charlotte.'

So Charlotte came, wearing an orange dress which Clara Mould had helped her to buy in a new shop in the King's Road. She wore her thick reddish gold hair loose and straight, scorned to wear make-up on her face, and gave in her bearing an effect of confidence and fire, only diminished and made to fluctuate by the inescapable fact of her youth.

She immediately saw the large neat man the other side of the room, standing alone, looking about him with a sort of patient amiability.

'Who is that?' she asked Ham.

'A painter, a man called Pennington,' said Ham.

'Oh.' She walked across to him, held out her hand and said, 'How do you do?'

'Rather hot,' he said. 'How are you?'

But she had realized that he could have no idea who

469

she was; nor could she now think of anything to say. She blushed, slowly. Confused, she said, 'I must go and find my sister,' and moved hurriedly through the crowd, pushing people aside rather rudely.

He watched her go, blinking with interest, and saw her talk to Penelope. He made his way towards them, and said to Penelope as if in passing. 'I'm just off. Too hot,' because they had been introduced earlier.

Penelope said. 'Oh but I must introduce you to my sister, Charlotte Dobson, Mr. Pennington. She's been longing to meet you. She's a great admirer of yours,' and with a meaning smile to Charlotte she turned into the crowd and left them.

Charlotte tossed back her hair, composed herself and said, 'I do like your pictures, it is true; at least, the ones I have seen. But I am not going to say anything about them because I don't know you well enough. Even if I did know you well enough it is still quite likely that there might be nothing for me to say about your pictures, to you anyway. But that was just Penelope, hoping to embarrass me.' She frowned, looking formidable for a moment, but then smiled and said, 'I have heard about you from John Mason who is a friend of Clara and Adrian Mould whose basement I live in.'

'John, oh yes. I like John,' he said. 'Everyone likes John. Do you like John?'

'Yes, I do,' said Charlotte. 'Except that he is too polite.'

'You don't like politeness?' He spoke in a round blurred tone with an accent which at first she thought he might have picked up from having recently spent two years in America, but which she later discovered to be the remnants of his native Northumbrian.

'I don't think it should go as deep as it does with Ian,' she said. 'I feel he would be polite in a really awful situation when it would be better to be violent.'

'You believe in violence?' he asked.

She laughed and said, 'Only for some people,' not willing to be drawn into being too serious, because she had taken to heart a number of recent hints that this was her tendency. 'I wouldn't mind some violence here, Guy Fawkes sort of violence. Or do you like politicians?'

'I only know one,' said Smith Pennington. 'I like him, because he bought a picture of mine. But isn't your brother-in-law a nice politician?'

'No, not at all,' said Charlotte. 'But my sister doesn't know it yet, and she is so blindly loyal that she may never know.'

'Perhaps that's fortunate,' he said.

'Yes, in a way,' she said.

'But you don't think so.'

'I'd rather know, wouldn't you? Almost anything.'

'Most things, I suppose,' he said. 'Not everything. But then I'm old, compared to you.'

'Yes,' she said.

'You should say, no, surely?' he said. 'Or would that be too polite?'

'I know how old you are. I saw it in some catalogue and it is old compared to me because I am unfortunately rather young.'

'I am forty-four,' he said. 'Is that what it said in the catalogue?'

'Yes,' she said. 'I am eighteen.'

'I know,' he said.

She did not question this, and so he went on, 'John told me.'

'He told you? But you didn't say so when we were talking about him.' She was unexpectedly hurt.

'I am sorry,' he said. 'I really am sorry. I thought somehow I ought to wait before I told you what he said to me. But you are quite right. I should have said it at once.'

'It's all right,' she said politely.

'He didn't tell me anything else about you,' he said appeasingly. 'I wouldn't let him. I didn't want to hear.'

'Oh, well, no, why should you?' she said, a little confused.

'He said, I've found just the girl for you,' he said. 'So I didn't let him tell me any more in case he was wrong. It was rather vulgar of him to put it like that, wasn't it? But then as you just said he is never vulgar.'

'I wonder why he said that,' said Charlotte, surprised. 'Was that all he said, he didn't say why?'

'I wouldn't let him.'

'I am surprised,' said Charlotte. 'Perhaps I have misjudged him.'

'Perhaps you have,' said Smith. 'He is quite perspicacious. But perhaps you are someone else's girl?'

'No of course not,' she said.

'Then shall we go?' he said, gesturing towards the door.

'Oh,' she said. 'Well, I was supposed to have dinner with my sister.'

'I see.' He was evidently sorry, but did not think of overriding the decision.

'Perhaps I could ask her if she would mind if I had dinner with you instead,' said Charlotte.

'That would be nice,' he said. 'I'll wait here while you ask her.'

He waited by the door, scrutinizing the passing people with the same amiable stare as before, a large man, but broad rather than tall, going a little bald, his face brown and lined round the eyes. He looked as if he could comfortably wait there for a week.

Charlotte came back and said, 'That's all right.'

They walked out of the House of Commons and along the Embankment.

'What shall we do now?' he said.

'Anything you like,' she said.

'I should really like to go to bed with you straight away,' he said. 'But I suppose it would be too soon.'

'Yes, I think it would,' said Charlotte. 'You might regret it.'

'I might regret it?' he questioned.

'It would be much harder to get rid of me.'

'I don't want to get rid of you,' he said.

'You might want to one day,' she said. 'It would be better to wait, really it would. You don't know me, you don't even know what it would mean to me.'

'No, of course, you are quite right. I told you because it was what I was thinking, that's all. We could go and see my wife. She lives along here somewhere, Pimlico.'

'Oh.'

'Didn't you know I had a wife? I thought you knew everything. I really did think you knew everything. How

could you? But it was so miraculous that I could believe
anything about you. I thought it was magic, you know.
We were at school together, and then we got married.
We haven't lived together for about ten years. She teaches
where I do. We see quite a lot of each other. She's rather
nice. We just didn't get on as married people.'

'Have you got any children?'

'No. We'd probably still be together if we had. But if
you haven't there's no point in struggling on when you've
lost touch with each other, is there? You get so oppressed
by the other person, it's madness, real screaming
madness. And rows and destruction. We couldn't work
it was so bad. Now it's all right. I suppose you could say
we didn't love each other or something, or not enough,
or not for long, I don't know.'

'But will you go back ever?'

'No fear. She's all right, though, you'd like her.'

'But you're not divorced?'

'We never got around to it somehow,' he said. 'But I
suppose we could if either of us wanted to get married.
She says she's put off it for life, though, and I've never
seemed to want to yet somehow. Nothing has felt really
permanent if you know what I mean.'

Charlotte nodded.

'I was a year older than you when I married,' he said.
'Nineteen. And Beryl was sixteen. We had no money. I
suppose that's why we did it, just to show off. But I wish
now we hadn't, because I can see you'd rather I wasn't
married.'

'No, you're quite wrong, I don't mind at all,' she said
firmly. 'You couldn't very well have got to your age
without something of the sort.'

'If I'd been born a little later, or a lot later, twenty years
later, I could have been faithful to you all my life. Would
you have liked that?'

'I don't know. I can't imagine it.'

'Perhaps we had better make do with what we have.
I'd rather talk about you. Let's sit on this bench. Your
father is a rich stuffy old business man and you have four
beautiful sisters. That's what you told John. Should I like
your father?'

'No, he is very hypocritical. But then you like more people than I do.'

'He certainly seems to have driven you to the extreme non-hypocrite position,' he said.

'You're laughing. Everybody does, I'm afraid. I am too serious, that's it, isn't it? I haven't got a sense of humour.'

'I love serious people,' he said. 'I do truly love seriousness. I am not serious enough myself. I am not able to be. I keep thinking I have reached a position of seriousness and then I find I have not been nearly serious enough. Somethings deserve more seriousness than I have ever felt confident enough to give them. I am talking about painting. My painting is completely trivial, do you know that?'

'No,' she said.

'It is,' he said. 'I don't know why no one's ever pointed that out. I suppose they don't care, they only want wallpaper designs. My painting is like John, in the best contemporary taste. I have good taste, did you know that, in my field. Colours and shapes, I'm good on them. But it is all quite trivial.'

'Perhaps it is a good thing for you to think so,' said Charlotte. 'But I don't believe it's true. The first thing that appealed to me about your painting was its directness, and what I thought at first was its mystery, because I didn't understand it, but now I think I see the meaning of it.'

'What is the meaning? No, don't let's name it. Anyway, there it is. We'll see. Or we won't see, more likely. I don't want to start messing about with meanings. All I can do is notice that there aren't any in my pretty pictures.'

'I never heard anyone say they were pretty. And if they're so easy and like wallpaper why do so many people dislike them?'

'Nobody does dislike them. I wish they did. Everyone's crazy about them. I'm rich, do you know that? I haven't got any actual things because I can never think of anything I want to buy, but I'm rich. By my standards, anyway, which are rather low. I'm a success, do you know that? The only people who don't like any pictures

474

are old diehard colonels like your father. He wouldn't like them, would he?'

'No, I don't think he would,' she said. 'Why do you go on painting them if you think they're trivial?'

'Because I don't of course. Not really, not all the time, not while I'm doing them. But I haven't done much lately. Perhaps the whole idea is dying on me. I don't know. You have to be awfully tough to go on trying. I think so anyway. But you're not trivial, are you?' He touched her face. 'Nothing about you is trivial, even your nose. Let's go on.'

They stood up, and began to walk slowly along the pavement, past other couples, and a cat, and seagulls on the wall of the Embankment, and a barge which hooted on the river.

Gabriel found out about Biddle's plans for the absorbing of Baker Boles by Oldhams Printing Machinery on a hot day in June in his office in Fenchurch Street. He had a room in the offices of a firm of investment consultants in which he was a partner, and he went there two or three times a week to deal with his correspondence, through the medium of Miss North, his secretary.

Miss North was a frizzy, wiry, little person of about sixty, whose absolute devotion to her employer was the mainspring of her life. It was a phenomenal devotion, watchful, selfless and unwavering. Gabriel, perfectly aware of it and not above playing up to it at times, was grateful for it and forgave her her remarkable inefficiency as a secretary.

Today she had brought four roses from her sister's garden in Upper Norwood to brighten up his office, a pink Madam Butterfly, a white Frau Karl Drushki, a spray of little yellow climbers, Mermaid, she thought, and a dark red Etiole d'Hollande. She told him their names to hide her confusion when he thanked her for them. She lodged with her sister, whose husband was a rose-fancier. Gabriel pushed his face into the flowers to smell them. His face was newly shaved, self-confident, smiling, tanned from reading in the sun at Harkwood last weekend.

This was the day on which he realized that he had been duped by Biddle. It was also the day on which Ham told Penelope that he, Ham, had been made a director of one of Biddle's companies and that prospects in that direction looked extremely promising. That was in the evening when it was getting cooler, and Penelope pulled an apricot-coloured shawl closer round her shoulders, eating strawberries on the terrace of the House of Commons. For Angel, it was another nameless day, better than some because it was sunny and under the weather's influence she wore a white frilly dress of the sort she used to wear a year or two earlier. She had lunch with three young men, and laughed a lot towards the end because she had drunk too much sweet white wine, for which she did not really care. After lunch the men went off on affairs of their own – to offices, perhaps, or to lie down somewhere? – so she went to the cinema, where it was very hot and made her head ache. For Selina it was the day that Brigid Knight sprained her ankle playing rounders and was helped from the field by a senior girl called Felicity. Brigid had what was known as a 'pash' on Felicity, so that Selina, distressed by Brigid's pain, must nevertheless watch in silence because this was a great moment for Brigid, and it would have been unforgivable to have interfered. This was the day Susan developed a slight heat rash and decided that Camomile lotion would be better for it than Savlon. It was also the day on which Charlotte, gritting her teeth manfully on a studio floor in Kensington, lost her virginity to Smith Pennington.

Gabriel had suspected for some time that all might not be well with his business relationship with Biddle, and these suspicions had been reinforced by one or two conversations he had recently had with people in the City. He had known before that Biddle, in spite of his success, was not well thought of in the true hard core of the City: he was thought to be too much of a manipulator, not a constructive business man, but this opinion was only held by a very small, though influential group, whose influence anyway was only likely to work against Biddle

were Biddle ever to be in trouble and to need help. It was
conceivable that Biddle might never be in serious trouble.
He had represented, too, for Gabriel, something new and
stimulating, a risk worth taking. Gabriel had felt able to
handle him; only for the last day or two he had been
wondering whether this confidence in himself might not
have been misplaced. It was in answer to some pressing
enquiries on his part that Biddle had written him the letter
he now held in his hand, and which confirmed his worst
suspicions.

Gabriel immediately moved into action. He sent for his
solicitor, telephoned the managing director of Baker
Boles, demanded to see Biddle and arranged to do so
that afternoon. The morning passed in lengthy telephone
conversations; he lunched with his solicitor, and in the
afternoon had an interview with Biddle from which he
felt he emerged the moral victor. It was only later, back
in his own office, where Miss North was waiting for him
though it was after half-past five, that he faced the fact
that a moral victory was useless.

He had known as soon as he read the letter that there
was very little he could do about it, but all day he had
been borne along by his own indignation and by the
knowledge that on one small question at least, that of
compensation for the directors of Baker Boles, there was
negotiation to be done. He had been shocked, too, by
Biddle's effrontery, and at first could hardly believe that
he could get away with it. Back in his office, he realized
that of course he could. He also realized, moving from
the general view which he held all day to the more
particular one, that he himself had every reason for mortification: Biddle had obviously weighed up the value of
his, Gabriel's good opinion and influence, and had
decided that it was dispensable. He had made, admittedly, a pretence of still caring about it. He had repeated
his offer, made at Harkwood, of a seat on the board of
his holding company.

'I meant it then, and I mean it now,' he had said, 'I
wish I could make you see this thing the way I do. I
repeated that offer when I saw the way things were going
because I valued your business knowledge and experience

so highly that I still wanted to be associated with you. Harvey Oldham is a young man in whom I have faith. I backed him some time ago for anything he cared to do. When you asked me for financial help for Baker Boles I didn't at first see how the thing would turn out. You must remember I'm new to some of this. I'm just a simple engineer whose father happened to leave him a business just on the point of booming. As soon as I saw what was happening I said to myself, I mustn't lose Gabriel Dobson. Apart from anything else. I value your friendship very highly, very highly indeed. I need your help, your advice, your experience. If you come on the board of Biddle Holdings we can do big things together, big things. There are only two others, an accountant and a solicitor. The job carries a big salary as I told you, and everything you want in the way of expenses – prospects are terrific, really terrific. There's this property business I told you about. Oldhams Printing will be just a flea, but a pretty safe and solid flea now, you'll admit that. With Baker Boles' business as well and no other competition, there should be some nice profits there, some very nice profits indeed. What I'm doing is offering you a share in them. I made that offer a few weeks ago, and nothing that's happened since has made me change my mind. The offer's still open, wide open.'

Gabriel looked at him sitting fatly behind his big desk, with his solicitor Jenkins beside him, a sleek sharp-nosed bodyguard in an old Etonian tie.

'What amazes me is that I believe you mean it,' said Gabriel. 'Not the stuff about my good opinion; but I mean that I believe you really expect me to take that offer seriously, to accept it, to associate myself with you. Have you heard of such a thing as business ethics? They are practised all round you, you know. You can afford to laugh at them, I suppose. Or probably you don't believe they exist. You think everybody's in some racket or other. Everyone has a price, even the Governor of the Bank of England. You realize, I suppose, that there are certain areas, quite large areas, of business life in this country – and not only in this country – where you have by this effectively cooked your goose. I think I may fairly say that my word is listened to in these areas. What can I say to your integrity as a business man. What can I not say of it? What shall I not say of it, at every opportunity? It will be my duty to warn people against having any dealings with you whatsoever.'

'It will of course be clear to them that you have a personal interest in making this warning, sir,' said the lawyer, detached.

'Personal interest has never swayed my judgment; this fact is completely beyond the comprehension of your maggot's mind. Fortunately for the honour of this country you are representative only of a tiny section of its business community.' He turned to Biddle. 'If you ask for a loan to increase your capital, how can I recommend the committee of which I am a member to advance you one penny? If you wish to be taken seriously as an industrialist in any field, in public life, in politics, have you considered the weight of any influence against you?'

Biddle shifted on his chair. He had been negotiating for a Conservative seat.

'Look here, you know, I think you're taking this a bit hard,' he said.

'My God, I'm taking it hard,' said Gabriel. Then he paused, and governed his rage, thinking that it would be wasted on them. 'But we have said all that we have to say. I needn't keep you any longer. My solicitors will be in touch with you on the subject of compensation. Good day.'

Biddle rose to his feet. 'I wish you hadn't taken it like this,' he repeated, his big face a picture of pained insincerity. 'I should hate to feel I've lost a friend.'

'I shall do my best to see that this is the least you have done,' said Gabriel.

But on the way back to his office in a taxi he thought, what does it matter to a man like Biddle what I and half-a-dozen others think of him? The odds are he'll always get away with it.

Back in his office he put his head in his hands and said, 'I am an old fool, Miss North, a pompous old fool.'

'Oh, Mr. Dobson,' she said, her heart bursting with pity and rage. 'How could you have been expected to know what he was doing, a man like that, too, who seemed so respectable?'

'Tomorrow I must go to Nottingham, to make my excuses to the men I have unwittingly betrayed. Will you put the necessary papers in my brief-case and ring up Miss Martin and say I shall be arriving at Harkwood tomorrow evening. I shall go straight on there from Nottingham – there's no point in coming back here. I will ring you up to find out what's in the post. And cancel that dinner engagement for tomorrow night. Say I've been unavoidably called away on business. Of course when all this comes out, I'm going to look an awful fool. But then I am a fool. I have been made a fool of. Would I have let this happen a few years ago? I'm slipping, Miss North. I'm getting old.'

'Oh, no, Mr. Dobson,' she said earnestly. 'Really you mustn't let it depress you like this. Why, only the other day I was thinking how well you were looking these days.'

He let her run on, while she found, dropped, lost, and refound his papers; but he could gather no comfort from her anxiety, which only seemed to feed his growing self-pity.

He walked to this club, where he was staying. It was a long walk, but he often did it: he felt it helped him to keep his figure.

He was tired. He thought, there's a great deal of wickedness about. Hannah used to say that, he remembered. She was often shocked by people's behaviour, or things she read in the papers, and they would discuss them, in the comfort of shared opinions, and she would end by sighing and saying, oh well, there's a great deal of wickedness about.

He walked across the park, which was crowded with people benefiting from the evening sun, lovers, children, dogs, old crones feeding the pigeons, noisy groups of boys. He felt the sensation, familiar ever since Hannah's death, of loneliness, which he now acknowledged. At first he had pretended to himself that it was only grief for her, but he had come recently to recognize it as total loneliness. In all my long life I have only had one friend, he thought; I have only been able to sustain one deep close personal relationship, and now that is over I have lost everything, for what is the point of a human being who cannot communicate? I should have died too. He marched on through the park, walking fast as he always did, a tall distinguished figure in his London suit and Homburg hat, his hand-made shoes, his brief-case and umbrella, his alert and handsome face. He began to think about his daughters. Why were they not companions to him? Perhaps it was his fault: he knew he was inclined to seem busier than he was. Perhaps he should make more effort with them. He decided to ring up Angel as soon as he reached his club; and then, walking up St. James's, he saw a telephone box, felt in his pocket for pennies, and finding he had enough, went in and dialled the number of Penelope's house where Angel was still living.

She answered the telephone.

'Angel?' he said. 'I was just wondering what you were doing tonight. I made a mistake about the date of a dinner, so I've got nothing on. It's a bit late for the theatre, but we might have dinner somewhere if you'd like to.'

'Oh, Father, well, I'd have loved to,' she said, sounding distant. 'But we're just off to some new restaurant someone's found in the country somewhere to get cool, with Roger Martin and some other people.'

'I see, that's all right then, I just wondered,' he said. 'I'll go on to the club then. I mustn't keep you. Enjoy yourself.'

He rang off. Heartless little wretches, he thought, continuing his walk. They pursue their own pointless pleasures all the time, without a thought for anyone else. What a silly life that poor child leads, what a wasted useless life, why doesn't she get married, or at least find a useful job? Part-time modelling, she says. God knows what that means. What I need is a dog. This thought came to him quite suddenly as he saw a handsome young man looking into the window of a picture gallery and holding a Great Dane on a lead. There is something rather nice about a man and his dog, he thought, stopping to stare. Now that really is a good relationship. A dog. His spirits began to rise. He would buy a dog, a good sensible man's dog, like that one. The young man became conscious of his stare, and moved on. Gabriel remembered a nearby dog-shop, and hurried towards it.

It was shut, but he could see a woman in a white overall moving about inside. He rapped on the window with his umbrella. She looked round and shook her head. He rapped again, importantly, and she unbolted the door.

'We're shut,' she said.

'And now you've opened, how kind of you,' he said. 'I wish to buy a dog.'

'Well . . .' she said hesitantly. 'We're not really open till half-past nine in the morning.'

'By that time I shall be in the train,' he said. 'What sort of dog do you suggest? I should like your advice.'

She turned back into the shop and he followed her. She was a short but gaudy blonde, with a big nose and a big mouth, heavily lipsticked, and bright brown eyes. She smelt of cigarettes, powder and dog.

'I'll stretch a point then,' she said more cheerfully. 'What sort of dog do you want? Is it for London, for a lady?'

'For London and the country,' he said. 'And for myself.'

'I see,' she said, looking at him curiously. 'But you haven't decided what breed?'

'I want a companionable dog,' he said. 'But a sensible one, one that can look after itself.'

'You won't find one that can look after itself entirely, you know,' she said, standing plumply in the doorway leading to the inner recesses of the shop, where the dogs had been put for the night. 'I mean, you have to be responsible for them, their food and exercise and so on.' She put her head on one side and gave him a jaunty look.

He was not sure that he liked her attitude.

'Of course, of course,' he said. 'I've been a dog owner all my life. Now what have you got to suggest?'

'We've a nice litter of Pekes,' she said. 'A lovely colour, good pedigree, nice little dogs.'

'No, no, certainly not, most unsuitable,' he said, following her through the doorway. 'Haven't you anything larger?'

'Dachshunds? poodles?' she said. 'Do you want a dog or a bitch?'

'Is this where they live?' he said, looking round. 'Rather cramped quarters, aren't they?

She was affronted. 'These are the healthiest and best cared for dogs you'll find in the whole of London,' she said. 'They have plenty of fresh air and exercise. Every weekend I pile the whole lot of them into my van and taken them down to my cottage in Kent.'

'Do you really? How splendid,' he said, peering into a box at a tiny shivering chihuahua. 'I don't like the look of that one,' he said. 'What's the biggest dog you've got?'

'What about a nice golden cocker spaniel?' she said.

'I've got one of those already,' he said. 'Only black.'

'You've got one already?' she said. 'Then you mean you want a companion for him? I thought you meant for yourself.'

'It is for myself,' said Gabriel. 'The spaniel is really more of a stable dog.'

'Oh,' she said. 'You have horses then?'

'No,' he said. 'Certainly not. Now what else can you suggest? My time is getting short. I ought to decide on something fairly quickly.'

He was annoyed by the recollection of fat black Bingo, whose existence he had until that moment forgotten. The whole scheme began to seem less promising.

'These Cairns are nice,' she said, helpfully. 'They're a man's dog, they really are, sporting as anything, tough, can go for miles, very friendly chaps too. Here, have a look.' She took one out, a creamy wire-coated puppy with bright black eyes and nose. Gabriel held out his hand and said, 'Hallo.' The dog looked suspicious and after a moment gave a small puppyish bark. 'I'll have that one,' said Gabriel.

'He's a nice little fellow,' she said. 'You wanted a dog and not a bitch, did you? There's a couple of bitches in there too. They're often more companionable than the dogs, you know, less independent . . .'

'No, no, this is the one,' said Gabriel. 'Just give me a collar and lead for him, will you, and I'll make you out a cheque if I may. Has he a name?'

'A kennel name', she said. 'People usually like to choose their own. He's Sago to us, isn't he, Sago boy? I'll give you his pedigree, of course. Twenty guineas, please.'

'Twenty guineas?' said Gabriel. 'Good Lord, is that what they cost these days?'

'I don't think you'd find one cheaper,' she said. 'He's pedigree of course. He's a beautiful little dog.'

'I don't doubt it,' said Gabriel, writing out his cheque. 'If you tell me that's what they cost, that's all right with me. I'm sure you wouldn't cheat me.'

'Indeed, I wouldn't,' she cried, rolling her bright brown eyes and seeming about to protest further. He interrupted her, however, and hurried through the process of paying, receiving instructions as to the puppy's way of life, thanking her, saying good-bye.

'I do hope you'll be very happy together,' she said sentimentally.

'Thank you, I'm sure we shall,' he said, and left the shop, the puppy under one arm and his brief-case under the other. Finding this uncomfortable, he put the puppy down and pulled hopefully on its lead. It sat down. He pulled. It scuffed along on its hind-quarters, looking miserable. Gabriel hailed a passing taxi.

When he went into his club he gave the puppy to the porter and said, 'Look after this for me, would you?'

It was not, of course, as simple as that; but after a good deal of talk it was decided that the porter's wife should, for a consideration, take the puppy home with her for the night and bring him back in time to catch the train with Gabriel in the morning. Gabriel went on into the club with a feeling of work well done, and spent a peaceful evening reading.

Charlotte and Smith Pennington bumped over a grassy track in his van. She called him Peter now. He had been christened Smith after his grandmother but had always been called Peter. She loved him violently. She loved the toughness of the weathered skin on his face, the mistiness of his slightly bulging grey eyes, the naked look of his lips; she loved his firm spatulate hands, his slurred voice, his musty smell; she loved the way in which he seemed to take it to be the object of his life simply to love and work and wait, wait for things to reveal themselves, which they usually did, in time. In believing this of him she was not quite accurate: although he was not introspective, he would in general have liked this to be his attitude to life, but it was only so when he was at his best. At the beginning of their relationship he was at his best. She also loved him for loving her, and for expressing his love physically and so introducing her to a state of delight. She was marvellously proud of their bodies for being able to express, and gratify, so overwhelming a love.

They came to the end of the grass track, in front of a ruined house.

'This was the house, as you see,' he said. 'It was vast and hideous and no one would buy it, quite rightly. So they sold the land and the lead off the roof and left it to fall down. We go this way.'

He walked round the ruin and through the remains of the garden. They came to a gate leading into a wood which grew at the slope of a hill. They went through it, and she followed him along a narrow overgrown path, down into the depths of the wood. It was cool and green, full of birdsong and the slow creek of branches in the slight wind. They passed a stone urn on a pedestal, half concealed by undergrowth and moss, and a little further on the mixture of trees gave way to beeches, and they could see the cottage. It had been a gardener's cottage, but it was in the middle of the wood with hardly a garden of its own, only a little clearing in front of it. It faced south across the valley, down the slopes of which the wood still stretched, to the smooth grass on the other side, where there was a farm with long stone buildings. The cottage was built of stone, too, and had some irrelevant castellations on its southern side, to provide a suitable sight at the end of a vista from a big house down in the valley, which could now no longer be seen from the cottage. The cottage had in fact once been two cottages, but half of it had been made into a barn-like room where Peter worked, and apart from that there was only a kitchen and one downstairs room, two upstairs rooms and outside lavatory. Water had to be fetched from a well near the ruined house.

'I haven't been here for a long time, as you can see,' said Peter. 'The whole place is falling down, but we can build it up again.'

Charlotte had walked slowly all over the cottage. She came out into the sun and said, 'It s beautiful.'

'It needs a bit of paint,' he said deprecatingly, pleased by her pleasure.

'I can do that,' she said. She put her arms round him and said, 'Thank you for bringing me here.'

'Thank you for coming,' he said, and kissed her.

A few days later Gabriel decided that it was his duty to recover his daughter from the wretch who had brought about her downfall. He drove to Somerset with that intention.

He had had a letter from her.

'Dear Father, I thought I ought to let you know that I am going to live with a man called Smith Pennington. He is going to divorce his wife, with whom he has not lived for a long time, and then we shall get married. We are going to live in the country until then. I am quite sure that I am doing the right thing. Love from Charlotte.'

He had been offended by this letter, which seemed to him inconsiderate and defiant, typical, in other words, of Charlotte. He read it in the office, and spoke to Miss North of the bitterness of a father's situation.

'You're quite right never to have married,' he said to her. 'As soon as one's thoughts start turning in that direction, one lays oneself open to such cruel arrows, such barbed and poisoned arrows, loosed by such relentless hands.' He sighed heavily. 'After all I have done for that child, this is what I get in return.'

He handed the letter to Miss North, who read it and blushed.

'Oh dear,' she said, uncertainly. 'I'm afraid this is a terrible blow for you.'

He sighed again. At the same time had had to admit to himself that he was not feeling the blow very deeply. Charlotte had never been his favourite daughter. He was angry, of course, and determined that she should be made to see her mistake; but he did not feel pain, as he had felt for Angel once. He sighed again.

'I seem to be always rescuing my daughters from undesirable assocations,' he said. 'They have no mother, of course.'

Miss North gave a sympathetic moan. Then she said, 'Perhaps Mrs. Hamilton, as the eldest sister, would be able to help?'

Gabriel rang up Penelope, who was practical as ever and undertook to find out where the couple was likely to have gone, and to let him know as soon as possible. He then rang up Susan, with the idea that it was his duty to inform the whole family of the misfortune which had befallen them. To his surprise Susan burst into tears.

'What's the matter, what are you crying for?' he said.

'I can't help it,' she gasped. 'It seems so sad. Oh, poor Charlotte.'

'She's not dead,' he said irritably. 'It's not as bad as all that. We'll find her. She'll soon see sense.'

'Oh dear, but it's so terribly worrying,' sobbed Susan.

'You needn't take it as hard as that,' he said. 'I'll see that she's brought back, don't worry. I only thought I should tell you in case you had any advice or suggestions to offer. I didn't realize you'd be so upset. Come now, it's no use crying. You were always too easily depressed, you know. One has to make a bit of an effort sometimes. You should get out more, that sort of thing.'

He rang off to the sound of her sobs.

'Silly fool,' he said crossly.

He decided that Selina was too young to be informed of the situation at this stage, and he did not know where Angel was, so he said to Miss North, 'We'd better get on with some of these letters,' and dismissed the matter from his mind for the time being.

When Penelope had found out the address of Smith Pennington's cottage from the gallery where he exhibted his pictures, Gabriel undertook to go down there the following day. Penelope offered to come with him, but he decided that that would look cowardly on his part and that he would carry more weight on his own.

'You will be careful, won't you?' said Penelope. 'I mean, you know how angry she gets.'

'I shall not use violence, if that's what you mean,' said Gabriel.

'I really meant, be tactful,' said Penelope.

'Of course,' he said, rather annoyed.

He drove down from London in his three-year-old Daimler. He was not interested in cars but had been persuaded by a salesman that this was a suitable car for a man in his position: having made it his he was convinced that there was none to better it. He drove fast and with conspicuous lack of consideration for other road users.

He had to ask the way to the cottage several times before he could find anyone who was able to give him intelligible directions, so that he bumped up the track to the ruined house in a bad temper. He found his way to the path through the wood and began to walk down it. He suddenly began to wonder what he might find. Supposing they were in bed together? Surely they were not likely to be, at lunchtime? But then you never knew; this painter fellow probably kept irregular hours, thinking himself very Bohemian: he knew those sort of people. For some reason he felt it necessary to make an effort to keep up his resolution. He fed his mind with inflammatory concepts, approaching the cottage through the wood. A married man, an unscrupulous bounder, totally without moral standards, abducting his innocent foolish daughter; could be put in prison; he'd have to frighten him; that long hot drive, as if he wasn't a busy man with hundreds of better things to do; poor child, her life in ruins, the scandal, no decent man would marry her now. But it was embarrassing to be approaching them unawares, as if he were spying. He should have brought his little dog, to run ahead and warn them, instead of leaving him in the car, which he had done because he had thought he would take away from the solemnity of the occasion. He coughed loudly, but there was no interruption of the bird-song and the breeze. He could see the clearing ahead of him. Without meaning to, he slowed his pace. He could see the cottage, its grassy slope in front of it, and the deep green circle of trees round it. The sun was bright in the little clearing and though they were silent they were there.

Charlotte was nearest him, with her back half turned towards him, carefully painting a window frame. Further away he saw the man, sitting on the steps, drawing, hunched and solid, his hand seeming to move very slowly over his paper. Having stood still, Gabriel could not now start walking again. He seemed to have forgotten how to breathe. Who were these people, in their circle of sunlight?

A voice dropped into the circle, sounding like a voice across a calm sea, quite but far-crying.

'Are we having lunch at all?' It was the man who had spoken, without looking up or interrupting the spidery movement of his pencil.

'Of course,' Charlotte answered, replacing her brush carefully in the paint pot and putting it down in the shade. She moved slowly towards Peter. 'It's been ready for hours.' Even their voices were slow, as if they were speaking in code and giving the other time to interpret the message.

'What is it?' he asked, putting his pencils into the pocket of his shirt.

She knelt beside him and said, 'Four hundred and eighty-two broad beans.'

He said, 'What a funny lunch,'

They looked at each other for what seemed a long time. Gabriel dared not moved. He thought, the moment they stand up I will move, but not yet. Their faces slowly drew together. They kissed. But this was incest.

He burst into the sunlight.

'Stop that at once!' he cried.

They jumped to their feet, Charlotte went completely white in the face and seemed about to faint. She clung to Peter, who put his arm round her. The dramatic nature of her reaction excited Gabriel.

'Leave her alone,' he said. 'Haven't you done enough

harm? Charlotte, go and fetch your things. You're coming home with me.'

She could not speak.

Peter said in his quiet voice, 'I don't think Charlotte wants to go home.'

What a frightful brute the man looks, Gabriel thought, and that accent, no one warned me about that.

'Come along, Charlotte, get your things,' he repeated briskly, ignoring Peter.

'I'm not coming,' she gasped. 'You don't know what you're doing.' She had begun to tremble violently.

'Of course I know what I'm doing,' he said. 'I am doing my duty as a father.'

'I'm not coming,' she repeated.

'Oh yes, you are,' he said. 'The law is on my side. I can send for the police and have you forcibly brought home and this man here put in prison, where he deserves to be. Hurry up, now, I can't wait much longer.'

'You'll have to wait for ever,' she said. 'I'd rather die than go anywhere with you.'

'You're making a fool of yourself,' he said, beginning to tremble too. 'You wretched girl, don't you realize how you're being taken in? I know these people. They live on women. They can't support themselves, too idle to do a decent job of work, they take in these rich young girls with a lot of foolish talk about living a free life and throwing over the conventions, and then they stick with them as long as the money lasts and no longer. You'll be discarded when the next one comes along just as the last one's being discarded for you. He thinks I'm a rich man. He's after your money, you poor fool.'

'You don't understand anything. You're so wrong that it's funny,' she said. 'It's you that's making a fool of yourself.'

'Is this how you speak to me when I have come here to save you?' He said, feeling his nostrils quivering uncontrollably. 'I might have washed my hands of the whole affair, left you to your fate, after that ungrateful, that brutal, that savage letter. Savage, that's what you are. God knows what has made you like this. After all I have done for you, all I have given you, to be treated like this, like an enemy . . .'

'Don't talk to me like that,' she cried, clapping her hands. 'You've done nothing for me, *nothing*. You weren't thinking about me when I was begotten, and from that day to this you have done nothing for me except out of pride or convention. You couldn't have *not* sent me to school, could you? And you needn't have sent me to an expensive one, I'd have been much happier at the village school. And you had to give me clothes and things, or you'd have been ashamed of me. But you never gave me anything else, love or friendship or understanding, or even your *interest* . . .'

'How can you say this, what are you doing?' he burst out. 'You speak like this to me, when I have provided you with a family background overflowing with interest and understanding and civilized influences? When I have given you . . . have given you . . . have suffered for you . . . oh, my God . . .' He turned to Peter and shook his finger at him. 'If ever you get a child, sir, in your adventures with women, drown it, drown it at birth. Otherwise you will see your generosity spurned, your hopes dashed to the ground, your love repaid with venom, venom. You speak to me of love.' He swung back to Charlotte. 'You have never *not* known love, you spoilt child. That's all you are, a spoilt child. And now you see a man you want, so you reach out your hand expecting to be given everything, regardless of other people, of your duties and obligations, of the moral code in which you have been brought up . . .'

'But I don't believe in that moral code,' she interrupted. 'I don't believe in God, and nor do you, only you're too hypocritical to admit it. God for you is just a voice within you telling you that everything you do is right. But it's not right to take me away from here, where according to the only moral code that matters I ought to be. You can't do it. I'm staying here.'

He had come rather close to her, and the possibility of violence between them was in both their minds, so that they were both half wanting it and half shrinking from it. They could not look at each other's faces.

'You're coming with me,' he said.

He made a sudden grab at her arm. She jerked it away violently, and in so doing hit him on the chin. He seized her by her arms in a ferocious grip and shook her backwards and forwards, his whole face dissolving into anger and grief.

'You don't know what you're doing, you don't know what you're doing,' he repeated wildly.

'That's enough now,' said a calm voice, like a policeman's. 'Come along.' Peter put a hand on each of their shoulders and pushed them firmly apart. 'This won't do at all, will it?'

They looked at him bemused, having more or less forgotten that he was there.

'I didn't know I was marrying into such an excitable family,' he said, in his slow voice.

She took what was meant to be cooling irony as mockery and turned away with a sob. Gabriel, shaken by how nearly they had come to blows, turned away too and walked a few paces towards the trees, clasping his hands as if he were praying.

Peter followed Charlotte, took her hands and turned her towards him.

'You mustn't think that any harm is done,' he said. 'I loved seeing you angry, though you will think that frivolous of me. Listen, I told you, we've been to these solicitors of John's, they're supposed to be the best in London. Beryl is divorcing me for desertion, it's the simplest case you can have. They say they can get the whole thing through in six weeks. That's no time at all. You'll have to go home with him, because he can call in the police as he says, but after that six weeks we're free. He'll see he can't stop us. Even if he tries we can appeal to some court or other. You may be under age but I'm not, and I can convince any judge of my respectability. Your father could be made to look an awful fool, and he'll see that pretty soon, I know he will, I'll come back to London and stay with the Moulds for a bit. We'll leave everything here exactly as it is till we come back again. The minute the divorce is through we'll get married. Okay?'

'If that's what you want,' she said, doubtfully.

'It's the only thing to do,' he said. 'It's a silly situation. Don't think I'm not absolutely with you over the rights and wrongs of it. I thought you were exaggerating when you talked about your father, but you hadn't told me the half of it. You go off now and write to me at the Moulds.'

She made an effort to be as calm as he was, and gripping his hand said, 'I am so ashamed of having caused such an awful ludicrous scene. Will you hate me for it?'

He kissed her on the cheek.

'I love you for it,' he said. 'But I can't feel the same about your old man, somehow. I'll get your bag.' He went into the cottage without looking at Gabriel.

'You're coming then,' Gabriel said to Charlotte.

She would not look at him, but said coldly, 'Peter has asked me to.'

'He's got some sense then,' said Gabriel.

They waited in silence, some distance apart, until Peter returned with Charlotte's small suitcase.

'I'll walk to the car with you,' he said to Charlotte, and led the way along the narrow path. They followed him without speaking.

When Peter opened the car door to put the suitcase in, the Cairn puppy jumped out.

'Hallo, funny dog,' said Peter. 'Is he yours?' he asked Charlotte.

'I've never seen him before,' said Charlotte.

'He's mine,' said Gabriel, shortly.

The puppy was bouncing about from one to the other of them, delighted to see them.

Peter began to be amused.

'How nice,' he said, quieter than ever. 'What's his name?'

'Trajan,' said Gabriel.

'Trajan, I see. What a big name for a little dog,' said Peter, addressing the puppy. 'So that's the sort of dog you are?'

'It was similar in sound to Sago, which was his kennel name,' said Gabriel, and immediately wished he had not spoken.

'I see. Sago, Trajan. Yes, so he knows his name. Good dog, good dog. Well, we can't dawdle here chatting about dogs all day, can we? In you get, my darling. I'll write to you, and I'll be with you the day I get that little piece of paper.'

She was able now to smile back at him.

Gabriel bundled the puppy into the car, got in himself and drove off quickly. He knew he should have told the fellow not to write, not to try to see her ever again, but somehow it had been impossible. Something had gone wrong with the whole interview, but he was determined not to think about it, not to face the fact, lurking somewhere in his consciousness, that he had looked a fool. He drove much too fast over the bumpy track, shaking the car and making the puppy whimper and try to climb on his knee. He pushed it over to Charlotte.

'Hold him, would you,' he said.

She took the puppy on to her knee, and they did not speak again until they drew up outside Penelope's house in Chelsea. Gabriel drove fast and maliciously, pursued by angry blasts on other horns. Charlotte sat beside him in a sort of dream, passive and distant. He could not think of anything to say to her.

Penelope came out to greet them. Gabriel said, 'Here is your sister. I should like you to be responsible for her until I can take her home tomorrow. I think the less said about her exploits the better. I must go now, because I am late for an appointment.'

He drove to his office, feeling a little better, because Penelope had looked impressed. Well, after all, he had brought the child back, hadn't he?

Miss North was waiting for him.

'I got her back,' he said briskly. 'Is Mr. Fortescue here?'

'Oh, Mr. Dobson,' she gasped in admiration. 'Yes, he's been here a few minutes. Oh, Mr. Dobson, I am glad for you.'

He went on into his room. Fortescue was waiting to talk about his investments, which were considerable and had increased appreciably since Gabriel had been advising him on them.

'I'm so sorry to keep you waiting,' said Gabriel, hurrying towards him with his hand outstretched.

Sitting down at his desk and drawing the Fortescue file towards him, he thought, thank God to be safely back.

Charlotte wrote to Selina at school.

'I don't know if anyone has told you the latest news. Father has really surpassed himself.

'I told you that I had met Peter and that it was all just as I had known it would be. So after that I wrote to Father saying that we were going to stay in Peter's cottage in the country until his wife had divorced him, and then we would get married. She is divorcing him for desertion so there's no "scandal" involving me to frighten Father. She is only doing it, indirectly, to please Father, since otherwise none of us would bother with meaningless formalities. However, he came rushing after us and there was a ludicrously awful scene and then Peter said I had better come back because there was obviously no hope of Father's seeing reason. So now I have to wait here for five more weeks until we can get married. Father has virtually retreated. He doesn't speak to me at all, but makes no protest about the letters and telephone calls from Peter. I think Martin is trying to bring him round to the whole idea, but I can't feel any interest in whether she succeeds or not. I can't imagine that Father could ever like Peter. Peter is too honest for him, so much so that I don't think they could even understand each other if they talked. The same words would mean different things. Also I don't think I could really forgive him for the ghastly scene he made. Peter could, but I don't seem to be a forgiving sort of person, especially where Father is concerned.

'The ridiculous part of it all is that I know it is obvious to any fool that the whole thing of Peter and me is perfectly all right. Martin was in a terrible state of worry when I arrived, but as soon as I had told her about it she saw that there was nothing to fuss about, and has been particularly nice since. She's even promised to come to Chelsea Register Office when we get married, though she hasn't been to London for years (Will you come?) Yet Father still pretends to be shocked; and there is Penelope with her horrible, hollow marriage – she can't still love that wretched Ham, or if she does that only makes it worse. I know there is Julian but she doesn't seem to care for him much, poor child. And Susan, really lost, being soothed by that sort of male nurse she's married, and Angel, who casually said the other day that she thought she would marry Roger Martin. No one paid any attention, because it's obviously absurd, so perhaps she'll give up the idea. But then Father makes a fuss about me!

'It might be after the end of term, the wedding, so then you could come, couldn't you? Love from Charlotte.'

Selina wrote back.

'Thank you for your letter. You and Father were always very dramatic together. You both swear you don't enjoy it, which seems a pity, as you do it so often. I expect he thought in clichés about your having "gone off with a married man." You say it is obvious that it is all right, but then he might not have had time to see that before the fight started. Of course he is very silly. I am glad Martin is on your side. I hope you won't be bullied by Father's opposition into marrying Peter if you suddenly find you don't want to. Now I expect you will tear this letter into shreds and stamp on them.

'Of course I will come to your wedding. Perhaps I will come without telling Miss Brace, and then I might be expelled. I long to leave this place. I am determined not to stay a moment beyond sixteen. Miss Fawkes says I am so amazingly intelligent that I must go to Oxford, but I can't see the point – it could only be like school again. Miss Fawkes has made Miss Brace hate me more than ever by insisting that I am clever because Miss B. now thinks that I am sinister as well as hostile. I wish I were. She doesn't know how helpless I am.

'Something odd has happened to Brigid today. I don't know what it is, but she keeps being sent for by Miss Brace, and so does Morag. Perhaps they have done something wrong, but she won't tell me. Brigid has been rather odd all this term. I don't understand her, but I am even more helpless with her than with Miss B. Miss Fawkes gave me a little talk the other day about letting my friendships interfere with my work, and not concentrating too much on one friendship, and learning to keep more in reserve there and less with other people. It was hideously embarrassing. Someone told me she is supposed to have a pash on me, Miss F., I mean – imagine!'

'We had house tennis tournaments last week. By some mistake I got into the Second House team, third couple. As you know this means you are very bad at tennis. However I had never been in any team of any sort before so I got rather over-excited and full of the spirit of competition and feelings about the honour of the house and everything. We practised for weeks. I was playing with Rosemary Wright, who is nearly as bad as I am. On the day I couldn't eat any lunch, so then I had terrible indigestion, and what with one thing and another and all the people watching, every ball I hit went either into the net or disappeared completely into the far distance. Most of them I missed, hitting myself on the leg or throwing my racket into the air by mistake. It was nightmareish. Afterwards Miss Brace sent for me and gave me a talk about team spirit and having a superiority complex. Sad really.

'Do write again soon. Miss F. keeps asking me what I want to do when I leave school. I don't want to do anything and yet I don't want to do nothing. I have leanings and am sometimes drawn by expectations and desires etc. (Trahearne), but I suppose that is just adolescence. I cannot bear the idea of competition – because I care too much whether I win or lose? – no, because madness and terror and outrage fill me at the mere idea of losing. We are all conceited, aren't we? – except Susan, and the idea of competition drove her to the opposite extreme – and sometimes I feel I am just waiting for the inevitable call to greatness, like Joan of Arc – at least to some great test, by which I shall either rise or fall. Do you ever feel that it is impossible – but out of the question – that there can ever have been anyone else like you in the world? But then, just occasionally, when I am reading, I think, now there's one . . . oh well, you will have been too bored to read this far. Do you think it is too late for me to take up the violin?'

When she had posted her letter to Charlotte, Selina felt calm and relaxed, but clear-headed. She thought, perhaps there are people who feel like this all the time. Immediately she became aware of some sort of discomfort: it was because she had written too much to Charlotte. Even to Charlotte she felt it unwise to commit herself on paper. She was afraid that in spite of her stern efforts at objectivity she had written things which were affected, and not true. The gulf between emotions felt and written down seemed unbridgeable, and the fault for this seemed to lie rather with the emotions than with the faculty of writing them down. The brief clarity over-balanced, to be replaced by a more familiar self-dissatisfaction. Then she saw Miss Brace.

Miss Brace was plodding up the village to see Miss Hunt at the Junior House. She was a familiar figure in the village, her white hair escaping from its bun, her droopy skirts, her stout legs and flat feet, the keen blue eyes, the jowl. She looked like an elder statesman in retirement, a legendary figure.

Catching sight of Selina, long-legged and thin, slipping quietly along the pavement and keeping close to the wall, she stopped and stood still in the middle of the road. Selina, seeing her, stopped too and looked round for escape. Miss Brace waited. Seeing the frantically turning head, she thought, suppressing a stranger emotion, that child's hair needs cutting.

Selina came on towards her.

Miss Brace said: 'Well?'

Selina tried to speak but could not. She could hear in her imagination her own voice, breathless and sycophantic, 'Oh Miss Brace I'm so sorry please Miss Brace I was just posting a letter to my sister Miss Brace,' but the words would not come. Fear possessed her, and beside the fear a feeling of defeat and helplessness which was oddly welcome.

They faced each other in silence. It was unfortunate

for Selina that Miss Brace should have just finished an upsetting interview with two of her girls, and was not feeling disposed to compromise.

'Well?' she said again. 'Where have you been?'

'To post a letter,' mumbled Selina.

'To whom?'

'To Charlotte.'

'Had you forgotten the rule that no girl is allowed into the village unaccompanied?'

Selina did not answer. Numbly she tried to ask herself whether or not in fact she had forgotten the rule. It was one which was perfectly well known to all the girls, so it seemed likely that she had not so much forgotten it as not actually called it to mind at the moment when she set out to post her letter to Charlotte: there was a distinction.

'Answer me, child,' said Miss Brace.

'No,' said Selina.

'You had not forgotten?'

'No,' said Selina.

'You deliberately chose to disobey?' said Miss Brace.

Selina looked down at the pavement helplessly.

'Well?' said Miss Brace.

'Yes,' whispered Selina.

'Come with me,' said Miss Brace.

She turned and led the way back into the school drive. Selina followed her through the gate and along a path which led to the games field, which was deserted. There Miss Brace stopped and turning towards Selina said, 'Why are you always so sulky?'

Selina felt a slight involuntary movement of her ears, which pulled the skin tight across her forehead.

'I don't know,' she muttered.

'You are the sulkiest girl in the school,' said Miss Brace. 'And do you know why?'

'No.'

'Because, you are always concealing something,' said Miss Brace. 'A secretive, underhand person is likely to have a sulky face, isn't she? Have you looked into your mirror lately?'

'No.'

'People who make a study of the human face say that

it has two parts, the upper part which reveals your inborn characteristics, and the lower part, which shows what you make of them. When you next look in the mirror, see if you notice the difference between the two parts of your face. Your high forehead shows the intelligence which you have inherited from your father, and your mouth shows your own character – a big sulky wilful mouth, selfish and self-indulgent – an ugly mouth, you know, had you thought of that? – and getting uglier each day that passes without your making an effort to forget yourself and contribute something to the society in which you live, that is to say, for the time being, the school.'

She paused, slightly surprised by her own strength of feeling. The extraordinary, and apparently unshakable, passivity of the girl in front of her was always irritating. As if to excuse herself, she said, 'How can people like someone who makes no effort at all be likeable? Have you thought of that? How can I like you? You have made no effort since you came into the upper school to make yourself a likeable person. The result is that I must confess I find it extremely difficult to be fair to you. Could you not make some effort to alter this state of affairs?'

Selina shut her eyes for a moment, then opened them and looked across the smooth green field to where a figure was crossing it on its way to the school.

'Miss Fawkes has told me the same,' said Miss Brace, following the direction of her eyes. 'She thinks that you could be a credit to the school if you would only give a little in return for what you take from it. She tells me she hasn't had a civil word out of you this term. How can she like you either?'

Selina did not speak.

'I shall be making an announcement to the whole school this evening which may effect you personally,' said Miss Brace. 'I am giving you a chance to show yourself willing to co-operate by asking you nothing about it now, but after the announcement I shall expect you to come to me and tell me everything you know about it. Is that clear?'

Selina looked blank.

'Do you understand me?'

'Yes.'

'Do you know to what I am referring?'

'No.'

'I shall expect you in my study after the announcement.'

'Did . . . did Miss Fawkes . . .' said Selina painfully. 'Did she say that?'

'Say what?'

'That I . . . that she . . . ?'

'Found you unresponsive? Yes. But not unkindly. She is very patient, Miss Fawkes, more patient than I am. But you don't give us a chance, you know.' And suddenly she gave her smile, a wise, kind, charming smile. 'I will leave you to think a little,' she said.

She turned away, and began to walk back towards the school. On the way she thought, I ought to tell her, it is only fair that she would be forewarned. She stopped and stood still between the box hedges. She heard birdsong and the distant sound of tennis balls. From the games field came uncontrolled wild sobbing. She turned back, and saw Selina lying face downwards on the grass bank, crying. She was slightly dismayed: why had the child never shown before that she minded about their good opinion? Or was that what she was minding about? How could one tell when she so steadfastly withheld her confidence? Selina looked up. A glance of amazed hatred, and then she was running, along the side of the field, round the corner and out of sight.

Miss Brace sighed. A difficult child. There had been a time when she had felt she knew intimately every one of the girls in her school, liking some, disliking others, but understanding them all. Now some of them seemed strange to her. Perhaps it was a result of present-day morals; they were so badly brought-up these days, even though they were supposed to come from nice families. She plodded back to the school with a heavy heart. This was a bad day, a black day in the history of the school.

The special school meeting took place in the afternoon. Miss Brace made her announcement.

'I have to tell you that Brigid Knight and Morag Fenton have been asked to leave the school. Their parents will be coming to fetch them tomorrow. Until then they will remain in the sanatorium and no one will see them. I have told you this because I want any girl who has any knowledge of this affair to come to me some time during the day and tell me what they know. Most of you, I feel confident, know nothing about it whatsoever, but I want any who do know something, who may have shared in any part of the activities for which these two girls are being expelled, to come to me, not so that I may punish you but so that we may clear the air and root out the trouble. There will be no more punishments. Everything necessary in that direction has been done. But I should appreciate a frank talk with any girl who feels she has anything to tell me. I am sure that you all agree with me that we must work together to keep the atmosphere of this school as frank and healthy as it has always been, and I am relying on the good sense and public spirit of those girls who know something about this evil thing which has come among us to help me to achieve this.'

She stood down from the rostrum, her face heavy with solemnity, and nodded to the head girl to signify that they might now march in order of seniority out of the hall.

Selina had no idea of what Miss Brace was talking about, but her first, indeed her only, thought, was that she must see Brigid.

This proved easy. Matron not being in sight, Selina simply walked into the sanatorium.

Brigid and Morag were sitting at opposite ends of the room reading. When they saw Selina, they looked shocked.

'You shouldn't have come,' whispered Brigid.

'I wanted to know what had happened,' said Selina, whispering too in case Matron should return. 'Miss M. said you'd been expelled. Why? What happened?'

Morag and Brigid exchanged glances.

'We'd better not tell you,' said Brigid solemnly.

'Don't be silly, of course you can tell me. What happened? Were you both in the loo together or something?'

Brigid was evidently suffering from extreme embarrassment. At the same time there was something about both of them which Selina could not quite understand. It was a sort of self-importance. Morag's face was blotched with crying. 'We can't tell you because it's so awful,' she said.

'We did something terrible,' said Brigid. 'That's all we ought to say about it. You'd much better forget about the whole thing.'

'How can I possibly forget about it?' said Selina desperately. 'What are you talking about? Of course you must tell me, it's only fair. I'm not just anybody am I?'

'Don't talk so loud,' whispered Brigid nervously. 'All right then, I'll tell you. Miss Brace came into my cubicle last night and found Morag in my bed.'

'What was so terrible about that?'

'We hadn't got any clothes on and she was lying on top of me because she wanted to see what it felt like before we had to do it with a man. So you see.'

Selina felt a slight dizziness, but went on, determinedly reasonable. 'Did you tell her that's what you were doing?'

'Yes. She was terribly angry. I'd never seen her like that before.'

'I don't see why she had to expel you,' said Selina.

'Because we might contaminate the others,' said Brigid solemnly.

'How silly,' said Selina.

'It's not silly,' said Brigid. 'We might. She's quite right. Once you start you want to do it more and more. She said so.' She did not seem altogether displeased at the prospect.

'Of course you won't,' said Selina scornfully. 'You haven't got a moustache or a man's voice or anything, for Heaven's sake?'

Suddenly Morag burst into loud sobs. 'What will my mother say?' she wailed. 'I don't know what to do, I don't know what to do.'

The door opened. It was Matron, starchily aghast.

'Selina Dobson!' she cried. 'Come straight to Miss Brace with me at once.'

'I'll write to you,' Selina said to Brigid, as she was shepherded out of the room.

There followed a long cross-examination from Miss Brace, designed to disclose whether or not Selina had been indulging in immoral practices. It filled Selina with disgust and shame.

For the rest of the term, she was in semi-disgrace. The other girls were particularly nice to her, and she comported herself with a sort of dignified melancholy which was considered very suitable.

She did not mention the affair in her letters home, nor did she discuss it with anyone until much later. She treated herself gently, like an invalid, prescribing for herself various treatments and distractions. None of them was immediately successful. She had been Brigid's best friend. If Brigid had wanted someone to lie naked on top of her, why had she not asked Selina?

8

CHARLOTTE was married in July. Miss Martin went to London, and found it much changed since she had last been there.

It seemed more prosperous, busier, newer, adjusting itself to becoming a modern city. Such people, in such cars; all so new and gleaming, telling of money, improvements in taste, enjoyment of the present, adaptability, know-how, stamina. Miss Martin felt old and dowdy. A restlesness took her; why did she never have her hair done, or go to the theatre, or take an interest in the latest anything? But a morning and a lunch were all she needed of it. The shop assistants were as unwilling as ever to part with their wares, the pavements were crowded, the traffic impossible, her large white cotton gloves filthy in no time at all. She had lunch with a friend, the headmistress of a successful girls' private school, who seemed, old friend though she was, boringly involved with her own organizational problems. There were little worlds in London too, for all its metropolitan air. The other people in the restaurant where they lunched interested her. She would have liked to have known some of them, for that after all was the amenity London really could offer; but then she reflected comfortably that she was getting old, and had had her time of excitement, of joining in, knowing people, caring, trying, living if you like, and had surely earned her right to her room at home, her books, her garden, her dogs, her children – for they were all as much hers as anyone else's or as she would allow them to be, valuing her detachment as she did. Selina would be at Charlotte's wedding: she had gone straight to London from school at the end of term, and was to go home with Miss Martin afterwards. Miss Martin would have been willing to join in again, and care and try, if it would in any way, at any time, help Selina; but otherwise she would rather stay at home and get on with things.

In Chelsea Register Office she found herself liking Mr. and Mrs. Mould. They had plenty of time to get to know each other because the bridal pair were half an hour late for the ceremony.

Gabriel paced up and down, making the space seem more confined that it was by turning on his heel each time some way before he reached the end of the room, as if a captive tiger might insist on his humiliation by using only half his cage, and so embarrass his captor. He was wearing what he would have worn for an important meeting in the City, black coat and pinstriped trousers. He looked correct and solemn, rather as if he were at a funeral.

Penelope and Ham, Susan and Bill Groves, were together in one corner. Penelope, making an effort, wore a pretty flowered hat, but their group was not a gay one because Susan was in a state of trembling nervousness and kept muttering, 'How sad, poor Charlotte, a registry office, where is she, oh, dear, I do hope nothing has happened. Bill, do you think you ought to go and see if anything has happened outside, I mean with the car or something, or perhaps she doesn't want to come in, perhaps she can't face it, oh, dear, poor Charlotte . . .' Penelope and Ham were annoyed, Bill solicitous.

Angel had brought Roger Martin with her, and was gossiping with him about some extraneous scandal.

Selina stood silently beside Miss Martin, half listening to her making friends with the Moulds, half waiting for any sound from outside which could mean that Charlotte and Peter were arriving. She was ready violently to criticize all the others for not really caring about Charlotte's happiness, and at the same time she was trying to convince herself that this did indeed lie with Peter. She had met him only the night before, and in spite of her anxiety to like him had found herself uneasy with him. Two things about him made her particularly nervous, that he was an artist and that he came from a social class other than her own: she felt he might see them both as good reasons for despising her.

At last they came.

'Sorry we're late, we were buying a hat,' said Charlotte.

They were breathless and confident, the only people at ease.

The hat was a joke. Hats did not suit Charlotte, who seldom wore them. This one was a white daisy. Perched on top of her golden hair above her beaming face, it had an absurdly festive look, like a cake decoration. It would hardly have seemed odd if they had put a candle in the middle of it, and the registrar had lit it as the climax of his otherwise prosaic act of unification.

After the ceremony, which seemed over in a moment, there was some talk on the steps, a few kisses, and then Charlotte and Peter climbed into their van and drove away to the cottage in Somerset, promising to invite them all to a party later on, in the autumn. They were left to disperse in an awkward anti-climax, depressed. There were two press photographers outside. Gabriel posed at their request on the steps, and his photograph duly appeared in the papers next morning beside a blurred impression of the bride and groom. It showed him apparently gazing after them as they drove away, thoughtful, moved, important, wounded. He was rather pleased with it.

'There is to be another wedding in the family,' said Ham to Penelope.

'Between who and whom?' asked Penelope.

They were sitting opposite each other in their little dining-room in Chelsea. It was a Friday evening, so Ham was not at the House. They had decided to go to the cinema, and were having an early supper.

'What do you think of this new wine?' asked Ham.

'Very good, of course. All your new discoveries are. Except the claret before last, which I didn't much like. But who is getting married?'

'Your beautiful sister Angel,' he answered.

Penelope put down her knife and fork. 'Not to Roger Martin.'

'Now don't get excited. Have some more burgundy.' He filled her glass. 'What's wrong with Roger Martin? He's my oldest friend, remember.'

'And your nastiest,' she said. 'Yes, even of your friends, the nastiest.'

Ham's thin face expressed his irritation. 'I fail to see why everything has to be made an excuse for being unpleasant about my friends.'

'I wasn't being unpleasant about them. I was saying that they are all nicer than Roger Martin.'

'Oh God!' Ham pushed his plate away from him. 'There's no point in going on with this conversation if you're in that sort of mood.'

Penelope drank some wine. They were going to quarrel and so far it was her fault. She made an effort. 'I'm sorry,' she said. 'I'm tired, Friday night. But surely it would be a mistake for Angel to marry Roger?'

'Why?'

'I don't think she really cares for him.'

'She wants to marry him.'

'Who told you so?'

'Roger did,' said Ham. 'But I have no doubt that Angel would confirm the story.'

'And why does Roger want to marry her?'

'Love?'

'Nonsense. If he was in love with her why didn't he marry her long ago? When she was pregnant by him, for instance. Wouldn't that have been a better opportunity?'

'She didn't want to marry him then.'

'She would have, for the child. I know perfectly well this is some plot of yours and Roger's. It's because you have decided Father is going to go in with John Biddle and become a millionaire, isn't that it?'

'Why should that make me anxious for Roger to marry Angel?'

'So as to let your friend in on a good thing, in return for all the useful tips you've had from him. And so that you and he can get together and make the money work – that's your expression isn't it? It's kind of you.'

'You have developed a very unpleasant way of looking at things.'

'Also you're no longer jealous,' she went on. 'Angel isn't quite what she was. She's been around a bit.'

'I don't know what has turned you into this sort of person. You are quite wrong of course. You think you are being worldly-wise and clever. In fact you are completely childish. It is childish to look at things in such an extreme way. Naturally I should be happy for my friend to marry a rich wife. Who wouldn't? I do also think it quite possible that your Father may accept Biddle's offer before it's too late. He's a fool if he doesn't, but . . .'

'In spite of the fact that he told you weeks ago that he wouldn't dream of it?'

'He protested too much,' said Ham. 'He's just trying to square it with his conscience. I told him at Charlotte's wedding that he's only to give me the word and I'll bring them together again. It's not too late if he hurries.'

'He wouldn't think it honest.'

'It's not a question of honesty. It's a question of business realities. I'll bet you any money he's on the board of Biddle Holdings a month from now. He told me he'd seen him at the club.'

'By chance.'

'Maybe.'

'Why should Biddle still want him? I should have thought he'd rather never see him again.'

'No, no. Business realities again. Your father would be a great help to Biddle, just by being there. All sorts of things would become much easier for him. Your father's name is very good, you don't understand – Dobson of the Dobson Report on Labour Relations – oh, yes. He could have a more or less nominal position if he wanted to. In fact it would probably suit Biddle better. Your father's not a very flexible business man.'

'You mean he's an honest one.'

'I wish you wouldn't speak in these absolutes.'

'I wish you wouldn't speak in these relatives.'

'Isn't there any cheese?'

'I'll get it. Oh dear, Nanny's been at it rather.'

'I've never known anyone eat like that woman. If you ask me there's something wrong with her. No one can eat as much as that and still look like a rake. She must have got worms.'

'Bread and cheese is all she eats in the evenings.'

'And chocolate biscuits. And cherries. And cream buns. And Horlicks. And just a teensy weensy whisky. And thirty-eight cigarettes.'

'She doesn't eat the cigarettes.'

'I wish she did. Then she wouldn't scatter the ash round the house with such abandon.'

Penelope laughed and refilled her glass. 'I wish I didn't hate you,' she said.

'You don't,' he said.

'I do,' she said. 'I really do. You are so unbearable, so shifty, so mean, so cold. Mean in mind, body and soul.'

'Why don't you leave me?'

'So as not to ruin your career?'

'My career would hardly waver.'

'Well then for Julian's sake.'

'He'd probably be happier. We're always quarrelling in front of him.'

'You are.'

'You mean you are.'

'It's always you who provokes the quarrel,' said Penelope. 'You know it is. I admit that sometimes I may be the first to crack.'

'Sometimes?' he echoed. 'I never "crack," as you call it. I belong to a sex which doesn't use hysteria as one of its weapons.'

'You know quite well that when we quarrel in front of him it is me he clings to and you he pushes away.'

'That is because he is still mother-centred. It will change. Perhaps you are wise to play on it while you may.'

'Play on it? How can you say that?' she banged her glass down on the table. 'I'd rather die than quarrel in front of him. I'd rather anything on earth. But how can I not say what I think and what I know to be true? Am I to let you say anything, however wrong, just because he's there? I have only to express the slightest difference from you and you're furious. You start snarling and sneering at me. Of course I lose my temper. You sneer at every-

thing. You were sneering at me just now for not leaving
you. You don't understand that I can't leave you because
it would be wrong after I promised to stay with you
always.'

'You didn't promise to stay and hate me did you? Surely
the least defence I can put up is to sneer. If I believed
what you say it would be terrible.'

'Is that why you don't believe it? Because I don't leave
you?'

'I know very well why you don't leave me,' he said,
his upper lip beginning to twitch slightly. 'You stay here
because you like it here, because you like being the
Honourable Mrs. Hamilton Maitland, wife of the well
thought of young M.P. Oh, yes, you do. And you like
the idea of being the mother of the future Lord Trent,
and having people pay attention to you for what you are.
You'd have had none of that without me would you? A
middle-class business man's daughter with a bit of
money. You had no idea of what being an old family with
a position meant, you told me so.'

'Shut up, shut up, shut up,' she cried, banging the table
with her fist. 'How dare you say such stupid, fatuous,
ludicrous, pathetic things. If you could hear yourself . . .
What in God's name is the advantage of being a penniless
son of a penniless disreputable dead peer? Position? What
position have you or your family got? . . . oh, how can I
argue with someone so thick-headed? Do you think I
wouldn't rather be married to someone the very opposite
of your useless pinheaded pseudo ex-aristocratic family if
they were capable of loving me?' She began to sob.

'Capable of loving you?' He laughed. 'You've got a child
to prove I am.'

'Don't be so stupid. I mean capable of giving something
instead of always taking . . .'

'I should have thought I gave the usual things.
However, you don't seem to be in a mood to listen to
reason.' He pushed his chair back. 'I shall go to the
cinema, though it will be half finished by now. I'll call in
on Lucy Greenwall and see if she'd like to come. It might
amuse her. Don't wait up for me.' He had gone quietly out
of the room before she had time to answer. She shouted

incoherently after him, realized it was no use, heard the door bang, bit her fingers with fury, cried and finally calmed down. She was left with the sore feeling of failure she always had after their quarrels.

She went upstairs, washed her face, renewed her make-up, combed her hair. Then she went into the nursery where Nanny was watching the television. She hoped that the noise of the television had concealed the noise of their quarrel, but to be on the safe side she wanted to show Nanny that all was normal, and that anything she might have heard had been of no importance, so she smiled a friendly normal smile, and was Mrs. Hamilton, calm, reasonable, busy, elegant, civilized, and said, 'Oh, Nanny, I'm not going out after all as I've got a slight headache and there's this wretched meeting tomorrow, so shall I pot Julian as I'm just going up?'

Nanny swallowed a piece of Crunchie rather uncomfortably and said, 'Well it's not really his time. I usually do it in about ten minutes and he's getting so nicely trained now it's a pity to change his routine, but still I suppose if you really want to, only I do usually do it in about ten minutes, that's the only thing.'

'Oh do let me. I'll wait ten minutes. I've got to get my book anyway.'

'Well, all right then, if you like. I don't usually wake him, you know, I just sit him on it on my lap and he doesn't wake.'

'I won't wake him up, I promise. Good night, Nanny.'

Upstairs, holding the warm heavy sweet-smelling child balanced precariously on his pot on her knee, she felt the exhaustion with which the quarrel had left her begin to turn into a more comfortable tiredness. Experience had at least taught her that Ham's remark about their neighbour Lucy Greenwall was an empty threat. She also knew that the quarrel would be made up without much difficulty, having been one of their milder ones; and that, though they might seem lost to each other for ever, there would be, next week or next month or some time, a surprising lightening of the atmosphere, and they would find themselves closer again. Each quarrel did harm, but they had had so many, and there seemed little harm left to do:

perhaps one day it would not seem worth the trouble of quarreling. Perhaps another child, she thought, laying the sleeping Julian gently back among his blankets. But she knew that the only way to sweeten Ham was to give him success. Success made him kinder, less bitter, more candid, less secretive. So, for a reason now less idealistic, she would continue to work for that.

In the meantime Angel married Roger Martin.

'I suppose I might as well,' she said. 'After all, one has to get married some time, and people have rather stopped asking me lately, what with one thing and another.'

Gabriel was not pleased. This was the fourth of his daughters to marry and he had not been pleased with any of their husbands: to that extent the shock was not wholly unexpected. But Angel was the beauty, and Roger Martin seemed a spiritless young man. When Gabriel asked him what his ambitions in life were, he said, 'To make money, sir,' with an air of conscious virtue.

'Nothing more, nothing less?' asked Gabriel.

'Not really, sir, no.'

'Don't young men want to be Prime Minister any more these days?'

'Not as far as I know, sir.'

Roger was terrified of Gabriel, whom he admired, unlike Ham. He admired a lot of things unlike Ham, though he did not always allow his admirations to show. He admired Ham, who was the greatest influence in his life. They had met at school, where Ham, though a few years older, had quickly seen in Roger a useful lieutenant, which was what he had remained. He had been so busy in this capacity at school, at Cambridge, in the Army (they did their National Service in the same regiment) and then in London, that he had hardly had time to develop any other interests. Indeed for someone of his age and intelligence he had remarkably few interest of his own. He knew enough about other people's to be able to talk about them, which was important, because his whole life was run on contacts. He had now left the gossip column business and gone into advertising, where he was doing well, owing to the contacts and also to his having proved remarkably sensitive to trends in taste. He had changed his job several times, each time to his own advantage, and was now earning a large salary.

He had been living in an expensive bachelor flat in Eaton Square, but now that he was getting married he had bought a house in Chelsea. He decided to marry Angel because he thought it was time he got married. His friends were mostly married now, and it seemed the proper next step. It could even add to his weight in his job. He was fond of Angel, and found her the most agreeable female companion he knew. They understood each other well; there would be no illusions to be destroyed. They had agreed that they should each have their own friends and go their own ways as much as they wanted, and that neither should ask awkward questions of the other. He found, however, that as the date of the wedding approached his feelings of pleasure at the prospect of their marriage surprisingly increased. He would spend a long time before they went out anywhere deciding what she should wear. He found pleasure in buying her little pieces of jewellery; and when they went to a party together he was pleased with the picture they made. When he showed Miss Martin round the house (she had come up to London to help Angel and had spent the morning buying sheets in sales) he pointed to a tiny room halfway up the stairs and said, 'And this will be Angel's sitting-room.' It was a sort of cupboard, with a tiny window of mottled glass.

'Oh yes?' said Miss Martin politely.

'Where she writes her letters, does her sewing, all that sort of thing,' he said.

'How very nice,' said Miss Martin, warmly, through Angel had never been known to touch a needle in her life and kept up an elaborate pretence of being illiterate.

Miss Martin said to Gabriel on her return to Lincolnshire, 'I don't believe he is as bad as we thought.'

Gabriel looked gloomily round the *Economist*.

'I've heard some very undesirable things about him in the club,' he said.

They were married all the same.

Angel insisted on the wedding taking place at Harkwood, which made the arrangements a good deal more difficult. It was on a Wednesday, which meant that only a few of their friends came from London. There were a great many local neighbours there, most of whom Angel did not know; nor for that matter did Gabriel.

'Who are all these people?' he said. They were out in the garden because the autumn day was mild. 'Are they friends of yours, Angel? Who asked them?'

'I've no idea but I think they're all terribly nice,' said Angel. 'Perhaps they're something to do with Martin.'

Gabriel went to find Miss Martin.

'There seem to be a lot of your friends here,' he said.

'My friends? I've never seen any of them before in my life.'

'Oh. Angel said they were your friends. If you don't know them, who does?'

'They were on the list we did together,' said Miss Martin. 'They're probably neighbours you've forgotten.'

'Perhaps that's it,' he said. 'Charming people, they look,' he added without conviction.

He went back to Roger's mother, whom he found himself liking. She was his idea of a nice little woman, well turned out and a good listener.

Angel glided between the guests on the lawn, spilling champagne from her glass and talking without stopping.

'How I love you for looking after me,' she said. 'What should I do without you? Fall flat on my face, that's the first thing. I don't know who you are either, which is so funny, oh yes I do, I know Johnny.' Johnny beamed self-consciously and filled his own glass. 'Doesn't Julian look heavenly, don't you think? He isn't hating it, is he, Penelope? Why doesn't he have more ice-cream? Here, have a sip of champagne, darling. Oh, Charlotte, I do wish Peter could have come. I know the dealer from America was much more important, but I'm sure he would have loved it. Or would he have hated it? Anyway I'm loving it. Where is Martin? Isn't it too sad about her and Roger not being related?'

She trailed on, and was seized by an enthusiastic lady in furs.

'Oh, Mrs. Bentley,' said Angel. 'And you gave us that heavenly tray, the one with the Peter Scott picture on it.'

'How clever of you to remember!' cried Mrs. Bentley, looking dazzled.

'May I, as an admirer of long standing, claim a kiss from the bride?' It was Mr. Shore, the father of Belinda and Sarah, once the horsey heroines of Charlotte and Selina.

'Oh, Mr. Shore, how kind of you, I feel terribly untidy,' said Angel affectedly. 'How are Belinda and Sarah? How wonderful, four grandchildren? Would you believe it? Oh, Simon, how lovely of you to come,' and putting her arm into the newly arrived young man's she walked him away from Mr. Shore murmuring, 'My dear, the strain. I must have more champagne.'

'You look a treat,' he said. 'I like the rocks.'

'Oh,' she put her hand up to her necklace. 'It was – it was a present. Isn't life sad, really?'

'You're pickled, my love,' he said.

'From a great great great great friend,' she went on. 'The greatest friend on earth. I hadn't seen him for an age and suddenly this came and I cried for three days. I mean, it's not as if he's rich or anything, and it's the most beautiful thing I've ever had. I almost thought I couldn't keep it. I really loved him more than anyone else in the world but it was all no good.'

A soft-faced girl, in feathers, came to kiss her.

'Oh, Lucy, you look so pretty, why aren't you married?' said Angel. 'Of course I can recommend it, it's lovely. Everyone is so kind to you and there's so much to drink. Oh, Sue, silly Sue, what's the matter with you? Whenever I see you you're either crying or having a sneezing fit.'

'Angel!' Susan expostulated, but laughed.

'When we come back from Majorca you're going to come and stay with us and have a lovely time without Bill,' said Angel. 'Yes, without you, Bill, you know you'd rather, because of all my lovers being spades. Oh, Roger, what a lovely surprise, how are you? I'm stinking. Oh no, please, I don't want to go, must we? You must all come and help me change then. Yes, everybody. Yes, all right, I'm coming . . .'

In the evening Charlotte and Selina went for a walk round the wood. Charlotte was staying the night and going back to London to join Peter the following day.

They walked slowly. The evening was cool and damp. They talked about Angel, about Penelope, about their father, and then about Charlotte herself. She explained how different life had become for her, how lost she felt the others to be who did not know what she knew about the right way to live. She talked about Peter, and what she felt he had taught her.

'Have you stopped painting?' asked Selina.

'Yes, I must, for the moment,' answered Charlotte. 'I should only paint feeble imitations of Peter. I am too much under his influence, I am still just absorbing. But I shall start painting again in a year or two.'

'Won't you be under his influence any more?'

'I think I shall have absorbed it, don't you? And be able to think for myself again, only in a new language. Then it will be worth trying to paint. But it may not work because of Peter being so much better than me, so that I might get depressed, but I don't think that need happen.'

'Is he so very good?'

'I think he's wonderful. He has this wonderful strong line. But has very precise and limited aims all the time, so that it's difficult in a way to see what it's all adding up to. This American dealer wants to arrange another exhibition in New York for him.'

'Would you go there?'

'We might. It wouldn't be for about a year.'

They walked on in silence for a few minutes.

'Do you ever go to a doctor for anything?' asked Charlotte.

'No, except at school,' said Selina with the right amount of indifference. 'Do you?'

'No.'

'Perhaps one should?'

'I don't really know any doctors.'

'There's old Mathews in the village,' said Selina. 'He was quite good about Father's ulcers wasn't he?'

'I suppose so.'

They walked on.

'What do you want to go to a doctor for?' asked Selina.

'Well, the thing is, it's awfully silly really, as bad as Susan, only I think there might be something wrong with me,' said Charlotte.

'I thought you were looking rather pale.'

'Did you? I have been feeling rather ill, terribly tired all the time and funny pains. Perhaps it's anaemia or something. Only I've got this sort of lump.'

'What lump?'

'Here.' She put her hand on her diaphragm.

'Let's see,' said Selina. Charlotte rolled up the man's black sweater into which she had changed after the wedding.

'You mean there?' said Selina.

'Yes,' said Charlotte.

There was a slight lump between the two curves of her lower ribs. Her right side looked a little swollen. Selina put her hand, brown after the summer, across Charlotte's white skin. They could feel each other's pulses beating.

'I can feel it,' said Selina.

'I know,' said Charlotte. They had unconsciously lowered their voices. 'It's hard, isn't it?'

'Yes.'

'What do you think it is?'

'I don't know.' Selina took her hand away and Charlotte lowered her sweater.

'Perhaps it's a hernia,' said Selina.

'Surely it's too high?' said Charlotte. 'One's stomach is lower down.'

'How long have you had it?'

'I first noticed it quite a long time ago. But I couldn't believe it could be anything that mattered.'

'Perhaps you're getting jaundice. Are your eyes yellow?'

'Have a look.'

The light was beginning to fade. Selina put her hands on Charlotte's shoulders to turn her round into what light there was, and looked into her eyes.

'They're not yellow,' she said.

'Perhaps it's nothing,' said Charlotte.

'I think you ought to go to the doctor,' said Selina. 'It's

silly not to. Go to Doctor Mathews in the morning. He'll
be able to tell you.'

'I was supposed to catch the early train.'

'Catch the later one. Was Peter going to meet you?'

'No,' said Charlotte.

'That's all right then,' said Selina.

'Will you come with me?' asked Charlotte.

'Yes. We'll ring him up tonight.'

'Will you not tell the others? There's no point if it's
nothing.'

'Have you told Peter?'

'No. I didn't want to. He doesn't like illness.'

'It's probably chalk.'

'Chalk?'

'A chalk deposit. From rheumatism. I have them in my
shoulders.

'Really? How extraordinary.'

'Oh yes. I had massage at school one winter.'

'I expect it's nothing,' said Charlotte again. 'When are
you going to leave school? Have you told Father?'

'Not yet. I'll have to wait till next year. But I won't stay
a moment after next summer.'

They walked on, talking away their unease, under the
beeches in the damp evening.

In the morning they went to see Doctor Mathews. He
told Charlotte that she should see a specialist in London,
and rang up one he knew and arranged an appointment
for the same afternoon. They heard him say on the telephone, 'I think we should lose no time.'

Selina arranged to stay the night with Penelope and
went to London with Charlotte, who still did not want to
tell Peter.

The specialist said that Charlotte ought to have an
operation. She asked if it was cancer and he said that it
was not and that he had every reason to hope that the
growth was not malignant. He asked if she would arrange
for him to see her husband.

'It's quite a simple operation,' he said. 'We do any
number of them. But it is a major operation and we must

take care of you. Now if you can bring your husband round to see me, shall we say on Wednesday at this time? Then I think we can arrange to get it all over as soon as possible for you.'

He saw them to the door, benign and comforting.

They walked out into Devonshire Place.

'We'll have to tell them now,' said Charlotte.

Gabriel remembered the corridor along which he walked; the brown linoleum, the lights outside the doors, the shrouded trollies and the smell of ether, or of fear. If it was not on this floor that Hannah had died then it was on one indistinguishable from it, in another building with a classical portico, a comic relief porter, and a lift in which one tried in vain to shut one's ears to the conversation of the other visitors. There was one of these coming towards him now, accompanied by a nurse, a pale prosaic little blinking man. Obviously the worst had happened, thought Gabriel, with a certain unreasonable satisfaction, otherwise he would not have had a nurse with him.

A patient was wheeled rapidly round a corner in a chair. Gabriel swerved to avoid her. She was an old woman whose face had shrunk right back on to its bones; the skin was so wrinkled that she looked like a throwback to a monkey-state, a fearful reminder a million years old.

'Steady, Nurse,' she now said with painfully clear enunciation. 'You'll be getting yourself more patients if you go so fast.'

She gave an appallingly cheerful smile. On her knee was a quart bottle of Guinness, which she was clasping with both claw-like hands. He had heard that in some cases patients were allowed whatever they liked to eat or drink, like prisoners in a condemned cell. The little pale man, who with his attendant nurse had stopped, and stood with his back to the wall to allow the wheel-chair to pass, although in fact there was plenty of room, joined in the joke, saying sycophantically to the nurse, 'You're busy enough as it is without making more work for yourself, aren't you, now?'

Gabriel walked on, looking for room 834. What always

surprised him was the cheerful resignation of patients and their families in these places. The little pale man had probably just seen his wife die in agony, yet he thought it in some way his duty still to make jokes with the nurses: even if, as he went out, the porter were to break the news to him that his only son had been killed in a car crash, he would walk on out saying, 'It never rains but it pours.' Things happened to them that would send him, Gabriel, shrieking and blaspheming down the streets, and they said, 'That's life,' 'Can't complain,' 'Got to carry on.'

When Hannah had died, Gabriel had first of all insisted on calling in several other passing doctors to confirm that life had indeed left her. He had then stayed beside her holding her hand for four hours, talking to her and weeping, trying to ease the pain of parting. Then when he had finally been persuaded to stand up, emotion combined with lack of food had been too much for him and he had fainted. He had had to be carried into another room and revived, supported downstairs by two nurses and a doctor, taken home in an ambulance with a nurse who put him to bed and stayed with him until his nearest available relation, Hannah's boring sister Beatrice, could come round to look after him. This seemed to him to be the proper way to behave.

He stopped outside Room 834, paused a moment, then knocked loudly. Charlotte's voice said, 'Come in.'

She was sitting up in bed looking sunburnt and healthy. The operation was not to take place until the following day. Peter was sitting on the window sill.

'My poor child,' said Gabriel, smiling expansively at her and spilling the parcels he was carrying on to her bed. 'I brought you one or two things. A game pie from Fortnums. I know these places, the food is quite uneatable, and you might as well have something decent. Tell them to take away the other stuff they bring you. Grapes, the real Muscats, very expensive. The taste is completely different from the ordinary cheap ones. I'll bring you some more of course in a day or two, those are just to be getting on with. And a really good peach, I picked it out myself, they let me take a good long time choosing it. Then here are some flowers, carnations, isn't that a deli-

cious smell? Now, we'll ring this bell here and get the
nurse to put them in water, shall we? Magazines, *Country
Life, Illustrated London News*, and then I said to the girl,
give me all the latest fashion magazines, *Vogue* and that
sort of thing, I don't know what they are and anyway
they seem to change so quickly these days, I hope you
haven't seen them all. And this they tell me is the novel
everybody's reading at the moment. Have you read it?
Oh good, I hoped you hadn't. I don't read them much
myself, as you know, they make me feel so old and out
of touch. Ah, Nurse, I am Miss – er – Mrs. – er – Pennington's father and I have brought her some flowers. Would
you put them in water for us? A nice big vase, don't you
think? But I can see you know all about it. I expect you
will bring back a masterpiece of flower arrangement. Well,
now, er, Peter, are you managing to keep her spirits up
all right?'

'She doesn't seem too bad,' said Peter, shifting his position on the window sill.

'It's awfully kind of you to bring all these lovely things,'
said Charlotte.

They seemed embarrassed. Gabriel noticed in passing
that Peter did not seem to have brought anything for
her, even flowers; but he was determined to show that
bygones were bygones in this hour of family crisis.

'I expect you're glad we managed to persuade you to
come in here in comfort rather than being in a ward with
a lot of others, aren't you? No insult to the National
Health, mind, nothing to offend your principles, but one
might as well augment the thing a little when one can,
don't you agree? It's quite a pleasant room, isn't it?' He
walked to the window. 'Not much outlook. But still, for
these places, not too bad. You got somewhere to stay, all
right?' He asked Peter.

'I'm staying with the Moulds,' said Peter.

'Ah, yes, the Moulds, I met them at your wedding. I
thought he seemed delightful, most intelligent. She was
a bit intense for me. Well, I must be getting on. You'll
want to be alone together, I only just looked in for a
moment to see if you were comfortable.' He bent heavily
over Charlotte, kissed her on the cheek, then gripped her

arm encouragingly. 'The best of luck for tomorrow, my poor darling, we shall all be thinking of you.'

'Thank you, Father. Goodbye.'

He returned along the passage. He had done what he had meant to do. He knew how a family should behave when one of them was in trouble. Hannah had been a devoted family woman. And now he had to go to the City for a meeting at three o'clock.

He became aware of brisk overtaking steps behind him. He stopped and turned round.

'Mr. Dobson? I'm Doctor Elliott. I shall be operating on your daughter tomorrow. They told me you were here and I thought I might just be able to catch you. I'll walk along with you if I may.'

'By all means.'

He was a round shining dapper man, who inspired immediate confidence.

'I've had a word with your son-in-law,' he said. 'He's going to make arrangements to get her home as soon as possible. She'll have to be here for at least four weeks after the operation, but he says he can make arrangements for her to be looked after properly when she's fit to come out. I'm afraid these things are a great test for a family to have to endure. I expect you'll all be able to help each other.'

'Yes, we're a very united family,' said Gabriel. 'Her sisters I am sure will help to look after her. It will be a long convalescence then?'

'I am afraid it may be a long business,' he said. 'Naturally I shall hope to get to the root of the trouble tomorrow, but until then one doesn't know how temporary an expedient it may be. There isn't really a great deal one can do, except of course relieve the suffering as much as possible. We shall certainly do that, you can be quite sure that the pain will be minimized throughout the whole business, that is one thing we can do. But otherwise, well, it may be six months, may be a year. Of course she's young and healthy and miracles do happen. The longer one goes on in this business the more one finds out. But as I say I feel sure that you will all find each other a great comfort.'

'Indeed yes,' said Gabriel, who had been listening less to the words than to the confident soothing voice. 'We shall certainly do that.'

They had reached the lift. Gabriel held out his hand. 'I feel sure that she couldn't be in better care.'

Doctor Elliott shook his hand. 'We shall certainly do our best,' he said gravely. 'I am glad to have seen you. I wanted to let you know what the situation was. But you may be confident that she will have every possible attention while she is here.'

'I'm sure of that,' Gabriel stepped into the lift, and was born down to ground level.

Doctors tended to speak in riddles, he found; they never wanted to tell you anything in case they should be proved wrong. Still, this one seemed an able enough chap. A convalescence of six months or a year, had he said? It seemed a long time. Poor Charlotte. Perhaps she ought to go abroad for a bit, get some sun. Would the husband see to that, he wondered? Perhaps he ought to offer to contribute towards the expense.

He hailed a taxi, and was driven to his meeting in the City.

They saw Charlotte after the operation.

It had changed her in the course of a few hours from a healthy person into an ill one. On the first day she was quite cheerful: they were favourably surprised. She looked pale and shaken, could not move, and was fed by a saline drip, but she was pleased that it was over and flattered to have been complimented by the doctor on being such a good patient. The second day was worse, and the third worse than that. She no longer seemed able to make the effort to speak to them when they came to see her, she only looked at them with anxious eyes.

The doctor said, 'It's not pain so much as discomfort . . . a severe shock to the system . . . we must expect this for a few days,' and after the second week she did seem to improve. She became cheerful again and began to look better; though she was still weak, she could eat, and read. Soon she was well enough to be taken home to the cottage. They had all begged her to go to Harkwood. The doctor, informed of the situation, did his best to persuade her that the cottage was not a suitable place for such a convalescence, but she and Peter had insisted that she would get better quicker there than anywhere else, and she had been moved there by ambulance, carried smiling down the path through the wood, and left there with Peter and a plaintive nurse.

When Penelope went down to see Selina at school at half-term she was able to tell her that she had heard from Peter that Charlotte had been up for an hour, and was getting stronger every day.

'He sounded so much more cheerful,' she said. 'They'd even been talking of getting rid of the nurse. You know they had to get another, the first one couldn't stand it, but the second isn't much better. Of course they're horrified by the place, being so isolated and having to walk to get the water and all that, they've never seen anything like it, and they never stop complaining. Apparently the doctor down there told Peter they'd have to go on having a nurse for some time, but they seem to think he may be wrong. Of course I can see why the nurses don't like it. They have to do more or less everything, I think. I mean, Peter in theory does the shopping and the cooking, and there's apparently some one who will come in and clean from time to time, but it must be pretty ghastly. She really should have gone to Harkwood. It would have been much easier.'

'One of us ought to go down there,' said Selina.

'But who?' said Penelope. 'Martin did go for the first few days, but then she had to come back because Father had the President of the Board of Trade for the weekend to talk about something. I mean she is meant to look after his affairs, and Angel's busy moving in to her new house and anyway is getting more and more impossible, and Susan would be worse than useless. I'm going to try and go next week for a bit, but it's difficult to go for long what with Julian and Ham and everything. It's going to be worse too, because Ham's going to get a job, I think. I oughtn't to tell you yet because it's a secret, but he's been offered a Junior Ministerial job and I think he's going to take it. It's actually rather a good one. It means giving up working for Biddle, but apparently he can come to some arrangement by which they still pay him something in a roundabout way and he does various things for them in return. I don't quite understand that part, but anyway he's frightfully pleased about the whole thing.'

'How very good,' said Selina. 'Perhaps he'll be Prime Minister.'

'I think he'd be satisfied with rather less,' said Penelope. 'But it looks as if he's well in now, and might get the things he does want in due course. But it does mean we'll both be busier, and I don't see how I can spend a great deal of time with Charlotte.'

'How long do you think it will be before she's better?' asked Selina.

'I don't know,' said Penelope, hesitantly. 'Did you – did you talk to that doctor at all, Elliott?'

'No, I never saw him.'

'He talked to the rest of us,' said Penelope.

'What did he say?'

'It's sometimes awfully difficult to know what doctors are saying,' said Penelope. 'I think we were all rather cowardly and didn't ask enough direct questions. I don't know. Father didn't seem to have taken in anything that he said to him. Perhaps he was more frank with me.'

'But what did he say?'

'He went on for a long time about how difficult for us all it was going to be, and how we must all help Father and Peter and how hard it was for them.'

'But didn't he say how long it was going to be hard for?'

'Not exactly. At least I took him to mean. . . . I don't know, it's so difficult. I asked him if he couldn't be more definite and he said he never liked to say such a thing absolutely definitely because you never knew and miracles did happen.'

'Miracles?'

'And he said the disease was far advanced.'

'But he said it wasn't cancer. He definitely said that to Charlotte, I heard him. Did you ask him again if it was cancer?'

'Somehow I didn't,' said Penelope. 'But, you know, I think sometimes they say it isn't when it is, because people are so frightened of it.'

'But she's too young. People don't have it as young as that, do they?'

'I think they do, yes,' said Penelope. 'But I think sometimes it is cured, you know, or at any rate cured for quite a long time.'

'I don't believe it. The doctor would have told us.'

'What else could it be?'

There was a silence.

'Does Peter know?' asked Selina.

'I don't know,' answered Penelope. 'You see, none of us have really talked about it. After all, I hardly know Peter. And Father won't listen. He simply refuses to talk about it, he's determined not to face it.'

'I must go to the cottage, mustn't I?' said Selina. 'Obviously I'm the only person who's free. She's got to have somebody.'

'But you've got to be here at school in the term time.'

'Why? I'm not doing any good here. I can teach myself anything else I need to learn.'

'But, Selina, don't be silly, you can't possibly leave school yet. I thought you were going to some university or something, and anyway you must get some sort of qualification. You'll have to, to get a decent job.'

'I can take a correspondence course,' said Selina.

'Oh dear, please don't do anything rash. Perhaps I ought not to have told you all this, only I don't see what good can come of keeping it all a mystery. But you must understand I may have got it wrong. After all, Charlotte is an immensely strong-willed person. I'm sure that makes a difference. Now, look here, I'm going to Harkwood the weekend after next. By that time I shall have seen Charlotte. I promise you that I will have a really serious talk with Martin then, and tell her what you've said and see what she thinks. Then we'll write to you at once, I promise. Now don't do anything rash will you?'

'No, I won't,' said Selina.

Penelope returned to London on Monday morning.

That evening Selina climbed out of her dormitory window, slid down a drain pipe, and walked to the station. She arrived at Angel's house at one o'clock in the morning.

There was a light upstairs in the bedroom, but when she rang the bell there was no answer. She rang again several times, until finally the bedroom window was opened and an angry voice said, 'Why the hell don't you use your own key?'

'I haven't got one,' she said quietly.

'Oh, for Christ's sake,' said the voice. 'I had three more cut for you the other day. What have you done with them?'

She saw that it was Roger who was leaning out of the window: she had not recognized his voice.

'Roger, it's me, I haven't got a key,' she said.

'I know, it's you. You can bloody well climb in.'

'Where's Angel?'

'What? What d'you mean? What are you talking about?' He leant farther out of the window. 'Selina? What are you doing here? Hang on a moment.'

He disappeared, and a few moments later opened the door.

'Well,' he leant against the door post. He was wearing a dinner jacket, his black tie was undone and his shirt open. He smelt strongly of alcohol and cigarette smoke. 'I thought you were Angel.' He made no move to allow her to enter the house.

'I've just arrived in London,' said Selina. 'From school. 'I'm going down to look after Charlotte but I thought perhaps I could sleep here for the night.'

'Of course you can sleep here for the night,' he said. 'Unchaperoned though we shall be, your sister being out with some lover or other.'

He still blocked the doorway.

'Oh, well, I just wanted a bed,' said Selina, hesitantly.

'Don't we all, don't we all?' he mumbled, finally moving aside so that she could go into the house.

'We shan't be alone, I'd forgotten,' he said, going into the drawing-room and turning on the lights. 'I found this here when I came in.' He gesticulated towards a figure on the sofa, and went over to pour out a large whisky and soda.

The man on the sofa was asleep, violently asleep, every part of his body seeming employed in maintaining that state. He was snoring irregularly, sometimes swallowing noisily and smacking his lips, his eyelids, perhaps affected by the sudden switching on of the light, were twitching and flickering, his hands, which were podgy and dirty with nicotine-stained fingers, were flapping spasmodically where they were resting on his enormous stomach, and one leg appeared to be affected with a twitch. He was wearing a filthy old battle-dress top, stained white trousers, thick woollen socks and sandals. Besides him on the floor was an ashtray, the centre of a heap of misdirected ash and cigarette ends, and an overturned bottle of vodka.

Roger held out the glass he had just filled to Selina. 'Have this,' he offered.

'No, thank you,' she said.

'Don't you want it? Why not?'

'I just don't, I don't know why.'

'Don't they give it you at school? What would you rather have? Brandy?'

'Well, all right then, just a very little, please. If it's a bore, I could easily go and see if Penelope would put me up for the night only she might say I ought to go back to school.'

'I bet she would, silly old cow,' said Roger. 'Sit down, take off your coat, make yourself at home. Delightful, delightful, I'd much rather see you than your sister. You're so pretty now, too, d'you know that? Of course you do. And so young, oh God. Don't bother about him. Nothing wakes him. Sit on him if you think you'd be comfortable.'

'I was only thinking . . . I mean, if there are people sleeping on the sofa, perhaps there isn't room for me.'

'Nonsense. There's a perfectly good spare bed upstairs. This fool has an absurd theory that it's less trouble to everybody if he sleeps down here and spills ash and vodka all over the sofa and is sick on the carpet, rather than shutting himself away decently upstairs. Also spending the night on people's sofas is part of his way of life, which spare beds are not. I wish they were. He never gets up till three in the afternoon.'

'Who is he?'

'A failed poet of about a hundred and ten. A man with absolutely nothing to recommend him except that he's always appearing in people's memoirs about the thirties. The last time he finished a sentence was in 1937 at the Fitzroy in Charlotte Street; now they all get drowned in spit and tears and he has to start again at the beginning. Angel likes to have those sort of people about because they're even more hopeless than she is. She leaves the basement door open for them and a bowl of milk, like the Little People, so that they can come in and foul up the house. If there aren't two or three of them here all the time she starts shrieking and saying that life has no meaning. Meaning. Christ. So you've run away from school?'

'Yes.'

'Quite right. Frightful place. I remember going to see Charlotte there once.'

'Penelope seems to think that Charlotte may be going to die.'

'No, she won't die,' he dismissed the idea with a wave of his glass. 'She's much the toughest of you, she'll outlive you all, you'll see. But you're going down there to look after her? How sweet of you, how terribly terribly sweet. And running away from school and everything, Oh God . . .'

'I was going to run away from school anyway,' said Selina shortly.

'No, but all the same it's terribly sweet. You always were supposed to be the nice one of course, weren't you? Penelope the bossy one, Susan the neurotic, Angel the beauty, Charlotte the clever one, and Selina the nice one, isn't that it? Selina, the little darling.'

'Don't be silly,' she said, standing up. 'I think I'll go to bed if you don't mind.'

'Mind? I'd be delighted.' He stood up too, but with greater difficulty. 'Delighted. I'd like to do everything in my power to help you, I'll show you the way, undress you, wash you all over with lots of lovely soothing soap, put you into your little white shift and carry you to bed, oh, how delicious.'

'Do shut up,' she said. 'I'll find the room myself.'

'No, no, a host's duties,' he mumbled and followed her up the stairs. 'There you are, isn't that nice? And I'm just next door if you want me in the night.'

'Thank you.' She tried to shut the door.

'Must show you the bathroom,' he said.

'I know where it is, I saw it on the way up,' she said.

'No, no, I must show you. You haven't seen where the bath salts are. Come along.' He dragged her down the stairs to the bathroom, pushed her against the wall and began to kiss her all over her face.

'Stop it!' She struggled and managed to kick him on the shin. He let go of her and rubbed his ankle. 'You are mean,' he said. 'You know you like it really.'

'Of course I don't like it,' she said furiously. 'It's perfectly horrible and you smell so foul that I can hardly breathe.'

'Smell?' he said, hurt. 'What d'you mean, my breath?'

'Everything about you,' she said.

'I have a bath every day,' he said. 'I can't possibly smell. What sort of smell? Not feet?'

'Everything. Drink and smoke.'

'Oh that, well, everybody smells like that at this hour of the evening.' He put his arms round her again. 'You had me worried.'

'Please stop it. Angel will be back in a minute.'

'Will she hell. She's probably gone for days. Kiss me. Please do.'

'I can't kiss my sister's husband.'

'I don't see why. She never does.' He buried his face in her neck.

'Do stop . . . I'll have to go and wake up that man.'

'You couldn't.'

'I could. I must.' She broke away from him and began to run down the stairs.

'It won't do any good,' he said. 'Even if you could wake him up, he'd most likely join in.'

She stopped, struck by the thought that this might be

true. Then she ran quickly up the stairs again and into
the bedroom. He followed her.

'Why are you being so difficult?' he asked plaintively.
leaning on the door post.

'Me being difficult?' she answered angrily. 'All I'm
trying to do is get to bed and go to sleep, and I wish to
goodness you'd leave me alone.'

'All right, all right, I can take a hint,' he wandered off
into the next bedroom and she heard him lying down
heavily on the bed. She undressed, looked at the door to
see if she could lock it but found there was no key, and
got into bed. He came in again immediately.

'Oh, God,' she said, sitting up furiously.

'Don't be cross, please don't be cross,' he said, sitting
down on the edge of the bed. 'You look so sweet in there,
you really do. I only want to look at you. I remember
Angel when she was your age, or not much older. She
had long hair too, didn't she? And she was so young,
much younger for her age than you are. She didn't know
anything about anything. You're much more serious,
aren't you? And I suppose you know all about sex, too,
they all do these days. Do you?'

'Do I what?'

'Know all about sex.'

'Well, I do in theory,' she said.

'Not in practice? You amaze me.'

'Oh, don't be so stupid. How should I know all about
it in practice? I'm sixteen, and nine-tenths of my life has
been spent in exclusively female society. I've hardly even
seen a man. If they're all like you I hope I never see
another. Do go away now.'

He leant towards her again.

'You don't mean it, I know you don't . . .' he began.

'Shut up!' she shouted, jumping out of bed. Evading
his grasp, she fled down the stairs into the bathroom, and
locked the door. He rattled at the handle.

'Don't be silly,' he said. 'You're only being silly. I shall
wait here till you come out. I only want to kiss you good
night.' She heard him sit down on the stairs. 'You'll be
cold if you stay in there,' he added disapprovingly.

'I'm going to stay here all night so you might as well go back to bed,' she said firmly.

There were a few old copies of the *Autocar* near the lavatory. Covering herself with towels to keep warm, she began doggedly to read them. Before long she used them as a pillow, and fell asleep.

She woke early, stiff and aching, and went down to the kitchen.

It was untidy. A pile of dirty plates and glasses surrounded the sink, and there was a smell of decaying meat. Following her nose, she traced the smell to its source. It was a very old chop which had fallen behind the refrigerator. With some difficulty and the help of a broom handle she extracted it, and put it into the dustbin. She found a tin of Nescafé and some bread, and made herself some breakfast. Later she found the morning papers on the door mat, and was reading them in the kitchen when Roger came down.

He was wearing a dark suit, beautifully pressed and brushed, a broadly striped shirt and a dark blue tie. His shoes were shining, exactly the right amount of white handkerchief obtruded from his breast pocket, and his hair was smoothed and flattened with an expensive-smelling unguent.

'Oh, you're up,' was all he said.

He made himself coffee and toast with surprising speed and neatness. Halfway through his consumption of them, he said, 'Sorry about last night.'

'It's all right,' said Selina coldly.

'Things aren't going awfully well here at the moment,' he said briskly. 'I daresay it will improve in time. If Angel comes back will you tell her I'll be back about seven?' He got up, put his plate and cup by the sink, and said, 'Mrs. Thing will be coming in later I think. She usually does on Tuesdays. If that horror upstairs wakes up leave him to her, she's good at getting rid of him. Stay as long as you like, won't you? Goodbye.'

He ran up the stairs. She heard him telephoning in the hall.

'Miss Powell? Is Mr. Manners there? Tell him I'm on my way would you, and will you give him that outline I roughed out yesterday to be looking at? And did you fix that lunch? Okay. Fine. See you in twenty minutes or so.'

The front door banged. She heard his brisk step on the pavement, the car door banging and the engine starting.

She went upstairs to telephone the station to find out about the trains, and to send a telegram to Charlotte since the cottage was not on the telephone.

As she turned to go up to fetch her suitcase from the bedroom she heard a key in a lock. It seemed to take some time to fit, but finally the door opened. It was Angel.

She was wearing a black low-necked dress, and had obviously at some stage in the previous evening been to a party. As much of her face as Selina could see through her hair and her dark glasses seemed extraordinarily white.

'Are you all right?' asked Selina, anxiously.

Angel gave a tremendous start, then leant back against the door which she had just shut.

'I didn't see you there,' she said, rather faintly. 'Have you been here long?'

'I came last night.'

'Last night? Did you sleep here?'

'Yes.'

'You should have let me know. Was the bed made up and everything?'

'Yes, it was. Do you want some coffee or something?'

'I don't know,' said Angel.

'You'd better, hadn't you?' said Selina.

'I suppose so,' said Angel. 'But perhaps it's better to have nothing. I've been rather sick.'

'I should have some,' said Selina, leading the way to the kitchen. 'Or tea, if you like.'

'Perhaps tea,' Angel followed her down to the kitchen, sat down at the table and put her head in her hands. 'Mrs. Ray hasn't been. Oh dear, I should have been here when you came.'

'You couldn't have known,' said Selina. 'Where have you been anyway?'

'God knows,' said Angel. 'Some party. Was Roger here?'

'Yes. He said to tell you he'd be back at seven.'

'At seven? Oh dear, I'm going to the theatre, I wonder when it starts. Did he say what he was doing this evening?'

'No.'

'Oh.'

'There's another man upstairs, asleep on the sofa. A fat man.'

'George, I suppose. Oh dear, I suppose it was all in a terrible mess when you arrived. Penelope will be livid if you tell her. I've had a frightful row with her. She really is too pompous for words these days.'

Selina said, 'I'm going down to stay with Charlotte for a bit.'

'Good,' said Angel. 'I am glad. I've been meaning to go myself, only it never seemed to be the right time of day to catch a train.'

'Penelope says she thinks she's iller than we realize.'

'Penelope is always so damping. They said at the hospital she was all right, didn't they? Oh dear, I'm not sure that tea was such a good idea after all.'

'Apparently they didn't really say that at all.'

Angel pushed back her chair and hurried out of the room. Selina began half-heartedly washing up. Angel came back, looking whiter than ever, and said, 'Don't bother about that.' She sat down and poured out some more tea.

'I thought you said tea wasn't a good idea,' said Selina.

'It's making me feel better really. It's a good thing to be sick.'

'Why are you being sick?'

'I drank too much.'

'I thought when you got married you were going to settle down and have a lot of babies. That's what you always used to say.'

'Well, yes, I know, but then as it turns out I can't have any babies. At least that's what the doctors say and I've been to two.'

'Why? I mean why can't you?'

'Oh well I . . . I don't know really. It's all my own fault. But it's all right. I mean, Roger doesn't mind.'

'You don't seem,' said Selina carefully, 'to be exactly the conventional idea of a happily married couple.'

'No, I know, but you see the thing is . . . Blast!' Her hand gave a sudden violent jerk and she spilt the tea out of her cup.

Selina mopped it up.

'It's all right really,' Angel went on. 'I mean, I'm sure it will be, in time. Everything will be better soon.'

'What makes you think that?' said Selina.

Angel moved uncomfortably in her chair. 'Oh well I mean things usually do get better don't they? Oh God my head aches. I mean, it's no use bullying me like Penelope does. She refuses to have me in the house now, because she's afraid I might shock some of Ham's influential friends. Honestly, the way those two work at it he certainly ought to get somewhere in the end. She was going to go and see Charlotte you know this week but she put it off because some Minister asked them to tea or something. I mean I know I haven't been to see Charlotte but it's only through inefficiency. I suppose that's as bad, though, isn't it? Or is it worse? Yes, it is, isn't it? Much worse.'

'I'm going now, anyway, so you needn't worry about it,' said Selina. 'In fact I must leave because I'm catching a train at 11.40. The only thing is, I wonder if you could lend me some money for my ticket?'

'Of course.' Angel stood up and began to search through the kitchen shelves, spilling a bowl of sugar and knocking over a vase of dead flowers. 'Here we are,' she said. She opened a cookery book, and took out several pound notes which were between its pages.

'Thank you. I'll pay you back.'

'No, of course you're not to. Honestly, it's supposed to be for buying food and things but we never seem to need any somehow.'

They went upstairs and Selina collected her luggage and telephoned for a taxi.

Angel peered into the drawing-room, said, 'It is George,' and came out again.

'No one told me you'd left school,' she said.

'No one knows,' said Selina.

'But surely it isn't the end of term?'

'No.'

'You don't mean you've run away? Oh you are brilliant. How did you do it?'

'I just climbed out of a window and caught a train,' said Selina, moving towards the front door as she heard the taxi drawing up outside.

'You didn't? How wonderful of you. I do think that's marvellous. I do wish I could do things like that. Oh is it here? Goodbye then, have a lovely time. Love to Charlotte and will you let me know how she is and if she'd like me to come and see her? Just send me a postcard and I'll come at once.'

Gabriel was walking round the wood, in the late afternoon, in autumn. He had spent the earlier part of the day dictating letters to Miss Martin, who acted as his secretary when he was at Harkwood, and he had arranged to catch the late train to London so as to be in his office early the following morning. While Miss Martin began to type the letters he had dictated, he had read the *Financial Times*, the *Times Literary Supplement* and the *New Statesman*. Then he had started his walk, his mind agreeably active.

He had had a letter that morning which, though not unexpected, had pleased him. It had asked him to be a member of a committee of four to consider and make recommendations upon the general economic situation. It was the sort of thing he liked doing, and meant several months of interesting work.

He swung his walking stick and breathed deeply. He said aloud. 'There's life in the old dog yet.' Life, he thought, life, I have an active mind, he thought; I'm alive, I exist. Most people of my age have let themselves go, got right away from the centre of living into unreality, dream, death. I'm still here, still at the heart of the fire.

He saw Miss Martin walking across the field towards him. As she approached he said aloud, expressively.

'An aged man is but a paltry thing,
A tattered coat upon a stick unless

Soul clap its hands and sing, and louder sing,
For every tatter in its mortal dress . . .'

He liked the idea of himself striding through his woods,
shouting poetry, at his age.

'Penelope's on the telephone,' said Miss Martin
breathlessly.

'Bother,' said Gabriel. 'I know it will only be to unbraid
me about something or other. Do you think Penelope is
becoming a scold?'

They began to walk quickly back towards the house.

'Selina has run away from school,' Miss Martin told
him.

'Selina? Run away from school? Why?'

'To be with Charlotte.'

'She can't possibly do that,' he said irritably. 'She hasn't
finished her schooling. Good heavens, what are children
coming to these days? How old is she anyway?'

'Sixteen. Nearly seventeen,' puffed Miss Martin.

'Hm,' he grunted, striding across the field. 'It will give
old Brace a bit of a jolt. Why didn't she stop her?'

'I don't know,' said Miss Martin. 'Penelope has spoken
to her, apparently. To Miss Brace, I mean.'

'She would.' He hurried into the house and picked up
the telephone.

'Father?' Penelope's voice came sharp and clear along
the wires. 'Look here, I think you'll have to take some
action. I sent Peter a telegram asking him to telephone
me as I wanted to explain why I couldn't go and see
Charlotte this week, and when he spoke to me this
morning he told me they had had a telegram from Selina
saying that she was arriving there today. I rang up Miss
Brace and discovered that she had run away from school.
Miss Brace had been trying to get hold of you all morning
but she didn't know where you were. It then transpired
that Selina had spent the night with that idiot Angel, who
had made no effort whatsoever to send her back. Angel
really is too ridiculous and irresponsible for words.'

'Which do you want me to take action about, Selina or
Angel?' he asked.

'Selina, obviously,' she said. 'Naturally, if you can do

anything about Angel, well and good, but I imagine she's beyond hope. But Selina must be sent back to school as soon as possible. It's quite disgraceful.'

'Yes, of course. I'll see to it.'

'What will you do?'

'What will I do? Well, er, I'll see she's sent back, I'll write to her. No, I know, Martin can see to it.'

'Martin can't see to everything you know,' said Penelope sharply. 'I think if you were to assert your authority a bit more. . . .'

'My dear, last time I asserted my authority it made no difference at all to the course of events. In the case of Charlotte's marriage I mean. I am the last person to whom any of you seem inclined to turn for advice, and I certainly can't use coercion. Martin and Selina have a very good understanding. I am sure she will be able to cope with the situation.'

'I think she should go today,' said Penelope.

'I will see that she goes today,' he said with resignation.

'As long as you understand the gravity of the situation,' she went on. 'I mean, she can't be allowed to go gallivanting all over the country when she's supposed to be at school. I know it may be to some extent my fault, because I did tell her that I took a serious view of Charlotte's illness, and I think that's what gave her the idea of going to be with her. That was obviously a mistake on my part, but I do feel that she should be made to realize that her responsibilities are to the school and to the people who are trying to educate her there, and to you who are paying the fees. Otherwise if she gets away with this she'll only turn into another Angel. I really begin to feel I'm the only member of the family with a decent respect for the conventions.'

'No one could accuse you of not having that,' he answered. 'I will see to it. She shall be sent back.'

He replaced the receiver with a sigh, and turned to Miss Martin, who had been listening anxiously.

'I am afraid you will have to go down and recover Selina,' he said. 'I have had enough of trying to rescue my daughters from that dammed cottage. It appears that the fault lies with Penelope. She led Selina to believe that

Charlotte was in desperate need of someone to look after her, and so Selina with her usual directness has gone to look after her. Perhaps it is her awareness of her own responsibility which makes Penelope so aggressive about the whole subject. What is the matter with Angel, do you know?'

'Penelope says that she leads a disreputable life, and quarrels with Roger,' said Miss Martin.

'No doubt Penelope has forgotten her own early days of marriage,' he said comfortably. Then as Miss Martin said nothing he went on unwillingly, 'Or do you think I should have a word with her, with Angel, I mean?'

'I think it might be nice if you would see her,' said Miss Martin. 'You haven't lately, have you?'

'I'll give her lunch some time,' he said. 'And you will deal with Selina as you think best? Daughters are a great trial, aren't they? A heavy load. What time is lunch?'

'One.'

'I'll be going through my papers if you want me before that.' He went to his desk, sat down, reached for *The Times*, and began to look at the crossword.

On the afternoon of her arrival at the cottage, Selina took Charlotte out into the garden.

The air was sweet with rain and wet leaves. The trunks of the beeches which surrounded the cottage were dark and glistening, like the flanks of sweating horses, and the leaves above them were red and gold. The clearing was mown now; at one side grew a row of vegetables. Immediately in front of the cottage some of the flowers which Charlotte had planted in the spring were still alive.

Her feet were very thin. Her old slippers hurt them, so Peter had bought her a larger size, lined with fur, and these were all she could now wear. She slid her feet into them slowly, sitting on the edge of the bed, then gently eased her arms into the old blue dressing-gown which Selina was holding for her. They had sent the nurse to the cinema in the nearest town; Peter was painting in the studio, which had no windows except in the roof, so that he was isolated from what went on around him.

Charlotte put her arm into Selina's and walked across the room. Her shoulders were very thin, but her stomach was distended, so that she looked pregnant. She walked hesitantly, concentrating. Selina more or less carried her downstairs and put her down in a chair to rest before they went into the garden. She was determined to walk into the garden. She had been looking forward to it for weeks.

The sun came out, then a cloud passed across it, and then it shone again. The sky was full of clouds, moving rapidly. To Selina, walking slowly beside Charlotte out into the sunlight, it seemed as if everything out there were in movement, the clouds, the trees, the drips of rainwater from the roof, the animals and insects in the grass and undergrowth, cows walking purposefully in single file across the hillside opposite, birds and aeroplanes, the earth itself; everything except the thin hand on her arm.

Charlotte was thinking, progress, this is progress. Here is the sun, these are the flowers I planted, everything is going to be different now, this is a milestone. It seems very noisy out here, perhaps it is the wind. I said I would do it and I have done it. Now I can go back to bed. How lovely the sun is. But how bright. I had better go back.

They stood on the grass, Charlotte leaning on Selina's arm. Selina coughed, to relieve her aching throat. Nothing that anyone had told her had prepared for her what she had seen in Charlotte's questioning eyes and ruined frame, in her room with its bottles and trays and bowls, in the nurse's callousness, in Peter's long withdrawals into his silent work-room.

'We must go back now,' she said quietly. 'You've done awfully well for the first day downstairs.

They sat in Charlotte's bedroom the following evening, Selina, Peter and Miss Martin. Charlotte was in bed, propped up on pillows.

Miss Martin was staying at a nearby pub. She had arrived that evening, and had said to Selina, 'I've just come to see how things are. Let's not discuss anything until the morning.'

Charlotte said, 'In the spring Peter and I are going to Greece.'

He was sitting by the window, dark against the light. They could not see his face. She watched him feverishly from her pillow. 'Aren't we?' she said.

'Yes,' he said. 'That's right. The Islands.'

'What a good idea,' said Miss Martin.

'We're going to take a long time,' said Charlotte. 'And stay as long as we like at each place. Peter has never been there either. He is not sure how it will affect his painting. Are you, Peter?'

'No, I am not sure,' he said.

'You know, the light,' she said.

'The light, that's it,' he said.

'I went on a Hellenic cruise, once, before the war,' said Miss Martin. 'We loved it. Have you books to read about it?'

Charlotte gestured towards a pile of books by her bed.

'I can't read yet really,' she said. 'I get so tired. But the doctor says soon I should be able to concentrate more. Only it seems to me that I get less able to concentrate every day.' On the last sentence her voice suddenly went high.

They all spoke at once.

'It's those new pills he's put you on to,' said Peter.

'It's always like that when you're convalescing,' said Miss Martin.

'You said you'd enjoyed that detective story,' said Selina.

There was a little silence.

'Perhaps you're all fooling me,' said Charlotte. 'But you wouldn't, would you?'

'Of course not.' Miss Martin stood up and approached the bed. 'Let's see what you've found to read.' She began to look through the books.

'Peter wouldn't fool me, would you, Peter?' went on Charlotte in her thin voice.

'Of course not,' he said.

She was getting tired.

'We didn't have much time,' she said dreamily. 'Much time to find out whether the other would fool us, when it came to the point. I hardly know you, do I?'

'You know all that there is to know,' he said.

'Isn't there any more?' she asked.

'No more,' he said.

'You said you would bring up some things to show me,' she said.

'I haven't done much. It hasn't been going very well.'

'I believe you only go in there so much to escape from this room.'

'I'm always like this when it is going badly.'

She shut her eyes. 'I can't escape from this room,' she said in the same dreamy voice. 'Sometimes I think I never shall.' She opened her eyes suddenly: they rested rather wildly on Peter's dark shape. 'But you will stay? If I never get out of this room, will you still be here?'

'But Charlotte, you have escaped,' Selina got up quietly and went to pour out some medicine. She spoke calmly, 'You have been downstairs and into the garden. Obviously that's the beginning of really escaping. If only it wouldn't rain so much you could go down again. Here's your medicine. I told Nurse I would do it at nine. Do you know what she's making all the time when she sits in her room listening to the wireless? A patchwork quilt. It's really rather pretty.'

'How clever of her,' said Charlotte. 'Perhaps I could do a bit of sewing.'

'We hadn't thought of that, had we?' said Selina. 'But at school you were terribly bad at it.'

Charlotte smiled faintly. Peter stood up. 'If it's really nine o'clock I think I'll just go down and have a look at something I was doing earlier. I'll look in again before you go to sleep.'

She moved her head from side to side. 'Last night you forgot.'

'My watch is working tonight,' he said. He bent over to kiss her, and went out of the room.

Charlotte said, 'Surely, if I died, Peter would be very upset?'

'You're not doing to die,' said Selina. 'Shall I read aloud a bit before Nurse comes?'

'I don't think I shall die,' said Charlotte. 'I'm sure people don't if they don't want to, not at my age, anyway. I should be very angry if I thought I was going to. It would be so wrong, wouldn't it, so unfair?'

'Do shut up, I'm going to read,' said Selina.

Charlotte was quiet, and closed her eyes.

'When Zeus had brought Hector and the Trojans up to the ships, he left them there with their enemies to the toil and agony of the unending struggle and turned his shining eyes away into the distance, where he surveyed the lands of the horse-breeding Thracians, the Mysians who fight hand-to-hand, the lordly Hippemolgi who drink mares' milk, and the Abii, the most law-abiding folk on earth. . . .'

In the morning, Miss Martin said to Selina, 'Your father sent me here to bring you back to school.'

'But now that you are here you see that I can't go,' said Selina confidently.

Miss Martin sighed.

'Not at all,' she said, after a moment. 'I see that you must.'

'But Charlotte,' Selina pointed out.

'I shall be with Charlotte,' said Miss Martin. 'I shall explain the position to your father, and come and stay here with Charlotte for as long as it may be necessary.'

'No,' said Selina. 'Father can't manage without you. He needs you for all sorts of things. You know the Italians are hopeless and you do most of the housework anyway, and all the organizing. Father can't even remember what he's supposed to be doing unless you're there to remind him. I'm the one person in the family without any ties at all so obviously I'm the one to stay here.'

'You have got ties. School is a tie.'

'Not to compare with this tie.'

'But we all have this tie. It is not yours alone. Look, I know what this sort of thing is like. I nursed my mother through her last illness and it was not unlike this. There isn't a great deal one can do. Doctors do all they can, and the pain-killing drugs make it more bearable for the patient than it seems to be to an onlooker. To an onlooker it is a very depressing business. Everybody has to go through it at one time or another but . . .'

'This is not everybody. This is me. And Charlotte.'

'I don't want you to be hurt . . .'

'Surely being hurt is the least I can do?'

Miss Martin began to feel helpless.

'What about your education?' she said.

'I'll take a correspondence course in anything you like while I'm here,' said Selina.

'I'll have to talk to your father,' said Miss Martin.

Foreseeing difficult interviews with Gabriel and Miss Brace, she nevertheless felt that there was one more thing she had to do before she left.

She went to see Charlotte and said to her, 'We are all thinking about you and worrying about you and feeling for you. But sometimes when you're ill you feel alone, and there is nothing anyone can really do about that. I know you never have relied too much on other people and have always made your own decisions, so you may be able to cope with this better than most people. Indeed. I think you are coping better than most people. But sometimes it's better not to struggle too much, to relax, to reconcile yourself . . .'

Charlotte looked at her with clear eyes.

'If you mean I should reconcile myself to dying, as long as I breathe I will never do that.'

Peter was sitting in his studio. He had done no work since the first few days after they had brought Charlotte home from hospital.

Since Selina had been there he had been thinking mostly of one thing only, that now she was with Charlotte he might go away. In the course of time he had come to believe what the doctor had told him; that Charlotte was going to die. He had asked the doctor whether Charlotte herself should be told and the doctor had said that he preferred to leave that decision to her family, but that in his own private and unprofessional opinion it was better not to tell her. He believed that his patients were happier in their last weeks if they did not know that they were dying.

Peter had imagined, in so far as he had been able to imagine anything, some sort of idyllic close to their love, in a spirit of calm regret, in the place they both loved. It had turned out otherwise. Three things lay between them; the apparatus of illness, the bitterness of Charlotte's resentment of her disease, and the lie about her condition.

He could not work. After what seemed an immeasurable period of time, of hopeless days and weeks, he had found this to be the most worrying aspect, and the discovery had made him say to himself that he must face the fact of his selfishness and rescue himself, rescue at least the part of himself that painted. Otherwise they would both die; and he felt an injunction upon him not allow himself to be killed. It was a moral injunction, of the same nature as the guilt he felt when he had no work in hand.

He could make no excuse for himself. He had sat for days alone in his studio, saying to himself, my wife is dying and I want to run away. I am a traitor. Whatever the cause, I am still a traitor. Finally he decided to go for a few days only.

He said to Selina, 'There's this dealer. I ought really to go and see him. I think I'll have to go to London for a day or two. I'll stay with the Moulds. You can always get me there.'

Charlotte took the news with surprising resignation. She would not look at him when he said goodbye, but she made no protest.

He rang up every day. The second day he said he had been asked to go to Cheshire to visit someone who had bought three of his pictures and wanted to commission some more. He thought it would only take a couple of days. A week later he was still there, ringing up every day.

Charlotte thought, when you need help, everything falls away from you and you are left with nothing. People disappear. Even when they are here you can't reach them, however•hard you try. Love becomes meaningless, it fails completely, it fails and fails and is shown up for what it is, true love, true love, true. And everything you ran your life by goes, principles and faith and art and literature, all useless, man-made comforters, irrelevant. God damn them all. God damn them all. There is no help. Only will is left. And rage.

Selina moved silently about the house, forestalling every wish of Charlotte's, fetching things for her, taking them away again, arranging her pillows, reading aloud, picking flowers, cooking tiny appetizing uneaten meals, making hot drinks, filling hot-water bottles, pouring out medicine; in total submission.

Time lost its usual meaning, it was measured out in medicine; the days were long and the nights very short. There were afternoons when the tears wandered endlessly down Charlotte's thin cheeks from under her closed eyelids. On one of these Selina said thoughtlessly, 'Sometimes I think it's worse for me than for you.'

The eyelids exposed the furious eyes.

'Nothing that is happening to anyone anywhere is worse than what is happening to me.'

Selina believed her.

One morning she seemed to be in a coma. The nurse fetched the doctor. He said she would die quite soon.

Selina went into the village and rang up the Moulds. They said Peter was back from Cheshire and they would try and get a message to him. She rang up Gabriel and Penelope. Then she went back to the cottage.

Charlotte was breathing with loud rasping breaths, and muttering. She seemed in great distress. Once she said to Selina, 'Don't let me die before Peter comes.'

'He's coming. He'll be here soon.'

'Oh God, oh God, oh God.' Her head moved violently on the pillow. The nurse gave her another injection.

'God damn them all,' said Charlotte. 'God damn them all.'

She seemed to sink into unconsciousness again. Later she muttered some more, but the only words which were distinguishable, though the voice did not seem her own, were 'Nobody, nothing,' and then again, 'God damn them.'

After a long time the noise of breathing which filled the room accelerated, increased in volume, became unbearable; then suddenly stopped. Selina's eyes closed for a moment over the tears which rushed into them. She thought, the presence of death. Death.

She approached the still figure on the bed. She hoped she might see that serenity and calm, even happiness, of which she had heard. But the face, though unlined, looked a thousand years old; a thousand years dead.

9

GABRIEL walked slowly up the steps of his club, nodded to the porter, pushed through the swing door, and looking straight before him plodded up the stairs and into the dining-room. He went to his usual table, sat heavily in his chair and unfolded his newspaper. He was aware of several glances in his direction, and became as a result of them minutely more bent and gloomy.

He could imagine the lowered voices: 'There goes poor old Dobson . . . daughter died of cancer . . . another in a madhouse I believe . . . it's aged him terribly . . . wife died young too . . . never remarried . . . an odd fellow . . . lonely sort of man . . . no real friends . . . was supposed to be going to do great things you know when he was younger . . . nothing much came of it . . . too late now . . . too old . . . finished now . . . oh yes, finished, I'm afraid . . .' But perhaps they were not interested even to that extent; perhaps they only said, before going back to their own affairs, 'What's that fellow's name? Always forget it . . .' Or perhaps not even that.

He ordered a lamb chop and looked at his paper, which he had read once already. He had not grieved for Charlotte herself so much as for the idea of her and of her death. There had always been a distance between them, an inability in each to appreciate the other. He did not like disputatious women; but it was not only that. She had had a special faculty for irritating him that only a member of his own family could have possessed. Now in retrospect her life seemed unbearably pathetic, in its urgency and immaturity, and in its total defeat. Her face and voice and gestures were vivid in his memory in the months after her death, causing him several times each day an access of intense regret and remorse. He told himself that he felt remorse because he had prevented her from marrying the man she loved for the space of two months, a period which seemed longer in the context of so short a life; but it was also because he had not been able to love her, and because he had begotten her, to no end.

To prevent these thoughts from recurring, he pulled some notes out of his pocket and began to look through them. The work of the advisory committee on the general economic situation was nearly over, but difficulties had arisen over the report. Gabriel found himself in almost total disagreement with his three colleagues; and he also found himself quite without his usual desire to compromise in order to make something workable come out of their deliberations. It was, he supposed, a diminution in his sense of responsibility and as such to be regretted, but was it not in his old age more important to preserve his freedom of thought? He had come to believe that the whole of the economic system within whose framework the committee was supposed to be making its recommendations was based on principles and assumptions of glaring falsity, economically quite apart from morally, and he had said so. The difference between him and his colleagues was that though they substantially agreed with him, they felt it to be possible and necessary to adapt and innovate in such a way as to make the present system workable. Gabriel no longer cared enough to agree with them, or at least he cared more for the saying of what he felt to be so. His colleagues understandably found him difficult to work with. He was considering resigning.

Re-reading his notes he was again filled with the impatience which he had experienced at the morning's meeting. Surely there was something of value in just that impatience?

After the meeting, Geoffrey Bolden, the chairman of the committee, a man he liked and with whom he had worked at the Ministry of Economic Warfare, had said to him casually and kindly on the way downstairs, 'Don't forget how badly we need you, old man,' taking his elbow just for a moment, and then leaving him with a cheerful smile and walking off in the opposite direction to his lunch. '. . . How badly we need you . . .' Then he must have let his bitterness show that morning; for it was true that he had been feeling for one reason or another separated from the others on the committee, not really one of them. It was partly the natural depression through which he was passing, but it was also the old sore about getting old and not having done enough, about feeling strong and not having the strength made use of: he ought not to have let that show. But then if Bolden had meant that, about their needing him, wouldn't it be wise to resign? Because there were after all things which could be done if only the others would admit the extent of their agreement with him. There was legislation which could be recommended and which might not be what was traditionally to be expected from a Conservative Government, but would do a good deal towards revivifying the economy. If he resigned it would show how much he had meant what he said. They would have to come after him, beg him to return, show themselves willing to compromise with him if he did; and then of course he would be reasonable, and they all knew from experience how eminently reasonable he could be. They would do that, surely, would come after him? His resignation, after all, would have the effect of more or less nullifying any report the committee might subsequently make without him. And it would be an action, a stimulus, something to jog him out of his dreary mood: one had to act, get things moving; then life filled up again, there was something on which to feed one's consciousness.

Finishing his lunch quickly, he went downstairs, telephoned a message to Bolden to say that a sudden indisposition prevented him from attending the afternoon's meeting, and went to the library to write his letter of resignation. It was a long letter, setting out in detail what he took to be the differences between his ideas and those of his colleagues, and when he had written it and put it out to be posted he felt pleasantly clear-headed and alert. He went back to have tea with Penelope with whom he was staying.

'Oh, there you are,' she said, as soon as he came in. 'I

didn't know whether you would be here for tea or not. I do wish you would remember to tell me what meals you are going to be in for before you go out in the mornings. I mean it's not just a question of ringing a bell whenever you want something like you used to when you had the flat.'

'Sorry,' he said. 'But please don't ever bother about me for tea. 'I'll just have a cup if it's there, that's all, nothing more.'

'Well, but it's all very well,' she said. 'You know that if there is any food you eat it all, and keep looking round for the cucumber sandwiches.'

'Ah, of course, if it's there,' he said. 'I must say, they give one awfully good cucumber sandwiches at the club. And sometimes I have a little toast, with Gentleman's Relish.'

'You see what I mean. Julian, leave Grandpapa's cup alone. I've told you before, if you don't stop fidgeting you'll have to go up to the nursery.'

'Have a lump of sugar,' said Gabriel politely to the little boy.

'Please don't give him sugar,' said Penelope. 'It's so bad for his teeth. Just that one and then no more, Julian. How's the committee today? Your meeting ended early, or didn't you have one?'

'I've resigned,' said Gabriel, drinking his tea.

'Resigned?' said Penelope. 'But, good heavens, I didn't know anyone ever did resign from those sort of things.'

'I found that I could not agree with the others as to the basis on which we were supposed to be working,' he said.

'Oh,' she said, doubtfully. 'Well, I hope you've done the right thing.'

'Of course I've done the right thing,' he said. 'Ham is not the only one who knows the tricks of the political trade.'

'It's a trick, is it?' she said. 'That's all right then.'

'Not exactly a trick,' he said. 'But I don't necessarily mean to sever my connections with the committee for good and all. It rather depends on them.'

'I suppose you know what you're doing,' she said. 'Ham says one should only resign if it's not a matter of

552

principle, so I daresay it's all right. Does that mean you'll be going back to Harkwood?'

'I detect a note of hope in your voice. Also one of fear. Don't worry. I shall both return to Harkwood and continue to pay the rent I have promised to pay you here, until Miss Martin returns from France and is able to supervise my domestic arrangements again.'

'I was not hoping or fearing anything,' said Penelope, irritably. 'You really are getting rather touchy. Of course you are welcome to stay here as long as you like, particularly as you are kind enough to contribute something towards your keep. Perhaps you may be back next week if everything goes as you plan?'

'Perhaps,' he said, smiling complacently. 'Perhaps.'

Selina and Miss Martin had been for a month's tour of France by car. Selina was withdrawn and unappreciative, Miss Martin patient. Selina began to look less pale.

When they came back to England, they went to stay with Angel for the night before going on to Harkwood.

When they arrived at her house and rang the bell at her front door, which badly needed repainting, there was no answer.

'We can probably get in through the basement,' said Miss Martin, leading the way down the cracked area steps. 'Though heaven knows what we shall find when we do get inside. She did know it was today we were coming, didn't she?'

'I sent a postcard,' said Selina. 'But she's quite likely to have forgotten.'

'It isn't locked,' said Miss Martin, opening the back door and walking in through the kitchen. 'This is all right anyway. The char must have been.'

They walked through the clean kitchen and up into the drawing-room. This too was surprisingly tidy.

'This is amazing,' said Miss Martin. 'Last time I saw this room it was like a pigsty. Something must have happened in the last couple of months.'

'Perhaps Angel's been away,' said Selina.

Then they heard her key in the lock, and she came in.

Her hair was neatly reduced to shoulder length and her arms were full of flowers.

'I'm going to have a baby,' she said.

'So that's what it is,' said Miss Martin.

'I haven't told anyone else,' said Angel. 'Penelope's so foul to me these days, we really hardly speak any more, and I haven't seen Father for ages. But it's quite definite, it's four months already. Roger's put it down for Eton, would you believe it? You have to pretend it's born already, of course, but it's the only way to get them in apparently.' She began to put the flowers into a nearby and rather too small jug.

'And you're pleased?' asked Miss Martin unnecessarily.

'Amazed, amazed, amazed,' she said. 'I'm very soppy and embarrassing about it, you'll see. The house is littered with tiny unfinished garments. You must agree it's a, well, a pleasant surprise, that I didn't, but didn't, deserve, and after Charlotte I feel I shouldn't be so happy, but she'd have wanted one to live wouldn't she, she believed in life, didn't she. . .? I'm going to cry.' She flopped down on the sofa, and took an enormous red spotted handkerchief out of her pocket. 'I cry an awful lot, what with one thing and another. I'm sure you must think me very self-indulgent.'

'We're delighted with you,' said Miss Martin. 'I'll go and make some tea.'

When she had gone down to the kitchen, Angel said to Selina, 'So I was wrong you see when I said that time ages ago that I couldn't have babies. Although the doctor was just as surprised as I was when I started. And Roger is so pleased too and so kind to me, you wouldn't believe it, and we're getting so respectable and boring already, you'd be amazed. Only not just to keep up appearances like silly old Penelope. And I haven't asked you one thing about France, doesn't that just show how selfish I've got? Was it fun and what did you mean about the Sorbonne on your postcard?'

'Martin found this friend of hers in Paris who's teaching there and we thought I might go if Father thought so. It seemed quite nice.'

'Do you want to?'

'I don't really mind what I do.'

'You will mind,' said Angel. 'I think it sounds a good idea. Listen, though, have you heard the latest thing about Susan, that she's going to some nursing home near them for all the week and coming home for the weekends, having voluntary treatment for her nerves? Have you ever heard anything so hopeless? I'm sure it's the worst possible thing for her to do.'

'It might be just what she needs,' said Miss Martin, coming in with the tea. 'But I was thinking that perhaps I might leave Selina here with you and go down and see her tomorrow and find out how she really is.'

'Do do that,' said Angel. 'Selina and I can do some lovely shopping. But I bet you anything you like you find her more maddening than mad.'

Susan was sitting very close to the fire when Bill came in. She was staring straight in front of her and did not look up. He hurried over to her, and moved her chair a little farther away from the fire, which was blazing brightly.

'Now, now, we can't have you burning holes in that nice skirt again can we?' he said. 'Come on, tell me all about it, I know what it is, Miss Martin's been here, hasn't she?'

'How did you know?' She turned wide lack-lustre eyes on his face.

'I met her in the drive. We had quite a talk. She said she was on the way to the club to look for me, so it was just as well I met her. But I'm sorry if she upset you.'

'Everyone upsets me,' she said fretfully. 'Except you and Doctor Dawnay.'

'What did she say?'

'She didn't seem to think I needed to go on going to Doctor Dawnay,' said Susan. 'She said they'd all been going through a terrible time after Charlotte's death, especially Selina. She went on about Selina, as if it was my fault. I can't help what other people are feeling, can I? I only know what I feel myself. They're all much tougher than me, anyway, they always were. I told her I wasn't doing it for pleasure, that I worried very much about the garden while I was away during the week, but I know she didn't understand. She wasn't unkind, she said I should go away, go up to Harkwood for a bit or something, but how could I possibly face Father in the state I'm in at the moment? You have to be feeling your strongest to be able to cope with him at all. But no one seems to understand these things. How I wish they wouldn't interfere and criticize all the time.'

'I'm sure that's not what she meant to do. Now, don't you worry. I had a long talk with her and explained everything. I told her this treatment of Doctor Dawnay's was just a temporary thing and that we hoped you'd soon be back here permanently, and that he was a first-rate man and there was no cause for alarm at all.'

'He is, isn't he?' she said, more eagerly. 'And he wouldn't take me on, would he, if I didn't need the treatment?'

'Of course he wouldn't,' said Bill. 'Now let's forget about all that and see what's going to be on the telly tonight, shall we?'

'Yes,' she said. 'But I wish people wouldn't make plots against me, and bother me.'

He stroked her hair. 'I love my gentle timid little mouse,' he said softly.

'It's so horrible,' she said vehemently. 'People who don't know how horrible it is don't know the truth.'

'To a sensitive soul, I'm afraid that's how it is,' he said, with a comfortable sigh. 'And that is why my little mouse needs her great big bear.'

'I do,' she said, looking anxiously up into his eyes. 'Oh, I do.'

Gabriel went back to Harkwood.

He received a letter from Geoffrey Bolden.

'My dear Dobson. You can imagine how much your letter has distressed us all. We had all enjoyed working with you and hoped that we might jointly produce something of value out of that work; but, as you say in your letter, the differences of opinion between yourself and the rest of the committee have become increasingly marked over the past few weeks.

'I feel confident that you would not have taken this step without having carefully considered every aspect of what is involved, and without having decided in your own mind that no compromise can be reached.

'I have therefore no alternative but with the greatest reluctance and regret to accept your resignation. Yours very sincerely, Geoffrey Bolden.'

He told himself that it was what he had expected, but it was not. He waited, however, for something else, a letter from Hollingsworth, the Financial Secretary to the Treasury, asking him to lunch, or a message from his old friend the President of the Board of Trade, offering him something quite different so that the Government could feel they had him on their side in spite of everything.

Nothing happened. The winter passed. A couple of board meetings a month in London, and one in Nottingham. A possibility that he might go to the United States for one of the firms concerned, but the situation changed and the plan fell through. Two of the big elms in the drive were blown down in a December gale. Susan was not well enough to come to Harkwood for Christmas. Angel and Penelope came but bickered, and a coolness arose between their husbands. After Christmas Selina went to Paris, Miss Martin went with her for a week to settle her in with the family with whom she was to stay. Gabriel was alone at Harkwood with the two Italian servants and the central heating went wrong. Faced with the prospect of its taking several days to mend he went up to London and stayed at his club.

He went to the theatre several times, and to the opera at Covent Garden. On the latter occasion he took with him an old friend of Hannah's, a nice sensible widow of sixty or so called Mary Penrose, but it was somehow embarrassing and he wished he had thought of asking another couple as well. On his way back to the club after dropping her at her Kensington flat he picked up a prostitute and went with her to a little room in Curzon Street. He had slept with prostitutes once or twice in his youth, to see what it was like, but otherwise he had not needed to buy sex. She seemed quite a friendly creature, and not unattractive, and he proved to himself that he had not lost his virility; but having proved that he felt he need not bother about it any more for the time being. 'I'm getting a bit old for that sort of thing,' he said to himself, and did not for once mind the idea.

But he was not too old for work. He let it be known discreetly that he was prepared to take on another directorship, but nothing happened. He even went so far as to say in a roundabout way to Ham that if Ham should happen to see old Morgan of the Board of Trade he might like just to mention the fact that his father-in-law had been asking after him, and was full of life and vigour these days. Nothing came of this either, though in fact some time later Ham did mention his father-in-law to the President of the Board of Trade and what Morgan said was, 'Ah yes, a very able chap, your father-in-law. Got a bit, well, idiosyncratic in his old age, hasn't he? Between you and me, I hear they had a frightful time with him on that committee. He ballsed the whole thing up, of course, Bolden told me he thought there was a good deal of just plain bloody-mindedness about it. Don't let that go any farther, though. And of course I admire him – Bolden does, too, told me so – but he's getting old, isn't he?'

'I imagine he was never the easiest person in the world to get on with,' said Ham.

'Well, he was fair, and a loyal colleague. But I've always known there was a strain of eccentricity there, though people didn't necessarily notice it.'

'Quite,' said Ham.

When Miss Martin returned from France, she found the house at Harkwood cold and deserted. The Italians had found another job and moved out, leaving an obscure but apparently offensive note. Miss Martin got the central heating mended and arranged relays of temporary domestic helpers of varying reliability from the village. Gabriel returned and was scolded. They settled down for the winter in a sort of harmony, Miss Martin dividing her time between the garden and the kitchen, Gabriel reading, going for walks with his dog, and making his periodical trips to London, where he had taken to spending money more freely than he had ever done before. He spent it on pictures (he had a good collection of English water-colours, and now no longer cared how much he paid for a new one) and on his own clothes, books, the latest gramophones and cameras, none of which he could work very well, and a new car. It annoyed Penelope, who thought he should be looking after his money more care-fully, but she missed a good deal of what was going on because she and Ham were busy in London and did not often come up to Harkwood.

February was a bad month, and he had a succession of nasty colds which made him feel low. He would some-times rant at Miss Martin, about politics, and the world and its dangers, and she would listen obligingly and occa-sionally contradict, whereupon he would fly into a passion and be rude to her. He decided to write a book on the economics of democracies and began to make notes for it. In March Angel had her baby. It was a girl and quite exceptionally pretty, with huge blue eyes and dark curls. Angel, losing her head completely, called it Sera-phina, and carried it round with her wherever she went with undiminishing delight. She announced her intention of having six more like her as soon as possible. Gabriel asked them often to Harkwood and found that after all there was something to be said for Roger. He had at least turned into a devoted husband and though he might be a bit slick and materialistic, he was no fool and quite helpful with the crossword.

In the spring Selina came home, thin and composed and grown-up. On her way through London she had looked in at an exhibition of paintings by Smith Pennington, but had come quickly out of the gallery, frightened by them. She had read in some paper that they showed an amazing advance on his past work, that they had the 'complexity of design and grandeur of conception of mature works of art,' and had gone with some muddled idea that they would be all Charlotte's love and suffering given a timeless meaning by art. She had seen only that they were huge and dark and full of some nameless incomprehensible movement. She hated them; and was ashamed of the vulgar weakness which had made her expect what she had of them.

It was a stormy spring. The world situation was worse than ever. Gabriel's scheme for his book on economics did not progress. He took to watching television, rather apologetically. He liked the programmes about animals; but *The Brains Trust* was agony to him because he felt that he should be on it himself. Witnessing his frustration one day, Roger said that he knew someone who was connected with the producer of the programme and would Gabriel like him to suggest that he might be willing to appear? A week later Roger wrote to say that the present series was nearly over, but that the producer had shown the liveliest interest at the mention of his name, and would like to meet him in the autumn when he started work on the next series.

Gabriel was delighted. He was going to be a television personality. It was a new idea, but one which he found increasingly appealing. He must not neglect his book, though. He ought to be working on his notes even now, but he was not, he was walking round the wood with the little dog.

He thought, some of my best moments have been in this wood. Trees, grass and water have meant a great deal to me, and yet I hardly know one tree from another, and have never so much as planted a daffodil bulb in my life. But it is perhaps not the names which matter, and one can participate without planting. Then he felt a flash of guilt, remembering how hard Miss Martin had worked in that wood and for how many years; and, willingly or unwillingly, the children, too, bossy conscientious Penelope, frightened Susan so overwhelmed at the thought of one bulb buried alone in the dark hostile earth that she put them in in twos and threes, Angel merely trailing her fingers in the lake, Charlotte in emotional turmoil because she had quarrelled with him at lunch, and solemn Selina, her mind on her never-to-be-completed book. And before any of them, Hannah, who had loved the wood.

He thought, after all I have let my soul live. He stopped in his usual place, by the big beech which grew closest to the edge of the lake, so that its roots on one side disappeared into the water, and stood looking across the lake at the field and the house. The dog started to dig a hole. I have let my soul live, I have not denied it. I have nothing to show for it, nothing much to show for anything, but I am something, even if no one knows me. Even if I never do anything more, if I don't finish the book, don't do the television thing, don't get offered any sort of job ever, here I still am.

He was standing with one hand on the trunk of the tree and the other on his walking stick, looking at the water, and quite suddenly he felt an extraordinary feeling of suffocation, and a sharp pain in his left side, and a moment later his arms and hands were seized by cramp. He gave a gasp, more of surprise than of pain, and then it was over. He leant against the tree, shaken. What had it been? Was that what a heart attack was like? Surely it had been too mild for that. But it had been something. What? A warning? An activity within himself quite outside his control. His body was obeying its own laws. He was suddenly flooded with emotion at the thought of this independence of his body. He felt the same sort of startled pride in it that he had felt when he first realized that he could ejaculate his seed. It must be that some time before long his body in the course of nature was going to die. He could only feel it to be amazing. As amazing as the living tree against which he was leaning, as the water on whose surface he could see, leaning over, the muddied reflection of his own face. He was filled with such an unreasonable joy that he had to remind himself of the pain, the pain that might be in store for him if he were indeed going to die before long, and the other pain, the immeasurable volume of pain not his. But he thought, there are the trees and the lake and the places on the earth where man does not go, where there are long-legged lemurs that jump from branch to branch and never touch the ground, and where the lioness has sheathed her claws to teach her young to play; and there are people like Hannah, and people like me. With extraordinary excitement he thought at least I have achieved this, that if I die now I shall die of love. I am on the right level.

At last the dog emerged from his hole, snorting and

spitting out earth, and hurried up to make sure that Gabriel was still there before returning to his digging. Gabriel called him and walked on slowly.

At the end of the lake was a flat piece of grass, framed by bushes, on which there had once been a stone summerhouse, all trace of which had now disappeared. Gabriel had sometimes thought of building another one there: it occurred to him now that he would like to build a folly, an extravagant, exuberant and useless folly, Gothic and picturesque. As soon as he had thought of it, he began to design it in his mind. He would start at once, and have it finished by the summer. He must get on to the builders immediately. It would probably be extremely expensive.

He walked back to the house, slowly because he was still rather breathless. As he came to the front door he shouted, 'Martin! I've decided to build a folly!'

Miss Martin was at the back door, scraping the mud off her gum boots. 'I'm just going to make it,' she called, not having heard what he had said and thinking he was shouting for tea.

Putting his walking stick carefully into its place by the front door, he said, 'How it will annoy them all!'

10

Two years later, a young man called James Ross hesitated on the platform at Paddington. His friend David Jones had said he would meet him but was, of course, late.

He should have known better than to have allowed himself to be met. He had so little time to waste. This was to be his last visit to London before he went to South America, a few days for making final arrangements, saying goodbye to friends, then back to his job as a schoolmaster in the north until it was time to leave for the jungle. He had just decided to abandon David, and was on his way to the Underground, when he saw him, an unlikely figure in a gleaming new Bentley, sweeping down the slope to the car park, an ugly little man with a mass of black hair and a delighted smile.

'Did you steal it?'

'Borrowed. From a maniac who thinks I know how to drive. Get in, we're late.'

'What for?'

'For Selina. Watch me try and turn this thing. It's like a dead whale. Frightful car.'

'Who's is it?'

'Campion's.'

'Campion? But what's he doing with a car like this?'

'Some uncle died, left him his money. It's turned him very mean.'

'He's lent you the car.'

'Not willingly. Not willingly at all. Are you still going on this expedition?'

'Yes.'

'You're mad. You're not the right sort of person to be

an explorer at all. You're much too highly strung, my
dear, you'll never stick it. How long for?'

'Two years. Maybe more.'

'You're going for the wrong reasons, aren't you? You
think of it as a test, a punishment.'

'No, I'm interested,' said James. 'Also I'd like to try a
bit of non-civilization, civilization not having proved quite
what I'd hoped.'

'You're looking for yourself, not some savage tribe. And
I can tell you you're going the wrong way about it. You're
being frivolous, for one thing. The rest of the expedition
are serious. You're also being romantic, you're also being
cowardly.'

'Cowardly?'

'You're afraid to join in, compete with the rest of us.
You pretend you're disgusted, when all you are is shy.'
He gave a shriek of laughter.

'That's ridiculous,' said James.

'It's easy, I tell you,' said David, accelerating. 'You can
fool anyone. It's much easier in London than it ever was
in Oxford. I'm a highly thought of young film critic,
known for my brilliantly paradoxical style and my filthy
puns. Any fool can do it.' He swerved to avoid an old
woman on a zebra crossing, scraped a good deal of paint
off one of the front wings on a keep left sign, and turned
into a side street with whining tyres.

'For God's sake,' said James.

'Sorry. Thought I saw a policeman. Anyway as I say
anyone can do it. Even Campion, now he's got some
money. He's doing well in the City, they say. And
Raymond, with that magazine. Oh, yes, anyone can do
it. The trouble with this car is that you can't drive it
slowly.'

'Try another gear. Where are we going anyway? I'm
meeting the others at eight at Graham's flat to make the
final arrangements. I promised not to be late.'

'We're going to a pub.'

'I don't think I've time, honestly. Can't I just leave my
things at your flat?'

'I told you, there's someone I want you to meet.'

'Who?'

'A girl.'

'A girl? I thought you didn't like girls.'

'Oh yes, new thing, you are out of touch. I'm mad about sex and very, very good at it.'

'Can't I meet her tomorrow?'

'She may not be speaking to me tomorrow. She's very difficult. Remote, I'm madly in love with her.'

'And she with you?'

'If she is she's got herself in an iron control. That's why I'm so mad about her. She's rich too. I found that out. I'm thinking of getting married.'

'It's an unlikely concept.'

'Her father died a year or so ago, and left quite a decent sum, even though there are a lot of sisters. The mother's dead too – no trouble with in-laws you see. One of the sisters died, too, not long before the father. And another's more or less mad. It's all on her mind, it's part of the whole thing about her. She's young and pretty and all that as well of course. Another sister's married to a smooth bastard called Maitland, Minister of Aviation, you know. Here we are.'

'I'll have to leave you in a moment, then, to go to Graham. I'll leave my case in the car till later. All right? Are you really going to leave the car just here?'

'Why not?'

David led the way into the pub, which was crowded.

Selina was sitting at a table in a corner, reading an evening paper. She was facing the door but did not look up when they came in.

James said in sudden fear, 'Perhaps I won't come in. I mean I am rather late.'

'What do you mean? You can't go now, you've got to meet this girl. No one's met her yet, not Campion, or Raymond, or Crab, or anyone. Come on.'

James followed him. She looked up. They were introduced. David bought drinks. A moment later a policeman came in to ask who was the owner of the Bentley parked across the entrance to a mews. David went out with him, protesting.

When he came back after having found somewhere else to park the car as well as having discussed at some length

with the policeman the proper duties of his Force, James
and Selina were talking intently, leaning slightly towards
each other. As he approached, Selina said, opening her
sad eyes wide, 'You must feel very free then, having
decided.'

'No,' said James seriously. 'I feel as if I were drowning.'

She smiled at him, slowly. 'You don't look it.'

'But you do,' said James.

'Oh, Christ,' said David, sitting heavily in a chair and
reaching for his drink. 'Isn't that just the way it is? My
best friend, the only girl I've ever cared for, a parking
offence, betrayal.'

'Oh, there you are,' said James. 'Have another drink.'

'You're late,' said David bitterly. 'You're missing your
expedition.'

'So I am, I must go.' James stood up, asked the barman
for another drink, paid for it, said to David, patting him
on the back, 'Sorry, David, mush rush, see you later,' and
leaning across to Selina, 'Tomorrow, then, at seven? You
will be there?'

'Of course,' she said.

'Christ!' said David again and swallowed his drink. 'I'll
have another of these. Oh, he overpaid you last time, did
he? Well, that's a bit of luck, isn't it? It's no use, you
know, Selina, he's going into the jungle for two years,
leaving any minute.'

'He might not go,' she said.

'Of course he'll go. He's said he will. He's given up his
job as a schoolmaster, turned down another on a magazine. Of course he'll go, it's too late for him to get out of
it now.'

'He said he might not,' said Selina, gently.

'He did, did he, blast his eyes. Shows what an unreliable sort of fellow he is, doesn't it? Ditching his friends
like that, letting them down, disgraceful.'

'He only said he might not.'

'Shouldn't believe a word he says if I were you. He's
completely unreliable, unstable really. Always has been.'

She laughed. 'We only said we'd go to the theatre. It
turned out there was something we both wanted to see.'

'Quite,' he said. 'That's all. You needn't think I'm not

going to put up a fight though because I am. You'll like
that, I suppose. Oh well, off we go. Have another drink.
I can see we're going to need it.'

'No, thank you.'

'Yes, yes, come on, of course you will. Let yourself go.
Celebrate. This is a great occasion.'

She smiled again.

'I know,' she said. 'I recognize it.'